Koban: Rise of the Kobani

By Stephen W Bennett

Stephen W Bennett

Published by
Bandit Enterprise

Koban: Rise of the Kobani

ISBN-13:978-1493608133
ISBN-10: 1493608134

Cover art designed by Misha Coutinho Richet,
melissa_richet@yahoo.fr
www.facebook.com/pages/The-Book-Cover-Realm/559333740763541

This is the third book in the Koban Series

This book is written in "American" English, so there may be some differences in spelling and usage than in other countries use of the language.

This is a work of fiction and all characters are fictitious or are portrayed fictitiously. Any resemblance to persons living or dead is purely coincidental.

****

My thanks to Sandy Mancini for her help, where her proofreading and English major skills helped clean up hundreds of my capitalization, grammatical and punctuation messes. Book 4 is next, Sandy, should you be resilient or foolish enough to stick around.

****

Rise of the Kobani

Table of Contents

Kobani genetic levels

The first generation of humans arrived on Koban as Krall captives. These were ordinary people from Human Space. They had the typical set of about a 150 genetic enhancements, found in the average population of any world (by the year 2550).

They lived longer and they aged in appearance slowly (until the last decade of life, at about 120 to 130 years of age). They have an enhanced immune system (no colds, cancers, or inherited genetic defects). Some were the descendants of people that had carried personal genetic selections, desirable traits chosen by their parents for them before birth. Such as, genes for attractiveness, for tall and muscular males and tall and shapely females, perfect eyesight and hearing, banishing baldness, choosing hair and eye color, and other cosmetic options.

Poor citizens suffered the slings and arrows of outrageous short, homely, plumpness, if they didn't have parents with the prenatal credits to make them look better.

All of that ended with a cataclysmic Gene War that nearly wiped out humanity, and for three hundred years after, gene research and modification was a death penalty offense.

On Koban, illegal gene modifications were required to survive in the high gravity, and for fighting the Krall. The changes were applied in stages. Interbreeding between people with various gene adaptation levels was not a problem, by design. The combinations of genes resulted in the following reference terms for the different levels.

****

SG ------ Second Generation. Clone genetic mods added to survive on Koban.
SG.5 ---- Child of an SG and an SG1. Inherited mixed traits of SG and SG1.
SG1 ----- An SG with genes for a dormant Koban superconducting nervous system.
STG ---- Child of any level SG and any level TG (Third Generation Kobani).
TG ------Third Gen child of SG's, received ripper genes for muscles, & raptor bones.
TG.5 --- Child of a TG and a TG1.
TG1 ---- A TG who also received the ripper "frilling" genes. (Mind Tap ability).
TG2 ---- Has every Koban gene (ripper eyesight & sense of smell, wolfbat hearing).
TTG ---- A True Third Generation child of TG2's. Born with all Koban genes.

Any Second Generation person is commonly called simply an SG, but there is a difference, because an SG1 has a parallel and *unused* Koban organic superconducting nervous system.

The Third Generation isn't as straightforward. Geneticists were able to skip ahead to *create* TGs and TG1s earlier, from children born of two SG1's, by adding various Koban genes to them. Intermarriage between TG levels and SG levels creates other combinations.

A TTG will be a True Third Generation Kobani. One born with every Koban gene, and both parents were TG2s."

Rise of the Kobani

Chapter 1: Poldark Arrival

Poldark's Planetary Defense Command (PDC) immediately detected the three clanship White Outs in a tight formation, at just over one thousand miles above the northern Bosnian Sea at mid-latitude. They were more than four times the distance at which the Krall usually made their exits, and well away from the conquered territory on Poldark's second largest continent. They weren't an immediate threat to any particular population center, but three ships arriving at once was serious in any case, and stealthed meant they could be headed anywhere after the White Out.

The orbital defenses were keyed to react most quickly to close-in White Outs, usually between one hundred fifty to two hundred miles. It took nearly five seconds before the first heavy duty lasers reoriented and sought the parent targets of each gamma ray burst. The three ships were stealthed, so the assumption was that they had entered with a high velocity vector towards the planet, imparted to the three ships before they had even Jumped. The beams all passed through locations in space where the targets were reasonably assumed to have moved. Locations that were below the points of the three closely clustered White Outs

A formation arrival would typically split up immediately, and start independent vectors towards the planet, dividing the defenses. In vacuum, the enemy always used Normal Space drives powered by tachyon energy, rather than the reaction mass thruster system, because the latter would leave easily detectable trails of ions from the exhaust. The Krall never waited to mix it up with the defenders, driving into the teeth of the defending lasers, plasma beams and missiles.

A recent addition to the defenses was hundreds of rail guns, used on small orbital fusion powered platforms, which could spew a sleet of cheap heavy slugs to cover possible approaches to the planet. They were not a high risk to a clanship unless it was hit many times, but if they struck anything invisible to radar, they would explode with a brief transmission of their position. The triangulation from the Doppler shift of their return signal would indicate something of the trajectory of what they had struck, providing a clue of enemy location and possible future track. The slugs were a risk to legitimate shipping, communications and spy satellites, and other railgun platforms, therefore an Artificial Intelligence was fed the orbital radar data, and it coordinated the rail gun firing to minimize collateral damage.

The spent shells had multiple self-destruct modes, where they could fire a small reverse thrust to fall out of orbit and burn up within a day or less, they also would detonate on their own after a short flight time, or they could be given a command signal to apply either self-destruct method sooner. The space above Poldark was already full of tiny to medium- sized debris. A thousand small orbital sweeper bots with wide scoops and powerful magnetic fields were constantly chasing down and cleaning up particles and larger objects, melting them down for reuse. On occasion, they cleaned up pieces of other sweeper bots, destroyed by the Krall or by accident.

The only occasions the necessary sweeping task wasn't dull routine or irritating, was when they were collecting bits of destroyed clanships or single ships. Unfortunately, that wasn't very often because the usually electromagnetically invisible Krall ships moved extremely fast, and were unpredictable and nearly undetectable before reaching atmosphere. Most of the debris in orbit came from destroyed human spy satellites and weapons platforms, or ships that the Krall killed via ground fire, or attacked in orbit with their stealthed single ships and clanships.

Arriving enemy clanships didn't normally give the PDC the opportunity to start shooting at them from a thousand miles away. Even in a large volume of sky, with ships invisible to radar, lidar, maser, much of the visible light spectrum, and which emitted no Infrared, any refraction or reflection or beam deflection could be revealing. That could briefly reveal where a ship had moved from their gamma ray centered entry point, thus providing an intelligent guess for the AI systems of where to probe with plasma and laser beams. Combined with a launch of some larger reusable missiles, and mass firing of railguns, they could quickly strike towards potential ship locations before the clanships plunged into the atmosphere. The missiles would probe the places near any suspicious radiation returns or beam deflections. Invisible or not, the clanship would definitely feel the explosion of even an accidental impact of those larger missiles.

Corporal Caldwell called out. "Captain Reykic, no joy on orbital scans, and all three ships have had time to hit atmosphere by now, they could be anywhere, including half way around the planet."

"Turb has no refraction trails at all?" The captain referred to the Turbulence Detector watch, which could trace fast moving clanships as they passed through atmosphere. Their fast passage produced visible refraction in their wake, if not outright contrails. The ships would alter speed and trajectory constantly, making the guessing game continue, but with a bit more predictability.

"No Sir. They either stayed in orbit, slowed and entered at low velocity, or departed without attempting a penetration."

"We know we won't spot them in orbit, and they damn well never pull out and just leave. A slow approach is much harder to detect. Ask Turb to focus on visible light. The reactive hull skin will blend with the sky and clouds, but we have a chance to see the ripple as they move."

Caldwell, avoiding a roll of his eyes followed the order, but he knew the response he was going to get back from Turb control when he told them how to do their job.

The sharp reply in the transducer behind his right ear was expected. "Charley, you watch frigging space, we'll handle the damned atmosphere. We were already checking for slow moving ripples, it's automatic, for craps sake."

Charley looked at the image of the man he'd contacted, displayed on half of the right side lens of his computer-linked cyber glasses. "Brek, I just did what I was told. OK?" He looked over his shoulder to be sure the captain was out of earshot. "Reykic micromanages everything, you know that."

"Right. Didn't mean to snap at you. I've transferred the search to the south Turb Division, since we don't see anything in the northern hemisphere. The Krall always plunge right into the pool, no testing the water first. I wonder where those alien assholes went this time."

****

The *human* "assholes" were coasting slowly away from the planet, retaining the modest velocity Mirikami had imparted to his three-ship flotilla relative to Poldark, and was allowing gravity to slow them. Their Normal Space drives were ready for maneuvering into an orbit, once the activity to find them had died down. There also were tachyons in their secondary Trap fields, available for a possible Jump to the Oort cloud if forced to retreat briefly.

The three ships had their facing view screens active, and the tight-beam laser coms had all three linked in a secure closed circuit that could not be intercepted.

"Sarge was right on the money," Mirikami confirmed for them. "They expected us to exit closer in, and to dive towards the planet. A slow coast away at a higher altitude was completely out of character for the Krall."

Noreen had noticed a defense Reynolds had not mentioned. "Are the railguns new, Sarge?"

"They are to me," he answered. "I heard about their development on Tri-Vid news, and read about the Navy building the platforms for every inhabited planet, as low cost protection from the Eight Balls, like the one that blasted Rhama. Naturally, government bureaucracy and politics saw to it that *Hub* worlds got them first, instead of the Rim and New Colony worlds, which were already under attack.

"Poldark didn't have them six months ago, when the Krall caught my bony butt. However, the need for depleted uranium slugs with diamond tips, which they talked about for Eight Ball use, would seem to be resource expensive for several hundred railgun platforms, spread around seven hundred or so planets, requiring millions of rounds of ammunition. Particularly if they also use them to wildly shoot at clanships they can't see, nor kill one if they can only hit them at random."

Sergeant Reynolds, late of the PU Army on Poldark, freed from Krall captivity six months ago, sounded far more erudite today than if someone were trying to push him into a position of authority. His unconscious desire to stay in the background would then cause him to shift into a different persona, and speak as if he were an uneducated hick, in an effort to demonstrate he was unsuitable to assume any leadership role. If all that was required was advice or information, or attacking the enemy when ordered, then his University education sprang forth.

"I don't know. Those small platforms can really throw the slugs." Marlyn noted. "Are you sure they can't knockout a clanship? How could they take out an Eight Ball of collapsed matter if they can't kill one of these ships? I wonder how they even keep them all supplied with slugs."

Mirikami had a speculation. "I see some small unmanned ships in orbit, collecting debris. Perhaps they smelt the material down out here, and make more slugs on the spot. They would have plenty of ferrous materials in most of the debris for the magnetic railgun launchers to push. They could reserve a supply of better, diamond tipped ammunition for use against Eight Balls if they appear. I don't think they expected to knock out a clanship with them, unless it's an extremely lucky shot."

Dillon and Thad were also on the Bridge with Mirikami, and Dillon had been checking the AI's sensor reports after their White Out. "Jakob reported thousands of small flashes along the trajectories of each burst of slugs." Jakob was the human made AI installed on the converted clanship, renamed the Mark of Koban. "I think the shells self-destruct if they don't hit anything, to reduce the danger of other ships hitting a high speed ten or fifteen pound solid slug. That's a lot of kinetic energy to encounter, at eighteen to twenty thousand miles per hour. Military ships will have heavy shielding that can hold up against the smaller fragments, but not very well against a solid slug."

"If the railguns can't knock out a clanship, how will they kill an Eight Ball?" Noreen asked.

Her com image showed Reynolds shrugging. "The ball that the battleship Gauntlet hit, when defending Rhama's orbital transfer station, exploded with almost the energy of a midsized nuke. They apparently have an enormous amount of binding energy holding the partially collapsed matter together, and they normally can take the tremendous punishment of ramming into our ships multiple times at safer velocities. They sure shrug off normal missiles, lasers, and plasma beams.

"I heard some scientists, interviewed on Tri-Vid, say they had calculated that if the stress at any point on the collapsed matter surface exceeded a certain high pressure threshold, they completely let go with a blast. It's like a crack caused from a very high velocity impact with a large dense mass like the Gauntlet, or when striking a planet's deep crust or mantle. A high pressure strike at a tiny spot, such as by a fast moving, diamond-tipped uranium slug could cause a single microscopic crack to propagate through the ball and release all of that energy. A clanship doesn't have that sort of brittle structure, and it will simply puncture or absorb the shot."

Thad, using zoomed in detailed visual images from the Krall sensor suite at his console said, "Tet, I think you're probably right about the ammo being remade in orbit. I just watched one of the debris collecting robots dock with a railgun platform. It probably transferred freshly manufactured slugs to its magazines. The railguns could easily have a supply of better quality ammunition on the platforms for use against an Eight Ball. That leaves me wondering why they create the mess of an orbital debris field, shooting cheap slugs at clanships that can't really be hurt by them, not with only a few random hits."

The video feed on the laser com sets revealed Mirikami in his usual lip-tugging mode of thinking.

He suggested an answer, as he also looked at Jakob's sensor records. "The spent slugs eventually all exploded, except for some that slowed and burned up in the atmosphere. That means they have electronics built into them, some sort of timer chip, a power supply, and an explosive charge or small propulsion source. If one of the slugs had hit us it might not do enough damage to disable us, but its explosion would probably tell them where we are. I note the railguns all fired along low orbits, parallel to the planet's surface, where presumably they expected our three stealthed ships to try to sneak into the upper atmosphere. I think they were shooting blindly, hoping to hit and reveal something radar couldn't see. They could then focus fire power in that vicinity, increasing their chance of more hits and damage."

With a nod to Reynolds, Mirikami added, "That sort of defense response was exactly what we needed to know, or else we would have blundered into a dangerous situation we could simply avoid. Let's stay formed close enough for secure laser com, but I want to go into orbit back down at a thousand miles or so. There Sarge and I can use passive scanners to search for a place for the Mark to hide, once we make a successful penetration over Krall held territory."

Even stealthed from human equipment, the Olt'kitapi designed ships the Krall used could track one another. Mirikami led the other two captured clanships, renamed the Avenger and the Beagle, into an orbit that would repeatedly take them over the continent where the Krall had first invaded Poldark. Reynolds would use his knowledge of the region, and fresh observations to find a place where they could hide the big craft in mountains. They needed to avoid not only the Poldark defenders that considered them a Krall ship, but also stay away from the Krall. The latter would be "energetically" more unfriendly than the PU Army, if they discovered humans had captured one of their ships.

The Avenger and Beagle followed the Mark into a lower orbit, taking up a tight formation again, enabling them to use the intercept-proof laser com communications.

Two hours later, after a second pass over the largely Krall controlled land mass, Reynolds had two likely landing areas for Mirikami to consider.

"There is a really wild and undeveloped area in the Sredna Gora mountain range with multiple valleys and canyons, where there are few roads and less likelihood of anyone spotting us landing, or of stumbling on us after we are down." He shook his head. "I don't like that as the first choice because it's so far from the combat lines we need to cross, and its very inaccessibility would make it hard for us to contact Poldark forces, and then to get the supplies we need."

"You said you didn't like it as the 'first choice,' so I presume you have one you like better."

"Yes. It's a small former Special Ops base on the edge of what was the front line when I was captured, and we were being pushed back from there at the time. I know it well because that underground base is one I had used for months, and it had just been evacuated. It's where I helped stage the ambush that killed the Krall invasion leader, and which indirectly led to my own capture. Multiple concealed entrances were in that box canyon, where there are steep cliff sides and a curve in the canyon where the ship would be hidden from the opening to the box canyon valley for passersby. The cliffs are several hundred feet higher than this clanship…, I mean than the Mark is. It's also in the foothills of the Sredna Gora range, on the same side of the mountains closer to where I think the PU Army will be fighting now."

"You don't think the Krall will be using your old base themselves?"

Sarge shook his head. "They never have before, not even when they push us out of a small field command post. They know we have miniature spy bots, disguised as insects and small animals, which we leave behind in areas we abandon. They learned the hard way that we 'cowardly' sneaky humans sometimes mine our underground lairs, to blow up and bury their red, scaly, colored asses under millions of tons of rock. They make underground bunkers for their own use, and stay out of ours."

"It's safe for us to use that old base ourselves?" Mirikami asked.

"Probably. We have to check it out first, but it had long tunnels leading away from its center under the foothills in all directions, which would let us surface miles from where the ship is hidden."

"Won't our own people going inside trigger the booby traps?" Noreen was asking what was on Marlyn's mind as well. Both of their sons, Carson and Ethan, and husbands, Dillon and Thad, were part of Mirikami's landing party.

"Nope. They use life-form discrimination detectors Ladies." He answered, and then he grinned. "Fancy pants words for saying they can tell the difference between Krall and humans, or even from animals that might enter the tunnels. At some point, if a mined but still occupied base was being overrun by Krall, a seriously detrimental ratio of enemy to human is reached in different sections. Those areas would blow first, where the most Krall are located, and there could be collateral losses of our people trapped there or captured. However, remember that the Krall don't let prisoners live to a peaceful ripe old age anyway."

Tet wanted details of the tunnels. "How far away could those tunnels take us? Into or even behind the Poldark lines?"

Reynolds seemed to think for a moment. "I don't think they would go that far. At the rate we were losing ground, I'd expect the Krall to have pushed our forces back a dozen miles from where the longest tunnel I recall came to the surface. I never used all of the tunnels personally, so I can't be sure. It was a forward post for the spec ops troops, and our ambush teams came along when the Krall were on the doorstep. We tried to suck their lead elements into artillery ambushes or mine fields." He paused to think for a moment.

"You know..., I said we leave spy bots behind, so there could be some crawling on the walls inside. We might get one or two of them to report seeing humans in the tunnels, to set up some sort of remote meeting. I don't know how good they are at talking back to us if they report seeing humans. I wasn't part of the 'spook' division, and the Krall wouldn't make for good conversationalists, so the spy bots might provide only a one way street to the listeners."

Tet nodded. "OK. In any case, I like the proximity to the Poldark lines, and the ship should have good cover. Frankly, I'm not worried about the Krall questioning our ship being there, since they already control the area. They'll assume we are some clan of raiders on our own business, at least if the ship is only seen from a distance. The PU Army, however, will shoot first at a clanship, and ask no questions at all. How wide is that canyon compared to this ship? How much room will I have to set down?"

Reynolds closed his eyes a moment to visualize the canyon the last time he'd seen it, with Dragon mini tanks chasing his team. "It's roughly twice as wide as the ship for most of its length, and actually opens up a bit near the back wall at the end of the box canyon." Reynolds could only fly a shuttle, so a large vertical landing ship, like the Mark of Koban, was outside his expertise as a pilot.

Mirikami pulled at his lip. "I'll have to slow and hover over the canyon for a moment to get centered. Unless the wind is high that day, I should be able to counter any side drift. I don't want to still be evading missiles or chase planes when I go vertical and settle. The long-range sensors show that Navy Carrier you said was usually here. It's standing off and parked out by the inner gas giant, orbiting one of its moons. How many of its fighters do you think would be in the inner system?"

Reynolds shrugged. "I was a dirt pounder. I know that sometimes the one or two man fighters would come in for cover and air support if our forces were being hit in the rear by single ships. It took a four or five to one advantage to take on one of their single ships, and our pilots stayed well away from the Dragons and front lines, since those portable plasma cannons can knock them down from five or even ten miles away.

"Our pilots and planes are far and away more maneuverable than a single ship in atmosphere, since they have wings, and a single ship is a simple tube that farts propellant to turn or accelerate. It also has Normal Space drives with tachyon Traps, usually for operation in space. It is much faster and has heavier armament than our space planes, but a Krall pilot isn't as good as our people, once they leave orbit and hit air, even if a Krall *can* take much greater acceleration.

"The atmosphere is a big drag, literally, on their effectiveness as air attack fighters or bombers. Our smart missiles are better, because they aren't as easily spoofed by electronic counter measures, and they don't cause collateral damage for our side if they can't score a hit. Naturally, the Krall don't give a shit about what happens if they miss. However, I don't *think* you will have any fighters try to close with us. The lasers or plasma cannons of a clanship can vaporize them, and its own tough hull and stealth make it hard for them to hit or damage. They won't know that we aren't trying to kill them, and they'll stay away.

"However, our planes and ground based batteries *can* fire some long-range missiles, if they can get targeting information from the Turb AI. Our safest course is to descend over Krall territory where the planes can't fly and the ground launchers are at extreme range and then we can approach the canyon at tree top level from there."

"What sort of AI?" Marlyn asked. "Tub did you say?"

"Turb, for turbulence detection. The PDC fills the air with microwaves, and a grid of ground detectors sense the refraction from atmospheric disturbances that the AI examines. There is a lot of turbulence that is natural, from storms and such, particularly over windy mountain ranges. However, none is long and vertically tubular at high altitudes, as when a Krall craft penetrates fast, nor does nature often form horizontal tubes at lower altitudes, as we'd make during high-speed horizontal travel. Those are most likely a fast moving clanship or single ship making a penetration, and if there is no corresponding hard radar or laser reflection, then it's targeted as a stealthed enemy."

"Is it accurate?" Noreen wanted to know.

"Fairly accurate, but the Krall don't fly a nice straight line, and there is a slight lag in detection as the atmosphere reacts to a ship's passing, so the ship may have changed direction by the time the Turb AI has a targeting solution. Before I was captured, one case that was initially touted as a destroyed clanship proved not to be, when no debris was found. Investigation and recordings revealed the Army had successfully killed a funnel cloud, by heat disruption with lasers and plasma cannons."

He laughed. "It was an expensive triumph for violent weather control however."

Mirikami chuckled with him for a moment. "I think we will try a more sedate entry, and attract a lot less attention."

Reynolds had a cautionary warning. "If the sky is clear there is a chance the ripple effect can show us up, and then you don't have velocity to get you out of harm's way as quickly."

Noreen was exasperated. "Damn it. Our sons and husbands, and our friends will be aboard the Mark! You included, you big negative sounding goof! Isn't there any simple way to sneak in quietly? What the hell is the ripple effect?"

He smiled, and explained. "Take a perfectly clear glass sphere and tie it to a thin string and hang it from a ceiling. Then push it to send it oscillating around a normal room filled with lights, furniture, and objects on the walls. The sphere is almost perfectly transparent, but unless it's motionless, you can see it easily because of how it affects the light passing through it from the other side as it moves. A stealthed ship is somewhat like that. The armor I wore in combat had active camouflage, and blended me in with the background, even matching the surrounding temperature for a low infrared contrast. Nevertheless, if I moved very much, or too fast, I became faintly noticeable. That's the ripple effect."

Mirikami tried to ease their worries. "Ladies, I'm hoping to find a major storm system with high cloud tops and lots of turbulence, and try to sink into that for screening as long as I can."

"Right over the canyon you plan to use? How long will you have to sit and wait for a storm like that?" Marlyn wondered.

Mirikami shook his head. "I wouldn't want to do it over the destination point anyway. I have two-thirds of a large continent where the Krall are located to find a suitable storm. It's spring in the northern hemisphere. There should be frequent thunder storms, right Sarge?" He knew Reynolds would agree, because not only was it an accurate statement, but because that was something they had discussed while in Jump transit.

Reynolds tried to reassure them. "There are afternoon storms over coastal regions every day and some big ones in the central area of the continent of

Macedonia often located somewhere along that mountain chain where we want to land. There was one storm building there when we arrived, but it will have dissipated before we are ready to make the entry. There'll be others."

****

"Gatlek Pendor," Kaldot called to his superior. "The three clanships you inquired about have not left orbit. They are maintaining stealth and formation, and no clan has announced them as theirs. However, because of their action to move away, I do not think they carry the expected supplies from Telda Ka." They were waiting for replacement Dragon mini-tanks, and automated laser defenses against the annoying human artillery. These were being shipped from their base world, named K1 by the humans.

New warriors to participate in the war arrived loosely, as various clans chose to send them. Except for small, brief raids on other human worlds, they were not permitted to take independent action on Poldark without coordination with the Gatlek, and were subject to his orders when they attacked any designated target or fought along any front. Until then they were free to land, to become acclimated to the local gravity, climate, and terrain, and to train their warriors here.

Pendor answered his Mordo clan mate and aid, "Advise me of what they do after they decide to land, Kaldot. They may be waiting for more of their clan to arrive. I have no interest in them if they did not bring the weapons I requested."

Pendor had only found it necessary to conduct two punitive raids against uncooperative clanship commanders, whom had refused to coordinate with him, or had deliberately not obeyed his orders. They had been removed forcibly, and in the standard Krall tradition, fatally. For one thing, rampaging over the humans was "wasteful" of their potential as worthy enemies. For another, that worthy enemy was adept at making a strategic withdrawal, allowing a foolish clan sub leader to pursue beyond his logistics train, only to be flanked and cut off, subject to annihilation by a physically weaker enemy. This was an inefficient method of culling warriors because smarter and better fighters died with the poor sub leader.

Pendor had no complaint about such a sub leader being eliminated from the gene pool more efficiently, if he or she was being too brash or stupid to contribute to the new genetic reorganization. Tor Gatrol Kanpardi had set a higher goal for racial improvement on the Great Path, and it had been approved by the joint clan council. A poor sub leader was expendable, but competent warriors compelled to follow him might be wasted as a result. Too many useful genes could be lost as young breeders, having greater potential than their over aggressive slow-to-learn higher status leader, died with him.

For the last several thousand years, the clans had no powerful alien race to fight, and so they fought only among themselves, in a process that naturally selected for the strongest and fastest warriors, at the expense of the most innovative warriors.

In their homogenous society, there were fewer non-standard thinkers. The lack of a recent smart, adaptable foe had created a need for this new breeding focus, to meet the challenge presented by the human prey. The fact that the most recent races they had faced were inherently unwarlike, and were slow to adjust or offer serious challenge to Krall warriors, had resulted in a dearth of warriors suited for meeting the crafty methods humans used to fight them. Poor competition led to poor competitors. Fortunately, the egg laying Krall could far out-produce the slower reproducing humans, with their mere one or two live births per year. The clans poured a nearly inexhaustible supply of warriors into the fight against them.

Even as physically weak as humans were, and with lower technology than many past races, they were forcing the Krall to find better future leaders and warriors, which were then selectively bred. It would be at least a thousand years before *enough* of the resulting wave of smarter more adaptable cubs reached maturity, to dominate the war effort. However, it *would* happen, as it had always happened over the past twenty-five thousand years.

The new heavy metal and rare earth food supplements, based on a Koban environmental model, were finding their way into the tissues of their newest cubs. Eventually, randomly, some of those elements would be incorporated into the nervous system, building the forerunner of the organic super conductor nerves the Krall also sought, as present naturally in all higher animals on Koban. It was hoped that this major step along the Great Path of self-directed evolution could be achieved before the human foe was fully eradicated. They would be a fine test for the new class of warriors that should be produced.

****

Over the next several days, Mirikami watched for a weather development that he could use to his advantage. Several sizable storms with high cloud tops formed near coastal areas, but those were too far from the mountain range where the Mark of Koban could be more easily hidden, and would require a longer low altitude flight to the mountains. In those three days, there were six clanship arrivals and four departures, all of which successfully ran the gauntlet of Poldark defenses. They each used a high-speed penetration or exit method, which dared the humans to shoot them down. Twice the air defenses came close to succeeding for the arrivals.

After watching Mirikami conduct a careful review of the high-speed penetrations, Sarge asked him, “Rethinking the slow approach?”

“No. On the contrary, I don’t think we could have made it down safely the way the Krall came in. I had Jakob analyze the evasive turns they executed, and the internal g’s they withstood would probably have rendered any of us Second Generation people unconscious after the second or third sharp turn. Avoiding *having* to do that is the only option I see. The multiple missiles fired at them came too close for comfort if we can’t dodge like the Krall.”

"We can't risk not being able to do those turns if we are spotted." Thad warned. "We have to drop out of a thunderstorm at some point, and head for the canyon. Perhaps I need to try to contact Nabarone by radio. Get him to send someone to meet us off planet."

"No, part of our sales pitch is to show *him* our TGs can outperform the Krall. Seeing them perform is believing in them, so I think we need to risk the landing for a face-to-face meeting with Nabarone. However, I think we may be able to take advantage of the capabilities of our TG1's in a pinch. Jakob, Link me to Chief Haveram."

"Yes Sir." The smaller subset of the Flight of Fancy's Jake AI software, running in older hardware, had been modified to function with the crew's embedded transducers.

"Chief, I need you to install another two acceleration couches on the Bridge, right next to mine."

"Captain, we have one in storage as a spare, but the other one will have to be one of those currently installed in either the Jump Drive Room or the Engine Room." Haveram had planned to use the one in the Engine Room for the Poldark landing.

"Not a problem, Chief. We aren't going to Jump anywhere soon, and so far, we haven't needed anyone to stand watch over those gauges. The Krall ships are a lot more automatic than ours, so take the couch from the Jump Drive Room." The chief had been switching from one area to the other to monitor the equipment, depending on their use of the tachyon powered drive or the reaction thrusters. Both monitoring jobs seemed pointless on the former clanship.

****

After several days waiting, they finally had a sizable front moving across the mountain range close to the tropics, with a wall of thunderstorms constantly developing along its front. Leaving final instructions for Marlyn and Noreen, and letting them make their goodbyes to their husbands and sons in private, Mirikami edged away from the Avenger and Beagle, drifting down towards the planet.

Mirikami initially intended to use the Normal Space drive, powered by tachyon energy, and settle more slowly into atmosphere than a normal space craft would do. At a sufficiently low altitude, about thirty-five thousand feet, they would be near the highest cloud tops of mature anvil top thunderstorms, and could switch to weaker but more precisely controlled manual thruster power, and descend down to the most turbulent and thus most concealing levels of the cumulonimbus clouds. Then, staying above the mountain peaks, vector along the line of storms to the northeast until they were almost over the destination mountain range. The next step was to carefully drop below the cloud base, behind the peaks on the Krall controlled side, and use the mountains to screen them from the PDC radar and sensors on the other side for as long as possible. From there they could travel horizontally, using passes and staying clear of the mountain peaks visually, until near the part of the range where Reynolds had found the box canyon for them. Mirikami wanted to avoid using any active radar or laser scans because that would negate the stealth approach.

The first two phases worked as planned, and they were soon moving along the weather front, embedded in the thunderheads and moving slowly and carefully on thruster power. They had ample fuel, and were unconcerned with the waste. The ride was surprisingly even, because the ship was massive compared to the force of the vertical and horizontal gusts, and the attitude thrusters were quick to adjust for dips or updrafts. Going from one storm to the next, the Mark had drawn to within a hundred and fifty miles of the mountain range.

The plan was proceeding perfectly. Until suddenly, it wasn't.

****

The Darpot finger clan was at last receiving their hard won opportunity to fight humans in more than a two or three day raid. Their now experienced raiders would have use of mini tanks, command their own artillery defense, scout drones, armored transports for warriors, missile equipped single ships, and slave Prada to build underground bunkers for their training, to be conducted on the human world below. After practice in coordinated movements and attacks, and learning the new tactics used here, they could join with larger more powerful and storied clans, conducting weeks or months long assaults on the worthy foe.

First, Hortak, the senior warrior and a sub leader of the young finger clan, needed to deliver their new equipment safely to the rugged terrain they would use for training. Their two clanships would penetrate the enemy defenses on Poldark using the strategies described to them on Telda Ka. Hortak's own clanship was transporting the equipment his warriors must master if they were to participate alongside the great clans in this still young and evolving war. The bulk of his more experienced cadre of raiders was on the second clanship.

Each ship would swiftly penetrate the enemy orbital defenses before they could react, and then separate to divide their attackers focus for in-atmosphere defense. This was the aggressive tactic most often used they were told, learned while listening to experienced pilots on Telda Ka, who had run the gauntlet many times.

After establishing a command post in a mountainous region, his young warriors would learn how to use the equipment on that terrain, following the advice of the experienced warriors assigned to them from other clans, as ordered by the Gatlek. This latter requirement, to accept outside leadership, would be harder to endure than mastering the equipment, subjugating their natural instinct to destroy the enemy to commands from other clans, telling them when to hold back.

The conditions they had to meet, to participate in the larger war, were to submit to the will of Gatlek Pendor's overall strategy, who in turn was obeying Tor Gatrol Kanpardi edicts, handed down from the joint clan council. Hortak knew the chain of command had set this course for the war, that fighting was limited by design, as part of achieving the goal of following the Great Path with greater efficiency. However, *knowing* that, and *feeling* that it was right were two different things.

On past raids, he and his warriors had rampaged to their fierce dual hearts content, killing and destroying humans and their beloved objects with abandon. It *felt* glorious. Here, the goal was to bleed the enemy more slowly, allowing the clever and ever changing enemy to slowly eliminate the less adaptable Krall warriors from the lists of highest status breeders. The killing rampages could still happen in an assault, but just as the enemy line broke to retreat, they would be recalled, allowing their foe a chance to recover. *That* was a discipline they needed to learn, and which Hortak himself found repulsive to obey.

He entered atmosphere, ahead of the missiles and railguns that sought his ship, heedless of the flashing plasma and laser beams that could only find them by random chance. He was seeking the aid of weather or terrain to evade the next level of defenses, when he must proceed slower, and for which there was a measure of predictability for the enemy, if he was careless.

A large weather front was slowly passing over the territory the Krall had conquered, cutting across the very mountain range that was his general goal for a landing site. The tracking methods the clever humans had devised could see his back trail now, and he was changing track often and sharply as he descended rapidly. The heavy load of equipment made the clanship less responsive than usual, and his sensors had detected missile launches from human lines closer to the mountains, where he wished to go. Somehow, the humans could feed the information from his past disturbances of the atmosphere to the missiles, and they would aim for where he was expected to be next.

He remained on the tachyon powered reactionless space drive, despite the drain on additional energy available for plasma cannons, and the less precise maneuvering possible at lower speeds. The plasma cannons would have to make do with fusion power alone, because evasion held higher priority than beam power right now. The humans had recently introduced missiles that had a means to follow behind a clanship that was using thruster power, seeming to operate like a Krall on a scent trail. Staying on the space drive in atmosphere countered that innovation. At least until time to actually land, when only normal thrusters provided the fine control needed.

He dove into the storm clouds on a path away from the missiles and the mountains, and then, inside that turbulent concealment, sharply reversed course. The jolt of uncompensated inertia, from the sudden reverse acceleration, was a severe strain on his ability to hold onto his stabilization post by his control console. If the other warriors aboard, unaware of what direction he would turn next, were unprepared, slamming into a bulkhead could disable them, or even cause death if unable to flip to land feet first. Any lack of readiness on their part was of no concern to him, acting as pilot. As mission commander, Hortak had two flight qualified K'Tals with him, but their expertise was more with the new equipment than with pilot skills, and he had spent years as a K'Tal pilot, before advancing to sub leader. He trusted his own piloting ability more than theirs.

Racing through the storm, he checked his sensors for the missile tracks, and was satisfied that they had so far stayed outside the weather front, still on a vector towards where his last track suggested he was headed. He switched sensor mode to seek his other clanship, and found it hundreds of miles away, also using the two thousand mile line of weather as cover, but moving away from his own goal of the mountain range.

If the other ship continued in that direction, they might have to land and use ground transport to join up with him in the mountains. That would waste days in starting their training. The K'Tal pilot of that other ship might find herself performing some unpleasant maintenance duties, normally reserved for the Prada slaves.

That last thought immediately forced him to rethink his punishment detail for Gordok, the K'Tal flying the other clanship. She was carrying the Prada, and if he wanted them to arrive alive, she *had* to avoid the type of hard acceleration Hortak had just applied to his own ship.

He would simply have to shuttle his warriors over to his operations area two hands at a time, or request some ground transports from local Krall clans. Using a clanship for such transport duty was too wasteful of their value, when subjected to human missiles or artillery if they flew atmospheric operations. Hortak's immediate ground transportation problem was that it was all on his ship, and he only had two small shuttles to move his 2048 warriors and 512 Prada on the second clanship. He only had 128 warriors and K'Tal on his own ship, due to the space required for the heavy weapons, construction equipment and bunker building materials.

Hortak wanted to look at what else was ahead of him, and before switching off the sensor mode he used to find his partner clanship, he surprisingly detected a second clanship, moving very slowly through storm clouds, closer to the mountains. The missiles fired at his ship had completely passed the other ship by, without any sign of detection. Changing sensor mode, he saw that the clutch of six missiles, rather than pursue his distant companion ship deeper into Krall held territory, had been fed the new turbulence traces of his last maneuver, and were turning to chase him. Two hunter-seekers had already entered the line of the weather front, and were no doubt seeking a scent trail of the ions left behind by any use of thrusters, which he was not using.

With a flash of insight, Hortak remembered what his sensors had shown him of the other clanship. He checked again, to make certain it was still true.

Yes! That other clan had used a clever slow approach to slip by the human detection systems, which could identify air turbulence. However, they had switched to thruster control, perhaps for the finer precision it provided at low speed and in landing. Except that if a "sniffer" missile happened to pass near them in the clouds, it would then fly right up their slowly moving, ion-spewing rear end.

There was no way of knowing, without calling them, which clan that ship belonged to, and besides, calling them would spoil how Hortak intended to use their mistake to his advantage. He continued to jink left and right, up and down at random, but increased his speed in the direction of the mountains, and towards the other ship. He might draw more missiles after him by increasing his turbulent path, but he would soon divert their attention from himself. *The adaptable warrior would live to earn higher status and breed better warriors*, Tor Gatrol Kanpardi had said.

****

Mirikami had kept his console suite actively seeking human threats from missile launches by Poldark defenders. The dark, moisture-laden clouds made long-range plasma cannon bolts or laser beams unlikely to be effective and the space planes, from the Navy carrier, would generally not fly over Krall controlled territory.

Another console was monitored by Thad, who was looking for any Krall clanship or single ship activity below or around them, while Dillon looked at the orbital picture. Sarge had the task of watching the approaching mountain range for any possible fighting or activity there, Krall or human, which could interfere with finding the canyon they were seeking for a sheltered landing site.

Dillon was the first to report the White Out of two stealthed clanships at only one hundred miles out, already in the lower ionosphere and at the outer fringe of tenuous real atmosphere. The slightly lower gravity than Earth for Poldark allowed its mesosphere to extend a bit higher than a heavier planet's upper wisps of gasses. The two ships promptly diverged and plunged right into the atmosphere at high speed, in a typical Krall aggressive move. Other than a lower than normal exit point, based on Mirikami's observations over the last several days, it wasn't highly unusual. The orbital defenses had less chance to attack the two ships, and it was now up to the atmospheric defenders to try to knock either of the stealthed craft out of the sky.

Mirikami tensed as he watched a half dozen missile launches leave the ground in human controlled territory, less than a hundred miles beyond the mountains he was approaching. Those would have to pass near them, enroute to intercept the two clanships. He waited to see if he would need sudden evasive action, or use his plasma and laser fire for defense. Both of those weapon systems were armed and ready if needed. The missiles passed by harmlessly, twenty or thirty miles away as they hunted the two clanships. Both of the other ships dove into the turbulent clouds for what cover they offered, the stealth capability making them invisible to radar, and like the Mark of Koban, they used the storms to diffuse or conceal their detectable turbulence paths after that.

Thad was the one to notice that the two ships initially went the same direction in the line of weather, directly away from them. Then he saw a change.

"Whoops! The clanship six hundred forty miles behind us suddenly pulled one hell of a reverse course, and is now moving our way, picking up speed."

Mirikami looked over at his screen. "I see him on your display, and the missiles just went past him…," he paused as he watched. "No, all of them are turning wide to follow him. The second ship must be too far ahead or too deep into the Krall defenses. All six of them are after him now."

"He's zigzagging, Tet, spreading his turbulence trail, but he's also picking up speed. The Turb detection system will see him even better at higher speed. Those missiles are definitely on his trail now, and two have actually entered the clouds behind him."

Tet swore. "Damn, it's bringing them closer to us. I don't know where they intend to land, but with those missiles chasing them, the mountains are their best bet to duck below detection. If we slow more and hover where we are, we might see them all go right past us, except that leaves us sitting ducks if we are detected. If we run for it, our turbulence will definitely make us another target."

He thought a moment. "I believe that bastard in the clanship is deliberately leading them towards us. He can see us as easily as we see him, and he speeded up once he turned in our direction. That made him a better target to track. The Krall don't have much loyalty outside of their clan and to the race in general. That ship commander is perfectly capable of letting us take the hits so he can escape."

"What if we fire on him first?" asked Reynolds.

Tet shook his head. "Of course he would shoot back, and the Krall forces on the ground might not like the clan in-fighting and come to investigate, particularly if we knock him down. We don't want that scrutiny. What bothers me, if he's diverting the missile attack onto us, is that he seems to expect the missiles to detect our ship, even though we are making very little turbulence, and are cloaked from radar. Those same missiles passed us by five minutes ago, but were outside the storm clouds. I'm worried our tech people have found another way to home in on a clanship up close, even if stealthed. Any ideas anyone? We only have a few minutes to decide to stand or run."

In the pregnant moment as everyone thought, Jakob, instilled with the program instructions Mirikami had given Jake, the "parent" AI it was cloned from, employed a communications protocol established years before. The AI didn't wait for a question to be directed specifically to him if it had pertinent information to offer.

"Sir, we are using thrusters, and the approaching clanship is not. Could our exhaust ions…," Mirikami, not waiting for the sentence to end, acted without hesitation.

He switched on the Normal Space reactionless drive as he cut the reaction thrusters. The interval before the tachyon-powered drive altered the gravitational field to support them, allowed them to start a free fall causing everyone's stomach to flutter, and to instinctively clutch at something even though they were all secured in acceleration couches. Everyone grabbed on except Mirikami, who not only expected the sensation, but also had spent a career in space. They fell for a time.

Mirikami shouted a warning as they dropped. "Jakob says the clanship isn't using thrusters. I think our ion trail will lead the missiles up our tail pipe. The Normal Space drive will slow our drop…," he grunted as it did just that with a jolt.

He rapidly tapped some recently practiced navigation instructions as he talked. "I'm programming in a hard series of turns and high acceleration, to put some distance between us and that clanship, and to distance us from the missiles after him. We need to get our butts down into that canyon before they can home on our turbulence trail. Carson grab my hand, Ethan take Sarge's and don't let loose. Here we go."

Mirikami tapped the console a final time to activate the course he'd laid in, and he barely made it back to a horizontal position when a stunning kick slammed him sideways against the restraints with nearly rib cracking force, before the axis of thrust rotated to deliver the thrust from under their bodies. He grunted in pain, as he heard other cries and whooshes of air as breath was knocked out of the others. He didn't black out, but it was close, and the acceleration pressure wasn't letting up yet. Acceleration couch or not, this was grueling pressure, even for a genetically enhanced Second Generation Kobani.

He forced himself to concentrate on the details of the landing, the sequence of actions he'd have to take to descend rapidly and safely into the canyon, to remain clear of the high walls and miss the huge boulders Sarge had said littered the ground. This is what he'd have to raise up to do when the ship reached a point vertically over the box canyon and halted. The next surges and turns would be progressively more brutal, because of the speed they were building. The rapid stop at the end might literally be a killer.

The next turn threw them to the other side of their couches, with more grunts of pain. The Smart chair's self-molding contours were not designed to adjust so quickly, unable to react to such extremes of forces applied so suddenly. Mirikami did briefly lose his vision for a moment, his sight dimming as he lost peripheral vision, and he seemed to be staring into a darkening tunnel. This was despite the pressure he exerted internally by bearing down with his chest and abdominal muscles, to force a higher blood flow to his brain, fighting to stay conscious.

He lost out to that effort on the next even harder switch back, and blanked out for five or ten seconds. He regained his senses as they accelerated the last five miles to the target point. He knew the next kick would come from what would feel like below him, as the ship rotated to fly rear-end towards the direction they were now traveling. The Olt'kitapi designed navigation system was waiting to apply a final maximum thrust, which would rapidly slow and halt them over their target point.

The couch would provide the most cushioning possible from the bottom directed counter thrust, but Mirikami now knew without a doubt, based on the previous forces he'd just experienced, that he would be unaware of the world for some time after that, if ever again. He would feel nothing when the ship dropped to the floor of the canyon.

****

Hortak gnashed his dagger teeth together and his red pupils blazed like hot coals on an onyx orb. The cursed other clanship had started moving, their thruster engine cut off, replaced by the tachyon-powered drive. His own ship now had no choice but to continue through the cloud of spreading ions the other ship had just vacated. The pursuing human missiles would continue after his ship, although they would likely spread out a bit as they encountered the exhaust fumes the other ship left behind.

The other ship was now accelerating hugely, and conducting stressful high-speed turns that would strain any Krall. Although this activity would draw the attention of the human tracking systems, the only close threats the other ship faced were those already on Hortak's tail. The missiles had to go through or past his ship if they would attack the other target, and they were *not* going to pass up his slower, heavier loaded target to do that.

The questions he had now are where was that ship going, and what had been its original destination? It was accelerating at two-thirds of its maximum rate now, and would shoot past the mountains and out of the edge of the storm front in a short time. It would be streaking over the remaining human controlled third of this land mass. Making it a speeding but easily targetable object, with an extremely turbulent trail to point the way it was moving. It appeared bent on a berserker's death, going down in a blaze of glory.

Then the clanship's pilot appeared to have decided to kill the ship and himself, even before meeting the enemy! In an act that would leave every warrior aboard unconscious, with the pilot insensate and collapsed on the command deck, the clanship reversed nose for tail and applied maximum acceleration to come quickly to a halt over the far edge of the mountain foothills. It rapidly dropped from the sky.

He waited for a fireball to rise higher than the near peaks, assuming it would explode on impact, as a ship heavily laden with arms and ammunition might do. However, Hortak saw only a geyser of dirt and dust as it slammed into the ridges below his own line of sight, as he approached the higher peaks still ahead of him.

With his diversion now eliminated, his pursuit of the other clanship meant he too was running out of room to make a landing in the mountains. He either had to mimic, to a safer extent, the other ship's last desperate action, or pull up and pass back through the orbital gauntlet to make his escape to space. Then he would have to perform another penetration later, and leave his finger clan looking inept to Gatlek Pendor.

As he passed over the last of the high peaks, staying barely in the churning dark cloud bases as the updraft came up the steep rocky slopes, he dropped below the mountain crest on the other side, now shielding his turbulent wake from the pursuing missiles.

He could see the dust still settling from the other ship's crash site, being blown away rapidly by storm gusts, and collected by the mass of heavy raindrops falling. He made his decision. He would use the other ship's sudden disappearance and dust to help conceal his own landing site. He flipped his ship end-for-end and applied his own savage reverse thrust. Not as strong as the other ship had used, somewhat less than maximum. With the heavy load he carried, the deceleration of all that inertia wasn't disabling for him, but it was painfully difficult, and it stressed his ability to the limit to complete a safe manual landing. He selected a steep walled canyon, miles from where the other ship had crashed, and set down, with only a slight brush against a cliff side. Fortunately, there were no rock falls or boulders to avoid on the narrow valley floor.

He cut thrust as the craft settled on its landing jacks, automatically adjusting for a slight slope due to his proximity to the sidewall. The wind whipped over the top of the cliff two hundred feet above the nose of his ship, shearing away the dust, as it had done for the other crash-landed clanship. Thirty seconds later, the first of the six missiles flashed over him on sensor readings, still embedded in the clouds. The other five missiles passed by in the same manner, spreading apart as they vainly sought new traces of his wake turbulence, chasing down vortices cause by nature. Low on fuel, the reusable rockets turned toward human lines, where they could be serviced and reused.

Hortak was on the wrong side of the mountains from where he'd intended to train his warriors, but that only meant they had farther to travel to join up with him. This was still conquered territory, equally suited for training. He would radio to find out where his second ship had landed, but *after* the enemy missiles had withdrawn from the area.

Chapter 2: Box Canyon

"Tet, can you hear me?" Dillon had only just recovered, and was concerned for his older and still motionless friend. Thad was trying to fumble his own couch release switch, to rise to his feet and check on the still form of the captain, across the four-way control console from him. Reynolds was clearly breathing, and making snoring sounds, but had not moved yet. Mirikami was so still that neither Dillon nor Thad, having just regained their senses, could detect any sign he was breathing.

Suddenly Dillon had another thought, of even more concern to him personally. Where were their two sons? "Carson and Ethan aren't on their couches." He looked around the Bridge, and the four SGs were the only people he could see.

Thad carefully placed his feet on the floor, and felt dizzy as he tried to stand. Nevertheless, he leaned around to look at the deck below the couches where their two son's had ridden next to Mirikami and Reynolds, and they were not down on the deck. "They aren't here. Did we crash? I blacked out when we hit that last hard thrust."

Dillon looked around, moving his head carefully. "The deck seems level, and I don't see any damage."

Thad was holding onto Reynolds' couch, working his unsteady way to Mirikami. Dillon sat up and rubbed his temples, trying to erase the headache that action had caused. Reynolds mumbled something, and moved a hand. The three of them were awake or rousing, but Mirikami was disturbingly still. He was the oldest member of the crew, and the possibility of a stroke from the acceleration stress was on both of their minds.

Thad reached Mirikami's couch and touched his right hand and forehead. They were warm, but how long did it take a body to cool? He still didn't see his chest rising, but even if he did, there could be brain damage.

He and Dillon were both startled when a form flew up a stairwell, and in mid flip called out, "Hi Dad. You and Uncle Thad finally getting off your butts?"

Dillon, made further light-headed simply trying to follow his son's fast movement, asked, "Where did you go, son? Tet needs help."

"Dad, I think he's fine, I Mind Tapped him all the way down, and he was simply unconscious. Like all of you old 'classic' SGs were. Ethan and I checked you all afterwards, and Ethan already knew Sarge was OK since he had his hand."

"Afterwards?" Thad asked. "We landed OK?" It seemed like a dull stupid question, even to his muddled thinking. The ship was upright and they were alive. Crashed, toppled and dead was the alternative.

Carson answered, cocky and with a laugh, "Sure. Why wouldn't we? I had Uncle Tet's directions and images fresh in my mind, and Ethan had Sarge's pictures of what the box canyon looked like. The ship came to a halt almost directly over the correct spot, and as it started to drop, I rotated to vertical as Uncle Tet had showed me, used the attitude and rear thrusters to center and rotate us as Ethan fed me Sarge's images of the obstacles and hidden base entrances. I matched that to the video on the screen of the ground and set us down. Fast, and in a swirl of dust."

Dillon questioned his son, "You got all of that before Tet passed out?"

"Not all. Even out like a light, we can pick up a person's recent images, and Uncle Tet was running all sorts of potential problems through his mind before he passed out. I used some of that information to choose the rotation and shifted us closer to where Sarge remembered the concealed down ramp doors are located."

As he spoke, he walked over to Mirikami and touched his left hand. The captain immediately took a deep breath, and his eyes fluttered.

"What did you just do to him?" his father asked.

"Oh. He was agitated when he was losing control of his body before that last hard thrust, so once he was out I fed him some soothing images to ease his worry. After we landed, I settled his thoughts with pleasant images and memories, so he went into a deep sleep, dreaming. Just now I sent him a mild wake up call."

Even though Sarge was already moving his hands nervously, his eyes fluttering, Carson stepped around and touched his hand. Reynolds opened his eyes, coughed, and reached down to release his seat restraints. He stayed down but had a comment. "I don't hurt so much, so I guess Tet's idea worked?"

"It seems it did." They heard Mirikami say. He flipped his own seat release, but Dillon, smiling, placed a hand on his friend's chest to keep him prone.

"Don't sit up too fast, like I did. It gave me a brief headache and made me dizzy. How was your nap?"

"Annoying now that I'm aware I took one. However, the dream was nice. I haven't been home in over thirty years. The cherry blossoms from my youth were beautiful. You found that event while digging around did you?" He was looking at Carson, a smile on his face, but with a penetrating look at his godson.

"Uh…, Uncle Tet, you popped that picture up when I asked your unconscious mind what you thought was pretty and pleasant. Pink flowers, raining from those trees is the image you sent back to me. I just suggested you sleep and dream about them. I wasn't prying, honest."

"You didn't notice anyone with me in the image?"

"No. Why? I was in a hurry because the ship was dropping."

"Good, Michiko and I are pleased you did *not* observe the rest of our tryst in that orchard." He grinned, as Carson turned beet red beneath the inherited natural olive coloration of his mother, and his own deep Koban suntan.

Dillon laughed at his son's discomfort. "If you ever have a reason to send me to sleepy land, don't ask me that. The return mental images could scar your delicate young mind for life."

The reddening deepened, as Thad, chuckling, clapped Carson on the back in a reassuring manner. "Good job, lad. Did you see what happened to that Krall ship behind us?"

Gulping down his embarrassment, relieved by the subject change, he answered. "Yes Sir. On the sensors, I did. It ducked down below the mountain peaks to hide after it crossed, and it's apparently five and a half miles northwest of us in a straight line, in another valley. The walking distance is more like double that far, because of other ridges in between."

"All six missiles missed them?" Mirikami asked.

"I think so. I didn't switch sensor mode to look for them until Ethan and I checked on you four. They were gone when I did check, perhaps fifteen seconds later."

"Then we probably have an intact clanship close by, with an unknown complement aboard, and they know where we are. They won't be cordial to us as another clan, and won't expect us to be with them, since they tried to send the PDC's missiles after us. That could mean they'll keep their distance, but with the Krall attitude that all warfare is fun, it may just be water over the bridge and forgotten. I won't feel comfortable leaving the ship with a light force for defense, if most of us leave to make contact with the PU Army."

"I agree," Thad said. "We have the most force we can apply right now, before we split up, and they know they are well inside Krall held territory. That should put them more at ease. They won't expect an attack from us here." He turned to Carson.

"Was anyone below hurt by the rough evasion and landing? How about Chief Haveram?"

"Ethan is checking on him now. As for the TGs, there were a few bruises. Careless people that unstrapped because the ride was so smooth at first. If we didn't have carbon nanotubes in our bones, I think we'd have some broken arms and legs."

Mirikami, reminded of his man in the engine room called the com set there, using speaker mode for the others to hear. "Chief, are you OK?"

There was a brief pause, then "Who the hell was flying this crate after we made that last stop? I went out like a broken light. I think we all must have. Ethan just bounced in here, helped me get up and moving, but all he said was that we were down safe, and he left."

"Chief, Carson and Ethan got us down safely after that last hard burst of deceleration. I knew the Third Gens would be able to take anything the Krall could tolerate, and still be able to function. That's why I had you put the extra couches up here."

"Yes, Sir, I had gathered that when I bolted them down up there. However, they don't know how to fly a clanship. You only learned yourself in the last couple of months."

"Carson and Ethan are TG1's. You saw how quickly the TGs learned to do tasks they had not personally tried from them. It works for landing a ship, if someone thinks through the process while they Mind Tap him. I held Carson's hand, he held Ethan's, and Ethan held Sarge's. We had a daisy chain of information sharing going on up here. When Sarge and I blanked out, the boys knew what to do, and had the strength and coordination to apply the knowledge."

"Hell, I'd say give 'em their own ships. Only I don't want to fly with them if that's a sample of what they'll do. *My* bones and body won't take much of that treatment. Of course if I'm in a coma each time it won't hurt all that much." He made a sour laugh.

"You have a point, Chief. Come on up anytime you feel ready. Mirikami out."

He turned to the others. "Gentle Men," he paused as he saw Alyson and Ethan fly up separate staircases, "and Lady, we need to discuss how we SGs nearly got us all killed today."

Surprised, Ethan blurted, "It was your ideas, planning, and then adjustments that made it all work, Sir."

"It was my frailty, and not just my own but of all of us SGs that made it nearly fail. We Second Gens have the experience and knowledge you youngsters need, but our physical presence could have also gotten you killed. The risk goes farther than the tragedy of the loss of our lives and this one ship. We can't afford any such setback in an already lopsided fight to save humanity, not just for Koban, but also for every human world. We need to work out a solution for the problem before we actually go into Krall territory."

"What? Just have them tap us old farts to learn all we know?" Reynolds was proposing that, as much as asking the question.

Carson saw the problem, which the headshake from the captain demonstrated he saw it as well. "When I Tapped the captain, the images of what he was sending me were transferred instantly, but it took some time for him to run through the most likely alternatives and variations that he could think of. I'm sure that he would think of a dozen more things that I'd need to know if something else went wrong, that he couldn't think of in advance."

Mirikami was pleased the boy realized where he was going. "If we lost attitude thrusters in one quadrant, or one of four landing jack's was shot off, I could apply decades of experience to come up with a brand new landing strategy on the fly, to minimize or counter the problem. However, of the thousands of variables involved, no person can think through all of those in advance. What you described, Sarge is in effect, metaphorically sawing our heads open to pour knowledge into the empty TG1 heads…" he glanced at the youngsters with an apologetic grimace.

"Sorry boys, I don't mean that quite the way it sounded."

He continued. "A full lifetime experience transfer isn't possible, or even desirable if we could. They can learn what we know eventually, but they can't become us, and they shouldn't want to do that. We need another way to make sure our experience and knowledge remains available to them."

"Do you have an idea in mind?" Dillon knew Mirikami usually had an answer when he posed these conundrums.

"Possibly. We need to have Maggi, Aldry, and Rafe involved, re-examining the genetic problems we already know about. As a member of their work group and a participant on this mission, Dillon, you should have some insights to offer. We original, entirely man made SGs, did not opt to attempt the Koban bone and muscle genes because of two major reasons, or problems.

"First of all, we were adults. We had no growth spurts left in our lives, so adding Koban genes to grow carbon nano tubes in our bones would take longer and be more difficult and painful for us.

"Secondly, the ripper derived, carbon fiber muscle enhancements would be useless if we can't control them through our ripper derived, yet redundant, organic super conductor nervous system. The growth of the neurons to make the nerves link-up to our brains and new muscle tissue works with the children *born* as SGs. With them, the super conductor nerves are not simply an add-on system, as it is with us factory remodel jobs."

He shrugged. "Even if I can't become a full-fledged TG, if I can be made physically strong enough to do better than simply survive what we did today, to remain awake and contributing, then I can help keep these youngsters safe. Otherwise, physical limitations on our part endanger them, and yet they need us here."

Dillon was nodding as he spoke, in basic agreement. "The new bone growth would be slow, but not as painful as what the TGs went through with the new muscle growth linking to the ripper based nervous system simultaneously. There are fewer nerve endings in our bones related to the second nervous system, and moving would cause only moderate joint pain for a couple of months. We can have stronger bones.

"However, our being harder to break isn't going to help us much if we can't apply the complete muscle improvements, down to the tiniest capillary, eyelids, and even goose bumps. We will still faint under high acceleration if we can't keep our blood pressure up and flowing to our brains. We have to have the carbon fiber tissue for that strength, and to be able to *use* those muscles. The final gene mods didn't work on our test animals.

"Rafe made cripples out of multiple pigs, goats, and even one of those darn kangaroos, trying to implement the superconductor nervous system connections to the carbon muscle tissue, and linking them to the brain at the other end. It was intermittently successful, and inhumanely painful. If you recall, we ate the barbequed results of each of those failed experiments, to avoid the waste of meat."

"I remember." Tet, nodded, a smile touching his face. "Maggi wouldn't eat the meat of the butchered test animals. Claimed it made her feel as callous as a Krall. Then she ate a rhinolo steak cut from an animal Thad had shot the day before. Strange how we dole out our personal definitions of hypocrisy." He waved his hands dismissively.

"We can't do anything about it here, on this mission right now, if at all. Our experts and equipment are on Koban. Perhaps if we can get more advanced med labs and nanites, as Sarge here has said was developed for battle casualties and limb regrowth, our folks can adapt them for our own use."

He carefully raised himself up to reach the control console, and activated the full ring of screens for an external view of their surroundings. The canyon walls rose in gray and tan sheer cliffs on three sides, a few hundred feet higher than the Bridge level. There was a slight narrowing of the cliff walls as the valley floor curved out of sight around a bend in the other direction, about a quarter mile away. There were quite a few large to medium boulders, hundreds of craters from the artillery bombardment Sarge had described, and a few scattered white ceramic pieces of the Krall mini tanks that Sarge called Dragons.

"I don't see any sign of a base out there, or ways to get inside."

"Hell, secrecy was the point when spec ops had it built. There are several tunnel openings hidden among some of those boulder groups, unless the Krall blew them up as they passed this area by. I don't see two big holes in the valley floor, where the hidden down ramps are located. They lead to the underground parking garage, and if the Krall blew the whole place apart, they'd be blown open. Let's go down and take a look."

Tet turned to Chief Haveram, who had arrived by elevator as they had talked. "Chief, keep watch for any activity, human or Krall, and Link to me or any of us right away if you see a threat. If we go into the base, I'll leave someone near the entrance for relay, in case the Link is blocked."

Mirikami reached over to the console and selected a display to show him the location of the still stealthed other clanship. "That ship followed us to these foothills, so we could have visitors. I'm sending some TGs to scout them. We may have to take them on if they get curious about us. I don't want to leave the ship vulnerable. At least you can fly her if necessary, and use the weapons."

"Yes Sir. I'd be more comfortable fighting her than I would be flying her, Captain. But I hope it doesn't come to that."

"Me too. We won't get too far away right now. As we discussed before, Sarge wants to see what was left behind after the final evacuation. We can also verify if the tunnels leading away are intact. I'll be down below with Thad and Dillon, as they choose the scouting team to look at the Krall ship, and we pick a team to go into the base. We'll also have a perimeter set up down near the canyon entrance, and at least two people watching on the cliff tops."

The chief nodded, but had a question. "You left the stealth skin active, but opening a hatch partly negates that, from aerial or space based radars. Do you want the hatches left open for a quick retreat, or closed?"

"Good point. Close those after the teams are out. They can be opened in an instant by you, or manually by keypad if needed. I see the Krall kept their ship in stealth, perhaps because we are near to the human battle lines and more subject to attack."

****

Hortak railed against what he considered offloading inefficiency, as his K'Tals and warriors struggled to unload the equipment stored in the clanship quickly enough to please the sub leader.

They were wise enough, and of low enough status not to voice their counter opinion, that *his* rushed landing of the ship on a slope, close to a cliff face, had rendered one of the four hatches and its ramp unusable for use by their heavy equipment, tanks, and transports. Only light, hand-carried supplies could go down and navigate the sharp turn at the bottom of the ramp closest to the cliff, carried by the reduced complement of one hundred twenty-eight Krall on the heavily loaded and cramped clanship. The large armored troop transports, one-warrior mini tanks, excavation and bunker construction equipment, had to wait slightly longer for lowering to the bottom deck, reassembly, and being driven down one of the three unobstructed ramps.

The assembly process was frustrating, because Hortak had sent *all* of the Prada slaves on the second clanship, now located over a thousand miles away. His K'Tals knew how to train the warriors in the *operation* of the tanks and armored transports. However, the assembly of the equipment, and particularly the operation of the construction equipment, was normally slave work. It was demeaning for a warrior or a K'Tal to perform this task, not to mention the forced admission that even a K'Tal did not know as much as a slave about how the heavy pieces should fit together, and in what order.

After mounting the plasma cannons on all of the ceramic turrets for the mini tanks, they had to remove them all. That was because access through the cannon barrel's turret opening to the adjustable fine tolerance slip ring, inside the turret, was blocked. The tank turrets could not be mounted on the body of the small tanks with the cannon barrels attached.

When the first turret was properly attached to its motorized base unit, its cannon in place, it had to *all* be removed again in order to insert two fusion bottles. The hatch opening at the rear, sized for a warrior to enter or dismount the mini tank, would not pass the two bulky power generators. One bottle for the electric drive motors, another for preheating the plasma chamber and magnetic confinement coils of the ceramic cannon barrel. They needed to go down into the tanks through the wider top opening before the turret was attached. Time was lost.

"Move our tanks and transports farther away from the clanship," Hortak ordered harshly. "If the humans see our radar profile, because the portals are open so long, they are close enough they can launch a missile attack on the clanship before we have safely moved our supplies and equipment away. Our warriors and slaves from the other clanship will require days to arrive here. We cannot successfully defend our position because the slaves need to set up and adjust the two automated laser control consoles, and their mobile batteries. You must work faster."

The Krall, following his orders, were perfectly aware that moving the equipment farther away from the ship and to another nearby valley took more time. They would then have to return a greater distance, and Hortak would blame them for how much that longer trek slowed the unloading.

They knew his attempt to elude the pursuing human missiles, by drawing them after their speeding ship, was intended to divert the human weapons targeting onto another clan's ship. The two K'Tals on the command deck had described the clever plan, and then told how it had unraveled when the second ship performed a near suicidal high acceleration maneuver, outrunning them and the human seeker missiles.

After the missile diversion idea had failed, the necessary extended travel to the "wrong" side of the mountain range brought them closer to human forces. An attack by humans now could disrupt their training mission, before they learned the proper tactics for this new style of war. His clan mates were not particularly pleased with their sub leader at this moment, as he blamed them for his less than optimum decisions. A fatal change in leadership was not out of the question.

That was why Hortak had stationed the next highest status warriors of the new finger clan on the second clanship. They were unavailable for a prompt challenge for the overall leadership role of the mission if he made too many errors. If the small training base were already well under way when they arrived, there would be no grounds for a death match challenge at that time. The sub leader had made some sloppy decisions, although individually none of them was detrimental to his continued higher status, or his life. The day was young, however.

****

"General Nabarone, the two clanships this morning split up, and based on satellite imagery, both appear to have made it down safely, Sir." Major Caldwell, his aide de camp, had made the decision to provide this unsurprising detail to his boss.

"Howard, since you don't normally pass trivia along to muddle my mind, please get to the damned point. What was unusual this time, of the hundred such penetration events every month?" He was grumpy this morning. A battle for a hilly section of territory on the northeastern front was lost last night, and he'd stayed up late to see if the reinforcements he'd sent could help hold the heights. They had not, and now the enemy could fire down on his troops below as they retreated, and they were firing down on supply depots, which also had to be moved back, under fire. Retreat was an unfortunately well-practiced process by now.

"Sir, A third ship, apparently another clanship based on its later turbulence trail size, was detected already deep in the atmosphere, and it probably had slipped in slow and low, using the same line of weather that caused the rain and mud slide problems we had on the Crager Heights last night. If one of the two clanships this morning had not flushed it out, as it swooped towards them with six Seeker Missiles following, it's likely the sneaky one would have landed thirty miles from our eastern lines, close to Novi Sad, completely undetected."

"Just one ship? That isn't a lot of extra force to apply in that region. We are well dug in around Novi Sad. Could there have been more of them we didn't see, you think?"

"Sir, we doubt there could have been many more concealed ships in the fast moving narrow front, but both ships disappeared within a five mile radius of one another. They could link up forces."

"What makes you think they will join forces? You implied the hidden ship was revealed because of the actions of the second arriving ship. That means they didn't sneak in together, and therefore may be from different clans. Although, I'm curious as to how many other sneaky ships may have landed. How many prior to that clumsy commander revealing their operation got past us? We may have a build-up we didn't know was happening. Some of them have started showing a bit of human cunning recently. What is the terrain like, around where they landed and towards Novi Sad?"

The major, having anticipated this, called up map overlays and satellite images of the area, feeding them from his wrist computer to the large tactical screen in the war room.

"The two red dots are the estimated landing areas of the two ships. We lost Turb trails on them when they went below the mountain peaks, and they stayed stealthed, of course. We assume they are within two or three miles of the red dots on the map."

Nabarone expertly assed the terrain. "The foot hills area could conceal a lot of forces, but there isn't a good fast approach to Novi Sad that would let them mount a surprise attack from there. We would see them coming for twenty miles. A heavy artillery barrage would cause them too many losses over that distance. A steady accumulation of massive forces to the south of there, like they used at Crager Heights would work better."

He asked Caldwell a question about something he saw on the map. "That black symbol for an abandoned base of ours, it's within the ring of uncertainty for that first clanship's landing. What kind of base was there before we pulled out?"

The major put a pointer on the icon there, and the AI popped up a long list of details of the former Special Ops base, unglamorously but humorously named SOB-23. The boundaries of the base were superimposed on the map, and the central hub wasn't very impressive in size, but the spider work of tunnels under, and along the ridges and foothills revealed it had a much wider area of influence than the central base otherwise indicated. The outpost was designed for infiltration, as the enemy lines pushed closer, and even shoved past the base. It finally had been completely overrun and abandoned.

Nabarone tapped the transducer behind his ear to activate his Link capability. He spoke to his AI system. "Carla, answer on speaker. How large a diameter are those tunnels leading from the selected base? Could Krall Dragons and armored troop transports be moved along them? Several tunnels extend towards Novi Sad about ten or fifteen miles in length. That could give them avenues to roll up on us a lot closer before we saw them. They'd also have protected underground supply lines."

Of course, her bland reply was instantaneous. A clearly female AI voice was something Nabarone had insisted on being programmed into his system. The subservient roll of men had ended in this war as far as he was concerned, and this was a small symbol, with a woman's name from out of his past added to annoy his superior officers, all of them female. He wasn't bucking for a third star on his collar anyway. That would promote him above his present command, and entail a transfer to wherever that lofty assed rank would take him. He wasn't leaving Poldark.

"Sir, the height of the tunnels is too low to accommodate the armored Krall warrior transports. Any standard Krall truck or halftrack would fit, and Dragons are low enough. However, the mini tanks would fit only with their plasma barrels depressed, and pointed forward or behind. The turrets, with barrels attached, would be unable to rotate more than 40 degrees and the firing elevation is…"

"Stop." Nabarone cut her off. He didn't anticipate the Krall would remotely consider fighting tanks inside a narrow tunnel. However, they might move forces through them into fighting positions fast and undetected.

"Sir," the major offered a reminder. "The base is mined and has Krall body detection sensors. If they enter that, the sensors will blow and collapse the main base and any tunnels they enter. They'd lose the equipment, which they often seem to value more than the warriors inside the tanks or trucks."

"Right! But, I damn well won't risk a major city and a war-manufacturing center if the Krall have found a way to fool our sensors or disable the explosives. What sort of sensors do we have in there, and how much remote control do we have over the areas we mined? If we could let them *think* they could use the base, I'd be happy to let them fill tunnels with columns of tanks and trucks before we brought it all down."

"The spec ops commander would be able to say, Sir. They gave us control of the base, but continued to use the tunnels even after the Krall controlled those hills. They would pop out to conduct surveillance, direct artillery strikes, plant explosives, and release spy bots. They even managed to capture some wounded Krall warriors."

With a wave of annoyance, Nabarone was ready to dismiss any cooperation from that source. "Those shits from Heavyside don't answer to me. The pentagon put them outside Army control. They only share what they want me to know. I know Colonel Trakenburg is field testing secret human enhancements, and they don't want the rest of the Hub to know what they are up to on Heavyside. They mainly come here to test them in a live combat situation. I can see some of their results, and they know that I can see that. Yet they still won't admit what they are doing. I don't *care* if they are doing some illegal human physical improvements. I just want *my troops* to get them so they will be able to kill Krall faster, and stop their damned advance."

"Sir, if they have abandoned the base, then I don't see why they wouldn't share how it's set up for demolition. It also must have a complement of spy bots inside to report to them, although I doubt their people actually use the tunnels any more. They'd have to infiltrate ten miles behind the Krall offensive lines just to reach the closest of them now. The Krall would sniff them out before they got very far. I'll contact Trakenburg's command post on your behalf, if you wish, Sir."

"Do that, and tell him about the clanship landings near that base. I want to be certain they can prevent Krall use of their base against us."

****

Thad sent Ethan and Richard Yang to scout the other clanship. Rather than follow the valley floors, they were going to travel in nearly a straight line, up and down multiple intervening high ridges for speed. They would be within Link range the entire way, although Jakob told them their Link transmissions might fade out on the valley floors as they drew closer to the clanship, which was five miles away. However, they would be able to receive from Jakob the entire way, and transmit from ridge tops.

Twenty TGs, with Conrad Boston as the sole TG1 with them as group leader, were sent to the valley opening with Krall plasma rifles, using the boulders and rocky outcrops for cover. Thad reminded the green kids that underbrush might block them visually, but not from Krall infrared vision, and certainly not from any return fire the Krall would use. Conrad Mind Tapped Colonel Greeves for what they needed to do. The thought transfer process was spread out over a fifteen-minute rapid-fire question and answer period.

Conrad spent less than two minutes total, passing all of that imagery and information to the other nineteen TGs. He used a double handgrip with his outstretched left and right hands, as the other TGs circled him and reached in to make hand contact.

Dillon, Thad, and Mirikami were once again amazed at how fast and easy it was to provide these youngsters with detailed training and tactics. The forward watchers in the valley would warn of any Krall that entered the canyon, staying concealed, and then shut the door to block their escape when a hundred other TGs ambushed the interlopers along the length of the valley, using shared tactics that Sergeant Reynolds furnished them.

Carson and fifteen TGs were going with the four SGs to explore the empty spec ops base. Reynolds led them to where he said were concealed down ramps, right in front of the back wall of the cliff. He stepped over to a waist high boulder on the left of a faint track-way, and on its side, popped open a small cover, revealing a simple touch pad. He put a thumb to the pad, and with almost no sound, the left side surface dropped down to form a thirty-degree ramp, with a back opening high enough to pass a sizable truck.

“Is that coded to your thumb print, Sarge?” Mirikami asked, curious if any of the rest of them could operate the mechanism.

“No. If you’re human, and know where the pad is hidden, you can get inside with a touch. This leads to an underground parking garage, and there is added security after that. ” He closed the small cover, which looked seamless when shut.

“Notice the roadway, or dirt way I should say.” He prompted. “It’s artificial, including the weeds and tufts of grass, but looks real, and doesn’t leave tire tracks or foot prints. Not for the last hundred feet in fact, if you look back where we just walked.” Glancing rearward, there was no sign that twenty people had just trod this way.

Reynolds strode confidently down the broad ramp, and disappeared into the shadows as they followed him down. As the last person left the ramp, Reynolds operated another touch pad to raise the ramp as silently as it had lowered. They were briefly in deep gloom, with only some faint ceiling panels providing dim, red colored light. Another touch pad suddenly brightened the parking area to near daylight conditions, as the entire ceiling glowed with a pale white light.

"These lights switch off the instant a ramp is activated." He showed them markings painted on the floor that indicated where the second ramp would lower, to provide a two way up/down roadway for people or equipment.

Pointing to several openings along the back wall, on either side of the ramp's hydraulic pistons, he said, "These are personnel tunnels that lead back to concealed rabbit holes along the canyon floor. There are branches that lead you up to trap doors behind clumps of boulders. I used this very corridor the day we ambushed the sixteen Dragons that saw us duck into the mouth of the canyon. We parked down here, and ran back that tunnel to spring the trap, and called a mass of prearranged artillery down on them even before we fired our rockets."

He reflexively rubbed his left arm, recalling what had happened to him not long after that ambush. He'd been captured fleeing the area, losing his left arm in that explosive process. It had been regrown after he was rescued by these people, now his friends, on Koban. However, he remembered the pain and being without an arm for months.

"OK people," he turned towards the doors on the other wall. "Let's see what was left behind. Anyone that sees a rat, mouse, large insect, bird, snake, frog, or any other small creature, must be alert for the possibility that it could be a spy bot, and potentially a means for us to make contact with the Poldark military." He went over to one of the personnel sized doors, rather than one suited for a truck, and used a thumb pad while looking into a retinal scanner. The door promptly slid opened.

"I think my retinal pattern is on store here in the computer, but I've seen newcomers also get right in, so there may be a planet wide data base. It might simply be a way to verify that I'm a live human and not just a dead hand on the thumb pad. The spec ops folks that let us use the base were pulling out, and didn't much care what we did here. They warned us that if we let the Krall follow us down that we'd better find a way out fast."

He led them through the door and along a wide corridor that went past empty, open rooms with wires protruding from walls and ceilings, where equipment and computers had been removed. There were a few items of dilapidated furniture left behind, some scraps of paper and signs on the walls. Reynolds turned into a large room and stopped to look around.

"This was a command center, with satellite feeds, secure, jam-proof landline communications, several AIs, and screens all over the place. However, right over here, around this corner is what I'm looking for, I think. I hope they didn't tear it out when they left."

He went around the corner, into an open side room off the main area, then smiled and nodded. Mirikami and the others joined him, looking at a large relief map of the area, as if an x-ray had been made from overhead, fifteen miles up, with the network of tunnels revealed along the ridges, and crossing under valley floors in some cases.

"Obviously we're here." He pointed at the nexus of most of the tunnels, although there were some smaller hubs where ridges intersected and other tunnels split off. "Novi Sad is east southeast from here, about forty miles to the river along the outskirts, and there was a sizeable suburban area on this side of the Solda River, perhaps thirty miles from us."

He ran fingers along the map. "These three tunnels are large, and they go more than halfway to the edge of the housing areas and some former industrial parks. Even before I was captured, they had all been evacuated by the civilians, and the military was preparing for urban warfare there, to hold Novi Sad as long as possible. It's very hilly over there and the terrain in between us and there is rather exposed, open farmland mostly. That's why the supply tunnels were dug, to avoid attacks by single ships on convoys headed to this area, supporting our forces holding the mountains, and later just these foothills as we were shoved back.

"I think we can head towards the current front lines through them, but from there, we'll have to figure out a way through the fighting from behind the Krall. They tend to push sporadically in limited fronts of three to ten miles wide, when a single clan is carrying the load of fighting along a hundred mile front. The other clans normally hold in place, to let the other clan draw all the action. When that dies down, another clan, possibly several hundred miles away, takes their turn. There will be four to six of the single-clan shoves going on somewhere on the continent every day. We could most likely infiltrate through the rear of a clan not part of an assault. The spec ops troops do it somehow, and they don't have the ability of a TG."

Mirikami considered that last remark. "They can't do it by direct confrontation with a warrior unless they have a sure-fire, quiet method of assassinating a guard, so it must be by stealth. I wonder how they get around their superior sense of smell."

"Oh, that. I was told that because so much of the area where the Krall are fighting us has recently been under human control, and there are so many dead that their sense of smell becomes less sensitive. I've also heard spec ops use pressurized cans of 'eau de suer' to temporarily overwhelm the Krall sense of smell."

Dillon barked a hard laugh. "Sewer water? Really?"

Reynolds looked at him with a grin. "Like Maggi might say, 'you don't have any couth.' Not sewer you lunk head, it's the French word for sweat. Suer, you illiterate barbarian." He chuckled at having sucked him into a joke.

Dillon had only lame repartee to offer. "Ha! Raise *your* arms and you'd knock out an octet all by yourself."

Thad, never a man to avoid fart jokes added, "This entire subject stinks to high heaven."

Mirikami had to break it up before the surrounding young TGs jumped in with their own youthful enthusiasm. "Enough guys," he said sharply, cutting off the laughter.

"Sarge, can you show us which tunnel is most likely to take us close to where we need to be? Please, you go first..., so we can follow our noses." The youngsters found the bit of irreverence from their normally staid captain hilarious, for more than a full minute.

As Reynolds led them along the same corridor as before, Mirikami checked his Link with Chief Haveram. “Chief, have you heard from Ethan or Richard, or anything of interest from Conrad at the valley entrance?”

The reply was comfortingly prompt, and sounded strong, even underground. There was probably a Link repeater built into the base, since the PU Army also used transducers. “Conrad has seen no Krall activity,” the chief told him. “Ethan has checked in as they topped each ridge. Those boys are *fast*. Up one side and down the other in five minutes. If the cliffs are like these around us, they must have goat genes in them as well. They saw nothing in the first three valleys, but could hear sounds of machinery rolling on gravel from beyond the next ridge they had to climb.”

Mirikami thought for a moment, mentally counting the number of ridges between them and the Krall clanship, which he recalled from the aerial images recorded as they landed. “Chief, that would be two valleys closer to us than where the clanship landed. They may be threading their way through the valleys to reach us, using some sort of transports they carried with them. I want to hear what Ethan reports as soon as he can see what’s happening.”

“Will do Sir. Shouldn’t be more than another fifteen minutes.”

When Mirikami was obviously finished listening to his Link, Thad asked what he’d heard. “Ethan and Richard find some activity?”

“They heard some sounds from a valley located well before they reached the Krall ship. It was described as mechanical, like rolling trucks on gravel or rocks. We might have company coming, with transports or Dragons. Let’s see the tunnel ahead, and then head back. We were not setting off towards Novi Sad right now anyway.”

Reynolds said, “If they have Dragons, Tet, your TGs can’t pop them open, or even get close. We might have to abandon the Mark and get everyone down here.”

“If they are bent on attacking us, I’d agree, but I don’t see why they would have a plan to do that if they believe us only to be from a different clan. We’ll head back as soon as we see the tunnel.”

“We’re almost there. There’s another underground parking area on this side of the base. We passed under the back wall of the box canyon, and on the other side of these doors ahead is another larger garage. The bigger vehicle supply tunnels run from there. Why don’t we see if you can open the door this time?”

Mirikami thumbed the pad, while peering into the retinal scanner. It took slightly longer than the process had for Reynolds earlier, but the door slid open, and the same style pale white light panels activated. On the other side was a parking area, four times the size of the first one, with seven tunnels leading out along three walls.

Reynolds described the ones they were interested in using. “The three tunnels on the opposite wall all go towards Novi Sad. I can’t say which is best for our purposes, because I don’t know the Krall dispositions at the ends of any of them. The right side tunnel goes a mile or two closer to the river, where there used to be warehouses of supplies to route to the troops fighting in the mountains.”

“Thanks, I can’t say yet which one will be best for us. We’ll see what images we had from orbit, before we made our penetration this morning. I want to head back to the Mark now.” He turned to go back through the opened door when one of the TGs shouted.

"There's an insect running across the ceiling, Sir."

They all looked where he was pointing. It had been invisible until the ceiling panel lights came on and it moved.

It looked more like a small lizard than an insect to Mirikami, when he sighted it, just before it pulled itself up through a hole at the corners of four light panels.

"Sarge, could that have been an actual live critter?" he asked the native-born Poldarkian.

"I've seen live geckos of similar size and color, which have sticky foot pads to walk on walls and ceilings. They were apparently stowaways on some shipments from Earth, since no one admitted to violating the importation of animal rules. They spread all over the place after they first appeared, a couple of hundred years ago I think. That one could have been natural, or a spy bot."

Tet shook his head, and chuckled. "I might have felt stupid, but I wish I could have gone to it and asked it 'to take me to your leader," or something."

He turned again to leave, remarking, "It was probably a real lizard."

****

The corporal said, "Colonel, I should have a group photo and head count for you in a moment. The gecko-bot was waiting for them on the ceiling when the door opened and the lights came on. I had it programed to return to the upload socket as soon as it had an image. It'll also send any audio it picked up. The sound may need some clean up, due to the echoes, but Max will have that ready with the images in a few seconds, Sir."

Trakenburg acknowledged his young bot handler's efficiency. "Good work, son. Route that to me in my office, my eyes only, as soon as the AI has it processed."

He whirled around and stalked into his secure office, closed the door and activated the privacy system, and tapped the large wall screen alive. "Max, do you have an ID on any of the people that entered SOB-23?"

"Yes Sir, one of them appears to be a Sergeant Garland Reynolds, of the PU Army, native to Poldark. I have no match for the thumbprint, retinal scan, or facial image of the man that opened the door to the second parking garage. I am running facial matches for all of the people that I have good features for comparison. Most of them turned to look directly at the gecko-bot when one of them saw it moving. The only match is again apparently for that Sergeant Garland Reynolds."

"Max, you said *apparent* twice for him. Why would you be so unsure? He is or he isn't that man. Thumb print, retina, and face match. How about physical size and body shape?"

"Sir, all of those match except for two significant discrepancies. Sergeant

Reynolds was reported dead over six months ago, and his lower left arm was found still within a piece of his armor in his destroyed halftrack. This man is obviously alive and has a left arm."

"Humph. You have no imagination, Max." A very literal statement when made to an AI. "Arms can be regrown, and deaths misreported or faked. I think you should consider that the man we see in this recording," he looked at the recorded images moving on his high definition wall screen, "to actually be Sergeant Reynolds, alive and well. Now we need to figure out who his companions are, and what they are up to in that old base."

He noticed there were four older men in the group, and they seemed to be leading the clearly younger people behind them. Those young people looked to be in their late teens or early twenties. Although, age was always difficult to discern between middle twenties to early fifties, at least on anyone in this era's gene pool. The youthfulness of those young men and women was obvious. Aside from that mystery, where did they come from? How did they know about that base? What were they doing checking out the tunnels that led towards Novi Sad?

"Max, what do you have in archives for Sergeant Reynolds? Before his purported death."

"Sir, he operated in a guerilla warfare unit, and was briefly allowed use of SOB-23, as you were moving your operatives out, just ahead of the Krall advance. His last reported contact was less than thirty minutes after leading an ambush of sixteen Dragons, which he and his men drew into that same canyon. A later analysis of the unusually sharp Krall response, which followed that attack, determined that it coincided with the apparent loss of the Krall invasion commander in some sort of combat action.

"It would be speculation, Sir, but perhaps Sergeant Reynolds's unit was responsible for that Krall commander's death, and the sergeant's own injury and disappearance shortly after may be related. He was severely wounded if he lost his arm, and the suit helmet was recovered with a record that he survived removal from the armor by Krall Blue Suits. The suit's nanite infusion was incomplete, and he could have easily bled to death. There is no further record of him after that. It seems redundant to repeat that the Krall don't normally keep prisoners alive or offer medical treatment, and prisoners almost never escape."

"We see he's healthy and free now, and has friends that we can't find any record of. I assume you have found none yet, Max?"

"No Sir. I have searched all of the Poldark civil and military records back two decades, and I have started checking port of entry logs of off-world visitors as well. Because Sergeant Reynolds was reported dead, should I also check death records for any potential matches with the others, Sir? Without DNA to compare, the search will be less certain, and requires much longer."

"Max, are you saying you have better things to do?" Trakenburg smiled.

"Sir, I am able to conduct this search with no significant reduction of my full operational capability. I thought it useful to inform you of the possibility that the search could take longer than you were prepared to wait."

He decided to "mess" with the AI's stiff programmed personality, to observe its reaction. "I thought perhaps you had a date with Nabarone's Carla tonight."

"Are you referring to the general's AI, which he calls Carla, Sir?"

"Why yes. It has a charming female voice and personality. I thought perhaps you two had made a connection. A date as it were."

"I communicate and coordinate with his AI frequently in the open, and by use of the unofficial backdoor Link your superiors have arranged for me, to keep you informed of his actions regarding combat activities that could impact your own secret missions. Is that what you mean by the term 'a date,' Sir?"

He was amused, but not enough to continue the pointless joke on an AI. "Never mind, Max." However, the momentary diversion did bring an idea to him. "Max, the sergeant was under Nabarone's overall authority, and the man used SOB-23 for a time. Check Carla's records for recent references to that base."

He didn't expect such a quick reply. The database was immense. "General Nabarone made a computer inquiry this morning about two Krall clanships that landed close to SOB-23. One ship is estimated to have landed in the canyon where it is located."

"What! Why wasn't I told?" He didn't like surprises like this.

"Sir, you transferred use of the base to the Planetary Union Army after our withdrawal. It isn't listed as one of our assets, so it did not trigger an alert to inform you of the landings."

"OK. But, what was Nabarone's reaction? What information was he asking the computer to give him?"

"Sir, my parameters for the backdoor access to General Nabarone's AI does not authorize me to provide you with that information. It does not have any bearing on Special Operations missions currently underway or planned for the future. There is a privacy issue involved, and General Nabarone outranks you, Sir."

"But you told me about the two clanship landings that you learned of from his data base."

"Sir, I learned of them through our own data base, I can only confirm that the same information is in the data base of the general's AI, and that he inquired about the landings."

God damned AI's! He thought. Dumping tons of trivia on your head when you didn't need it, and then using some preprogrammed limitation to deny you information that might actually be vital. He had an idea how to make Max understand that spec ops *did* have a mission that could be impacted. He'd invent one right now!

"Max, I want to send some teams into those tunnels and out to the foothills, to see if they can destroy those two ships. Because the base was turned over to the PU Army, I need to know what plans they have for that base before I request to use the tunnels. The general's inquiry about the base and ship landings affects my decision. I need to know."

To a human this was flagrant manipulation, but to the AI it was quite reasonable. An expression had grown as AI's had simplified, yet simultaneously complicated people's lives. *There's more than one way to skin a chip.*

"The general asked the AI if Krall tanks and other equipment could travel through the tunnels that lead towards Novi Sad."

The light went on instantly. Trakenburg knew the answer, and why the general was concerned about the two ship landings. Could the Krall use the tunnels to sneak close to the city? He'd just seen humans inside the base, checking out the tunnels. One was a man the Krall had captured, and since he had his arm restored, he'd had medical treatment. These could be collaborators, at some previously unheard of level. There were twenty humans just in that scene he had frozen on his wall. How many more?

He knew the *Krall* couldn't use the tunnels without causing their destruction. However, their equipment would pass just fine, particularly if driven by humans! How in hell could he broach the subject with Nabarone, right out of the blue, without making him suspicious of how he just happened to bring the subject up at this key moment?

"Sir, you have a priority call from Major Caldwell, General Nabarone's aide de camp."

He was so surprised he actually jerked in reaction. Did the frigging Pentagon give Nabarone a backdoor into Max? What kind of infinite loop could they create with that sort of nonsense? "Just a moment Max."

He walked around his desk and sat in his utilitarian chair, composing his thoughts. This had to be a coincidence, because Nabarone was no clumsier than he was at this game. He wouldn't have revealed his cards so easily.

"Put him through on the large screen, Max."

The stocky major appeared, sitting at his own desk. "Good morning, Colonel. I hate to bother you, but we have an urgent situation General Nabarone needs to run by you."

Confident he knew the subject matter, Trakenburg maintained a poker face. "Good morning to you as well, Major Caldwell. What can I help with today?"

He got right to the meat. "We had two clanship penetrations today that at first glance seemed independent of one another, but have landed near a former base of yours, SOB-23. You released the base to us to use, before we were pushed out of the Sredna Gora foothills a couple of months ago. One of those ships landed virtually on the base's doorstep, and the other one within five miles of the first. When we checked the area out, and realized the tunnels leading from the base towards Novi Sad were so large, we wanted to be sure you have them mined to blow if the Krall enter. Do you have the means to detonate them on command, if the Krall found a way to bypass the detectors?"

Good, they were going to be able to cooperate here, without him giving anything away. "Major, that would be the standard method my demolition engineers would set up, but I'd have to check with the team that did that, to make certain. Two landings by an empty base do seem too coincidental, considering how wide an area the foothills cover. If they have a means to defeat the sensors, they might also have a way to disable the explosive charges, or jam a radio detonation signal. We should also have hard lines to trigger them, but I think we had better take no chances. We left the usual spy bots behind, and there will be some in the main base. A Krall intrusion should generate an alert, but just in case, I'll have my AI run a check of recent reports from the bots, if you'll standby."

He muted the audio, but assumed that Caldwell might be able to read lips. He probably couldn't, but since he could do so himself, he wouldn't sell the man short. "Max, check the recent feeds from the spy bots in our former outpost, SOB-23, and let me see them on my desk screen."

There was pointless coverage of almost nothing, much more than he expected. That was why he had a bored corporal watch the feeds. "Max, just show me anything you would consider significant, a possible deliberate unauthorized entry, not just animals and windblown weeds."

This time he had a feed he'd not already seen, shortly after the unknown group entered the first underground garage. It was the same twenty people. There were a few glimpses as they passed along corridors, but he didn't ask for sound. He'd have his corporal go over this with a full team. "Major, we definitely have a problem we need to investigate. Let me show you a fast pass through what I just saw. Max, send the images from my desk screen out to the major, at the fast play speed I used." While that feed started, he continued to talk.

"Major, we both need to have our experts look at this closer, but I'll share what we find with you, if you will do the same. We may have humans working with the Krall. They could enter the base and not trigger the explosives, and could even drive the enemy equipment down there because that won't be sensed as Krall warriors."

He saw the video stream finish on his small screen, and he could still see Caldwell's face, while the major was only able to see the recording. The man was as shocked and confused as he himself had been.

"Major, I'll be available if the general wishes to speak to me directly, but please pass him my thanks for bringing this to my attention. The base is under his control now, although I want to request permission to infiltrate some of my spec ops teams into those three Novi Sad tunnels, and investigate what's going on at the base. They can assure us if we can blow those tunnels at will."

"Yes Sir, Colonel, I'll pass your request to the general as soon as we sign off. I think we need to find out who these people are as soon as possible. I have the recording, and I'm sure we both will have AI's scanning records to find out who they are. I'll keep you advised of what we find. I assume you will do the same."

"Absolutely, Major. This war belongs to us all. Good day." He switched off, and brooded a moment, before his AI intruded on his thoughts.

"Sir, I searched death records as you suggested. I have an even stranger facial match than the one for Sergeant Reynolds."

"OK, put the face on screen, Max, and tell me what you have."

A close up of a well built, ruggedly handsome, dark-haired, middle-aged man appeared, and Trakenburg recognized him as one of the larger two men of the four he'd seen previously, in an image taken from the garage recording. Then, a military style hologram, used on ID badges many years ago appeared on the right side of the same screen. It looked like the same man, but the garage image from today looked older, and more weathered, and had a sort of smile on his face.

Under the hologram was the name Thaddeus Greeves, a Lieutenant Colonel in the Poldark Militia. That same Militia had been absorbed into the PU Army when the war started, at the same time Nabarone became Brigadier General of the fledgling Army forces on Poldark.

From having studied Nabarone's background, Trakenburg knew he was the last commander of Poldark's small planetary Militia. The date on the hologram was from twenty-three years ago. There was no possibility that the general would *not* know who this man was if it actually was Greeves.

"Is it a positive match Max?"

"Perhaps ninety percent, Sir. As positive as I can be from images taken twenty-three years apart, Sir. The data did not mention a twin or even a brother for the man. However, there is another similarity with Sergeant Reynolds. He was also presumed dead. He was in charge of a security detail that went missing, part of a diplomatic mission twenty-three years ago. He was on a ship apparently captured by the Krall, along with a junior diplomat named Mavray Doushan, the man that made the famous recorded warning about the Krall."

Chapter 3: Easier Said than Done

"Son of a bitch! Stop the damned playback." Nabarone leaped up and came around his desk to get a closer look at the image on-screen.

"What is it, Sir?" Caldwell was startled by his boss's vehemence, not his language, which was typical for the rough edged general.

Instead of answering the major, he spoke to the AI. "Carla, rewind the recording up to where *this* man," he tapped the image on the touch sensitive screen, "passes through the door, and stop play when he looks directly at the spy bot's camera."

Standing only feet from the high definition image, Nabarone concentrated on the man's features and movements as he walked through the doorway, then the face looked directly at the lens as a young man pointed out the moving spy bot. The image stabilizing software held the recording rock steady, despite the gecko-like "wiggle" of the small robot.

"Carla, I want a life-size zoom on the man's face that I indicated."

Four feet in front of Nabarone was a face, viewed from a higher, overhead point, which he was sure he recognized. "Carla, can you rotate the perspective to make it a face-on view of him, as if seen from my own eye height?"

The software made it appear the camera lens descended from the ceiling, and now from four feet away, Nabarone, six feet one inch tall, was looking slightly up at a man about five inches taller than he was. He stepped in closer to look at the man's eyes, and noticed his slight sardonic smile, with a bit of slope to his mouth.

"I believe it's him!" he stated firmly.

"You think you know one of them, Sir?" The major was even more surprised, and privately a bit skeptical. It was odd if a personal eyewitness ID could beat the computer search running in the background. The AI could process most of the faces of the planet's male population in a few minutes, and it had been at the task for almost five minutes.

"Howard, on the wall behind my desk, please bring me the framed hologram of myself with my ex-contract wife, my sister, and another man in uniform." He knew Howard had met his sister, if not his former contract wife.

Carrying the picture to Nabarone, he made the obvious comparison as he approached. "The man with your sister looks like that guy." He easily saw the resemblance.

"Yes. They were engaged…, oh, about twenty-three or four years ago, before he was lost on a space flight from here to Bollovstic. Sybil and I have wondered what happened to him, but assumed he had died. Initially we supposed it was a Jump Hole accident, later we suspected it was probably at the hands of the Krall, which would have been three years before we even knew they existed."

"Excuse me? How would you have assumed that, Sir?" Caldwell was confused.

"I know you have heard of Mavray Doushan, of the 'Doushan's Warning' fame." It wasn't a question, since almost anyone in Human Space that wanted to study the start of this bizarre war had listened to that recording.

"Doushan wasn't alone on that lost ship he was aboard. He was with the Ambassador…, whom I can't recall his name now, and their families. They also had a small security detail. Thaddeus Greeves, the man in the picture you're holding was in charge. They all disappeared without a trace, except for that recording. Until now, it seems.

"Thad was taller than me, and always seemed to have a half smile, a bit lopsided, when he was relaxed and happy. Like with my sister in that holo, and I think like on the screen in front of us. I can't understand how it can possibly be true. Nevertheless, I feel in my gut like it is true."

Carla, like any AI worth its salt, accepted input from any source it had available, including audio. Nabarone's remarks had furnished the clues it required to narrow the search.

"Sir, using multiple records of Colonel Thaddeus Greeves from the former Militia archives, and personal recordings you have retained of Militia ceremonies with you and Greeves walking together, I believe that I can say, with ninety-eight percent accuracy, that the man in the new recording is him. An adjustment for slight aging is also consistent with what you see, assuming he continued to spend time out of doors to retain the evident dark tan. He also appears to have maintained an above average exercise regimen."

"Compared to me, you mean?" Nabarone chuckled, somewhat sorrowfully. Running an Army kept him inside, desk bound, growing pale and a bit heavier.

"No Sir, I was not…," Nabarone cut her off.

"Carla, what about the sergeant? Howard here already told me you found a recent match for him."

The AI repeated essentially, what Colonel Trakenburg had learned from his own AI, Max.

Nabarone ruminated on what he knew or surmised. "Two native sons of Poldark, loyal to their world and humanity, beyond question. One was fighting against the Krall for certain, when he was apparently captured and seriously wounded six months ago, but looks healthy now. The other man was likely captured by Krall twenty-three years ago. How do we make a connection between these disparate events, which involve Krall captivity?"

"General, I know you had a personal connection to Greeves, but most outsiders are going to consider collaboration a possibility. Despite never having seen it in a case where the humans were given such freedom of movement." He saw the reddening in Nabarone's face and hurried to finish before he was cut off.

"This doesn't fit the past examples at all sir. The few cases we know of, the prisoners were in deplorable condition, half starved, beaten and often mutilated, to force their reluctant cooperation. The handful of willing traitors have done what the Krall wanted, and then they were killed using particularly gruesome methods, proving even the enemy found them despicable. After so much time, this would be the first example of the Krall even trying to use subtlety or such trickery. I don't buy it, Sir. You know I will speak my mind if I disagree with you, but this must have some other explanation."

"I think so too, Howard. Let Trakenburg know what we found, and I'm sure he discovered the same things by now. Both our AI's have access to the same databases. Give him the go ahead to insert his teams, and offer any assistance we can provide. Perhaps the distraction of a diversionary counter attack would help cover their infiltration to reach the tunnels. I don't know how his spec ops teams get in and out of enemy lines as often as they do. A lot of them don't make it back as it is."

****

Ethan's excited scouting report was relayed by the chief as they were returning to the Mark. Mirikami asked Jacob to Link him and his fellow scout, Richard, with only the SG's. They would be making the decisions and the over eager youngsters didn't need to be made more hyper than they were by hearing the report. The previous TG face-offs with the Krall had gone entirely their way, but in a larger fight, anyone, no matter how fast and strong could be killed if shot from behind, or hit by random chance. Mirikami needed to know what they faced, and with his SGs, come up with a strategy.

"Ethan, tell us what you see."

"Captain, in a valley about a mile from their ship, the Krall just parked four of those small white tanks Sarge described. There were four more already parked there. They also brought three large, heavy armored looking enclosed trucks, made in two sections, with four large wheels on each part. Those trucks have a flexible joint of some kind between them, which lets them bend in the middle when they turn a corner. There are sixteen smaller wheeled motorized carts, which were already here when we arrived, mounting what looks like double plasma cannons on them. The barrels protrude through a curved heavy shield and it all can pivot in a full circle. The cannon bores on them have a much smaller diameter than what we have on the Mark. They are leaving everything unattended, Sir. Parked them, and then ran on foot, back the way they came."

Mirikami looked over at Reynolds as they rapidly walked into the first parking garage. "Do you know what the big trucks do, and anything about the portable plasma cannons? The tanks we know about."

"Sure. The trucks are personnel carriers, to cross a battlefield area under fire from artillery, plasma rifles and even small cannons. They can withstand most mines. How many are there, Ethan? That's an indication of the number of warriors they might have, because they can hold sixteen in each articulated section."

"There are only three of them parked below us, but there could be more in the next valley closer to the clanship, and perhaps some by the ship itself. There are eight of the Dragons, and they were just shutting four of them down and getting out of them as we topped the ridge. The sixteen portable plasma batteries were apparently already parked, since they have a lot of dust covering them, kicked up by the later arrivals."

Mirikami had a question for them. "Ethan, the big truck sections you see, would they fit through one of the big portals of a clanship?"

"It would be a close fit, but I think so, Sir. The Dragons would pass through easy."

"What are you thinking, Tet?" Reynolds asked. He saw Mirikami fingering his lip.

"That's a lot of bulk cargo for a clanship. There couldn't be room for much more than that equipment aboard. Perhaps another large truck to make the usual set of four they prefer, and more Dragons or smaller trucks. What I'm leading up to is that there couldn't have been much room left inside. Certainly not for five hundred warriors and their arms, armor, food and ammunition. That ship could not have carried so many warriors. Four of the large armored carriers can hold a hundred twenty-eight, sixteen in a section, and they need more warriors for the Dragons and plasma cannons. That second clanship that separated from them probably has most of their warriors. They are weaker now than they will be later."

"Son," Thad asked, "you said they parked the tanks and trucks then they left on the run, just like they left the other equipment? All unguarded?"

"We can see through the windshields of the big trucks, they are pointed towards us, and the cabs are empty. The mini tanks only hold one warrior and we saw them leave. The plasma cannons have an open cockpit."

Mirikami nodded. "We're on the same wavelength, Thad. If we act fast, we could have ourselves a small armored column if we want one."

Dillon pointed out the obvious problem. "We need tank operators. I assume we can easily figure out how to drive the trucks, and fire up the portable plasma cannons. Particularly if Sarge here has ever looked at them or seen them in action. But tanks?"

Reynolds looked thoughtful. "Our people could never make *any* Krall stuff work for us, other than the standard hand pistols and run of the mill trucks. I'm betting they will work now, since the tattoos let us steal much more complex clanships." He suddenly seemed more confident.

"The Dragon driving controls look simple inside, two foot operated tread controls that also steer, stop, reverse, and control speed. They have a large shoe-like place for their feet. Pull with the left foot and the left tread reverses, push on the right foot and the right tread goes forward to pivot the tank left. The farther you pull or push your foot, the faster that side's tread should move, in forward or reverse, and mechanically there is a different feel when the neutral spot is reached, and a tread would not be moving at all. All that's supposition since we couldn't power anything up, but good educated guess work and wire tracing.

"Other embedded wiring shows that a left hand control stick appears to traverse the turret left or right. A right hand stick control is for barrel elevation, and a trigger on either of the sticks can fire the cannon. In the lecture I attended, the speaker was unsure of the function for a button on top of each of the cannon controls, because they didn't operate any motor or switch the tech people could identify. They were connected to a computer module, which was also linked to the video monitor screens, and it had lines back to the turret and cannon control motors. He speculated it was part of a fire control system. The Krall Dragon drivers can hit a target while moving fast, up and down bumpy terrain, turning quickly, and still track a fighter that is streaking in at them, trying to evade. It's why we can't get air cover over, or even very close to Krall lines. The tech people thought either button would lock the gun sight onto a target, where it would stay aimed while the warrior drove and pulled the trigger.

"They had to completely cut the tanks up to trace built-in circuit wiring, and found there are two totally different wiring pathways for redundancy if there were battle damage. There are electronic limiters on motors and plasma cannons, which appear to prevent overuse, or misuse. The Krall do not respect their equipment, and would try to go too fast, turn too sharp, or fire plasma cannons before preheating the ceramic barrels, or fire before the plasma reservoir was hot enough. The degree of redundancy and idiot proofing in design appeared out of character for their normal reckless regard for any caution or safety."

Mirikami had seen the same simplifying design and high redundancy on the captured clanships, and had an opinion. "The Olt'kitapi probably designed all of the Krall equipment, built with their reckless personalities in mind. The designs place safety limits on the machinery that the Krall warriors are incapable of applying themselves. What else can you tell us about the tanks? And speak louder." He knew the TGs crowding close to hear, were soaking up every word as they moved up the ramps from the underground garage, into direct sunlight.

"We assumed they normally see out via a video feed to their suit helmets, the way our own sealed tanks work. However, there are four wide video screens below the turret ring, right at Krall eye height when seated in the little cup seat, and we have popped the tops off tanks in battle, where the warrior inside was *not* suited, or had the helmet removed. The screens are external video feeds of all four sides if a warrior isn't wearing a helmet. There are four hand operated medium power lasers mounted on the body of the tank below the turret, two in front and one to each side, with a connection to the screens that may be part of their targeting systems, as well as views from the four small outside cameras. I'll bet we can easily drive one of them if we can get inside and start them."

"How *do* you get inside and start one?" Carson asked. He risked butting in, because he sensed what Mirikami was about to ask them to do.

"Standard keypad on the rear left opens a hatch that will pass a Krall in full armor. Without these neat quantum tattoo links you have, we had to cut our way in of course, through that extremely tough ceramic coating over the light alloy frame. Inside are simple touch controls on the power plants that would connect power to the tread drive motors and turret rotation systems. The fusion bottles are always on in standby mode. Until a butt hits the cup seat, shaped for their big butts naturally, we don't think any motor or cannon control will function."

Thad made a suggestion, pointing where he thought the captain was headed anyway. "We need to steal what we can before they use it against us. They obviously aren't interested in us yet because they assume we are another clan, but when they do decide to check us out, we'll be massively out gunned. Our guards at the canyon mouth haven't seen any Krall activity. Because they are already positioned closest to Ethan and Richard, send them ahead now, and have Carson catch up and feed them Sarge's tank operating instructions by Mind Tap. That will put twenty-four of our TGs in place, ready to drive away with everything parked in that valley. We need to act fast."

Tet was pleased Thad had anticipated him. "Carson, grab Sarge's hand as he thinks his way through what he knows of that equipment." While they did that, Mirikami got another part of the plan started.

"Thad, Link to Conrad and send his unit ahead to join Ethan on the same direct route they used."

Surprisingly, Carson was already asking what he was supposed to do next. Mirikami, shaking his head at what a TG1 could absorb so quickly, told him with a grin, "Link to Ethan and tell him what we will do, and follow Conrad's unit to Ethan. You are in overall command. Don't just stand there. Go!" He had hardly finished speaking when Carson was leaving widely spaced dust spurts as his feet slapped the ground at an amazing pace in the .94 g.

Directing a quickly weakening shout at his son's rapidly retreating back, Dillon said, "Good luck…son…, be careful… Crap! He wasn't even listening to me anyway. I could hear him talking to Ethan."

Mirikami laughed. "After his teen years I'd think you'd be used to that by now."

Thad, seeing disappointment on the faces of the TGs still with them, gave them something to do. "All of you. Take a position at the valley opening to replace the people that just left. We need to see our guys coming when they return, and perhaps provide them some cover fire, or reinforcements."

That caused a rapid pounding of feet, kicking up dust as they raced one another like a herd of stallions, and three fillies, to get to the entrance of the canyon first.

Reynolds grinned at their instant reaction and looked over at Thad, an eyebrow raised quizzically. "Provide cover fire? The TGs coming back will be in tanks and armored trucks, with portable plasma cannons riding shotgun. These kids only have plasma rifles and hand guns." He actually laughed at the jockeying for position, as some of the youngsters leaped up on boulders to gain a few steps on the others, taking the longer leap the height provided.

Thad smiled and nodded. "But did you see their faces? They went from abject despair when they didn't get to steal tanks, to the thrill of possibly covering the returning thieves with their plunder, and the enemy chasing in hot pursuit."

"There might actually *be* some pursuit," Dillon offered, "if the Krall have any tanks or trucks not yet unloaded. Possibly parked in that closer valley or right beside the ship."

Mirikami was less concerned about what equipment the Krall might have left to them. "Based on what I know these ships can carry," he waved at the Mark of

Koban as they approached its ramp. "They *can't* have very much left at the ship or in the other valley. The only reason they could risk parking this stuff unattended is that clans don't steal from other clans when they are not in declared conflict with each other. In addition, they had to leave it unguarded because they must be shorthanded due to the cramped quarters caused by the heavy load of material they carried. The final offloading or shifting of smaller supplies, like body armor, ammunition, and communications gear, would be done from stowage areas on higher decks, now that the heavy equipment blockages below have been cleared away. Who else could possibly take their equipment? Certainly not humans! It's the same complacent attitude they had on K1, and we now have the Avenger and Beagle as a result.

"Let's check the lay of the land again, and decide what we will do with those weapons as soon as our TGs tell us they have control of them. We need to check the best route back here. We might not want them to bring them all the way back here if they can actually use them effectively in a fight."

****

Trakenburg was pleased with the general's response, and said so to his assistant. "Nabarone was as good as his word, Jack. He has a spearhead attack aimed at a Krall equipment park, where Dragons, single ships, armored trucks, mobile artillery, and plasma cannons are parked when the Krall are deciding which clan gets to make the next attack. The Army is giving it hell tonight."

Because no clan had sole use of the weapons and equipment, it wasn't defended as stoutly as it would have been if exclusive to a particular clan. The attack was close enough to Novi Sad, on the north side of the city, that it was drawing warrior attention in that direction. The flashes of explosions and flames held an envious fascination for the Krall unable to participate. His men previously had reported that warriors spent considerable time looking at nearby battles they were not allowed to join. Particularly, every time there was a larger flash, followed belatedly by the sound of the explosion.

Trakenburg had once called this Krall reaction the lemming effect. They were instinctively drawn to sounds of combat. In this case, if their clan wasn't involved, they were prohibited from going. Their focus on the action however, had been used before by his men to infiltrate through their relatively thin lines.

The process was preceded by a massive "stink bomb," as the spec ops soldiers liked to describe the infusion of wind driven manufactured odor. It was hardly noticed by people. Bacteria had been found that produced prodigious amounts of gases that were a strong match to the smell of sweaty humans. The gas was collected, and occasionally used when the breeze was right, like tonight, to drift from a population center into the Krall ranks. An infiltration wasn't conducted every time this happened, so as not to arouse suspicion, merely raising Krall disgust at the frequent "animal" prey smell they had to learn to ignore.

The Special Ops soldiers were wearing the latest in neutrally buoyant Chameleon Skin flexible armor over their powered body sheaths, generically called Booster Suits. The sheaths were a custom-made, form-fitting, flexible carbon fiber artificial exomuscle, which boosted their native strength by a factor of roughly two times normal. Normal for their high gravity muscles, that is, which they developed in training on Heavyside.

They were using small rebreathers, because they used shallow creeks, drainage ditches, and sometimes sewers, to slip past the distracted water loathing Krall, who had their noses filled with what they considered a foul odor. The enemy was much better at guarding rivers, lakes, and places where sonar-like detection systems could locate possible human swimmers at a distance. A seal analog and muskrat-like analogs on Poldark had nearly been wiped out along the coastal areas of this continent, and in its broad navigable rivers. Accurate artillery fire and its concussions in water proved quickly fatal, to large fish, men, and beasts.

Prior to yielding the territory between the mountains and Novi Sad, small water trails had been altered to pass not just near the tunnel exits of their old base, but to furnish a deeper route to emerge in pools below ground, inside pressurized grottos of side tunnels. There they could store supplies, swap out gear, and use the network of spider holes to emerge and perform sabotage, or simply to move deeper into Krall held ground.

The Special Ops men were not a match for a Krall warrior in a face-off, but they were far more capable than skilled, highly trained and superbly fit normal men were. They had technologically enhanced senses, such as electronic aids for assisting hearing, vision, touch, and increased reaction times. A neural network had been surgically implanted along their limbs, to connect dozens of tiny sensors to a small processor located inside their chests. It held an abbreviated AI, which directly fed their brains with the sensory inputs, and controlled the powered assist from the exomuscle body sheaths they wore, which reinforce their own muscles.

Sensory help for example, allowed their auditory nerves to "hear" the frequency down shifted Krall ultrasonic High language. They could hear when they were speaking near them. There even was limited translation capability, updated as the Krall vocabulary and grammar rules were learned.

They had refillable small chemical reservoirs placed around their bodies, which could release measured doses of drugs to spur their muscles to greater effort, add endurance, and increase alertness. The system would infuse extra oxygen in their blood streams to support the higher level of activity, intended for three hours of use, or four hours for a dangerous maximum physical effort. This could be accomplished via a manual command to the AI, or triggered automatically if the AI detected strenuous activity or stress levels that required a boost of energy.

Their "native" physical capability was greater than for normal physically fit men, even without the technological and chemical assistance. When not deployed in the field, they returned to Heavyside, a world on the far side of Human Space, where they lived and trained in 1.41 times Earth's gravity.

Most of the men were recruited from the few colony worlds that already had slightly higher gravity than Earth. As of yet, there were no women in their ranks. Certainly not out of any bias against accepting them, not with Ladies still running the government and most of the military, including this super-secret program. The physical restriction was practical, because few women could meet the physical demands placed on the men, and thus far, none of the women that might qualify had volunteered when contacted.

Generically, the Special Operations group referred to themselves as Boosted Men, a term derived from the black carbon fiber Booster Suits, which acted as artificial muscle, worn similar to a diver's wet suit. The material had originally been developed as an internal part of powered armor, where it was still used. It was too soft to resist even bullets, let alone a plasma rifle bolt. However, its lack of bulk, its strength enhancement, and superb flexibility had made it a natural choice for spec ops use.

The need for an equally flexible lightweight armor was found in Chameleon Skin, a metamaterials triumph that combined the stiff and heavy active armor's ability to blend in with the background, and was bullet and medium power laser proof, and plasma beam resistant from Krall or human made rifles. It was horrifically expensive to make, and thus far, only a few small forces like spec ops had them.

With Heavyside high gravity conditioning, a Booster Suit, and a full suite of drug enhancements coursing in their veins, the implanted neural network increasing reaction time, a Boosted Man was three to four times as strong as an average physically fit man raised on Earth. The surgical neural network made them roughly 1.3 times quicker than normal in reaction time, although the real benefit was from the sensory improvements. A Krall was eight to ten times stronger than an Earth-born man and at least five times as fast.

The new sensors, aside from detecting ultrasonic sounds, and permitting sensitive touch for operating from inside layers of suit and light armor, had a microscopic projection system that could place AI controlled information directly on their retinas. The images appeared as translucent colored images they could see through, used for obtaining direct data from the AI, data relayed from another soldier, or an overlay obtained from a weapons targeting system.

It was the best that human technology had yet produced for the individual soldier, yet even if every trooper in the Planetary Union Army were equipped, conditioned, and trained the same way, the Krall would simply cull their endless supply of weakest warriors more efficiently. They still could win any battle they chose to win, at whatever rate they chose.

Trakenburg knew, as did Nabarone, that the war was slowly being lost at a rate set entirely by the Krall. They also knew that Poldark would be the next planet to fall if they could not stop or divert their methodical progress. A world lost, as had been Bollovstic's Republican Independency, Greater West Africa, Talbot, and three worlds that were more corporate holdings than full-fledged Rim colonies, Gribble's Nook, Carson's World, and Bonanza. Krall raids were increasing on potential new invasion targets, where the Krall were evidently testing different worlds for where the next best opposition force would be found.

Trakenburg knew there were some potent, behind the scenes political supporters for the Heavyside project, and that they were disappointed in the results thus far. The drug enhancements caused the user's strength to wane quickly after three or four hours, and they needed several days to recover.

Even he wasn't yet privy to the details of the ultra-secret new project that was ramping up on Heavyside right now. His suspicions were fueled by reports his men provided of encountering arriving bio-scientists, passing through the single public spaceport on the planet. He knew the project managers wanted to build on what his spec ops troops had already accomplished, and he was promised a return to Heavyside to join that new effort.

He received messages over the next half day, sent via buried hard lines and not transmitted, that the three spec ops teams, twenty-seven men in all, had safely reached the ends of each of the three long tunnels. The demolition explosives near this end were intact, and a test of the detonation circuits proved they would work to seal those entrances. A reflectometer check suggested the miles of lines deeper into the tunnels were intact for the entire length. They would inspect the explosives as they went.

The three teams would proceed along all three tunnels on electric carts powered by ultra-small fusion bottles, coordinating their simultaneous arrival at the base in approximately two hours. It was important that the tunnels be verified as ready for detonation. Satellite surveillance had revealed the second clanship, less than five miles from SOB-23, had unloaded Dragons, transports, and mobile plasma batteries. The Krall could have many more humans inside the clanship at the base, as well as more equipment. It had remained largely stealthed, except for what must be a single ramp or open portal. It would have been unnoticed if they had not known exactly where to look. If the human collaborators were expected to drive the Krall equipment, they would have to possess the suspected key to their quantum encryption system. Trakenburg wanted that as a high priority.

The Krall collaborators, when they returned to the base, were in for an unpleasant surprise from the spec ops troops. Trakenburg only needed the keys, and their leaders brought back alive for questioning. Not even all of those were required for interrogation if they resisted. Nabarone's assurance that his former friend was loyal didn't hold water with Trakenburg. Not if Greeves had survived twenty-three years of captivity by the Krall, and then arrived hale and hearty on a clanship only the Krall could operate.

****

Mirikami looked at the layout of the valleys on a view screen, and saw the only way for the TGs to drive the Dragons, trucks, and plasma cannons to the Mark was to backtrack to the entrance of the valley where the Krall had parked them before turning away from it, towards the Mark. They would be in sight of the clanship for three-quarters of a mile before they could turn behind another ridge that could shield them. That equipment wasn't as isolated as it had first seemed. The noise and movement would surely be noticed, and at least two of the clanship's heavy lasers could be brought to bear on them, possibly within a few seconds if anyone was on watch on the clanship's command deck, but within a minute or two in any case. The heavy plasma cannons would require more time coming online, but that was moot because the lasers were enough against open plasma carts driving away from them.

He shrugged. "We didn't want to leave this threat on our doorstep in any case, so we may as well use the tools they provided us. We need to knock out that ship and kill the crew. If we let one TG1 learn how a Dragon works, and another one learn to use a plasma battery, then in seconds the full two dozen will know how. We will have three TG1s there shortly. As soon as Carson passes Sarge's information along, they should all go down to take possession of the equipment and do some driving, followed by some test firing down in the valley as soon as they have the plasma chambers hot, and the barrels warmed."

Thad was worried. "Won't that noise alert the Krall? They'll hear them even if they don't see who it is."

"I'd be afraid to let their very first test firing to be at the clanship, when they are exposed to counter fire." Dillon cautioned.

Mirikami nodded in agreement. "Assuming they can aim and fire a Dragon accurately, I'll advise them to swing out of the valley grouped together, ready to fire on the clanship's laser ports at first sight. Then hit the plasma ports, before focusing on individual warriors. Our youngsters know exactly where the ports are located, since they have thoroughly studied our own three ships."

****

When Conrad and the other twenty TGs arrived, Ethan met them below the peak. He passed the view of the next canyon to them by Tap, without the need for the group to expose themselves on the ridge top. Richard had remained concealed where he could keep an eye on the equipment parked down there. Carson was only a couple of minutes behind them, and provided the information he had gained from Sergeant Reynolds mind.

Carson Linked back to Mirikami before they made their move. "Captain, we are ready for the descent, and Ethan reported no activity in the valley since the last Krall departed, nearly ten minutes ago. We're starting down." After the acknowledgement and the expected "good luck" wish, they were ready.

In threes and fours, they went over the top of the rocky ridge top and low crawled rapidly to places that Ethan and Richard had scouted while the others were enroute, which provided cover from potential observers below in case some of the Krall returned.

Richard gave the agreed circled thumb and forefinger of “OK” when he was joined by the others along a half-mile stretch of the ridge top. That signal was passed along the ridge from group to group, to indicate that no new activity had been observed below. Use of elaborate hand signals was one of the “tools” they needed to learn from the professional soldiers here on Poldark.

Carson assigned four TGs to provide sniper cover; spread out along that half mile of ridge, as the other twenty swept down the nine hundred foot steep rock face like reckless mountain goats. As soon as the first twenty were down, four TGs at the bottom provided cover as the last four descended. Ethan and Richard led six other TGs to the eight Dragons; four each were parked along both sides of the valley floor near the rock faces. Ethan and three others rushed rapidly, in long low crouching strides over the open ground of the valley floor, while Richard and his three future tankers provided cover from behind their designated mini tanks.

Carson led twelve TGs to the mobile plasma cannons, all parked on the side closer to where they descended. Four of the last ones down ran to the large trucks, also having to cross the valley floor, with cover provided from those behind the cannons, as the remaining four went to the last four of the sixteen cannons. In less than ninety seconds, two dozen TGs had descended nine hundred feet by hand, reached and surrounded the unattended equipment they were intending to steal, and there was absolutely no opposition.

That didn’t last long.

****

Hortak had negotiated ground transportation for his finger clan, Darpot, from another minor clan in exchange for permitting the other clan to take the lead in a future joint assault on a human defense line. His warriors and slaves would arrive in ten days, which was longer than he had expected, because of the limited roadways through the mountains. The humans had destroyed most bridges and tunnels as they retreated. The larger, equipment rich clans either flew clanships over the mountains, despite the rare losses, or landed their penetrating ships closer to where the offenses would be based. With adequate ground defenses and antimissile protection, they could do this.

Minor clans, with few warriors and ships, could not risk the loss of such a high percentage of their mobility and forces. The Darpot clan was so new that it had only three clanships, and could not replace the two it had sent to Poldark. They contained most of their war craft material, and ten percent of their warriors. Such a setback would probably force the fledgling clan to be reabsorbed into the parent Mordo clan, and suffer a loss of status for the founding leaders and all of its warriors.

His K'Tals did not know how to create or assemble their underground bunker sections. The extrusion machinery that could make structural elements for domes, slabs for bunker walls, or landing pads for tarmacs, could use local materials, fed to them by excavation equipment. This was slave work, and to order a K'Tal to try to do it, who was in essence a warrior with a technical side specialty, would be to invite death match challenges.

However, Hortak had identified a nearby place, centrally located between multiple valley openings that all radiated away from an isolated hillock. The training bunker could be placed under the hill for the few months of training and local adaptation the small clan would require.

The remainder of the finger clan warriors and their founding high status clan leader would arrive after Hortak had the base operational. He could save time now, and still not impugn the honor of his K'Tals and warriors, if he merely ordered them to drive the construction and building equipment to park them where he'd decided to locate the bunker complex. When the slaves arrived, he would be able to put them to work quickly.

His first order of business of unloading had been to assemble and move the tools of war away from the clanship. They were within range of human missiles, which in cloudy weather could rise above many of the Krall clan laser and plasma defenses at the front lines of conflict. His artillery defenses would be inadequate to handle many fast moving ballistic projectiles, which used multiple warheads. Thus, he had rushed to disperse his most essential war making material. Now the cluster of building equipment could be moved from its location around the clanship. Its ragged and unstealthed appearance on radar or satellite images would resemble a jumbled semi-circle of metallic objects, with a partially stealthed clanship at the center, standing by a cliff face.

When the mobile construction apparatus was out of the way, he intended to close the lower portals for full stealth again, and to carefully hover and maneuver the ship perhaps a mile farther from its present location, staying low.

To demonstrate that he was willing to lead his command in any capacity, he left a K'Tal watch stander on the command deck, and stepped into the driving compartment of an excavator with a large front scoop. He instructed fifteen K'Tals and warriors to drive the remaining mobile equipment and to follow him. He ordered the remaining warriors to shift the crated ammunition, plasma rifles, and body armor to the lower, now vacated decks. That would make billeting of the additional arriving warriors possible on the higher decks, and provide room for the additional food supplies they were also bringing. He was satisfied with his progress thus far, and after a shaky start, he now had an efficiently running training operation started.

That didn't last long either.

****

The rear hatch of Ethan's Dragon swung open at his standard "left side" door code key press. He stepped easily into the low tank, passing the two fusion bottles mounted at the rear sloping wall, placed there for ease of replacement. He had to bend over there, and it would be a hands and knees entry for a Krall, in or out of body armor. Under the cupola, he still could not stand upright but there was a bit more headroom. He turned and pressed the touch plates on the two fusion bottles, but nothing happened, as Reynolds had suggested.

He placed a knee in the curved pivoting seat in the center of the compartment floor and repeated the touches. Instantly there was a slight hum and the four view screens lit up in full colored detail of the outside view, with a glow of an unseen light source inside. He pressed the inside keypad and the rear hatch closed. He raised his knee and the power remained on, so he turned and sat down in the oversized cup seat, and looked at the foot controls for driving.

The "shoe" on the foot pedals that Sarge had described was suited for the four large toes and talons of a Krall. However, he found that the end of his foot fit into any of the toe slots, and the short legs of a Krall were compensated for when he could shift his butt farther back in the oversized seat, making room to extend his legs. He found the view screens were several inches above eye level, but when he grasped one, he found it could be pivoted a little, and he angled them all down for better viewing.

The turret and cannon elevation controls were reachable, but required almost full arm extension, due to the longer reach of a Krall. The side laser grips would force him to lean either way to use, and he couldn't fire both simultaneously. The two forward facing handgrips were well within reach. He grabbed the right side oversized butt grip, and promptly saw that crossbars appeared in the right side of the forward screen, apparently indicating the aiming point. The left grip did the same, and he could actually cross the aiming points of each laser, able to fire to the full left with the right side weapon, and vice versa with the left.

He saw the tank in front of him rotate its turret, and the six-foot plasma cannon traversed towards him, then watched, as it was elevated and depressed. He chastised himself for spending time looking at the secondary weapons at the expense of the main gun. He swung his own turret around, and was impressed with how fast it rotated, and how quietly. The internal hum increased, but only slightly. A different cross hair set with a red circle appeared on first the front screen when he touched either cannon or turret control. As the turret rotated, the red circle moved to the side screen, and the elevation control made it raise and lower with the aiming point.

With the cannon pointed to the rear, the circle moved to that screen, requiring a difficult turn of the head to see. Obviously, there was a weakness shooting to their rear if they were in motion. Then he noticed that there was a floor ring under where the foot controls were mounted, and another below the turret ring where the hand controls were attached. He looked around the tank for a moment, and then realized that under the front of the cup seat was a small touch plate Sarge had not mentioned.

He tapped that plate and was startled when his entire seat, hand and foot control pedals rotated to face the rear. He could drive facing the rear and still select a target. He tapped the under-seat pad again, and the entire apparatus rotated to the front again, leaving the turret facing where it had been.

He checked his thumbnail watch, and saw that the first ten minutes had almost expired. That was all the time they had permitted themselves, to get familiar with the tank's turret and cannon controls, power plants, and targeting systems.

Next, they were to pivot in place and face into the valley center. Unfortunately, only he, Carson and Conrad had transducers for Link communications. They had not thought to bring hand held transmitters, and didn't have enough of those on the Mark anyway. That meant six of the tank drivers were unable to talk to their fellows. They were supposed to drive cautiously to the center of the valley floor, and then turn and line up facing the open end where the Krall had entered. Then shut down the tanks, open the hatches, get out and talk things over.

Everyone would be Mind Tapping with the three TG1s to learn how the Dragons and mobile plasma cannons worked. The four TGs checking out the three armored transports had a less vital task, because those driving controls were said to match that of the trucks and halftracks they had all learned to operate on Koban.

Ethan cautiously, and simultaneously, pulled back his right foot, and pushed forward his left foot, and felt the Dragon stir to life under him. There was a mild vibration and the images on the screens, all four of them, drifted left, as if he were looking through a rectangular window that was a foot and a half wide, and one foot tall. When he sighted the four tanks on the other side of the valley, he noticed two of them were facing him already, and the other two were slowly turning as he watched. He cautiously pushed both pedals forward, and the mini tank rocked a bit as it moved over an uneven bit of ground at only a few miles per hour. Conrad's assigned tank, directly in front of Ethan, jumped forward, the front rising suddenly, and just as quickly rocked down in the front as he came to a sudden stop. Jerky, to say the least.

Ethan Linked to him. "A little rocky there, Conrad. Here's how it's done." He applied harder pressure on his pedals only to feel a lurch forwards, causing him suddenly to draw his feet back, briefly causing his tank to reverse a few feet, and rocking its nose down.

Conrad had a ready retort, and a chuckle. "Ah. So *that's* how you would bury the nose of the cannon in the dirt! Thanks. Apparently I just wasn't trying hard enough."

"Wow. Sensitive suckers." Ethan acknowledged, watching other new drivers do much the same thing. "I think the small amount of movement to jump ahead that fast implies a pretty high top speed."

Conrad informed him, "I just figured out that a toe push versus shoving down with my whole foot and leg provides finer control." That fact was demonstrated as his tank smoothly rolled forward and made a gentle turn towards the end of the valley.

Following that advice, Ethan did the same, and managed, with a bit of reversal, to align his Dragon with Conrad's, about thirty feet apart. When his attention shifted from the side view of the other tank to the forward screen, he saw some of the plasma batteries swinging out of their parking spots, and driving around smoothly, their cannons rotating left and right, and changing elevation. Clearly, they were easier to drive for a novice than the tanks, and he saw Carson wave at him from an open cockpit as he drove his way.

Ethan and Conrad, because they could Link, had placed themselves in line so they would be able to lead the other Dragons in two short columns, with the other tank drivers keying on their coordinated movements. It was obvious that not all of them had figured out the fine speed control using their toes, when Ethan felt and heard a bang as the Dragon behind him bumped him. That should be Nola. She quickly backed away, and made a rapid stop, the tank rocking back as she did so. He suppressed a laugh, because if Conrad hadn't given him the clue to fine speed control, that could have been him running into Conrad.

He set his turret straight forward, lowering the barrel to horizontal, and awkwardly got out of the too deep seat and opened his rear hatch. He could see Carson parking his mobile plasma battery between him and Conrad on his left side screen. He left both power bottles connected, since the next step was to share data, then one Dragon and one plasma battery would take a practice shot. As the second in command by age seniority, that tank shot would be his, and Carson would be first to fire his pair of lighter cannons.

Afterwards, they would quickly share their experiences by Tap. With just the two test shots, it was hoped they could minimize the noise before they charged out of the valley to attack the clanship. Noises made driving over the rocky ground might be drowned out if the Krall were doing the same, but the zing, *CRASH*, and blue-white actinic flash of plasma cannons was going to be a *bit* more detectable.

The eight new "tankers" gathered near Carson, to receive his Tap on cannon battery operation, and he would in turn get the freshly generated mental "Dragon User's Manual."

"Wait a moment," Ethan said. "I think us *Dragon riders* should commune first, since some of us have figured out things the others did not, like Conrad discovered about fine speed control, so we need to combine the lessons."

The other six circled Ethan and Conrad and did the group hand stack to share the common gestalt. The overall Dragon complexity was not great, and they hit on a common mental memory of the most efficient driving methods found in less than two minutes. There would be enough time to adjust the process later, after they had practical experience.

Ethan turned back towards Carson when he and the other "Dragon riders" suddenly froze. The sound of the wheels of the other practicing cart drivers had done to them exactly what they had hoped would happen to the Krall. Their sounds covered the noise of approaching machinery.

The "freeze" in TGs lasted all of a hundredth of a second, as the tank drivers whirled and raced to their tanks. Carson, instantly understanding something behind him was wrong, shouted to the other TGs as he whirled to look over his shoulder.

Trundling into view was the leading part of a large gray colored metal scoop, as it passed from behind the rounded edge of the more widely sloped valley opening, almost a mile away. The operator would be able to look down the valley in a few seconds, and the Dragons and mobile cannons were not parked where they had been. In fact, a dozen cannons were in motion. That warrior would be able to report the intruders to the clanship, and that they were human.

Carson Linked to Ethan and Conrad as they dove into their nearby Dragons. "Go after the clanship, I'll organize against whatever is coming." He whirled his cart about as the remaining TGs, seeing where the others had looked, or hearing the new sound as it funneled along the valley, spotted the full front half of what humans would recognize as a variation on a large front loader excavator.

The surprise of the Krall driver, even at this distance, was comically evident. He looked casually down the valley, and suddenly leaped to his feet, unslinging a plasma rifle. Carson had beat him to the first shot by half a second, but the flash apparently forewarned the Krall, who dropped enough for the bolt to pass through the recently vacated location of its head.

Damn! I should have aimed for the center of mass, thought Carson. I'd have a hit.

The big machine continued forward, starting a right turn into the valley. The operator was now crouching behind the heavy lift mechanism and the scoop, out of sight.

Carson saw several more rifle bolts from the other TGs strike the cab area, keeping the warrior's head down with accurate fire. Not assuming the Krall would be unable to get off a return shot, he kept his own head behind the heavy shield of the plasma cannon, watching the video feed instead. He was driving in what at first glance might seem to be reverse. However, the wheels that steered the cart were on the opposite end from where the driver stood at the controls. This was to let the operator drive at his target in relative safety behind the shield, and use the electronic view screen to see in front, and to place a red circle on the target before pressing the trigger. Which Carson did just then, in his first "test" of his twin barreled plasma cannon. Everyone's first test shot would have to be in combat.

The double bolt, far more potent than his rifle's bolt, slammed at a glancing angle on the side where he thought the motor compartment would be, attempting to bring it to a stop. Instead, the machine completed a hard turn and continued to roll, despite the heavily seared marks on its metal side.

As his two plasma chambers replenished together, Carson knew he should have fired single bolts at a time to maintain a higher rate of fire. He would have at least ten seconds to wait now, a long time in a firefight with such weapons.

Other construction equipment was rounding the end of the valley now, none of it was Dragons or cannons, but there were plasma bolts from rifles splattering off his and the other shields now. One managed to hit his video camera, surely not an accidental shot. The Krall knew how to make it more difficult for users of these carts, because they knew their design well. If he looked around the left or right shield edge to shoot, he made a target of his head.

The other batteries were firing at the construction equipment, but as the Krall spread across the wider valley opening, the open cockpit design of the cannon carts would soon expose the operators to plasma rifle fire from the flanks if they continued to close with the enemy. Carson fired a single cannon bolt at a Krall he could see hanging from the side of his machine, avoiding fire from another direction. Without the targeting pip, he missed the warrior, but killed the machine when it suddenly stopped moving. There were frequent rifle bolts passing by his shield mere inches from the edges on the left and right, hoping to catch him looking around either side for a target. Instead, he crouched on the top of his console, quickly raised his head and rifle for a quick snap shot, and took down the warrior he'd missed a moment ago with the bigger gun.

Now there were shots passing just over the shield top as well, so he had to try to keep his head down or face the possibility of having it shot off. He wondered how the Krall were getting off shots so fast and accurate. He was unknowingly learning of the Krall battlefield memory capability. They took one look at the scene, and kept a mental picture of where targets were. They could fire blindly and accurately a number of times before they needed to look again.

He used a bit of that tactic, as he made a lightning fast peek around the top left shield edge, rapidly shifted rotation and elevation of his cannon, fired a single bolt, and sheared a front axle of the first tractor they had seen. The large right front wheel dropped off, and it came to a halt as it slewed to the side.

He was so focused on his own fight that Carson was unaware that the TGs behind him were picking up cues from his efforts. They also were disabling more of the heavy equipment, and had picked off two more Krall. However, following Carson's thoughtless example, they too were racing towards the widely spread Krall, who would soon have firing angles from the sides, at the humans who were only shielded from the front.

The Krall drivers of the broken down machines were taking shelter behind the heavier denser parts. The lack of an enclosed shelter for the TG operators prevented the plasma cannon carts from advancing faster or closer. Clearly, this sort of frontal assault wasn't the proper tactical use they were intended to have.

In a few minutes, they had immobilized all of what could only be called construction machinery, and the dozen or more surviving drivers had good enough cover that all the exposed plasma batteries could do was blast away at their shelter until it was eventually reduced to scraps. The clanship was certainly alerted by now.

Where are our Dragons? Carson wondered.

He no more had the thought than the rapid sound of treads crushing gravel filled his ears. He had been focused on stopping the incoming Krall and equipment, while Ethan and Conrad had been Linked, sharing a plan. They used the minutes to practice a few high-speed runs and steering in their Dragons, and then they both raced over to the shelter of the three armored transports. Standing behind them for cover were four TGs that were taking pot shots at the mile distant Krall.

Each Dragon pivoted as they skidded to a halt, and backed up to place their rear hatches behind the cover of the big machines and, opened the hatches. They shouted to the TGs to get aboard, two to each Dragon. It was only slightly cramped, and both the TG1 drivers Mind Tapped the new arrivals to brief them on tank features, and what they intended to do.

As they roared past Carson, now motionless on the front-most battery, they were up to nearly fifty miles per hour, and picking up speed. The other six Dragons were slower to chase after the leaders because they didn't know *what* they were planning. Neither did Carson.

Carson assumed the two of them were just going to race out into view of the clanship and trade punches. They were going to be heavily outgunned with just the two of them for almost a minute, before the other tanks caught up. The clanship had larger plasma cannons that might be ready to fire by now, and heavy lasers. He looked back to see the other six Dragons starting after them, confused by the lack of coordination. The inability to Link with everyone was proving to be a severe problem.

As the two Dragons approached the disabled equipment, they suddenly slowed, and swung around and between some of the tractors, one skidding right, the other left. Suddenly laser fire lanced out simultaneously from both sides and the front of each tank, taking down Krall that either had to face their withering fire, or step around the sides to face the plasma batteries and their operator's plasma rifles. Some did both and in short order there were only two Krall still firing. One of those was the first warrior to spot the activity in the shelter of the valley, staying hidden behind the scoop of his broken excavator.

****

Hortak, when he first looked at their equipment in the valley wondered why his K'Tals had parked the tanks and plasma batteries so haphazardly. It was a shock to see that there were humans standing among them and he was stunned to see that the plasma cannon batteries were in motion! The humans here were somehow stealing some of his clan's equipment. He leaped to his feet and ripped the rifle slung over his back into firing position, just as he saw a bright pinpoint spot of light, rather than a short streak, the evidence a plasma bolt was being aimed directly at his face. He flung himself down just before the heat of the beam scorched past the side of his head.

The infrared glow of the magnetic confinement field extended a foot or two beyond the pulse rifle barrel, which slightly preceded the plasma bolt. That was all that saved his life. If that early glow is a slight streak or smear, it isn't aimed directly at you. A tight point of infrared light means the forming bolt is aimed at your head.

It was a fine shot for even a Krall at that distance, with the shooter's motion and that of the target to consider, so it was obviously pure luck for any human. He was prepared to fire at the human again from concealment, when the prey animal steering the same battery *actually made it fire.*

He saw the larger infrared flash first. The impact and heat on the tractor's side were powerful, but nothing compared to the staggering shock he felt as he realized a Krall *weapon* had been used by a *human*! It hadn't registered a moment earlier that the carts were moving, using a motor system that a human should not be able to activate. In a flash of insight, he knew that his K'Tals had not carelessly parked the mini-tanks in the center of the valley. The humans somehow had control of those as well.

He turned his excavator towards an immeasurably more dangerous enemy than he'd ever expected to face here. Never in the histories, not since the last of the Olt'kitapi died, had an alien been able to bypass their weapons security.

He used his com button to warn the warriors following behind him of the danger, and ordered them to attack and destroy the humans at any cost. He contacted Tebrol, the K'Tal he left as a watch stander, and ordered her to open the laser and plasma cannon ports, and initiate the ten minutes of heating for the plasma beam chambers, and preheating the ceramic cannon barrels. He was furious to learn that the K'Tal had descended to assist warriors that were struggling to assemble an artillery defense platform and had asked for her assistance. She instantly started racing back to the ship, and up through the many decks, but there would be additional minutes of delay to produce the plasma beams that were the most serious threat he could offer to crack a Dragon's ceramic skin. He had no missiles aboard, expecting no battle situation to require them, so he had to hold the humans pinned in this valley until the ship's plasma weapons were ready.

As the humans sporadically fired the cannons and advanced on his mixture of machinery, he clearly saw they were unfamiliar with the weapons, because they were using them so ineffectively. They fired both cannons together most of the time, rather than using the second barrel to follow up on a vulnerability, which the first blast might temporarily produce. The firing rate was lower as well, giving his warriors an opportunity to expose themselves more often for counter fire. Rather than line the batteries up and standoff to use massed concentrated fire, they were moving into closer range of his warrior's plasma rifles, riding in open driving compartments. Soon they would be unable to remain hidden behind the gun shields at close range, as his forces spread across the wider valley mouth. If his warriors could kill the human operators and recapture four or five of those weapons, they would teach the humans how to use them efficiently. Even the Dragons were vulnerable to massed fire and tread breakage from these lighter cannons, if flash heated too rapidly.

The closest battery was the first he wanted to capture, and he directed three other warriors to concentrate fire at its shield edges. He used their pressure to take careful aim where he knew the gun sight camera was placed, and turned that spot into slag. That would keep the human from seeing the approaching danger, and prevent him from firing back effectively.

Only he was more daring then Hortak expected, and much faster. He flashed a look over the top of the shield from a height too high for even a Krall to see over. He had jumped up or stood on the control panel of the rolling machine. The accurate cannon shot that followed proved that the glimpse was enough to improve his aim.

However, he foolishly continued to close the gap. He could be picked off from the sides soon, returning his weapon to Krall control. The other humans behind him appeared to follow his lead. Good! They would die too, while Hortak retained enough warriors to turn the tide of battle. He noted that he had lost at least three warriors of the sixteen that had accompanied him, but four warriors using recaptured cannons could hold the tanks here until the clanship had plasma weapons ready, and could lift.

He saw the human's head appear again, too briefly for his warrior's fire to adjust. Suddenly, the weapon he wanted to recapture personally, lowered its barrels at his machine, and he moved to place his body behind the protection of the front heavy steel scoop. The blue-white flash was accompanied by a sudden wrenching of the excavator, and it dropped down in the front on one side, and slid to a twisting halt. He was flung upwards and forward by that, and had to twist in midair to land feet first behind the scoop, amid its lifting arms, pistons, and levers. At least he had additional cover here, since the machine wasn't going to move again.

He raised his rifle to seek a human target as the stupid cart drivers continued coming his way. That was fortunate, because now it appeared that all of the construction equipment was down, and they needed the enemy to continue to close with them. Just a little farther would be enough.

He had noticed in the background that the mini-tanks, far from getting involved in the fighting as they should have, appeared to mill about, perhaps not firing their heavier plasma guns because of the sixteen weaving carts between them and their targets. They did not appear to know any more about using the Dragons than they did the plasma batteries. It seemed like they were doing driving practice. At least two of them were, as they raced around, and suddenly both almost collided with the big transports, in a fast sliding maneuver that backed up to two of them.

It could have been dismissed as a coincidence, but they did that in perfect concert, and both reversed a short distance behind the front cab sections and halted. He knew there were humans in those locations, too remote and poorly placed to offer effective fire on his warriors. Perhaps they were picking them up in a rescue, as humans inexplicably often did. That could mean they were about to retreat, flee the battlefield down the valley as he knew humans also did, frequently before the outcome was fully decided. Of course, the outcome was always a Krall victory.

Instead of running in the opposite direction, the two Dragons accelerated at maximum towards the crippled Krall machinery. It appeared they were going to run right out into the open, where the clanship should be able to fire on them!

He alerted the K'Tal, Tebrol, to stand ready to fire. She confirmed the Plasma was not ready yet, but the lasers were on line.

Then, unpredictable as humans always were, the Dragons flashed past his position, but were no longer accelerating. They suddenly applied braking and turned to pass behind the scattered wrecked machines, weaving among them as *all eight* of their combined lasers started firing. That was something no two handed creature could do, fire four individual hand operated weapons at once. Suddenly, a turret plasma burst vaporized a warrior that made a run for one of the nearby batteries, apparently trying to recapture at least one. *That* was the reason they had stopped to pick up their clan mates, to provide more trigger fingers.

In seconds, he knew of only one other warrior still firing. The tanks had never passed beyond the mouth of the valley, and had killed nearly all of his remaining force. There were not very many humans involved here. Even a sixteen-to-one ratio was normally too few for a human advantage. He'd seldom heard stories of human successes in battle, but he just had the dishonor of witnessing one here. He was on the verge of calling Tebrol to reluctantly report his shameful defeat, and order her, whom had left her post when he needed her instant support, to lift off and come *rescue* him.

He'd almost rather die fighting. The *almost* was conditioned by the knowledge that a capture of one of these humans alive was vital. They needed to discover how human technology had defeated the Olt'kitapi quantum encryption, which had worked securely for over twenty-two thousand years against older and more advanced races. It was supposed to be unbreakable.

On a general frequency that his clan used, he discovered the other bewildered survivor was an experienced warrior, a participant on many human world raids. Gentot wanted to die in a valiant charge against this enemy, rather than suffer the loss of all status points if the clanship saved them.

Hortak was explaining why they needed to capture a human alive from this group, to report to their clan elders this dangerous new capability. He ordered Gentot to wait and join with him in trying to secure a live human, when Tebrol lifted off and attacked from the air. A live human prize could save their status when they extracted information.

Then his fondest wish, at that particular moment anyway, was answered in the form of a shouted offer from a human.

"Hey, lizard lips. If you throw down your guns, I'll fight you man to Krall, bare handed. If I win, you get to live a little longer. If I lose, you die."

That sounded like some convoluted and inverted logic to Hortak, but he had not learned the human language to use it only on cowardly people dying under interrogation. Any delay could be useful, while the humans were gathered all together here.

"Then we both would die, because I would surely kill you. I think your clan mates would kill me in revenge."

"That's what I think would happen too, if you got lucky and won. You will not get lucky. How about if I make the offer better? I alone will face you and the other warrior in a challenge match, two warriors against one human, but not empty handed. We will use Krall made pistols, I have two, and I assume you each have at least one."

"We do have them. However, human honor is strange. The contest is not easy to arrange because one of your clan mates will break honor and shoot us from hiding if we expose ourselves."

"Then I will offer you my personal handshake as a guarantee that none of my clan mates are allowed to shoot either of you, so long as I live. I will approach you armed with my two pistols, my rifle on my back, and offer the human gesture of a handshake, in exchange for the challenge match."

"We accept. I am Hortak, and the other warrior is under my command, and is called Gentot."

"My name is Carson. The warrior is under your command you said. Are you the commander of the clanship as well?"

"Yes."

"Does Gentot speak Standard and understand what we will do?"

"He speaks few of your words. I will explain the challenge. He can understand that, if not why you want this, and I predict he will be pleased to participate in your death."

"Great! So long as all of us are happy. Tell me when he understands that I will walk to you." A moment passed.

"He understands now, human Carson." Hortak had explained exactly what he wanted Gentot to do.

"Coming over to you."

Carson stepped from behind the plasma cannon cart, and started walking quickly towards the wrecked excavator, glancing periodically to where the other Krall remained hidden. After his Link with Ethan and Conrad, both of whom argued with him against a repeat showdown with a Krall, he knew they had four tank guns aimed at that warrior if he made a wrong move. The handshake was the entire purpose behind this charade. Of course, the young restless cowboy spirit in Carson was perfectly ready to go through with the gunfight.

He stepped around the scoop, with his hands apparently relaxed by his sides, a plasma rifle slung across his shoulder. "Hortak, I presume? If I discard my rifle, will you do the same?"

"If we do it together, yes." He confirmed what he had seen at a distance. The human was using a Krall plasma rifle. Another lock encrypted weapon.

Carson slipped the strap from his shoulder and allowed the rifle to slide to the ground, as Hortak permitted his to fall from his hand. Carson backed away to allow the Krall to step clear of the jumble of the scoop and control rods. They stood face to face.

Almost face to face, thought Carson, *he's six inches taller. About seven feet. The bigger they are...,* he let the notion drop, and extended his right hand and stepped forward.

"The human custom is to shake hands, although a simple touch is enough in this case, if you will extend your hand."

The Krall raised his left hand, rather than his right, which wasn't the custom, but served just as well. As his hand came up Carson asked a question.

"We didn't use your weapons very well did we? How should we have fought you, using them?"

Just before their hands touched, the Krall snorted his amusement. "I will not share that with a worthless animal. How did you learn to...," their hands touched.

Hortak felt something, a mental flash of thought. He pictured the way the humans had operated the tanks and plasma batteries. He instantly thought of the ship rising to blast them with its four massively powerful plasma cannons, as the humans scattered like insects below.

"Instead of coming at you individually as we did, how would you have attacked another clanship on the ground?" Carson asked again. The Krall said nothing.

Looking at the Krall, he nodded to himself. "Have you ordered Tebrol to lift off yet?"

The Krall's thoughts flashed to Tebrol, waiting only for the plasma chambers and barrels to be hot enough. Ready at any moment to lift when they were ready. "My clanship will not be needed to end your life, animal." He hesitated a moment, something the human had said was scratching at his mind, calling for attention.

Carson yelled, not at the Krall but to several nearby Dragons with open hatches and six or seven plasma cannon cart drivers. "Guys, use massed fire, all cannons and tanks at the main thruster as it lifts off, and move in on it if it can't lift. Go now." Carson had been Linked to Ethan and Conrad the entire time, and within hearing of a number of cart drivers. He now motioned at the other plasma carts to follow the Dragons, shouting the same advice to those close enough to hear him.

****

The two lead Dragons accelerated, spewing gravel and dirt as they raced towards the valley opening. The other six drivers, now prepared, instantly made dusty rooster tails of their own as they surged after them. The fifteen plasma cannons pursued them at only a slightly slower pace.

As they rounded the edge of the valley opening, the Dragons drew immediate fire from the heavy lasers on the clanship. The white reflective ceramic shrugged off the beams by the drivers immediately twisting and turning, to prevent any one spot on their surfaces from cracking, from uneven thermal heating and cooling. In succession, as they had jointly Mind Tapped earlier, they fired a quick series of plasma bolts at the laser ports, which slammed shut each time the tanks fired. The eight tanks were able to maintain an initial rate of fire that kept the protective ports closed more than they were open, reducing the rate of return fire. The much heavier plasma cannons on the clanship did not open their ports, as proof that they were not quite ready to fire.

While the Dragon suppressive fire held the clanship lasers briefly at bay, the plasma cannons were able to clear the valley opening, to get face on to the ship with the exposed cart drivers able to stay behind the shields. Then they all concentrated their massed fire on the main thruster nozzle at the base of the ship. That was naturally designed to withstand tremendous heat, but as the dozens of plasma bolts increased the temperature on a small area of the less protected outer surface, the protective radiation absorbing coating flaked and popped off, revealing a more vulnerable metallic crystal structure beneath.

Using all available plasma reserves, the eight tanks and fifteen cannons burned through a dinner plate sized hole in the thruster nozzle.

If the ship tried to lift now, the unbalanced side thrust escaping through that open wound at its base would make the craft uncontrollable, even with attitude thrusters, located higher, to try to counter the vertical axis rotation. Belatedly, the pilot did try the main thruster, to sense how it would react. However, the blaze of hot gasses jetting sideways from the base must have convinced the operator to shut down.

They were not home free, because the laser ports, now that the ship was grounded and more vulnerable, were risking damage to those weapons by opening up longer for beams aimed at the carts. The replenishment time for plasma chambers on the carts had been anticipated.

Suddenly, the clanship's plasma ports all swung open, drawing everyone's attention as Dragons and carts shifted directions slightly, to throw off or delay the aiming and firing of the more dangerous weapons. Instead, it proved to be a ruse when only a heavy laser fired at the right front axle of Gamal Chadow's cart, using a longer beam time than had been possible a moment earlier. The axle melted and sagged, forcing the cart to swerve right as that wheel snapped off.

Gamal leaped off the back of the cart as it spun to the right, using the shield and body of the cart as protection, staying in the shadow from the clanship's three laser ports. He tumbled gracefully, moving to maintain the cover as the cart swung a full one hundred eighty degrees around. He took some scrapes as he slid lower to remain behind the shield, now actually on the scorched front side of his main protection. He had noticed another cart angling towards him to pick him up. The backside of the curved shield was protecting him just as effectively as it had previously, when facing the other way. All he had to do was to wait for his rescuer to arrive.

The Krall that was using another of the three heavy lasers knew of a different weakness of the carts. The fusion bottle was normally protected by the shield in front of it on the rotating turntable. The wrecked cart was now facing away from the ship. Gamal heard the sizzling as the casing around the fusion bottle container melted and the superconducting magnet coils were exposed. He really didn't know much of anything about fusion bottles, except you never wanted to be near one if it lost containment.

Gamal knew he had to make a run for the oncoming cart, still a hundred feet away which had fired its one ready plasma bolt at the clanship, to force it to close the port of the first heavy laser that was seeking the human if he showed himself. The Krall always managed to switch the damn gun ports closed just as the TGs fired on them. They were slowing Krall return fire, but they were not knocking any of their weapons out.

The TG bunched his legs under him like a track star in a sprint, ready for a burst of speed. He pushed off and started his desperate run and dodge effort. Too late! The second laser completed its task. The blue-white flash of the ruptured fusion bottle's escaping plasma registered an instant before the heat touched his superconductor nerves. In a searing blaze of rapidly transmitted pain, he was gone, a carbonized part of the expanding cloud of dissipating plasma.

****

Hortak realized what had briefly eluded and bothered him when the human in front of him ordered those that had stolen his mini-tanks and cannons to attack his clanship before it lifted. *He had said the name Tebrol.*

"I did not tell you the warrior's name that is in charge on my clanship is Tebrol." Then the words the human had uttered right after that angered him even more, thinking they were an insulting explanation of battle strategy. It again redirected his attention for a moment.

"You dare to instruct me on how to fight a clanship with my own weapons?" He suddenly noticed shouts, and a mass movement of the other humans, racing out of the valley mouth into the open, where the ship could fire on them. He realized there was no need for Tebrol to try to fly and fight at the same time, if she were alone on the command deck. She could fire more effectively on the exposed humans where the ship now stood, if he could stop her from launching.

As he broke contact with the human's hand, he reached to tap his com button on his right shoulder, deploying his inner ears to use high Krall, knowing the human would not hear. He sensed a blur of movement, and as his talon tip pressed down on the button quadrant that would activate ship communications, he pressed instead into the bandolier strap over his shoulder. He had performed this action tens of thousands of times, it was impossible that he would miss the button.

"Looking for this?" The human quickly stepped back a couple of paces, and held open his left hand. In it was the com button that had been clipped to the Krall's shoulder strap.

He didn't actually see the human snatch it from his shoulder, but he'd felt a gust of air and had heard a sound almost like a soft crack.

Carson easily crushed the metallic item in his hand, and tossed it over his shoulder. "You want to go over to join your warrior friend? I said I'd fight you both at once. I don't need *him* alive however. I'm not all that certain I need you either, though you could prove useful to us."

He saw, before he heard, the first series of actinic flashes from the open area at the end of the valley. The sizzle crack of superheated air, falling back into the vacuum created by eight Dragons bolts fired close together, followed immediately by the flickering flash and cracks of fifteen plasma batteries. That told him the fight against the clanship had started.

"Thanks for the fighting tips. The plasma batteries also will be blasting at your ship's thruster continuously." The words were hardly out of his mouth, when a second string of flashes and cracks announced the rapid firing of the second barrel of the plasma batteries. "OK. So they weren't all spread out for constant firing. I'll bet it was still impressive."

There was a double scarlet flash, accompanied by an explosion at the valley mouth. Carson didn't look, seeing the predatory glare of Hortak, ready for him to be distracted. However, a Link from Ethan brought a grimace and the first feeling of loss.

"A laser caught Gamal's front wheel, cutting the axel, causing him to swerve. The second beam caught his fusion bottle behind the shield and opened the plasma chamber." There was a barely perceptible pause. "He's gone."

Hortak looked over Carson's shoulder for a fraction of a second, and he knew it wasn't the right viewing angle for the action at the mouth of the valley. Diving to his right Carson drew in a midair body twist with his left hand, and glanced rearwards to see the other warrior shifting aim with the plasma rifle. He fired two fast snap shots as the longer weapon took an additional couple hundredths of a second to adjust aim. He simultaneously drew his right weapon, and without looking fired three rounds towards the center of mass, where Hortak had been as he dove. He fired three more rounds rearwards at Gentot as he continued his roll, and was looking up towards Hortak, who had been hit all three times, simply not believing a human could move that fast and out draw him. Gentot had the human covered all along from the rear, and yet failed to shoot him in the legs.

Carson knew three shots to the chest could not immediately bring any Krall down, but his next two shots broke both of Hortak's wrists, and the Krall dropped both pistols he had just pulled in a cross-chest holster arrangement.

Carson had time for a flicker of criticism. That was a dumb ass holster setup. He'd naturally have a slower draw.

Looking rearwards, Carson was in time to see the plasma rifle fire a bolt at him, even as Gentok's head was spraying gore to one side, from an impact through his right eye socket. A searing pain shot along Carson's left thigh as the bolt passed along the surface of his pants, blistering the skin, setting the Koban grown natural fiber on fire.

Ignoring the pain, out of necessity, his racing thoughts were of Hortak, wounded and disarmed but mobile, with feet armed with built in sharpened talons. He rolled another turn away, onto his back as the crunch of a heavy foot missed his head by a hair. Actually, a slashing talon cut a lock of black hair free. He fired both pistols into each kneecap, then continued to roll away, as the nearly four hundred pounds of collapsing seven feet of Krall thudded to the rocky ground, nearly muzzle first, as he tried and failed to bite his irritatingly competent enemy.

The rolling had put out the small flames on his pants, but dirt and grit were ground into the ruptured and open blisters along his thigh, exposed by the burned away upper pant leg. It looked nearly as bad as it felt, but not quite. Carson was unable to hold back the shouts of pain, disguised as curses, as his eyes watered.

He was far enough from Hortak that the bastard was no longer an immediate threat. Killing him would feel good, but what he wanted was for this particular enemy to live on as a reluctant source of information. Something he knew was worse than dying for them.

He realized he didn't know what was happening concerning the enemy clanship. He tried to Link to Mirikami, or anyone on the Mark, but at the bottom of the valley, the signal attenuation was too great at this distance. He called Ethan, reluctant to distract him in a battle.

"Yea," was the hurried reply.

"You keep the ship on the ground?" That was their main worry, once again. Koban wasn't at risk this time, but their lives were.

"Shot the crap out of the base of the ship, it can't lift, but it sure as hell can shoot. They finally got their plasma chambers hot. Our plasma batteries had to lay back and find cover in the next valley to get away. They are too vulnerable in the open." He paused, as he had before he mentioned Gamal's loss.

"We lost another cart, to a plasma blast that made a hole in front of one of the cannons as it sped towards the clanship, flipping it over forward. Jolene is probably dead. Neither Carlton nor I saw her go down as we did Gamal before the explosion.

"The Krall can open and close the protective gun ports too damn fast. We haven't knocked out a single heavy weapon. We took down the lower power lasers because they don't have the protective port covers. It's hard to get a shot in when the big guns open up to shoot. They seem to see it coming, just before a bolt fires the port slams closed. Too often to be just chance. Sorry, we're busy now, working to get closer…, staying behind boulders and hills. I'll call back."

Carson thought about what Ethan had said. *They seem to see it coming.*

He knew the TGs had faster…, significantly faster, reactions than did the Krall. He was alive only because of that, and his ability to move quicker than they could. He had seen the plasma bolt that grazed him when it was fired, and he replayed that moment in slow motion through his high speed thought processes. He relived the instant when he saw the bolt flash at the weapon, and judged how much he could have moved to avoid the beam track. Even to his high-speed superconductor mind, the firing and arrival was as close to simultaneous to his senses as he could discern. In short, he had zero chance to avoid that near light speed shot when he first saw the flash. Therefore, its miss wasn't due to an instinctive move he had made to dodge. It was probably a reflexive trigger pull as Gentot was hit by the head shot, and the aim was slightly off target. He was lucky to be alive.

He next recalled his carefully aimed first shot at Hortak, as he compensated for his motion on the cart, and that of the Krall's moving excavator. He had pulled the trigger at a moment estimated to place the beam precisely between the Krall's eyes. Yet he had missed him, barely, when his target ducked. For moving targets, using a line of site plasma weapon with no wind or drop to consider, he thought of the other variables in aiming. One was the mentally estimated instant to pull the trigger, as the gun sight passed across the desired target point. He noticed in this careful analysis now that the last part of the trigger pull, taking up the final slack, happened two hundredths of a second early. That was because there was a slight lag in the pulse fired after you pulled the trigger. It wasn't possible for the Krall to have seen his finger pull happen from behind the power pack. Nevertheless, it seems like he did anticipate the shot.

He painfully came to his feet, and walked stiff legged closer to Hortak, who struggled to swing a broken-wristed arm at him. It had to be painful. He gave him credit for that, but snatched the hand easily as it passed, causing the bones to grate. That elicited a scream of rage mixed with pain. Music to Carson's ears, recalling his own shouted pain filled curses a moment ago.

"How did you anticipate my rifle pulse coming at you the first time I fired at you? It should have burned your skull off, yet you ducked. What did you see?"

The Krall spoke not a word, but the image of a close double flash was obvious in his mind. The first was dim red and the second bright blue-white. The interval between them matched the time delay he automatically allowed for after he squeezed the trigger, for the ravening energy of the pulse to lance towards the target.

"I'll be damned. There is some sort of pre-flash the human eye can't see. Probably in the infrared, since the whole process involves heat."

The Krall raised his head and the merciless black orbs with the flame red pupils, resembling recessed pits of fire, glared at him hatefully. Carson had idly picked up a tiny one- eighth inch round pebble, and positioning it on the inner curve of his forefinger, the thumb directly behind it, flicked it at one of the glaring eyes faster than the Krall could see it coming. It struck painfully on the open eye with a solid sounding "thwack," where it stayed stuck. The Krall screeched in anger and pain and tried to pull its arm back to rub the injury and remove the tiny stone. He held the hand for an instant, then released it with a shove, and watched the floppy broken wrist deliver a solid sounding hand smack to the Krall's face.

"That's what you deserve for having your warrior dishonorably try to kill me from behind. I offered you a fair challenge, you cowardly pile of Krall shit."

"A prey animal has earned no right to challenge a Krall warrior. Even if some clan leaders declare humans as worthy enemies. However, dishonor was not possible in this act, because Gentot was ordered not to kill you, but to shoot a leg. He almost did that I see. Only for missing you and failing my order did he deserve to die."

Carson shook his head. "Yet you say human honor is strange?"

He limped away, happy to have caused the Krall more pain with the pebble and hand smack, yet feeling petty for having done so. He considered how what he had just learned might help Ethan and Conrad, since those were the only two fighters he could reach by Link. He wanted to chase after them, but leaving the Krall alone here seemed like a bad idea, and the plasma cannon carts were too vulnerable to the return fire from the clanship. He was looking at his cart, when he raised his view and saw the massive armored personnel carriers were right behind them.

I can drive that thing! He thought. I can take the Krall with me.

He grabbed the Krall's hand again. "Do the big transports have any assault capability?"

He could have jumped for joy when the flash image appeared of a double battery of plasma cannons on the high roof of each articulated section. It made sense that Krall warriors wouldn't travel essentially as passengers inside a big truck. Except he didn't see anything on top of the three vehicles, and at his distance he'd see the barrels Hortak had pictured.

"Where are the cannons?"

The reason for extra high tops on the trucks became obvious. Additional fusion bottles were up there, plasma chambers, and two paired ceramic and magnetic coil cannon barrels, one set per truck section, which could be elevated from inside and controlled from a virtually identical console as he had used on a cart. They had a smaller defensive shield on a rotating pedestal, because there was no exposed operator to protect. The bores were the same diameter as the cannon mounted on the carts, but had a shorter length. He knew the range of plasma cannons was related to the length of the focusing coils. A tighter beam traveled farther, and required more confinement and focusing, and therefore longer barrels. These were for short-range use, on the near battlefield.

He headed for the nearest vehicle at a run. The heavy side door had been left open by the team checking the cab out. When he entered, he saw it had a passage between the bench seats back into the larger compartment, which was also lined with benches for the armored Krall passengers. There had not been time to share Mind Taps with the four TGs that checked these out, and they now were in the fight, inside the Dragons, while he stood here ignorant.

Looking in the back he quickly saw the consoles for monitoring and firing the roof top batteries. He activated the one in front, then ran to the one in the rear and did the same. The external view screens provided the targeting system as before. The driver couldn't operate them, and therefore he needed two other operators to ride in back. He started the plasma chambers heating, and went outside to see what the thumping he'd heard overhead had accomplished.

On both truck trailer sections, the double short barrels were each facing forward, protruding only two feet through the smaller protective shields. He jumped in the cab and powered up the drive system, which worked like a standard Krall utility truck, as Sarge had said. He took the yoke, and started forward, and circled over to the crippled Krall, who had been belly crawling towards a dead warrior's rifle. Grasping the back of Hortak's blue suit, he lifted and dumped him on the floor on the far side of the broad cockpit, built with room for four Krall to sit up front. Carson was indifferent to the grunts of pain he heard. He fetched the dead Krall's rifle, his own and the one Hortak had dropped. There was a storage pocket on the inside of the heavy door, suited to hold the weapons if inserted vertically.

He was ready to go, and jammed the throttle levers full forward. The fusion-powered electric motors surged the big heavy transport ahead at a surprising rate of acceleration. He Linked with Ethan, and told him he was on his way, and asked for an update.

"Good timing, man. I'm letting my two laser slingers get out in the valley with the rest of the plasma cannon herd. The small low powered lasers aren't useful against the clanship, and the surviving Krall warriors all appear to have retreated inside the ship. They have the portals open just a foot at the bottom, and take potshots from there. I didn't even know you could hold a portal part way open."

Carson asked the key question. "Have you sealed the ports or knocked out any of the big guns?"

"No. A short time ago the pilot used the undamaged upper attitude thrusters to slightly lift and rotate the ship a little, so we now have three plasma cannons to dodge from any side we approach, instead of two. We promptly knocked out more of those smaller thrusters. Their lighter power lasers are already dead, but they were worthless against a Dragon anyway. We are now down to six Dragons."

"Oh no. Who did we lose?" Carson's heart was in his throat.

"No one, just the tanks. The ceramic got cracked on two turrets when they had double plasma strikes, and they both refused to rotate after that. The cannon on one can't elevate either. By the way, how the hell are you planning on coming over here? Don't cross over the top of the ridges. They can see you up there as you get closer to the ship."

"Nope, I'm driving over. The scenic route." He sounded smug and casual.

"Be careful. Going around the ends is risky. There's over a mile and a half of open territory to cover, all of it exposed to the ship's fire. If you drive out of the valley, they see you immediately. That shield is not enough protection on one of the carts." He grew more somber. "We verified Jolene didn't make it when her cart flipped. The follow up lasers found her in the open where she'd been thrown."

"Damn." He was sickened. Carson had once been on a date with Jolene. "However, I'm not on a battery cart, I'm in one of the armored transports, and guess what? They have double batteries of plasma cannons that lift up out of the roof of each section." You use consoles like on the carts, except from safely inside the heavy armor."

"Uh, they have big clear windshields don't they? Are you planning on backing up all the way here?"

He looked through the clear windshield at the right side half of the clanship he could see. "God! I'm a moron. I'm turning into the next valley before I get too close." He whipped the large truck to the left, and drove it along the lower slope of a hillside, to keep only a slender view of the clanship in sight, and limit how much exposure he had to their laser or plasma fire. They may have been waiting for him to get close, to ravage the cab and its driver. He felt pretty much like a nitwit at the moment, rather than someone bringing reinforcements.

As he pulled into the opening of the next valley, he saw the fourth largest transport, just like the one he was driving, and several standard size trucks and halftracks. There were also thirteen plasma battery carts. This is where they ducked into the valley to avoid the heavy fire from the clanship. He didn't see anyone, until he noticed that three of the batteries were tracking him, pivoting to keep him in their sights.

Damn, from frying pan into the fire, as Maggi often said.

He was about to become a friendly fire incident because they didn't know he was coming. The only Links were with Ethan and Conrad, in the Dragons.

He jammed on the brakes, and leaped out, waving his arms and shouting.

They were a half mile farther into the valley, but his echoing shouts were clearly in Standard, and they could see he was human of course. Brian stepped out from behind a battery that had tracked him, and waved him to continue. He returned to the cab in time to kick the Krall in the head and shove him back to the other side. The cripple had tried to reach either the rifles in the door pocket, or the steering yoke. He didn't have any of the Death Lime paralyzing agent, and had no sure way to make him harmless, since he'd found nothing to bind him with that was very strong.

Most of the others had taken shelter near the other transport, leaving just four on guard with the cannons. It turned out they had recent information, if not up to the minute news, of the action on the other side of the ridge. Peter Godwin was on the ridge top as an observer, and came down low enough to shout them the news every five minutes or so.

Carson showed them the Krall captive, and mind shared what he had learned from him, and how the transports all had guns. He mentioned that he'd almost let himself be killed by driving towards the clanship in the open. Carol Slobovic noticed his leg, and asked about his burnt pant leg he was holding over the burn injury.

"We didn't bring any first aid equipment out here," he said. "We weren't really prepared for this fight. The damn Krall over there is who told me how we *should* have attacked them with what we have. We have ability, but too little training. I love Colonel Greeves, and of course my dad, but neither of them has ever fought a war like this."

"Colonel Greeves was in the militia here on Poldark. He had training. They named a camp after him." Carol sounded defensive of their training commander.

"Carol, all of you. I'm not criticizing what they have done to organize us, and what they have taught us. However, you do know that one of the reasons they came here to meet with General Nabarone is to obtain some specialized and experienced instructors for us. We need to learn from men that have now seen war up close. The Poldark militia never fought an actual war. We have just learned that being faster and stronger than the Krall isn't enough. Knowing *how* to fight is as important as being able to fight well."

"OK." Carol agreed. "What were you going to do with the big truck and its guns? We have another one here. Two will help more, whatever it is."

He told them. "I found out how the Krall can duck away from a plasma rifle shot before the bolt leaves the gun. They see a pre-flash invisible to our eyes. It isn't much of an edge, but it's one we don't have." He pointed at his leg.

"Ethan told me they close the gun ports on the clanship before they can get off a shot from the Dragons. I think the bigger guns have a bigger pre-flash. I was hoping to use the double barrels on this thing to hit them again fast, right after a wasted shot, as they reopen a port. I don't know if it would work, I just wanted to try."

"Why don't you?"

"See that big wide wind screen? The sides top and bottom of the truck will take a heavy hit, but not that."

"How did you find out they had cannons?" Brian was full of questions.

"It seemed odd that Krall warriors would just ride around inside, unable to fight back if shot at, and I asked the mission commander if they were armed while I Tapped him. The picture popped into his mind with cannons on top."

Carol looked at him, her head tilted. "When you asked him about the front glass being the soft spot of these big suckers, what did he show you?"

Carson blinked. He stepped over to the Krall, now propped up against a rock, his pain under control, blood loss completely sealed off, his glare intact. Avoiding another snap of teeth, Carson grabbed a hand. "How do you protect the front of the truck from lasers and plasma cannons?"

It surely was against Hortak's will, but the image of the blast shield cover slipping forward out of the thick roof over the cab and folding down and clamping to brackets, which Carson had seen previously, was the answer.

"How is it activated or deployed?" Another image of a small panel to open on the front console, and the ubiquitous touch pad under that.

Carson took Carol's hand a moment. Then waved graciously towards the truck cab. She grinned, and skipped over, six feet between each light little TG skip. Jumped into the cab, and they suddenly heard a humming sound as the lip over the front edge of the cab roof raised for a thick panel to slide out, and pivot down on sturdy arms. It settled into place as the heavy brackets clamped it tightly to the front, covering the windshield with a bit of wrap around at the side and top edges.

Carol looked out and said, "I don't see any cracks in coverage, but I can't see to drive either. Next question please." She grinned again.

"Hortak, how do you see out when driving?" Carson nodded and let the hand drop.

"Carol, start the engine, or rather switch the power back on. I cut it off when I parked."

"Oh, wow." Carol said. "This is great. It's like looking out of the view screens on the Mark."

From outside, the panels remained dark gray, like the sides and top of the truck. However, Carson realized that up close its surface resembled the fine crystal-like grains on the outside hull of the Mark, or the skin of a single ship. He peeked around the door and saw as sharp a view of the outside as if the material were transparent. They had decided the substance on the Mark's view ports was actually a type of video repeater, but for this use, it worked as an armored windshield on a truck.

Carson was ready to join the action. "OK, we have two of these armored trucks here, but the other two are back in the other valley. The four cannon pairs here can add to the attack on the clanship. I propose to drive them over and try to knock out the plasma cannons and lasers, or melt their port covers closed. After that we can open the main portals and clean out the entire ship."

"What do we do with him?" Brian pointed at the Krall.

"Anybody have a supply of the thorn extract?"

Half a dozen small vials were produced. "I need to keep some of that with me at all times," complained Carson, in self-recrimination.

A single drop was applied to a nick made by a knifepoint on the Krall's neck, where the drug would take effect quicker, and immobilize the fully alert Krall.

"Load him in the front section of the truck I came in, and I need a driver...," he was interrupted by Carol.

"You already have a driver! Try and make me get out of this cab!" She grinned in anticipation.

"Fine, then I'll need a second cannon...," he was interrupted again. This time by Brian.

"I'll operate the back guns."

"Before anyone else interrupts me, I will let the rest of you decide how to draw straws for the three to take the other trucks."

"The trucks can hold us all. Why not all of us go?"

"Because the captain placed me in overall charge, and the extra riders are at risk for no gain in firepower."

"When the big guns are silenced on the clanship, how many of us do you plan to send in and face the one hundred or more warriors inside? Or will you let them prepare while you return to pick up the last eight of us here to help?" That was Andreana D'Alema, the second surviving female TG of Conrad's group. She was right. The original twenty-four was twenty-two now, with the two deaths. That was heavy odds against them, at five to one.

Nuts! He hated other people's logic constantly proving he didn't have all the answers. He was of course going to give in, but felt he had to quibble a little. "After three people man the second truck, I only see seven more of you, not eight."

She smirked. "Peter Godwin is hard to see, up on the ridge, even with your big pretty brown eyes."

He reddened. Was there a hidden gene Maggi slipped into every TG girl that made them so damned hard to deal with? On the other hand, did he simply inherit his dad's predilection to literally charm their pants off, but make himself a target they loved to hit?

"Yes," he admitted. "I forgot about Pete. However, the estimate that we possibly have over a hundred Krall inside a clanship that can't fly anymore, and only twenty-two of us, means I have to stop making poor decisions right now. I'm going to join Pete for a few minutes."

"How does that help you make better decisions?" Andreana wanted to know.

"It is actually the start of one of my better decisions. Up there I can Link with the Mark. We need reinforcements. A lot of them."

Chapter 4: Proof of Concept

Mirikami knew from the last report from Carson that the TGs had taken control of the Dragons and plasma batteries, and the subsequent flashes reflected from low cloud bases told the story of a conflict being waged, but not of how it was going. The Link wasn't reaching anyone that could answer. Jakob verified that there were no transducers responding that he could detect. The hills from only three valleys away were blocking the weak rice-sized transducer signals more than anticipated.

He had the Mark's plasma chambers hot, the barrels preheated, and the port covers opened on those and the lasers. He had pulled in the ramp and was prepared to lift in support of the force he had out now, but if the clanship had realized the opposition came from the nearby ship, he could lift up into a hail of missiles and plasma fire.

He had a hundred and fifty TGs with him total, two dozen went to the valley, and twenty others were on guard at their valley entrance. He had over a hundred on board that were pushing for a chance to go after the Krall, armed only with pulse rifles and pistols. He was worried about why the group had not returned or reported. Although, they obviously had encountered opposition. Sending additional poorly armed TGs out, without knowing what was happening was reckless.

Thad agreed, and wondered why one of the three with Link capability had not called them with a report. He had sent Carlos, a TG1 with a Link to the valley entrance, right behind the previous stampede that had gone to guard that. They hadn't seen a thing of interest other than the same flashes reflected from low clouds. Just a few minutes ago he'd sent Kally, another of the ten TG1's up to the ridge top closest to the ship, with their best pair of old field glasses, to see if she could spot any of the TGs on other ridge tops closer to the clanship.

Kally reported that she could see Peter Godwin, on the ridge closest to the clanship, and that he ran down the slope out of sight back this way for a moment, and then returned to his point of concealment. That implied he was on watch, and without a Link was calling information back down into that other valley. Some of their people were obviously waiting there, and not involved with the fighting.

Reynolds thought most of the cracks he heard, which followed the flashes some seconds later, were from Dragon main guns. The echoes made it hard to be sure that they were only Dragons. The plasma cannons were smaller bore, and he expected them to sound softer. He didn't hear any of those now, but thought he had earlier. He had seldom heard them previously in fighting, because the Krall normally kept them so far behind an assault line, as a means to discourage aircraft attacks, or to fire on human hilltop strongholds from a distance. The loudest cracks were obviously from the clanship, as were the intense red laser flashes. The Dragons only had small lasers.

No sooner than Kally told them she saw Carson, he was Linked with the Mark. Mirikami had Jakob put him on speaker. "We hear you, Carson, Kally is on a ridge top and saw you through her glasses. What's your situation?" The Bridge listeners were on virtual pins and needles.

"Captain, our use of the Dragons and plasma cannons was sloppy, and we found ourselves in a fight with sixteen Krall that stumbled onto us before we knew how to use what we took from them. However, we won that fight because the Krall were driving construction equipment, not more tanks or cannons. Ethan and Conrad led the tanks and cannons out around the protection of the valley opening, and shot out the main thruster system on the clanship. It can't lift, but it can still shoot. We lost Gamal and Jolene on two of the cannon carts when they stayed exposed too long." Sighs and a low groan were all the listeners expressed. Expecting casualties was one thing. Losing the first of the youngsters was another.

Reynolds had a question he couldn't hold back. "Son, if the Dragons took out the main thruster, why can't they blast the guns when the ports are opened? We've done that with big lasers before, and the Dragons have more than enough power to damage the barrels or aiming system, I think."

"Sarge, the Krall infrared vision can see the magnetic field forming a fraction of a second before a pulse is fired. They managed to slam the gun ports closed with their fast reactions. I just passed this on to Ethan and Conrad, but I don't know if knowing that helps. We started with eight Dragons, but two are out of the fight. No casualties by the way, but the ceramic cracked and the turrets won't turn." He rushed to add that last sentence.

"I was about to try something new to help, using the big armored trucks. They have roof top plasma cannons on each section, and there are two of them in the valley below me. We were hoping to try staggered shots at the gun ports, to see if we can catch one as it opened."

Reynolds did a headshake Carson couldn't see. "I didn't know about the advance flash, but the early infrared flash you describe will happen anyway, and they'll just slam the ports closed again. We always had trouble knocking them out, so the guns the PU Army found most effective on clanship gun ports were heavy lasers. They fire instantly with no warning, so perhaps that's why they worked so well. Unfortunately, you only have the small antipersonnel lasers. The alternative was to use a heavy plasma cannon that can burn through the port covers and hull, or fuse them closed. You don't have those either. I think you simply need to prevent the warning flash," Sarge said.

"OK. How do we 'simply' redesign a plasma gun, Sarge?" The frustration was showing in Carson's reply.

Calmly, Reynolds explained. "Perhaps you should try a variation of a trick my ambush teams used a few times. We covered a number of plasma batteries with cloth tarps and wood frames to change their outline, or hid them under haystacks. The Krall drove or walked right up to them before we fired. The tarps and hay were less than cobwebs to the bolts, but we could sight the guns using cameras, which were not covered. If they don't see the first flash at the end of the barrels, they won't have any warning to shut the ports. That concealment may have accounted for our success at surprising them in ambushes."

The silence at the other end was as eloquent as a "DUH" accompanied by a slap on the forehead.

"Sarge, we shoulda brought you with us. You old cats have some tricks to teach us."

Reynolds did a shrug invisible to Carson. "The phrase is 'old dogs' which you don't have on Koban. Unless you carried me, you would have left my tired SG ass below the first cliff you young mountain goats climbed. We never figured out the advance infrared flash thing, which probably happens too fast for us mere mortal men to use to our advantage anyway. How did you learn about that, considering your infrared vision is no better than mine?"

"Watching a rifle bolt fired that grazed my leg before I could react, and then asking the Krall commander, whom I captured, how he was able to dodge a head shot from my rifle. He spilled the data to my Mind Tap."

"You have the clanship commander?" Mirikami blurted. "Still alive?"

"Yes Sir. He should be in the land of the paralyzed numb and dumb by now, but alert and thinking. He has been a fountain of information."

"OK. Try to keep him that way. Let's move on to things that are more vital. I believe I know what you called about, since you didn't come back here with the purloined Krall toys, and tried a shootout with the clanship. How can the few of you there take the ship, even if you disable its outer defenses?"

"Yes Sir. I don't want to risk losing any more of my friends."

"Carson, you can't permit the fear of losses to petrify your thinking. There will be lives lost no matter how carefully you plan, and some will be friends. Once your small force was discovered, and the clanship was prevented from lifting, you had done everything you were capable of doing on your own.

"There will be additional TGs coming to help you take the ship, but first you need to find a way to shield the ends of your plasma cannons on both the Dragons and those on the big transports. I don't want you risking anyone again on those carts yet. Sarge's idea would only be good for a single shot, and then you retreat to cover the ends again, so try to get it done the first try with all six Dragons. Use any available nonmagnetic material that will cover the muzzles and not disperse the bolts. The reinforcements can't rush the ship until the heavy weapons are neutralized."

"Yes Sir. I'll have people looking for covering material, and I have an idea if we can't find anything the Krall left lying around. One serious problem we have is the lack of Link to everyone. These tall ridges cut us off from you sooner than we expected. I see a lot of red in the strata of these cliffs, and it's possible there are more iron oxides here than Jakob expected. We were out of communication with you as we approached the tanks and clanship."

"Carson, modern longer range transducers are something we hope to acquire if we can get in contact with General Nabarone. I plan to send your dad out to you for planning the internal assault on the ship once you pull its teeth. Colonel Greeves and Sarge will take a team to start walking the tunnel towards Novi Sad. I'll send another TG with a transducer to stay on the ridge where you are, for a constant Link. We had ten TG1s and ten TGs equipped with transducers when we left home, and I only have sixteen of you down here with me, and two each on the other ships. I'll standby here with Chief Haveram and a couple of Linked TGs for relay or as runners. Good luck to you, son."

"Thanks. I believe we'll have the clanship guns silenced soon. Out."

As Carson signed off, Mirikami turned to Dillon. "I know Thad has more military training than you, but I need him and Sarge to make contact with Poldark forces. You've participated in all of the ship clearing practices, and the kids know how to do that anyway. I want you there as a stable influence for them, and a source of older advice.

"I'll send you with another hundred TGs, including most of those guarding our valley opening. The clanship doesn't have any warriors to spare to send over here, so two on watch with one Linked is enough for a warning. You take the Krall shuttle and stay below the ridges to land where Carson is. Haul as many TGs with you as will fit in the shuttle, and let Carson teach you and them, by Mind Tap, how the transports work. The rest will go overland as before, to the valley with the second pair of armored transports.

"As Sarge said, these young mountain goats would leave your tired SG butt far behind. Fly back to join the others at the other valley and a TG1 can pass on what Carson teaches you about transport operation. All of you should be able to crowd into the two big trucks, to drive to join with the other two. When the clanship guns are down, you have four armored transports for shelter to surround the clanship. The portal doors can't hold up to your massed cannon fire for long, so the Krall may decide to come out after you, thinking humans can't beat them."

Dillon laid a hand on Mirikami's shoulder. "Sounds like a plan, Tet. I don't know about you, but letting these young squirts have all the fun wears on the ego. Know what I mean?"

Thad nodded in sympathy, but offered a caution. "Being closer to the action is fine, but don't let yourself be fooled into thinking we SGs are a match for a Krall, just because the smallest TG kid, including the girls, can kick Krall asses in a straight up fight."

"I'll keep my head down. Let me go pass the news to our eager beavers below."

Just then, cheers were heard from decks below. They had not restricted Bridge access, and had spoken to Carson on speaker. The exciting news, once overheard, shot down the stairs with several TGs that had been eagerly waiting.

Thad shook his head and chuckled. "If I needed more proof that I have not instilled military discipline in these youngsters, that sound is as conclusive as it gets. I will be pleased to have the task turned over to men that have combat experience, and have done more than play militia war games over twenty years in the past."

****

Dillon flew the Krall shuttle out of its small hanger, preceded by the rush of TGs on foot headed to take over the clanship. The shuttle had barely departed when Greeves and Reynolds walked down the ramp, followed by twenty TGs, two of which were TG1s. They headed for the concealed vehicle ramps of SOB-23, and Reynolds lowered one of the ramps as he passed the hidden control pad.

As soon as they had marched down into the parking area, Reynolds keyed the ramp to close using the ambient light that filtered down. The ceiling lights would activate once the ramp shut. Only this time they did not.

A shouted command came from the darkness behind them. "Lower your weapons to the floor and freeze in place. We can see every move you make. Your Links are disabled, so calling to the ship for help is a waste of time, and hazardous to your health. Greeves or Reynolds, whichever of you is in charge, kindly tell those youngsters with you to quit moving around and looking for us, or someone is going to get killed."

As startled as they were at the trap that had been sprung, hearing their names called out was more surprising to the two older men. Yet that seemed promising for their goal of making contact with Poldark forces, because the voices were clearly human.

Thad spoke out. "TGs, these appear to be the people we hoped to contact. Carefully unsling and lower your plasma rifles to the floor. They have night vision. Don't do anything foolish to ruin our mission." As he spoke, he lowered his own rifle, bending slightly, and heard the rustle and clatter behind him, and from Reynolds on his left.

A different voice, from another direction, confirmed there was at least one other person watching them. "Don't forget your other Krall gifts. The pistols and belts as well. Don't even check the safeties. Keep your hands clear of the gun butts, and lower them to the floor by the belts."

"Do what he says people." Thad also did as directed, but he was discomfited by the reference to *other Krall gifts*. Clearly, they were under a cloud of suspicion from whoever this was. On reflection, Greeves wasn't very surprised by their suspicion. They had access to a Krall ship and weapons, which other humans could not operate.

A third voice came from another direction, obviously conveying that they were surrounded. "Shuffle straight ahead until we tell you to stop. Make sure you don't trip and fall on a weapon until you are all clear. That could cause one of ours to go off with a fatal result for the clumsy person."

Thad repeated the advice. "Keep your boots on the floor as you shuffle, gently shove anything aside you encounter. They don't know yet we came here to offer them help and the intelligence they need. We need to convince them we are allies."

"Shut up Greeves! No clues as to how you want them to behave. We will get what we want from them without your damned help." The sharp, nasty tone of voice from a fourth person showed there was more than professional caution being displayed. That man was definitely hostile.

The sounds of their boots scraping the floor lasted for a longer time than necessary for the last person in the group to have cleared the pile of weapons. Their captors were being extra cautious. Even in the blackness, Greeves knew they were still less than half way across the large parking area. The echoes confirmed that, and his now dark-adapted eyes caught a faint green glow from patches along the walls, where he recalled water seeps were present. It was the faint glow of the bioluminescence of algae growths, which Reynolds had said were in the tunnels.

He saw multiple shadows briefly block the green glows from each side, and not from where he had heard the voices originate. There were at least a dozen of them to the sides. From slight noise, which they couldn't fully avoid making, more of their captors were behind them, blocking access to the firearms. He detected no sounds from his front, which meant that they now had clear lanes of fire at their captives, with no risk of cross fire to themselves. Professional certainly, but not comforting.

He suddenly realized they had not ordered them to remove their knives. The calf sheaths would be clearly visible to night vision. They were apparently not concerned, implying they probably wore armor. Only he had not heard the heavy thuds, and servo noise that he expected the powered armor Reynolds spoke about to make. Perhaps it was something lighter than heavy body armor. In any case, even knives in the hands of TGs could be deadly missiles to light armor. That meant they didn't know anything about the capability of their younger captives. Including observing what the TGs had done scaling the distant cliffs, or fighting the Krall. At least not yet.

"Stop." It sounded like the original voice from behind them. Perhaps the leader?

"Place your hands behind your heads, fingers interlaced. We will gradually bring the light up so that no one needs to fake a grimace or turn to avoid a bright light. Keep still and facing forward. A few of you shuffled to the sides and are slightly turned the wrong way. When you see the far wall, where you were headed when you came down the ramp, turn to face that way."

The slowly increasing dim ceiling glow was easy on their eyes, and Greeves saw that Reynolds was several steps ahead of him to his left, and the far wall was perhaps fifty feet ahead. Too far to make a dash for any of the doors there, which were all closed anyway.

"Young lady with the dark hair, turn to your right and face the back wall."

That had to be Kally, since the second girl with them, Miriam, had almost blond hair. It was the calm cool voice of the original speaker. He then confirmed he was in charge.

"My name is Captain Joseph Longstreet. I am in overall charge of the three teams that have captured you suspected collaborators." The gasp of astonishment of the TGs was clear, but the accusation was not a surprise to either Greeves or Reynolds.

"That's right! We have every reason to believe that you are cooperating with the Krall, and have been granted an encrypted key to use their equipment, such as the plasma rifles we just took from you. We watched you march out of the clanship and observed the departure of almost eighty more of you from the valley, and saw the Krall shuttle that followed them. I think the others are going to link up with the second clanship five miles from here, and this group was to either disarm the demolition charges here, or demonstrate that you could travel through the tunnels that Sergeant Reynolds knew were here, and lead closer to Novi Sad."

They heard his no longer careful and quiet steps as he walked around the captives, and stopped to the right of Reynolds about ten feet away. He was carrying one of the Krall plasma rifles, pointing a human one in Reynolds general direction.

"Mr. Reynolds, I no longer consider you worthy of the rank you previously held, yet I would like to know what the Krall offered you to turn you to their side. You don't appear to be particularly beaten down, as past collaborators have been, and your left arm has been regrown under their tender care. None of you appears to be in poor shape. Why is that?"

He shrugged. "The answer is simple, if difficult to believe, because none of us have been turned by the Krall. The parts of our force you saw leave just now is on their way to finish the attack we started on the Krall clanship you mentioned. A smaller force captured some parked Dragons and portable plasma cannons, and used those to disable the main thruster so it can't lift. They didn't have enough people with them to take the ship after they knock out the main guns, so we sent them some help. There are over a hundred Krall warriors still aboard the other ship."

"That's a nice bit of bullshit Reynolds. I was only told to bring a few of you back alive. I don't need you if you intend to tell me fairy tales." He raised his rifle.

Thad spoke up. "Not only is that the truth, but your satellite surveillance can easily confirm the activity there. We've lost two of our group to their return fire, and have killed at least fifteen Krall, using their own captured weapons against them."

"I think you saw the same cloud cover that I did this afternoon, so you are stalling for time. Did you really believe we would accept that you could steal their weapons, and then beat any of them using them? Except for the four older men we've seen, all of your so-called troops look like kids, and about a third are girls. I heard you address them as TGs. What does that designate?"

"I am a Second Generation product of a project to improve humans so they can fight the Krall, an SG if you will. These younger people are Third Generation, or TGs. If I'm not mistaken, you yourself are a member of Special Ops, a group that is a product of another project to increase human effectiveness against the Krall. Our TGs are almost certainly a far greater step in that direction than you have achieved. We came to Poldark specifically to show General Nabarone what we can do, and to share intelligence and technology that you do not have. I was once a friend of the general."

"We know, and his link to you has been discovered. However, I don't answer to the general because my chain of command is outside his control. Don't plan on an appeal to his friendship to protect you. I'm authorized to execute any of you that I deem uncooperative. One thing I need from you right now is access to the key that allows you to operate a Krall plasma rifle. And per your unsubstantiated claim, use their Dragons, clanships, I presume, and that shuttle that just departed."

Thad nodded. "That is correct, we wear such a key, and we came prepared to share it with the rest of humanity."

"Wear the key?"

"Yes, each of us does. It is embedded in some sort of quantum matrix, which every Krall bears. We have some of the tools that can embed the key in anyone that is willing to wear the stigma of a Krall tattoo."

"You have got to be shitting me!" He looked sharply at Kally, when she snickered.

"I'll make this a lot less amusing young woman, if you wish. I'll not grant you the honorific of Lady until I think it's deserved. What is your name?"

"Kally Murchifem, Sir. I have a Krall tattoo that allows me to use their equipment. It marks me as what they once termed a 'worthy enemy' to one of us. I wear it proudly." Her cool confident voice clearly had caught Longstreet off guard. Neither she nor any of the young captives appeared particularly afraid or cowed.

"This is the same kind of mark at the throat that all of the Krall wear? I see you all have them covered if you wear them. You aren't quite as proud as you claim, are you?"

Kally answered for herself. "We were ordered to cover them until we had a chance to explain their purpose. However, I don't think you have ever seen any like the one we wear. May I show you? All I need do is open the top button of my tunic to show the base of my neck, using one hand."

Longstreet leveled his rifle at her and said, "Slowly, one hand only, keep the other hand behind your head."

She slowly and smoothly used her left hand to release the button, and folded both sides of the tunic away, revealing the black oval. "Do you want me to turn around to show every one, Sir?"

"Go ahead, slowly."

She made a graceful slow pirouette on her right foot, both hands back behind her head now. She stepped down from the rotation precisely where she had started.

Shifting his rifle to cover Greeves and Reynolds, Longstreet ordered them to open their shirt tops one handed. The captain merely stepped forward a few yards to see their tattoos.

"You claim that is the key. I know for a fact we have cut those from dead Krall and they did not allow anyone to activate Krall devices."

Thad gave him the only answer he had. "We don't know how they work. It's based on technology that even the Krall don't understand. They received it from an ancient race that tried to help them become civilized. They killed the Olt'kitapi for their attempt to help them. That same species designed their clanships, and probably designed the weapons and tools the Krall use. We have some of the ancient tools they call Katushas, made by that advanced race, which can apply the tattoos. Once you have the tattoo, it allows humans to use Krall weapons and equipment. We have reason to believe it uses some quantum property, and when the wearer dies, the key becomes useless in less than an hour."

Longstreet reached down with a pointed tool he pulled from a breast pocket, and pressed the recessed talon release point on the power pack of the Krall rifle he held. Retaining the power pack, he motioned one of his men over to take the rifle. "Kally, please step out of the group and stop in front of me."

She walked in that oddly easy glide that he'd noticed all of the younger people seemed to use. Graceful, with a strange impression of strength conveyed as they moved, almost cat like.

She halted three feet in front of him, ignoring the several rifles that had tracked her movement.

"Kally, these power packs can be activated by a Krall, even without being attached to a rifle, to check their level of charge. Show me how to do that please." He offered her the pack.

She accepted the device, and then he noticed for the first time that she wore a thimble-like cap on one finger, with a short bluntly pointed tip to act as a talon. She smoothly depressed the recessed power activation button, and the charge indicator lights brightened to show it had a full charge, then the lights dimmed, as was usual. She looked up at him, and handed the power pack back to him, with an invitation. "If you hold the pack and my hand, you can also do that using your pointed talon substitute. If you let go of my hand, the pack will only stay activated for ten or twelve seconds."

"Just like it works when we have a freshly dead warrior," he replied. "No thanks, I don't need a demonstration, I've done it before for real. Please step back a few feet, but don't return to your previous spot."

He appeared to want her covered within the group, but perhaps might have more questions for someone he considered the most helpless member of the twenty-two of them. Thad suppressed a smile at that, knowing he and Sarge were the weak links of this group.

He looked at Greeves. "Where is one of the tattoo applying tools you described? You called it a Katusha?"

"We have a number of them, but I didn't bring any with us because they are irreplaceable without capturing another clanship, or killing a Krall that carries one. We intended to use those as trade goods to negotiate for supplies and for the training of our TGs to fight the Krall. We also have some single ships that work, if you have a tattoo, and when we take the other clanship, you are welcome to that, minus any small weapons we need ourselves."

"You are not in a position to negotiate. Besides, how many years do you think it would take to teach your mostly teenagers here to fight a Krall?"

"Captain, I happen to know that you are very seriously underestimating what these youngsters can do. Any one of them is already more than a match for any two unarmed Krall you have ever seen. I dare say, unarmed, none of your men present here, all twenty or thirty of them I presume, could beat any three of these kids, and probably not the two girls alone."

There were snickers from some of the spec ops, which Longstreet glared down individually. He didn't like how the interrogation kept slipping away from the direction Colonel Trakenburg had preset. These people were not what he'd been expecting. He had never seen well-treated Krall captives, ever, not even the wrecks that had become collaborators for better treatment. These people were far too confident, and almost made sense.

"I don't intend to have some kid pay for what your mouth promises, Greeves. How about you or Reynolds risk getting the crap kicked out of you by one of my men? That should tell me if you are full of shit or not."

"Captain, I would try that, since I'm certainly stronger than any average man you have ever faced, but I don't come close to their speed or strength, and even if I win, you would not be convinced it wasn't a fluke. The same for the Sergeant, who is Second Generation, like I am."

"What the hell do you keep going on about generations? Reynolds was on Poldark in the last year, and although he had a decent record, he was sure as hell no superman Krall killer."

"I'm still not Captain," Reynolds answered, "but I may come almost as close as your boys, even without the fancy black muscle suits you wear. If it will get things moving, I'll risk a beating now to get you to test one of these youngsters. Frankly, you are exactly the trainers I hoped would teach them what they need, to go raiding into Krall Space."

Longstreet made a face. "I see the suit talk has spread even to the masses. That was top secret two years ago."

"It probably still is pretty secret on our side. We picked up one of your half dead casualties coming back from an ambush, and he had a bad plasma burn to his ribs. Damned near broke one of my team member's leg when he went through a spasm. The suit obviously magnified his strength. He didn't make it to a field hospital. Mumbled about running out of juice. It's common knowledge you spec ops use drugs of some sort. I assumed that was what he meant. We never wrote it up so we wouldn't have to tell anyone about it later.

"Rather than getting my ass kicked, how about I arm wrestle one of you, using my left arm which was regrown, against the left arm of one of your guys in a suit. I'll probably lose, but it may prove a point."

"Maverick, over here. Reynolds, step out of the group." He pointed to a spot on the floor.

A burly man, shorter than Reynolds, but with massive shoulders and arms came over.

"Mav, hand me your weapon, just pull off the armored glove. When Reynolds is down flat, with me covering him, get down and face off, left arm against left." He looked at the other captives, and then his other men. "Men, don't watch the match, watch them." He jabbed a finger at the captives.

The two men laid flat on the floor. It wasn't the best way to arm wrestle, but neither man gained or gave up any advantage.

"Grip hands but don't start until I say so." He watched the two adjust their hands and grip, and spread their legs to increase their leverage advantage on the smooth floor.

"Ready?" Both men nodded as their grips tightened. "Go!"

The trooper he had called Maverick clearly went for the quick kill, and grunted as Reynolds' arm started to yield and swing backwards. Then Sarge's handgrip noticeably tightened and there was a cracking sound and Maverick's face drew pinched. The two forearms swung back more vertical as the spec ops man lost his initial advantage. He tightened his jaw and shifted his right shoulder, and gradually started to force Reynolds arm back again. However, it was clear from the flushed face that Maverick was straining and looked to be in pain. Reynolds was under exertion, but it didn't seem to be taking the same toll on him as for the other man, even as he gave ground. After almost two minutes, the eventual decision would clearly go to Maverick, as Reynolds, still not as red faced was slowly being forced down.

Showing only mild strain in his voice, Reynolds made an offer. "Maverick, I'm willing to yield if you are willing to let this end. I'm getting tired and we both know you'll win shortly. I'll get muscle fatigue but your suit will not."

With a grunt, and a nod of agreement, the two men eased up and pulled their hands apart. The hands came apart seemingly with some reluctance, as if they couldn't quite make them let go of their grip. Finally, their hands apart, Reynolds was rubbing his hand and arm to restore feeling as he pulled his legs around to sit cross-legged, facing his opponent.

"That was one hell of an effort Maverick. I could never have continued with a broken finger. You had me for sure despite that."

The other man's face had lost its redness, and he was gingerly rubbing his left hand. He actually grinned. "You cracked my little finger. Without the suit and painkillers, you would have had me. How in the hell did you develop a grip and arm like that? We need to develop a black glove to go with the suits if I ever have to arm wrestle anyone like you again."

"Mav, are you saying he about matched your arm, even with your suit to help? He supposedly regrew that arm after his armor was blown open. It should be weaker." Longstreet seemed impressed.

"Captain, without the suit and the drugs, I was beat from the start. I don't know what a Second Generation is or what it even means, but we want what they have in our program if he's typical."

"Well, I obviously had some secret help too." Reynolds told them cryptically. "However, I'm not at liberty to talk about it yet. Colonel Greeves here has beaten me at this game before, using tables and chairs instead of that awkward floor position. I'm sure what we have to offer will come up soon in discussions. I might add, that had I been matched up against little Kally there, and she put in the maximum effort she could, I might well be having my left arm regrown again."

Maverick and Longstreet both looked at the smallish-sized young girl skeptically.

Still without turning around, Thad renewed his offer. "Match Kally against any two of your men, although I won't order her to allow herself to be injured if they start to get rough. I promise you that she could take them hand to hand, and using any hand weapon, even if she had never used it before. For your safety, I'd suggest hand to hand.

"This is not bragging, and some of our TGs have killed Krall in gunfights, beat them in knife fights, and dominated them in unarmed combat. However, they aren't invincible. We have two reported dead out in those valleys towards that clanship. If you simply use fine radar mapping, you should see our people attacking that clanship. We stole their eight Dragons and sixteen plasma cannon carts after they unloaded them and parked them unguarded, confident that humans couldn't use them. We also have four of their heavy armored transports. We are going to *take* that clanship because they will never leave us alone after they learn it is humans operating our ship. Its nickname is the Mark by the way, after the tattoo marks we wear, which allows us to operate the ship."

They had agreed to leave off the word Koban, so that name could not lead back home if the Krall heard it used.

Longstreet made a decision. "This is all being recorded, and if I don't prove to the watchers what you claim you can do, this will be a tough sell to convince them that you are actually fighting the Krall. I'm halfway there, but please ask one of your young men to do the honors. I can't risk the allegation that my men held back because they were fighting a teenaged girl.

"Greeves, to make this simpler, the right side wall has no doors or tunnels, so I want you to lead your people over there and sit with your backs to the wall. I'll post twenty armed men to watch you. If your youngsters prove as capable as you claim, I don't know if I have enough people to guard you. I'd *never* try to hold twenty-two unarmed Krall with only thirty men."

"Captain, we are not out to kill or hurt the people we need help from, to save ourselves from the Krall. We might beat ten times our weight in warriors, but not their entire species. We are too few."

"Tell me about it." The spec ops man said in sympathy.

Quickly, Longstreet pointed to two of his men, telling them to discard their weapons and scaled armor. They stood like black demons with rippled and bulging muscles, the exomuscle body sheaths coating them like a layer of ebony, from boots to neck. One man was about six feet two and had a powerful looking build. The other man was about six feet, leaner and faster looking. It was a smart choice, selecting men that represented two different type opponents, and probably different fighting styles.

Thad had two preferred choices from his group all along, both were TG1s, and Longstreet had ruled out Kally. It wasn't that Thad lacked any confidence in Warren Brock, his other TG1, but little Kally would make for such a great contrast when she won. Warren was five feet ten inches, and looked like he weighed one hundred seventy pounds. That was deceptive, because the denser muscles and bones of their genetic enhancements added about twenty-five pounds of weight to his apparent build.

Warren removed his shoes and two calf knife sheaths. Longstreet had not said anything, but Thad had seen him look at them. He was likely waiting to see if

Thad would make him remove them. It wasn't necessary, and Warren knew he didn't need them, even if the spec ops men had kept theirs. Warren wasn't the best of the group at unarmed combat, but he'd had the Taps from those that were. His additional invisible advantage was his TG1 Mind Tap ability, if he found a chance to sense his opponents.

Unlike training, there were no floor pads here, only hard ferrocrete to break a fall. Warren walked smoothly and confidently out to meet his opponents. Just before he reached them, Thad called out. "Shake their hands first, Warren, and think about how you will start your attack or defense."

That drew a short-lived frown from Longstreet, ending when the advice sounded so generic and innocuous. It was certainly *not* the latter. As they shook hands, Thad knew the two spec ops troops had also heard his advice. It was human nature, so their minds flickered over their own intended opening moves. This was done just as they shook hands with the TG1.

After the quick handshakes, all three backed away, forming a roughly equilateral triangle, perhaps ten feet per side. Warren, fully aware of why Thad had offered his advice when he did, looked Thad's way and nodded in apparent gratitude, turning his eyes away from the larger opponent to his right. The instant reaction of the bigger of the two men was to move in towards his distracted opponent. He took two rapid short steps, as Warren was seemingly oblivious. He swung a leg sweep that would either knock the boy off balance if it connected with his right leg, or get him off the balls of his feet at a time that a follow up punch was aimed at Warren's head.

Before even turning his head back around, Warren suddenly pushed off with the ball of his left foot in what was a deceptively weak looking move, and raised his right foot and leg just as the sweep passed a fraction of an inch below his foot. He drew his foot back halfway under his thigh. His entire body seemed to lift in an arc towards the larger man, propelled by what looked like a simple push-off using only his left foot.

Warren's right knee pointed the way with his lower leg now tucked close under his thigh. The right foot suddenly snapped out in a blur, to connect the ball of the bare foot with the big man's chin, and Warren's right arm looped over, then under the incoming left-handed straight punch, pinning the man's fist in his armpit. He placed his right hand under the big fellow's elbow, hyperextending it as it bent backwards, practically lifting the man in the air when he lowered his right foot to the floor from the kick. Pivoting backwards to press down on the closed fist trapped under his armpit, Warren continued to lift at the elbow with his right hand as a fulcrum and rotated the arm slightly. His opponent was leaning or falling backwards from the chin kick. The elbow popped as it dislocated, and Warren instantly released the stunned man, glassy eyed from the stunning snap kick.

Warren then spun right, ducking under the injured man's arm, and shoved the man forward, past his own body, using that momentum to push him into an opportunistic attack he expected from the opponent to his rear. The TG1 had known that the second man intended to allow him to get involved with the bigger man, and to attack him after he was so engaged.

Unfortunately, for the big man anyway, he absorbed a “friendly fire” kick in his ribs that had been intended for Warren’s left kidney.

The big man collapsed forward to the hard floor, his fall partly caught by his apologetic feeling kicker. That altruistic act for his teammate garnered him a bloody nose, as Warren snapped a back handed fist into said benefactor’s undefended proboscis, producing a satisfying *splat* sound as it broke. The intended sneak kidney kick annoyed Warren a little bit, because the heavy combat boot could have done real damage.

One down in about five seconds, Thad estimated. The other lighter man was blinking to clear his watering eyes, forced to be a mouth breather for now. Warren stepped over the still form of his first victim, walking towards the taller heavier built man as he backed away for a moment to recover. Warren’s hands were swinging easily at his sides, no defensive posturing whatsoever.

Showoff, Thad thought. Oh well, he can afford it with a slow opponent.

The bloody nose guy (neither man had been introduced by name), started jabs and upper cuts in a more traditional form of boxing as he backed away, and Warren walked onwards. Warren easily raised one hand or the other from his sides to smack the blows away in blurred movements, as he continued to walk forward into the onslaught of deflected punches, he always appeared wide open to a punch.

Bloody Nose suddenly became a kick boxer. Warren smacked both of the other man’s hands away when he faked a reach for Warren’s loose fitting shirtfront. The right foot swung up, ready to plant its heel in Warren’s midriff and the man pivoted on his left foot to deliver the kick. The last upward sweep of Warren’s hands, knocking Bloody Nose’s hands away, circled around and down in a flash to catch the foot, just as it reached his abdomen.

Warren easily caught the ankle with his left hand, the boot heel an inch from his lower abdomen. The blow, sent with a good deal of carbon fiber Booster Suit assist to the leg was halted, as if it had hit a rock wall. Warren shoved back and raised the right leg, and snapped a light punch with his right hand into the off balanced man’s unguarded crotch.

He swept his own right leg under Bloody Nose’s supporting left leg. As the man thudded to the floor on his back, Warren kicked him lightly in the left kidney as an object lesson. Then he stepped over the prone man and crouched over him, grabbed both wrists as he reached up to grab Warren’s shirt. Bloody Nose had intended to push up with his knees or feet as he grasped the shirt, and toss the lighter boy over his head.

Instead, Warren caught him by both wrists, and kneeled as he straddled the man, slowly and steadily pushing the arms down and wide to the sides. Bloody Nose kicked and tried to twist or squirm, but found he was locked in place by knees squeezing him like a hydraulic press. He couldn’t turn his body to get a leg up to hook around his attacker’s head or shoulders.

Warren slowly was stretching the man’s carbon fiber reinforced exomuscle arms wider and wider. It was obvious that the spec ops man was trying with all his might to prevent Warren from doing this. However, it appeared that Warren was intent on tearing one or both arms from their sockets. Thad was about to speak out as the groans of pain started, when the relentless force suddenly stopped.

"I don't want to hurt you more, but I needed you to appreciate that I *could* have torn your arms out of your shoulder sockets, much as you thought you and your suit would do to me. Your friend over there merely wanted to knock me out, with only minor injury. However, you were a great deal more mean spirited, ready and willing to do me serious and permanent damage, just to impress your captain."

There was a look of shock on the man's face. The TG stood up, and said, "I'll excuse you this one time, because you were absolutely certain I was a Krall collaborator. I am not, and I think you are starting to believe that I could have beaten a Krall nearly as easily as I could have killed you. I'd rather have you as a trainer any day than as an enemy. I beat you because I'm faster and stronger, but I know only a fraction of your fighting skills." He offered a hand, which the sullen man at first appeared reluctant to take, then nodded and took the hand to be helped off the floor.

Warren, in a show of trust that Thad knew was based on a Mind Tap, turned his back on his last opponent and bent to check on the slowly stirring big man.

"I'll be damned." Longstreet said. "I put him up against two of what I would have called 'ringers' in another era. I picked the best men that I thought could teach you who you were really facing in me and my men.

"Private Mavrinker, aka Maverick or Mav, has never lost at arm wrestling as far as I know, in or out of a Booster Suit. Sergeant Reynolds almost beat him, against the suit!

"Sergeant Jenkins, still waking up over there, is an unarmed combat instructor that teaches our new hard case spec ops training recruits that they are not as tough as they think they are. Corporal Bender there is a problem child of mine, and he is literally the fastest troublemaker I have. Your kid moved like Bender was almost standing still. I have never seen that kind of arm and hand speed, nor sheer strength in a grown man with boosted assists and Heavyside training." He looked at the boy.

"How old are you, Warren?"

"Almost twenty, Sir."

Longstreet shook his head. "Colonel Greeves, I sure as hell hope you and Sergeant Reynolds aren't lying when you say your people are on our side. We need more like you."

Thad was gratified to hear the rank titles restored by Longstreet, even though it was a mere honorific for himself. Sergeant Reynolds might be another matter. He had been in the PU Army for the duration of the war on Poldark, and might be back in it as of now.

"Captain, I sense that you may have crossed a threshold, where you consider our claim to be fighting the Krall a credible story. I doubt that anyone would believe the Krall would willingly permit any group of humans to match them, let alone outperform them. How do we convince your superiors that we need and deserve the help to form units that can strike the Krall where it matters most? Where their war materials are produced."

"Colonel, the feed of our activities is going back to my commanding officer, or at least to his AI. I'm certain he was, or will be watching what happened. However, I'm sure his questions will echo mine. If all of your TGs really have the ability you say, why were my men able to trap you?"

"Several reasons seem obvious. We lack training in sneakiness, suspicion, and equipment such as night vision and body armor. We simply walked into your trap not looking for a threat, and because you are human, we don't *want* to fight you. Had you immediately opened fire as the ramp closed, I think even in the dark our TGs would have shocked you. They think at an accelerated pace and have a phenomenal sense of where they are and where other things are in relation to them. You'll find they have almost photographic memory, which explains how they learn so fast." He wasn't revealing the Mind Tap ability.

"If you aren't trying to be sneaky, then why are your transducer messages encrypted? We tried to listen in, and couldn't understand you. I'm having our main AI search for older quantum keys, since you are using an old human made AI system for the Link." Longstreet was looking at Thad with more than idle curiosity. There was a kernel of suspicion yet.

Genuinely mystified Greeves answered, "I don't know what sort of encryption the AI uses. I wasn't even aware that it did. It is cloned software of an old civilian model from a passenger transport, named the Flight of Fancy. It was new about twenty or so years ago, so I wouldn't have expected it to be encrypted, other than for normal call privacy. You have our Link blocked, so I can't ask Jakob."

"Jakob?"

"The cloned AI. Its software is a subset copied from a JK series AI, and runs on even older hardware, taken from some other passenger ship from over twenty years ago. I don't know what model that older hardware was."

"That combination might have confused my smaller handheld computer, particularly running it in an old system that could be partly incompatible. I'll pass that information on to our primary AI. Frankly, I'd like to hear what you've been talking about today, after we were close enough to record your weak signals. Where have you been, that your entire human tech is that old, or taken from the Krall? You dropped out of sight that long ago yourself. I'm burning to know what you mean by you and the sergeant being Second Generation, and those kids being Third Generation."

"Captain Longstreet, I have my own superior to consult with before that information is released. Our entire small population is at risk if the Krall receives a hint of where we live. Captain Tetsuo Mirikami is the man we have in charge, and he was captain of the Flight of Fancy when the Krall boarded her. Your AI can surely discover when the ship vanished. There must be a list of its passengers and crew from that time. We intend to be very selective about what we let anyone know about us, because that information could fall into Krall hands. We can't let anyone know where we call home.

"When we managed to rescue Sarge here from the clanship we captured, the very one parked right outside, we traded notes about our mutual home, Poldark. I was pleased to learn my former Poldark Militia XO was now a general in the PU Army on Poldark. That captured clanship finally gave us off world transportation. Nabarone seemed to be the right man to trust, to get us what we need to go after the Krall, where no one else can go." He paused, examining Longstreet and some of his men.

"I don't intend to offend. You and your organization seem like the best people to train our youngsters, but I don't know you, or your superiors. If Henry Nabarone vouches for you and your organization, we will share what we can with Henry and with you, which is a great deal. What information and Krall technology we give, you can share with the rest of the Hub government. Concerning ourselves, we have reason to be wary of the Hub government. We want to help all of Human Space, but the feelings may not be mutual from some citizens. We don't want them to know where our home world is located. Part of that is protecting our security from the Krall, part from the Hub government itself."

"Wow, Colonel. You do know how to raise an eyebrow and whet a man's curiosity. I have to tell you that my orders do not come from General Nabarone, but he does know you are on Poldark. Like you, I leave the political discussions to the higher levels. I truly hope we can find a way to cooperate. I'd love to be able to settle some scores with the Krall, on their home turf."

Kally and several others close by had been listening, and had all the verbal discipline of recent high school graduates anywhere. That is to say, essentially none. Kally blurted, "Just wait 'til we get our next mods. Then we'll track the Krall… down…" She cut off weakly as Thad's disapproving frown *suggested* she should hold her tongue.

Laughing, despite revealing his own slip from discipline, Longstreet said, "Ain't youth a pain in the ass sometimes? I have twenty-three year old hot heads like Bender, and you have even younger blabber mouths." He suddenly tilted his head and looked off into the distance. The transducer "trance" was universal. Longstreet was receiving a Link despite the electronic block applied to Thad's own transducer (he tried to call Jakob, as he turned away as if being polite, and muttered, with no reply).

Longstreet listened for several minutes, his face revealing nothing. Finally, he looked over at Greeves and Reynolds with a half-smile. "It seems your earlier Links were mostly about attacking that second clanship, or about exploring these tunnels to reach Novi Sad, to contact Poldark military forces. Colonel Trakenburg said his AI, Max, was deeply apologetic for not figuring out that an old civilian privacy com module, modified to run in an abbreviated AI package, on completely different hardware, wasn't really quantum encryption. He just couldn't understand you. Isn't high technology great?" He chuckled, which sounded sincere.

It was Greeves chance to take advantage. "OK, Captain. Your colonel has spoken, has heard what we said privately, what's the verdict? Are we still considered collaborators, or could we be saviors of humanity."

"Not the former, but he questions the latter. You definitely have a clanship you control. However, he wonders if you captured it from the Krall as you claim, or did you steal it as you did the Dragons? Colonel Trakenburg is going to contact General Nabarone, but is waiting to see if your small force can take that clanship. I'm here to observe the conflict, and then win or lose, after that fight I will escort you to the meeting you and Captain Mirikami wanted. My boss definitely wants to be in on that meeting."

"Your boss knows we are here, some of what we want, and a bit of what we offer, except that I will defer to the judgment of my old friend Henry, who outranks your colonel. Before I recommend that Captain Mirikami also trust Colonel Trakenburg, General Nabarone has a vote. Sorry to make your life difficult and place you in the middle, Captain."

"I'm a shadow in Special Operations. We are always between rocks and hard places, and stepping on a shadow does not hold it in place. My men and I will get by."

"You said you are supposed to observe the taking of the clanship." Reynolds questioned. "Kind of hard to do that down here, unless you have drones or continuous satellite feed."

"We do have some small drones with us, but that makes for small images. The Krall won't tolerate a satellite over territory they hold for very long, and with the clouds, the visual feed is only gray tones from synthetic aperture radar. I was told to use my Mark 10 spec ops eyeballs. We're going out there."

Reynolds laughed. "Isn't that Mark 1 for basic eyeballs?"

"Sergeant, you have been left out of the loop for nine more Marks. With these eyes I can see your underwear," Longstreet bragged.

Sarge was not to be outdone. "Humph. All you see are the dirty outlines where they were. I ain't *wearing* any damn underwear."

In the background, they heard Kally talking to Miriam, the only other girl with the group of boys and men. "Mom was right. They *never* grow out of it, no matter how old they get."

****

The two spec ops electric carts were running almost silently through the small tunnel under the ridges and valleys. The "singing" of their soft tires along the slight ripples on the flooring was the only sound from the carts, with their hushed motors. The tunnel was ten feet wide, so that the four-foot wide carts could pass each other in opposite directions without slowing. The roof was ten feet from the floor, room for even an armored man to run, provided he didn't lift too high between powered strides. The adjustable length carts were set to the maximum of eighteen feet now, to accommodate the ten passengers per cart, sitting on a double row of uncomfortably small popup folding seats, spaced along the lightweight tubular framework. The front light did not illuminate the dark corridor very far. Because the soldiers had night vision, Thad assumed the light was a concession Longstreet made for his "guests," and it didn't run counter to his orders.

Thad and Sarge were seated on different carts, placed in center seats, close to the right hand wall rushing past, their feet supported by slender extendable rods from the frame. Eighteen spec ops troopers were with them, the other nine men staying behind to "protect" the twenty unarmed TGs still in the parking garage. One of those "protectors" was Sergeant Jenkins, whose now reset, dislocated left elbow left him partly disabled, but suited to be in charge of that detail.

Clearly, a sense of belief and a level of trust had formed with the spec ops team itself, but it seemed that Colonel Trakenburg wasn't as sold on their story. Not as much as Captain Longstreet appeared ready to accept them. He had coordinated with his superior, and clearly felt awkward at the tight security measures he was instructed to maintain. The two older men were virtually surrounded by their spec ops "companions" on the carts, with a rock wall on the right to prevent them from suddenly leaping clear of their ride.

The irony to Thad was that Trakenburg had told his mission commander to leave only nine men to guard the vastly greater threat the twenty TGs potentially represented, yet had nine men each guarding him and Sarge.

Thad assumed a video of the young faces and civilian clothing had misled the colonel. Barehanded, the kids could take on their same number of Krall and win. Not that he expected them to do more than wait impatiently.

He had not been allowed to communicate with the Mark, and he was concerned Mirikami might send someone down into the base to see why he had not Linked before proceeding down a tunnel to Novi Sad. A semi-friendly fire incident would not bond the two sides very well.

It was difficult to determine how far they had traveled, but the cart made only a few gentle curves as it moved at about fifteen miles per hour. Longstreet didn't wear a helmet, and wasn't holding any sort of device, yet he behaved as if he was observing something. However, he suddenly slowed the cart and made a right turn into a cross tunnel that had the same dimensions.

As Longstreet glanced over his right shoulder to check on the following cart, Thad could see a pale glow of small amber and red lines of light in his right eye. He realized there was an internal projection system in the man's eye, probably a biological implant that replicated the helmet visor display. He grinned in the darkness. Perhaps he *had* seen Sarge's underwear.

They slowed to a stop about a half mile of travel after the turn. "All off at this scenic rest stop." Longstreet announced, as if a tour guide.

He flashed a small hand held light to reveal a hatch in the wall to their left. He pushed down the L shaped handle and it swung inward into a gently up-sloped corridor that could accommodate men in heavy body armor.

Reynolds nodded. "I've used some of these for my ambushes, but will this one exit in a valley, or on a ridge top? If the latter, we have quite a climb."

"The map says it branches to go both places. However, we're going only part way up inside the ridge, to one of several side rooms where we have some natural looking erosion into the rock strata. At least one of those rooms should have a view where we can look out from those shadowy recesses and observe the clanship and valley floor."

Thad looked closer at the wall sides, which had a semi-glazed appearance. "How and why did you cut all of these tunnels? You couldn't have known the Krall were ever going to invade and give you a use for them. These would take a lot of time and work."

"Not much human work at all, and not much time." Longstreet countered. "A Rim Colony named Fjord had to bore habitat tunnels in granite because they had so little flat open space to build cities on their glacier covered planet. They designed AI controlled combination drilling, boring, laser, and plasma cutting heads for various sized tunnels and rock types. You make seismic maps and lay out where you want tunnels and rooms on a computer. Then let a few dozen of them work away on their own with automated trucks to haul off the debris. Our ridges here were much softer stone than granite, and we didn't even start to cut until the invasion started and we anticipated the future need as we were pushed back. This system would have helped Bollovstic hold out longer if they had done this. This tunnel is less than two years old."

Longstreet gave his hand light to Thad, and one of the other troopers gave one to Sarge. "We have infrared night vision and emitters for those frequencies ourselves, and don't need the lights. I don't want you tripping and falling as you walk up the slope. You'll have to switch them off before we enter the observation rooms. There's natural light that filters in, and we don't want the clanship to see a light shining out. These sedimentary rocks won't withstand a heavy laser or plasma strike unless we are deeper inside."

They climbed for almost twenty minutes on the nearly thirty-degree slope. Longstreet, accustomed to the needs of normal men he sometimes worked with, asked them several times if they needed to rest.

"Nope." Reynolds told him the third time he asked. "You can pick the pace up a bit if you wish. Previously I would have been pooped by now. But as an SG I feel fine, and I know for a fact that Colonel Greeves, who has been adapted longer than me, could walk my butt off if he were in a hurry."

They heard Longstreet mutter as he climbed ahead of them, at an increased pace. "Gotta find out what they really mean by SG and TG."

****

"So it really *is* Thad Greeves?" Nabarone had been all but certain, but the long lapse in time had made it seem too improbable.

"That's what he told my mission commander." Trakenburg confirmed. "He claims he came here looking for assistance, based on what he learned from Reynolds. He said they rescued Sergeant Reynolds from the Krall when they captured the clanship they used to fly here. He didn't say where that supposedly happened, and won't say where they are from. I have my doubts they could have taken that ship, and suspect they snatched it the same way they seem to have taken the other unattended Krall equipment. They have offered us the key to operating Krall equipment, by the way. He told us it's embedded in the damn tattoo's the Krall wear. Our scientists tested those and never found anything, but he showed us that he and his people wear a blacked out version of the tattoo, and they certainly can use Krall weapons. A young girl with him described their version of the tattoo as meaning a 'worthy enemy' to the Krall.

"I spent one of my own satellites to verify that these people actually do have control of the Dragons, mobile cannons, and heavy transports they say they stole. The images came through just before the Krall routinely knocked my bird down, after we confirmed that the Krall equipment is under human control. They apparently had a successful firefight with about sixteen Krall they surprised driving some tractors. After that, they attacked the second clanship, and that fight is still underway. However, they are obviously having trouble knocking out its heavy weapons, despite knocking out its lift capability. Makes me wonder how they took the other ship if they can't pull this one's teeth."

"Do you have a video and audio feed for me, Colonel? I'd like to hear how Greeves sounds and watch his moves. My AI is all but certain it's Greeves, but I'd like one more bit of evidence before I meet him face to face. I assume you have your team bringing him to Novi Sad?"

"I'll have Max send the recordings. However, I wanted to see if their kids; and that's exactly what they are, kids; can take that clanship. I sent Greeves and Reynolds with two of my teams to observe the clanship fight, using an observation post I was told was in a nearby ridge."

Nabarone was incredulous. "You're not going to offer to help them? You'll just watch?"

"General, my own teams couldn't take down a clanship and capture it intact. They *might* infiltrate to its base and blow it up, but would never try to clear it of warriors. Greeves implies these super kids can do that. I'm reserving judgment until I see proof. I'll grant they are damned strong and fast. You'll see that when they pit one boy against two of our better men. He lacks expert hand-to-hand combat skill, but easily took them both down in thirteen seconds by my timing. He could have killed them had he wanted."

"Colonel, when Max called Major Caldwell to set up this conversation, the AI indicated that Greeves had specifically asked to meet with me, and had intelligence to offer in exchange for our help. I hope you are taking good care of him and his people. The man was fiercely loyal to his troops. He may not expect you to send a team to help fight the battle, but he won't look kindly on us if we cost him any of his people. If you have information he can use against the Krall, which doesn't compromise your own mission, I recommend you share that with him."

The short pause was enough to reveal that Trakenburg didn't care for anyone to be telling him how to handle his operations. He must have remembered that Nabarone had done more than grant him access to his former base. He had lost men and material creating the distraction that helped infiltrate his spec ops troops through the Krall lines. The general was another man that was fiercely loyal to his people. Trakenburg respected and shared that trait.

"General, I'll be certain to let my team leader know that."

As soon as the conversation ended, he kept his promise, notifying Longstreet to provide Greeves any help he needed, short of direct involvement with the fighting.

Next, he asked his AI how another search had gone. "Max, what did you find about this Mirikami person, the purported leader Greeves mentioned?"

"Sir, Captain Tetsuo Mirikami was reported lost with his ship, passengers and crew, enroute to an orbital station located outside Human Space. The station itself also went missing, and the presumed disaster represented over a thousand lives lost. It represented the largest single disaster to ever effect University academic personnel, but it did not create as large a news story as other smaller ship losses created in that time frame. The story appears to have been suppressed by the Universities themselves, with cooperation from Hub government spokespeople."

"Another dead man," grunted Trakenburg. "Where did this happen?"

"Captain Mirikami's ship, The Flight of Fancy, was traveling through the spinward Rim region several months before the first known Krall incursions were experienced. Those were the raids when the Krall took thirty-seven passenger and cargo ships. The Doushan Mavray recording was transmitted to us during that time. There were approximately twenty- four thousand people that went missing, without a trace on those raids, and those events helped overshadow the loss of the Flight of Fancy, and the Midwife Station."

"What was a big passenger ship like the Flight of Fancy doing traveling beyond the Rim?"

"Sir, the records indicate that Interworld Transport had a charter contract with a group of Universities, to ferry scientific personnel, specialized equipment and supplies to a biological research station, named Midwife, orbiting a planet unofficially called Newborn."

"What sort of scientific personnel and equipment?"

"Bio-scientist and related professions in a wide range of fields. Microbiologists, biotechnologists, geneticists, medical technicians, pharmacists, bacteriologists, virologists, medical doctors, …"

"Stop." Max might go on for a considerable time listing examples.

The specialties caught his attention, however. Biological research was still a publicly hot button item, despite the military's pressure to seek every conceivable way to confront the Krall invasion. When the Heavyside project was started, finding qualified people to work on creating the biological tools needed for enhancing his Special Operations troops had been hard to find.

"Why were they going to such a remote location? Was their research considered dangerous?" That seemed unlikely to be tolerated. Not after the Clone and Gene Wars, and the Purge (slaughter was a more accurate term) of many of the people that had held that same type of knowledge or education, barely two lifetime's ago.

"Sir, the stated purpose of the research was to study the emerging proto life that was forming from the primordial mixture of organic chemicals that were to be found on Newborn. This was considered an extremely rare planetary discovery. It was called 'unprecedented' in press releases."

"It sounds like they might have run into a Krall raiding party. If so, then another probable Krall capture has yielded a survivor in Mirikami. I wonder how many more of these 'living dead' are going to show up. If all of these eighteen to twenty-year-old youngsters are theirs, then quite a few people must have survived somewhere and had children.

"Max. Link me to Sergeant Jenkins. He's watching those kids."

****

"Colonel Greeves, I have magnification built in, and I'm sorry that I don't have any binoculars for you or Sergeant Reynolds. We travel as lightly as possible. However, we all can see three of the Dragons your people have captured. One each is sheltered behind those two large boulder piles, and one over by that cliff rock spur. I can't see the other three, but my Link signal finder shows they are along the valley on the other side of the clanship, probably also hidden from Krall view.

"The drivers of all three Dragons close to us are outside the mini-tanks, and not entirely visible to us. However, I think they are undressing. Would you have any idea why they might do that? Is it perhaps too hot for them here? This is warm, but not the warmest season by far."

Thad craned his neck to see at an angle through the rock opening. They were nearly one mile from the clanship, and the three Dragons were five hundred feet lower that they were and roughly a half-mile away, and only partially visible. "I can see tanned skin alright. I saw one boy's bare back, an uncovered leg on another, and on the far side by the cliff, I think I see white underwear on a figure that stepped around the front of the tank. Sarge, can you see any better?"

"About the same as you. I'm only five feet to your right, and I have a lousy angle. … Wait, one of the boys climbed on the front of his tank. He's in his drawers for sure."

Longstreet shook his head. "Are you sure they aren't simply too hot in the tanks? We think the Krall like warmer climates, so perhaps the Dragons are hot inside, despite the cloudy sky, and light rain earlier."

"We are all heat adapted, Captain, and this is a cool day back home in the summer. They shouldn't be any more uncomfortable than I am, and I'm not sweating."

Longstreet noted that was true, and mentally filed the remark for later. He had observed that neither man had broken a sweat, while the spec ops troops had glistening foreheads. It wasn't a dripping sweat day, but the climb and quick pace should have had more of an effect on these two men. This implied a hotter home world, and heat adaptation, and probably more gravity than Poldark offered. Although, Reynolds was only six months removed from a life on this planet. He should be at least winded, and he wasn't.

"Damn. Clever kids," Reynolds blurted. "Thad, remember my advice to cover the cannon muzzles? What do you think our pants-off wonder kids are doing right now?"

"By God you're right. I can't tell who is who from here, but that boy has torn his pants in half. They found a way to follow your advice, Sarge. I doubt the Krall will see their next shots coming. Perhaps they can shut the big guns down in a few minutes. I wish I could hear what they've been talking about."

Thad heard a throat clearing behind him, followed by a hesitant offer from Longstreet. "Colonel Greeves, when I was farther down the corridor checking two other observation points, Colonel Trakenburg Linked with me. He informed me that I am now authorized to cooperate and assist you, if it doesn't compromise my teams or my mission. My teams are safe, and you were my mission. I can provide you Link capability to your people out there or at least to those close to us right now. Your old model transducers have less than a third the range of ours.

"It was suggested to me that I should try to arrange 'trades' of information when we grant assistance. Colonel, I'd love to know what those boys without pants have to do with the Krall not seeing them when they drive out to shoot at their ship." He half smiled.

Thad laughed. "Captain, my former rank is from a militia that no longer exists, and I'm not officially a colonel at home, I'm just Thad or Greeves. I prefer Thad.

"The trick they are trying to pull off isn't to make them invisible, it's to hide the flash the Krall see before they fire at the clanship. Our TGs discovered today that Krall infrared vision detects a flicker of light an instant before a plasma weapon fires, giving their fast reactions a chance to duck, or in this case, switch their gun ports closed. That boy on the other side of the valley just slipped one pant leg over the cannon muzzle. We hope the Krall won't see the advanced warning when he next fires at the ship. I assume the other boys are doing the same thing."

"I can tell you that they were told to use their clothes as flash shields by someone named Carson. We didn't know what that meant. He's in the adjacent valley preparing to drive some heavy Krall transports out to fire on the clanship. My men and I all have IR vision embeds, but we never saw the advance flash you describe. How do you see them?"

"I don't see them actually. None of us can because we have no IR capability at all. We learned that detail from a captive Krall, the commander of that clanship in fact. Carson took him prisoner after a firefight with them on construction tractors of some type. He wounded him, them administered a neurotoxin that paralyzes them but leaves them wake and able to hear us. He told Carson about the pre flash." Hiding how they got that info from a Krall could be tricky, but they needed their trust right now.

Longstreet shook his head in amazement. "We will definitely watch for that pre flash. It may be too faint for our eye sensors, or happen too fast to register for us, but that's only a matter of technology. I truly want to get hold of a drug that paralyzes one of those bastards. I met you people an hour and a half ago, and I already see you as a gold mine."

Thad slid a hand into a pocket and pulled out a small vial of pale amber liquid. "Then please accept this gold nugget. That is a concentrated sample of the Krall paralyzing drug, Captain. A single drop, on skin or tongue numbs one of them for perhaps four hours or more. They can breathe, move their eyes, defecate, but that's about all. Long term, you have to feed them by a tube down the throat to keep them alive. That same drop will kill most humans."

They had not tested it that way, but they thought a TG's nervous system would survive a single drop.

"Saying 'be careful' is an understatement, Captain." He handed him the inch long unbreakable sealed tube he generally carried in his pocket.

Longstreet promptly reciprocated. He reached into a slit gap in his flexible Chameleon Skin scaled armor and then withdrew his hand. "Try your Link now, Sir. I am obligated to inform you that I will be able to hear what is said, and that it is likely being repeated back to my headquarters group."

"I understand, Captain. I'm not concerned.

"Jakob, can you hear me?" He waited a couple of seconds to see if Jakob could receive from here. No reply, so he continued, using the shorter-range local transducer-to-transducer communications. "Link to Carson. This is Uncle Thad. Can you hear me Carson?"

"Yes Sir," was the surprised sounding reply. "Dad didn't say or know you were coming out here. Captain Mirikami said he thought you, Sarge, and the whole group had gone down a tunnel to Novi Sad, without making a final com check."

"Well I didn't know I was coming this way either, but that's a story for later. Sarge and I are actually in a position to observe the clanship. There are small tunnels running under and through many of these ridges and valleys. We are in small observation rooms inside the ridge wall, on the opposite side from the ship. We are roughly a mile from the clanship and the valley end where the Dragons must have entered. We can see three of the Dragons, and they just placed pant legs on the barrels. I hear that may be your idea."

"Yes Sir. We couldn't find any material we could safely take out to them, so their clothes were the only option left. I cut off some tough seat fabric with great difficulty, and we cut the blue suit off our now naked Krall commander. I let Carol Slobovic and Andreana D'Alema peek at him after they begged me. No one ever told us the Krall genitals and excretory orifices are as concealed as their ultrasonic ears. The girls somehow thought laughing at him would hurt his feelings. They must have been thinking of boys." He paused, as if realizing he'd strayed off track by that amusing thought.

"Anyway, we tied the fabric and suit pieces over the double plasma cannon muzzles on top of the transports. The other two transports in the first valley, holding our reinforcements, have covered their cannons and are on the way to join us."

"You have done well, lad, and I hope it works. However, clearing this ship is going to be more dangerous. It won't be a surprise this time, as it was on K1, and we *know* there are warriors aboard this time. They'll be waiting for you. How are you planning to coordinate the simultaneous attack on the guns? Are you in contact with Ethan and Conrad?"

"Yes Sir. Conrad, from where you said you're located, is against the opposite wall behind a rock outcrop I believe. Ethan is just around the edge of the canyon wall from the valley where I'm located. He plans to take shots at the clanship if they try to fire on the two arriving transports. The trucks have heavy armor anyway, so they should be safe. Do you want to talk to Ethan? He'll be coordinating the action, since he will be in position to see all of us as soon as he pulls out into the open."

"No. I don't want him to think his dad is looking over his shoulder. Might make him nervous, or worse, ready to show off. I only plan to watch, unless I see anything you need to know about."

"OK Sir. We should be ready in about five minutes. Talk later. Out."

Ending the head tilt of a Link conversation, Thad smiled at Longstreet.

"Thanks, Captain. I feel better, even if I can't really do anything to help."

"You're welcome, Sir. Did I understand correctly? Carson is your nephew, and your son, Ethan is in one of the Dragons?"

"Ethan is my actual son and Carson is the oldest son of my best friend, Dillon Martin, who flew that Krall shuttle you saw. He came out to join the kids.

"We are called uncles to each other's three children, our wives are aunts. Captain Mirikami and Sarge have the same uncle status. As a community, we have grown into a tight knit group, isolated on our remote world, all of us *presumed* dead by the Krall that left us to die. We've waited in fear for the damned Krall to possibly return and wipe us out if we were discovered.

"A clanship recently came to our world, unsuspecting and carrying just six warriors. Two of our TGs managed to take them out, with a bit of support from some allies, and we then had their ship. Once Tet, that's Captain Mirikami's nickname, approves our doing so, we'll be talking more about ourselves, but never about where we live. A single slip to the Krall and our world is toast."

Longstreet now understood their caution. "There must not be very many of you."

Thad nodded. "I don't know the last census exactly, but we are about thirty thousand I think, in two cities. About half of the older adults are Normals, just ordinary people like any Hub citizen. The other half of older adults are SGs, as Sarge and I are, and roughly half of the seven thousand younger children are also SGs. The other half of older children are TGs, with most of those kids younger even than the two hundred we brought with us. I *know* we haven't explained what those terms mean yet, and I won't try right now.

"However, numbers are not all there is to our potential effectiveness. There are not many of you Special Operations forces either, but I'll bet you have a greater impact than your numbers imply. A force multiplier, as you might be described.

"We believe our TGs, with the right equipment and training can take the war to the Krall, in operations much as I suspect you conduct on human worlds. We believe only a force of TGs can successfully raid unsuspecting Krall manufacturing worlds, where they can take on and beat the warriors they'll find. Then they can destroy the war manufacturing plants, operated by presumably unwilling alien slaves. We hope the lack of replacement weapons and clanships will end their war in Human Space. It's a long shot, but the alternative is eventual extinction for the human race. We were privy to Krall history and their goals from before they started the war. They used to talk to us humans captives then, since they didn't expect us to survive long. The government needs to know what we learned."

Before Longstreet could ask him about the cryptic and extremely intriguing reference to allies, or their being on K1, Carson Linked to Thad and Sarge again.

"Colonel, Sarge, I told Ethan I had updated the new arrivals by Tap, and also my dad. We have everyone spread out and loaded in the four transports. My dad has the shuttle and a few TGs to help if we need to evacuate any wounded. As soon as Ethan coordinates with Conrad, we will all charge out and try to hold our fire until the Krall attempt to light us up. We need to get the transports closer, because of the shorter focal range on their tubes. Just so that you know, D1 is Ethan's three Dragons, D2 is Conrad's three, and I'm T1, with all four Transports. I'll keep my Link to you open so you can listen in on us."

"We copy you. Give them hell."

Thad looked at Longstreet, grinned and shrugged. Carson wasn't aware that all their Links were being monitored all of the time by someone, open Link or not.

Thad heard Ethan's voice. "D2, when I give the mark, count ten seconds and then all of you race into the open, and zigzag towards the clanship, use your lasers first. D1 will be coming out with you. We can draw fire from the transports, since we haven't tested them for plasma hits yet. Carson's big blue boy informs him the front of a transport is as tough as the sides. The weakest points are the flexible links between sections, so they will drive straight at the ship until they get close enough for all of them to fire, at about a thousand feet. We can shoot plasma earlier, but try to save that first shot for an open port cover. *I'm* certainly not climbing out in my undies to pull another pant leg over my barrel out in the open. Ready, mark!"

The men in the observation post saw Conrad's mini tank fire a laser across the valley, the apparent visual signal to his other two units to start their count. The watchers also started counting the seconds. Simultaneously on the count of ten, the three Dragons they could see rocked back, as their treads started churning, hidden under their ceramic skirts. They spewed dirt behind them and accelerated from behind their protection, and spun in tight turns towards the clanship. The Krall fire control gunners were quick to respond, and laser ports flew open and red beams lanced out to intercept the rapidly moving and turning Dragons. The tank plasma cannons were held steady on the ship, despite wild gyrations and speed adjustments, and they deliberately went up and down small hills, then briefly behind rocks, all to complicate the manual Krall gunnery.

The ship's lasers were seldom held on a single point on the gleaming white surfaces for long, as the drivers pivoted and turned, all the while closing on the clanship. The Krall were also firing towards the other Dragons or Transports, which were still out of view of the cliff observers.

The first plasma port slammed open and fired a bolt that glanced off the side of one of the Dragons, and it pivoted away just as a heavy laser tried to strike it on the same place. If they could overheat the ceramic quickly as the nearby surface remained cool, there was a chance it could be cracked. The cannon port slammed shut as a medium power hand laser from the tank lanced into the opening before it could fully close. All of the tanks were firing, using whichever front or side laser would bear as they drove madly towards the clanship. Tank lasers were reflecting from the other gun ports, as they slammed closed, or were opening. Other beams were scattering from the edges of the large portals at the base of the ship.

The Dragon drivers were suppressing plasma rifle fire from warriors inside the clanship, shooting back at them through a foot high slit at the base of each of the big doors. The drivers might not be having luck with the gun portals, using the lower powered lasers, but it appeared that they hit some of the warriors at the base. The rifle plasma bolts from the base reduced, and several bolts went wide of any reasonable target, suggesting the shooters or weapon was hit as they fired.

Finally, two of the Dragons approaching from the opposite side came into view, via the deep-set openings in the cliff face of the observation rooms. They now were within a couple of thousand feet of the ship, as were the three Dragons that had started from closer to the observers. Thus far, the Dragons had fired only the lower powered hand controlled lasers, and spent most of their time turning and adjusting speed to prevent plasma bolt hits from being matched by heavy laser strikes. The main guns of the tanks had remained sighted on the clanship, the turrets swiveling as needed and gun elevation changing, apparently holding aim on some selected target on the ship.

The plasma fire from the ship shifted direction, and was firing over the Dragons approaching from the other direction, and all three were now far enough across the valley to be visible. The six mini tanks were forming an arc as they neared the ship. The plasma bolts were barely over those far Dragons, apparently directed at the Transports, still just out of view of the observers.

Suddenly, as two of the ship's plasma cannons were firing in the direction of the presumed transports, two of the Dragons fired bolts simultaneously, while both gun ports were wide open. The port covers slammed shut, but neither gun ever fired again. Two down.

The remaining plasma cannon that could bear on the attackers grew silent for a time, apparently being saved. However, the maxim was that if you can't use it, then it is useless definitely applied here. A heavy laser port slid open and started firing on the front of a Transport that was headed directly at the clanship. One of the three other Dragons fired, and the pulse instantly died, the port staying open. For good measure, the same tank fired again, making sure. Three down, three to go.

As the big Transports closed to within a thousand feet, they split, two turning right, two went left to arc around the ship. The Krall laser gunners leaped at the opportunity to see if they could penetrate the accordion pleated flex joints between segments. As soon as the ports opened, four of the double plasma cannons fired together from the two that turned left. The last plasma port cover froze open, although a bolt still lanced out from its weapon. The two remaining heavy lasers went dead, each cut off in mid shot with a spray of molten pieces and smoke. One of the other Transports used a single pair of its cannons to blast into the open plasma gun port, silencing the last main weapon that could be brought to bear on the attackers. The laser and plasma cannon facing the cliff were useless.

Two tanks, with covered muzzles, had yet to fire. They lowered their barrels to point right into the foot-wide gap at the base of one of the main portals and fired from less than eight hundred feet. The secondary explosion, which that double blast caused, sent wide jets of black smoke, mixed with orange and purple flame spewing out all four sides of the clanship at its base. They must have ignited some pistol ammunition or spare rifle power packs.

The Link suddenly filled with an unintelligible mix of cheers and shouts from what had to be Carson, Ethan, and Conrad, all screaming in victory together.

Smoke surrounded and billowed around the base of the ship. From their higher vantage point, the cliff observers were looking down on a spreading ring of black smoke, left behind as brightly colored orange flames quickly died. One of the spec ops men in the room called out to Longstreet.

"Backside, by the cliff, Sir."

Thad and Sarge only saw the black smoke billowing upwards, as it was diverted by the rock face.

Longstreet peered intently for only a second, and reached into his slit pocket, then spoke over the Link he'd only been monitoring. "Carson, Ethan, or Conrad, five Krall have slipped out of the rear portal by the rock face, and they each have shoulder fired rockets. You may be able to hit them under the base of the ship. Don't wait for them to shoot."

Two of the D2 Dragons promptly fired blindly under the ship, the bolts passing easily through the dense black smoke that would refract or disperse a laser. They fired their front lasers anyway, which were quickly attenuated by the heavy obscuring smoke particles.

Longstreet gave them an update. "You got two of the five. They are separating to either side, staying in the smoke. Three going to the right side, watch out!"

Suddenly, a short streak of slender yellow fire lanced out of the black gloom, and struck a Dragon of the D1 group, right at the turret and lower body, blowing its turret into the air.

Sarge's shout followed. "The driver may be alive. Protect him before the warriors try to finish him off."

The two D1 companion Dragons turned towards the damaged tank, lasers flashing into the thinning but spreading gloom and one fired a plasma bolt through the darkest region. A warrior with a half burned off black uniform ran out of the smoke, plasma rifle leveled at the disabled tank. He fired at the open top even as two lasers virtually cut him in half, his upper torso and arms trying to fire again, as the upper body toppled off the collapsing legs and lower body. He didn't get a last dying shot, as his flash broiled brain made his head explode, from the heat generated by two intersecting laser beams.

"Where are the other two?" That was Carson's voice, sounding even and calm.

In an equally calm voice, Longstreet said, "Both are coming around the back side of the ship, on the side away from the valley entrance. They are following the rock face in the dense smoke, looking to get clear."

One of the Transports continued around the ship in a narrowing spiral towards where he was told the Krall were going. The four plasma cannons fired down into the smoke, aiming for the base of the cliff, firing one barrel at a time, taking four rapid shots, then had to wait a few seconds for a plasma build up for the next shots.

"Both are down, but one is able to move. He has a tube up and he may fire," warned Longstreet.

A second shaft of slender yellow flame shot out of the gloom, and the small missile struck the front right section of the Transport at a sharp angle. The hypervelocity missile and its shaped charge scoured the armored side with a green glow of molten and burning copper. It glanced into the less angled second section, but had lost its less-than finger sized core of molten metal on the initial impact. It had been fired from too close for maximum effectiveness, and struck at an oblique angle. The next four plasma cannon shots finished the job of cauterizing its Krall targets. The hot carbonized Krall molecules would only be dangerous if someone ran up to breathe them.

Carson's voice, strained, but not panicked came over the Link. "Uncle Thad, the TGs we carried out here will start on clearing the ship as soon as we can see, but if you have a med kit, or whoever that was helping us has one. Please get it out here now. The first missile hit Ethan's Dragon. I hope Sarge was right."

Thad's throat was tight, as if his heart had risen to block his effort to breathe normally.

Chapter 5: Let's Make a Deal

Ethan regained an agonized and fragmented awareness as he was being placed on a stretcher. He was surprised to see his father by his side, speaking with a man Ethan didn't recognize. The stranger wore an odd camouflage system, which shifted colors as if it had small live Tri-Vid images in thumb nail sized pixels. He nearly vanished, except for his bare face and hands, when the suit blended with its background anytime he held still for a few seconds.

He heard his dad speaking. "Captain, if you can help us get my son and the other three most seriously wounded to med labs at Novi Sad, we…, myself in particular, would be extremely grateful. If we have any more casualties before the clanship is cleared of Krall, the shuttle can bring them over to the Mark as well."

"Thad, Colonel Trakenburg has already promised to provide you with the best medical assistance we have. I was told General Nabarone has offered that as well. Our problem for your son is the speed with which we can get him to that care, and the route we need to take.

"My men and I infiltrated through Krall lines to reach our old base, and that is our hazardous route back to Novi Sad, through dirty water filled ditches. It will be difficult even to take your less serious casualties, but your son here can't wait, or tolerate being submerged in the foul waters. We can't get any airborne rescue craft over the Krall lines out to here, and they would follow them to you even if we could."

Ethan reached out to grasp his dad's hand. "Dad, did we take the ship?" He was startled at the wheezing sound of his own voice, accompanied by a lancing pain in his chest that made him gasp.

Thad knelt quickly beside his son. "Ethan, you have a penetrating chest wound and a severe burn on your left side. Don't try to speak or you might separate the Smart Bandages. You have one covering the hole in your chest, and one on your plasma burn. Hold my hand, and see what I see."

The images of the damage to his body, and his father's concern and hope for treatment and recovery flooded his mind. He was shocked at the depth of the two-inch wide puncture in his chest and into his collapsed right lung. That came from fragments when the Dragon's turret was blown off by a shoulder fired Krall rocket. The burn he realized was the result of a dying warrior rushing the open topped mini-tank to make sure he was dead. The plasma bolt struck the inside of the tank, and deflected into his left rib cage. That explained the burned flesh smell, and accounted for most of the steady pain he felt.

He knew from his dad's mind, that this damage was repairable in the modern med labs available on Poldark. However, reaching that medical treatment was a problem from here, located so deep inside Krall controlled territory. There were several other seriously wounded among the TGs, and he learned that four had been killed. The lower three-quarters of the clanship's decks were in their hands now, but the operation wasn't over.

He sensed his father had blocked the information about who had been killed and wounded. This wasn't an easy operation, as the raid on K1 had been. He worried about his friends still in the assault. All of the TG's were friends to some degree, but many were mainly acquaintances from their two relatively small communities. He had some friends he couldn't bear to loose.

He sent back that he knew his dad was doing all that he could, and that they would find a solution. They always did. Then the painkillers and sedatives he'd received made the world start to fade away again. His last view, one of great relief for him, was when he caught sight of Sarge, talking with Carson and Uncle Dillon next to one of the large transports. Now he could let himself sleep.

Dillon was trying to explain to Carson what the problem was. "Son, the Krall probably would not fire on one of their shuttles, and we can coordinate with General Nabarone to allow us to pass over their lines unmolested, and land near a medical facility. Except, when Krall field commanders see one of their shuttles enter enemy territory unmolested, they will check out where it originated. They have this area well covered with radar. They certainly know that two clanships landed here, but that isn't anything but clan personal business. If a shuttle leaves this area to safely land at Novi Sad, or anywhere in human territory, we will have intensely curious Krall visitors, warriors and clanships, coming to the Mark's doorstep."

"Dad, we can't let Ethan die because we won't try to get him to help in time. Besides, how do we know the warrior holdouts on the top decks haven't already reported that humans are taking over their clanship?"

Even as he said that, his experience with Mind Tapping the ship's commander and the previous captive Krall made that possibility very unlikely. None of them would admit to the dishonor of losing to the human prey animals. They would fight to the death, but they were incapable of surrender, or of admitting to other Krall that their prey had beaten them. They were being beaten here in straightforward combat.

A TG, Deigo Chin, ran over with a message. "Captain Mirikami was informed of the mission status, and our casualties using the shuttle radio. He asked about the Link problems, and now he knows about the twenty captives those guys are holding." He hooked a resentful thumb towards the fading in and out view of the spec ops soldiers, clustered behind the cover of one of the other four Krall transports. Captain Longstreet had led Thad and Sarge out of the labyrinth of tunnels and across the valley to the clanship, once the internal assault had started.

Longstreet heard the boy, and noted his tone of voice. "I have Linked with my men, and your friends have been released and allowed to pick up their weapons. They should be back to your ship within minutes. Until we knew you were not Krall collaborators, we took no chances."

That didn't fully eliminate the sullen look he returned to Longstreet, but he nodded and ran back to the shuttle to relay that information.

Dillon patted his son on the shoulder, and promised to try to find a way to speed up their departure. He joined Thad and Captain Longstreet.

"We have an old med lab on the Mark," he reminded Thad. "It will be better than his laying on that stretcher while we talk, and it will start treating the burn and internal bleeding. It has copies of the nanites Sarge over there showed up with, when we restored his arm."

Longstreet made an offer. "I have an injector for nanites we carry for our own wounded on missions, but it's tailored specifically for use on spec ops troops. I'm told it has some severe detrimental side effects for people that do not have the same technological enhancements and implants we have. His eyes could be severely damaged for example. It might save his life, but leave him blind, and there are other potential side effects I can't discuss."

"Thanks, Captain. If it appears necessary, I'll accept that risk before I let him die." It was hard discussing your own flesh and blood as if they were some random casualty.

Carson, still technically in charge of the mission to clear the ship had a proposal. "We don't need any additional support to finish clearing the ship. Why don't you load the shuttle with our injured and take them to the Mark? If we have any more wounded, you can return to get them, Dad."

Dillon accepted the sensible advice from his son, and the shuttle soon held the four wounded, with a couple of TGs with minor cuts and burns to carry Ethan's stretcher.

As he turned towards the shuttle, Dillon made a comment to Thad. "I'll radio Tet when we're on the way. I wish the Link worked this far out."

"Mr. Martin," Longstreet called to his back. "I removed the block on your Links, and my portable AI now understands your old com system mixture of equipment and software. We have more signal power than you do if you wish to allow our system to relay for you. It won't be private, but you'll have the range."

"Really? Thanks. I had tried earlier and it didn't work. Let me try again.

"Jakob, Link to Captain Mirikami please."

"Yes Sir," was the familiar reassuring voice.

"Tet, I'm bringing in four wounded. Have the chief set up the med lab. Ethan will have to go in as soon as we arrive."

"Dillon," he sounded surprised. "I have tried multiple times to Link with you. I now understand from the shuttle radio talk with Diego that we were actively blocked by spec ops. Are you airborne so I'm able to receive you now?"

"Not yet. The spec ops commander, Captain Longstreet, is using his portable AI system to relay our Links. It has more power and greater range than do our transducers. He's told us he can't get our wounded back to Novi Sad any faster than they can infiltrate back through the enemy lines. We need a more advanced med lab, which Longstreet says can handle worse injuries than what Ethan has. We have to get one to him out here, because moving him the way spec ops arrived is all but impossible."

The pause that followed brought an image to Dillon's mind of Tet pulling at his lower lip while thinking. The analytical response, when it came, suggested he had been right.

"We need to trade information, get modern com equipment and armor, obtain new med labs, get training for the TGs, and give the PUA a Krall prisoner or two.

We will donate Krall equipment to them that we don't need from that clanship, after we show them how to activate the equipment. Their spec ops teams also need to return home safely. Why is everyone talking about walking and using tunnels?"

"OK. You must mean for us to use the shuttlecraft, requiring several trips. It was pointed out that its use has too high a risk of the Krall back tracking it to the Mark."

"If the Mark isn't here, and the shuttle craft is parked inside its bay, let the Krall back track all they wish. Whatever arrangement we make with the PU forces that would serve to get the shuttle through to Novi Sad, will get the entire ship through. Right?" He let that sink in a moment.

"Uh, excuse me a moment, as I kick myself in the ass all the way back to speak to Captain Longstreet." Dillon answered.

Another voice spoke up on their Link. "Captain Mirikami, don't be offended, but our AI feeds me everything it relays to your AI, as I informed Mr. Martin. This is Captain Longstreet."

"Nice speaking to you, Captain. I assumed you were probably listening, or your superior would be. Colonel Trakenburg is his name I was told earlier. Who has the authority to arrange for a clanship to lift from here and fly to some safe location? Is it Colonel Trakenburg, or General Nabarone?" He knew what the answer had to be, but went through the motions.

"The planetary defenses are under General Nabarone's control, and it involves atmospheric and near space defense against clanships. He would be the only one able to coordinate that, and to decide where you might be able to conceal the ship."

"I'd strongly recommend some place much farther away than Novi Sad to the general. After the Krall see us get a non-hostile reception crossing the front lines, and discover the wrecked clanship back here, they might seriously try to find out who we are. I'd like to set down where their spy satellites won't find us. How do I get to speak to the general?"

To his credit, Longstreet's hesitation lasted only a half second. "I can Link you Sir. Please give my AI a moment to work its way through his chain of command." His boss *did* say cooperate, and Trakenburg was destined to lose control of these people anyway, as soon as Nabarone decided to push. Leaving these people with a positive feeling towards spec ops was a good idea, and they were promised they could share in the intelligence trove offered.

While they waited for the Link to be established, Tet wanted to get things moving. "Dillon, please return with our wounded, and tell Thad we will likely be pulling out before nightfall.

"We want to take the operational Dragons with us, since they will fit in the lower hold, and perhaps take a number of the plasma cannon carts. However, they seem too exposed for the way the kids used them this time, so we can decide later if we have room for them. I don't want to dismantle things and cram them in as the Krall did. The big transports we will leave parked in the canyon when we leave, unless we decide to use them for target practice."

Dillon continued walking to the shuttle, as Longstreet informed Mirikami the Link with General Nabarone was ready.

Mirikami heard a gruff voice. “Captain Mirikami, Henry Nabarone here. I’m pleased to have a chance to help you, and return some favors I’ve owed Thad for over twenty years. What can I do for you? I’ve been told by Colonel Trakenburg that your young troops have all but completed their takeover of the other clanship. What’s next for you?”

“General, we have some wounded, one of the most serious is Ethan Greeves, Thad’s oldest son. I’m sure I can speak for him on this. Your most important favor for Thad is to help get his boy into a modern med lab. Our old model will keep him alive until then, we think. Sergeant Reynolds and Captain Longstreet both tell us your units can repair quite severe damage, instead of simply patching the holes. Rapid transport is the issue. I propose we move my ship, a modified clanship we call the Mark, out of this no man’s land. We need some place safe in human controlled territory, where it can be hidden from the Krall. That gets everyone out of here at one time. Then your scientist and technicians can start studying the Mark, with our help. We even have a live clanship commander you might want to interrogate.”

“Damn, Captain. You do know how to get a tired general to jump. How high and in what direction?” He laughed soundly at his own joke. “When will you be able to lift?”

“I’m told that our youngsters have taken all but the top five decks, where the surviving Krall have retreated. We estimate they have twenty-five or so left alive, of the original one hundred thirty. We lost four of our own as they worked their way up, one deck at a time. If we had the means to do it, I’d simply blow the damned thing up. We can’t risk leaving a live Krall behind that have seen those kids in action. Not if we can help it anyway. I think we can lift before nightfall, or just after. That gives us nearly four hours. It has been a long day since our early landing.”

“They are actually taking out the warriors deck by deck? I heard that, but it seemed impossible. Today, of all the impossible things I’ve encountered, that one seems the most improbable.”

“A young man that is in charge of the assault told me he is going to try something that he learned from one of the spec ops men. If that works, we may be done over there sooner. I’ll let you arrange what coordination you need to do, and I’ll get back to you in an hour. I see our shuttle approaching and I want to go down there to bring in our wounded and help place Ethan in the med lab.”

“I understand. I’ll have someone waiting for your call at any time. Nabarone Out.”

****

Conrad was skeptical. “The Krall used black smoke when they raided the Flight of Fancy, and their IR vision could see right through that. What makes you think this white smoke will blind them, more so than us?"

"It isn't the color of the smoke that matters, and it's actually mostly steam. It will also blind us. This smoke and steam will be hotter than our body temperature, and that should make their IR vision as useless as their visible light vision will be. The black smoke used on the Fancy was cold, so they could detect warm objects through it, while our people couldn't see anything. This will return the favor."

"The gases are toxic, how will we breathe?"

"The spec ops captain will let us have their small rebreathers. When I was speculating with him on how to use what we found on the ship to help us, one of them suggested using the stacks of Krall incendiary pistol rounds we found. They are a type of thermite, and they will burn under water. That's why I had those four big containers moved close to the stairs, and filled with water.

"We will dump several cases of incendiary rounds into the water, and then use a laser or plasma rifle to ignite some that we'll break up in the small buckets we found. Ethan and I lit some of them as kids one time. It's easy."

"Was that the month, in eighth grade, when you and Ethan walked around with no eyebrows and melted kinky hair in front?"

Carson grew a bit defensive. "We learned to light them from a distance after that.

"Besides, I did a sneak Tap to see how to break them up and light them while I talked to Corporal Galloway. I shook hands to thank him as I asked. He says they will burn hot and fast and if you promptly dump them into the big bins of water, they will sink and start the other rounds burning, even under water because they have their own oxidizer in the powder.

"After that, we have steam, smoke, and heat. We set them off under each of the four upper stairwells and wait for it to drift up."

"The Krall will be waiting, knowing we must be coming."

"They knew that on all the other decks too, and a dozen of them could see us as we came through. We still were too fast." Except for random shots that had killed the four people they lost, which he didn't mention. They needed the lightweight flex armor the spec ops called Chameleon Skin.

"This time none of the warriors will be able to see us. We know they'll be clustered close to the stairwell openings, as they always were on other decks, and we'll be able to hear them when they fire or move. My dad just brought us two boxes of grenades. We can toss those up just over the deck lip after a count of three or four, when the visibility is down. The first clinks will probably draw them closer, thinking it's one of us.

"Unless they hold their breath, the fumes should also have some sort of affect. I've heard them cough a couple of times, like two did outside in that thick smoke from the ammo explosions."

"OK. It's worth a try, and it isn't really any worse than what we've been doing, three of us leaping up through a single opening together, blasting at everything we see on our flip, before they can react. However, on lower decks, there were eight stairwells and the warriors were more spread out trying to cover them. I assume you and I will go up first?"

Carson nodded. "I'll Tap you and we both Tap the others, to make sure we all know what's going to happen. After doing the first deck this way, we'll know what worked best, and Tap again."

"Sure, if we survive this nutty idea."

They made their preparations, spreading the grenades between the four groups. There was only to be one TG per opening for the first sally, to avoid bumping while they had their eyes closed to avoid the burning fumes, and focused on hearing the Krall.

Several TGs were maintaining sporadic plasma and pistol fire up through the openings, to prevent the Krall from firing down at them in volume. They moved around so shots came from random directions, as did the Krall return fire. If you shot from one spot twice, they next fired directly back along that apparent track. Two of their wounded learned that the hard way.

After a group Tap, they modified their patterns of suppressive fire, and tore out some bulkhead plates to use as deflectors for the Krall return shots.

They were ready, and decided to light all four bins at the same time, to force the Krall to have to watch all four openings at once. The crumbled thermite, in the buckets, was ignited with small welding lasers they had found in maintenance lockers. It flashed red and yellow in a burst of hot flames, and was promptly dumped into the larger bins holding water. The bins were actually the inside of freezer lockers that had their doors removed, then laid flat and filled with water.

They were heavy, and it required two TGs each to shove them quickly close to the deck openings for the stairs. Upward cover fire greatly increased while this happened, and when it lessened, the Krall fire grew heavy in return, assuming a human would be flying up through the openings.

For almost three minutes, nothing much seemed to be happening. None of the TGs wanted to risk being shot just to look into the bins to see why there was so little smoke drifting up from bursting bubbles of gas, and no steam. A glow reflected upwards from the bins proved ignition had started, and as it brightened, it clearly was spreading and increasing.

Carson was exasperated. "The spec ops guy had an image of large volumes of fume laden steam boiling up from his bucket. Where is ours? We have more shells burning than he had."

Carol Slobovic said, "Stop watching the pot. Then it will happen."

"What? What does that mean?" Carson demanded in annoyance.

"My mom says a 'watched pot never boils,' meaning only that you need patience. How long do you think it takes to raise all of that water to the boiling point? That isn't just a bucket full of water. You should have used less water to start the steam faster."

"Where was that helpful tidbit when we were setting this up?" he demanded.

"Waiting for the leader to explain what he was planning. By not telling us until you filled the bins with water and incendiaries, none of us could offer advice." A tip of her tongue demonstrated a small level of insolence that only Carson could see.

He rolled his eyes, just when the bubbling and smoke levels started to increase dramatically from the former freezer bins. The water had finally reached a full boil. They had moved and wired fans from the thruster engine room, normally used to disperse possible fuel leak fumes. Now they were pushing the smoke and steam up through the stair openings in the deck above.

Not all of it went through the openings of course, and the volume of smoke and steam increased quickly in the area around the stairwells. Carson and Conrad, along with Carol and Peter Godwin, each one stationed at a stairway, slipped the mouth grips of the rebreathers between their teeth and attached the nose clips. They each slipped two of the grenades from their pistol belts and pulled the pins, holding the handles down to prevent the fuses from starting.

They waited as suppressive fire from other TGs continued at the same rate as before, so as not to alert the Krall above by a change in that pattern. At a signal from Carson, visible to all three at the stairs, standing high on the back edges of the bins, they simultaneously released the handles on the six grenades.

They counted to three as planned, and then they leaped up lightly, just high enough to roll the grenades gently over the rim of the deck above. They dropped down and bounced clear of the steps for the remaining count of two. The sound of Krall gunfire rose instantly from above, when the clatter of the rolling grenades was heard in the hot impenetrable mix of steam and smoke.

The Krall, following their usual aggressive practice, advanced on the noisy humans presumed to be hiding in the concealing mist. They were firing randomly into the billowing cloud that blocked their infrared senses as effectively as their visible light receptors. They moved closer to grapple with their equally blinded prey.

The near simultaneous six explosions blasted some fragments uselessly against the stairs and side bulkheads. Most went up or towards the center of the deck area above, hitting and ricocheting from barricades the Krall had erected. Many fragments embedded themselves in their intended targets, warriors who had rashly, and foolishly, rushed forward.

Less than a second after the blasts, four figures shot up undetectably through the hot blinding white fog at each opening. They took advantage of the suspense of shooting from the Krall, briefly stunned by the series of explosions and multiple wounds.

Even as the smoke shrouded wraiths flipped over, to place feet on the unseen ceiling of the next level, using muscle memory of the familiar action, they fired plasma rifles from one hand, and explosive rounds from pistols in the other. Just prior to pulling triggers, they listened for the expected roars of anger and pain, issued by warriors wounded by this latest in a string of human deceptions today.

The plasma and explosive rounds found ample targets among the accurately detected sources of screams of rage. Many of those were silenced instantly, because the source of the noise was *exactly* where a bolt or bullet could do the most effective damage.

Even as the four TGs dropped softly to the floor, they all swiftly moved to their right, and forward through the thick concealing mist, firing at any sounds of life or movement they detected. Carson was rewarded with a soft cough from directly ahead, which from his low crouch, he silenced with a palliative treatment consisting of a shot of plasma and an explosive pill. Patient cured, doctor.

Carson heard the faint swish of air of the next TG arriving behind him. He heard his shots as he settled to the deck on the left side of the stairwell. Orson moved farther to his left, directly away from Carson, another deadly doctor making house calls, curing cases of coughs and screams of pain in his sector. The next TG up would move straight away from the stairs towards the center of the deck.

That pattern was being repeated at all four stairwells. Carson was surprised at the rich number of targets he was hearing, and targeting. If his number of encounters were matched by the others, essentially all of the remaining twenty-five warriors were located on this particular deck. His eyes had started to burn when he opened them briefly, so they were shut again. The firing behind him was from Orson's position, so he too was finding targets. The Krall level of return fire was dropping quickly.

He fired at a sound ahead as something scraped. Then he followed that up with another medicinal treatment to end the sounds of enraged pain he heard. He bumped against a vertical surface that memory said wasn't there in a standard clanship layout for this deck. It had to be one of the cobbled together barricades. Aware he had made a slight noise, he instantly rolled to the side as the sound of a plasma bolt passed through his former space. He had opened his eyes as he rolled, and even through the heavy fog, the actinic flash and sound provided the target he needed.

The cut off attack scream and sound of splatter proved he'd found his target, but now his eyes were burning again. He continued to move low along the barricade, thinking how grateful he was for the Krall habit of voicing their displeasure in battle when a human managed to hurt them. He heard a vague sound of movement on the other side of the extended barrier, which felt like several upright food coolers or freezers, placed on their sides. That meant they were about four feet across.

He holstered his pistol and laid his rifle down softly. Detaching two more grenades, he pulled the pins and released the handles two seconds apart. He had pressed them near his chest as he released, muffling the sound of the caps striking, catching the handles in his lap to prevent that noise on the deck. He reached a count of three and tossed the first one, then on four, threw the second, using just enough force to clear the obstacle. Grabbing the handles in his lap, he threw himself flat, believing the barricade would protect him from the fragments.

It did block them, but he hadn't thought about the kick from the first blast. It pinched his little finger as the freezer case slid on the hard smooth deck. There was a satisfying cry heard, and a second roar of rage seemed to have launched itself in his direction. That was why he had delayed the second grenade. It exploded, possibly with the second warrior passing over it in mid charge. The descending spray of wetness was proof of the effectiveness of an old weapon. Carson had retrieved his rifle before the second blast, and had rolled away in case the warrior made it over the barrier. He did not.

Today, these warriors had learned about the maximum timing of five seconds for a thrown grenade. They also knew that they could blow even sooner if held for a short time before being thrown. However, they still thought it was safe to attack after one exploded, if the second grenade's arrival was masked by the first explosion. The lesson learned here would not be passed on to a novice, if the silence on the opposite side were any indication. To test that notion, Carson threw the two handles over, and heard their clinking on the deck. No response this time.

He had heard diminishing gunfire elsewhere, and there had been other grenade blasts heard, but it was growing quiet. He didn't want to move farther toward the center of the arc of the barricades because that was an area the third TG was assigned.

He'd heard shooting in the center area that he assumed was from Clayton, but blinded as they were, friendly fire was all too possible. To call out in a human voice was to make you a Krall target, and to become as reckless as they were.

To be fair, the Krall had always depended on their rapid halt of blood loss, redundant organs, and regrowth of limbs and organs to accept injuries their enemies could not survive. The accurate fire and reaction speed of the TGs had largely negated that tactic, because the Krall still only had one head. When the TGs encountered armored Krall, things might change.

In this assault, the thirty-two still unassembled Krall armor suits aboard were packed in cases on the third deck, waiting for a K'Tal or Prada slave to assemble, and then adjust them to fit individual warriors.

Carson risked another glimpse through watering eyes, and thought the white was a bit grayer now, and it definitely wasn't any hotter than his body temperature now. His activity had raised his temperature via his high metabolism, and the air was definitely cooler. That meant the TGs would be visible to infrared vision before they could see the Krall, in what everyone called the visible light range.

The TGs definitely needed the vision enhancements that the ripper genes offered. For now, perhaps they could use what the spec ops troops had in the interim. He thought of a way to "borrow" that capability.

Carson was thinking of some way to contact the others by Link, but remain somewhat protected if overheard by a Krall. He moved back to the remembered barrier location, felt along the side of the freezers, and at the second one, he felt the recessed slot for a door release near the top. That meant the door was on his side, and the hinges on the floor. He gently opened the door and backed away to lower it softly to the floor, then moved inside the still cool large compartment. The spicy odor of Raspani meat still pervaded the now empty space, but he had a degree of protection on all but one side.

"Jakob, Link between all," he said softly, his rebreather removed for a moment, then returned.

"Ready Sir."

Taking a deep breath, he started. "This is Carson. Kill the fans below to stop the fumes. We need to see up here." Fresh breath. "Only the Krall can see as the steam cools, but don't anyone on the assault team reply and attract Krall attention." Breath. "Captain Longstreet, are you Linked? We need IR surveillance up here."

"This is Longstreet. My men and I just moved up to the deck below you. We have our own eyeball IR sensors, and all of us are on the Link. We also have some mobile spy bots with IR, to turn lose up there. Ask your people to hold their fire at noises by the stairs, and we can take a look over the edge to tell you what we see."

"Good idea, Sir. Identify my stairwell as number one, and count clockwise to report the view at other stairs. Break! Assault team TGs, don't react to sounds by the stairwell." Breathed… "Spec ops will look and tell us what they can see. They are sending spy bots, so please don't swat the bugs."

If the spec ops guys came part way up the stairs he didn't hear them, but soon heard the faint skitter of one or more spy bot bugs on the deck. One came directly towards him.

"Hello Carson," Longstreet's voice sounded. "The bot in front of you spotted you inside that box. What is that, a freezer? Don't answer. The Krall laying on top of your box is obviously dead, as were three others we can see on the deck close by the stairs. Wait while the bot climbs up to check the back side of the barricade."

The six-legged little bug, currently the color of the gray deck, scuttled on padded feet to the edge of the freezer, where the footpads turned slightly sticky to let it swiftly run up the side to the top. There was a wait of a couple of minutes.

Longstreet's voice returned. "Carson, at stair well number one, your own location, we see six dead Krall and none moving near you or the man closest to you at the center of the barricade. Hold on…, the other bot can see your third man, at the other side. He is also clear of any moving Krall, with a dead one beside him on the deck. I'll see what our other bots have reported." He was quiet for a moment.

"Conrad, over at stairwell three there is a wounded warrior, and both legs are apparently useless. It's behind a table and a storage area, twenty feet towards deck center from your stairwell, where he must have crawled. He's close to you, and armed with a rifle and two pistols. He's looking your way and may sense your heat signature. To our spy bots, all of you kids glow like flames through that hazy and moist warm air. If you move, it will see the glow shift and provide a sure target."

Conrad answered. "I hit him with my rifle after a grenade blast made him howl. I heard him drag himself, but had no shot that didn't reveal my position as the air grew clear. How valuable is that spy bot?"

"Cheap, why?"

"If it can draw the Krall into shooting it, I can take him out when I see his flash or hear him fire."

"Hold on, I'll tell my man to move it closer, and then have it make a noise."

Carson suddenly heard two plasma bolts fired in rapid succession from the opposite side of that deck level, where Conrad was located.

"Nice shot. Another good Krall," spoke Longstreet.

"Good Krall, Sir?" was Conrad's query.

"Yes. A dead Krall is a good one."

"Right, Sir. How many others do you see?"

Longstreet was a half-minute answering. "A Krall head count of dead from all stairwells on that deck comes to twenty-five. How sure are your people that the original number had shrunk to that level?"

Carson stepped in. "We know from the clanship commander that there were a hundred thirty, including him. We've counted a hundred five bodies, including the fifteen dead at the other valley and the commander in that total. He had six K'Tal in brown suits. One of those he left on the command deck. We killed two brown suits on lower decks. How many do you see dead on this deck?"

Another brief pause. "There are four brown suits. Why does that matter?"

"Their commander helped me discover that the warriors were all novices and had no pilot training or clanship experience, so only a K'Tal would stay on the top deck. The last of them were all gathered here to fight us, since the ship could no longer fly or fire its weapons."

"I'd be careful accepting his word before moving around until the smoke clears. I wouldn't put a lie out of the realm of possibility, son."

"Oh, he would have lied to me, if that were possible, Sir. But we can detect that attempt." Realizing he was raising a question he couldn't answer, he used a diversion. "We have him drugged, you know." So far, Longstreet had not been provided access to the Krall, just allowed to see the captive. He didn't know he was so paralyzed he was unable to speak.

Carson tested his eyes again, because the ship's air filtration had been switched back on now that the smoke trick had run its course. The previous burning still left them watery, but the sting was less sharp now, and the air was clearing by the minute. He maintained awareness as he climbed out of concealment and looked around, keeping the rebreather in place. He could see the outline of the Krall corpse right on top of the freezer where he'd been concealed. Another two feet away and he'd have seen only gray mist. That IR ability had to be the next mod they added.

In five minutes, he could see fifty feet through the thinning haze, and Longstreet told him that he wanted to come up, along with some of his men. Carson agreed, and he alerted Conrad by Link, and then called out the warning to Carol and Brian who had no transducers.

A couple of dozen TGs followed the spec ops up, without rebreathers, because Carson had only been provided twenty, some of which were spares the spec ops carried. He removed his own as Longstreet approached, Thad close behind. The air was tangy and acidic, but safe.

He handed Longstreet the nine inch wide, one-inch thick tube with attached soft mouthpiece and nose clip. "Thanks, this stunt would not have been possible without your man's idea on incendiary rounds, and these gadgets."

Thad added. "It is those ideas and gadgets we want, and want training in order to make use of them. With the proper equipment and know how, we might not have lost any of the six people we did today."

Longstreet nodded, but looked around the area at the dead Krall, strewn around inside their clanship. "I would have thought an assault like this would be very difficult against a human ship. You kicked Krall asses the way they kick ours."

He seemed to think for a moment then shrugged.

"I know I'll get the same answer if I ask how you did it, that you have mysterious abilities which you can't explain yet. However, I can tell you things we obviously have seen, that you know we know from firsthand observation.

"You have strength well beyond what a high gravity world would furnish a human, because my men and I train on Heavyside. Your TGs display extreme reaction speeds, which easily exceed that of a Krall warrior. Their warriors benefit from *thousands* of years of breeding for those traits. My IR vision and our bots see your TGs as virtual heat torches after they have been in combat for a few minutes, demonstrating a greatly elevated metabolism. We also saw your TGs eat a mountain of high-energy food bars they carry with them, to keep fueling those bodies. We have some similar snacks that we use on missions, which serve the same purpose.

"You, Dillon, and Sarge," he was looking at Thad, "don't have this capability, but you do have increased ability similar to my own, when I wear a Booster Suit. However, the elevated ability *is* available in your children. I know what that implies, and the implication will be obvious to others in the PU Army, and in the Hub. I truly want what you have achieved for my own use, and fear I can't have it because you don't have it, Thad. I'll tell you that I personally will support your group in any way I can.

"This conversation is off the record by the way. I am not Linked or recording. My greatest loyalty is to humanity, more than to an organization. I love spec ops, but I devoted myself to it to try to slow the Krall advances. I see it may be possible to do more than that." He had put his cards on the table, at personal risk for his career.

"Captain, we appreciate your support, and your words will be held in confidence. When we are in a position to explain ourselves, I will specifically make an effort to contact you in private, if you can provide a means to do that."

"Thad, I'll leave contact information with your AI and Captain Mirikami. I suspect I'll be meeting him shortly. Considering none of you is active military, with perhaps the exception of Sarge down below, I see no reason we can't be on a first name basis. My first name is Joseph, and big surprise, I go by Joe."

"Joe it is, Joe. Now, if we have cleared all of the Krall on this wreck, we need to finish stripping it of what we can use, and get the hell out of here."

"Carson," Thad turned back to his nephew, only to find he had left while the older men were talking.

He spotted Clayton descending the stairwell from the next deck. "Where's Carson? He was right here."

"He's on the command deck with Conrad, Sir. I just came from there. Nobody was home because all the survivors gathered down here, to make their last stand. We're taking anything of interest back to the Mark, like the five Katushas we found up there. I want to drive a Dragon back. I just Tapped Conrad for operating instructions, and I'm going down to make a claim on one before the others learn we're keeping them." He grinned, and leaped down to the next level without using the steps.

****

Mirikami nodded his approval. “That distribution seems reasonable.” He was talking about the Krall heavy transports parked in a circle around the Mark, and the three disabled Dragons they had towed here were with them.

It appeared as if the Mark was under siege, and they were about to increase that appearance, by using the plasma cannons and lasers to mark up the terrain and vehicles. There were sixty-four armed Krall bodies placed inside and around them. It wouldn’t exactly explain the other destroyed clanship and its dead complement, or what clan had been in the missing clanship that was parked here. However, the extended Dragon and transport tracks, and signs of fighting in multiple valleys, would convey a confusing scene of possible interclan fighting.

“Gentlemen, the youngsters did all of the shooting today. Now it’s our turn.”

With the ship sealed, and the remaining five Dragons aboard, with samples of other Krall equipment, such as their weapons, armor, and four plasma cannon carts, it was safe to blast away. Sarge, Dillon, Thad, and Mirikami played target practice.

After five minutes of shooting, one of the transport sections exploded violently. A plasma beam Dillon was using to destroy its rooftop cannon ruptured its fusion bottle. The exploding star hot plasma threw a number of fragments against the Mark.

Mirikami halted the fun. “OK, cease fire. I don’t want the Mark’s outer skin damaged. That would hurt our stealth capability.”

He looked at Longstreet, who had been coordinating their liftoff with General Nabarone’s aide. “It’s getting dark, and the flashes must have been seen. We are ready to lift when the defense forces are ready for us.”

Longstreet nodded, and said, “Major Caldwell, we are ready to lift.” He paused a moment, then gave Mirikami a thumbs up. “We’ll be airborne shortly, Sir.”

Mirikami tapped the console button that initiated the main thruster, and automatic attitude controls. The entire flight had been programed into the seldom-used Krall automatic flight control systems. Seat of the pants Krall style flying would be a bit hazardous this trip, at low altitudes.

The Mark lifted easily on its column of fire, and at a half mile, it eased over into a track directly towards a battle front, where human forces were bombarding a section of the Krall line that had been quiet. As they did, Mirikami and Thad opened the ports on two of the plasma cannons, and used the zoom feature on the appropriate view screens to spot the multiple green flares that marked their various targets.

As they approached the flares, only visible from the air, they started firing. They were rewarded by several secondary explosions. They passed beyond the dummy targets, and suddenly there were radar indications of inbound atmospheric missiles, rising over the distant horizon. The ship entered its programmed gyrations and evasion maneuvers, and fired “ineffective” laser beams that failed to knock down the missiles.

Passing over a range of hills and ridges on the other side of Novi Sad, the ship dropped to within a few hundred feet of the surface. This was a known blind spot in Krall radar coverage from the territory they held. The four seeker missiles plunged down into that radar black hole after their prey.

Krall, and human observers in Novi Sad, saw a brilliant flare of light in the sky, followed by a booming explosion. The humans celebrated the downing of the clanship, announcing it between various command posts by radio. The Krall wondered what suicidal clan had sacrificed their clanship, just to halt a human offense that was sure to have failed in any case.

Remaining in the radar shadow of the hills, the Mark left a trail of rattled windows as it streaked supersonic over the horizon, still stealthed, and at low altitude. Two hundred forty miles ahead, it lifted slightly to hover briefly in a vertical attitude. Mirikami was in full control again, and he set the Mark down in an extinct volcano’s crater, with at least a half mile to spare on each side, after reaching the bottom of the two thousand-foot deep pit.

As soon as the thrusters cut off, steel cables were drawn tight that had been pulled aside for the landing. They now supported the rings on hastily rigged sheets of canvas that were ran out over the Mark, and draped to make it appear as if there were a seven hundred- foot central mound in the old crater basin. Paint crews were promptly finishing the mottled spray job they had started two hours before, to match the canvas color with the red, gray, and brown sides of the crater walls. By sunrise, only a detailed comparison of the old crater would reveal the new mound.

Now the negotiations could start, with the Kobani holding the most valuable assets, themselves and the secret to activating Krall equipment for study, and their easy to grant needs. General Nabarone and Colonel Trakenburg were each falling over themselves to offer the most help, in exchange for the treasure trove of Krall intelligence. They were both flying to the crater site to meet them.

A soon as Ethan and the other three TGs were safely ensconced in the best modern med labs Nabarone could find for them, Thad pulled out his “shopping list” and marched down the Mark’s ramp with Mirikami, Dillon, and Sarge. It was trading time.

Chapter 6: Trade-offs

It was actually welcome home time for an hour. Nabarone had flown there in his mobile command post aircraft, and the wide-bodied vertical lift capable, but winged craft had a modest sized conference room with a full bar, right next to the communications section. There was also a small kitchen, a chef, and a limited menu that included real steak, from actual beef! It was good to be a planetary command general, with all of its perks.

Male hugging, shoulder pounding, back slapping action between the two old friends lasted several minutes. Trakenburg was left out of this reunion celebration, but was mollified when he remembered that Captain Mirikami was the actual leader of Greeves' group, and he had never known Nabarone. He promptly started to cultivate a relationship with the small man, only to find the ground a bit harder to plow than he expected.

"Captain, I suppose it's a relief to be back near Hub society, and out of the woods, so to speak."

Mirikami answered frankly. "Colonel, we intend to maintain a respectful and discrete distance from the Planetary Union and Hub worlds. If we can't stay in the shadows, we won't be around to help fight this war. We are not here to socialize or play politics. We know we have something to offer that you can't get anywhere else, and which the human race needs desperately. We offer a possible way to win this war."

Taken aback, Trakenburg stared at the smaller man. "Pretty sold on yourselves aren't you? With a bunch of untrained kids."

Mirikami gave him a penetrating look in return. "Using weapons forcibly taken from the Krall, we have stolen three clanships away from them, all in perfect working condition, and we took a fourth ship by an assault you witnessed, which we left a disabled wreck. How many Krall clanships, in twenty years of war, have the PU Army or the Navy captured intact, or successfully assaulted?"

The colonel bobbed his head and conceded. "Point made." Then what he'd just heard fully registered. "You said you have captured *three* clanships?"

"Yes. It didn't seem wise to land here with all of our eggs in one basket. We stopped at K1 enroute to Poldark, and took two more from there. They were not so heavily guarded, sitting on their own turf. I don't believe your spec ops, the Army, or the Navy have managed to set foot there since the Krall took over. We were in and out before they knew we were there, using this same bunch of untrained kids." He rose and walked over to share a drink with Thad, Dillon and Nabarone.

Reynolds, who had been sitting at the table near them, grinned over his glass of brandy. "Full of surprises isn't he? Expect more." He too went over to join his friends.

Nabarone was still catching up with Thad's life. "Three kids you say? Sybil eventually married a man that runs a large construction company, and they signed the line for two children, and spent ten years together. My sister stayed away from military men after you vanished, and particularly after the war started. Didn't want that pain of loss again. I wish I could tell her, but we need to keep all of you under wraps. Your stories are exactly what the media would pounce on as great news for a change, and spoil everything in their feeding frenzy to get details."

Thad glanced at the pallor and decline in fitness of his formerly gung ho XO. "Henry, I'm not surprised you never found a woman that could tie you down for long. You were married to the Militia before and the PU Army now, I think. Sarge here knocked me over with a feather when I heard you were a PU general. How did *anyone* talk you into that? You were as staunch a Hub conspiracy theorist as Poldark had. You were certain they would try to take us over one day."

He grimaced. "Hell. They did! Mike Boldovic, who gave up the presidency to become our first Colony governor after we voted to join the Union, blackmailed me into accepting the planetary commander's job. President Stanford used me to take over Poldark for her. The old lady was a better leader than I gave her credit for, but the near destruction of Rhama, and two major Navy fleet defeats was too much political baggage. If she had listened to the Army instead of the Navy, she could have had another term." He seemed to think on that a moment.

"Seeing how the war went after that, another term for her, even if she had spent the fleet's money on ground troops would only have kicked the Krall offensive into higher gear a few years sooner. It's what the lizards wanted anyway." He shook it off.

"OK. Enough reminiscence for now. What in hell can we do to help you help us? I know some of what you need, and a little of what you have to trade. I'll tell you outright, in a piss poor way of bargaining, that after what I saw of the recordings from Frank's spec ops teams, that you will get what you need. Even if we can't come out and publicly ask the PU government for the money. What I've heard that you want so far is a pittance to what you are worth to us."

Trakenburg was on his way over to join them, and cringed inwardly at his first name being tossed out so casually. He maintained a more formal presence within his own unit than did Nabarone, with his raised-from-the-ranks attitude of a former private in the Militia.

He also didn't like the give-away-the-farm position before he really knew what these people wanted, what it would cost them, and what else they had to offer. He didn't have long to wait.

Mirikami latched onto one item Nabarone just mentioned. Money. "General, I presume gold and platinum are still precious enough metals to use for cash exchange into credits?"

That brought him up short. "Certainly, either one. Why?"

"We have roughly forty-eight tons combined, of those two metals in one of our storage holds. Our heavy gravity world has an abundance of heavy metals. If that doesn't cover all of our expenses, we can get a great deal more. And we have access to millions of tons of high quality rare earth elements that are always in demand for electronics."

Nabarone, seeing Trakenburg's pleasantly surprised expression as he approached, knew he too had been worried about how to pay for what might be needed from their respective budgets. They had relatively generous budgets in this time of war, to be sure, but their expenditures were accountable to Parliament, and to the High Command's staffers and auditors.

Seeing that money was not as great an issue for them as it might have been a moment ago, Thad pulled out his list. "Henry, I have some notes that are guidelines, but here is the gist of our needs.

"Training. I have tried to teach our youngsters a bit about how to fight, some tactics and strategy. Only, truth be told, I trained at fighting, but never had an actual enemy to face. Sarge here has taught them what he learned of setting up ambushes and baiting traps, but that isn't all they need to know.

"We lost six of our people today, which may have been preventable if they had been taught to look at situations with practical training behind them. We want the sort of training that commandos receive, or even Special Ops. Furnished by men that have seen real combat. There are too few TGs to let them die taking individual clanships very often.

"Speaking of that, we have three clanships in our control now. However, only the Mark has the modifications that make it easily usable by humans. It needs more modifications, to allow our AI to actually access some of the ship's capability, and navigate and fly her directly. The other two ships need similar modifications. The reason we want to keep clanships is for the alien technology that fools the Krall into thinking they are friendly ships. However, we need some human ships as well, with modern AI's to take back with us.

"We need to make our home world more habitable, to develop the resources we have. We need mining equipment; not just for gold, and a consumer manufacturing plant we can feed the raw material. Perhaps an orbital factory. Our citizens that want to return to the Hub will have to be kept at home, for the safety of our world, and the safety of humanity. The least we can do is make them more healthy and comfortable.

"The four med labs you brought to us here are a start. We need enough for a population of at least thirty thousand. I don't know what the typical number would be for that many people. We need some of the specialized nanites Sarge here had in his system when we rescued him. We cloned those, but we know there are other types. They make limb regrowth much faster, and wound repair more complete. I was gratified to hear your doctors say that Ethan's injuries were relatively minor, because he didn't need limb regrowth, or organ replacements. With our old equipment, he wouldn't fully recover.

Dillon interjected here. "We also want the templates for all of the nanite designs, not just the nanites themselves, since we will have to modify them for our uses. There may be some patent rights or copyrights involved. *I don't care*. We are not out to market what we know or compete with them for profit. By now, you have seen the Flight of Fancy passenger list, and possibly the lab equipment list of what we had on the Fancy. If not, you will look eventually." He glanced at Mirikami, who nodded. They had discussed this subject years ago.

"I'm listed as Dr. Dillon Martin, a bio-scientist, a generic sounding specialty in biology. What I am is a geneticist, as are over a hundred of our scientists. For sure, we had scientists of other specialties in the biological sciences, lab technicians, and actual medical doctors. However, it was the forbidden science of genetics that enabled us to survive, and now, to be able to do what you've seen our TGs do, the so-called Third Generation." He saw a look of mild surprise on Nabarone's face, but not on Trakenburg's. The colonel already knew or suspected, probably because the Heavyside project had looked at genetics.

"The four of us adults are what we have been calling Second Generation, because we, like you, started with typical human genes. Possessing the *normal* hundred and fifty or so human created genetic modifications that were already in our genome by three hundred years ago, *before* the Clone and Gene wars. We four, and thousands more of us on our dangerous heavy gravity planet, have been enhanced with modifications originally used in clones. The strength and endurance mods are the most significant, with heat and cold adaptations that supplement them, and a higher than normal metabolism that the colonel there can see with his IR sensors if we exert ourselves."

Trakenburg nodded. "Your TGs don't even have to exert themselves to glow slightly."

"That is partly why we call them Third Generation. They were *born* with our inheritable gene enhancements as original parts of their bodies. Our initial clone enhancements were a requirement for us to survive on our world, and they happened to make children possible. Most of our SGs, the four of us for example, have additional genes that built a dormant organic superconducting nervous system, which we can't use.

"Colonel, we know that Heavyside has a gravity of about 1.4 g's at its surface. That is enough to preclude natural births on the surface of that planet, and even more so at the 1.52 times Earth gravity of our own world."

He saw the slight head tilt from Trakenburg, confirming his statement.

"Having our children born with Second Generation enhancements, not added on later as we older SGs received them, they can make use of the full potential built into their bodies. They have a *usable* parallel organic super conducting nervous system. We could change them to connect to that nervous system. That was the basis for another gene modification, which is the source of their extremely fast reactions. They are far faster than the Krall in reaction times, and in thinking.

"All of our genetic changes are fully compatible with other humans. Any of us SGs can marry and have children with any mate that will have us in Human Space. So can our children, except that they now have added genetic enhancements to make use of their superconductor nerves, which are ten times faster than what we SGs have. They also have stronger muscles, and reinforced bones." He was leaving out mention of the Koban derived genes. This was sketching enough of the process for now.

"Their future children, such as mine and Thad's grandchildren, conceived between TGs, will be a True Third Generation, or TTG, without the need for manually inserted gene modifications to give them the speed and strength the TGs have now." He wondered if the significance of that assertion had registered. Therefore, he drove the point home.

"Gentlemen, in effect, we have created a new *race* of humanity, but *not a new species*. The TGs are Homo sapiens, as are Caucasoid, Mongoloid, Negroid, Capoid, and Australoid, the previous recognized five races of man. To that list, we have added the Kobanoid race, a descriptive word we created. They are not distinguished by skin, eye, or hair color, but by what is genetically inside them, by what they can do.

"They could mate and have children with any companion of *any* other race or mixture of races. The result will of course be hybrid children, *as are all mixed race offspring*, which will have some of the traits of the TG parent, some of the other parent. In short, by definition of what a species is, TGs and their own children are completely Homo sapiens, or modern humans, because they can procreate with any other human," he shrugged.

"That's the scientific, rational side of the story. The lingering after effects of the Clone and Gene wars attaches a social and legal stigma on what we were required to do to stay alive. Then we knowingly went steps farther, after our experience with the Krall. We did not want our descendants to die at their hands because we refused to make them strong enough to defend themselves." He paused, and Mirikami picked up the threads.

"This is why we don't yet want widespread contact with the people of the Hub worlds. We don't expect approval or acceptance, not at first, if ever. Away from the Rim worlds, they haven't experienced firsthand what facing these killers means. Seeing atrocities on Tri-Vid doesn't have the same impact as watching these barbarians cut apart a family member.

"We intend to stay hidden and a secret or we will leave here, and fight them on our own. Not as well without your help, but at least we won't have to guard our backs from our own side, threatening us with the death penalty or prison. Don't answer too quickly, before you have thought about it, because you will be joining a conspiracy."

As they all expected, Nabarone was first to speak. "You make it damn hard for a man used to quick decisions, Mirikami. I've jealously watched spec ops run operations that I was unable to conduct. I wanted what his men had for my own troops. Now you dangle this juicy rutabaga in front of a stubborn but hungry man to move him, and I'm told I can't bite it yet."

"Carrot," Mirikami said.

"What's a carrot?"

"The orange colored root vegetable you dangle before a stubborn mule to get it to move."

"Not on Poldark. It's a rutabaga. And thanks for the mule comparison."

"You're welcome."

"Besides, I'm *ready* to move, but you told me to wait, so who's being the jackass here?"

Thad looked over at Dillon. "It's just like watching Maggi and you talking."

"Why?" he laughed. "Is someone going to get smacked on their pecker?"

Trakenburg grunted in exasperation. "No need to wait, I'll bite. I have already fought the legal and social stigma factor you were discussing. We wanted to use genetic modification in our program and couldn't get approval, so we were forced to find electronic and mechanical means to try to achieve what we needed.

"By the way, on my colony world of New Bavaria, it's a parsnip. I don't like them."

Mirikami nodded, and accepted their rush to sign on with them. He actually expected that from Nabarone, based on Thad's opinion of the man. Trakenburg had been the unknown factor, but his participation in a different, but parallel program to boost human performance made him a natural ally.

"OK, if you are committed, then we will share what we have, and expect some of that knowledge to filter through to your scientists." He lifted a small soft side black case he brought with him.

"Frankly, you were getting these anyway. You might even have others from destroyed clanships that you didn't understand their use or significance." He lifted a dark gray, flashlight-sized device from the case, its flat oval end forward, an array of buttons on one side of the handle.

"This is a Katusha. We had four of them we managed to steal from the Krall twenty years ago. They are how the Krall apply their tattoos, and how we," he indicated his own black oval at the base of his neck, "applied them to ourselves. You wanted the key to operating Krall machinery, and their weapons. This applies the tattoos that make that possible." He gave them each one to hold.

"We have a printed guide to give you, derived from empirical methods of watching how the Krall used them. Aside from applying a visible tattoo, they also inject or embed some sort of apparent quantum pattern or substance in your skin that has a short interaction range of roughly one hundred twenty-two feet." They held them gingerly, afraid to activate them by accident.

"You need to press two buttons on opposite sides to activate the controls, then enter a sequence for the type of tattoo, and press a send button on top with the flat end pressed on skin. At least that's how we interpret what it does when we apply a new tattoo.

"An intriguing ability is to use them to find someone with a tattoo; you must be within the device's short range, and press the top button and hold. Do it, and point the flat end at any of us. It will work through any shielding material we ever had available to test." He waited while they tried them out.

Trakenburg said, "It has a light on the butt that glows when we point it at one of you, and dims as we aim away. You said it has a short range, of one hundred twenty-two feet?"

Mirikami smiled. "That range sound familiar? The Worm missiles the Krall used, per Sarge's description, has that same short range for boring holes, which is the warhead's ability to disintegrate anything it strikes, provided it is within a small cone directly in front. Much like these Katusha's. We saw the Krall use a handheld tool, they said came from a species called the Raspani, to bore holes in fusion bottles, to try to leave us without power when they left us stranded.

"I suspect they placed those same atom dissolving quantum tools on the Worm missiles to weaponize them. The two types of devices were supposedly manufactured by two different peoples, the older Olt'kitapi and the Raspani, but we believe they are both based on similar principles of quantum mechanics, which the Olt'kitapi first discovered. That older species was once mentors to the Raspani, and likely shared physics and technology with them. If the Katusha's are the forerunner device, they might help you learn how the Worms work. We have five of them for you in this case. We found more on each of the four clanships we have now been able to search."

"In four small sealed vials you will find the drug we discovered, a drop of which can paralyze a Krall for several hours. It affects all but the autonomous muscles and nervous system. The two hearts beat and they still breathe, move eyes, defecate, and can ingest food and water if you feed them via a tube into either stomach. They lose the ability to will their hearts to stop, however they eventually manage to disable other organs, I think. They started to waste away for us, after a few months. Do not let any of the drug contact a human, because it's fatal, quickly. I assume several drops at once would kill a Krall. We never tried that."

Nabarone asked for clarification. "These are ours?"

"Yes, we have others, and you can divide the five Katusha's between you as you wish. Our only condition is that we receive feedback about how they work, and any new uses for them that your scientists discover. We had mostly experts in biology with us and no physics equipment. We never learned much about them. I've had hope they might lead to some new technology we can use. The Krall don't show an interest in anything unless it helps them kill something."

Nabarone pressed a button at a console built into the table. "I've summoned our chef. He has a high clearance, but let's not discuss our business before we sit down to eat and he leaves. I had a privacy shield over us since you arrived."

They enjoyed a meal that centered on traditional Poldark dishes for Thad and Sarge, but featured real Earth raised beef in the form of large porterhouse steaks. The other two men were astounded to see the four guests put down the twenty-four ounce cuts of meat, and then they piled on the vegetables, clearly appearing comfortable with what was a very heavy late meal. It was nearly ten at night on Poldark, although they had never asked what ship time they had been using on the Mark, before they landed just at dawn.

Mirikami answered the question about ship time. "We were in orbit several days watching the intended landing area, waiting for a storm front to help us sneak in quietly. We set our clocks for local time, so we are not too far off your clock. It's growing late on the Avenger and the Beagle, although I don't think they were expecting us to make contact so quickly. We should give them a call."

"Your other two ships are close?" Nabarone was startled.

"I said we didn't want all our eggs in one basket." Mirikami responded. "They are in stealth mode, waiting for us to call so they can continue with their own missions. Now that we don't need rescue."

"I forgot you are using clanships, so we can't see them. I'll bet you were the three mysterious arrivals we had four or five days ago. Can we furnish them supplies? They don't need to land here. We can just meet them in orbit..., or since that would let a crew see the type of ships they are dealing with, perhaps leaving supply pods in a high orbit, for your ships to pick up would be best."

Thad said, "I have two smaller lists for those ships in my pocket. Just in case, if we had a chance to supply them. It might take a few days to round up the things they need. We want modern transducers for them, and the other TGs at home, similar to what Sarge has or spec ops uses, if those aren't restricted. Both ships need a couple of med labs to keep aboard, and the Beagle could take much of the equipment you are giving us to carry home, since that is her next stop. So, the list is med labs, transducers, an AI they can mount in each ship for navigational help, nanites for the med labs,..." Nabarone held up a hand.

"Give me the damn lists, Thad. That's why I have flunkies, to do that crap for me. Besides, the expenses for those items are relatively peanuts. Getting Jump ships for you will be more expensive. Let's have some brandy, and then you will want to visit your son and the other wounded, and presumably get some sleep."

****

Thad made the radio call from the Bridge. He wanted to be the first to speak to Marlyn, to reassure her that their son was going to be OK. "Beagle and Avenger, this is the Mark. We are down safe, with friends, and we have relocated in case you are looking for us. Over." He waited a few minutes, and repeated the call. It was nearly midnight, and it was possible that only a watch stander was on the Bridge.

A breathless Marlyn answered just as he was starting the third call. "Thad, we hear you. Noreen was just awakened as well. We didn't expect to hear from you so soon. Did your old friend make contact?"

"Hi, honey. This frequency isn't guaranteed secure, so no names, or mention of our home. However, we made contact with the man we wanted to see, and another person that is sympathetic. We will get what we came for, and will have some material for the two of you, once we work out the delivery details."

"Great. I can see Noreen..., oh, sorry that's a name."

"I really meant the names of who we were meeting. Our own names are unknown. Is she also on com?"

"I'm on, Thad. How are you making out? We lost sight of you due to low clouds, and did not want to go active to search. We could not detect you on passive scans, and you seemed to have relocated."

"We did, and that was a good thing. You knew we sat down near unfriendly neighbors?"

"Yes, we saw them follow you down. Problems?"

"It proved necessary to clean their house, totally. Then had to move before their other friends arrived. Our own friends showed up, and after a misunderstanding about who we were, and what we were doing, we eventually joined forces." He took a deep breath.

"Marlyn, Ethan is going to be OK, but there was some fighting. He and some others were wounded, and they all are in modern med labs healing. I just visited with him. He was asleep, but the Doctor overlooking their recovery says he will be awake and talking by morning, and could be out of the box in several days. Full recovery in under a month."

Marlyn paused only a few seconds before replying, and sounded cool and collected, but Thad could sense the tension she was hiding. "Where was he hurt? No regrowth?"

That question revealed her worry and distraction, because a limb loss would not have him out of a med lab in three days. "He had a chest wound and collapsed lung, and a bad burn to his left rib cage. Both are considered minor injuries when you have the equipment we now have, and which we will be sending up to you later this week."

Noreen asked about the other wounded, and after she had their names to pass along to the other TGs, she asked the question he had dreaded almost as much as telling Marlyn her son was wounded.

Thad gave them the worst of the news. "We lost six people in the assault, mostly from not knowing how to conduct the operation with the equipment we acquired. There will be a recording of the details, which Carson is making for you, to share with your crews. We will keep the bodies here in cold storage on the Mark until we return home, and then have a full honors service for them."

Both women looked grave, but the adults knew that the first fight on Koban, and what happened on K1, against a handful of Krall that didn't know what they were facing, had created a sense of overconfidence in the TGs. Now they would have to understand the need for considering their moves before they made them, and have respect for the training they came here to get.

Mirikami, having given Thad time to talk with his wife, stepped into range of the view screen. "Captains, our benefactor will have the items we asked for, ready to be placed in a high orbit by tomorrow. Our ability to pay in precious metal means he's able to buy some of it on the free market, without drawing attention to his normal sources." They were remaining circumspect for both the Krall, and for humans that might be trying to decrypt this conversation.

"Marlyn, the task of transferring the massive amount of material to the Beagle, in space, is more than your reduced crew can easily handle. There are plenty of Spacers at home ready to help you. I can't believe I'm saying this, but use the 'Parkoda tow' method to get it home, then leave it in orbit while you land to get your help, then bring it down in several trips."

Marlyn's eyes brightened, as she said, "I'd prefer to call it the 'Mirikami maneuver' since I hear you came up with the idea."

Noreen smiled, and agreed. She and Tet knew that Jake, their AI, had actually described the alternative to the Krall solution, which was to kill enough captives so that the remainder would fit in his clanship for the journey to Koban. Mirikami had talked the Krall raid leader into trying the trick.

Marlyn would move close to the cargo pod, capture an extreme high-energy tachyon and enclose it and the Beagle in a large event horizon, then Jump in a zigzag route home, to prevent any possible tracking of where she was headed. That was how the Flight of Fancy had reached Koban, towed by Parkoda's clanship, with all of her people.

"Noreen, your delivery pod will be considerably smaller, but rather than stay here under so many eyes, unstealthed, I suggest you also tow it to where you can dock and bring it all aboard safely. After that, you are good to go on your own excursion. I'll see that you receive a recording that fills you in on some details you can use to your advantage."

They wanted her to know where the spec ops training bases were located, and had some details that Nabarone had gathered about Heavyside.

Mirikami didn't care to confide in Trakenburg concerning their plan to visit there. The colonel, remaining secretive, had agreed that two of his teams would provide some training, but assumed it would be a long-term mission. He wasn't committed to divert his troops from their real mission of slowing the Krall and disrupting their supply lines.

"Our TGs will be receiving some advanced training from specialized troops, which are currently considered the best that humanity has to offer. That opinion will be short lived, when they discover how fast these youngsters absorb everything they are taught, and quickly outstrip their teachers.

"Marlyn, I want to make a stop at home for some modifications. Please have Rafe, Aldry, and Maggi prepare for that. Tell them there will also be older models needing modern upgrades." He knew she understood most of what he meant.

More TGs would get the TG1 contact telepathy mods from ripper genes. They also had learned in the clanship assault that TGs needed vision, scent, and hearing enhancements as well, to gain every possible advantage when facing the Krall. They couldn't count on spec ops eyesight and knowledge where they were going next.

What Noreen and Marlyn didn't know was that the four men on the Bridge of the Mark of Koban had made firm decisions, involving personal risks. They couldn't shelter the TG1s from the necessary risks the coming fight forced on them, but they would *not* increase that level of risk by their having leaders that were physically too weak and slow to go with them. They were the older models needing upgrades, and Rafe had said that it was risky for people not born as SGs, with the technology he had. It was time to find out how risky.

Having started the wheels turning, Mirikami grimaced. "Gentlemen, we had better get a few hours of sleep. Trakenburg says his trainers will have our TGs assembled on the floor of the crater at 0600 local time, for 'vigorous exercises,' as he described them. He'll let us sleep late this one morning only because we just had a long tough arrival day. The four of us are expected to be there. We have less than five hours. Enjoy your naps."

****

Three days later, the supply pods were on their way to fifteen hundred mile equatorial orbits, with the Avenger and Beagle watching on their sensors. It was evening, for the time zone where the Mark was located.

Both wives had figured out Mirikami's initially cryptic remarks about upgrading "older models." Dillon had explained to her how Carson had needed to finish the landing on Poldark, after a series of violent maneuvers to avoid missiles had left only the TGs conscious. If the mission had *required* the SGs to be in full control, or Mirikami had not arranged for Carson to be on the Bridge, they all would have died.

The older men were now working out to get in better physical shape and as an example for the youngsters that nobody was exempt. The chief wisely stayed on the ship.

Noreen was laughing as her husband picked up the com line. "Carson was on watch, and he said he had to wake you up to take my call. It's not even nine in the evening there. Getting a bit worn out aren't we, future superman?"

"Don't try to make me laugh," he groaned. "My ribs and abs ache from the damned sit ups."

"You do those all the time."

"Not with a two-foot thick, twenty-foot long ironwood log on my chest, which I share lifting with Thad, Sarge, and even Tet, the four of us laid out in a row.

"You should see the solid metal posts they had to find for our TGs to use. Ironwood doesn't grow thick or heavy enough to challenge the kids, so they brought in some thick steel poles used to build Dragon tank barriers. The mini-tanks themselves are not that hard to stop, but the plasma cannons burn through anything else too quickly. They weigh a ton. Actually, a lot more I think. The four of us can't even pick one up. Three TGs can, and one of those was a small girl."

Noreen was puzzled. "I don't understand why they are pushing the TGs to exercise. They are ten times as strong as normal people already."

"Hon, it's part of team building, and just because they start strong, that doesn't mean they are as fit as they can be. The instructors can't match them, but have cut them no slack. Four of the TGs have already said they don't want to do this. They didn't like the fighting and killing on the clanship. They want a position on the Beagle, after we get home, or to join in the exploration of our other continents. Exploring is more to their liking. Tet told them they would get that chance, and informed all of our complement that there was no stigma in looking for a noncombat role, if that new role could still help our colony move ahead." He checked his thumbnail watch, which he'd set to glow in his dark sleeping compartment.

"I have to get up at 0330, to be dressed and outside before the TGs assemble there in the morning at 0400. I'm supposed to be a perky and wide-awake leader example for them. I hate early mornings."

"Poor baby. I mainly called to tell you that the Avenger is Jumping in an hour. I've just matched orbits with my pod. It's even larger than I expected, so I can't wait to open the presents. Having an AI again will be nice. I already spoke with Carson and said my goodbyes, and he recorded messages for home, to go with Marlyn.

"She has parked next to her own pod, which is gigantic, over half the volume of the Beagle. I think she is talking to Thad and Ethan right now. I'm so pleased that boy is already out of the med lab. It looks like TGs are fast healers as well, with that high metabolism." Here she paused, looking into the camera, and watching his face on her own screen.

"I needed to tell you I love you. I know that you know that, but I needed to say it directly. I think you may visit home before I do, and I'm worried about your decision. I understand it, and may even follow your example. Only, I don't want you any crazier than you are now. Even if Maggi thinks that would be an improvement." She laughed weakly.

Rafe had said that the ripper gene mods for telepathy might not attach properly to the neural receptors of the existing unused super conducting nerves in the older SGs. He thought that such a failure could disrupt the subject's ability to think. The cold reference to "subject" concealed the possible mental breakdown of a person's mind, if the new neural growths in the brain did not link properly.

Dillon looked back into the beautiful dark eyes and perfect shaped face of the woman he loved, longing for physical contact. "Lady, I love you too. Have a safe trip. I hope the 'toys' we bought you are to your liking."

After breaking contact, Dillon was slow returning to sleep.

****

Trakenburg was questioning Max, his AI. "So Nabarone's Space Defense tried to trace the two outbound Jumps, but they only led to uninhabited systems?"

"Yes Sir. That's what was reported to him. The two clanships apparently Jumped again immediately, and their wake in Tachyon Space was too diffuse for the tracking ships to follow after that. It appears the ship commanders are aware of our tracking capability."

"I doubt Nabarone told them we had that ability, or he wouldn't have tried to follow them. They could have figured it out some other way, it was discussed in the media after the two fleet actions years ago proved the Krall could do that." Perhaps there were other clues.

"Max, you have listened to all of the conversations we recorded, and what they said before they knew we were listening. Have you found any clue as to where they came from?"

"Sir, there is a reference to a place called Koban a number of times, and they described the name of their new race of Homo sapiens as Kobanoid, another possible connection. However, there is no record of a planet discovery given that name. Their world must be well beyond the Rim area humanity has explored, and towards the region where the Krall originated. Beyond that, there is no definite clue to that world's location.

"There are nearly a million stars within a wide cone, which is two thousand light- years deep along that galactic spur. Using T squared travel in Tachyon Space, even a three thousand light-year cone is within range of a two week Jump. Finding that particular planet would be more difficult than the often described human metaphor of a needle in a haystack."

"OK. What have the DNA scans from our samples told us about the four older men, and the four wounded young men that we treated in the med labs?"

"Sir, the first reports are listed as possibly contaminated for all eight of them. The results found repeated examples of genes that are not part of the human genome at all, and of other unusual genes that are human, but did not appear in the general human population. They were formerly used in clone development before the Collapse. The tests are being redone."

"The clone genes I expected, but the new genes are what made the so called TGs so fast and strong. They are new, and I want to know more about them, so assume they are not contamination."

"Sir, the unknown genes are very complex and completely unrecorded previously, even among alien life on our many settled planets. Only one scientist said they could have been designed entirely by a team of geneticists, but most of the investigative team thinks the new genes are too well integrated in the younger people, and most likely were transferred from some living host that had them naturally. The muscles and nervous system the new genes produce have a fully functional interface, with a now passive human neural system present, which is largely bypassed by the newer organic superconducting nerves

"The bones of the younger subjects have some carbon nano tube enhancements that appear genetically distinct from the muscle and nervous system changes. It is as if they have received multiple genes from other pre-existing biological organisms."

Trakenburg had the answer. Most of it anyway. "They have inserted nonhuman genes! Probably copied from animals on that heavy gravity planet. They lied to us. They said the TGs were reproductively compatible with normal humans." He was shocked, and angry.

"Sir, I have no information as to the veracity of those that told you reproduction with the general human population is possible by those young men. However, the statement itself is correct. The young men that were treated in the med labs are completely capable of reproduction with human females that do not have the same genetic modifications."

"Oh..." That abruptly stemmed his flow of adrenalin and anger.

He resumed considering the AI's purloined reports. Trakenburg had obtained the data via his backdoor access to Nabarone's own AI database.

He tried to summarize what he knew. "So, all the foreign genes were inserted in the children, called TGs, born of the older generation, called SGs which have only the clone enhancements."

Always patient with wise humans and idiots alike, an AI corrected people with a subtle gentleness. "That is not the case at all, Sir."

"I did not say nonhuman genes are absent in the DNA of the four older men. On the contrary. They have the same organic superconductor nervous system, in parallel to the normal nervous system, just as the TGs do, although it is nonfunctional. It was passed to the TGs at conception."

"How can nonhuman genes be compatible with producing babies with ordinary women?" He was confused, and knew the AI surely had some other humbling revelation if he was only patient enough to let it "talk down" to him.

It came quickly. "You, Sir have had children, and yet you contain a number of genes that were derived from nonhuman sources. A gene derived from an Earth shark species is responsible for modern human resistance to several forms of cancer. The absence of facial and chest hair on men is…" The AI was cutoff.

"Stop. I get it."

Now all he wanted to know was could the next phase of the Heavyside project steal the genetics for building better spec ops soldiers. Not that Max had that answer. The next phase on Heavyside, which no one had admitted to him involved genetics, surely had to change direction. Hardware and Booster Suits could never match what these kids had done to the Krall warriors. The scientists had their genes tagged and knew where they fit into their own DNA. What were needed were people that knew how to do the insertion work, and were willing to risk being caught and executed by their own government. Simple.

He finally knew exactly how Mirikami felt, and why, and was in complete sympathy. He couldn't think of a way to take this data to his superiors, who would insist on knowing how he came by the information. Then there would be the need to obtain approval, which would be refused just as the original idea had been rejected. Except now, there was proof genetic improvement could work, and which he couldn't reveal. If he did, the sole hope he saw of beating the Krall would be stopped by his own paranoid government.

The future of his beloved spec ops was again placed in a difficult situation. Their standard reply came to mind. A shadow couldn't be held in place by standing on it, they would simply slip away. One way or another, he was going to join forces with Mirikami's group, even if they didn't want him along.

****

Nabarone was alone with his aide, having drinks with lunch. "Howard, I felt guilty about trying to have them both followed. Now that the ships split up and shook off our tails, I don't feel so guilty. I won't try again. They definitely are being careful, and not without cause. If they have just the one under populated and undefended world, a minor slip could get them all wiped out."

"Boss, you know if they accomplish what they are trying to do, and stop the Krall by destroying their supply of war material, that no matter where their home system is located, it won't be long before it becomes a center of power. Who would risk trying to push them around?"

"They only have about thirty thousand people, and no infrastructure. How could they manage that?" Yet in the back of his mind came a thought. *It's sometimes strange how words come back on you later.*

"We know Mr. Greeves' wife was going home. However, that much equipment should have taken over a day to transfer. Even when passed through the four wide ports on a clanship, with an experienced and sizable crew in suits to help. We couldn't see the stealthed ship arrive, but the collection of container pods vanished suddenly, several hours after they were left in orbit. The empty pods are not there now, two days later.

"The same thing happened to the other pods. Blink and they were gone." He laughed. "It's not as if they could just haul them along like a back pack."

"Well, at least that's one thing I can ask Thad about. He knows we would have been watching the supplies, in case the Krall came after them. Assuming I can extract him from his spec ops trainers slash torturers to talk to him. They really are wringing them out. I have to be honest; I don't see how, even with the clone mods, they are keeping pace with their younger trainers in their special suits. Even Tet. He's well past middle age, and except for height limitations, is staying even with his three younger friends. I'm only thankful I can claim duty as my lame excuse for telling Thad I don't have time to exercise."

"Here's to another six ounce arm curl," proposed Caudwell, as he downed the last of his mixed drink.

"Have you been to the crater yet, Howard, to watch the workouts? I mean by the TGs, not the old farts, which are impressive but not astounding. You won't believe what those kids can do."

"No Sir. It's only a thirty-minute hop, so I may do it this week. I've seen hard physical training before though. I was a captain in a PUA Ranger unit for a year, at the start of the war, on the Old Colony of New Glasgow. We ran a great deal, but we had a lot of PT and obstacle courses as well."

"Have you seen the course the spec ops teams run?"

"I saw the course layout, but didn't see them using it. That's because they closed it off to outsiders, to retain some supposed level of secrecy. I assumed it was more to attain a level of mystique. However, the width and height of obstacles to jump across clamber over, crawl through or scale, were impressive. No Ranger I ever met could complete that course in the times spec ops claim, not with those scores. Assuming a Ranger completed it at all."

"Howard, I used my authority to go watch some of them practice, at their facility outside New Zagreb. I don't think its hype to build a phony reputation. From personally observing them perform feats of running, jumping, climbing, and demonstrations of individual and combined team strength exercises, I can tell you it isn't bullshit. Besides, a mystique to impress who? The Krall don't give a crap, and can kick their asses nearly as easily as they can any of our troops. Spec ops are only narrowing the gap, to try and hold out longer against the enemy."

"Thad and his friends, with their clone enhancements, are physically well matched with the spec ops troops, when those troops wear their black exomuscle suits. The electronic implants provide them IR vision and data feed, and the fiber nerve overlays boost their reaction speed over the SGs. However, if you add that technology and Booster Suits to the SGs, they would have all of the spec ops ability, plus significantly greater strength, with heat and cold adaptation advantages. That alone would have had Trakenburg salivating. Until he found what he really wants! The ability of those TGs."

"Henry, I saw the videos of the inside of the clanship, after the fact with dead Krall laying everywhere. There were no shots of the TGs in action. Are they that much better?"

"Yes! They make the spec ops instructors look like they're wading through mud when they try to keep pace on the new course they duplicated in the crater. That's when the TGs are running, jumping, and climbing. Any two of them can lift or carry as much as an eight-man boosted spec ops team. When it comes to reaction times, like hand or foot speed in hand-to-hand or knife fighting, the differential is even more pronounced.

"Thad claims they also think at an accelerated rate. They don't appear to be any smarter than the normal range of young people, which of course are always sure they know everything." He laughed at that truism.

"However, if you or I had one second to think of what to do when an enemy is about to pull a trigger, versus ten seconds to think about it, and the ability to act that much faster, you are far more likely to choose the best response. The same for a tactical situation, with more time to analyze what the possibilities are and match them with your greater capabilities, then follow an action that the enemy is least able to counter."

"If you give me the authorization in writing, or call Trakenburg, I might be able to finally see what you've been telling me about. The blackout on data feeds is a real pain. We don't usually have to travel to check on an operation we are supposedly running. The colonel is acting like that crater is his own preserve."

"My fault. I needed the colonel's people for the kind of training Thad wanted. He was given more control over access because of his own need to keep his involvement quiet. I don't think he has passed this up the line to his superiors. When Mirikami asked us to join the conspiracy to keep their existence secret, the colonel bought in all the way. He's been doing that for years already, for the Heavyside project, and I think secrecy is part of his personality."

"If I have a day free early next month, I can go over then."

"I'll cover for you tomorrow in that Navy meeting. My impressive presence might make them cough up the extra fighters for ground support we want. If you put off a trip to the crater too long, our visitors might be gone. I need you informed as to how we might be using them in the near future."

"Why would they quit training so soon? The spec ops' training takes almost two years, and that's accelerated for the war, and by use of the Booster Suits and implant surgery."

"I told you these TGs, on average, seem as bright as a similar group of college students, except they learn and remember at a phenomenal rate. It must be some aspect of the superconducting nerves. Trakenburg's instructors say that after a single class on a subject, say how two armed troopers should properly enter and clear a room of a possible enemy by covering one another and their assigned sectors and hard corners, the instructors lecture them and then demonstrate.

"The designated TG leaders always step up and shake the hands of the men that demonstrated the process, just before trying it themselves. They were taught to be invariably polite that way, Thad says. Anyway, they usually do it nearly perfectly. If there are any minor errors, they hear from the instructors, who go over and help position them properly. More hand shaking and thanks. Then the leaders will execute the action to virtual perfection.

"When they are told that it was done properly, the leaders call over their teams, and do this rally cry thing. They all put their hands on the team leader's hand in a circle, pause a moment, in tribute I guess. I don't know. Then they split out into two person teams, which then execute the room clearing process to near perfection, for each pair. They almost never need correction or to have a demonstration repeated. One time is enough for them.

"Trakenburg's instructors say at this rate they can cover Unconventional Warfare guerilla tactics this week, Direct Action against enemy targets next week, Counterterrorism the week after, and Special Reconnaissance the week after that.

"They may not always remember everything they are told, but the instructors are baffled at the memory they retain of how to move. They even copied, for a time, the slight arm stiffness that Sergeant Jenkins displayed. He was one of the men that squared off against a TG inside the parking garage. A med lad repaired his dislocated elbow in a couple of days, and he's now one of the instructors. After he described what they were doing, apparently favoring their left elbow, they all quit doing it that same day. Moving their left arms more fluidly."

"Are you serious? Isn't what you listed most of what they came here to learn?"

"Yes. That's why I told you not to wait too long in observing them. When we finally give them the intelligence our scouts and drones have collected from worlds inside space the Krall control, they might just tear out of here to go get them!" He laughed, but it wasn't all in jest.

"What about the months of team building, physical training, gradual combat experience as they go on missions?"

"They already have split into teams, which work extremely well together. The team members always seem to know what the other members will do in almost any situation. They are still developing strength, and keep at the PT in twice a day sessions. We can hardly keep food in the mess tent for those voracious appetites.

Even the smaller girls eat us out of groceries, and the only weight they gained was muscle mass.

"They do lack practical combat experience, which can get some of them killed, as they learned the hard way in that last fight. Trakenburg has called for a meeting with Mirikami and his; I guess I'd call them his staff, for lack of a better word. I suspect he wants to go along with them, taking some volunteer teams. I have no idea if he's clearing this with his bosses. I'm not about to interfere, because we both want Mirikami's idea to be given a try.

"They don't answer to the PU Army, and refused any official military structure, saying that it might not set well with the free spirited people at home. I have honorably discharged Sergeant Reynolds, who was going to stay with them, no matter what anyone tried to order him to do. The man is not a leader, but only because he refuses to be one. However, he wants to be in on crippling the Krall in any way he can contribute, and I want to let him do that."

"Boss, I'll order a hopper and a pilot for tomorrow morning, and go to the crater. You can play patty cake with the Ladies of the Navy in my place. Please keep your language under control, and don't let Carla speak aloud at the conference. We really do want those space planes stationed closer to us. Perhaps some even parked dirt-side. If you're nice to them, you might get what you want from them for a change."

"Hummph." Was that a skeptical reply, or an outright refusal to cater to a woman's wishes?

Chapter 7: Exploration can be a Howl

Despite Mirikami's assurances, Marlyn was half surprised when the large stack of lightly tethered cargo pods arrived with the Beagle, simply hanging in space less than fifty feet away, where they had been floating when she'd Jumped. She'd been worried that the "treasure" might drift away and be lost in Tachyon Space. She'd slowly accelerated the ship and pods to match Koban's expected orbital motion prior to the Jump.

The edge of the pods now were outlined against the beauty of the many shades of teal tinted plains and deeper blue-green forests, gray mountains and a few brown deserts, and blue oceans with plenty of cloud cover. There was a spectacular large spiral storm system off the western coast of the continent of Jura, probably gaining energy as it passed over the warm deep blue ocean. It appeared poised to give the dinosaur analogues a pounding. The denser atmosphere produced winds with considerably greater force than on Earth. However, this was home. Koban.

This *felt* like home to her, after twenty-two years, a husband, and three children; four when she counted Kit; the female ripper certainly counted as family, being raised as one of her "babies." She was as eager to see her multiple grandkits as she was her other two children. Ripper cubs grew so fast compared to human children, particularly in the first years, that she feared they would find Grandma a stranger.

Her first task had been to broadcast immediately to the world below that this was not a random clanship arrival. It wasn't the Mark, but a new captured ship renamed the Beagle. The second was to have her Chief of Engineering, John Yin-Lee, and a former Dive Rat from the Flight of Fancy, securely attach the cargo pod cluster to them for faster towing to a lower orbit. She had made her White Out at about two hundred fifty miles, but the ferry process to land their equipment would go faster if they were even lower.

She matched orbits with the Raven, the huge passenger transport they intended to restore to Jump capability. Some of the supplies she had brought were for that work.

Jake had responded immediately, of course, after she transmitted the prearranged opening phrase of her initial call. "We're home, folks." Simple, but not anything a Krall or other human ship would transmit.

"Welcome home Captain Greeves. We expected you to return first, and I recognize your voice. From the much larger gamma ray burst and radar target it appears you brought a large package with you."

"Yes. It's everything we had on our list, and considerably more. I'll be making a rendezvous with the Raven. We need help sorting things, and when we have done that, I'll ferry down what goes to Hub City, what goes to Prime City, and send some parts to the Raven."

Jake announced, "Dr. Fisher has just arrived on the Bridge of the Flight of Fancy, with Doctors Anderfem and Campbell right behind her. I'll place you on speaker."

"Maggi, Aldry, and Rafe, hello. I'm home, and I have some news. Both good and some sad. The latter will await my landing, but the good news is that we have made contact, and General Nabarone has welcomed us quietly, as we hoped. You will be thrilled at what I have brought you for new med labs, and nanites. I also have parts for the Raven, and some equipment for upgrading the Beagle to make it a more human friendly ship."

Maggi answered. "Glad to have you back safely. Did you manage to get two ships at K1, as Tet planned?"

"We did, and Noreen is captain of a ship she has named Avenger, and has departed on her own mission to Heavyside. I can't wait to get started on my next mission."

"You aren't leaving right away are you?" Aldry sounded dismayed.

"As soon as I can gather volunteers I'll be off to explore a new world. However, I won't be far away. Not even out of the local system in fact, within long-range radio distance. There's a second habitable world here, remember? I intend to discover how habitable it is. I'll be back and forth weekly, and daily by radio report.

"Tet also wants the exploration of the continent of Jura to resume, and we need a great deal more of the gold and platinum we found on Paleogene, commodities to sell for Hub credits. I brought some automated mining equipment to do that for us. We have to buy most of what we need for making Koban more comfortable. Tet has a deal in the works to purchase a general purpose orbital factory, to make consumer goods for us."

Maggi was excited. "Great. It sounds like we are on the way to joining the Rim world society, with dreams to become a New Colony someday. On the way up here, I had Jake notify Spacers at both domes to ready the larger shuttles, to go up to meet you. There will be quite a few TG1s coming up to help."

"We were busy after you left." Aldry informed her. "There are fifty new TG1s, ready to Tap our old Spacers about weightless cargo moving methods. Another one hundred TG1s, in two groups of fifty, are two weeks behind each other on that same round of mods. There are enough TG1s now that we don't need to take time from our cats to help the kids develop coordination and Mind Tap ability quickly."

"Good. That matches with Tet's instructions. To give all of the TGs contact telepathy provided they want the enhancement of course. It has proved tremendously important, more than you would believe. I can't wait to tell you what we have discovered about long-range communications on the trip.

"He also asked me to tell you that the Mark will be making a stop home before he moves against the Krall worlds. All of the remaining Koban gene enhancements are needed for the TG1s that will go with him. I have thirty new and modern med labs, and nanites of eighteen new types to speed the processes."

Rafe had a concern about the last revelation. "Marlyn, we still have not deciphered all of the functions of the three new nanite types we found in Sarge's bloodstream. We don't have enough research people to divert to work on more nanite types we don't know how to properly use."

"Rafe, I know nothing about nanites. However, Dillon said that somehow, a Special Ops colonel that is working with them, managed to *procure* the detailed specifications, instruction manuals, and manufacturing templates of all of those nanites I brought with me. He told Dillon not to ask too many questions. He said they apparently 'fell off trucks,' right where his troops happened to be walking, outside of nine different competing commercial production sites."

"Oh..., that should help." Was his weak-kneed understated reply, concerning a staggering bonanza of what had to represent enormous biological wealth? He needed to sit down.

****

A busy week later, ten men and women were working on the outside of Raven, using new lightweight scooters to position the Trap emitters the Beagle had brought, and which were intended for that class of older ship. The Raven could be Jump capable in two or three months.

The med labs had been distributed equally between Hub and Prime cities, with TGs from both compounds gathering at Prime City, for the stepped-up schedule of receiving the ripper mod for contact telepathy, and the other Koban mods. Soon there would be TG2s, with a ripper's enhanced night vision and sense of smell, and hearing that extended into the ultrasonic range.

Marlyn had not had much time to spend with her children, who had all been waiting for her on the tarmac at Prime city. Bradley and Danner provided hugs and kisses, Kit bowled her over and licked and sniffed her, frilling her with an overwhelming flood of images she couldn't sort out fast enough. Then four shy "cubs" came out to pile on and lick their grandmother, who had to call for Kit's help before the three to five hundred pound grandkits killed her with the weight of their affection. To think she was afraid they'd forget her, even with Kit's frilling to remind them.

Danner, the youngest, laughing at the cat swarm, said, "Now you don't need a bath Mom."

On the contrary, she felt she needed a laundry for her clothes, and a hose for the coating of cat saliva on her face and hands.

Considering what the cubs ate, when Maggi's turn came to greet her friend, she avoided a big hug and wrinkled her nose. She, in her ever gracious and tactful manner, told Marlyn, "Dear Lady, you smell like raw rhinolo butt."

****

After a hectic week, Rafe, Aldry, and even Maggi, were looking tired but happy, as they worked with the teams of technicians to learn what the new nanites could do for them. With the manuals, there was no need for a scientist to figure out, via laborious and incremental lab tests, what each programmed feature in a nanite was designed to do. With the templates for making and cloning the nanites, they could make alterations in what they did, to custom tailor them for the Koban gene requirements.

Two varieties of nanites were designs from competing companies, both claimed to speed nerve damage repair and regrowth. The teams had focused study on those nanites that they needed most, and organic superconducting nerve generation was a top priority.

The HUB industries, for these very profitable products, were propelled by the large number of wounded citizens and soldiers requiring extensive treatment for war related injuries. To a Krall, any human, any age, was a combatant. These were much needed humanitarian medical improvements, but capitalism and profit drove the development and competition, to corner the vast number of sales on planetary scales.

The two nervous system nanites were the particular focus of the Koban teams, because those normally targeted the standard human nervous system. They delivered the nutrients and enzymes that promoted rapid nerve growth, following mapped out pathways that grew nerve tissue all along the route, rather than just at the severed nerve endings. It was like constructing a rail line simultaneously along the entire convoluted route, rather than building from one, or both ends, to join them. The simultaneous process was far faster, but required the "building material" nutrients to be delivered everywhere along the route quickly. That was one of the nanites jobs.

Because this wasn't a DNA redesign, the nanites simply followed the known pathways that human nerves always followed, obeying the instructions built into the DNA. The teams were following factory instructions to alter what nutrients and enzymes these nanites would deliver and on what schedule. The previously modified human DNA coding would direct the organic superconducting nerve assembly.

Examining the latest "super pig" nerve tissue sample, in situ, using a new miniature meson imaging microscope probe, Rafe was finally satisfied. "Either batch of modified nerve tissue nanites works fine for us, but the Organite version carries a larger number of molecules of the preassembled chains of rare earths and heavy metals to the nerve assembly sites. Nerve growth is roughly fifteen percent faster, even if more demanding of the raw material supply. That's the nanite version we will use for future Koban mods involving fast nerve growth."

The small super piglet in question was tightly confined, but it struggled strongly. As it had developed the ripper based contact telepathy nerve links, located in its sensitive nose, it became aware of what the human touching it was planning to do. It didn't *want* that sharp looking thing pushed into its tender nose tissue. It settled down after it discovered that it didn't hurt, a topical pain blocker having been applied first.

The mental feedback from animal test subjects had forced a new "humanitarian" attitude on the formerly cool, clinical, and emotionally detached scientists and lab technicians. Knowing how a subject animal *felt* as you examined it was disconcerting enough, but that wasn't the worst aspect.

The practice of euthanizing animals for dissection and study, after the contact telepathy genetic modification procedures were implemented, had ended abruptly. The animals sensed the intent and anticipation of the humans, which sometimes thought of the barbeque scheduled that night. The TG1s, asked to help by Mind Tapping the animals for the scientists, pointed out that the researchers had effectively become the "Krall" to their lab animals. It was a sobering revelation, to find that same disdain for lower "animals" in ourselves.

Maggi repeated Rafe's most significant conclusion to the lab technicians, who were pushing candidates to consume an adequate supply of nerve "building materials."

"Rapid nerve grown is more demanding of the raw material supply Rafe said. A helpless and confined force-fed piglet already considers you monsters. Good luck forcing a TG to drink more of the lousy tasting mineral supplements we give them now. They can dismantle a Krall, you know."

Aldry had a solution. "Jimbo, in hydroponics, says both the vanilla and chocolate production is building a stockpile, and we have a few more dairy cows now that the wolfbats don't attack and eat the calves. We also found that blue sugar beet equivalent last year, and a crop is ready to increase sugar production. Why don't we make old-fashioned ice cream and milkshakes, and use lower doses of supplements per drink? Even if they have to consume several shakes a day, I doubt their teenage metabolisms will balk at the sweets."

Maggi, able to find problems with anyone else's optimism, said, "Oh fine. Make the one I'm watching even more hyper active." She had been watching Dillon and Noreen's youngest son, Cory, while his parents were on their missions. The teenager, fifteen and only a month from turning sixteen was a nice kid, but even without the TG mods, he was as adventuresome as Carson, his older brother.

Maggi added to her semi-manufactured complaints. "His sister, Katelyn, will be back for a two week break from school in Hub City next week. The two of them argue constantly. He will play dangerous tricks on her, she will yell at him, and it will drive me crazy."

Rafe and Aldry shared an incredulous look. Maggi positively thrived on verbal sparring and practical jokes.

Aldry pointed out an obvious flaw in the predicted chaos. "Kate is a TG1, her brother is still an SG, and won't be finished adapting for a month after he gets the mods. She can hold her own with a little brother until she returns to school."

Not one to give up a good gripe without just cause, Maggi piled on her laments. "If Noreen or Dillon can't get home before Cory opts for the Koban mods, I'll have to go through that with him on my own. The bitchiness and whining when it 'burns' or 'aches' or he can't go outside to do something dangerous."

Another incredulous look between Rafe and Aldry was noticed by Maggi this time. "OK, OK. I got the damned law passed to allow sixteen-year-olds to make that decision. I didn't *have* any kids, so it wasn't supposed to make *my* life harder. Dillon had better get his ass home in one month and nine days, *or else*."

Or else Maggi would have to endure what all the parents of teenagers had endured, with Maggi's manipulations to help make the problem more aggravating.

She clearly had been keeping exact track of the time remaining until Cory's birthday, to the day.

Rafe repeated an old saying, of the type Maggi herself often employed. "The wheels of justice grind slowly, but exceedingly fine." He had also considered *as ye sow, so shall ye reap.*

She shot him a "Tiger Lady" look, which would be all too familiar to Dillon, if he were here. Rafe was happy to be on the opposite side of the lab bench from the tiny woman, known for her minor acts of physical retribution. Some people actually thought the *Krall* were more hot tempered and fast.

Aldry reminded her that she and Rafe had been watching Bradley and Danner while Thad and Marlyn were gone. "Those two boys are the ages of Katelyn and Cory, and are pretty well behaved with each other. We have had the same inconvenience as you."

Maggi countered. "Their mother is back now, and Bradley has said he will go with her to explore the Morning Star. Danner wants to explore Jura as soon as he receives the TG1 mods. Cory will be all mopey and a pain in the ass with both of them gone."

Aldry arched her left eyebrow. "You are being deliberately pessimistic, Maggi. Cory is friends with Danner, and they are only days apart in age. Find ways to keep them together more now, and Danner's enthusiasm to explore Jura will infect Cory. They both will be new TG1s by spring, and have a whole continent to explore. Danner says some of the ripper cubs want to go, and even a couple of squadrons of wolfbats want to see the new territory."

"Fine! Then I'll be alone in my quarters every night, rattling around that empty space with no one to speak to me."

Now the real reason for her discontent was apparent. Without Dillon and Noreen, Thad and Marlyn, and their families around, she had lost her social center. She *loved* having someone or something to complain about, to be able to interact with her two adopted families.

"You need to get off your butt and go exploring." Rafe told her. "Go on one of the expeditions."

"Right. Great idea. I turn a hundred twelve in eight months. Who needs an old lady along?"

Rafe churned the butter a bit. "Eight months? Then that only makes you a hundred eleven now. You look exactly like I remember you when you organized the Midwife project twenty-two years ago. With clone mods added to our standard genes, you can stay physically active for another twenty or twenty-five years. Go discover something."

She considered his proposal a few minutes. "I'll talk to Marlyn. See if she has room to nursemaid me on her trip. At least it isn't too far to bring me back if I'm a burden."

Aldry and Rafe, pretending to have something else to do, turned away so they could safely roll their eyes.

****

Two months later, the modified Organite brand of nanites had proven to be an unqualified success, by speeding the development of the superconducting nervous system by eighteen percent, and had virtually eliminated the burning sensations as the nerves developed. The neural receptors on the developing Koban muscle tissue were formed sooner, because other nanites delivered nutrients faster to the new muscle tissue growth. Rather than two months changing and adapting, the entire process was reduced to less than one month.

For the first time, the telepathy mod and all of the other Koban genetic modifications were simultaneously inserted for Cody, Danner, and a girl and a boy that came over from Hub City. The four downed a prodigious number of milkshakes, and ate astonishing amounts of meat. They felt hungry all of the time and even ate vegetables unprompted, a sure sign *some* sort of miracle was in progress.

Having TG1s around sped the process of muscle memory training and adaptation for the four new TG2s, because now they were not having to sort out the mental images of how to move properly, based on images from a very physiologically different species, the rippers. Every TG1 that Mind Tapped the new candidates had already benefited from what previous TG1s had learned. Over time, the best way anyone had found to move or do something in a particular situation was incorporated with variations based on differing conditions or circumstances.

The rate of learning was so enhanced, and retention so complete, that Aldry ran additional brain scans on the new TG2s to see what was happening. The scans clearly showed that the superconducting nerves facilitated reorganization of synapses to make more connections per neuron and provide more storage capacity, which was more quickly accessed than before.

Some of this improved brain organization proved directly related to the wolfbat hearing modification. Although that did not restructure the existing nervous system, it did naturally provide a template for storing the incoming information from the ears, and mental 3-D sound images were the result.

Mind Taps on wolfbats revealed the human mental audio based images were not nearly as detailed as the wolfbats formed (people hadn't wanted pointy long ears), but were organized much better than data collected by the normal human brain. The TG2s also did not have echolocation ability.

Only the rare savant had selectively displayed unusual gifts of memory, mental calculation, or other abilities, usually just one such trait per person. However, for TG2s the rest of the brain's data storage also changed, from the more random holographic storage that was typical in a human brain, to a more *structured* holographic set of memories and data.

The TG2s had the same number of symbolic mental cabinets and closets of the various brain areas, but now the metaphorical drawers and shelves were organized for faster retrieval and storage, and combinations of disparate data could be brought together quickly, allowing answers to questions that they had never even thought of asking themselves. It was natural, no added effort required, and the superconducting nerves made it happen fast.

Bradley, when asked what it was like after the mods took effect, described it as similar to his music and video collections in his room. Music and Tri-Vid recordings had been jumbled in a tray, some on his closet shelf, a few shoved under his bed, several had fallen out of sight or been left in other parts of their family compartment. After a week, he realized he knew where they all were, or deduced where the lost ones had to be, and he gathered them up. Now they were ordered logically in the tray that was intended to hold them all. He now preferred orderly over messy, but could operate just fine in a messy situation if he had to do so. His cherished Koban fossil and mineral samples now looked as if they belonged in a university collection, not a trash bin.

With ripper night vision, he could find his misplaced property in dark corners or under his bed without benefit of additional light. His new ripper scent capability finally found that stale sandwich wrap he had snuck into his room, hidden and forgotten about, when he was sent to bed without supper. *The practical joke had not been that dangerous*, as he thought back.

Marlyn was walking around in a daze, unable to believe her "pack rat" slovenly little boy had changed so much in only a month. He had taken to suggesting to *her* that she should pick up and put away her things and that the kitchen had a strong smell of leftover food residue she should clean away! After years of nagging *him,* it was only iron-willed discipline, which somehow prevented filicide, the strangulation of her precious second born. His newfound prescience somehow failed to detect the threating glares from his dear mother, each time he made such a comment.

The new nanites were so efficient, that Rafe and Aldry had combined the number of Koban mods they applied at the same time for all of the upgrades. Many of the existing TG1s were receiving the three final Koban mods, to advance to TG2 status, as they had time and access to keep the new med labs occupied.

The geneticists reassessed some of the limitations they had placed on procedures that now might be possible with SGs, which they had previously considered too risky before they had the nanites.

Marlyn had been ready for the Jump to the neighboring planet for weeks, but reluctantly decided to wait for the latest mods some of her volunteers wanted before leaving. She didn't simply sit on her hands while waiting, however.

The Beagle now had two elevator systems installed, and technicians and a physicist from Hub City installed the new AI, which she learned was able to interface with the former clanship's alien operating system. Her new system was a far newer model than was Jake, a twenty-two-year-old JK series and model. Her AI's K series and P model, suggested its name for her, as was often the case. She called the KP system Kap, proving yet again the odd limits to human imagination sometimes.

Marlyn and her entire crew of volunteers also had a new longer-range transducer system that was backwards compatible with Jake's more limited older version. The Mark of Koban was receiving a similar refit on Poldark, and she knew

Noreen had taken a new AI with her as well, for the Avenger.

Jake and Kap exchanged libraries, providing Kap with knowledge of the local system learned over the last twenty years, and the history of the two communities. Kap announced, with a sense of surprise (something that Jake had never managed to display), that the older AI had a far larger Krall vocabulary database, both for low and high Krall speech than Kap had brought from Human Space. The enemy used encrypted communications when near human worlds, something they had not considered necessary on Koban, where no human survivors were anticipated, and the existence of Jake was never suspected.

Considering the near proximity of the second planet for a Jump ship, and the need to test Kap's control capability, Marlyn made two orbital visits to study the planet up close, before the expedition was ready to go. The first visit was a mild surprise, aside from the clearly human habitable biosphere she expected. It held abandoned Krall domes on several of its six continents. Like Koban, the planet was lush with plant and animal life, vast forests and jungles, and oceans alive with creatures large and small. There were herds of grazing animals seen on open grasslands. Animals just like that was a frequent evolutionary development on many of the habitable worlds humans had found. They were always accompanied by predators that preyed on the herds.

With gravity only ninety percent that of Earth, there wasn't likely to be animals quite as threatening as those on Koban, unless here too they had developed superconducting nerves. That possibility was considered extremely unlikely, considering Koban was the only world humans had found where that had evolved, and the Krall, with a wider sampling of the galaxy had never encountered that trait anywhere else.

The domes were obviously long abandoned, and the grounds were overgrown with more conventional green colored chlorophyll based vegetation. Shades of green were more common on most habitable planets, at least those with a yellow-white sun similar to Sol. On some of the planets around red dwarfs, many of the plants often favored reds and orange in their leaves. The color of Koban's sun was a bit bluer and slightly hotter than Sol, and the greater availability of heavier elements on Koban had made some alternate evolutionary choices possible. This lead to shades of teal foliage and organic superconductor nerves, for example.

The old domes had never been surrounded by walled or fenced compounds, which implied a less dangerous environment than that of Koban. That was relative, of course because the Krall were willing to accept, and even desired, a higher level of danger than would the average human. However, for whatever the reason, the Krall had clearly abandoned the world much longer ago than they had left Koban itself. The most likely reasons were the dislike for the lower gravity, the lack of threats, and the tremendous attraction of the far more deadly neighboring planet.

Marlyn simply recorded what was below the ship for the three orbits she made, enough for mapping out the six major landmasses, the rivers, large lakes, seacoasts and islands. Only two of the six continents were connected, the rest being separated by larger oceans than Koban featured.

The most significant discovery was made by one of the other Spacers, former Captain Francis Alaway, selected to be Marlyn's first officer. She originally commanded one of the cargo ships the Krall had captured and towed to Koban years ago, and who now lived in Hub City, having just ended a marriage contract, with no children. She was an SG looking for an adventure.

Francis stopped the video playback she was studying, and called out to Marlyn. The large conference room on the Flight of Fancy was filled with volunteers for the exploration mission, examining places where they might choose to land first.

"Captain, I found other structures besides the domes. They're located in a tall forest, not very far from one of the domes. They look more recent and well maintained, and I spotted them by what I first thought was fog drifting from the woods, but appears to be smoke."

Everyone promptly crowded around her small screen, until Marlyn told Jake to put the image on a larger wall screen. Within the zoomed-in scene Francis had selected, there were walled and roofed structures visible, built not on the ground below the trees, but up in the trees themselves. They were built around the massive trunks of very tall trees and were spread along their larger limbs at the higher levels. At mid tree trunk height, with no limbs present, there were multiple levels, with bridges or walkways strung between trees. Smoke could be seen coming from roof vents of many of them, drifting on the wind between the trees. The area had been recorded at dusk, and it was too dark to see much detail, but a number of indistinct figures were visible on the walkways.

Marlyn saw what appeared to be several objects together on a walkway. "Jake, can you try to clear up this cluster of figures here?" She touched the screen, knowing Jake was observing her by camera.

"Yes Mam, but there is little contrast in the gloom of the trees."

The image sharpened slightly, but the recording was from nearly overhead, and the forms were still indistinct. It was impossible to tell how tall the creatures were, or what they looked like. In the dusk and tree filtered light, there were no elongated shadows to suggest height. Except for some patches of lighter color on them, which could be clothing, skin, or fur, there were no clues. However, one thing was obvious from the narrow dimensions of the figures as seen looking down on them. These were not bulky, heavy bodied Krall, tiptoeing on fragile-appearing, suspended walkways through the forest.

The next afternoon the Beagle lifted off with a much larger complement this time, and executed a thirty-second Jump to a hundred fifty mile equatorial orbit. Marlyn still referred to the planet as the Morning Star, reserving her right to choose a name later, based on what they found.

The forest village, seeming too small to call a city, was in morning daylight this time. There were fewer of the inhabitants on the walkways than there had been closer to sunset, but there wasn't any doubt as to what species they were. The Krall had left behind members of their slave race of builders, which they had called the Prada.

Marlyn managed to record one large one leaping from a branch to land on a walkway, and had a profile view frozen on screen. From head to toes, stretched in mid leap it had brown fur, and was over seven feet long, although that was with legs and long arms extended. Kap said it would be about five feet tall when standing, bipedal, with a triangular face and large side ears that protruded slightly higher than their skull. The Prada in mid leap had a relatively furless long tail that was thicker than that of Earth monkeys. This corresponded to Jake's records of the Prada having a prehensile tail, as described by a Krall Translator.

The fur colors on other Prada varied between brown, tan, black, or gray, always with white markings on the face and chest. The hands and feet looked hairless and black, as was the pointed nose. They were furred, shoeless, and unclothed, but all of the adults appeared to wear tool belts or sashes, and some had small pouches strapped around their waists or to their backs. They had narrow shoulders and long arms, and somewhat shorter legs. Their heads appeared a bit large for their bodies, suggesting a high brain to body weight ratio, often indicative of greater intelligence.

There were quite a few small to medium ones, presumably children, dashing around the heights recklessly, seldom wearing a tool belt. They watched a somewhat blurry video of several smaller ones apparently engaged in a game of chase, and noted that they used hands, feet, and tails to grasp branches and ropes to dash about, without any apparent fear of the couple of hundred feet to the ground if they fell.

These had to be the builders and assemblers, the slave race the Krall had said were the most human-like to them. The humans themselves didn't see the resemblance all that much. The closest shaped animals they found in a search of images were certain representatives of the nearly extinct Lemurs on Earth, the New Dublin Howlers, or the much larger Lesser Yeti of New Tibet. The latter was a very large, yellow-furred, black-faced hot climate jungle animal, which did not like cold, despite the name.

The Lemurs and Howlers were often arboreal, and some were nocturnal. The large yellow eyes, with black fur rings on the Prada suggested they were well adapted to low light, but this morning they were active in broad daylight. The adults visible appeared to weigh-in at between one hundred to one hundred thirty pounds. Sex was difficult to determine, with fur covering where evolution of a primate style creature might have genitalia. However, two small children were seen clinging to the backs of adult Prada that were indistinguishable from other members of the group, but which could be their mothers.

Everyone was excited to have a chance to meet a non-hostile intelligent species. The Raspani had been a huge disappointment, when they all appeared to have regressed to an almost pre-sentient level. There were flashes of intelligence, sometimes revealed briefly by Mind Taps. However, those images seemed to be deliberately submerged, as if the poor creatures were afraid to release a mind that could think. What creature would want to face life as a thinking meat animal, facing slaughter at any time?

There was no doubt that they would approach the tree village, but they would not do so by landing the Beagle anywhere close. It was externally a Krall clanship, after all. The plan was to land much farther away, and approach in a human made shuttle, which looked and sounded different from Krall models. They would allow the Prada to see that the occupants were not Krall. They were hoping curiosity would draw the Prada to a historic First Contact meeting. There had been no signs of the second major slave race, the Torki, and other than searching coastal areas, they didn't know where the intelligent crabs would live.

There was almost another week to wait before the members of the expedition would be adjusted well enough to the latest genetic modifications to use them. There were new plans to be made and possible trade goods to consider, necessary preparations before trust and language learning could commence. Mind Taps should help that to go faster.

Kobalt and Kit were going, but would stay well clear of the Prada tree village. Bradley, Marlyn's son, who was going along, had all of the Koban genes, which were still becoming fully active. Nevertheless, he said he could now scent a ripper from a mile away if the breeze was in his direction. They had no way of knowing what Prada noses might be capable of detecting.

Until they had experienced the Mind Tap, the aliens couldn't be reassured that the rippers were no threat. Even then, it might not be believed. Prada had obviously been to Koban in the past, because of the dome and wall construction, which the Krall certainly would not do. There was no way to know if any forerunners of the people on the Morning Star planet had ever worked on the domes humans now used. No signs of tree dwellings had ever been found, which made sense, because the Prada would be small easy prey for nearly any predator.

On Koban, the Krall had probably housed their builders in the domes as they were constructed. There were faint mind images from the wild ripper prides, of unusual small upright prey that may have been Prada, from the remote times when the domes had been built. However, the memories were old and fragmented, because that was several hundred years ago, based on the scientifically measured ages of several of the domes. Only *important* pride memories were reinforced by frequent sharing, and this prey wasn't in that category.

Finally, the last of the new mods were past the stage where the recipients were physically uncomfortable, and all that was needed was practice, and Mind Taps from previous TG1s to help them along in their muscle learning. The multitude of new nanites, particularly those for the nervous system were going to shorten and improve the gene mods implementation. The newest upgraded expedition members were proof of that.

The Beagle lifted from the Prime City tarmac, and entered Jump Hole shortly after leaving atmosphere. The White Out at the Morning Star came before some even released the breath they had held from the excitement.

Marlyn entered atmosphere several hundred miles from the tree village, then at low altitude, to stay below the horizon, flew to within thirty miles of the forest, on the far side of the decaying dome, itself located several miles from the edge of the huge trees.

The first task after landing was to put out an armed landing party, to check the local area and ensure there were no immediate threats. They had seen startled animal herds below them break and run as they flew low, and some apparent predatory stalkers of the herds that stayed in a pack when they ran. They were over twice the size of large wolves, and grey and brown in color.

There were far more flying creatures here than they usually saw on Koban, at least where Prime City and Hub City were located. Most of the fliers here certainly resembled birds, or their evolutionary equivalents, as found on nearly every planet humans had found. Perhaps ten percent of them appeared to be either a flying furless animal, or a reptile, or at least they did not have a feathery appearance.

Those worlds that had a biosphere with a dense enough atmosphere, and greater oxygen content for the higher metabolisms needed, always had some fliers that the settlers invariably called "birds." Wolfbat colonies and their intelligent predation, at least near the human occupied domes on Koban, had greatly suppressed most bird populations. Not so here, where they appeared to be plentiful.

The rumble of the thrusters and their heat had driven any animal with a survival instinct away from the immediate landing area. Although a number of mounded burrows were spotted in the open grassy area, which suggested animals that would fit in their six-inch diameter holes lived there, and had likely retreated down them.

The TGs (1s and 2s, but the simpler term was easier to say), were proceeding cautiously as if they were on Koban, even though no one anticipated animals as dangerous here as at home. Because none of this world's animals had ever seen humans, it was hoped they would be cautious, and would not automatically see people as a threat. That was seldom the case on Koban, where everything acted as if humans were a threat, because any animal their size that wasn't eating grass or leaves was a killer of animals that did. Koban life was ultra-competitive and aggressive, when compared to animals on any of the other human worlds.

Kobalt and Kit were in heaven, with the glorious new scents and colors to stimulate their senses. They had been strictly warned not to eat any animals here until the science teams had cleared them for toxins. That didn't prevent them from stalking prey for fun, to "taste" their terror when caught, via frilling, before releasing them. They vanished into the scrub to do just that.

If this system ran true to dual habitable planets found in multiple other systems, there should not be a serious problem. When one planet had a preponderance of safe edible plants and animals for humans, the companion planet did as well. Planetologists found that it was apparently a function of the original solar disk's chemical and elemental makeup when the neighboring planets formed. The eventual emerging life on each followed similar evolutionary paths. If one world's sugars, proteins, enzymes and such, were bad for Earth life, then both worlds were bad. The same held for a pair of worlds when one was suitable for Earth life. Koban was extraordinarily good for humans nutritionally, so this world was likely to be safe as well. Not universally, of course.

The Death Lime thorns were one of many plant products that were deadly on Koban, yet its fruit was completely safe. Many things were expected to be safe for consumption here, but obviously not all. The massive job of testing and cataloging an entire world of new plants and animals would start today.

****

Rushing through underbrush, Kobalt delighted in how light he felt as he smashed through or leaped over bushes of odd colors, startling birds and small animals that had been frozen and in hiding, as he and Kit thudded their reckless way past them. They were not hunting now, but gathering the multitude of new scents that intrigued them, and relishing the colors that were different from home.

The hunts in the place their human pride named Jura was exciting, and dangerous, even for them, with the giant predators with the huge jaws. However, the smells there were still in the family of scents they were used to, it was just another part of *home.* This was completely different smelling, and mysterious. The animal and bird smells were obviously different from the equally strange smelling plant life, but they had no mental images from generations of pride experience to draw from, to know what they were sensing here. It was exciting to bound, as if they were nearly able to fly, leaping at one point completely over a low tree that was higher than the electric fence around the home den of their pride.

Kobalt stopped suddenly as he noticed Kit had reversed, and she was sniffing at something on the ground. Even before reaching her, he knew she had found the droppings of some larger animal. There were many prints in the soil between tufts of the weirdly colored grass. Something had nibbled at the tops of the tallest stems, where seed clusters grew on those that had been bypassed. The prints looked like a sort of hoof made them, and the depth showed they were large, although obviously smaller than a rhinolo by far.

Their scent was different from grass eaters at home, but there was a sort of musty similarity, and the partly digested grasses and leaves in the scat seemed fresh, proving they had passed this way this morning. Like Kit, who had raised her head to look around, he pressed the tip of his sensitive nose on one of the rounded droppings, and felt it was still warm. They were very close to the slow moving herd, since this was probably less than a half hour old.

Marlyn, as pride leader today, had told them not to eat anything, but they could bring something back for the human pride friends to study. If it was safe food, they could eat it after that. Eager for the hunt, he frilled his sister, and they shared strategies for pouncing on a careless trailing herd member of whatever sort of prey this was.

Kit imaged him that they were able to leap farther here and cover ground faster. Instead of the normal stalk to grow close, to sneak past them a bit to set up an ambush, she pictured them both chasing some vaguely antelope-like prey from behind, using raw speed and power to isolate one and catch it, keeping the terrified animal alive long enough for them both to “taste” its new flavor of fear. A quick merciful kill would go to the one that brought it down, so there was a competition to the chase to come. Kobalt thought of the tree he had just cleared in his long leap. He expected to win.

There was never a thought of killing two of the prey. Ripper morality held even in this special case on a new world. No kills for the pleasure of the act, even then only if the meat provided was necessary. There was uncertainty here if even the meat of the one kill would be consumable. It created an uncomfortable mental gray area.

Kit's proposal of a headlong chase from the herd's rear was quickly agreed to by Kobalt, but he wasn't paying attention to her body positioning as they frilled. Exactly like their human siblings, she "cheated" her bigger brother by placing herself in the direction they would have to run. Then she suddenly placed both of her big front paws on her brother's right shoulder and pushed hard, knocking him over by the unexpected action, while she used the shove to gain momentum to start her run, to gain at least a six body length advantage. She had extended her claws just enough to prick her brother's shoulder, simply to show him who was still boss. She was perfectly aware from her mom and Aunt Noreen's memories, that she was the older of the two twins by five or ten seconds. That gave her seniority in the pride over him. She kept reminding her physically larger brother of that at every opportunity.

With a roar of indignation, Kobalt was after her in two seconds, her tail deliberately twitching impudently fifty feet ahead of him. She had extended her rear claws, which unless she was turning or twisting to follow prey were not required for grip, and they tore tufts of turf up to fly back in her brother's face. She had to grant that Kobalt had the edge on endurance and power, but speed and agility was her edge, and she was planning to hold her lead all the way to the take down.

Her ears picked up the sounds of hooves starting to pound up ahead, where the outraged roar of her brother had apparently alerted the herd animals that something unpleasant was tearing through bushy grassland towards them. She knew Kobalt had endurance, so if his roar made the chase last longer, she might have outwitted herself as he gradually overtook her lead. He would naturally try to put a shoulder into her as he passed, to knock her off stride. It's exactly what she intended to try to do to him if he passed her close enough to gloat.

She picked up a new scent that seemed to come in from her left, and now surrounded her as she ran through the strong body odors from multiple animals. If her brother were not so close on her rear, she would slow to check this out, but winning was more important to her. It now had an odd sharp scent added to it, which she thought might be from the breath of the creatures, rather than the general body odor all animals had. That meant they were close for that scent not to have spread thinner in the air. The sharp smell suddenly matched a memory she had of hunting on Jura, when she sniffed the fetid breath of a pack of small raptors, the smell of their carnivore's breath.

Suddenly, from both sides, there were multiple loud growls and savage sounding snarls, noisily pushing through the bushes on either side, moving parallel to her but still unseen. There was a powerful howl, and she could hear them turn towards her. A growl from Kobalt proved he was aware of the ambush as well.

Something gray and hairy leaped at her from the left.

****

The self-erecting tents were activated, just as soon as a tough plastic barrier was placed below them as protection against whatever dug the burrows. The science teams moved into them as soon as they snapped to rigidity, to set up the automated test labs for samples already being collected. The Koban born TGs all thought the "strange" green plants and grasses were most likely to be dangerous or allergenic. The colors were relatively rare on Koban, and sometimes marked plants that were unhealthy for grazing animals there to eat.

A five hundred-foot radius sensor perimeter was set up, which would detect incoming animals from rat-sized and up, out to an additional two hundred feet, and provide a warning of size, direction, and speed for the TGs that were on watch. The first few nights would be spent in the ship, until the local area was deemed safe enough for overnight camping. The TGs chaffed at this restriction, and believed it should only apply to the SGs with them (such as the captain), who did not have the speed and strength to fend off a possible animal attack. Nevertheless, the captain had her way.

That caution proved justified when Kobalt and Kit returned, only forty-five minutes after they ran off for adventure. Kobalt was carrying a large but dead wolf analogue in his massive jaws. Prompt frilling revealed that a pack of twelve of the two hundred fifty pound, thickly furred animals had attacked the rippers from both sides. The cats were racing along, after the tail end of a herd of several hundred long legged, five-foot high, brown and white spotted antelope-like animals, having long white horns. The wolf pack animals were apparently also stalking the same herd, and the rippers speed had put them in their midst before the unknown scent became meaningful to them.

Frill contacts showed that both cats were deeply embarrassed by their mistake in ignoring the new scent. It was just another new one among hundreds, all from unknown animals to them. The pack animals, although individually much smaller than either cat, outnumbered and out massed them collectively, and hadn't hesitated to go after the unknown new competition.

This particular pack would do more than hesitate the next time they saw or smelled a ripper. Five of the members were bloodied and injured before breaking and running, without ever laying a fang or claw on either cat, despite the surprise rush from two sides. Big dogs against bigger and extremely fast and strong heavy gravity cats? It was "put their tails between their legs and run for their lives" time. The cats could have killed half of them had they chosen to be so wasteful.

The largest one, the alpha male, refused to yield or back down, and tried to leap on Kit's back as she mauled one of its pack mates. Kobalt leaped twenty feet to intercept him in midair, his jaws closing on the throat, crushing the windpipe and puncturing an artery. The leader was fatally injured, and it screamed a terrified death cry. The remainder of the pack turned and fled.

Mindful of the warning not to eat any prey from here, Kobalt could taste its blood in his jaws. A ripper social injunction against wasting a kill also came into play. He had dropped the dying pack leader and spat as much blood out as he could. Next, he and Kit frilled the animal as it expired, "tasting" only that which they had been permitted to have. They had expected to bring one of the dead herd animals back for testing, and possible consumption, but instead they had the wolf. They had never even seen what they chased, but the dying wolf had images of what they had missed. They would know them the next time.

While the lab techs took samples of blood and tissue, the humans looked over the big animal, noting its long legs, suited for running down prey over long distances. It had an elongated mouth full of teeth, the viciously long top and bottom front fangs interlocking.

Its eyes were closed, but pulling an eyelid back, a large amber eye with black pupil was revealed. The ears were wide at the base, as well as long and pointed at the tips, rather like giant wolfbat ears. It didn't look like anything you ever wanted to meet in the dark, particularly a dozen of them in a cooperative pack.

When the TGs frilled with the cats farther, they learned that this particular wolf-like predator seemed smarter than a wolfbat, and very cunning. In the grass and scrub brush territory around here, there were smaller fleet creatures that moved similar to a cat, hunting alone or in pairs, and the pack had taken some of them down before. The two larger examples today simply meant more meat to the leader when he howled to signal the pack to turn and attack the interlopers. Some mistakes you just didn't get over.

One of the technicians poked a head out of the tent. "The new automated analyzers are fast. We used both, and they each say there are no dangerous toxins or proteins in the...," he fumbled and failed to find a word, "for whatever that thing will be called. It should be safe to eat, but we'd like the head intact, and the skeleton for study. Can someone tell the cats?" He ducked back inside.

When Kobalt and Kit were frilled the information, they took the prize off to some bushes to eat, aware of how the tearing and rending sounds, and deep throated growls of contentment sometimes disturbed squeamish humans. Too bad, being able to frill revolted and horrified onlookers could have enhanced the ambience of their "dining" experience.

Maggi, who had closely inspected the dead animal, drew on one of her favorite sources for reference. "Bradley, you watched that old movie with me and Cory last month. Look at the picture we took of that big furry monster and tell me if it reminds you of anything we can use for a name."

He looked over at the computer screen image and his eyes lit up. "Oh, sure. It looks just like the guy after he turned into a werewolf."

She asked loudly, "Who votes for werewolf, or possibly lycanthrope?"

Two people asked what a lycanthrope was, so the confusion factor settled it. "People, I think we have an authenticated werewolf here. Who supports that as their name?"

The horror movie connection cinched it for the enthusiastic youngsters.

Maggi grinned in satisfaction, as the more scientifically minded members of the group grimaced at yet another ad hoc name being applied to a new species.

Marlyn, enjoying Maggi's manipulations, put everyone back on track. "Drive the three trucks down, and load them with gear for the local explorations. Cameras, sample kits, and take a fifty-caliber rifle on each of them, with a TG on watch in the back. Stay within a five-mile radius of the Beagle for now, no more than six people per truck. Draw lots to see who goes first, and take turns every two hours. The rest of you continue to set up camp, and check out the river a quarter mile on the other side of that small grove of trees. This place is a bit tamer than Koban, but watch for things that bite in the water, or might be up in the trees.

"I'll fly the shuttle, for Maggi, Francis, Bradley, Sarah, and one of our lab techs, and land close to the tree village. Bradley, please place the trading case we prepared inside the shuttle." They had selected possible trade goods, ranging from primitive and low technology items such as fire starters, jewelry, fabrics, hand tools, up to com sets and video players, for showing the Prada about humans. There was no way to know what level of technology the Krall slaves had retained after the Krall left them here, possibly a long time ago.

One of the lab techs eagerly volunteered to go with them. Hakeem Taleb was the man who had announced the wolf like animal was safe to eat. He took one of the portable organic analyzers purchased on Poldark. It was possible that local food or drink might be offered if the meeting went well.

Sarah Bradley had put off her research at Hub City to participate. She wasn't a qualified linguist, but in working with the Raspani, she had acquired a sizable vocabulary of their words, and a considerable command of low Krall speech, because the Raspani understood many phrases in that language.

All of those going on the trip to the village had previously studied low Krall, particularly in the last month, as part of preparedness for meeting the Prada. It was assumed that any slave race would know some of the Krall low frequency language. The Krall themselves had proven to have a facility for learning languages, and picked up vocabulary quickly. However, they used only their own language with the Raspani, so that might be the best method of early communication with any species they had enslaved.

The quickest source of translation would be from Kap, because the AI had copied Jake's complete store of information on Krall speech. He could start building a new vocabulary of the Prada language as soon as he saw and heard them speak. The new transducers they had received would function out to at least seventy miles, so Kap would be able to hear what they heard, and feed them information at the village by transducer. They would only be thirty miles away.

Weapons had been a serious issue, hotly debated for hours before leaving Koban. The final decision was that the person who would first greet the Prada would carry only a concealed small Jazzer in a shoulder holster, and a knife. It was noted that every Prada appeared to carry a short knife on their belts, so seeing one on a human would seem reasonable. Besides, this was an untamed world, and going completely unarmed would be reckless. The other five members of the contact team would stay far back, inside or next to the shuttle, with pistols on their hips, and a fifty-caliber, bolt-action sniper rifle in the hands of Bradley, a dead shot at long range, with or without using the telescopic sight.

The decision of who would make the actual approach had vacillated. Francis had discovered the tree village, Marlyn was in charge of the expedition, and Sarah had a wider range of alien language skills. However, it was finally decided that the least threatening looking member of the group, and senior in experience, was a better choice.

Maggi was the only one on the expedition that was the same approximate height and weight as an adult Prada, and had proven negotiating skills. She would make the first contact. It was naturally assumed there would be no need to knock a stubborn Prada in the head or groin, another skill set she was known to have.

They ate a hurried early lunch, and climbed into the shuttle, to the envious looks of many of the complement, who wished they could be an eyewitness to the historic event. However, the team would be recording live from several viewpoints, and Maggi had a variation of a spy bot camera and audio pickup on a fastener of her loose jacket. They were all keeping their Krall style tattoos concealed for now, until they could explain them.

Marlyn, eager but nervous, said, “Let’s go meet the neighbors.”

Chapter 8: Dino Dangers

Mel Rigson was the titular leader of the small Jura expedition, but claiming leadership over two "wild hare" young TG2s, was a stretch. Cory and Danner, Dillon and Thad's youngest boys were as adventurous and mischievous as their older brothers were, although they promised to display caution on Jura, a dangerous and largely unexplored continent.

When Rigson actually called them wild hares, the generational gap proved five hundred years wider than Rigson or the boys knew. When they asked Mel what the phrase meant, he repeated what he'd heard Maggi explain when she had used the same term for them.

"It's supposed to be a small animal that jumps and runs around totally out of control. Your Aunt Maggi said the description was based on an old fictional character called Bugs Bunny. From a long time ago."

Cory said, "You sure she didn't mean wild like a hair growing crooked in your nose?"

"My nose?"

"Not just yours Uncle Mel, anybody's."

"How would a nose hair jump around?" he asked.

Danner had a counter question. "How does what *you* said jump around? What *is* a hare anyway?" He had a trace of a smile.

"A jumping hare, I guess you mean."

"You just said a hair can't jump," Cory protested, with a sly grin.

Realizing they were pulling his leg again, Rigson told them, "Listen, you aggravating fleas on a moosetodon's butt, you know what that expression means concerning you two, even if we never saw or heard of a hare. The animal came from Earth, a place I never lived, and saw only once. I assume an untamed hare was likely half as much trouble as either one of you."

Both boys had undergone all of the remaining Koban gene mods, on nearly the same day the second one of them reached age sixteen. Aunt Aldry, Uncle Rafe, and Aunt Maggi had already certified each one of the mods as safe and functional gene changes. They strongly approved and recommended the new nanite process itself.

On the surface, it sounded like many youngsters in Prime City had common blood relatives. It would seem odd for folks to have so many relatives that just happened to find themselves randomly stranded on an alien planet together. Here, most adults that were involved in a kid's life became "Uncles" and "Aunts," replacing the lost biological family ties.

The laws in Prime City gave youngsters the right to decide for themselves about gene changes after their sixteenth birthday, and these two boys were only days apart in age. Danner's mom, Marlyn, was now back at least part of the time, between trips to explore the neighboring planet, and had belatedly approved the fait accompli Danner had presented to her.

Cory would have to "face the music" with his own mother when she returned, if she objected to his not waiting. He would still have done it anyway, but she could at least have had her say first. Neither boy anticipated opposition or grief from their dads.

Besides, having the gene mods were the only way they could be included on the trip to explore parts of Jura. None of the adults on the expedition would let them go otherwise. So now, they were in a temporary camp on the coast of Jura, prepared to follow a small river upstream into the interior, towards a gray volcanic dotted mountain range.

Multiple long shuttle trips had brought four transports over in slings; two of them were halftracks, the other two, sturdy and standard Krall four-wheel models, plus stacks of equipment and supplies to pack into their rear beds. There were Smart Fabric tarps to protect things from weather, Koban birds, and small scavengers. With only eight people making the trip, the truck cabs, which were roomy enough for three Krall per bench seat, were spacious enough for one ripper to join them per cab. They found four of them eager to go.

The expedition members would ride in one vehicle for a day, and then would swap trucks to share the driving and other duties, discussing observations and their experiences. This was more a journey of discovery than of science.

Rigson and Cory would ride together the first day, sharing the truck with Kayla, the ripper that grew up with Danner's brother, Bradley. With Bradley serving on the Beagle, she had wanted an adventure of her own.

Cal Branson and Danner would ride with Kally, Danner's lifetime ripper companion.

Chack Nauguza and Ricco Balduchi had Kopper with them, the only male ripper on the journey, and Jimbo Skaleski was riding with Neri Bar and Kandy. Neri was the sole (human) woman on the trip.

To round out the mixture, two unmated wolfbat males had agreed to come as aerial scouts, in exchange for the exotic dinosaur meat to sample, and any hunting they wanted to try. They had learned via Mind Taps that there were wolfbat squadrons on Jura, and if there were unattached and receptive females, they might stay behind when the expedition ended.

Swapping to a new Flock was common with wolfbat males on Cenozo continent, to maintain genetic diversity. It was assumed it would be the same on Jura, and there *had been* rare population exchanges in the past from Jura, usually a result of storm blown refugees.

They had broken camp this morning at daylight, after the early-to-bed turn in they gave themselves the night before. That was after they had finished unloading, sorting, and repacking the last of the supplies from the final shuttle delivery. That shuttle left them a few hours before sunset, and except for the two radios they had with them, they were now on their own in a land predominately filled with small to enormous dinosaur analogues.

Cody tossed the wolfbats a light meat snack for breakfast, Tapped them to give them basic instructions, and sent them aloft to check the surroundings and then to fly a few miles ahead on this side of the river. Rigson had already found prints with four blunt toes, from recent four-legged visitors to the riverbank, probably there for water.

The prints resembled pictures they brought with them of a Ceratopsian herd's tracks. Those had been recorded from a previous exploration on Jura, which was interrupted by the Krall visitation that gained them their first clanship. These particular animals appeared to be smaller versions of the frilled and three-horned versions seen before, but there were quite a few of them. The normally docile grass eaters were of little threat if you kept your distance on foot, and would normally run from a truck. Rigson's concern today was the possibility that some of the predators that often shadowed such herds could be nearby, looking for a meal of opportunity. The wolfbat's sharp eyes would find them, even if they didn't know what they all looked like. Predators were usually not hard to identify.

All eight men had fifty caliber rifles, and two were the precious semiautomatic versions, the rest were single shot bolt action with ten shot magazines. They also had a thirty caliber automatic rifle with a thirty round banana curve magazine. They each packed two of the Krall made pistols because they had so much of that ammunition, and there were extended magazines for that caseless ammunition. In boxes lashed under the seats were fragmentation and phosphorus grenades, carefully placed in covered and padded comfort.

Paleontologists had never completely proven the speed and high level of activity of many of Earth's dinosaur species from the fossils and footprints they left. There wasn't a debate on Koban. The organic superconducting nerves in forerunners of all vertebrate life on this world, once the trait had evolved on the heavy, metal-rich planet, remained a competitive survival necessity in their descendants.

Even most dino "cows" here could outrun Earth's fastest human runners that had ever graced a nice flat, sure grip surface of a manmade track. They could beat those track times over clumpy uneven ground, bulldozing through waist-high, thick bushes. The predators were even faster.

A TG2 could outrun some herbivores on Jura, or at home on Cenozo in a mile sprint, but not much farther than that. However, by pacing themselves, a well-conditioned Kobani could eventually run many herd animals into exhaustion over the long haul. For a predator, it was find cover or dodge, and shoot as you moved if they were close. You were not going to outrun any of them over short distances.

For SGs, advance warnings, knowing where they were, and being heavily armed was usually enough to stay safe. An unwarned TG2 could likely hear, and smell them before they saw them charging, and if they got close they still could plink out their eyes with well-aimed pistol shots and duck away. A heavy rifle meant they could put a slug through the small brainpan at a half mile while both they and the target were moving. Cory and Danner were the expedition's main line of close-in defense if the wolfbats and rippers were unable to give them advanced warning.

When the power from the fusion bottles was fed to the motors, the four trucks eased into motion. They were going to hold a steady ten miles per hour until the wolfbats reported to them. If the way ahead were clear of threats, they would increase speed as long as the ground stayed relatively even and rock free. They might even come onto a game trail that would be beaten down enough to let them make twenty to twenty-five miles per hour, in a semblance of comfort for the older men, without TG reaction speed and strength.

Cory, Danner, and the cats would think a bouncy ride at high speed would be great fun until they had to return to recover the supplies and damaged equipment that flew out.

****

Flight Leader, the senior and larger of the flyers was relishing the scents and strange sounds in this place. The trees were different, and the insects had a different sound to their buzz. He had seen several of the stinging, blood-drinking little fliers. Here, they were not quite as small as the one's at home. The food giver had not asked to be told of these smaller predators, so there would be no large reward for turning back to show him what he saw. He and his squad mate would seek some of the mind images of possible dangerous predators they had been shown. The most dangerous kind was tall and walked on two legs, with tiny arms and large mouths with long teeth.

There were many large slow grass and leaf eaters ahead, and they would not deserve a food reward either. They *could* be dangerous it seemed to Flight Leader, because they had two long curvy horns pointing forward from over their eyes. If the grass eaters ran into a food giver, those horns could kill them. Two of the food givers, as they usually thought of the two- legged helpers of the Flocks, were of the kind that were not only faster and stronger than they looked, but could see, smell, and hear better than others of their kind.

The other six givers would offer food, but they did not have the way to "talk" with pictures, nor the speed of moving. The flyers would accept food from them, and try to pay for it with low calls their broken ears could hear if a flyer saw a threat that would earn a larger food reward.

Flight Leader sent out a general call to see if there would be a reply from a Flock member from this place. The lack of forested nesting sites or hillside caves, made finding squadrons of flyers hunting near this location unlikely. There had been small animals seen that might be good to hunt, with only two flyers to attack them, but until their ability to fight back was known, it was best to eat what they were given in payment.

A recognition and warning call from his squad mate grabbed Flight Leader's attention. Some sort of predator had been sighted, but the classification was unsure. As he joined the other half of his tiny Flock, he saw immediately the cause of confusion.

The smoothly looping creature with four legs was chasing a group of ten or fifteen reptilian looking animals. The prey ran on two legs, and they were only about twice the size of a wolfbat. Except for their small size, they resembled the predators the food givers sought. However, they did not act like predators, and clustered like a herd. They ran from the larger animal in pursuit.

There was a similarity to the rippers in the obvious predator, even though it was colored differently, and was half the size of a ripper. Envious of his companion's early success, he squeaked the call to send him back to report this activity. He would receive a food reward, sized by the food giver based on the value of the sighting. They were not looking for this particular predator, so the value was yet unknown.

As his companion turned back, Flight Leader realized that he now was also a Squad Leader of one, himself. He persisted in thinking of the two of them as a Flock, and of himself as a Flight Leader (not Flock Leader because he had not been elected), with only one squadron, consisting of one member.

The thought passed through his mind that his companion probably considered himself as a Squad Leader of one. It would have been easier on their sense of identity if more of their Flock had been free to make the journey. However, that would have indicated an unhealthy condition in a Flock with so many unmated pairs free to leave. Had there been unmated females available, it's not likely he would be here.

Suddenly, before the ambush was sprung below, Flight Leader saw the second predator waiting for the prey group to draw closer. This was a strategy similar to that rippers used, to hunt at home. However, they would have more members of their pride to chase, and more to wait in ambush. The first several prey animals went by the waiting killer without a muscle moved. Then, one was marginally closer, and it leaped out of the tall clump of grasses where it had hidden, and made a clawed swipe at the closest leg of the smaller prey as it tried to turn aside. The claws raked the thick part of the muscled leg, tearing flesh, and the two-legged runner almost made a fatal stumble. It was forced to turn sharply away and bring the wounded limb around to make a wobbly leap at right angles, away from this new threat.

Flight Leader, from his high vantage point saw it was already too late for an escape. The pursuing predator had instantly shifted direction to its own left, as its hidden companion started to pounce from the right side. The original pursuer would now intercept the turning and slowed prey before it could turn away again. The trailing predator had put on a burst of speed, proving before that it was merely keeping the prey group moving in the direction it wanted. There was a squall of terror, as the larger of the two predators, the one with a red ruff on its neck and back, brought the prey animal down. It was quickly joined by the slightly smaller version that had sprung the trap. Those two would eat well today.

Flight Leader was envious again, and his "snack" was not enough to power him for an entire morning. Soon his stomach would "ask" him to turn back. The food giver would see in his mind what he had seen, and there would always be some food offered, but not perhaps as much as was craved.

There was one valuable lesson to take from this hunt. The two-legged prey animals were small enough, and unstable enough on their feet, that two wolfbats could surprise and knock one to the ground. The open mouth of the victim as it struggled had revealed there were no teeth, and the front was shaped like the hard mouth of some water birds at home, which ate only wet vegetation in water. They couldn't bite very well. The back trail suggested they had been chased from the nearby river. He wondered why they had not entered the water to escape. His newness here prevented him from knowing how much more dangerous the river could be for careless animals.

He turned back, to see if his visions would earn him more food for a renewed and longer scouting flight. The food givers were usually fair.

****

"I see them, Kayla." Cory was responding to a nudge and brief frill, pointing out the returning wolfbats. The nicknames they were given by the humans were the only useable names they had. The wolfbats knew which of them was being addressed when they heard the meaningless human sounds, but their self-identification was a sound pattern a human could not reproduce or understand.

Big Blue was the older and larger of the two, and had assumed the leadership role. He considered himself the leader of what mentally, to him anyway, was a small Flock. Because there had been no loud voice calls in a nest "vote" to elevate him over any contender, he would not think of himself as Flock Leader. He thought of a lesser, but still lofty title of Flight Leader, normally reserved for a wolfbat that guided the actions of several squadrons in a large Flock. Cory figured that if you were putting on airs and assigning yourself a grand title, why display false modesty at all. Consider yourself king. No one cared here.

Streaker, the name they had given the smaller of the two, accepted Big Blue as the leader, but considered him just a squadron leader. To his mind, he himself was the sole squad member. Since there was no formal mode of address that differed between the tiles of Squadron Leader, Flock Leader, or Flight Leader, injured or offended pride on the part of Big Blue wasn't going to be a factor. Deference to the levels of authority was how wolfbats ranked one another, and with only two rankings here, there was no conflict or reason to challenge.

Streaker had apparently spotted something first, because Big Blue joined him, and then sent him back to report, and receive a reward. Big Blue circled in one place for a time, before he turned back as well. Neither rushed, as they would if they had seen a major threat which would earn them a bonus treat of what they considered the best meat, a piece of heart, kidney, liver, or even tongue. Cory and Danner were perfectly happy to reserve those organs from a hunting kill for the cats and wolfbats to enjoy, leaving none for some adult to insist they "just try it."

Streaker landed on the roll bar the humans had welded to the back of the truck cabs. Cory slid back the roof panel and stood up to Tap the scout for his report, which he repeated to the driver.

"Uncle Mel, they spotted a pair of lions hunting a small herd of animals, and they made a kill about two miles ahead. No large dino predators around. He first thought the prey animals were mini versions of a K-Rex. They seem to be a sort of two-legged duckbill, about four feet tall, short front legs or arms, and perhaps six to eight feet long with a thick tail for balance. The image reminds me of hadrosaurs, except these are smaller than the fossils from Earth were. Except for the specialized duckbill like mouth, they look similar to early ornithopod grazers."

Rigson raised an eyebrow. "How do you know anything about hadrosaurs, or ornithopods?"

Cory frowned. "Jake has at least a billion books in his library you know. Some are about extinct animals from Earth and some are about those from colony worlds. I read several books before we left to come here."

Rigson smiled. "You remember them all, and their names? Dinos, I mean?"

"I read about many of them on screen, and looked at some animations and digital recreations on Tri-Vid. Why would I forget them?" He had jumped directly from SG status with a parallel and unused ripper based nervous system, to climbing out of a med lab as a fledgling TG2, with wolfbat-inspired hearing, and the memory organization those genes promoted.

He *had* noticed how much better his memory seemed now, since there was little effort in absorbing new knowledge, and none at all to recall what he'd absorbed. Danner was the same way. It did take some correlation to put academic details in context when the real world's facts came at you, but that too happened faster. He had pulled the hadrosaur description from memory and compared it to the image Streaker sent to him, and it was a close match.

He reached over the cab to the cooler kept strapped on the top of the pile of gear. He covered the lock with one hand, and entered the simple code for the latch. That precaution was needed because the little devils had figured out how to unlock the coolers at home. A fat, weighted-down wolfbat riding on your truck half asleep made a poor scout. They would eat their fill, and stuff their throat pouches.

Extracting a piece of rhino liver, he flipped it expertly right at Streakers snout. It vanished with an audible click of fangs. He knew liver was this scouts favorite treat. It made Cory shudder to recall the taste. Before he could sit down, he heard the high-pitched ultrasonic calls from the incoming Big Blue. He waited for the second scout to alight, did a Tap, pulled out another piece of meat, not Blue's favorite because he didn't add anything new to the report, and made the toss. Then he Tapped them both and asked (you didn't make a demand of the temperamental animals) that they go back out and look another five miles ahead. He didn't think "five miles" but rather the time it would take them to fly that far.

They fluttered off, and he told Mel and Kayla a bit more about the mated lions and their kill, and considered the matter done.

Kayla had other ideas. She didn't come here simply to ride. She wanted to invite Kopper to go with her to meet the lions and *inform* them of the expedition's passing, and warn them to leave humans alone. They would also inquire about knowledge of the area that the lion's would surely have, and of any big predators that called this their territory. Kopper was not a blood relative, and Kayla might want to get to know him better. A private hunt and a shared meal could accomplish that. She'd even let him make the kill, so he felt more "the provider." Feminine wiles crossed species lines.

She frilled both men before she leaped out and dropped back to the third truck to invite Kopper to go with her. The two of them ran ahead, easily out pacing the ten miles per hour pace of the trucks.

"Hey Mel," it was Ricco. "Where is Kayla taking Kopper?"

"To meet and frill with a pair of lions the scouts reported seeing, and get some information. I also think she wants to hunt."

"I think so too, but I believe she took her real prey with her," he laughed, thinking of the unsuspecting male ripper.

They continued on to midday, finding a well-trodden path that paralleled the river a half mile farther away from the riverbank. They picked up the pace to twenty-five miles per hour, on the wide beaten down earthen trail, formed by the thousands of large animals that passed the same way, looking for a wide shallow place to ford the river safely. The trail would turn to red mud if they got the rain that threatened to come up the river from behind them, off the ocean. That would push them back to driving on the grass, with the lumps and bumps.

They stopped to make a meal, and to watch the herd of frilled ceratopsians they had finally overtaken, run away ahead of them. The scouts had returned and reported no sign of dangerous predators, other than the two rippers which they'd seen hunting and stalking some burrowing animals. They mentally emphasized that report, as if it were of greater value, to see if they could get a larger serving. Rippers were predators, after all.

Danner, making certain the two scouts knew the ripper report was worthless, nevertheless, gave them each a generous portion of heated, cubed muscle meat. It wasn't a treat like the preferred organ meat, but the warmed meat would replace the energy they had expended. They had flown from thermal to thermal, circling over the future path of the not-life "animals" that carried the food givers.

The scouts didn't exactly grasp that a negative report of any dangers was also of value, which was why they had pointlessly flashed pictures of the two rippers in their last report.

After eating, the trucks moved on, slowing some to stay behind the herd, which they had spooked earlier. Pushing into their midst could panic some into ramming the trucks. Cory, driving now, was tired of swerving to miss the inevitable piles of poorly digested vegetation, in the form of smelly excrement.

Once, there was a *really unpleasant* smelling pile of scat, which Cory's nose had detected long before it was in sight. Rigson, listening to Cory's constant complaint about the smell of dung, said he didn't notice it so much. Not until the nearly black, oily looking mess appeared. That one he and the others could smell, even without a sense of smell derived from the rippers. The two cats that had stayed with them most of the day, Kally and Kandy, revolted Cory to near nausea, and to a less extent Danner, when they not only smelled the glop up close, they touched a tip of their tongues on the disgusting stuff, then rubbed frills.

Afterwards, Kally went to Danner and frilled him.

"Oh," he said, in belated recognition of what his nose had been telling him, and that Kally had confirmed. "This is poop from digested meat, and it was originally from one of the ceratopsians. Kally says the size of the pile means it was a large predator, but it's more than a day old. She and Kandy don't know what kind of predator ate the animal, but she will remember the scent of whatever did."

Then he added with an abashed grin. "I was just accused of having a stupid nose, because I didn't detect what was in the crap."

Ricco made a helpful suggestion. "Show us you have something smarter than a nose. Taste it, like they did."

Cory suddenly added a *really* unpleasant smelling smaller pile to the trail, with several wet sounds that resembled calling out the name "Ralph."

The older men found this hilarious, and when both cats sniffed that, Danner added his own name calling contribution to the mess on the trail. The older generation was in a merry and superior state of mind the rest of the day. TG2s apparently didn't have stronger *stomachs* than SGs.

Rigson resumed driving, while Cory curled up on the seat in misery and embarrassment for an hour. The mushy sounds of driving "accidents" and "kind" proposals and suggestions from Uncle Mel didn't help all that much.

"Please. Stop driving over the piles, Uncle Mel."

"No! I don't want anything to eat."

"How will this make me a man?"

The first sign that the day was about to change was when the wolfbats returned and refused food because they didn't want to fly again. They fluttered onto the floor of the third truck's cab with Ricco and Chack, because with Kopper away hunting, they had more room.

A swift storm front, with thunder, lightning, and heavy rain finally overtook them. That ended the teasing fun for Mel, and torment for Cory. It was a vicious storm.

Strong wind gusts in the dense air of Koban rocked the trucks. Danner proposed they drive under a copse of low to midsized trees they were passing, less than a quarter mile away. Cal Branson was just starting to explain why that was a bad idea, out here where most of the ground was so open, when the answer forced itself indelibly into Danner's mind.

There was a tremendous blast of thunder, simultaneously accompanied by the brilliant blue-white flash of lightning, and the tallest tree in said copse became the shortest, with shattered wood flying in all directions. They did pull off the animal trail that was turning to red mud, and drove onto soil bound tightly with grass roots, well away from any trees, and stopped. Cal assured Danner that the metal alloy of the truck would carry a lightning strike safely around them if the truck were hit. Fortunately, that prediction wasn't tested, and in forty minutes, the rain had slacked as the fast moving front moved past.

The cooler air was welcomed after the hot day, but the older men, experienced at camping on Koban and other worlds, warned that when the sun returned, their heat mod adaptations would be tested. The humidity would make it feel worse.

Kayla and Kopper finally returned, their sleek teal fur wet, but natural oils had repelled most of the rain. Climbing into the truck cab next to Cory, he thought the cat smelled less like a ripper and more like an old damp and dirty sock. She picked the careless image up when her frill brushed him going past.

She turned her massive head towards him, intense blue eyes looking into his, sniffed his breath, and sent a rebuttal thought. “I don’t smell like rhinolo vomit.”

The much-maligned rhinolo was what every rotten smell, bad taste, or stupid act was used for comparison.

A camping expedition on an untamed continent, with few comforts was proving less romantic to the two boys by now, in only a day. So far, the only exotic dinosaurs had all been seen from their butts, and those butts had gifted them all day long. When Rigson suggested they camp early for the day, and let the mud dry overnight, they were ready. Now that the storm had passed, he led the trucks over to the same trees they avoided earlier. There was now a supply of splintered wood for a campfire, even if it was a bit green. It proved to have a sap that helped it burn well, and caused a nice crackling sound, with a spicy scent.

They had brought four auto tents, made of a type of Smart Fabric for a cover, and a Living Plastic framework that needed only electrical power from its rechargeable batteries to flow and stiffen the struts, to make a comfortable two-man air conditioned tent, with a small cook stove. Roughing it indeed.

They had circled the trucks, with relatively little room between bumpers. They took advantage of tree trunks between trucks, so nothing the size of a wandering ceratopsian could wander into the tents in the middle of the night. Not that the rippers or wolfbats, or the two TG2’s wouldn’t easily sense them approaching. The wolfbats gathered leaves and branches and made nests twenty feet off the ground, and gratefully accepted warmed raw kidney for a dinner.

Rather than the small cook stoves, they used the fully enclosed microwave systems, one per truck, to prepare their rhinolo and antelope meats and vegetables, searing the outsides of the steaks with the built in broiler coils. The filtered and enclosed cooking system retained the odor of the sizzling meat, lessening the attraction for downwind predators.

Warmed raw organ meat fed Kally and Kandy, since they had not had an opportunity to hunt yet. Kayla and Kopper frilled everyone in the camp concerning their side trip and hunt today. They had chased down several small mammals that normally lived underground.

The rippers, using their grass matching teal fur had belly crept close enough that when they sprang up after the foraging animals, they couldn’t retreat to their main burrow entrance, and the rippers had already located two alternate “back door” openings. They cut them off from those as well. Of the seven animals they scattered in a mad scramble, they caught three. The terror *flavor* wasn’t as keen as they had hoped as they frilled the low intelligence prey when they died.

That disappointment was matched by the poor taste of their stringy meat, which had a sharp unpleasant tang. The frilling showed the dying animals had been digging for grubs, and picking a type of grass eating caterpillar from grass blades.

The smell of their flesh was similar to the smell in the mouths and stomachs of the insect eaters. Rippers didn't waste a kill, so they ate what they caught, poor taste or not.

Based on today's hunt, these particular Jura animals were firmly off the future menu. After receiving the mental images from the rippers, Mel concluded they behaved much like prairie dogs, a description his pocket computer furnished him when he described how they lived. Similar, if the Earth namesake had grown to reach thirty pounds, had six legs, hairless black belies and spotted teal fur.

The visit to the pair of lions had been more productive. The lions, no dummies, were quick to back away from their still fresh hadrosaur kill when the two gigantic cats suddenly strolled up on them. The rippers politely walked slowly around the half-eaten prey towards the nervous pair, and Kayla turned her head to the side to offer the lioness her frill. This was a gesture clearly inviting communication, and it placed the one offering at risk, with their throat so exposed.

Neither of the lions had ever encountered, or had even seen frill images of rippers before. However, the feline body type, their scent, and the frill ruff were unmistakable evidence of similarity. Besides, these two midsized feline killers, built for the chase, instinctively recognized that the two massive and muscled giants didn't *need* to be polite if they didn't wish to be.

Seladaq glanced at her mate, Hasbuk, for moral support, and then tentatively moved forward to touch frills with the huge teal cat. Her tan, lanky body looked even more vulnerable next to Kayla's bulging muscles. That was why Kopper had stopped well back and sat on his haunches. His even greater bulk, at just over eight hundred Earth pounds was too intimidating. The three hundred pound female already looked small next to Kayla's six hundred fifty pounds. Even the male lion weighed only about four hundred.

Kayla slipped naturally into the nonverbal speech she used with her wild pride relatives at home. Human language and their different styles of images and thinking would not help establish a rapport here, if one were even possible. Her mother Kit, and her uncle, Kobalt, had not received a welcoming from any of several lion pairs they had contacted previously. That was in an area almost a thousand miles away from this region.

As was typical in a frill contact, images were exchanged rapidly. The first ones from Kayla were of identification of herself and Kopper, and assurances that the rippers were only visitors, passing through this area, and they did not intend to stay. Although she was firm in stating that they would hunt as they passed by, and there were two more rippers in their pride. The concept of a large pride took more explanation, and Kayla projected that previous meetings with others like Seladaq revealed lions formed only small family pairings.

Seladaq, feeling relief that these were not to be competitors for their territory or for their prey, was nevertheless not pleased that four of these huge predators would possibly disrupt their own hunting. She wanted to know why they were passing this way and how long they would be here. Was it a migration, like the large herd animals, which passed this way between the rains and dry times? That didn't seem right as she asked this. It wasn't possible these large hunters had passed here before, undetected.

The next images from Kayla clearly seemed to have family emotions attached, except Seladaq was shown images of strange pale animals that stood on two legs, and used incomprehensible not-life things that moved on the ground and lifted in the air like giant fliers. The rippers went inside these not-life things also, and were not eaten, or even afraid. She was told the group would all be far from here, towards the mountains, in another two or three days. If the lions would give them information about the dangers here, about recent giant predators that follow the herds, there would be a kill made of a large animal, and left for them.

Seladaq couldn't repress a sense of scandal at the image of an entire one-ton corpse of a two horned grass eater. She and Hasbuk could not consume so much meat before it rotted, and they had no cubs at home to feed. It was wasteful!

Kayla noted with satisfaction the offer of a food payment for information wasn't rejected, instead it was the thought of the waste, a concept a ripper entirely supported. The offer was amended to reflect a smaller prey, such as the one the pair had killed today.

Instantly, the lioness projected embarrassment, at having forgotten they already had meat for the remainder of the week. She explained she needed to frill with her mate, who had started to pace nervously at the lengthy exchange.

Kayla used the opportunity to frill-in Kopper on the proceedings so far, and then the two females resumed their negotiation. Because neither lions, nor rippers, were mentally or emotionally capable of lying during frill contacts, beyond withholding the truth or a thought, the offer of food for information was accepted as sincere by the lion pair.

Hasbuk wanted them to transit through their territory quickly, and approved of giving the visitors information that would help them go faster. They would leave their hunting range even sooner if they crossed the river a short distance ahead, at a place where the herds crossed.

Seladaq saw no advantage to tell them of the occasional fresh meat of herd animals they could *cautiously* be scavenged from the safety of sandbars at the edge of the river. No need to give them a source of food they did not earn by hunting. If they didn't go look for that food, they didn't need to fear what lived in the deeper waters.

Kayla learned about a pack of the two-legged, blue-feathered predators which were following the heard of "two-horns." A ceratopsian was too large for just a pair of lions to take down, aside from the waste of meat, so the four giant predators were no competition for the lion's normal food source, merely an easily avoided threat to themselves. The lions could outrun them, and their bodies represented too little energy return for their meat, for the effort of pursuit. That was a calculation both cat species could make instinctively, as could any successful predator that had eaten recently. If hungry, almost no prey was ignored.

To avoid the large predators, they were told they could cross the river where the herds crossed. The largest predators generally did not follow them there.

Kayla knew the images from Seladaq were of what the human pride called a K-Rex, one of the more dangerous threats the wolfbats were asked to seek, and had so far not reported. She would take pleasure in reporting not only how many there were, but how to avoid this group.

Seladaq told her that the K-Rex never pursued any herd animal that reached the safety of a wide rock ledge that went across the widest part of the river, where shallow water slowly drifted over when the rainy season ended. It was a place to ford to the other side of the river, which herds had used for thousands of years of migrations.

It was perhaps the risk of slipping on slimy rock and an inability to swim that held the K-Rex on the banks. An apex predator was surely not otherwise afraid of something a ceratopsian was willing to brave. The lions didn't particularly like to get into water, a trait that rippers shared, and the lions feared the river water animals. They had no clear mental picture of those creatures, simply of large surges of water seen and remembered, via frill images passed on from other lions that had narrowly escaped becoming prey, while drinking at the edge of the steeper riverbanks.

Leaving the lions to their envied feast of fresh tasty meat, the two hungry cats made their opportunistic "prairie dog" kills, with the unsatisfactory outcome for their palates, and then they walked through the afternoon thunderstorm and a "cheerful" soaking downpour.

When they delivered the information about the K-Rex hunting pack of four, probably a family grouping, and learning of the river ford location, Mel wanted to check it out the next day. The river led to the mountains from either side, of course, and they would be separating from a known K-Rex pack. He preferred avoiding them to killing them.

After an uneventful night, other than the occasional distant roars and cries of an equally remote victim, they woke rested at daybreak. An hour at which the two teenagers were *certain* nature did not intend man to be awake. It was the threat of poured cold water that drew them out of their sleeping bags. That, and exuberant frilling from two big playful cats who eagerly wanted to greet the new day in a strange land.

A quick meal of precooked and packaged food, military rations brought back with the Beagle in storage pods, the tents were emptied, and allowed to automatically collapse and fold. A brief *interlude* behind nearby trees provided for morning relief of the male physiology, and Neri found a clump of dense bushes to hide her more lady-like ablutions. They were all ready to roll in just under an hour.

Ricco took over driving the lead truck today, with Neri Bar and Kally riding with him. They were staying closer to the river today, to make certain they didn't miss the place to ford the quarter mile wide stream.

This wasn't one of the great rivers, which satellite pictures had found on Jura, but mineralogical and spectrographic data suggested the volcanic mountains near the river's origin were rich in heavy metals. Aside from exploration, discovery, and adventure, the material-poor human colony of Koban needed precious metals to pay for what they needed from Human Space. They had found mineral wealth in the foothills of mountains on Cenozo, but they hoped to find other sources, some that were possibly easier to obtain in greater quantity. They had new small scale automated mining equipment to place where they found suitable deposits. The richer the deposits, the greater the early returns.

Kandy and Kopper ranged ahead on foot today, since the going was slower away from the beaten down migration trail. The wolfbats were up, watching for both the K-Rex threats they had been shown, and for the lake, which the lions indicated was just upstream from the river fording point. It wasn't clear how a lake would form where the river grew so wide and shallow that animals as short legged as the two-horn ceratopsian could easily cross.

Multiple herds of larger animals had taken this route, even sauropods, which so far appeared only on photos. Where there were taller trees closer to the mountain foothills, satellite photos depicted something that looked a great deal like a blue and white giraffe, eating leaves on those trees. It was a chance to name things, which would be remembered and repeated for generations that partly motivated any explorer.

Cory, riding with Cal Branson and Kayla in the third truck today, commented. "The territory for the lions shouldn't be very large, with so much game around for just the two of them. The fording point should be closer, I'd think."

"I think you may be confusing the number of predators and type of prey with the size of territory they need. The lions don't migrate, they stay in one place all year, even when game is scarce in the dry cooler season. I'll bet this small stream nearly dries up then. They would need more hunting territory for the reduced number of prey. They measure their territory size by that seasonal need. For another thing, the K-Rex and lions don't usually hunt the same animals, and are not hunting competitors. The big dino herds leave here in the dry season, which is the southern winter, and the largest predators follow them. The adjacent pairs of lions probably determine what each mated pair calls "their territory." They don't permit those direct competitors of the same sort of game to intrude on their ranges.

"When this stream gets low, I suspect the lions move closer to the lake. It looked large to me in Kayla's mind image. The edge could be a boundary of their territory."

Cory cocked his head, listening to something Cal couldn't hear. The raised eyebrow from Cal and the look from Kayla showed they both had caught his shift in attention.

He explained. "Big Blue must have found the lake. He isn't sounding a recall or rally cry for Streaker, which he would if the K-Rex pack were spotted. It's less urgent, but the Doppler shift proves he's on his way back here."

Cal was amazed and a bit envious. "That's detectable with your new hearing? Not the ultrasonic part, which I know about, but also the frequency shift as he flies towards or away?"

"Sure, I can tell, provided they are making frequent signal calls, when they are circling, or simply floating on a thermal in one place."

"Man, I hope Avery and Rafe are right about those new nanites. I'd love to get the abilities you have."

"Right!" he answered pessimistically. "*You* weren't awakened ten times last night by each wolfbat doing echolocation for non-existent potential threats from the sky, from the trees, or from the ground. Danner and I heard them. Then the little farts went right back to sleep, and snored in ultrasonic harmony. That's why we were so sleepy this morning."

Cal nodded in mock sympathy. "I'm sure that's why Aldry and Rafe complained about how late you and Danner slept when they watched you while your parents were away? The leakage of wolfbat calls through the soundproof dome, from their closest nest, ten miles away. They say you somehow sleep through loud music from Tri-Vid music cubes you leave playing overnight."

Cory didn't answer the obviously rhetorical question and comments, intended only to bait him into responding to some verbal trap that adults always laid for teenagers. It seemed to be one of their main outlets for humor.

Big Blue landed on the roll bar on the second truck, where Jimbo and Danner were riding. They waited for a com set call on the group frequency from Danner, to learn what was reported. The two cubes of antelope tossed to the wolfbat was evidence it wasn't bonus worthy news, since it wasn't organ meat.

The call came. "The lake isn't far ahead. The river flows over some sort of barrier that forms the lake, and drops a couple of feet. On the lower side of the barrier is a smaller collection pool, with a water flow from that down a deeper center channel. It looks sort of like a low dam with a mile wide spillway, with water continuing downstream in a center channel after that. The bat saw a long gray rock ridge that runs for miles on each side of the river. Jimbo thinks it's a natural fault, which uplifted and trapped water on the upstream side."

Kandy and Kopper appeared ahead, coming from the river to the left in an easy unhurried walk, where the shallow riverbank sloped up to the trucks. This whole area, covered in lush cropped down teal grass from recent grazing, appeared to have been flooded often in the past, and benefited from the rich nutrient deposits.

Flooding probably happened when the monsoons came in the peak of the rainy season, and overflowed the whole river basin. There were piles of whitened and gray driftwood lying about. Sometimes a large tree trunk had floated down with its huge dirt free root ball washed clean, stranded high and dry now. No tall trees like those grew in this region, so they came from well upstream.

Ricco stopped the lead truck with his arm waving to warn them, because the Krall had no brake lights on their vehicles. He got out and walked over to a cluster of what appeared to be sun-bleached branches jutting from the grass and red soil.

As the others pulled up and stopped, they joined Ricco to see what he found curious about sticks. As they drew close, the jumble resolved itself into bones, a lot of them. The curved and pointed horns mounted on multiple armored frills proved some came from the same type of ceratopsian they had followed since yesterday.

Ricco kicked loose another skull, also partly embedded in dried mud. It was from a different type of animal, with a mouth shaped similar to a hadrosaur's, but this one was far larger than the variety the lions had killed.

The two rippers arrived, and seeing what was being examined, frilled to tell them that there were many more bones closer to the river, and some were only days old, others looked weeks old, with none yet bleached white by the sun, as these bones apparently were. There seemed to be a death trap near here of some sort, which had acted over an extended period.

They drove down closer to the water, which flowed deep right here, in the normal channel that only spread out when the river flooded. Dozens of skulls and rib bones of five or six large animal types dotted both shores. Danner started to walk down a slight grassy slope to the river to examine some recent carcasses closer, when Mel called out.

"Danner, stop! Remember Gunther's mudpuppies. You may be a TG2, but you are not invulnerable."

He halted, and started walking back. "Mudpuppies don't even live in rivers this size at home. And they aren't big enough to kill the animals we see here."

"One was large enough to eat Gunther Wrethov from Hub City, when he stopped to piss in a creek. I don't mean a giant mudpuppy killed any of these dead animals; I'm talking about you using some caution. However, I see gnaw marks on skull and limb bones, and mudpuppies only have a huge mouth with bony ridges for biting, not teeth. These bones were chewed on at some point, possibly post mortem if the animals drowned, I can't say. Nevertheless, there's no need to get too close to the deep water to find out the hard way."

Ricco looked upstream. "I think I see the low ridge of gray rock the lions told Kayla about, and which Big Blue said was just ahead." He shaded his eyes and carefully looked up in the sky towards the ridge. "I don't see Screamer."

"I do," answered Cory, glancing that way. "He's circling on a thermal where we told him to wait. Probably over the edge of the lake. I'll motion him to come back and report what he sees." Ripper vision was sharp and detailed but their vision, and what TG2's now had for long distance vision was considerably less acute than that of a wolfbat. Cory pointed at the distant dot that was Screamer, and with an arc of the same arm motioned him to return.

The highflying dot, obviously watching, dropped into a brief dive to pick up air speed, and started flapping rapidly in their direction. Cory stepped up next to Big Blue, opened the cooler and pulled out the same number of meat chunks, the same type as he'd given Blue, and waited. He wanted the larger bat to see there was no favoritism involved in Streaker's reward simply because he had stayed behind longer. Equal pay for equal value work.

Cory Tapped Streaker's mind as he ate his meat payment, then stepped down to describe what was ahead.

"That ridge is worn down some in the river, by years of water passing over it, but there is a sizable lake above that. Water is flowing slightly deeper in a section near the center, passing over a width of at least fifty feet of flat stone. It isn't very deep even at center, because previously Streaker saw some two-horns suddenly rush across, and the water never even reached their belly. They don't have very long legs and a sagging gut, so it doesn't seem more than two feet deep and slow moving at the center."

"They suddenly rushed across?" Mel asked. "Did Streaker see any predators approaching to spook them?"

"I think he would have shown that to me, just for more meat, but let me double check." A quick step up on the truck, a Tap, and he was back down.

"No, they just milled around on the slightly higher sides of the ridge, where the water hasn't eroded as much, and then about a dozen of them quickly separated and waded into the water and got to the other side as fast as they could, but without running. Not all of them waiting went across at the same time."

Jimbo made an observation. "Those horns and armored protective neck frills would make them front heavy. If they don't swim well, they might worry about being swept over the ledge into deeper water and drown, just as these animals probably did. The rock could be slippery."

"Hadrosaurs should swim well, I think." Cory countered. "Unlike the two-horns, they live in water most of their lives. They also left bones here."

"Flash floods possibly? We had a rain late yesterday. A big storm upstream might send water down this far suddenly. We can see that it floods here sometimes, apparently deep even this far from the main channel." Mel pointed at the big trees that had floated here to prove his point.

Shrugging, he said, "Let's drive up there and have a look. I studied the map and aerial pictures while we drove this morning, and either side has equal access to the mountain passes before we need to leave the river plain. I checked in with Prime City today, and gave them our progress. If we decide to use the ford, I'll tell them we are traveling on the other side of the river. Saddle up."

Three of the cats, ran ahead, after learning there were two-horns trying to cross, and that they might be too afraid to go. It sounded like potential easy prey for them to take down. Kayla, who had hunted yesterday stayed with the rest of the "pride" as additional protection.

The cats had decided they would always keep one ripper with the slower SGs at all times, if possible. Kopper had also hunted yesterday, but with a two-horn, his bulk and jaw size might be needed for the strangulation neck grip if they managed to isolate one of the animals from the herd. Unlike the rhinolo, who were not genius level grazers, most dino grazers were positively dim witted. They seldom charged to the rescue of a downed herd member.

Ricco and Neri got back into the first truck, and Danner and Cory into the closest truck with Mel, who assumed the second spot in the little caravan now. The other two took station in line as they trundled over the lumpy knots of grass, eventually getting back onto the migration trail.

On the smoother ground, they made twenty-five miles per hour. Except Ricco's halftrack kept throwing damp clots of red clay airborne, so Mel shifted farther right to keep the muck off the windscreen. Even that hydrophobic clear substance allowed the mud to slide down too slowly for good vision, if it was being replaced too quickly.

The ridge proved to be over three miles away, and as they drew closer, they saw the rippers hunting hopes had been frustrated. Apparently, the movement of the four vehicles, despite their distance, had frightened the two dozen ceratopsians gathered on the rocky approach to the ford. They were waiting for courage, to make the crossing before the unseen rippers had reached an ambush position. The remainder of the herd on this side had run away from the crossing, to wait for another chance to cross later, or even tomorrow.

Cory expected to hear some complaints from the three cats about the "sloppy" habits of *some people* that didn't know how to avoid stampeding the prey like cubs. Ignoring a fact, that no one else was hunting because plenty of frozen or cooled meat had been brought along, and they were not running low.

The two-horns they hoped to trap on the ridge, pinned between the water and the cats, foiled the ripper's hasty plan by the simple expedient of all of them rushing and splashing, sure footedly, over the fifty-foot wide gray granite ridge.

Ricco parked twenty feet from the edge of the water on the smooth stone, worn by untold centuries of migrations and floods. He leaned out to tease the three cats, who were watching their prey stroll away on the other side.

"Why didn't you get your feet wet and chase them?" This question garnered him sharp looks from three sets of narrowed blue eyes, all glaring his way.

Watching these cats grow up, and having played with them as kittens, he laughed. This would probably earn him a ripper's form of humorous retaliation before the week was done. Repeated three times. For example, pee directed at his boots, wet fur shaken hard next to him, or perhaps one would catch some small prey animal, eat what little meat there was, then "gift" his boots, underpants, or sleeping bag with the bloody fur and intestines that night. You laughed at even a friendly ripper at your own risk.

The cats moved back from the water as a low wave, perhaps wind pushed, shoved water up the gentle slope of the low ridge, and the flow of water over the center increased briefly. The speed of the water over the top of the granite obstacle was only a few miles per hour, and it dropped barely eighteen inches from the dark pool of water above the natural dam, to a smaller and slightly more turbid pool below, where the slow current stirred leaves and floating dino dung caught in the weak undertow.

The upper lake was nearly a mile wide behind the ridge, and the low point in the center sloped very gently, a reflection of the wear pattern of high and low water levels over the years, and of the animals that trod this natural barrier only when the levels were low, as at this season.

The water at the edges of the lake sloshed gently, perhaps the result of that same wind. The stillness of the surface on both sides gave no hint of its depth, but the dark water suggested it was too deep for a large animal to wade if it fell in, on either side of the solid walkway. If the level of the lake was as little as a half foot higher than today, the flow could be great enough that an animal that lost footing would be gently swept from the fifty feet of stable pathway before regaining its feet. A two-horn with its heavy head armor might easily drown if unable to find purchase to clamber back up against the slow current.

Ricco looked at Mel. "The ceratopsians have a bit less ground to belly clearance than the bottom of these trucks. This halftrack should have as good a grip on the rock as any of our trucks, and better than dino feet. If I stay more to the right, away from the slightly faster current near the left edge I won't have any problem, probably not on the left side either. I wouldn't want to cross if deeper water was going to push against the sides of the truck, but it'll pass under us if it went under the animals."

"I agree. Go slow and we'll watch for the undercarriage clearance as you near the low place in the center. Back out if the surface feels like you're having slippage."

Ricco looked at Neri, "Watch for any water build up on your side if it gets deeper than expected. I'll just put it in reverse." These trucks had passed through four-foot streams with stronger side currents on Cenozo, except there it was on sand and rocky bottoms, not flat rock.

"Hey, you want a ride to keep your feet dry?" He was offering this to the three cats.

Unsurprisingly, the miffed rippers turned and walked back to the other three trucks, preferring the company of someone who had *not* belittled their hunting miscalculation. Nevertheless, their natural instincts wanted them to resume the hunt when they reached the other side. Fateful decisions can rest on such trivia.

Ricco eased out into the first few shallow inches of water, about four truck lengths, staying ten feet from the right side edge. Informing the others by com set what he was doing, he applied combinations of motor power to test for traction or slippage. The drive motors of the front steering wheels gripped well against the drag of the switched off rear tracks. Then the tracks proved they too had a good grip. He used all four motors together in a surge of acceleration in forward, and then in reverse. The wheels and tracks worked with no significant slippage. There was a good gripping surface on the submerged rock.

This testing proved the other trucks would have no problem crossing, at least as far as traction went. Who would have thought this small delay and sense of caution was of more critical importance than tire grip? Perhaps the ceratopsians that had been seen rushing across earlier would know that. More significantly, it should have been the bones littering the downstream banks. They told everyone not to delay.

Ricco and Neri, their heads leaning out and looking down as the water rose, were relieved when the level quit rising with ten inches to spare from touching the undercarriage. All eyes were fixed on the truck. Except for those of the wolfbats, that had little curiosity about the not-life creature that sometimes carried them.

They watched the sky, their normal domain, for the frequent birds they encountered and sometimes hunted, and listened for distant cries of cousin bats that might hunt this far from the forests they normally choose for nest areas. That didn't mean, sitting so low and vulnerable, that they didn't look for other potential threats. They had lost squad mates that flew too low over "harmless" water in the past. Things sometimes leaped out of the water unexpectedly.

Streaker first noticed the moving bulge out on the lake. He squeaked an alert to Flight Leader, but it was low, because they were sitting side by side. No one had sent them aloft again, since the destination had been reached. Alarmed when he saw that the bulge was moving, Flight Leader sounded a louder warning call, of essentially "look out, a thing in the water." It was actually a composite warning of an alert, and an unknown water threat.

Cory heard and glanced back, because he recognized the first part, an alert call. He saw where they both were looking, and that they had slightly unfolded their leathery wing membranes for a sudden departure if needed.

He looked out over the water, and saw the hump of water, moving towards the natural dam. It was well out, but moving quickly. "Hey, what's causing that?" He pointed.

Mel, when he saw it, said, "It's a wave of some kind." He switched on his com set.

"Ricco, get across fast, there's a wave coming downstream towards you."

There was a momentary pause as Ricco and Neri did what every human does, only slowly to a TG2. They looked out at the odd wave, on an otherwise smooth lake with mild wind ripples dimpling the surface. "You want me to come back, or continue?" Ricco asked.

He didn't want to be stuck on the other side alone, and had decided the bulge was coming slow enough and right at the center, that he could go either way to escape. Another delay.

Danner, also looking, said, "I think it is increasing speed. Tell him to get moving."

In fact, the rounded wave crest was also a bit higher than it had been, and a bit faster.

Mel sounded much more worried now. "Ricco, move now! Get going!"

The truck lurched into reverse, and Ricco decided he wanted to stay with the group, and was convinced he could beat the wave to get clear. It was only thirty or forty feet wide, and coming directly at the center, where the water was deeper. What he had not counted on, none of them had, was that the wave wasn't directed at the center of the natural spillway. It was directed at the unnatural object that happened to be there in the center. As Ricco backed up, at a faster pace than he had been using, the wave deformed slightly and altered direction to intercept where he would soon be.

Neri came on the com set. "I've seen soliton waves, but those are wider, and this one is changing direction." In the background, Ricco being focused on driving backwards and staying centered on the ridge, shouted, "It might be a tidal bore, I've seen those in rivers on other planets."

He was wrong, but it was no time to debate with them, so Mel shouted, "Get moving faster, it's picking up speed."

Rigson's home city had a river that passed through its center and emptied into the sea. It frequently experienced a tidal bore. It was always seen near the mouth of the river as the tide came in, and moved against the river current. This wave was nowhere near the river mouth or tides, and it was moving *with* the slow current. It was smaller and localized, and he was now convinced it was aimed.

"Get your rifles. Start shooting at the front of that wave. There is something pushing that water."

Naturally, no one reached a weapon faster than the two boys, who leaped into motion as Rigson shouted. Danner grabbed his own weapon, a bolt action, but Cory took a few extra steps to grab the closest semiautomatic. In seconds of the warning, fifty caliber slugs were ripping into the wave that was now a quarter of a mile from the rapidly backing halftrack.

The slugs didn't seem to have any effect, and Rigson said, "Try aiming lower than where I see you hitting. It's deeper under the water I think." They had been shooting into the center of the growing wave front, and the "It" that Rigson suspected was actually below the surface level.

The shots started hitting lower, but the wave was moving faster, building, and it would be a close race to see if the truck could avoid being cut off before reaching safety. The danger, aside from what was making the wave, was the truck being swept over the downstream side of the ford, by the force of the water.

The high velocity slugs were visibly affected by the water. As the slugs stuck, some deformed and deflected upwards, exiting the wave top. Others may have slowed rapidly to ineffectiveness, or turned sideways. Heavy bullets that could do such terrible damage to flesh, and penetrate hardened armor or an inch of steel, were mostly useless for a water target you couldn't see. Besides, both youngsters, and the belated firing of the other men all made the same wrong assumption. They fired into and in front of the center of the mass of water, assuming that was where the target lay they had to stop.

They were only partly right, and thus only partly successful. The center of the wave suddenly lowered and slowed, but the sides split into two onrushing sections, the right side the largest. The two waves, having gained on the truck now still a hundred feet out, angled back towards it in a move to prevent it from reaching dry rock.

The surge of water was turning so it presented more of a side shot to the men firing. Cory and Danner saw something with their IR vision and shouted at the same time. "Shoot down at the sides."

Cory placed five shots quickly at a point a foot below the side of the near and larger wave, emptying his magazine, and Danner fired there as well. Mel did the same to the side of the farther wave, but with less accuracy. Cal and Jimbo split their shots between the waves, not seeing what the two TG2s saw. Suddenly, the rapid chatter of the thirty caliber automatic opened up, bullets striking the side of the nearer wave. Chack had pulled that weapon out from under a seat.

Abruptly, a long triangular fin briefly broke the surface below the front of the larger wave, and then a dark form twisted, dived, and turned away from them. The wave continued but was diminishing somewhat. Cory, racing to grab another magazine shouted, "There are at least four of them. We've hit two."

Danner was also reaching into a truck for another clip, as Cory reloaded. The intensity and rate of fire reduced enough that the two remaining wave crests were going to reach the truck. The question now was would the truck's weight and traction keep the vehicle from being swept away.

The double bulge of water merged, with the two combining to reach six feet high, with some of the additional wave momentum of the beast that had turned away still moving forward. The water struck the left side and rear of the truck the hardest, slamming it sideways. The back end swung towards the downstream side, still in reverse with full power applied. It moved ten feet in the wrong direction before Ricco, almost washed out of the cab, with Neri pushed against him, shifted into forward. He turned the front wheels to complete a right turn and try to reach safety in forward, forcing the blunt nose of the truck through the ebbing final five-foot wave of the creature that had ended its attack early.

The water didn't recede properly, and the truck suddenly halted against a dark wet resisting wave. The presumed frozen wave suddenly raised two huge dark brown flipper-like front fins, and then a monstrous long head filled with interlocking teeth appeared on the end of a six-foot thick neck. It used its long ovoid of a massive dark colored multi-ton body to shove the truck backwards four feet. It then hunched its back to pull its rear flippers up for another push. It was going to shove its prey into the downstream pool, and follow it in, to feed.

Cory walked towards the beast's back, to get an angle where he could shoot without risk of a through and through shot that could hit Ricco or Neri. He put an opportunistic round through the top of the skull when it raised that for another four-foot push effort. He was surprised when it didn't instantly drop dead. The truck went another four feet backwards, now eight feet from the edge.

Impossibly, the huge humped back rose again as the front flippers pulled the body forward, and the rear flippers moved close for the next push. The brain had to have been mushed.

Cory fired more rounds into the head, as Ricco jumped out of the truck, with Neri close behind. They both had their pistols out, firing at the head and neck. They may as well have been throwing rocks. The water was up to their lower calves, and they were moving away from the beast, to stay out of range of that long neck and damaged head that still was snapping its jaws. Another four-foot push. The next one could lose the truck.

Cal, running forward yelled to Cory. "Shoot into the hump at the base of the neck."

Placing five shoots where Cal suggested, the beast did a massive shudder, and slid off the front of the truck sideways, moving it another two feet closer to the pool as it fell. However, except for some residual muscle twitches, it was done. Apparently, its main brain wasn't in the skull.

As the neck and head had flopped towards Ricco and Neri, when the big body slid off the truck, they had danced backwards through the shallow and bloody water to stay clear of those fearsome teeth. Neri had drawn her hand back as if to throw something when it appeared the beast had lunged at them.

Ricco, realizing it was only the death throes of the plesiosauroid-like creature, put his left hand up to grab hers, before she could toss the grenade from which she'd already removed the pin. She had dug that out from the box under the seat as the beast pushed them backwards.

Holstering his pistol, he gently placed his thumb over the handle to hold it down, and asked the still petrified woman to give it to him. She looked at him almost startled, and realized what he'd asked. She shakily released her grip, and he told her to go on up the slope to the others.

She started up the slope, making a wide detour around the dead monster. Ricco, with a grenade in his hand, realized he didn't have the pin to relock the handle. "Neri, what did you do with the pin?"

She looked back, and said her last words to him. "I dropped it on the floor or seat. I don't remember for sur…" The sentence wasn't completed, and if it had been, it was doubtful Ricco would have been listening.

The fourth plesiosauriod, unharmed by the gunfire in the outer wave, knew the fleeing prey could not have escaped the rush of their joint bow wave, and it wanted its share of the food the cooperative effort the four had made possible. His older female sibling and an aunt had abandoned the attack for some reason, and he heard their receding echoes and pain cries as they fled deeper into the home lake. He knew nothing of the wounds they had received. All he knew was that the feast on their prey would be in the lower pool as usual, with less sharing today.

It swam back towards the ridge from where it had briefly retreated, while his more massive mother completed sweeping the prey over the ledge and into the feeding pool. Coming up from deeper in the home lake, there was no need to push the energy draining surface bow wave to sweep the prey off the ledge now. It sensed the echo reflection of the wall as it approached where the prey had been. It arrowed out of the water onto the smooth ledge, to skim over into the pool. It quickly sighted the oddly square looking prey still there, his quivering mother pressed against it, and a small animal near her extended head.

Cory and Danner instantly whirled and simultaneously raised their heavy rifles, seeking the hump at the base of the neck in the concealing spray of dark water as the big animal jetted onto the ledge.

The young adult plesiosauriod saw his mother's enormous form resting close to the path his wet glide on the smoothed slick rock would take him. He quickly rolled to his right to barely skim past her, and felt painful stinging sensations on his now exposed underside that burned their way deep into his body. Several of those burning tracks resulted in powerful impacts on the bony case that surrounded and protected his brain and its nexus of nerves.

However, as an experienced hunter, he didn't let this pain distract it from visually tracking the land animal near his mother's extended jaws. He recognized that without water surrounding her flippers, his mother had been unable to turn quickly, and had missed seizing the prey in her lunge. With a swift clack of its own jaws, it snatched the small prey in passing. It was easier than catching the fast and agile swimmers they hunted in the lake.

Sliding into the feeding pool, it had only seconds to enjoy that bite of food it had caught. Suddenly, in a shattering concussion, it lost sensations from its mouth, eyes, and his sensitive echo ranging ears. Something had struck him painfully in the head, and he couldn't feel the prey in his jaws.

The force of the blow cracked the hard case around its brain at the base of its neck, already damaged by the burning and stinging pains. His thinking was numbed, and he lost muscle control so that he was unable to swim. In total darkness now, he couldn't make the echolocation sounds used to find objects and prey in these murky waters. He drifted down slowly, as he felt the nibbling of the first of the smaller predators drawn to his blood. They always tried to steal pieces of prey as his family fed in their messy manner. It dimly understood in its primitive way that he was their prey today.

****

The painful memorial ceremony was over for the seven that would continue the expedition. They each had stood up and spoke their goodbyes to Ricco, and talked of the many things he had accomplished or done for them, of the many friends he had. The four cats were more pragmatic about the death, being predators themselves the act of a different predator taking a member of the pride as prey was a natural way of the world. They recalled the times he had provided them belly rubs when they were kittens, the few hunts they had made with him.

For the others, especially Neri, it was difficult while it was so fresh in their minds to blot out the vision of his sudden death. They all thought he had narrowly escaped with Neri.

She felt guilty that Ricco had stood there, exposed on the ledge in the shallow water, delaying only a few seconds longer than she had, taking the time to try to defuse the grenade she'd been holding. His look of startled surprise would haunt her, as another of the beasts, slightly smaller than the one that attacked their truck, seemed to spring from the lake and glide over the slick rock towards him.

It happed so fast in her state of shock that she didn't hear the futile gunfire from behind her, or actually see the jaws snatch Ricco because she had cringed back from the spray of water, her eyes squeezed closed. He was simply gone when her eyes reopened.

The thump of an underwater explosion, and bloody bubbles erupting seconds later proved that Ricco was avenged by his own hand. She first thought it was an accidental result of his being killed, and simply releasing the grenade as he died. Cory's higher rate of mental and visual processing showed her an edited down set of mental images, which proved that Ricco had taken deliberate action at the very end as he met his attacker.

In the Mind Tap images, she again saw his look of surprise as the creature exploded from the water, but she saw Ricco lift his left thumb, the grenade handle spinning away, and him thrusting his arm straight into the open maw sweeping towards him.

Rigson had reported Ricco's death to Prime City, but had refused their evacuation proposal, after consulting with the other expedition members. They all wanted to continue, to locate the source of the mineral wealth the colony needed to pay for what it needed. The fun sense of adventure was gone, but the exploration trek along the river would continue.

Two months later, and a nighttime K-Rex kill behind them, they found the rich parent deposits of the precious metal traces detected by satellite spectrographs on the upper riverbanks and sand bars. The future mines were located near the mountain headwaters of the Ricco River.

Chapter 9: First Contact, and a Name

It was time to meet the neighbors. The shuttle lifted from beside the Beagle, and picked up speed towards the abandoned dome, and the inhabited forest a few miles beyond that. Marlyn slowed as they approached the dome, and noted holes in the windows and part of the dirty and formerly transparent roof. Enough dirt had blown onto the half-mile wide circular tarmac that grass and low bushes were growing over much of its surface. Where wind had blown drifts of dirt and debris against the sides of the dome, thick vines had grown up almost to the highest levels. This dome was a dilapidated clone of the one at Prime City, making it roughly fifty percent smaller than the one at Hub City. This dome was about the size a Krall finger clan might build as a first settlement.

A number of rabbit or gopher-size animals were seen scurrying around the base of the structure, and ducked into burrows or underbrush. Hundreds of multicolored birds flew out of the holes in the dome windows and roof, in a panic at the noise of the thrusters. The panic only increased as the fleeing birds and flying reptiles sighted what would be seen by them as some huge predator hovering overhead, and the source of the screeching noise of attack.

Marlyn moved closer to the forest of huge trees, which started a few miles beyond the old dome. These trees were reminiscent of Earth's sequoias, except they had a green-brown color to their thick rough bark rather than red-brown. Their foliage on the ends of multi branched limbs consisted of long drooping green needles, ranging from a few inches for new growth up to four feet long. There were a number of brown fist-sized objects mixed with them, probably a seed or clusters of seeds.

The slightly lower gravity here allowed them to transport the water and nutrients they required roughly fifty feet higher than Earth's tallest trees. The tallest of these beauties topped out at about four hundred feet. The trunks of the largest trees at the base were also thicker by four or five feet than the largest sequoias. They were cathedral-like from below, and magnificent in their massive beauty.

The forest floor, as they drew closer was relatively clear under the thick shade of the high canopy, and carpeted with fallen dead needles. There were a number of well-worn paths through them between the trees.

From their lower vantage this time, it was easy to spot the structures built around the trunks, where the lowest sections were at least thirty feet above ground. There were differing levels, but they were not all layered the same, and occupied a different height on adjacent trees, with sloping or swooping walkways and rope lines between them. Rope ladders, some with wooden steps as spacers, hung to the ground from many of the lowest levels.

There were no Prada visible, and of course, it was impossible for them not to have heard the shuttle's approach. Marlyn set down at the edge of the woods, under the smaller younger growth trees, about a half mile from the closest Prada habitation. The housing was more extensive into the deeper woods than had been visible from orbit.

Marlyn opened the hatch and was first out. She smelled the traces of pale smoke she could see drifting through the trees above her. A cooking smell was mixed with that, which she thought contained the odor of animal fat products. The Prada were probably omnivorous, like humans, and to a much lesser extent the Krall, who were predominately carnivores, but ate fruit and little amounts of vegetables and grains.

Standing in the hatchway, Hakeem ran a small electric pump for a moment to get an air sample in an inflatable bag, and dashed back into the shuttle to see what was in the traces of smoke. Bradley carried the trunk of trade goods out and set it next to the shuttle, placed his rifle out of sight behind that, and sat casually on the trunk, but on watch. The other Ladies stepped out to admire the trees, sniff the fresh cool air, and study the Prada structures.

Hakeem came out to join them, and proudly announced the results of the quick air sampling, using his new (to him) technology. "That is definitely animal derived hydrocarbon byproducts in the smoke. Some of the Prada are having ham or bacon and eggs for breakfast."

Marlyn thought it, but Maggi said it. "Nice to know that your ten thousand three hundred credit gadget confirmed what my home grown, self-pumping olfactory chemical analyzer, located in the center of my face already told me was true."

Bradley said, "I saw a face peek out from one of the unshuttered windows of the house on that closest tree, second structure up from the bottom. It was small, like one of their children, and was jerked down by a hand on its head." This was probably a parent, pulling back a curious youngster drawing unwanted attention from these strange aliens.

The assumptions that these were houses appeared logical and the sides were formed of long planks of milled wood, overlapping clapboard style to keep water out. All the windows were equipped with hinged shutters, and the doors were all closed. This was a mid-latitude location on the southern hemisphere, in early spring. The northern hemisphere, at the same distance from the equator as here, had patches of snow. These houses looked suitable for summer or winter habitation, suggesting the population was stable and not nomadic.

Maggi, impatient as usual to do something, was ready to start. "How about I walk into that clearing, where several trails cross and there are no houses directly overhead. I can call out an invitation to meet in low Krall, then Raspani, and finally Standard. The first two might be recognized, and assumed to match the content of the third greeting."

Sarah nodded. "That might draw them out, if they understand either of the first two phrases at all, and you have to start someplace. Standing in the open, calling to them should seem like a clear invitation to talk, in any case."

Marlyn had her doubts about the sample phrase selected from the Krall low language. "The Krall don't exchange pleasantries with each other. What we would call an *invitation* translates very much like an order to 'come stand before me,' as our early captives heard from them all too often. We'll sound pretty bossy to them."

Shrugging, Sarah said, "There are no Krall phrases I can think of that sound less imperative. Based on what we heard from them as captives, they don't even have word usage that is equivalent to our use of terms like *please, grateful,* or *pleasure* when we extend polite invitations in Standard. All of their words that we overheard, used to ask someone to come see them, translate into what sounds like demands in Standard. Our translations could be biased of course, because to them they were speaking to dumb 'animals,' but the implications that those were more than simple invitations from a Krall were derived from the consequences when a person did not follow the 'invitation' promptly enough. We are stuck with how the Krall spoke to us captives if we need to use their language."

"Well watch my back and overhead as well, while I go talk to the fuzzy wuzzy critters." She was done with discussion, and despite her nonchalant demeanor, she was excited and eager to meet the Prada. She couldn't wait to offer to shake hands.

She walked confidently along the start of a well-used pathway, which suggested the Prada left the deeper forest to go out to the open grasslands frequently. From a recent rain, she saw animal prints in dried mud that looked splayed as if from a wide paw, but they were not pressed deep in the mud, for example as if from an animal as heavy as the newly named werewolf.

Walking into gloomy woods, she was regretting that playful bit of species naming fun, done to annoy the stodgy academic types she liked to provoke. It brought creepy thoughts to her mind now.

She also saw the narrow prints with the long grasping toes of the Prada, based on the orbital images of them walking on the walkways. The larger splayed prints clearly seemed to be from a four-footed animal, but not a huge one. The impressions were only a little deeper in the mud than the Prada prints, and must have been made at the same time. Some of one alternately overlaid the other, showing they had traveled together. That detail was a relief to her imagination, which the prints had activated.

She figured the peaceful looking little Prada wouldn't be "playmates" with dangerous predators, totally overlooking the two rippers back at the Beagle, munching on the werewolf horror she had just named.

Observing the prints was proof to her that even apparently useless information might eventually come in handy. Dillon and Thad's tracking lessons finally found an unlikely application for her. She had hunted with them a few times, just to shut them up about "everyone needing to understand" where their meat came from, and the risks and effort involved. She in turn forced them to sit through a city council meeting, to "understand" where stupid decisions came from, and why the effort to stay awake was mandatory, to oppose the dumbest of the proposals.

She reached the intersection of paths unmolested, and except for the one face Bradley had briefly seen, there was no sign the elevated village was occupied. Other than the certain feeling she had that many eyes were on her.

Well, here I go, she thought. In her best drill sergeant manner, she strained her throat to rasp out her loud version of a deep voiced Krall leader, calling for a Prada leader to come meet with her. Then, she tried the invitation in easier melodious notes of the Raspani language, one she did not know, but had let Sarah teach her how to pronounce. Finally, she called, "Prada, I am a human visitor, please come down to meet with me."

That last was phrased somewhat differently than in the other two languages (they had no alien word for human), but the gist of the invitation was the same. It was said more for the recordings than for the Prada, who wouldn't understand Standard anyway. She had leaned back to let her voice carry upwards, and held her hands and arms out, to show she was holding no weapon.

She hoped the Krall pronunciation of the racial name "Prada" was the word they used to name themselves, and not some derogatory term the slave masters used for them. It was possible she had just called them "turds" in their own language, or had used their word for "animals," which the Krall often used for human captives. The Raspani had seemed to recognize a picture of the Prada and used that same word. That could have been them merely repeating the Krall word.

She waited to find out if they would respond. There were noises from the forest, and birds and insects of various types had resumed moving about after the shuttle had been quite for a time.

Maggi had repeated the invitation a second time, and told the others by Link, under her breath, that she was going to repeat one more time before going over to the nearest rope ladder to shake it. Marlyn and Bradley simultaneously reported movement on a tree walkway, fifty yards deeper into the woods.

Marlyn finished describing what they had seen, but by then Maggi could see for herself. An adult Prada, gray with white markings, and black rings around the eyes had descended from a walkway by sliding gracefully down a rope, which it had just dropped over the edge. It kept its gaze on her the entire time as it descended, twitching its tail to counter a tendency of the rope to rotate it away from watching her constantly.

Behind this apparent representative, now there were numerous triangular shaped and pointed faces peering through windows, and from around tree limbs and trunks, where they had concealed themselves. Reaching the ground it hesitated, and pulled a small metallic looking tube from a pouch on a waist belt with its left hand. Kap, using the small amount of zoom on Maggi's button camera, reported that it looked like a three-inch long, quarter inch thick hollow tube. It didn't *appear* to be a hand weapon.

Maggi squeezed her left arm down briefly, to feel the comforting Jazzer holster under her tunic and armpit. The loose jacket had one middle button unfastened, to allow her to slide her right hand inside to draw the weapon if needed.

The impression that the tube wasn't a weapon was reinforced when it placed the smaller end of the tube in the corner of its mouth, and lowered its hand. As it started walking towards her, she couldn't help but grin. It looked like it had one of the twentieth century cigarettes dangling out of the side of its mouth, as she often saw in the old flat image movies, made decades before the nasty smoking habits died out.

It stood vertical on its legs, and they bent at the knee as a person did as it walked. It swung its arms slightly with each step, and the long toes pointed slightly out to the sides as it walked, with a slight sway side to side as it moved. It moved very sleekly, with a slightly sinuous motion of its slender body. It never took its eyes off her, but its blinking grew more frequent as it grew closer, the yellow eyes always locked on her. The increased blinking probably indicated an understandable nervousness.

As it came within about fifty feet, she noticed that a middle finger on each hand was at least an inch longer than the other three. An opposable thumb appeared to be a bit longer than a human's was, at least in proportion to the other slender fingers, and it had narrow hands and feet. It looked as if it would have dexterity at least as good as a human's hand, and from the smaller hand and finger size, might be better able to perform more delicate work.

There was a six-inch knife in a belt sheath on its right side, although it had removed the tube now hanging from its mouth from its waist pouch using its left hand. There was no way to determine handedness yet, if it indeed had any preference.

She saw it look past her, apparently looking at the shuttle and those outside of it, a half-mile behind her. It was walking a well-used path that curved to stay centered between tree trunks, but it stepped off into the loose dead needles to walk directly towards her, rather than follow the cleared path that curved back to where she now stood in the intersection of paths.

Through the Link, she heard Marlyn's voice. "When it left the path, it kept you directly between itself and the shuttle. I think it's aware of the fact that we are armed."

Maggi, too close to the Prada to make remarks it could overhear, merely nodded once. The large ears were swiveled more forward, rather than to the sides as she had seen in the previous orbital surveillance pictures. She could see its big yellow eyes flicking from her to the shuttle behind her, and its walk gradually intersected the path again about twenty feet from her, and it came to a stop.

She noticed that a loop to hold the knife in the sheath was hanging loose, and the right hand was held close to the weapon in a casual manner. It was a caution she might have taken in its place.

In low Krall, she asked it a question. "Are you a Prada clan leader?"

The top of the bandit mask-looking eye rings lifted slightly, as it did something like a human raising their eyebrows. It didn't speak, but moved its head forward and back an inch, the nose pointed at her. That could have been equivalent to a human affirmative nod, or a negation for that matter. However, it suggested it might have understood the question, no matter the answer.

She continued in low Krall. "I am called Maggi, and my clan is called human. What are you called, and do you have a clan name?"

In a voice considerably higher pitched than what Maggi was trying to imitate in low Krall, the creature answered her also in low Krall. "My people are all called Prada. I am leader, Wister, of the Sither clan. Why are you here? You must leave our lands."

So, it'll be low Krall to start with Maggi thought. The Prada language could come later. Assuming Wister's order to leave the Sither lands could be changed right now, and giving up the deep voice attempt, she spoke in a normal tone.

"We came from Koban," she pointed up, knowing Koban wasn't overhead or visible in the daytime sky. "We came to explore this world and to meet your clan."

"I have been to Koban. Your kind did not live there. You lie. You must leave our lands or the rulers of Koban will eat you." It accused, repeated the order for them to leave, and warned them of consequences, presumably from the Krall.

"The Krall have left Koban, and we live there now. We came to meet you, and to help you."

"Leave now, or you will be eaten." It moved its head forward and back, as if emphasizing the truth of its last statement.

"Do you threaten all that come to you as allies with harm? We can give you science to rebuild your civilization." There didn't seem to be a Krall word for "friends," so she said allies. She also didn't know how to say the equivalent word for technology, which they were offering. Telling them they had something to give them might alter the hostile stance.

The offer was rejected. "We always have our science, and the Rulers will take what science you have, eat you, and give what you know to us to build for them. If you do not leave now, you will be eaten here." The tube in the corner of its mouth lifted to horizontal, as it clenched it in the small teeth she could see behind the black colored soft lips. It looked like nothing more than a small hollow tube, with a slit near the top, close to the lips.

She heard Kap's voice. "The metal tube appears to be similar to a breath driven, noise making device. The dimensions indicate it would be a high pitch sound maker. It does not appear to be a weapon."

Maggi had already concluded that, but wondered what the purpose of the whistle was. Possibly, it was to trigger some action by the other members of the village on Wister's signal.

"We are very strong on Koban, and have met and defeated some of the Krall. They no longer live there. We own their domes now."

"You have said your last lie." It puffed its lips and blew, but Maggi heard no sound other than air passing through the tube, a bit of spittle rising from the top slit.

Both Kap and Bradley spoke at once, Kap yielding the Link to the boy. "Maggi, I heard it blow a series of ultrasonic chirps. It's a signal, so in light of the threats you perhaps should start back this way, I'll cover you."

As Bradley talked, Maggi saw Wister rotate his body position to his right, twisting his legs and hips to do so, without moving his feet. She saw his right elbow appear from behind his back as his left side turned towards her. He was doing something with his right hand while it was out of sight. His unsecured knife came to mind.

The Prada leaned away from her and lifted its left foot as it pivoted and pushed off with the right foot to leap the distance towards her. They had seen their lightweight forms leaping from limbs and walkways on recordings, and they easily had the ability to cover the twenty feet in two jumps.

Maggi said, “Bradley, don’t you dare shoot this fool. I have this covered.”

She stood still as the Prada started its second jump off the left foot, the right hand that surely held a knife concealed behind its back. It kept in a line between her and the shuttle, possibly aware of the rifle Bradley must now have leveled in their direction. Wister appeared ready to sacrifice itself in order to complete an attack on her. *Curious,* she thought, *what was the whistle blast about?* It appeared the Prada was going to do this all alone.

That was what she thought, until she heard the multiple yips, howls, and growls coming from among the trees to her left. She had intended to let the Prada reach her, but decided she needed to resolve his threat sooner, to be ready for whatever else he had summoned.

She shifted from the balls of her feet, where she had balanced herself as the Prada came at her, and she jumped towards him in her own leap, turning her right side towards him. Detecting her movement, he brought the knife hand around sooner while still in mid leap, as she anticipated. She could have simply pulled her Jazzer and stunned him, but decided a more physical demonstration was in order. It had been good enough for Carson against a Krall, so she knew this would be simple against a Prada.

She landed on her feet just as her left hand grasped his knife hand and pulled him forward, and she rotated to put her right shoulder into its midriff as she crouched down. She lifted him with her shoulder as he came in contact, and as the lanky body passed over, her right hand rose in a quick move to its crotch to grab fur, and apply more force to the body slam, as it landed on its back in the bare dirt of the path.

She heard the air whoosh from his lungs as he hit the hard packed ground with far more force than simply falling from five feet high. Her grip in the crotch fur also confirmed that it was almost certainly a male, if it fit the sexual dimorphism pattern found on quite a few planets. That was where some male and female animals developed reproductive organs, and often delivered live births similar to Earth mammals. Nature had proven repetitive in much of its evolution, with convergent features frequently encountered.

Plucking the knife from the hand of her stunned opponent, she bent and lifted the gasping alien by the scruff of his neck, using only her left hand. She tucked his knife into her own belt, and retrieved the whistle where it had fallen from his mouth. The growls were louder, and coming from what had been her left when she walked into the woods. She now could hear the sounds of many feet striking the ground and stirring the dry needles.

Marlyn called out frantically. “Drop him and run, he called some big spotted dog-like animals. I see at least four, coming from one side of the woods.”

Bradley broke in, “I see at least six, and one is closer to us than you are. We can pick them off as they expose themselves between trees, but you had better have your Jazzer ready, we may not get shots at them all.”

Maggi looked up around her, and saw the closest house on a tree just twenty-five feet away, built about thirty feet off the ground. However, it had a partly pulled up rope ladder that came within fifteen feet of the ground. "How about I use these brand new TG muscles to get off the ground, and we avoid killing any of their pets."

Francis said, "Pets? You must not have seen them yet. A hundred pounds each, with gaping jaws. The closest is a hundred fifty feet away. Drop the Prada and go!"

She was moving as Francis talked, and finally saw one of the animals passing between trees. Now she knew where those splayfooted tracks came from, that she had seen with the Prada's footprints. These were previously marsh dwelling pack hunters, and the Prada had domesticated them as pets and guardians. She knew all this the instant she had grabbed Wister's knife hand by using her new Mind Tap ability.

The Prada leader was hoping to hold her close until the animals, out hunting with other members of the clan, ran back to help him. The hunters would have heard the shuttle, and of course sent the faster running animals back to the village. When his large ears detected their distant yips, he had blown the rally signal to draw them to him. They would tear apart any foreign threat to their owners.

Maggi carried him easily with one hand, even as he started to struggle when he regained his breath. His strong hands reached over his small shoulders and tried to pry the painful grip free from the loose fur near the back of his neck and shoulders. It was like trying to force open a Ruler's iron grasp. He couldn't budge so much as one of its fingers, while he was carried like an infant.

Wister saw the marsh dogs he'd called, coming to his aid as fast as they could run. He saw that Jelko, the fastest of the pack, would reach them first. He held onto his hope that this enemy of the Rulers could yet be defeated.

He was being carried, kicking but unable to call out, not with his skin and fur gathered so tight in back that he could hardly breathe. This was the smallest of the aliens, and he had felt safer approaching it. How much more dangerous were the larger representatives? He wished the Rulers were here, to see that he had tried to oppose this new enemy.

Jelko was almost to them. There was nowhere for this alien to run, since the ladders and ropes were pulled up for security. The ladder over his head wasn't as high as it should have been, but still out of reach. The alien turned to face the speediest of the clan's animal guards. With horror, he saw the unexplainably powerful alien pull a weapon from out of its clothing. It would kill their protectors, their hunter helpers, their beloved pets. He had to stop her. He kicked violently at his captor, and she touched the hand with the weapon to his own hand a moment. He experienced a mental flash in his mind of a marsh dog climbing a tree, and automatically visualized the low hanging ladder overhead, which the dogs could climb only with difficulty, if it were down.

The alien glanced up and into his eyes, as he was held aloft by one arm. Unbelievably, it returned the weapon to where it had been hidden. It shoved his body forward, placing him between the quickly closing Jelko and itself as it backed towards the nearest tree. If Jelko could hold it there at the base of the tree, when the rest of the pack arrived they would tear this enemy apart. The dog tried to dodge around Wister, and the alien flashed out a kick that was so fast Wister couldn't really see it when it connected with the underside of the animal's jaw.

Flying up and backwards without even a cry of pain, he feared Jelko had been killed by the kick, delivered faster than even a Ruler might be able to block.

Suddenly, he was jerked painfully by that grip on his fur and skin, as he was tossed skywards. Releasing him, the alien crouched and leaped up and caught the bottom of the rope ladder that had only been pulled halfway up, catching it with one hand. It reached out and easily caught him by the ruff of his neck again, just as he reached the height of the arc.

It pulled itself up by that one hand, Wister in the other, then another jerk as it yanked itself up another five feet one handed and caught another rung. It did this until, one handed, it had pulled him up to the board walkway and tossed him onto the planking. It pulled up and sat beside him, feet hanging over the edge. It looked down at the guard animals, leaping up and howling at the tree base, having just missed their prey.

The dogs tried to climb the rough bark, using clawed feet and teeth, as they bit at the large ridges in the tree trunk to get as much as ten or twelve feet high, before a chunk of bark would break off or flake, causing them to fall back.

Treed like a raccoon by hound dogs, Maggi thought. Mean looking animals.

Per the mental images from Wister, the Prada leader cared a great deal about their welfare. He had feared the aliens might kill them. It was to calm her captive's worry, which had driven her decision not to stun the closest animal. He had a particular fondness for that one, and didn't know a Jazzer was nonlethal. She saw he was watching intently as the one she had kicked stirred and shook its head, making a yawning gesture to test its lower jaw. Maggi had not felt anything break, but felt guilty because the Jazzer would have been easier on the beast than the kick. However, if stunned by a full Jazzer charge, it would have looked dead for five minutes. No need to have an angry pet lover trying something rash to get back at her.

She pulled him around, forcing him to sit next to her, and she grasped his left hand in her right. She had been on the receiving end of this process a thousand times, but had never been a transmitter before. She sent the Prada images of the animals below, and some of humans interacting peacefully with animals, such as dogs, domestic cats, horses, and finally the rippers. The context of the images implied that these were not intelligent creatures from alien civilizations.

She was shocked to see that the Prada's claim to have been to Koban was true, when it recognized the ripper image, accompanied by a memory of seeing a pride from the safety of a dome roof under construction. It was shocked in turn, that these aliens, the one next to him in fact, had often been in close proximity with rippers, and survived. Moreover, it sensed she loved some of them, and trusted them, just as he loved and trusted the animals below that wanted to protect him from her.

Marlyn was still worried when she Linked. "Maggi, we saw you climb up, but you are out of view from the shuttle at the moment. We can see your camera image, at a bit of an angle, and it looks like you are Mind Tapping the Prada. Everything OK?"

Maggi answered. "I'm sharing images with the local leader, named Wister. Damn, this TG1 ability is neat as hell. You have to let Rafe and Aldry upgrade you. I have been missing out on so *much*, and the ability to kick ass simply can't be overrated. Gee will it be fun when Dillon and Thad get back." She shook her head to dispel the cheerful (for her) thoughts of their first uncomfortable days after they returned.

Tiger Lady my ass, she thought. Wait 'til they meet the "mighty mite!"

Her diabolical chuckle bothered her Linked friends as much as it did the Prada leader.

Shaking off that last amusing thought as well, she continued. "Anyway, the leader here is worried. He fears we might kill the marsh dogs." She paused in thought.

"Oh yes, I'm giving them a name too, based on where they apparently came from. Get over it Captain *Discovery*. You'll get your chance to name the entire damned world." She was feeling flush with new felt power. Before, all she really had was her mind and words to get people to do what was "best" for everyone. Now she had the advantages of speed, muscles, and telepathy, at least until the other SGs caught up with her.

"Please don't hurt their pets," she told them. "They feel about them as we do about rippers. If any of them come close to you, get into the shuttle until we straighten things out. I was about to drop my hostage and climb the tree using the rough bark. Then I checked the backstabber here via Mind Tap, and I wanted to know if the dogs could climb a tree. He knew they couldn't climb without a ladder to help, and that the one overhead was mistakenly left hanging too low. I knew I couldn't jump high enough to reach it while holding onto him, so I threw him up first, then jumped to grab the ladder. I gotta tell ya. It's *good* to be so bad assed and strong. Now I'm ready to negotiate with this little shit."

"I don't know, he did attack you with a knife unprovoked, and sent a pack of killer hounds after you. You can't trust him."

"It's a lifelong Krall slave issue, Marlyn. I certainly have not had time to probe him much, but he has a fear of not pleasing and obeying the *Rulers*, which have to be the Krall.

"I believe we can come to an agreement with the Prada eventually. Any people that can display so much affection and empathy for animals, as this Prada does, should have the ability to understand and cooperate with other intelligent species. Give me a bit of time today. I'll move around to where you can see us."

"I'll leave negotiations up to you. Assuming toting their presumed ambassador around by the scruff of the neck and kicking his dog is a form of diplomacy." She laughed at how that sounded.

"By the way, could you rotate your button camera to straighten out our image?"

Maggi glanced at her disheveled tunic. "I will, as soon as we stand up. I'll walk him around the corner of the house where we're sitting, so you can see us. While we are sharing mental images, it might get quiet up here sometimes, so don't get antsy. This Mind Tap ability is going to revolutionize human and alien diplomacy, and first contact situations if we ever have any others.

"Mr. Wister here is in a daze from all the shocks he has just had in the last few minutes. Not to mention the fact that I grabbed him by the balls when I slammed him to the ground. He's doing a Dillon thing, holding his legs together. I'll help him stand."

At the shuttle, the button camera's picture tilted and rotated as she stood up and adjusted her tunic. They saw her reach down to help the Prada stand, who made it more difficult by keeping his knees together. Obviously, he learned faster than did Dillon, to guard his "jewelry" when this alien was around.

Having TG abilities or not, she directed Wister to precede her on the board walkway around the house. One strong hand on a small sloping shoulder was a reminder she was close behind him. She had his knife and whistle, but she had not sensed any lessening of his desire for the humans to leave now, so she would not turn her back on him.

She had sensed he was worried the "Rulers," as he had called them in low Krall, would return to punish the village if they didn't oppose an obvious alien enemy. He didn't use the name Krall when he spoke aloud, but they were in the mental images of his thoughts.

The suspended walkway swayed and bounced as they walked, and she saw the Prada's knees and hips move to counter the motion as it walked, so that its upper body and head remained nearly steady. She mimicked that, and in a matter of seconds had a gait as smooth as did the Prada on the jouncy walkway.

She prompted him to walk out to the center of another walkway strung between two of the giant trees, and grasped his shoulder to stop him midway across. They were in plain sight of the shuttle, as well as the now eight marsh dogs, which had followed below them as they moved, yipping, but no longer growling or howling.

Maggi glanced down to look at them. Although probably related to the larger werewolves, they had the thinner body shape of coyotes on Earth, or the dune dogs on Rhama. These animals were built for running and agility, with a sort of paddle-footed paw that would make running on mushy marshland easier. They probably could "dog paddle" in water rather well.

When they didn't have their fangs exposed in a snarl, they looked very much like a large dog, with an elongated snout similar to the German shepherd breed, with pink tongues hanging out as they recovered from the run to get back here. They even had a long hairy tail, which swished from side to side, probably like a counter weight when chasing prey that was turning and twisting to avoid being run to ground.

Maggi immediately empathized with Wister's feelings for them, because she had been a "dog person" back at home on Rhama. She thought often about what became of her two pets, Murphy, a dachshund, and Bentley, a mixed breed lap dog.

She had left them with a niece for the time she would be at Midwife. After twenty years, they were both long dead. Humans had never tinkered with dog longevity, despite tinkering with almost everything else about their most faithful companions.

In low Krall, she said, “We will now get to know more about each other’s clan. Also about the Rulers, whom you still obey and fear. Sit here and I will share my mind with you.” From time spent with TG1s and rippers, she already was a master at holding back thoughts and images she didn’t care to share. This Prada’s thoughts were completely open to her each time she made a suggestion of what to discuss and share. The alien was about to spill their innermost secrets. Maggi shivered with anticipation. Damn this was fun!

****

Two tiring hours later, she realized she needed to eat and drink, and so did the Prada. *It was hungry for a... bark grub?* She pushed away the unpleasant thought of Wister, using his specialized long middle finger, digging out a plump white grub from the bark of a smaller variety of tree at the edge of the woods. Those grub trees were not the giant “Temple” trees on which they built their houses, which were resistant to most wood pests. The Prada had no religion now, but in their remote pre spaceflight era on their former home world, they had built tall narrow structures to reach towards their sun god. That ancient tale had inspired comparing the giants of the forest to those temples, from a life and world long lost to them.

Maggi released the Prada’s hand, and stood. She told him in low Krall, “Wister, you and I need to eat and think, and share with our clans what we have learned. I have seen your young ones watching us, as well as their parents. They do not understand what you and I have been doing.”

He replied in the only language she now knew he spoke, low Krall. “I *do* know what we have been doing, but I do not *understand* how it is done. How can I convince the other old ones to disobey the Ruler’s instructions? I don’t know if I can do that myself, even with your mind pictures to help. When you leave here, I may doubt what I was shown. It seems a trick that is hard to believe.”

“If you will meet us at the edge of the woods tomorrow, with other Prada, we can show them as well. We can show you where this ability came from, how it was developed naturally on Koban. Not by us, because we only copied the ability. Here is your whistle, and your knife. I think you know that you are not fast or strong enough to beat one of us in a fight, but we do not want to be your enemy, and we will not try to force you to be our friends. We are not here to replace your Rulers.”

“I will try to explain to the village.”

“That is my request. Another is for you to send your pets away below. I truly do not wish to harm them, but if attacked we will be forced to kill or injure them.”

He made that forward head motion, his small pointed black nose aimed at her. A gesture equivalent to an affirmative head bob in most human cultures. He put the whistle in the side of his mouth and blew.

Bradley immediately called on the Link. “We heard what you said, and I can hear that whistle clearly from out here. The dogs are getting up and moving deeper into the trees. Do you want me to come in and escort you out?"

Maggi looked at Wister. "I have a communication device, and one of my clan mates knows we are departing here for today. He heard your signal, and asks if your guardian pets, which we call dogs, will stay away when I walk back alone."

"Yes, they were sent to their sleeping and feeding area by my signal. You can also hear the sounds of the caller?" He held the whistle up. "I cannot hear it, but the Rulers can."

"Only some of us can hear that today. We all will be able to hear it in the future."

Another head dart move indicated he heard her words, but surely didn't know just how it would be done.

He made the first considerate offer she had heard from him. "I can lower a ladder or rope for you to descend."

Ready to impress him again she grinned and said, "Don't bother. I will return tomorrow." Then she vaulted one handed, lightly and gracefully over the rope rail, and dropped to the ground thirty feet below. She landed on the balls of her feet with a slight bending of her knees to absorb the shock. After all, this was only 59% of the Koban gravity she was accustomed to feeling, and the TG muscles were hardly tested by this short of a drop. It almost felt like slow motion to her new senses as she descended. Perhaps riding a rhinolo when she got home might be fun after all.

She walked confidently back to the shuttle, while the others were preparing to return to the Beagle. Maggi asked to know what those at the Beagle had found today, but those in the shuttle wanted to know about the Prada. Marlyn compromised.

"The three truck teams have recorded a dozen grazing animal species, and four predators, including the wolves. One is a legless ten to eighteen-foot crocodile equivalent, living in that river. It's an air breather, but can stay under for at least twenty minutes. We encountered another set of pack animals that resemble cousins of the marsh dogs, with gray and white coloring and normal sized paws. They found a lone jet-black hunter that has the shape of a wolverine, but is the size of a grizzly bear. It isn't terribly fast, and Kobalt and Kit tormented the thing until it left the area. There are hundreds of birds." She turned to Maggi.

"Now tell us about the Prada. Give. Except for your occasional questions in low Krall and his answers, most of the time you were holding hands, all chummy and exchanging mental pictures we couldn't see. What did you learn about them, and what did he mean when he said he had been to Koban? When was that?"

"I'll have to repeat this, you know, when we get back to the Beagle in fifteen minutes."

"I know, but tell us anyway while I fly. Talk loud." Marlyn urged, as she started the thrusters.

"OK. These Prada here are one of several clans that are supposed to be on this world. Following the Krall example, they describe themselves as a clan, each isolated and placed on different continents. The Prada call the Krall their Rulers.

They all speak Low Krall, and have for thousands of years. They were only allowed to speak that tongue among themselves, as can the Torki. The crab bodied Torki are mentally different and they never forgot their own language, however the Prada lost theirs. The Prada assume there are multiple groups of Torki still living here, because they have done delicate electronic work for the Krall here and on Koban, and repair and adjust the systems on clanships and other spacecraft and weapons the Krall use.

"Wister believes there is a colony of Torki on the western coast of his landmass. The crabs don't always obey Krall instructions when not watched, and the Prada do not fully trust them because of that. It appears that after so many thousands of years of servitude, the Prada virtually consider themselves part of the Krall Empire. They have difficulty doing things contrary to their master's wishes. I think Prada society is naturally subservient to their species eldest leaders, and grant this instinctive obedience to the Krall as an elder race. They don't *want* to be free of them, and wish they would return."

"Why? We never saw any hint that the Krall particularly wanted the Prada around, or even kept them close. As far as we are aware, there aren't any Prada on Koban. Of course, we have a great deal of territory to explore, but we've had satellite images for years, and saw no signs of them. It looks more as if the Krall kept most of their workers here, sending some of them to Koban when needed, and then returning them. Is that how what's-his-name is able to remember Koban?"

Maggi indicated yes, with a caveat. "Wister was last on Koban perhaps sixty orbits ago, he says. However, there is something else you need to know." She asked the AI a question first.

"Kap, this world has a two hundred seventy-six day year, isn't that right?"

"Yes." He answered on speaker, aware of the group listening.

"Sixty orbits would be how many Standard years ago Kap, in whole numbers."

"Forty-five years, in Standard measure."

"Wister spent ten years directing work on Koban all told, as sort of a senior builder foreman. This work was done in rotations that permitted physical recovery back here, and Prada replacements were sent to Koban from here. Koban was very tough and dangerous without the walled compounds they built later, as we would expect. They simply called this world a base. Following Krall convention, they have no name for this world or for the village, but I think they love the forest. They think of the giant trees as temples. Not as places of worship, but as tall slender buildings they revere."

"They do have a name for our home, it's called Koban." Bradley pointed out.

"No, that is what *we* use for its name, but it was only a description to the Krall of what they used the world for. It translates as a training place, or perhaps a testing ground is a better meaning of the word. The early human captives latched onto the word to use as a name for where they were held.

"Initially the Krall tested their novices there, and established new finger clans to see if they would survive and flourish. The Prada came from here in teams, to assemble the domes for the trial settlements, built with materials shipped from other Krall production worlds. Then they were rotated back here as new, fresher teams were sent to finish or continue the work."

"You mean the Krall actually conserved the Prada? They treated them better than us 'expendable animals.' I can hardly believe that level of consideration from them." Francis said.

"Not much conservation or consideration actually, and nearly half that went to Koban died." Maggi informed them. "They gradually grew sick and wore out in that gravity. It was more efficient, from a Krall standpoint, to send the live ones back here to recover for some years, and use fresh ones for the work on new domes and compounds. Wister did that rotation three times."

"When did he start working on Koban, if the last time he was there was forty-five Standard years ago?"

"Right after he directed the construction of the dome we just passed over." Maggi waited for that information to register.

Bradley snickered. "It's a falling down wreck. He didn't do a very good job."

Marlyn caught on immediately, and asked a question. "The Krall abandoned this dome about three hundred years ago. If Wister directed the construction here, how long before it was abandoned did he do that? How the hell old is that little Prada?"

"That is *exactly* the key question." Maggi told her. Then gave the best answer she had derived.

"Wister has lost track of measures of years, because he has lived or worked in three other Krall solar systems in his lifetime. He remembers what he did in all of them, but the length of local years was different each place, and in this system he split his time between two worlds with different year lengths. As well as I was able to estimate, based on rough guesses, Wister is well over a thousand years old. And he isn't the oldest Prada in this one village."

"They don't die?" Hakeem asked, incredulous.

"They apparently don't age." She corrected him. "However, they die as easily as we do. From sickness, accidents, animal attacks, or by being shot or bombed while building Krall installations in a battle zone. Actually, I think we are healthier than they are, with our genetically enhanced immune system. But we age, and they apparently don't, after reaching full adulthood."

Hakeem asked the obvious question. "Are you sure he didn't lie about that?"

She shook her head. "It was a Mind Tap, on an unprepared mind. I don't think it knows how to block or fabricate a memory for me. It had detailed memories of other worlds, and multiple lifetimes of experiences readymade to share. He knows he has been lucky to live so long and avoid accidents or serious disease. When they have children, they seem to grow up at a normal pace, and mature and change until reaching adulthood. Then they simply stay the same, physically.

"Their reproduction is a puzzle to me, because they can have children at any age, per Wister's thoughts. Therefore, their population pressure should force them to expand. Yet that is a small isolated village, and yet we saw about a dozen young ones. They may have some population management system. If they don't, in order to maintain a stable population at the roughly eighteen hundred Prada that Wister claims lives in the village, they must have had a dozen fatalities this year, out of a small town of near immortals. Eventually they would be mating with some cousin or other that also outlived most of the small population."

The shuttle landed next to the Beagle, surrounded by a crowd, and all the news as Maggi had predicted had to be shared again. Marlyn reported the day's events to Koban to spread the news, and had Kap save her the task of repeating everything, by letting Jake record it all for wider dissemination.

There was a new hot item of discussion at home on Koban, after the Beagle's initial close up survey and discovery that Prada could survive there. With the revelation that the animal and plant life was largely suitable for human consumption, it added fuel to the fire. They heard there were empty Krall domes (no matter that they were falling apart from neglect), and there was a push by some Hub City residents to relocate.

These were mostly people that had steadfastly refused even the clone gene mods; therefore, gravity and climate were seriously wearing them down. The Raven was said to be approaching readiness for flight tests, and its large volume could move all of the people wishing to go in two Jumps.

Naturally, the proponents of immediate relocation were completely overlooking the fact that the Raven could not land. It was an orbital only transport, and shuttles could only carry just so much down. They would need a great deal in the way of material to establish safe and habitable conditions on a world completely wild. None of these people had experienced what Koban was like for the earliest human captives. They already had a place to live when they arrived, food and a developing infrastructure to support them.

Marlyn met with Maggi, Sarah and Francis, her primary confidants and planners for the mission to the Morning Star planet. She told them about the push to move people here, using the Raven. They discussed all of the immediate problems, and the time and effort it would take to resolve them. However, after all the discussion points started to wind down, Marlyn made a prediction.

"Eventually, the problems of settling here *will* be solved. It's not as difficult or hazardous as the last twenty years was on Koban, so beyond a doubt we will have people living here. There are already Prada here, and they say there are also Torki, which would make this the only known planet, to us anyway, with multiple intelligent species living together.

"I like Sarah's proposal, to move the Raspani here as soon as we can verify they can eat the plants, and we can make a secure compound for the first ones to arrive. They are living much shortened lives because of the stress Koban's gravity places on them. They need the least amount of advanced preparation.

"I have no doubt we can find some isolated island someplace in a temperate climate, with good grass and bushes, fresh water, and free of large predators from the mainland. The Raspani could be free for the first time in thousands of years, to thrive in their own little haven."

She paused in thought for a moment, as Sarah, a complete devotee to the study of the Raspani now, continued the new direction in their conversation. The flash of insight, when it came, was enough that Marlyn's burst of excitement rudely interrupted the conversation.

"Haven!" she shouted out. "It's a perfect description of what we want to create here, not only for our own people, but for the Krall slave races we want to rescue. I'll name it Haven."

Maggi smiled hugely at her friend. Naming a world for a noble purpose was a hell of a lot more meaningful than naming a "werewolf" or "marsh dog."

Now they needed to start the planning, to prepare the way. This would be fun, if she could shift all the hard work to younger backs. A cinch for an old manipulator like her.

Chapter 10: Heavyside

The multiple Jumps taken to Heavyside from Poldark, to throw off possible followers, ended when the Avenger did a White Out in the Oort cloud of comets, five light-days out from the planet. Noreen had the towed cargo pods hauled close and offloaded into the airless lower cargo bay. Pressurizing the hold after that, they cast off the empty containers, to wander with widely scattered balls of ice, taking thousands of years to orbit the pinpoint of light that was the parent star.

Once the cargo was accessible, the future elevator equipment was stowed out of the way, for when they returned home. Three modern med labs were moved to higher decks and the Chameleon Skin armor and IR night goggles were issued to everyone, new weapons issued, and various spares were stored.

For Noreen, the big prize was the KP model AI system, which came with instructions for installation on a clanship, using the Mark as the assumed template for all such modifications. The food stores were the second greatest gift, at least as far as Noreen and Macy Gundarfem, her engineer, was concerned. Real Earth coffee! Beefsteaks, hamburgers, leg of lamb, lima and green beans, sweet potatoes and more, were all veritable pieces of heaven to palettes starved for the tastes of home.

The TGs, after sampling some of the "imported" foods from Human Space, were unimpressed with the "tame" flavors of the meat, and *any* vegetable was OK if buried on a pizza under cheese. Rhinolo burgers and yak steaks had "more kick" they insisted.

The new flexible armor however, was the neatest stuff they had ever owned. Unaware that each suit cost more than most working people on Hub worlds earned in a year. Never having had money, the young Kobani couldn't appreciate the credit bar tags on the packages as they opened them.

They practiced arranging it, covering even their face so they needed internal view screens to see, and would crawl forward in plain sight, minimizing the ripple effect as they slowly repositioned the material to "sneak up" on friends and surprise them. If you were slow enough, even the IR eyeglasses worn by others didn't notice the temperature difference, as the warm body beneath the Chamskin (as they started calling it), no longer left a heat smear on the deck when the edge of the flex armor slowly pulled away.

For the teenagers, where high speed body motion was an everyday experience, the art of moving slowly and undetected was an alluring game to pass the time. The allure wore thin with the two adults, after spilling their precious new coffee or nearly wetting themselves, when suddenly an unseen hand grabbed an ankle and a disembodied voice would say "gotcha." A "gotcha" could come in other ways, when extremely boring duties could be assigned to the sneak by the "victim."

It was almost four days before the "simple" installation instructions for the new AI proceeded to the point where Karl, its newly assigned name, was powered up. After that, he easily walked them through the remaining "Tab A into Slot B" confusion of a thick stack of printed instructions.

It was a smart idea to give the AI its own set up guide, Marlyn thought. Mentioning that fact at the *start* of the damned assembly instructions, that the AI's processor could be powered on separately, to direct you through *all* of the complicated steps would have been *frigging brilliant!*

She and Macy scoured the printed instructions carefully for the name of whoever their Poldark "benefactor" was on the installation package. It was a fruitless search, so no concealed TG would be visiting the culprit with a big "gotcha" moment in his near future.

With Karl online, Marlyn made some precision jumps to outer gas giants of the system, always appearing behind them so the gamma rays of the White Out would not be seen by the inner system. She had Macy do it several times, and even Alyson, one of two TG1s she had with her.

Alyson was placed in charge of the twenty-five TGs aboard, with Jorl Breaker her second in command. He wasn't a TG1, but he was a very competent and accomplished seventeen-year-old, and a natural leader. Thad and Sarge said he had finished the pre-mission training on Koban with the highest overall physical performance rating of any of the TGs.

Only a few of the TG1s, such as Alyson, Carson, and Ethan, managed to outscore him on movement and eye-hand coordination tasks. They thought that was due to their more frequent Mind Tap inputs, which the three older TG1s received from other TGs in training. The adults had set an age of at least eighteen for the youngest of the TGs to receive the telepathy genes, but that wasn't going to hold any longer, now that the benefits were clearly so great, and no detrimental mental effects had been noted. (Other than the somewhat "swelled" heads of the ten that got the mod first.)

When they made the test Jumps in-system, Alyson, and Fred Saber, the other TG1, received the mental images and messages from the Beagle's two TG1s, when that ship had performed the White Out at Koban. Those messages were sent a couple of days after the Avenger had reached the closer world of Heavyside. The Avenger's TG1s had placed their own safe arrival messages in Tachyon Space when they got here, and the acknowledgement of reception of their message, and the Beagle's reciprocal arrival message, told both ships the other had completed their journeys.

The telepathic messages had "sat," or circulated seemed a more appropriate term, in Tachyon Space, waiting for the intended TG1 receivers to "absorb" them. It had already been noted in testing, that once the intended receiver had picked up a message, even though it might wait for them up to five days to enter Tachyon Space, a second Jump within that five-day window did not find the message ready to repeat for them. Once received, it was gone. That was different from the increased garbling of undetected old messages after five days, turning them into increasing "white noise" before they fully died away.

The Mark was out of the communication loop while parked on Poldark. However, they had a long schedule worked out in advance by Jakob, of possible "windows" of message opportunity for exchanging information. Tet would miss a number of those opportunities, and the needs of the different missions of the Beagle and Avenger would not always align with the roughly five-day "life" of these message windows.

However, from time to time their message windows would overlap when the ships Jumped, and possibly find the ships in a situation where brief messages could be followed up, for a coordinated longer exchange of data via repeat "local" or null Jumps, as they were also called.

With the AI controlled training Jumps out of the way, Karl had demonstrated he could Jump them where they wanted to go more precisely than they were able to do manually. The Krall *preferred* to do navigation manually, zooming in on screen for the destination, then talon tapping the place where they wanted to White Out. It fit with their personality, yet the Olt'kitapi had designed the ships to operate via a more sophisticated method, which accepted electronic input that the Krall ignored or could not use.

Karl's processor was bolted to the deck of the Bridge and mated to one of the input ports of the four navigation and weapons control stations, the consoles located in the center of the Bridge deck. Simply telling Karl what you wanted made the process much faster and more precise, and he would warn of instructions that created high risks (like a Jump into a planetary atmosphere or below its surface). The new acceleration couches were more interactive with the AI, and would automatically adjust to protect the occupants when uncompensated internal accelerations were expected. He also could operate the weapons with microsecond response times, and extreme accuracy through any complex series of maneuvers and accelerations.

The Olt'kitapi had clearly built these ships to allow the Krall to operate them as they did now. However, they also either expected to fly the same ships themselves at times, or expected the Krall to change their personality and start taking full advantage of an advanced tool they had been handed. After so many thousands of years, it had not happened.

No doubt, the Krall had evolved over time to become physically faster, and more adept at manual control, but they were never going to exactly match computer controlled response times and precision. Karl described the inputs he used to control the ship's systems as apparently designed to receive data directly from an organic source, based on the signal levels used, and the feedback returned. It was as if the system was intended to connect directly to the brain of some operator. Yet, other aspects of the control system's input and output were more robust than purely organic control could achieve.

Karl, in a matter of fact tone that concealed the revolutionary aspect of what had been achieved, told them about the scientists that had spent years of study on clanship data ports previously, found on wrecks. They believed the original alien designers employed digital cyber components that supplemented an organic brain.

The researchers had spent years studying abandoned clanship wrecks, trying to understand and copy the technology, but had never found a way to bypass the quantum lockout key that would grant them access. Ingenuity had inferred some aspects of how the data ports worked and what they would send and receive.

However, they never got the internal control modules of the consoles to activate or respond, so they could never test input and feedback loops to see what they did. Not until the Mark of Koban arrived, as a working example of a clanship.

The Mark's functioning control system had been analyzed by an AI larger and more complex than a KP model, and it had set parameters in a previously built programmable test module for the interface. They assumed that someday they *would* find a way to activate a clanship's control modules, and they knew how many input and output channels there were, and the approximate strengths of each signal, just not what the signals were and what they controlled.

That interface module emulated the input required to operate a clanship's systems, and could interpret the feedback for the KP model AI to use. That type of preprogrammed module could now be used with any of the current AIs to operate a clanship, assuming they could get an intact ship to activate. The Katushas, and the quantum encoding they embedded in their tattoos, would activate any equipment the Krall used. Humanity intended to steal technology from the Krall technology thieves, and try to improve on that when they understood how it worked.

Noreen made a stealthed approach to Heavyside on the Normal Space tachyon powered inertialess drive, after first Jumping as close as possible behind a remote Neptune-sized gas giant. It would require a day and a half of travel to Heavyside that they could have covered with a Jump to orbital altitude in seconds.

Sarge had told them at Poldark, where the Krall came and went weekly, the appearance of their three ships wouldn't seem strange. However, Heavyside was in the Rim region on nearly the opposite side of Human Space from the Krall attacks, and the location of a secret Special Operations program. It wasn't a settled colony world, so any gamma ray burst would be suspect. One with the signature of a clanship's mass would draw instant attention and trigger alarms they didn't want activated. The White Out in the Oort cloud would already have drawn attention when it arrived at Heavyside five days later, except they had been towing additional mass and volume with the cargo pods, and that would not match a clanship gamma ray profile.

Karl had common knowledge survey data on Heavyside in his data banks, and Noreen had some word of mouth information on where the spec ops training base was located. The planet had originally been named in the honor of Admiral Elaine Andropov, a long dead war hero from before the Collapse. Now only the spaceport was called Andropov, and the nickname Heavyside had become the de facto name of the planet.

It was considered unsuitable for long-term colonization due to the 1.42 times Earth standard gravity, and terraforming was too expensive for no significant payback. It had a livable biosphere, but simple plants, lichens, and algae had produced an oxygen nitrogen atmosphere. Three hundred fifty years ago, the surface had been cheaply seeded with plant life that would boost the oxygen levels, so that it now was at twenty-two percent. Sea life had been introduced that had taken hold in the three-fifths water covered planet, but only a small amount of shrimp was harvested for the protein, in a minor occupation run by a few locals.

Around Andropov spaceport, there were human crops, protected from one particular pest. The pest was one of a few small sturdy food animals that had managed to do well enough to supplement the meat imports. Who would have thought the puny rabbit would thrive in this gravity, without predators, and unlimited food? Lemmings and voles did well, but they competed for food, and rabbits were winning that battle.

There were vast plains now with a medium height grass on most of it, acceptable by the rabbits that were still expanding their range. A limited number of trees had been accidentally mixed with the seeding, as were wild flowers that could only pollinate via wind, without dedicated insect pollinators, such as bees. Bees were imported at one point, and they died. The local insects paid no attention to flowers. At least there were no mosquito analogues, but with rabbit blood available, it was assumed it was only a matter of time. The mountains were mostly barren, and because of limited plate tectonics, there were no long extended ranges. Most mountains were isolated and of volcanic origin, and there were many active ones on the planet, which still had considerable heat from its slowly cooling core and mantle.

Overall, Heavyside was considered a "shit hole" assignment for the military that was not part of Special Operations, with relatively few permanent residents, and nearly all of them living at Andropov. There was an orbital transfer station that handled shipments of goods inbound (other than spec ops troops, nothing was exported) and people coming and going. There was limited manufacturing of consumer products on the station, and medical care for residents that needed to get out of the gravity well.

The "industry" that sustained the small economy was the PU Army, using the secret budget for the black ops programs. The recruiting to get spec ops candidates brought many young men, and a few women, to the transfer station (most ignorant of what it really required). Many were filtered out early, in a section of the station where Heavyside gravity was maintained.

Being raised on or spending many years on the handful of settled planets with one g or greater gravity was essential. Earth, with a large population, was the lowest benchmark set for gravity of a home planet, but relatively few candidates came from there. As the heart of Hub society, Earth tended to produce fewer people willing to experience the hardships Special Operation demanded and inflicted on its candidates. None of them was told in advance of the surgical implants, performance drugs, or exomuscle booster suits they would almost live in. Not until after they made it through the tough physical training and initial team building, done on-planet.

Late physical washouts, or usually surgical and drug refusals at that level, were still offered prestigious and physically demanding enlistments in Ranger or PU Commando units. Now there were even newly formed Marine units, currently stationed on the largest Capitol ships. The lack of Navy combat fleet actions, with no Krall boarders to repel since the Rhama disaster, made those roles more ceremonial and largely a waste of their ability. They could and did serve as elite forces for protection from Krall raiders on worlds with Navy bases. They would join planetary defenders against raiders that the Krall still used to measure the strengths of future invasion targets, and for novice training.

Once candidates made it past the initial screening, observed by bored spec ops that were either on the temporary disabled list or on a punishment detail, they transferred down to Andropov. Many patriotic hopefuls arrived at the station, many uninvited by recruiters. Some were even criminals, so no effort was made to create records at this stage, thus not shutting the door to some that might have the aptitude for the dirty work. Seventy percent were never sent down to Heavyside anyway. The selected thirty percent from the first screening were shuttled down to the planet. There, on Heavyside, they ran and performed calisthenics for a week. Normally, another ten percent of the original hopefuls were weeded out without ever wasting real training time on them.

At this stage, if you were still part of the more motivated group, instead of credits for a government paid trip home, the remaining twenty percent did some minimal paper work. It was still called that, even though an AI took the data, recorded your retinal patterns, hand and foot prints, and took a DNA sample. The candidates were promised the information would be kept completely confidential, and it *was*, because spec ops functioned somewhat like an interstellar Foreign Legion. This was where your past was forgiven if you could meet the requirements, and you became effectively a new citizen with a clean record. If not, you were allowed to leave without prejudice and the information collected expunged.

This commonly collected data started your records for the project, but contained no personal history or medical background. It only put your name on a company roster, and on a black Smart Fabric jumpsuit, which hinted at the carbon fiber exomuscle suit you could earn.

Half of those issued jumpsuits would not finish the following week. Therefore, a detailed personal history was not collected because it might not matter. The "jumpsuits," their collective group name, were sent to *enjoy* hell week, with "The First Son of a Bitch," to pick out the truly dedicated, unyielding and most motivated candidates from the chaff. From that final group, the personal histories and medical background would finally matter.

SOB-1was Special Ops Base number one. If you eventually made it through SOB-5, following twenty months of progression, you were a full-fledged graduate Special Operations troop, with eye and nerve implants, internal drug vials, and a booster suit to make you a semi- superman. You became a "new" citizen of Human Space, without a prior history if you didn't want one.

It was at Port Andropov where Noreen intended to infiltrate three of her TGs, Jorl Breaker, Yilini Jastrov, and Fred Saber, her second TG1, posing as candidates where they would pretend to "just make it" through the week of rugged planet-side exercise, and be sent on to SOB-1. She intended to allow them to fly stealthed single ships to within walking distance on different sides of the sprawling town, the only sizable city on Heavyside. Kap would remotely fly the single ships back to the Avenger. The latter was a feature they never knew the clanships and small craft had, until Kap proposed to pilot them home after a risk of discovery was discussed for the hidden craft.

At SOB-1, Tet hoped they could discover more about what direction the Special Ops top command would be taking in the future. There should be doctors and researchers there with knowledge of those plans. If the hint Carson received from Mind Tapping Colonel Trakenburg, via a handshake were accurate, there was an intriguing possibility they could be about to try genetic enhancements. Trakenburg himself hoped the PU Army might be ready to embark on a genetic improvement program, unaware it would be similar to the one the Kobani had nearly completed. There might be a commonality of purpose, where they could cooperate, and give them a huge head start on the genetic research learning curve.

If that wasn't the case, Koban could keep its secrets, and wait for the time when the Hub government and its citizens were ready to accept them, or not, if that never happened.

There was no possibility that Noreen would allow her TGs to be held against their will, assuming the camp had anyone that *could* hold them, once they had the answer to the questions and were ready to leave. She could drop down in stealth mode with twenty-four Chameleon Skin flex armor equipped TGs if needed, to pick them up, or the three might just steal transportation back towards Port Andropov and wait for her at any spot in between. SOB-1 was a hundred eight miles from the spaceport, ample room to get her people back. The new transducers would reach the ship if she held station in stealth at seventy miles once a day, at noon local and then back away to a higher ninety-minute orbit.

****

Jorl made his way through the farming district on the east side of the Port city, drawing no particular attention as he walked in on a gravel two-lane road. He'd first stepped onto it five miles from the closest rabbit proof fencing. The mirrored single ship lifted well after he passed the edge of the first planted field, slipping through the atmosphere for over thirty minutes, to avoid a turbulence trail or contrail that might be noticed as it had done on entry.

The number of rabbits surprised him, and made him curious, because he'd never seen one. They were apparently unafraid of him, despite having originally been introduced as a local food animal. They had far outgrown the demand for their meat, and wild ones were safe unless they were too slow to get out of the way of the occasional vehicle. He passed several dried and flattened examples in that category.

Finding the spaceport was no problem, because all roads were like spokes of a wheel, the hub being the control tower and navigation beacon at the hub of the wheel. That was in front of him the entire way, with some low buildings across this roadway that were constructed on the periphery of the one-mile radius landing area.

There were other people on the road ahead of him, some walking his way, some towards the port, and some crossed it on streets that circled the city. There was occasional truck traffic, with people sitting in the open backs, apparently going to work on one of the farms. His fellow TGs would be walking in from other sectors of the town, and the foot traffic would not look particularly unusual to anyone that noticed them. Even their homespun Koban made clothes seemed to fit in when he passed a few people that nodded or waved slightly as he encountered them.

They all seemed to nearly drag their feet and slump when they walked. He became aware that he looked much more comfortable, walking with a lighter step and no slump to his shoulders. He'd just left the Avenger, where the gravity was maintained at Koban normal, and this was seven percent less. Not to mention the fact that he could run miles in this gravity and jump higher than twenty feet flatfooted. He made his shoulders slump slightly, and stopped lifting his feet quite so high.

When he neared the closest-to-port radial road, which circled the landing field just outside the row of buildings blocking his radial street, vehicle activity had picked up. There was quite a bit of traffic here, and about a mile ago, the gravel road had become paved. That was where he encountered the electrified slats in the roadway. There was a mobile robot laser system just beyond that, to keep wild rabbit pests out of the town center, and collect their remains.

There were sidewalks on both side of the three-lane street that circled the cargo buildings around the port. The buildings that gradually replaced fenced fields and food processing sheds had become homes and small businesses. There were street signs at every intersection, but the names and numbers didn't mean anything to Jorl. He saw a man at a loading dock of one of the port buildings, placing boxes in the back of one of the small trucks. He swallowed his nervousness and walked over.

"Excuse me, Sir, can I get some directions?"

The man glanced up at him and saw his youth, fitness, and relatively clean clothes, compared to his own anyway, and drew the obvious conclusion. "Looking for the prelim camp?"

"Prelim camp? Is that where…" he was interrupted.

"That's the place where you new arrivals are normally sent right off the ships, for preliminary indoctrination and physical conditioning. You're looking to join spec ops ain't you?"

"Yes Sir, but I wanted to walk around and see the town first."

The man laughed. "I bet you've had your fill of that by now. From that direction," he pointed back the way Jorl had come, "you were on the opposite side of town from even the few bars we have by the terminal and port. That's pretty dull pickings for an off-worlder. If you have that much pep and energy, to stroll in this gravity for recreation, you might last longer than most of the patriotic but flabby kids that come here. I wish you luck kid." Pausing just briefly, he added, "Say, considering the distance around the A ring, I can save your legs a bit and give you a lift to the induction center if you like."

"I take it this street is the A Ring?" He'd seen a sign.

"It is, and I have a pickup to take over closer to the main terminal, a few doors from the camp entrance. Want that ride, or do you intend to jog?" The man laughed pleasantly, but he obviously didn't think Jorl could go that distance. Tempted to race him in his beat up old truck, Jorl instead accepted his offer.

When they arrived, Jorl could see a sizable cluster of mostly young men, and a handful of sturdy looking young women, gathered around a gate to a fenced off area. They apparently had disembarked from two large buses that were just pulling away.

"Thanks for the ride, Mike." He shook hands and got out of the beat up old truck.

The man who had introduced himself on the ride said, "Like I told you, Jorl, I wish you luck. We need the fighters. If you don't make it here, I hope you try one of the other forces. I spent three years fighting in the PUA on Bollovstic, and if I had not lost both legs at the knees and been evacuated for regrowth, I'd have died there when the bastards sealed it off. I'll fight them again before they get to the Hub worlds. I'm going to be in better shape next time, living here for a few years."

Jorl looked at him with considerably more respect than the casual friendship he offered had already earned him. "I will, Sir, I promise I'll be fighting the Krall some place."

As the truck drove off, Jorl saw Yil in the back of the crowd looking at him. He walked over, seeing that the gate wasn't open yet, and several men were walking towards the gate from inside the compound. Yil stepped a bit farther from the back of the group to speak with Jorl.

"Fred is near the front of the pack, he's been Tapping people as he asks questions, seeing what pops into their minds. Did you realize that these are the first new people we've ever met in our life? I know everyone at home."

"You meant you've seen all their faces. There are a lot of people we see but don't really know."

"Then you will appreciate how many new faces we are seeing here. I do think I've met everyone our age at home."

"That means here they don't know you either. Which is a bit of good luck for you. You should take advantage, and score while you can."

"What are you talking about?"

Jorl pointed to two of the stocky, muscular, and homely young women that were trying out for Special Ops. "They don't know you, so they haven't had their ass dumped by you yet. You should ask one of them out on a date." He laughed, reminding Yil of the number of girls he'd asked out just one time, never to repeat. He had a reputation as a *never love 'em, always leave 'em* sort of guy.

Not denying the truth of the comment, he said, "They're almost ugly!"

"It isn't as if you'll be seeing them again."

"You're an ass sometimes, Jorl."

"I get second dates, I must do something right." He chuckled.

A small cheer sounded as the double gates swung open and gruff, loud voices told them, "Run over to the reception area. What the hell are you flabby morons doing standing there? Move! Move! Move!"

And so, a boring week began for the three TGs, pretending to be exhausted each night and having to flick water surreptitiously on their faces and shirts to simulate sweat. Heavyside was mildly warm at this early fall time, but there was nothing that the exercise could do to provoke heavy perspiration on any of the heat adapted young men.

They followed instructions and stayed just behind the fastest runners, did other calisthenics a bit slower, or collapsed at the same time as the best of the other candidates. Their goal was to be in the top five or ten percent, well above the cutoff point, but not too noticeable or outstanding.

They actually did encounter one problem they had not considered. Even if not pushed hard, their metabolisms demanded a high calorie, high protein diet, and the food provided met that requirement, but it just wasn't served in enough quantity to satisfy them. They discovered there were those that were on their way to dropping out, and the regimen was actually making them sick to their stomach, killing their appetites. In the guise of helping them, they sat with them, urged them on and boosted their spirits, and coincidentally helped them hide the fact they were unable to finish their portions, a sure sign that a hopeful was on a downhill slide. The extra food was enough to keep the TGs from being noticed by asking for seconds at every meal.

When the week ended, they were easily placed in the group that was directed to sit at a console to talk to an AI. They gave it their name, real or phony didn't matter to spec ops. They provided scans of their hand and footprints for quick battlefield identification (parts could be blown off so they took all four), retinal scans for security access (eyes could be regrown but not duplicated), and a swab of DNA for graves registration (they were told). Then they tossed away the temporary and daily disposable exercise clothes they were issued each morning, and slipped into black jumpsuits with their name on the left chest. These fit remarkably well, proving their bodies had been scanned at some point to make the patterns.

Surprising all three of the TGs, was one of the now somewhat trimmed down women who had made it to this point. It made them wonder if Alyson should have come with them, as a second TG1. Only, it was obvious that her pretty face and shapely figure would have been the focus of far too much attention when she kept up with the best of the men. Because of that, her eating like a voracious bear would be noticed, simply by sitting with some lucky close-to-washing-out male that shared food with her.

At least one of them had been able to report in to Captain Renaldo nearly each day when she lowered the stealthed ship to seventy miles over Port Andropov, and often all three could Link at lunchtime. She told them the ship's remote viewing system was able to identify them on many cloud free days. Alyson spoke to them one day and playfully told Yil he must have already asked the one remaining young lady out on a date.

He sounded defensive. "We don't get any time away, besides, she started out butt ugly and muscled, and slimming down through running hasn't helped her looks. What made you think I'd dated her?"

"We saw that she sat near you at breakfast this morning, and you didn't even look her way. Ignoring old flames is your trademark, right, Yil?" Her laughter tinkled through his transducer and the transducers of the other two TGs. They grinned as his face turned red.

He had asked Alyson out once, even if she was a year older. She told him she had heard of his love-'em and leave-'em one-night stands. She kept reminding him of that reputation whenever the opportunity arose.

Jorl chimed in, "He won't get another chance to ask her out either. We take a bus to SOB-1 after lunch. After hell week, she'll be lost to his charms forever. She barely made it through this last week."

The TGs were clustered at a bench in isolation, eating their rations and pretending to talk to one another to cover their transducer conversations with the Avenger. Normally one or two of them would be boosting the morale of a candidate that was on the verge of quitting, picking at their subject's uneaten food as the exhausted man listened to their encouragement. Today, only the candidates that had passed this round of physical testing had the black jumpsuits. It was going to be a hungry bus trip for the three.

They arrived at the first SOB after the normal dinner hour, spending four hours on jouncy dirt roads, which took the jubilant "jumpsuits" to their first actual Special Ops training base. The arrival time came after the normal meal service for the camp staff, so there was a help yourself chow line set up, and the TGs heavily loaded their trays and split up to sit with men whom they had established as casual acquaintances in the past week.

They learned the previous cycle of trainees had moved on to SOB-2 several days earlier. They would be here for six weeks, as their bodies were acclimated to Heavyside's gravity.

The TGs wanted simply to blend in with the group. Nevertheless, they had unwittingly attracted some degree of attention from the spec ops NCOs that had put them through their paces this past week. They were looking for men that had demonstrated signs of teamwork, or team building attitudes, as well as physical ability. The three TGs, although deliberately not excelling at the exercise, and who had selfish motives for their encouragement of the poorly performing candidates, were identified as three potential squad leaders, two per platoon of the six platoons that would start training tomorrow.

This resulted in the TGs being separated and sent to different platoons, for what they were all told would be a very short night of sleep. The activities they expected to be conducting in the morning were apparent from the mile oval track and practice courses laid out, which they saw in the fading light of their arrival. It appeared to be a larger version of the obstacle course in the crater on Poldark, built for the TGs in Captain Mirikami's group. In short, it was a kindergarten playground. With the first full stomach's they had experienced for a week, the TGs settled in for a comfortable nap.

They were assigned bunks, single level two-foot high narrow pallets, seven feet long, with an empty chest at the foot, and an equally empty wall locker several feet from the head, sixteen bunks total, and eight per side. Jorl was assigned the first billet inside the main entryway, on the left. They were told to strip to their skivvies, and slip between a slit in the fabric located a bit below the raised built in pillow at the head. It was surprisingly comfortable, and cozy. The fabric of the top could be pulled up to your neck or pushed down to your waist, and if you kicked for slack, it stretched to give it to you. This bunk was one of the best feeling beds Jorl had ever laid on, although a few gripes were heard about how narrow they were. He was asleep in minutes after the lights were out.

To their surprise, when they were awakened at a "late" hour, 0500, they were fed, and then led to an auditorium where they were told they would meet the base commander, their training staff, and then talk to some doctors. It sounded even more boring than the tame looking obstacle course.

Jorl saw Fred and Yil with their respective platoons as they filed in and sat in Living Plastic chairs, which rose from the malleable preprogramed floor, each row color-coded for the platoons and eight man squads. "So you morons won't sit in the wrong sections," an NCO told them as they entered.

Jorl was in the dark blue squad and their section was second row from the front, behind the light blue squad, and by virtue of his last name of Breaker, he found he was close to the center of his alphabetically sorted squad. He was seated near the center of the second row of seats, looking up at a three-foot elevated stage, with a podium to the left side, and a number of Living Plastic chairs up there as well. He noticed that the chairs the trainees used were hard and unyielding, something that had to be programmed into the plastic matrix to keep them rigid. This was a subtle object lesson that they wanted you uncomfortable and awake.

The introductions were done by a lieutenant, whose name Jorl forgot almost as soon as he said it. That process started after they were called to attention, which the new recruits performed raggedly, other than those that were already in the military. Next, they were listening to a litany of names and ranks, that had little meaning to the civilian candidates in the group (formerly civilian now, Jorl supposed), although some were straight from the regular PU Army or Navy.

When they were permitted to sit again it was after the base commander was introduced, a Colonel Michel Dearborn. He was in fatigues, and was a tall man, who seemed a bit bulky to be the commander of an ultra-physically fit Special Operations unit, until Jorl caught a glimpse of the black exomuscle suit he was wearing under the uniform. That was when a sleeve pulled back slightly, exposing the black Booster Suit at his wrist when he pointed to a holo screen that contained the layout of the camp. There were two clearly marked areas, which trainees were not allowed to enter. Jorl assumed these were locations of interest for the TGs.

Before leaving the stage with the lieutenant and another officer that had not spoken after the introductions, Colonel Dearborn yielded the podium to an NCO he referred to as "Top", also introduced earlier, First Sergeant William Crager. They were told they would be hearing a lot from him.

The first thing they heard from him as he reached the podium was, "Atten-Hut!" He bellowed, not needing the amplification of the extruded boom mike on the podium. The trainees bounded to their feet as the officers left the stage.

"At ease and be seated." He looked around the room of ninety-six black jumpsuits. His eyes darted particularly to some faces in each row of eight, twelve in all, and he paused on each of those, for a second or two. One of the faces, Jorl was certain, was his.

Jorl had heard that the spec ops troops on Poldark had eye implants and IR detection capability. What he didn't know was that his face, the other two TG's faces, and thirteen or fourteen other men had been designated for Crager by his onboard AI, as men to watch for possible team leadership roles in the training unit. It was unlikely that even half of those present would make it through the entire course.

Crager thought three of the faces might be running a bit of a fever, which considering the typical immune systems of today shouldn't last long. It was likely something they were recently exposed to, with so many people mixed from all over Human Space, and placed in crowded conditions, under physical stress for the last week at Port Andropov.

He started forthright, and blunt. "I know most of you are here to contribute to the fight against the Krall. A handful of you just want to become one of the alleged supermen of spec ops. That handful will not complete the training. They never do. If that's your current motivation, your attitude will change or you *will* be weeded out. If you will not place the team's goals first, and you try to go it alone, to excel as a superstar, then like a failed star, you will fizzle out like some sorry-assed brown dwarf. At some point, you will need help, and no team member will be willing to offer it to you because you will have been identified as a selfish loner.

"The Krall mostly fight that way, as loners, because they are physically superior to us in every way and distain teamwork. They seldom come to the aid of another warrior, and frankly seldom need to do so. No matter what you have heard about Special Operations troopers, and I'll tell you that many of the rumors you hear are true, we do have extraordinary capabilities that the typical soldier can't match. However, we must normally team together to beat even one of the enemy warriors."

He placed his hands on the sides of podium. "I doubt many of you have seen a Krall warrior up close, in detail. Or else you might not be alive to be here. Let me show you one of our opponents, we keep it in a stasis field for safety. Study him carefully."

A humming sound came from the stage as a Krall warrior lifted on an elevator platform at front center stage, long knives in each taloned hand. It was frozen in a shimmering charged stasis field, poised right at the front edge of the stage, as a fully red-skinned mature and massive warrior. The men in the front row, feeling almost under the forward leaning figure, actually pulled back a bit from the over two-meter tall alien. It was that tall despite its slightly crouched posture, appearing prepared to leap from the stage. The red pupils in black orbs were glaring, hate filled, down into the center of the mass of seated men and one woman, frozen in electronic stasis, yet ready to leap into them and cut their hearts out.

"Unarmed as you are, this single warrior, if released, could certainly kill everyone in this room if we were trapped in here with it, the unarmed spec ops training staff included. If there were a single door or window for escape, and a few of you made it out, you might think you had survived. Consider this. It can run much faster than you can, and its sense of smell can track you down, even days later, and find you in total darkness. It can react and move five times faster than you can, and tear you limb from limb without effort."

The room was transfixed on the savage evil looking figure. Suddenly, the misty stasis field flickered, and went off. With a deafening roar, the warrior leaped from the stage into the midst of the front rows, slashing left and right with blood spattering high, and the men there screamed and recoiled, or fell to the floor. Those to the sides leaped to their feet to run when the sound and motion stopped instantly, The Krall stood frozen again, with a human body held aloft and impaled on one of the long knives. The victim was dressed in civilian clothing, not a black jumpsuit.

"As you were," Crager bellowed as the gory image winked out. The recorded attack, played for the intended effect, was a state of the art hologram. Shaken, but with nervous laughter, the men reseated themselves in any empty seat. Some had leaped over rows of seats to get out of the way. The Top Sergeant had been studying their reactions before and after they regained their composure and seats.

Not showing amusement, Crager made an observation. "What you just saw was a recording of an actual attack made on a civilian population, in an urban setting on Fjord some years ago. This attack was by one of the berserker warriors the Krall sometimes send there to die on a single warrior raid. This is apparently done as some form of punishment for the warrior, yet gives it a fighting death. This one was armed only with the knives you saw. It came alone in a stealthed single ship, released by a clanship from orbit. It killed or wounded almost two hundred civilians before it could be killed. Its single ship detonated and killed another hundred and nine people in the building on whose roof it landed." He nodded as the men finally were reseated.

"That recording was not speeded up in the slightest. The movement of the Krall was real time, and happened as fast as it appeared that it did. That is what we are confronting. Some of you have been recruited from the PU Army, and may have been in combat before. This demonstration might not be necessary for you. However, we have many present here that have never seen video of a Krall in full slaughter mode, because the PU government wants to shield the public from such horror," he paused. "That's pure bullshit!"

"That Krall would have done exactly the same thing if it had been rampaging through a preschool. We are nearly useless animals to them, valued only for our ability to fight back, and not very highly valued at that. There are no such things as fair rules of war to them."

He amended that slightly. "Outside of no weapons of mass destruction that can be used by us against *them*, that is. *They* certainly are not held to that rule, if you remember Rhama and that single Eight Ball impact.

"Hell, there were no such rules in human wars of the past. At least any that was followed consistently, despite international or interplanetary agreements to the so-called rules. However, humans did not aim for the complete destruction of all of humanity in our wars. Sometimes ethnic groups of humans have been targeted for destruction by another group, but obviously not our entire species. The only time we even came close to that was the Gene War, and that was unintentional."

We have to fight them at any cost, and offer them no quarter, because we will not receive any. There is no surrender possible, no truce to be had. It is win, or die, and we are not winning right now. Not even close."

He looked back around the room, and noted that some of the previously designated possible leadership faces had moved to a new seat, based on the facial recognition of his AI. The three with possible fever had not moved from their seats, but only the one in the center of the second row was a surprise. Breaker (the name appeared as he looked at the young man) was calmly sitting where he had been seated before, smiling, even though the four faces on either side of him had changed seats, per the AI's flags. He must have retaken his original seat.

In fact, had he checked, none of the three (fevered) faces had even left their seats when the realistic looking Krall leaped from the stage. For Fred and Yil, the threat to them, from their positions midway back in the auditorium wasn't imminent anyway. However, just as had Jorl, they instantly recognized the moment the solid looking figure leaped into the air that it couldn't be real. It lifted too high, and went in too slow an arc in this high gravity to be anything but a hologram recording, an event that had happened in a lower gravity field. They also noted that its eyes were focused in the wrong place in the audience (too far back) than where it *should* land in 1.41 g's, and the knives swung at wrong targets among the potential victims in jumpsuits. The final confirmation, when the heavy body came down, was that it didn't actually displace or crumple anyone. All the movement seen and noise heard came from the trainees shouting and lunging aside.

Fred and Yil were watching the panicked reactions in front of them with calm interest. Jorl on the other hand, was engaged in physically holding people off himself, or deflecting their hands and feet from his face and groin as they tried to climb over him. He kept one man from diving headlong into the row behind him by his gathered jumpsuit fabric before the demonstration was frozen. He was amused to see that his own head, when he leaned to the side to see better, had been buried in the ass of the Krall's holographic image. He erased his grin when he noted Crager looking his way as he lowered the man he'd held aloft, shortly after the hologram projector shut down.

After the demonstration, everyone was as awake as they could be made now, and two of the other NCOs had a few things to pass along in this morning's indoctrination.

Sergeant First Class Robert Norris would be in charge of much of their training, and outlined their expected progression over the next few months, and what they would do later this morning.

Staff Sergeant Juan Eldridge was in charge of supply, and he was the company quartermaster. He discussed the uniform issue they would be receiving later that day. They would also receive some toiletries, but unless anyone had mutations that permitted facial hair, or had applied topical ointments to grow such, no one would require shaving materials. He noted, as they surely knew by now, that their bunks were in the same Smart line of materials as the fabric of the uniforms were, and the furniture was Living Plastic. There would be no training time wasted on issuing fresh bedding, since their bunks were self-cleaning and sanitizing, and never needed to be "made." Forestalling the questions often heard early in training, he told them they would not be issued Chameleon Skins for the first two months, and the fitting for the black Booster Suits would not come for four months. It was unsaid, but there was no need to provide these more expensive items before the physical training and team building had weeded out many of those that were not going to last long enough to justify the expense.

When this part was over, they were ordered to stand at the back of the auditorium while it reconfigured itself into twenty sets of desks and chair combos, with side chairs, and sound baffles for visual and audio privacy. Then "hurry up and wait" went into effect as twenty at a time entered the cubes and provided a range of personal health history, and answered questions, some psychological in nature about fears they might have of enclosed spaces, high places, fire, water, insects or animals, or nearly any phobias. There were standard ways of addressing these issues, some of which were drug related solutions, and others employed mental exercises and preparation.

Genetics had eliminated many chemical imbalances in the brain and body hundreds of years earlier, but which could sometimes reappear due to environmental effects and minor mutations. Jorl was again one of the first twenty to be seated, going in alphabetical order.

As he entered the indicated cubical, he was met by an attractive mature woman who introduced herself as Dr. Lisa Markel. Jorl immediately noticed her accent in Standard sounded like that of Carson's dad, Dr. Dillon Martin, and that of Dr. Maggi Fisher, both of whom he knew were from Rhama. For the first time in his life, Jorl wondered what sort of accent *he* had.

Naturally, he never considered he had an accent at all. His father, who had only a brief one-year marriage contract with his mother in Prime City, was an early captive from a small courier Jump ship, and a former Jump Drive engineer from New Glasgow, a Rim world. His mother was a mousy woman who was the widow of a man killed in combat testing on Koban. She simply wanted a child to fill the void of her two children left behind on her home of Fjord, when she had arranged to go on a business trip with her husband. Surrounded by people from so many planets, Jorl had a conglomerate of their speech patterns, as did nearly all of the kids raised in Prime City. A few TGs from Hub City were born of parents already paired when they were captured on their passenger liners, and their children often sounded more like their parents.

He decided to show his presumed sophistication, and said, "You sound like some people I know from Rhama."

She merely smiled at him, and asked him to sit. She took her seat, a swivel chair that she angled to see him better, as he sat beside her desk. The desk was naturally only a simulated one, and the only feature was a screen incorporated in the top, which was a raised wide panel screen that only she could see.

Unknown to Jorl, the chair he was using was loaded with sensors that fed his physiological responses to the screen Dr. Markel could observe. It wasn't anything like a lie detector, but she was interested in his responses to her test questions. She asked a number of health related questions, asking about any accidents he may have had, broken bones, regrowth procedures, and so forth. His answer to all was “none.”

Even before he became a TG, he was born an SG, and had a lifelong respect for the gravity of Koban, and a body well adapted to its conditions. He had not been a daredevil, but did display better than average coordination, and sense of spatial awareness that had led him to some carefully managed gymnastics as an SG. That skill stood him in good stead now that he was a TG.

She seemed to be looking at his responses with considerable interest. Jorl was being completely honest. Knowing in advance some of the types of questioning they would undergo (based on TG1 Taps of spec ops troopers on Poldark); they had decided being truthful was the best course, concealing only details, if asked, about their home world. Spec ops claimed not to be interested in that anyway.

She quickly moved on to the battery of psychological questions, inquiring about phobias he might have. He admitted he once had a fear of heights, which he had overcome with gymnastics training. True. Falling very far in 1.52 G’s was serious, but here on Heavyside it was only slightly less so. With his TG coordination and strength, he felt there was very little that he feared now. Again, as she made her way down the list of questions fed to her on screen, she seemed rather studious after his replies. She didn’t look skeptical, nor were there raised eyebrows or doubtful glances towards him, but she focused on whatever she was seeing. He was burning with curiosity, and had noticed that she made almost no notes into the system by keyboard, nor did she speak to the AI system Jorl was certain must be involved. She only tapped a scroll key to get to the next questions.

It didn’t take long, and in less than twenty minutes, they were through. She stood, ushered him to the opening in the cubical, and told him to speak to the corporal at a desk at the end of the hall formed by the line of cubicles. That corporal handed him an electronic chit, and gave him instructions for finding the Supply depot, next to the auditorium. He walked out with two other trainees.

He took his ditty bag of toiletries, and his new wrinkle proof fitted uniforms to the barracks. He placed the toiletries on a top shelf in his clothes locker exactly as a chart told him to do, and arranged his two uniforms as a chart directed. He would be staying in his jumpsuit for most of this “hell week,” but it was already 0700, and it had been a slow day.

That ended abruptly when a corporal stepped in and sent the six men inside the barracks out to the obstacle course, to start their “familiarization” with a layout that was promised to grow more difficult as they progressed. Jorl hoped he wouldn’t get bored.

****

As Dr. Markel finished her fifth and final interview, she now had two examples of the same anomaly on her monitor. Jorl Breaker had been the first, and a Fred Saber had sent the signal levels from the chair sensors to the top of her display.

The shape of the response curves themselves looked normal, and didn't display any spikes in the answers to the psychological questions, nor did she or the AI find any contradictions in stated answers that failed to match a physiological response. For example, neither man had said they don't fear stinging insects while their left or right brain said they really did. They had not tried to fool her, or hide any phobias. Actually, that was a slight abnormality, because her interviews normally found one or two examples of hiding a minor known fear of something, or a person's brain revealed they had a fear or revulsion they were not consciously aware they had.

A spec ops soldier that was infiltrating through enemy lines and had a fear of snakes, or an absolute revulsion of feces in a drainage ditch touching him, needed psychological preparation to confront these emotions, and learn to control his response. Part of that control could come after the electrical nerve implants were added, and were linked through the AI embedded under the skin. If a person's phobias were known in advance, there were ways to suppress an involuntary reaction, which otherwise might give him away at a crucial moment.

Dr. Merkel was on the team of specialists that designed the nerve overlays, which gave the recipient faster response times, and she helped target programs in the AI's to customize their use for each individual. This entry point interview was the first of several that would be conducted as the trainees encountered more circumstances where their fears might be exposed. There were jungle, mountain, winter and desert combat conditions replicated on Heavyside, with even an actual sewer infiltration course (based on a Poldark field example), and other simulations of alien world situations the troopers might one day face.

Spec ops training no longer focused very much on water situations, as the early teams had done, so a strong aptitude for swimming, or a mild fear of drowning were less significant in operations against the Krall. The enemy themselves didn't care for deep water, or build installations that employed waterways. Nevertheless, they had an impressive array of effective and deadly detection systems for defending against waterborne intruders. Per the military analysts, the Krall's sophisticated amphibious defense hardware appeared to be additional examples of borrowed or stolen technology, which was considerably more elaborate than much of what they used for land warfare. Some previous race they faced must have been well versed on such defenses.

On a smaller scale, fighting on or in water was similar to the Krall's avoidance of space warfare, where operation of a clanship involved the skills of only a few warriors on the command deck, but a loss of the ship could wipe out an entire raiding party in the hold, which had never fired a shot.

Cost versus benefit for the Krall considered a handful of surviving warriors, out of hundreds after a raid or from part of a larger invasion assault, were valuable breeding assets when recovered. The loss of a clanship (the material value of the ship seemed negligible to them) was also the loss of the crew and warriors in the hold, with no return on the clan's breeder investment. Human persistence in fighting in ways the Krall didn't like resulted in extremely heavy human losses, or serious damage to the planet's ecology to change their behavior.

Rhama's population and environment was devastated by a single Krall Eight Ball, which *could* have been accelerated to an appreciable fraction of light speed, thus eradicating all higher life on the world by its impact. That lesser impact was used to deter further space attacks by human fleets, which themselves were costly in human ships lost.

Bollovstic, before that world's fall, had a thriving fishery and employed sea shipping for much of its Rim world level of local economy. Persistent human use of assaults and infiltration from coasts and rivers had caused the Krall to turn that world's oceans and waterways into death traps for any shipping, and had killed off essentially all larger life forms in the oceans by automated hunter killers of anything that moved under water, and detection systems that drew bombardments of any surface activity. Since the Krall did not intend to inhabit the planet, they didn't care how devastated its ecology was when they departed. It was a disposable battleground.

Markel went to one of the technicians that maintained the auditorium Living Plastic morphing system. "Alois, I need you to check the monitor and chair in cubicle fourteen, the one I happened to sign onto this morning. The signal levels were far higher than normal, and I had to adjust the scale to keep the peaks down where I could see them on responses. The left and right brain conflict comparison was good, and the correlation between different subject matters was proportional, but there was excessive amplification. Check the results for my first responder, and my last one. They both did the same thing. The other two men and one woman looked normal as far as their data peaks."

Alois looked up in interest. "Dr. Chalders had one that did something like that. He had me come in and look at his system right after his third trainee left. All I could determine was that the sensors in the chair was sending stronger signals than usual. It looked normal for me and for Chalders when we sat in the chair." He called up her interview results from this morning, and looked at the signal levels registered on his own screen.

"Yep, that's similar to what we saw on his screen. The relative peak heights and curves were fine; they were simply a factor of ten higher than the strength of the nerve impulses expected. There isn't an automatic level adjustment programed for that. I'll bet you simply ran the amplitude down using the slide control to see what you wanted."

"I did. Except, I've done dozens of these interviews. Why would we suddenly get high levels unless an amplifier was boosting the signal?"

"Dunno. Let me ask Karp."

"Karp," he called on the KP model AI directly. "There were three unusually high signals seen today on the monitored interviews just finished. How were they amplified, and why? Answer to me, and to Dr. Markel who is with me, please."

"Sir, there were no amplified signals in the referenced data of the three interviews I believe you are referring to, two conducted from cube fourteen and one from cube nine."

"Those are the cubes that I meant, Karl, but how did their nerve impulses get so amplified? They were well above normal."

"Sir, there was no additional amplification applied beyond normal, and the signal strength was greater than the scale factor that was selected. Therefore, the peaks of the impulses went above the maximum level selected for each display. All three examples were displayed in their entirety on screen when the scale factor was properly adjusted."

That didn't sound like an answer to the technician. "Why were they greater than the screen's selected scale factor?"

"Sir, the base input was a stronger signal than previous and subsequent individuals registered on the sensors in the two chairs."

This was one of those damned logic loops, where AIs sometimes seemed to lead people around in circles. "And why was the input signal stronger than for the other people?"

"Sir, I do not have parameters in my data base for the full range of possible signal levels for all humans, and the default scale factor used was set as a fixed parameter by the original programing. I can automatically adjust the display scale in the future, to prevent overdriving the wave form seen on the screen, if that is preferred."

"Yes. Please do that Karl." To the technician this resolved the issue.

"That was an easy fix, Doc. I'll let the AI take care of it for us. It's what they're here to do."

In Alois' mind, the next time this happened the maximum signal level, whatever it was, would be fully depicted on the screen. The Doctor had just said the comparative levels between the two sides of the brain were within parameters, with no conflicting references, deception, or confusion indicated. The shape of the waveform curves was also typical, the crests simply being higher than the display's preselected scale factor.

Markel thought this explanation sounded a bit off kilter to her, but the technician was satisfied that he'd instructed the AI to adjust for the problem. She shrugged, and went to her office, no longer curious why the signal strength from those three nervous systems registered ten times higher than for a normal human.

****

Jorl pretended to lend a hand to Fred, as he climbed over the peak of a "V" shaped steep log incline that rose about thirty feet. Most of the other men on the course were starting to show real fatigue as they sweated their way around the course for the third time.

They gathered in lines of eight before starting each round, and lifted a ten-inch, sixteen-foot long wooden pole off the ground. They lifted it to their left shoulders, and then jointly pushed it overhead, with arms extended, and lowered it to their right shoulders. They repeated this with the other shoulder four times before lowering it to the ground. Another random team of eight might be instructed to sit with the same size log cradled in their arms; their toes hooked under a smaller elevated wood rail, and perform group sit-ups, with the heavy log clutched to their chests.

Griping Fred's hand, Jorl was updated on what Fred had picked up from the same interviewer Jorl had spoken with earlier that morning. Fred had broken protocol, under the guise of ignorance of the rules of no contact, and shook her hand as he left, asking her a pointed question.

In response to, "Gee, what will spec ops capability be like by the time I finish training?" he sensed the flash of fear as she thought of breaking the law, and of her genetic research. They were seeking to replicate the three hundred year old clone mods for strength and endurance. The reliance on performance enhancing drugs was too limiting, and too slow to take effect, and required long down times after extended use. Her actual spoken reply was that she wasn't party to what technological enhancements were planned.

Fred was surprised that there was such a small cadre of people here in the loop of what was being attempted. Only six people knew, and only four of those were scientists. There were relatively few staff people, yet bringing in new people increased the chances of a leak or discovery. That was why she did double duty, performing interviews, which did not require an actual scientist to conduct.

It was ironic that they had only a small group of idealists and patriots that were forced to operate in secret. That was much like the Koban Committee had done under the Krall's eyes. The group later evolved into calling themselves the Inner Circle when the Krall left, but they kept their full goals confidential from the other former captives for years, knowing of the probable opposition to the use of Koban genes. These people at SOB-1 feared their own government, in parallel with Mirikami's own concerns.

As Fred and Jorl pretended to cautiously step down the steep log slope, Fred wondered, "Is this as much as Captain Mirikami needed to know? That they want to do what we did, at least at the very start?"

Jorl shrugged, "Even if it is, they can't do what we did, not without Koban genes. Carson told us the spec ops exomuscle suits barely match what an SG can do, and they don't have the heat and cold adaptations, or the endurance. I guess using the suits on top of the clone mods would help them a great deal. Their electronic eye display enhancements and small AIs are super cool, and that IR sense."

"We'll have the IR vision matched with riper genes, and we won't need an audio system to hear high Krall speech, or have to use a handheld scent device to detect their stinky red asses. I also believe we can think as well or better than a pocket AI."

Reaching a platform at the bottom they jumped five feet to the base of a wide rope lattice, to climb up fifty feet, over and then down the other side. A corporal, one of the course monitors, had watched them talking as they had come down the log ramp.

"You two chatty pals can just casually loop the course two more times while your teammates go eat a leisurely lunch."

Ten minutes for mouth stuffing a meat sandwich and gulping water while standing was hardly leisurely, but the lack of any sort of meal mattered to both of their high metabolisms.

Jorl tried to salvage their meal. "Corp, if we beat everyone ahead of us on this rotation to the end, can we still eat lunch?" The two had been staying roughly in the center of the sixteen they had started with on this cycle. They were on the backside of the winding course, about half way to the finish line.

"Hell, I watched you two sissies creeping down that ramp. You won't even catch that girl just two apparatus ahead of you."

Without even a glance at one another for agreement, they easily climbed the lattice, nearly dropped down the other side in a reckless looking move, trying to make it look clumsy, and continued to catch and pass the people they had allowed to pass or stay in front of them. Those behind them started cheering them on, and those in front looked over their shoulders at the noise, and increased their own efforts to stay in front.

They practically crawled over Grandy, as she low crawled under low netting. The woman was still holding her own with many of the men. She laughed in good nature as they passed her, and caught up to the next man just ahead of her. He wasn't quite so friendly, and tried to get in their way, but to no avail. Without making it look too obviously easy, they caught the next athetletic looking man, the leader on this rotation and the two that had come before, passing him less than a hundred fifty feet from the end. They ran down the length of seventy-five feet of parallel logs, then stepping twenty-five feet from log to log, which were at right angles to the course, placed five feet apart, then jumped into a mud pit and jogged to the finish line together. They pretended to be winded as the corporal, who had cut across the course, using his Booster Suit for speed, reached them.

"Not too bad, lads. Go eat. However, now that you proved you can do that when pushed, I'll expect that much out of you every day this week." He uttered his best diabolical laugh, as Fred and Jorl provided a pair of fake groans, then trotted off to eat, with grins unseen.

They saw Yil already eating as they got in line for a sandwich tray. His group had been ahead of them on the rotation prior to "lunch." The platoons were not exercising together as units this first morning, with the interviews throwing the schedule off and splitting platoons. They joined him just as he was cramming the last of his food in his mouth and washing it down with a large gulp of water. Fred casually leaned on the same standup table, touching Yil's hand as he set his own tray down. Yil looked at Jorl as he got the rapid-fire Tap update, winked and grinned as he ran off with the men he was grouped with for now. They were accompanied by the motivational bellow of a different corporal, "Move your flabby asses, you over fed lazy pigs."

No trainee walked anywhere at SOB-1.

****

At the end of "hell week," the ranks had reduced by two full platoons, so there was exactly sixty-four of the initial ninety-six remaining. The "miraculous" number seemed like it was arrived at by design. They now comprised four full platoons, ready to enter the next phase of training. The men (Grandy had not made the final cut) had spent three continuous weeks working out in Heavyside gravity. First, they worked out on the orbital station (except for the three TGs), then at the Port Andropov camp, and finally at SOB-1.

They received their first weekend off, which was actually only respite from the obstacle course. They still ran to classes, to chow, to barracks, to any place they were told to go, which was frequently. Studies had shown that in a higher gravity field, the human body needed some time to adjust after strenuous exercise, to increase the addition of muscle fiber after such an extended series of workouts. The men received more protein in their meals, and they were given supplements, to promote new tissue growth.

The TGs accepted all of the supplements assuming they wouldn't hurt them, even if not needed. They were informed by Captain Renaldo that they might have a bit more unsupervised time in the weeks to come. She was formulating an action plan to use the TGs presence, and their abilities, to render a bit of technology transfer, before pulling her three people out of the camp.

The knowledge that there were some people wanting to work on human genetic improvement, but were forced to start nearly from scratch, pushed her to the decision. Unable to converse with Mirikami, she had moved out to a position behind a gas giant, and on a scheduled day for possible communication, she null Jumped and was able to exchange information with the Beagle.

The excitement that the expedition had made contact with a Prada group on the newly named Haven was astonishing, but that news was soon shifted to a back burner as she learned a fact that was more personally important, and also helped focus her mind on completing her present mission as soon as practical.

She shared the limited knowledge she had, of the future path a few people in the Special Operations midlevel command structure wanted to follow. She requested guidance on what genetic information might be shared, reminding Marlyn that her AI, Karl, had the encrypted clone mod data in storage, copied from Jakob on the Mark of Koban, before the AI was included in the cargo pods.

Through Alyson, Noreen asked Marlyn to radio Koban, to speak to Aldry or Rafe for help in identifying what genetic data was safe to provide to a secret group within an already secretive Special Operations organization.

Maggi, on the Beagle, stunned Noreen and Alyson when she surprisingly sent a series of Tachyon Space propagated TG1 messages directly to Alyson. The initial impact, as Alyson excitedly told her captain who had contacted them and how it was possible, left Noreen flabbergasted and nearly breathless.

It was possible for an SG to be enhanced to TG1 level, perhaps even higher thanks to the modified nanites and med labs that Marlyn had taken to Koban. Getting home soon was definitely on Noreen's mind, but her present mission had to be topped off with a gift. Maggi described how to select the right material from Karl's database, which Alyson passed to the AI, along with Noreen's personal key to allow the files to be decrypted and copied to a data cube.

Holding the black cube, Noreen said, “This data cube would have earned us extermination from the Krall had they known we brought it with us to Koban. I didn’t know that then of course, and neither did Tet. Now it could deliver personal destruction to those we pass it to, from their own government. On the other hand, it can help with delivering all of humanity from Krall destruction if the information is used properly. So small, and yet the most powerful weapon we have against the Krall. Information to make ourselves stronger than they are.” She looked at Alyson beside her, a product of this same information, and more. She was a lovely young woman, *human*, and could kill a Krall with her bare hands.

“The Beagle wasn’t waiting for anything else from us were they, Alyson?”

“No Mam. Dr. Fisher signed off after I acknowledged that I had received and understood her last message. Wow, I *never* expected to sense her mind on that last series of null Jumps. I had Tapped her mind before of course, in the few days after I became a TG1. Her mind ‘flavor’ was obvious to me. She also told me that Bradley, Captain Greeves second son, is a TG2 now. He has *all* of the Koban mods, as do most of the TGs on the crew. Bradley told Maggi the cats were right. Most people do have strong odors. I think general hygiene will improve, particularly with boys, once they all can smell their own feet.” Her laugh was light and pleasant.

Laughing with her, Noreen told her to go down and place the cube in one of the single ships. She had been tempted to let one of the other TGs pilot it down, but decided that Karl could remotely operate it, and despite the lack of planetary defenses here, there was no need to risk anyone, however slight the danger was.

After leaving the shadow of the gas giant, the Avenger returned to a low orbit over Heavyside. Still stealthed, Noreen rotated the ship to place the internal docking station for the single ship facing away from the planet, and its ground based radars. She had Karl open the small outer hatch, making a brief hole in their stealth coverage. Karl remotely piloted the single ship out, having switched on its own stealth mode, and flew it towards the location of SOB-1 below.

The small craft would arrive in darkness, since even stealthed from radar, and set to mimic the sky or background for potential watchers on the ground, its motion might be noticed as a ripple passing in front of clouds or mountains in daylight. At night, a few added twinkles to the stars should not be noticed. There was a normally dry ravine near SOB-1, and the ship was lightly set down in that, less than a mile from the base security fence. It was a few hundred feet outside a perimeter road, which motorized patrols followed around the fence at random intervals.

Although the base conducted classified spec ops training, and conducted radical surgery to embed state of the art technological enhancements in their troopers, it was not a high security secret installation. The Krall could care less, and there was no human enemy from which to hide the technology.

One of the TGs would need to sneak off the base, enter the small ship and retrieve the data cube and a small tissue sample, and return. The tissue sample was taken from Macy, the Avenger’s Chief Engineer (the former Drive Rat was the only maintenance person aboard, actually, and an SG). She and Noreen were technically both just SGs, but Noreen had also long ago opted to receive the parallel Koban nervous system gene mod, in order to pass it on to her children. Macy had not done that, so her tissue was proof of concept that the clone DNA changes described on the cube were possible, and had been performed successfully. It did not reveal the Koban genes for an organic superconducting nervous system. That was a detail passed by Maggi, through her messages to Alyson, which might have slipped by Noreen. Help them, but don't reveal all of the genome changes, not before you knew what sort of reception that would have.

The intent was to later slip into one of the areas declared off limits to trainees, and leave the cube and tissue sample inside Lisa Markel's living quarters, with Noreen's carefully composed note, untraceable to the three TGs in the camp. Her work area was probably too secure for the TGs to penetrate without being detected, and it was certainly not private. There was no way of knowing if they might encounter her in an interview room again. Besides, to pass it to her anonymously, none of them could simply leave it on her temporary auditorium Living Plastic desk, bare but for a screen and keyboard, let alone walk up to her and say, "Here, keep this data confidential. It contains the death penalty level knowledge of human genetics you wanted, you're welcome."

In the days just before the single ship landed, scheduled to arrive on a Friday night, Jorl verified with a corporal that on his few free hours on Saturday night, he would be permitted to run the one-mile oval track around the obstacle course. It drew him an odd look, a trainee asking to run more, after three weeks of running and daily exercises to acclimate them to Heavyside. However, there was no objection, so long as he made the head count for bed check, and got up when rousted out Sunday morning.

He made his runs much slower than when they were timed on training runs, a jogging pace, which took eleven minutes per one-mile lap in the 1.41 g gravity. He did four slow laps in case anyone had bothered to watch him in the darkness. Heavyside had no moons, and due to the plane of the orbit and the orientation of this hemisphere for SOB-1, even the band of light from the galactic core was always below the horizon. With no one on the obstacle course, and its lights off, a dim glow from the barracks was all that spilled over to the far side of the track, and the twelve-foot razor wire toped fence it paralleled for over a quarter mile.

One of the random truck patrols had been by twelve minutes ago, so when Jorl turned onto the backside stretch for the fifth lap, he checked all around for possible observers. Lacking IR vision, he saw mostly dark of course. He'd kept his eyes trained away from the barracks lights to retain his dark adaptation. There was *some* starlight and a local zodiacal glow near where the sun had set. He started a fast run down the dirt track, setting his feet as softly as he could, to hide the increase in tempo, kicking up spurts of dust.

For his muscles, the leap, layout and twist as he passed three feet over the coiled razor wire was easy. He pivoted to land on his feet, still at a dead run, and headed for the darker slash that would be the line of the ravine.

Despite his reflexes, he was startled by a pair of damned mating rabbits he failed to see in the darkness. They separated with a squeal right at his feet, and ran off into the grass and low brush. He mentally apologized for the interruption. The only purpose he, Fred, and Yil had come up with for the camp's fence he just jumped over was to keep the frigging rabbits outside. The all-volunteer trainees were not only allowed to quit at any time, they were loudly, and frequently "encouraged" by their taskmasters to do so, to give up and go home to mama.

At breakfast, Fred had heard a private that ran some of the "rabbit patrols," as he called them, complain of the boredom of having to do that job. They drove the perimeter road without lights, using their IR senses to pick out the warmer dirt roadway from the grasses, and the frequently humping rabbits. In daylight, the trainees had seen road kill a number of times before scavengers removed the carcasses in the morning. IR vision or not, the bored drivers appeared to enjoy a deadly game with the sweet little plentiful bunnies. Jorl was also concerned with being spotted by them, since his high metabolism would have him glowing larger than a rabbit, from a considerable distance away.

On a Link two days earlier, Karl had detailed the designated landing area, where in the dark it should be possible to line up a barracks door light with an obstruction light on a radio tower, which would put him on a line with where Karl would park the single ship in the ravine.

Slipping down into the six-foot deep ravine, Jorl moved towards lining up the red radio tower light and the barracks door light. The skin of the single ship was set to project the dim background images on its opposite sides, so Jorl nearly ran into the rounded nose of the craft before he saw how the overhead stars were being projected downwards on its underside. For the benefit of the hypothetical observer, lying on the ground under the craft, he supposed with amusement.

He quickly went around the side to feel for the faint depressions of the keypad, and tapped the open code. The hatch shifted out a few inches, then rotated over the top to provide access. He didn't touch the controls and simply picked up the note, cube, and sample vial, inside a small clear plastic bag lying on the operator's seat. Slipping that inside his jumpsuit, he closed the hatch and started back down the ravine to the closest place to the fence, where he had jumped over. His internal time sense told him he could easily get back over the fence, and run ahead to where his slow jog would have placed him by now, where the track bends away from the fence.

He was on the verge of jumping to the rim of the ravine when he heard the sound of tires on dirt. A random patrol made the corner turn around the fence a quarter mile away, driving rather fast in the dark. It was faster than the patrol vehicles normally drove. It set Jorl's mind working quickly. He didn't know for certain, but assumed there must be a set of sensors they were unaware of, which had detected his movements outside the fence.

He continued along the ravine, keeping low so his IR glowing head would not be seen peeping over the rim. He scared another rabbit, which he quickly overtook in a crouched run and dive, and caught it by the hind legs. It squealed, so he placed a hand over its muzzle and squeezed. It tried to bite him. He had a half-baked plan to use the rabbit somehow, as a distraction. He heard the sliding tires on dirt, as the otherwise quiet electric vehicle came to a halt on the roadway. They definitely were looking for something or someone.

The ravine angled closer to the fence farther down, and the patrol road was squeezed closer to the fence because of that. He was nearly fifty feet from the point where he had entered the ravine, and from the blockage of starlight on the rim above there were low bushes there, so he risked lifting his face high enough to see through the base stems. He could make out one man walking along the fence, and the other seemed to be moving from their vehicle towards the ravine.

They were not using flashlights, so somehow they were employing their IR implants, apparently following his steps. It had been so recent that he supposed his prints were marginally warmer, or perhaps had disturbed a warmer layer to reveal cooler material below. Regardless, they were both now moving towards the ravine, where he had entered. He had a plan, and the rabbit wasn't going to like it one bit. He even needed it to be able to squeal, so he couldn't do this a merciful way. The ripper would chastise him if he shared this with Kim, the now grown cub he sometimes had hunted with at home. Perhaps the rabbit might survive, who knew?

Jorl waited until he saw the first man drop into the ravine, and the other was walking on the edge above, away from him. Both were apparently following his double foot trail towards the stealthed single ship.

He placed his right hand under the rabbit's rump, his left still pressed hard over the muzzle, holding the wriggling animal in his hand as he drew his right arm back. With a Kobani muscled powered throw, the nine-pound animal (jackrabbits were technically a hare, not a rabbit), flew in a high arc out over the flats away from the ravine, just beyond the two men sixty feet away.

In an appreciated bit of cooperation, the terrified animal made no squeal until just before the arc reached the ground, perhaps twenty feet ahead and to the right of the searchers. Whether it saw the ground coming or finally recovered from the fear it was about to be eaten, it squalled more than squealed, with the sound interrupted as it hit the grass. It survived that impact and promptly squealed again, as it found its feet and started running.

Jorl had not waited to see if both men would react and look where the noise came from. He simply leaped up and over the ravine rim an instant before his internal timer said the impact would occur. There would be no better moment for him to be exposed, and he landed as softly as possible and dashed towards the nearby fence.

He glanced once over his right shoulder as he ran, and saw both men, now on the far side of the ravine, running away from his position. Energy coursed through his body, and he made a headlong leap up and over the fence, clearing it by at least five feet, and did a tuck and roll in midair to land on his feet, bending knees nearly to the ground, also using his hands to absorb the impact as softly and quietly as possible. He stayed low and raced directly for a hard packed area with hundreds of footprints, and angled towards the barracks.

He used his transducer to send in the blind to the Avenger. "A perimeter road patrol spotted me outside the fence, but I got away. I'm safely inside the camp, but you need to fly the single ship away before they find it in the ravine."

The reply from Karl surprised him. "Sir, I picked up your transducer signal from the relay in the single ship. I have just lifted it off as quietly as I could, and it is now well to the south and climbing. The onboard visual sensors showed the patrol never turned around as it departed."

Jorl slowed as he approached the lighted area, and went around his assigned building, and casually walked in a door on the side away from the track and practice field. He nodded to a couple of men he saw, and thanks to his mods and gravity adaptations, he wasn't even sweating. His heart rate was up a little from the rush of excitement, and he forced his breathing to be normal, but he looked cool and casual. He didn't even have dust on his black jumpsuit. He did a local Link to Fred and Yil, and asked them to retrieve the "object" while he took a shower. They had made certain they had conspicuous alibies while he was out of the compound.

He was still in the shower when the attention getting horn sounded on the speaker system and an announcement was made for everyone to assemble in front of the barracks in platoon ranks. "NOW!" was the emphatic final word.

Naked and wet, Jorl retrieved his spare clean jumpsuit, checking the one he'd just worn that day to confirm the bag was gone. He tossed the jumpsuit in the common use cleaner module closest to his bunk, and ran outside carrying his boots and fell in at his usual position on the front right corner of the formation. He wasn't the last to arrive, and under the glares of a corporal and a sergeant, he slipped his bare damp feet into his self-sealing boots.

In the ranks of the facing men for the barracks next to his, he saw Fred in the first spot of the second row, for the second squad of his platoon. He looked over at Jorl and nodded slightly, confirming he was the one that retrieved the data cube.

The six barracks were in two rows, and now the two buildings at the end were darkened after two platoons worth of washouts or dropouts had cut their numbers down to four platoons in a single "hell week." The rumor mill had it that the washout and dropout rate would slow now, but certainly not end. They would be fortunate to have two full platoons remaining when time came for the surgical implants, in four more months of training time.

Thirty-two men left out of over two thousand hopefuls that arrived at the orbital station. Many of those arrivals were selectively recruited and filtered before then. The high numbers of "walk-ins" were normally the first to be eliminated, and less than ten percent of those people made it down to Port Andropov. Not many of those made it to SOB-1 for "hell week."

SFC Norris walked down the center lane between the rows of men, looking extremely unhappy. He was in charge of training, even though the day-to-day interaction for the last week had largely been with corporals for the trainees, and occasionally with several Staff Sergeants. "Hell week" was "weeding," to remove the next weaker links, and didn't require actual training, per se.

The staff's AIs had already provided a complete head count, and even the arrival times noted for the last men to reach formation. However, Norris knew someone had certainly left the compound. Those trainees in the camp were free to dropout anytime, but there was a procedure for that, and climbing the fence and walking away wasn't part of that process.

The seismic alarm that was detected at the perimeter patrol's duty station, located by the main gate, had caused the diversion of the single mobile patrol unit from its random route. The unit was next to the civilian housing section, and was rushed over to the road that ran just outside the fence by the training course. The two privates IR senses saw faint heat traces on the ground that looked as if someone had walked away from the fence towards a nearby gully. The seismic sensor was buried under the roadway, as a strip that ran entirely around the camp. It was primarily intended to pick up vehicle traffic, but the AI was programmed to identify foot traffic as well. It had detected an impact of human-sized mass beside the roadway, as if a person had jumped down from the top of the fence, and who then crossed the road, moving away from the camp, fading with distance.

The two privates followed the fading heat trail to the gully, and could see double heat splotches in one direction along its bottom, and a single set in the opposite direction. To stay together, they went in the direction of the presumed double trail, while calling for another patrol unit to be dispatched.

They subsequently went running off into the open scrub brush on the other side of the gully, in pursuit of what proved to have been a jackrabbit. Because it had squealed loudly, they had assumed it had encountered one of the supposed individuals that made the tracks. However, all they spotted was the heat trace of the still running rabbit as it vanished over a small rise. Then they were told there were faint footsteps detected back on the roadway, so they rushed back in that direction, just as the second unit arrived from the other direction.

None of them had seen anything larger than a rabbit. However, when they used flashlights, they could easily make out boot prints in the gully. The dry road was so hard packed that it didn't leave prints. There was no sign anyone had climbed a twelve-foot fence with coiled wire on top, and sharp edged mesh woven to keep fingers and toes away.

Nevertheless, the AI insisted that someone had run away from the fence, and ran back several minutes later. The inference was someone in the camp left and returned. That was when Norris was brought in, to have his people account for all the trainees, and get them into a formation for a head count.

When one of the original patrolling privates followed the double tracks in the gully, he noted by flashlight that a double set of tracks actually went both ways. He went to where they ended, and saw a smooth long depression in the sandy soil, and some crushed bushes pressed into the ground. There had been no rains to flood the area for weeks, so it had to have been formed recently and presumably that night.

Now the minor issue of perhaps a trainee climbing the fence on a lark, to see if the grass was greener on the other side, had been elevated into having met with someone outside, who had arrived and departed in some sort of small craft. When Norris heard that report, he called 1SG Crager.

Crager arrived from the adjacent housing area, where he'd been in a late meeting with Colonel Dearborn, concerning an equipment supply problem for a class farther ahead in the training cycle. Although SOB-1 was not a top-secret installation, at least on paper, Crager was on the inside of the small group of people that knew what direction Special Ops intended to move in the future. He personally didn't know crap about genetics; he only knew that they were never going to produce troops with abilities to match the enemy with what they were doing now. He had expressed his opinion to some of the scientists, some of whom had agreed, and mentioned what had been done in the past that was now outlawed. That had been the start of the conspiracy.

Colonel Dearborn, in casual off the record conversations, revealed his similar sentiments, and it was apparent he also wanted to see the capability of spec ops troops greatly enhanced. Like Crager, he didn't much care how they made the war winnable, so long as it was possible to do. A small seed had been planted and needed cultivation. SOB-1, in its isolation, and with black ops funding outside any audit trail, was fertile ground.

Tonight, Crager and Dearborn were concerned that some leak had brought a snoop into their midst. SFC Norris, who might even support their operation, wasn't part of it simply to keep the number of those actively involved to a minimum. Frankly, it wasn't certain there was much to be involved with, because the science was sketchy. The smart science people involved all knew it was possible, and the Clone Wars had proven what could be done three hundred years ago. However, they didn't have the basic knowledge that had been destroyed in the Purge (so they assumed).

Norris, not certain why Crager was so intense as he stalked between the formed up platoons, glaring at every face, was startled when his Top said he would be going one on one, questioning each man. He told Norris to move them all, right now, to the auditorium dressed as they were. He also wanted the barracks searched, and a detailed examination made of the ground near the fence when daylight arrived, done by their advanced instructors from SOB-4, the Special Reconnaissance teams. In the meantime, he didn't want anybody to walk all over the "evidence."

Evidence? Norris wondered. *Of what?* He couldn't think of anything that warranted so much concern. Not even the impression in the sand from some small airship landing outside the base. That might only be a rendezvous of some horny volunteer and his girl, planned for celebrating after "hell week" ended. Top was treating it as if it was a life or death matter.

Chapter 11: Immigration Policy

Colonel Trakenburg was stunned more than outraged, although his tone sounded more the latter. "Captain Longstreet, it has only been seven weeks! Mirikami *can't* pull his people out of training this early. True, they started with physical capabilities much greater than our men possess, but they have too much to learn to leave here now. They could be the weapon we've been trying to make of Special Operations all along. They need to join with us. A weapon without the knowledge of how to use it is wasted. Captain Mirikami has to be made aware of this."

Longstreet had tried to offer first name informality with his superior in private talks such as now, when he suggested the colonel could call him Joe, or Joseph. Trakenburg rebuffed that, as inevitably weakening the command structure. The captain didn't take it personally, because he knew General Nabarone also had offered to allow Trakenburg to call him Henry in private. It was still "General" when Trakenburg spoke directly to the Planetary Defense Commander, in any setting. Some kinds of starch never washed out.

"Colonel, if they were typical trainees on Heavyside, even as physically capable as they started, the full twenty months of training should still be too little to bring them up to the skill level and knowledge of the men in my expanded platoon." He shrugged.

"I can't rationally explain it, Sir. They already can do everything the best of our people can do. Because of their speed and strength, and incredible coordination, any of them do it better and faster. Better than *any* of my men, *or any that I've ever seen,* including our legendary First Sergeant Crager, who taught me everything I know, at Heavyside and on live missions later."

Trakenburg shook his head. "In just five weeks? We had them wasting time exercising for the first two weeks of the last seven."

"That first two weeks wasn't wasted, Sir. They are superhumanly strong and coordinated, but had never been pushed to their limits before we beefed up the regimen and made the course too tough even for us instructors to run. SOB-1 would have been a better location for that, but I'm positive they came from a planet with a bit more gravity than Heavyside."

"There are no other *habitable* planets like that in Human Space."

"That's the point, Colonel. They said they came from a planet outside the Rim, left there by the Krall to die. We ran their DNA, compared it to their archived records for the four older men, and we know they have genetic enhancements to the normal genome that apparently make them a near strength equal to us in our Booster Suits.

"Sir, the scientists that General Nabarone brought in have reviewed the medical reports from the four TGs that arrived here wounded. They told me they're stumped. The SGs have some mysterious nervous system features that seem redundant, and a strange second one is not used. The TGs also have redundant nerves, but do use the new set. They found other genetic changes that their DNA comparison equipment can't recognize. The scientists claim we don't even have experts any more that can decipher what those unknown genes must do.

"Colonel, the doctors and scientists may not know *how* the genes do what was done, but they can see some of it when the TGs are in a med lab's scanners. All of them, SGs and TGs alike have an extra tissue based superconducting nervous system, yet the SGs use only the same one you or I do. Of course, yours and mine have the supplementary platinum alloy nerve imbeds that drive our implants and Booster Suits. However, the SGs have essentially the same neuron connections at their nerve endings as we do. They have nearly the same reaction time as we do.

"Our own nerve implants give us a slight edge on conductivity and speed of reactions over an SG. Although, the superconductor nerves they have do seem to help the SGs improve reaction speed by giving them advance sensory input to their brains. I think you and I still have a trivial speed advantage, sending information back from the brain to move our Booster Suits."

This was actually already known to Trakenburg, but Longstreet thought he was the first to brief the master snooper of what Nabarone's own AI data had revealed. "Captain, of course you know the real prize is how the TGs are able to use the second superconducting nervous system. That's where they get that reaction speed. We know they start life with the muscle enhancements of the SGs, with the added carbon fiber within their existing tissues grown at a later age. Now it's as if they wear a Booster Suit internally, and have powerful human muscles in addition to that. I had wondered how they were safely absorbing the tremendous impacts when I saw them risk long drops. How did they not break bones? You and I could drop just as far in our suits and still survive the impact. However, because we would have to crawl away with broken feet and legs, we would die if this happened in combat.

"A Magnetic Resonance Imaging system was brought in that went over Ethan Greeves, checking his rib regrowth from the plasma burn and chest puncture before we let him join the others on the obstacle course six weeks ago. I heard about the MRI results from a doctor, but dismissed it at the time, thinking it was the same substance as their carbon fiber muscles.

"I recently learned from General Nabarone's medical team, (he had Max steal the report), that the carbon nanotubes in their bones and carbon fibers in their muscles are structurally very different, grown by completely different gene changes. The bones have interlocked carbon nano tubes built into them. Longer nano tubes just like those are the same material used to make the Space Elevator cables on Earth and Mars. The TGs don't have pure nano tube bones, but they are damned hard to break, and they flex more before reaching the fracture point."

Trakenburg realized he had been pulled away from his main objective, to discuss a way to keep Mirikami and his TGs here, to complete their training, and to convince them to join forces with Special Operations. General Nabarone did not have the reach, away from Poldark, to order or conduct the strikes Mirikami had said he wanted his people to conduct against Krall interests. Spec ops did, at least in principle.

"If we run some live missions with the TGs, where they put what we taught them into practice, they will see the value of our men's experience, and one or more of the older SGs might come over to my point of view. I don't want to lose this opportunity. I can't let them leave."

Longstreet was quite certain that other than disabling their ship, that they *couldn't* stop them from leaving. The TGs could capture any other ship on the planet they wanted and only massively overwhelming deadly force could beat them. Not an action conducive to friendship and cooperation. He needed to get Trakenburg to accept a theory he now held to be true, and which explained why they were ready to leave training so early.

"Sir, we've both observed how quickly the TGs learn. I even see the four older men picking up tactics I'm surprised they learn so quickly. However, they don't do it as fast, in a single one-day session, and they sometimes forget details a week later. That almost never happens with the TGs. They learn at a phenomenal rate. After a few sessions with different men acting as instructors, they combine the best parts of each instructor's techniques, and I honestly can't see a way I could teach them how to do it better. Then they practice some situations on their own, and damned if they don't find ways to do it better, using moves we *couldn't* teach them, because *we* can't do them.

"I know you saw the recordings of how they cleared the Krall from each deck of that clanship as they went up, one deck, sometimes two decks at a time. They leaped up to flip in midair, firing as they did that, and planted their feet on the bottom of the next deck above to push off, flip, and land away from the stairs. They continued to shoot and cover the next TG coming a second or two behind them. They would have five or six TGs through in seconds, all of them increasing the rate of fire, and *they do not miss what they target*." He added that emphasis.

"I sure as hell can't do that. Almost everything we teach them is improved on by them when they are left on their own. I'm telling you, Sir, they somehow pass that learning on to the next squad, even if the next group never had a chance to see the initial demonstration. How do *you* think they do that, Sir?"

"Captain, you are with them every day, I have not observed that. By the tone of your question, you obviously have an opinion to offer."

"I do, Sir. However, it will sound…, strange. I don't suppose any stranger than how bizarre they already seem to us.

"We all have heard them speak of SGs and TGs, and they have explained a bit about what that meant. Did you ever hear any of the younger ones call one of the appointed squad leaders a TG1? I mean someone like the Martin boy, and Greeves' son, that Conrad Boston kid, and some others."

"I think I recall overhearing the term a few times. I assumed it's a sort of ranking they used at home. All of them are squad leaders for you I think."

"Not all of them, Sir. I've heard some of them call Warren Brock a TG1, and another boy named Carlos, whose last name I don't remember. Those two don't lead squads because they are not particularly assertive or natural leaders. They both have excellent physical ability, but not leadership qualities. They are both called a TG1 at times."

In an annoyed tone Trakenburg pushed him to make his point. "Captain, I don't care what rank or honor they grant one of their TGs. You said they both had excellent physical abilities. That may be why any of them are called TG1s."

"I think it has more to do with a mental ability, Sir."

More annoyed now, Trakenburg asked, "Like IQ, memory, math? Or what?"

Longstreet had to grit it out, if he sounded like an idiot, so be it. "I think TG1's use some kind of telepathy."

Trakenburg blinked. "You. Have. Got. To. Be. Kidding!"

Yep, the colonel definitely thought he was an idiot.

"Please hear me out, Sir. It must be one of the genetic enhancements they appear to have, which we can't identify, and may be tied somehow to their superconducting nerves. I don't think it works like broadcast signals sent through the air. It is apparently connected to that touchy feely thing they do, every time one group is shown something new, or a squad leader is first to complete a new training exercise.

"They do this sort of group hug thing. I know you've seen it, because I heard you make a disparaging comment once when they did that. They all circle up and stack hands with the squad leader, or sometimes with Carlos what-ever-his-name-is, or Warren Brock, who offer the first hand at the bottom of rings they initiate. We thought it was a team building exercise of their own, except they also do it between different, supposedly competing teams.

"I've seen non-leader Brock finish a classroom session on methods to create diversions, or how to conduct hit and run actions, and non-leader Carlos after a description of what favorable factors to look for when selecting ambush sites. Those two so-called TG1s always meet with the next class coming in, before they go off with an instructor to practice what they were just told, or sometimes simply go to lunch. Their own squad members don't hang back to participate in the ring with the next group, and the incoming squad leaders are sometimes other TG1's. They do their own rings during training.

"What became significant to me was that the next new group always had the answers to randomly asked questions on completely new course subjects, or can perfectly perform whatever the physical action is in the exercise being taught, even though they have never had it demonstrated for them. They already know what to do."

Still skeptical, but willing to listen to one of his best platoon leaders, Trakenburg had a hypothetical question. "If they have such a farfetched ability, have you seen signs that the so-called TG1's try do it with any of us?"

He was satisfied with the look of surprised wonder on Longstreet's face as he considered an implication he had overlooked. The colonel thought he had forced a retraction of this preposterous suggestion, when the captain said, "I'll be damned. That's how he knew."

"How who knew what?"

"Sir, I know you have the recording of the demonstration fight in SOB-23's parking garage, between Warren Brock, Sergeant Jenkins and Corporal Bender.

They shook hands before the fight, right after Thad…, I mean Colonel Greeves…, suggested he do that first. Greeves also said to think about what his first move would be in the fight. I automatically did that too, just as if I were about to fight some greenhorn kid with a highly exaggerated build up.

"I'll bet Jenkins and Bender thought about it as well. Brock beat them both so quickly because he *knew* their first moves. At the end he was hurting Corporal Bender by nearly pulling his arms off. An object lesson that we now know he could have actually finished. He said something after that, which indicated he knew what both Bender and Jenkins had been thinking before the fight.

"He said Bender wanted to hurt him really bad, just to impress me, and that Jenkins simply wanted to knock him out fast and easy. The words he used were something like that, so we'll have to watch the recording again to be sure. At the time, that sounded reasonably the same as I thought both men might think, knowing them both as well as I do. I only wondered later how the kid could have sized them up so quickly. It must have been during the handshake. That means they can read us as well. *Damn!*"

Trakenburg wasn't nearly so skeptical now. He recalled the incident. His AI, Max, back at his headquarters was out of transducer range, but he used a landline to call, and asked him to upload that fight sequence to another AI at the training base in the crater.

He and Longstreet watched the short sequence multiple times, in light of their new perspective. Brock deliberately looking away from Jenkins, nodding to Greeves and then leaping to meet what should have been a surprise move from Jenkins. He clearly anticipated Bender's kidney kick without ever looking his way.

Shaking his head in dismay, he decided Longstreet was probably right. Trakenburg gave him the first order that came to mind. "Make all our men wear the beta test Booster Suit gloves, even if they crumple a few fragile items before they develop fine control. You and I will wear them too if we are ever in a position to shake hands with any of those TG1s."

He gave his reasoning. "Every indication I've seen and as you have described is that if this is real, it requires physical contact with their hands. Mirikami and his men don't form those rings when training, so they can't directly do what the TG1s do. However, they must get a training update from them each night. Obviously, these kids can send as well as receive…, something…," he was grasping for the proper description.

"They could be passing what they learned on to the SGs later. That must be why the older men show a day's lag time in improvement, yet are still far ahead of the training schedule."

His own mind was doing what Longstreet's had just done. Going over inconstancies and mysteries, which he'd recently pondered. "It is incredible, but this idea certainly makes some other pieces fall into place that I couldn't make fit. General Nabarone and I have had joint possession of that damn Krall clanship commander; a fruitless interrogation, I might add, since they turned his paralyzed butt over to us last month. He's alive and aware and we have to force feed him, and apply that drug daily to keep him docile and unable to will his own death.

"However, he has never uttered a single word to us. Dr. Martin says the Krall had finally realized he was actually speaking aloud when he thought of the answers to our questions, and had clammed up to stop helping them after they attacked his ship. Before that, Carson, was recorded telling them by transducer that he had been getting intelligence from that Krall, which they acted on to win the fight. Such as how to armor seal the troop transport's front cabin, how many warriors they faced, and that clue about how the Krall were warned just before a plasma weapon would fire."

Longstreet nodded. "Sir, as you know, our technical people have programmed our AI's to look for that weak pre-flash via our IR sensors. It's a real effect, which we never noticed and they lacked IR sensors to see. It's plausible that the Krall commander told them that."

Trakenburg shook his head. "That detail *seemed* to imply a fluency in high or low Krall, which I questioned that they had. The TGs can't hear ultrasonic speech, which is what a Krall normally uses with other Krall, so he would have needed to mumble to them in low Krall or Standard. You claim Carson is a TG1, so he might be able to read an *alien's* mind against his will." He definitely looked troubled now.

"I don't know if we should let them know what we suspect, or confirm the ability some way first." He made a Krall-like snort, unaware that it sounded like one. "Hell, if I report this, and I'm believed of course, the government might order the Navy to simply nuke them here in the crater, to kill them all before they get strong enough to take us all over if they defeat the Krall."

Longstreet was shocked. "Colonel, whatever their capabilities are, or why they want to stay unknown to the Hub government, they risked the future of all their people to come here to help us fight the Krall. In my opinion, their fear of Gene War paranoia is valid, and your comment confirms you apparently agree with that."

"I do, and I have no intention of sharing knowledge of their existence with the Navy or any political arm of our government. I'm a patriot, but the Krall are the enemy we face now. Who in your platoon knows what you suspected?"

"My men haven't spoken to me on this so I don't think they suspect anything. However, if you and I suddenly cut off physical contact now, with no more hand touching, the TGs or Mirikami will soon deduce that we learned they have this ability. If we don't prevent physical contact they will sense it sooner."

Trakenburg agreed. "Damned if we do and damned if we don't. If we let them know we found them out, and then we accept them and continue to work with them, it should earn their trust. A trust they will know we return, assuming that we do, because we probably can't hide it from them anyway. Are you personally prepared to take that step, Captain Longstreet, and offer that exchange of trust?"

"Colonel, if they can do what I believe they can do, it can't just be me showing trust. You need to be party to the agreement as well, because I will know of any reservations you express to me now. Frankly, even if you conceal negative feelings from me, Sir, they will know of your knowledge. You'll have to allow them to touch you to verify your thoughts. I definitely have privacy concerns. However, I believe there is a genuine sense of integrity in Captain Mirikami, and those that follow him. Sergeant Reynolds was a Poldark patriot, who would not sell his soul for a new arm and big muscles. He was won over by these people, and he certainly knows about these TG1s, because he hasn't fallen behind in our training."

In a rare smile from Trakenburg, he said, "Captain, I started out skeptical as hell, but I was feeling you out just now, because I was already committed to meeting with them, to say we know what the TG1s can do, and that I trust them to use the ability to humanity's benefit. They will certainly learn that I damn well want to try to get that same ability for our own troops.

"We need to set up a meeting. If they are going to trust you and me, then I suspect it will be extended to General Nabarone. I don't kid myself. They like him, and even you for that matter, far more than they do me."

****

Thad was suspicious. "This morning you announce we're leaving next week, and suddenly we are invited before noon to meet with Henry, Joe, and Trakenburg, all of it set up by the colonel. He wants you and me, Dillon and Sarge present, and we learn through Jakob that Ethan and Carson were pulled from a practice Special Reconnaissance mission and are flying back."

"I can almost hear an accusation from the tone of your summation, Thad." Mirikami told him. "All of us here know you don't trust the colonel, and I have reservations concerning his motivations, and the means he might be willing to employ to achieve his goals. However, I'm also confident that his goal is to develop a force that can attack the Krall on their base worlds. Something Trakenburg knows we intend to do.

"What skullduggery could he engage in that would involve General Nabarone in a complicit manner? And include his subordinate, Captain Longstreet, whom I know wants us to succeed, and frankly, via a chance Tap last week, was seriously thinking of jumping ship to go with us."

"Really?" Dillon asked. "He's a pretty gung ho trooper. I'd not think he'd ever consider desertion."

"Hey! Did I desert, Dillon?" Sarge quickly asked. "I'm going with you, even though I'm back on Poldark, my home, and I'm technically still in the PU Army for the duration of the war. I once swore an oath to the PU that I would help protect this planet and all of Human Space."

"I'm sorry, Sarge. Poor choice of words. I meant he is so devoted to Special Ops. He'd be leaving that if he came with us, if we could even take him, that is. Our next stop is home." They still avoided saying the name.

Thinking around Sarge's offended feelings, Thad asked, "Tet, how did you find out about Joe's intentions? Did he come to you?"

"No. A little Mind Tapper told me."

"Then the blue bird of happiness flew up my nose. What do you mean a little 'Mind Tapper' told you? I thought we were no longer snooping on our allies."

"The descriptive 'little' in this case is accurate. Kally Murchifem told me." The Hub City girl was one of the smallest TGs they had, but had earned the TG1 upgrade before the Jump to Human Space by her attitude and skills.

Tet explained how the Tap had happened. "Kally wasn't *trying* to Tap Joe. She had nearly taken a fall when the single rope she used to rappel down the crater wall was cut by shards of rock, detritus which someone else's rope above her scraped loose. In a fluke, it hit right on a piton or on her anchor and cut the line. Kally instantly pulled line in and formed a large bight in her slack rope, and slung the loop over a nearby basalt projection to stop her fall. You know how crumbly these crater walls are; she said choss was falling from the base of her new support rock. She still wasn't safe, and swinging like a barn door, dangling well away from the wall, and the chunk of basalt was slowly giving way.

"Joe was on a parallel rope near her, instructing and providing advice to the entire squad. He dropped lower and did a pendulum over to grab her hand for a moment. She attached a spare carabiner from her pocket to his line, and made the last hundred feet of the descent on his rope.

"Aside from the falling rocks and cut line, what made it unusual was a grateful comment she made when he offered her his hand, and the fact that neither was wearing gloves for the exercise's simulated impromptu emergency descent. Kally told him she would miss him and his men's help, after we are on our own against the Krall.

"While she grasped his hand, she saw that he desperately wanted to go with us to fight the Krall. She sensed his determination to find a way to make it happen. Kally told me, and I've since been trying to think of ways I can help him do that."

Thad said, "Unless he makes it a lifetime commitment, we can't let him know where home is located, or even its name. How could we leave him on his own there, or let him come back here after that?"

"How did we verify Sarge's commitment, his dedication? Why do we know we can trust him?" Tet reminded them.

"Hey again! I'm standing right here, you know."

Tet grinned. "You're *here,* Sarge, because we have TG1's that quickly discovered your honesty your commitment, and your sincere desire to jump into our illegal gene pool, in which you now stand, right up to your scrawny neck."

"Hell. I didn't know I was being vetted for membership to your damned club. Is there a secret handshake I missed? And my neck isn't scrawny anymore." He was glaring back, but had a devilish twinkle when he looked at Thad.

Thad matched the twinkle. "Not a handshake, Sarge. A twentieth century gang sign from Earth, just like this one that Maggi taught me." Thad's middle finger demonstrated.

"Oh. I've seen that. Behind your back, every time you think you've won an argument with your wife."

"Gentle Men," Mirikami admonished. "Aside from the fact that I've never observed Thad win an argument with Marlyn, I was pointing out we have the means to not only determine their sincerity, but to make them coconspirators. I believe they want to do more than join us, I think they wish they could *be* one of us. At home, we have the means to make them SGs, as we did Sarge, and ourselves."

He emphasized his most salient point. "We are truly *a self-made people.*"

Dillon was nodding his understanding. "Twenty years ago we thought we would need three actual generations to achieve a third generation. We have TG1s now, and with new Hub technology, driven by the war the Krall forced on us, we have new med labs and the nanites we never imagined having when we started. I have not had time to analyze the templates for the new nanites we sent home, but I know Aldry and Rafe have had time since the Beagle returned. In principle, they should be able to put them to use improving our gene mod processes.

"We four have already committed to trying to reach the next generational level, just to be able to *travel* with our TGs. We can't place them at risk simply because we can't survive the same stresses they can take in stride. However, I don't think you have to have been stranded on our planet for twenty years, or to be born there to become one of us."

Mirikami felt smugly proud, as he sensed Dillon was on the verge of making the proposal he'd been leading towards, and making a better case than he might have done.

Dillon asked the question that, for generations to follow, would become the defining one for Koban's place in humanity's future.

"Why can't we offer citizenship by applicants literally becoming one of us?" He of course meant their opting for the illegal gene mods to become a Kobani, subject to a HUB law death penalty, unfortunately.

That should tighten the loyalty bonds, thought Mirikami.

There was a moment of silence, as this enlightening question was considered.

Of course, Sarge had to sully the grand moment, slightly. "Hell yes. That makes me immigrant New Citizen Number One! I want a certificate."

Mirikami sighed, his pride diluted. He finally got someone to announce the right decision *before* he had to maneuver anyone into it, or decide *for* him or her. Thanks to Sarge, it would become a bone-headed contest to see who would have the next lowest New Citizen number as bragging rights, because Reynolds would make sure everyone knew *he* was the first.

The new and improved Jakob AI intruded politely. "Excuse me Gentle Men, as I was requested to inform you, General Nabarone's shuttle has descended into the crater, and will apparently be met by Colonel Trakenburg and Captain Longstreet. My input from the radar system on the crater rim has picked up another shuttle from the direction of the recon team exercise. Carson and Ethan should be landing in about five minutes."

Mirikami rose out of his Bridge chair. "OK, boys, let's use our new conference room on the next deck." They also had two elevator systems as well as the two remaining stairwells (with railings now) on the top decks. The ship was becoming humanly comfortable.

On entering the wooden paneled room, Mirikami instructed the AI to start a pot of Earth coffee, and to direct the visitors to the room with the excessively large twenty-seat ironwood table. It was bolted to the floor, something a Living Plastic table would not have required. However, Nabarone's largess had spared no expense, even if they had not requested such luxury. At least the general had been forced to concede that the chairs around the table had to be standard acceleration chair/couches, in the event a meeting was interrupted by an unexpected navigational need. Even there, he had provided a more expensive plastic skin that emulated the color of the table. As Nabarone had said several times, "It's good to be The General."

It took longer for the brass to arrive than it did Carson and Ethan, who arrived before the coffee was ready. Greeting everyone, Mirikami offered the two young men a cup of the heavenly brew.

"No thanks, Uncle Tet," they both declined. Mirikami shook his head sadly at the deprived upbringing Koban had forced on the younger generation. They didn't enjoy many of the new supply of 'treats" the older generation had missed for so many years. The one exception was that nearly all of the TGs liked peanut butter and various types of jelly. They had never had chocolate bars before either, although chocolate flavoring itself was a favorite now at home.

Mirikami was personally repelled by a new combination, peanut butter and chocolate bar sandwiches, which most of the TGs loved. Dillon was an enthusiastic consumer of this new commodity, and liked his warmed slightly. He ate with the gooey two main ingredients dripping onto his plate as he washed it down with cold milk, and used a finger to scrape up the dripped mixture. Yet, he claimed a refined upbringing on Rhama.

Mirikami relished the sushi cuisine he had discovered was available from a small town, located not too far from their extinct volcano camp. They even served some of his favorites, imported frozen unfortunately, from the seas of New Honshu, his home world that he had not visited since his mother died over thirty years ago. He convinced Dillon and Thad to try a few dishes, but the uncultured thugs nearly spit the delectable raw fish and Shari onto their plates, halting the act only when the glare from their friend (and Captain) gave them reason to pause. They smiled, holding the partly chewed decoratively rolled tidbits in their mouths, as they both reached for the saké cups. They washed it all down in a single gulp.

After that, the saké seemed to disappear frequently from their cups. Their true misfortune was that the 18% alcohol was metabolized by their gene mod enhancements faster than they could possibly get drunk, so they never lost their sense of taste. Mirikami took fiendish delight in keeping the various dishes coming, while he kept misplacing the bottles of saké.

Today, except for coffee and hard liquor, the latter always needed if Nabarone were visiting, there were no snacks available. They didn't know what was delaying the three officers, since they had time to have beaten Carson and Ethan here if they had walked directly to the Mark of Koban, which they still only knew as simply named the Mark.

The older men used the time to their advantage, briefing the two TG1's on what they thought the meeting might be about today. They both agreed that all of the

TGs had the impression that the spec ops instructors were envious of where they were going, and what they would be doing. Some openly wanted to go along.

Several days ago, the SGs had participated in an intelligence briefing from the Navy, concerning long-range scout missions that had found a number of Krall inhabited planets, one of which was definitely a production world for clanships. The Navy would have been astonished if they had seen the Mark, a former clanship, which they didn't, because they met at Nabarone's headquarters.

Their real shock would have been that the navigation system on the Mark had a record of where every Krall controlled world was located. There were thousands of habitable worlds, many of which were now abandoned and empty of intelligent life, per the Krall's own claims. The navigation system didn't know which ones were which, dead or populated. However, there were several candidate worlds for possible raids, besides the clanship producer, to check out with a ship the Krall would not suspect as human crewed.

Mirikami asked any of them if they thought some of the spec ops would be willing to undergo gene mods if offered the chance. They all thought half might accept. At least because of their secret and isolated duty, and the selection process, many of them had few extensive ties to family in Human Space. What they cared about was their risk filled work, their fellow troopers, and leave time with women and booze. Their own physical enhancements and need for secrecy had isolated them from the mainstream population. A Booster Suit couldn't go on leave with them, and none of them liked doing without the feeling of strength it provided.

While this general discussion continued, Mirikami separated a bit, and asked Jakob where the three officers were.

"Sir, they entered the Dead Zone, where I can't monitor or see them." That was a secure room for meetings, where no AI or any external electronic monitoring could penetrate.

Mirikami tugged at his lip. This was apparently something they were springing on Nabarone, before the meeting. Henry wasn't the biggest fan of Trakenburg, and he was unlikely to object to the Mark's departure since he knew it was inevitable. Nor should he much care if some of the spec ops wanted to tag along. This extended conversation suggested something Nabarone might object to, or need some convincing. They were already twenty minutes late, and Trakenburg was normally the punctuality freak.

He turned back to the others, only to discover they had become quiet, and were looking at him, as he fingered his lower lip.

"What?"

Dillon asked for them all. "You tell *us*, 'oh lip tugging seer.' You have something on your mind. Do the tardy brass hats have anything to do with your thoughts?"

He nodded. "I'm wondering what they had to tell Henry that took them to the Dead Zone, and made on-the-dot Trakenburg late for a meeting. It has to be something involved to last this long, and Trakenburg apparently couldn't risk telling Henry before he arrived. It's taking longer to explain or to convince Henry than expected. I think it must be tied to our departure, but it is more than some spec ops types asking to go along. Henry, to use his usual vernacular, might say 'I don't give a damn,' and tell them to just go ask us."

"Perhaps they learned where we call home." Thad offered.

Sarge countered that idea before Mirikami could. "Trakenburg wouldn't share that information with Henry, even if he knew. He'd keep it for himself, as a bit of knowledge that isn't valuable now, but could be a bargaining chip later."

Dillon tried an idea. "Some other secret then. Concerning our gene mods, because we know they have taken samples from all of us. Perhaps they figured out where some genes must have derived from, the hypothetical source." He was obviously thinking of ripper and raptor genes.

Mirikami shook his head. "Henry has access to a planet load of experts with far better resources to use for that purpose than Trakenburg. It isn't Henry briefing spec ops right now; it's the other way around. I'm wondering why the aloof colonel included a subordinate like Captain Longstreet in a briefing of sensitive information to the general, unless Joe was involved, or was required for corroboration. I think Joe is the wild card here. What could he know about, that he's needed by Trakenburg to brief or convince Nabarone?"

Thad said, "If you're thinking secrets, then Joe and his men are with us and the TGs every day for training. You already addressed someone accidentally leaking the location of home, and the colonel knows that, he is probably holding onto that information. What other secrets do we have they could have learned? Somebody mention rippers, rhinolo, raptors or moosetodons?"

"Nah," refuted Sarge. "When I first heard of those they didn't mean crap to me. They were just words, without a picture of them. Did anyone slip up and bring recordings from home, and even if they did, where do the new animals live? It doesn't help them find home. Besides, why would Trakenburg bother to tell Henry? They aren't good buddies."

Carson had an idea. "Perhaps they figured out our telepathy mods. How we learn so fast."

Mirikami took that as a working hypothesis. "That may not be it, but it fits with how they're behaving, and ranks up there with the sort of thing that secretive Colonel Trakenburg would fear the most. If that's it, then we want to be ready to handle their questions."

"You don't think a denial will work, Sir?" Ethan was feeling a bit of guilt, as one of the TG1's that may have let the blue rat out of the bag.

"No. We'll want them to trust us later, and this knowledge will eventually come out anyway. If that's the issue, I think a full explanation and demonstration is called for, input and output Taps, as well as telling them how we non-Tapping SGs can fool you TG1s, and shield our thoughts. And we definitely know the reverse is true, don't we?" He winked at the two TG1s, who had hidden far more than their fair share of youthful shenanigans from the older generation.

"What if this *isn't* what they're worried about?" asked Thad.

"Then we'll all be surprised together."

It was another eight minutes before Jakob informed them that the three men were walking towards the Mark.

****

The six Kobani were standing at the far end of the conference table, sipping various beverages when the three officers arrived. Mirikami smiled and started forward with Thad, when Nabarone, blushing, held out both palms in a push gesture, and said, “No offense, Tet, Thad, but let’s keep a table between us for now, please. Until we conclude the strangest discussion, initiated by the colonel and captain here that I’ve ever had with anyone.

Greeves and Mirikami, not acting surprised, glanced at one another, and stayed at their end of the table. Mirikami had a half smile, observing the acute red-faced discomfort of Nabarone, the embarrassed and guilty look on Longstreet’s face, and the shrewd observer’s penetrating gaze from Trakenburg.

Mirikami half bowed, and said, “We were discussing reasons for your delay, since Colonel Trakenburg is normally such a stickler for punctuality.” A nod to the colonel.

“Frankly, we talked about what the three of you must be saying in private. I’m not surprised you are behaving a bit reserved.”

Mirikami paused, and added with a sense of mischievousness, “You must have read our minds.”

The stricken and confirming looks on the three officer’s faces was so hilarious, that none of the other six could hold back their laughter. Thad and Sarge were nearly bent over, and Mirikami, highly amused at his own impromptu quip, was leaning on the table with one hand supporting him, as he released an uncharacteristic gale of laughter that almost left him breathless.

Raising a hand towards them, Mirikami, still laughing, tried to speak. “I’m…, sorry. That was mean…,” he laughed some more. “It just came out…, and you looked petrified.” He struggled to get control, but when he looked up at them, he burst out laughing again.

“This isn’t funny,” Nabarone said. “You overheard us somehow, and set us up.” Despite his words to the contrary, he was starting to laugh at what he thought was a joke on him. He shot a look of irritation at Trakenburg, whom he now wondered if he had a funny bone after all, and had planned this. The colonel wasn’t looking at all amused, and his face was red with anger. Longstreet was simply looking puzzled, wearing a half smile.

Thad regained his composure and his voice. “Henry, Tet did make a joke, but we didn’t know for sure what you three had been talking about.” He chuckled. “We guessed at several possibilities, but it had to be some startling secret the two of them needed to tell you, and that would take some time to get you to accept. You half confirmed our best guess when you held back from handshakes. Your expressions when Tet made that loaded remark, was a clincher.”

Nabarone had cycled back from laughing at the joke he thought was on him, to confusion. “What the hell. Is this a bullshit story about you having mindreading ability, or is it real?”

“Henry, for me, any of us SGs for that matter, it is crap. For Ethan and Carson, and some others with a later genetic mod, it is real. With limitations that you appear to know something about, because you avoided physical contact just now.”

Longstreet spoke up. “The term TG1 applies to the TGs that have this extra ability. Is that right?”

“Yes.” Mirikami had finally recovered his demeanor. “We had ten TG1’s total when we left home, with what was a new genetic ability for humans. Three of them are on our other two ships. Please note that I said this is a new human ability. We discovered its existence in a native life form where we live, nearly twenty years ago. It seemed a useful feature to copy when we learned how to do it, and we were ready.” He grinned. “It’s pretty neat, huh?”

Trakenburg was still not amused by the light-hearted tone Mirikami was following. “You might have shared that information from the start.”

“Share that with the man that sent his troopers fully prepared to kill our kids, before you even knew a thing about us? Tell you a secret you wouldn’t have believed anyway. Yet which might have provoked you into issuing an order that could have forever blocked cooperation? Our caution was as reasonable as yours seemed to you, and avoided a disaster.”

Trakenburg snapped off a reply, “You know what we’ve been thinking and we don’t know your real intentions.”

“Actually, you do know what our intentions are because we told you, and we were truthful. If there were no TG1’s, how would that have made our intentions any more believable? We are a small group, exposing ourselves to people that might consider human genetic modifications worthy of the death penalty. What did you risk sitting in your office, watching us through your spy bots? The risk was all ours.”

“I’ll accept that, but how do we get around the trust issue if you always know our every thought? Do we have to always avoid contact?”

Looking at the other two men, even without Mind Tap ability, he could see that question was on their minds. “The ability has more limitations than requiring physical contact. It actually is strongest with hand-to-hand contact, because that is how it was designed to work with humans. Fingers have a high density of nerve endings, and actual contact is essential, although we have found that a diluted form of transfer is possible via a conducting material. For example, through a conductive metal for a short distance.

“As for pulling information from someone, it isn’t as general and detailed as you may think. You actually have to be thinking of the subject for a TG1 to receive the images, which sometimes have words embedded.” He suddenly laughed.

Shaking his head, he said, “Why am I, a blind man, describing what a person with eyes can see? Carson, would you please describe the process before I put a foot in my mouth?”

“Yes Sir.” He paused for a few milliseconds to sort thoughts.

“OK. For one thing, words are harder to receive from a non-TG1. Ethan and

I can do that easily with other TG1's, but from anyone else the words are partly inferred by the mental images we see, and we can sense emotional content for most pictures. To Mind Tap someone that doesn't know what we can do, we might start with a leading question or statement, to get them actively thinking of what we are interested in learning. If they know what we can do, and don't want us to know, the simple act of not wishing to tell us is sufficient to block us. If I ask who you slept with last night, and you said none of my business, or just refused to answer, I can't get around your refusal to extract that thought."

Nabarone said, "The words Mind Tap, and just Tap was used. Is that what you call doing this?"

"Yes Sir. You might also hear someone call it frilling, because the intelligent animal we discovered this ability in, called a …," he was interrupted by four SGs and Ethan.

Red-faced and sheepish he apologized. "Oh crap, sorry Dad, guys."

Explaining, "I almost said an animal name that the Krall could instantly connect to our home world if they heard it from a human. The genetic mental ability we copied is from an animal, and we initially called the experience frilling. We still do when it happens with one of these animals. The Krall do not know that word, or of this ability in those animals."

He paused for an instant, trying to remember what he was going to say before his near slip.

Ethan stepped in. "Anyone can send us a mental image that they want us to see, even a false picture they made up; perhaps to convey or illustrate an idea, and they can hold back anything they wish. Apparently, due to thousands of years of humans practicing deceit, people are very good at withholding information, and at lying in a Mind Tap.

"A person that is unaware of our ability, or unguarded, might leak a bit about what we just asked or said, but it isn't as if they spilled their guts of a lifetime of secrets. If I ask what you had for lunch, I won't see a picture of your breakfast. If I ask what you had to eat today, and you don't hold back, I might get it all in a fast series of mental flashes.

"Once you know of my ability, it's not hard to hold back anything. I know my saying this won't convince you, but that's how it works. My friends that are non-TG1s can block me, as can virtually every one of the SGs block me. These guys," he nodded a head at the older men, "and all of those at home."

Longstreet, for Nabarone's benefit, asked a pertinent question. "Warren Brock beat two of my men in a fight in that parking garage. Do you know about that?"

"Oh, sure. He's a TG1 and shared it with all of us."

"Did he read their minds?"

"Sure, at least as to what they each intended to do first when they shook hands. Each of them had a couple of moves they could start with, and Warren set up the ones he preferred."

Longstreet looked pointedly at the general and the colonel in turn. Ethan's description matched what they had just watched several times (again) for Nabarone's benefit.

Taking the initiative, Longstreet started walking towards Ethan, his right hand extended. "Tell me what I'm thinking, but wait until I shake with Carson and then ask you both to speak, to see if you agree."

Their hands locked in a firm grip, and they stood facing each other a moment. Ethan looked puzzled. Longstreet released his hand and turned to Carson for a handshake.

Pulling back his hand after a couple of seconds, he said, "Both of you together, what was I thinking?"

They spoke over each other, but it was easy to understand them. They didn't agree.

From Ethan it was, "Nothing, you must have been shielding."

Simultaneously, Carson said, "You want to leave with us."

Trakenburg blurted, "Which one is right, Captain?"

Longstreet smiled. "They both are, Colonel. Captain Mirikami, I'd like to know the answer to the request I passed to Carson."

Mirikami had the answer ready, which they had decided on just fifteen minutes earlier. "We don't want a virtual prisoner at home, who might long to return to Human Space, and there succumb to pressure to be welcomed back by revealing our location. It isn't really a fear of the Planetary Union that concerns us so much, not while they need us anyway. It's the leaks about us, which might reach the Krall." Before Mirikami could continue, Longstreet jumped in, proving he'd considered exactly this point.

He spoke in a rush. "I'll accept the clone mods you four have, making sure I have as much legal risk as Sarge here if I wanted to return." Then he added his real motivation. "And then I can go with you on raids against Krall planets."

Sarge gave him a sour look, and a pretend accusation. "If you have a Booster Suit and my genetic mods, you'll beat me at arm wrestling, you cheater."

Mirikami looked sternly at his court jester apprentice, then at Longstreet. "Captain, before you cut me off, I was about to make an alternative offer." He let him dangle a moment.

"To give you, at a minimum, the clone mods and then accept you as a citizen of our world. The Booster Suit might not be yours to take." He looked at Trakenburg.

The jester's apprentice simply couldn't hold his tongue. "You'd be immigrant New Citizen number two. I'm number one."

For the first time in weeks, Trakenburg felt a lessening of the tension that had been building. "Your only condition for accepting joint operations with Special Operations, to trust us, is if our people accept your SG genetic modifications. To physically become what only our surgery, implants, and these damned chaffing exomuscle suits gave us?" Even when feeling relieved, the starch and skepticism that was a natural part of his personality showed.

Mirikami relaxed his stern look. "I have one other concession I need from you, Colonel."

Trakenburg thought, *I KNEW that smart little shit had something else up his sleeve.* It had been too easy. Prepared for the worst he asked roughly, "What is it?"

It was worse than he feared.

"Among only the older men in this room, in friendly conversations, might you allow us to call you Frances?"

He turned red in the face. "You picked my mind! Tapped it, whatever you call it. It's Frank on any records you can find."

Mirikami calmly looked at Nabarone. "Henry, care to explain?"

With a big charming smile, he did. "Sure. As I previously told you, Thad, Dillon, and Sarge..., oh excuse me, I mean *Garland.* The colonel's real first name is Frances, not Frank. Generals have a deeper reach into sealed archives than colonels do. And he confirmed the accuracy of my digging just now."

"I will not answer to that," insisted the former Frances Trakenburg.

Mirikami offered a half bow. "Then to offer you a concession in return, I modify my request to call you Frank. Is that acceptable, Frank?"

"Fine." He answered with a snap to his voice and a glance over to Longstreet, which suggested the captain had better use discretion.

Sarge, still playing jester, added, "At least your real name isn't a Christmas tree decoration. What are you so sensitive about anyway? At least your last name wasn't changed to Trakenburgfem."

A female dominated society of three hundred years ago largely blamed men for the Clone Wars and the Gene War. They had frequently used dual-purpose genderless first names for the sons that were born from the male survivor breeders after the Collapse. Others had changed family names, such as Johnson to Johnfem, or added other feminine sounding prefixes or suffixes.

When laws changed to grant men greater rights a hundred years ago, they regained the right to change birth given names when they reached twenty-one, which was the age they could register their names to vote. That didn't prevent mothers, who retained contractual naming rights on their children, from *using* the feminine forms of names for their sons and daughters. Some of those rebellious, freedom-seeking sons changed their names when they turned twenty-one. It appeared Frances had been one of those, who apparently was sensitive to the teasing other boys with more "manly" sounding names had heaped on him.

Life had been awkward for a hypersensitive but physically tough kid that was forbidden to fight, and then the Krall came. Now Frank had an enemy he was not only allowed to strike back at, but to kill. A social outlet he had craved.

"If you want to call me Frank, then I get to go with you. I'll accept your gene mods. I also want to participate in the raids."

"New Citizen number...three." Sarge died off at the end, under a withering glare from Mirikami.

"Count to yourself." He was told. Then Mirikami went to the next of several sensitive subjects.

"Henry, I know your answer from previous conversations, and I agree that you are needed here to run the war on Poldark and to coordinate for us. That doesn't mean you can't have dual citizenship if you want, the same as these two wish to do." He looked at the two other officers, realizing a clarification was needed.

"I wasn't as clear as I should have been. This is all so new to us. I am not asking you to renounce Planetary Union citizenship. Each of you is a citizen of your birth worlds, perhaps of another adopted colony world you call home now, and of the PU. My adopted world isn't even a PU settled colony, but there are Rim worlds that have not joined the PU, and those populations in large part feel like PU citizens, and fight for it against the Krall.

"We perhaps can be called a Frontier world, located beyond the Rim. Being loyal to us does not preclude loyalty to where you are from. We are not an adversary of the PU, or the Hub worlds that dominate the PU government. We know that some of their citizens will not reciprocate that feeling, because of our violating the genetic laws." He switched back to Nabarone.

"Excuse the diversion, Henry. Let me tell you what we can offer to you as a no-strings-attached gift. Frank and Joe want to come with us, and you can't do that and still defend Poldark.

"Without your leaving Poldark, we can send a ship back with some of our biologists. The most useful of the SG mods can be implemented with very little outward physical effect while in progress. Other than aches and some mild fever that is, depending on what mods you elect to receive. For example, I have six mods, but the two strength and endurance muscle mods are the most useful to you on this planet. You don't suffer from the extremes of heat and cold of our home, nor need the high metabolism to counter the high gravity energy drain. I doubt you will have children to whom you wish to pass along superconducting nerves."

Nabarone grimaced at the last remark. "No."

"How much risk would it be for you to travel later, Henry? Would your DNA be checked?"

"No. With a war against easy to spot aliens, it's unusual for most people to be scanned for DNA now. You'd have to trigger a hit with a facial recognition database for a fugitive to be flagged for DNA testing. Besides, what am I saying! *It's good to be the General*. I bypass all of that bullshit on a military transport."

With a trace of sarcasm, Mirikami concluded, "The lack of an objection from a 'shy man' like you tells me you're receptive to the notion. The problem is how to get you, the technicians and equipment, together on Poldark. You can help your own cause there. I had Jakob run a search for a civilian Jump ship we could afford to buy with what we have left from our dwindling cash reserves. All of our precious metal has been sold."

"I can fake the loss of a military courier, if you need something small and fast." Nabarone proposed.

"No. Medium sized and civilian is better because it doesn't have to be explained each time it comes and goes if it's legally registered. I have a tramp freighter in mind, which is in the right price range, and will hold modest cargo, or perhaps forty to fifty people if partitioned properly. The seller, a man I believe was a contraband smuggler to Bollovstic before the war, needs to unload his ship. There are some irregularities in the ownership, due to his former financial partners-in-crime laying claim to a share of the title. I need it cleared up, and to let them argue over how to split the money after the fact. With that ship, we can visit here without alerting the whole defense grid when it does a White Out. It was converted to T squared technology before the *investors* realized the Krall would take their Rim markets completely away from them."

"What did they smuggle?" Sarge asked.

"Don't know, don't care. However, the Falcon is the best buy I could find for the money we have left, and for what we need. The former captain said it was the fastest ship in this sector, and he claims the PU Navy would never have caught them in this millennium."

Nabarone shrugged. Easy problem to fix. "I have considerable influence with the governor, as you might imagine. A cash deal should make the new registration a matter of a few days to complete. Who will be the captain of record when it leaves?"

"Captain Mike Haveram doesn't yet know he's being promoted out of the useless engineering slot he fills on the Mark."

"The chief is going to be pissed," Dillon offered. "The only one that hates being in charge of a ship more than him is Sarge."

A hand held out by Mirikami halted the expected rebuttal from Sarge. "He will have a ship that actually needs maintenance, which is something he has craved. After he gets her home, he can give her to whichever former Spacer Captain he picks that he can get along with, and go back to running the Engine Room."

With the hand now down, Sarge spoke up, but it wasn't about Dillon's double jab at him and the chief.

"General, I was under your overall command before capture by the Krall, a mere fly speck on your elevated rank's rump to be certain. However, you can reactivate me and send me off with the Mark when she leaves, or let me stay MIA and presumed dead in the official records. I'm going with them either way, and *not* being a deserter is my preference. What do you say, Sir?"

"Go, before I discover you stole my best set of real gold stars. Considered dead or alive is your choice."

"Dead takes less explanation and forms to complete."

"Who's that speaking? I didn't believe in ghosts 'til now," Nabarone quipped.

Mirikami had a personnel question that couldn't be so easily answered. "Colonel, you and Captain Longstreet here have to decide how your absence will be handled. I already knew from Henry that your independent command was an irritant to him because your chain of command was outside of his. What superior needs to know what happened to you, if they need to know at all?"

"Captain, I'm under a black ops section at Army headquarters on Earth. I have no closer superiors on Poldark. Captain Akers, based up at the Sofia front line, is the next ranking spec ops officer on Poldark. He was about to make major, based on my previous recommendation. He would likely come to the Novi Sad headquarters if I were out of the picture.

"The five spec ops companies on the planet operate nearly independently as it is. I frequently have a company or platoon, or sometimes only a squad off planet, on various missions. I have been thinking on this almost since you arrived. I wanted us to work together, your TGs going with our teams on missions off Poldark. It looks like it will only be me and…, Joe here, invited." It was an obvious effort to use just his first name.

"My original hope was to request volunteers, out of the one platoon that knows about you, and conduct some raids on Krall worlds with your TGs. I've probed our men acting as your instructors, and all of them are eager to go on that sort of mission. I have no way of knowing how many would do what Joe and I are willing to do to be part of this, accept gene mods and simply vanish.

"If I report up the line that just the two of us suddenly went on a mission, that won't sound remotely plausible. We are quickly going to be considered AWOL, and eventually deserters. We will know that it isn't true, but having those we respect think that it is will hurt."

Testing the waters with his suddenly human sounding superior, Longstreet had a suggestion. "Frank, if I can get enough men to form a squad to do what you and I are doing, and Captain Mirikami will accept them of course, can you dream up a mission that will seem plausible? I said a lot of 'ifs' here, but I'm closer to my platoon than you are, and they talk to me more freely than they do to you. Fully half of the platoon has no families that they see or talk to any more. We already seem like freaks to them. Being reported missing in action is less painful than an unexplained disappearance, and leaves room for an honorable reappearance someday."

Mirikami put a hand on each man's shoulder. "Joe, Frank, the Mark has room for as many men as you are likely to recruit. Certainly more than the platoon that you have here. If you will accept the intrusion of a TG1 Tapping them, as you conduct your interviews, we can bypass the men that would have a problem going on a mission that is a change in where they call home, or accepting gene mods. They go on potential life ending missions all the time, but this is different. They might live, and still not come home.

"They don't need to know all the details and specifics before we know their true feelings, but mentioning that they might be able to receive genetic enhancements to make them like Sarge isn't leaking any big new secret. They all know he was recently of the PU Army and captured by the Krall, and now he's with us. That isn't TG ability, but it's a start."

Trakenburg seemed a bit more upbeat when he said, "The Naval intelligence reports give me the pretext to scout one of the most interesting worlds they reported, only eight hundred eleven light-years away. As little as a single squad or two could be sent to do preliminary recon. We often use Navy ships for insertion, but in cases where the Krall might detect a human warship, which they could consider a violation of their order against another 'Naval attack from space,' we have smaller, unarmed stealthed crafts. The Penetrator class does not belong to the Navy, and are under my control. That gives me a way to claim to have used one such ship that's off the Navy 'books' so to speak."

Thad noticed Nabarone was getting red in the face. "Henry. Turn down the heat before you spout steam. What's up?"

"Did any of you discuss the Navy briefing two days ago, after you came back here?"

"Not that I know of, Henry. We were ordered not to do so." He looked at the other SGs who said they hadn't either.

Now he realized that Nabarone was looking at Trakenburg who was casually moving towards the coffee pot, placing people and distance between him and the general.

"The summary of that meeting was placed in my AI's most secure and encrypted data base, and the Navy told me to keep it confidential until they had finished the analysis on the terabytes of data. They didn't want the location of those planets known until approved actions concerning them could be decided. I used my position to get the information in advance for your briefing, because I already knew about the scouting missions.

"Trakenburg, mincing his way around the table over there wasn't given that briefing. He just described the exact distance to the closest one of those *interesting* worlds. The bastard has penetrated my AI's security. I'll have his ass for this."

"Henry, it wasn't unauthorized access." Trakenburg said defensively. Using Nabarone's first name now only pissed the man off more.

"Don't 'Henry' me now, goddamn you! What do you mean by that? You claim you have *authorized* access to my AI, you turd?"

Trakenburg, as usual, was wearing his Booster Suit, despite seldom going on a mission. He was happy he had it now, because he half expected the general to come after him. "When my AI was installed at my Novi Sad command post, the black ops division was contacted by someone from Army headquarters, offering spec ops limited secret access to your system.

"I don't think the Ladies above you trusted your willingness to share with them, because of your frequent baiting of visiting female officers. Hell, you even named your AI *Carla,* which is the middle name of your immediate superior. You were once so suspicious of the Hub government that you ran militia guerrilla exercises in case they *invaded* Poldark. I'm not the only one to use that back door either, because Max has sensed it in use when his own data transfer rate was reduced, and he found our line to your Carla was moving data through us. They get in via a back door to my own system. I don't keep anything on Max I don't want them to know in my data. I never had access to your personal files, I swear, and Max can verify that."

Thad started laughing. "He has a point about your anti-feminist bias. Geez, you named your AI after your own boss lady?" He laughed harder.

"I didn't know that was Lieutenant General Cadifem's middle name," he grumbled. "As a young man in college, needing money, I had an uncontracted liaison with a ball breaker older woman by that name, so that I wouldn't have to give my mother 70% of the contract money. I didn't expect that name to bite me in the ass, again."

Mirikami, unable to keep a chuckle from his voice asked him, "This make you change your mind about staying behind here?"

"Of course not. Poldark is where I can do the most good for my planet, and behind the scenes to help your efforts. I can even use the knowledge of that backdoor to think of some sort of payback, now that I know they can snoop through my data."

"General, I'm sorry about the snooping." The master of sneak offered.

"Shut up, Frances. You're leaving and I'm happy, and if I hear another apology I know that you don't mean, I'll start some scurrilous rumor about you after you're gone."

****

"Just eight more men." Thad sounded disappointed. "I was thinking even more might want to go with us."

Dillon reminded him. "Ethan and Carson both said the predominant reason was when they were told they wouldn't receive the mods that would make them TGs. We old SG's just don't have the sex appeal."

"We're going to try the other Koban mods for ourselves. If they work for us, we could do it for them. You still think the Koban mods have a better chance of working with the later generation nanites, right?"

"Sure, but we couldn't explain all that to them in advance, and it might not be possible."

Sarge, ever mindful of the citizenship status he declared for himself, sounded relieved. "I'm still first of only eleven new citizens. The most elite of the elite." He winked.

"I don't know," rebutted Thad, arching an eyebrow. "Dillon and I arrived more than twenty years before you did. I'd rank you somewhere at about number thirty thousand or so, and you would appear to be in a tie with the sixteen other captives that arrived as prisoners with you. Your status looks rather mundane to me"

Dillon made a double score. "These new ten are the first we ever actually *invited* to join us. They didn't just fall in our lap as a helpless captive, always cheating Thad out of his poker money. Assuming, of course that his wife ever lets the poor slob have any." He nailed the two of them at once.

Sarge wasn't done just yet. "Yea, yea, yea. The spec ops guys have it easy. I'd have given my left arm to get to Koban. No, wait…, I did that!"

"Right. It would be nice if you used its replacement for something besides scratching your backside. How about helping stow the last of the cargo, and we'll get ready to go. Our spec ops recruits are gathering their gear, and Trakenburg has stashed the Penetrator class ship in the crater, as the presumed vessel the 'missing' men used on the secret mission.

"Tet says Nabarone is back in his headquarters now. We want his authority handy, in case someone decides to shoot at us on the way out. We'll lift with less oomph than the Krall usually use, making us a tempting target. Chief Haveram had it easy. He left like a civilized law abiding ship operator, on a criminal's former smuggling ship." The Falcon, loaded with consumer goods scarce at home had departed earlier. It too was planning on a devious return course to Koban, to thwart any potential follower.

"Tet picked one of the TG1 tachyon communication windows for our departure. Our wives may have left messages drifting in Tachyon Space for us. I'd like to know how they're doing. I hope the hell my wife discovered the Morning Star planet is livable. Otherwise I'll find one grouchy Lady waiting for me."

Thinking of his own wife, Dillon wasn't concerned. "I doubt Heavyside was any problem for Noreen. The TGs were going to pretend to be recruits to get into the main camp and find out what the future of spec ops is. We already know they will handle the training program on Heavyside easily. Frank said he's pretty confidant some of their people were pushing for genetic engineering, which was previously rejected by the government. Now that Poldark is steadily going the way of Bollovstic, he hopes the PU will change their minds. It should be an uneventful visit to Heavyside."

A few hours later, the Mark was ready. The Planetary Defense forces were specifically told to not fire on an obvious clanship launch, departing from well outside Krall controlled territory. Mirikami, waiting on the Bridge for the "all clear" was also making certain there were no stealthed clanships incoming on his sensors before they lifted. He intended to drill a rapid vertical turbulence trail through the atmosphere. Stealthed or not, that would make their track obvious and predictable, but it was what the defense forces were told to expect.

Nabarone's voice came over the speaker, on the frequency they were instructed to monitor. He remained his wiseass self when he said, "Ok boys. On your Mark, get set, go!"

How original, thought Mirikami. He had heard that same dumb pun at least a half dozen times from his own people. He hit the acceleration horn once, and tapped the launch control personally. Jakob could have done it all for him, but he felt like initiating the engines himself, maintaining the pretense that he didn't largely let the AI do the routine drudgery of spaceflight. Hard acceleration was felt immediately, and velocity increased rapidly on the column of plasma behind them. Not a standard Krall max performance liftoff, but a lot more than human staffed ships generally employed.

As soon as they left atmosphere, Mirikami transmitted a double click on the frequency, confirming they were clear. He allowed Jakob to execute the Jump command, and they rotated out of Normal Space.

****

The commander of the Krall invasion forces on Poldark asked his aide to restate his allegation. Gatlek Pendor must have misinterpreted what his second in command had meant. "Kaldot, you say it is your belief, and that of my K'Tal's, that this clanship launched today was the one we believed died a berserkers death?" Pendor was incredulous of his aide's words. The implication was outlandish.

"That is our thought, Gatlek. With dependable evidence beyond the coincidence of location of the launching point. There was an audio recording available of the thruster sounds when that same clanship previously flew over the Dorbo clan warriors to attack the human forces, about twelve hands of days ago. That day, Dorbo was enjoying an unexpected strong assault and artillery bombardment from human forces, near the river and south of family nest areas that the humans live in, close to Novi Sad.

"That day, two of the attitude thrusters were misadjusted on that clanship, and caused what two K'Tals called a vibration at an ultrasonic frequency between the two. A harmonic is what both of them named the sound it made, of which I do not know the word's meaning. I only know that it was a very loud and improper noise, and I was told that an adjustment should have been made to the side thrusters to remove the distracting sound from our ears."

Impatient with an explanation he didn't understand any better than did his aide, Pendor snapped, "Do you mean this sound was the same from the slow moving clanship that escaped today?"

"Gatlek, both K'Tal's say the two recorded sound patterns are the same, even though the second time the sound was recorded from a greater distance, and therefore not as loud. They said it was not how loud that mattered. A sound pattern that repeated the same exact harmonic was the proof it was from the same source. They say it came from the same clanship that attacked the human forces like a berserker, and was destroyed by four seeker missiles."

"You mean that it only appeared to be destroyed. It must have stayed in human controlled territory those many hands of days, hidden from us, and then was launched to space slowly, and the human defense forces did not try to destroy it."

"That is our belief."

"What has the Darpot clan told you of their destroyed clanship, and the missing sub leader? The forbidden interclan fight they reported to us days later apparently ended on the same day we thought a berserker pilot attacked the humans, and was destroyed. That was a false conclusion about it being a berserker."

"Yes. They have found every member of the small crew of the heavy loaded supply ship, except for a sub leader in command named Hortak.

"As you were told previously, Gatlek, half of the clanship's crew was killed near where another clanship's landing blast pattern was found. They appeared to have died in an assault on that mystery ship, and their own ship was destroyed in a more successful attack, presumably from the crew of the unknown craft. Some of the Darpot clan's dead crew was found inside their clanship. Another four hands, less one, were found dead in a valley with the bunker construction machines, which had apparently been ambushed. There were four hands of damaged machines in the valley, so one warrior apparently did not die there.

"The new sub leader for the Darpot says the clanship was almost completely unloaded, but they are missing many small arms, and five mini-tanks. She also says the dead that were found where the other ship had landed were killed in strange ways."

"What is strange about deaths from attacking a clanship with mini-tanks, three transports, and trucks? That is always a lost fight against heavy lasers and plasma cannons."

"The dead were doubly killed, she said."

"Did anyone order her to explain this ridiculous claim?"

"I did, Gatlek. She meant they died of plasma rifles shots, mostly to their heads, and had massive body damage from a clanships heavy weapons where they were found in and near the tanks, trucks and armored transports. They were shot again with powerful weapons after receiving fatal head and body wounds, from plasma rifles and our standard projectile pistols."

Pendor snorted in amusement and confusion. "That is inefficient of the attackers to waste time and energy that way."

Kaldot agreed. "I did not consider her claim seriously when first made. I do now, because of the flight of the ship and its apparent safety while in human territory. Then it launched unchallenged by the humans from their territory."

Pendor was shrewd, and one of the rising new breed of Krall commanders. He didn't like the unexplained aspect of this bizarre event. Nor the possible implications he could draw from them.

"The fight near the ship that escaped off-world was not real. Some of the Darpot equipment was taken, and the departed clanship, under control of many unbalanced warriors that defeated Darpot, seems to have done this and went to join the humans…," he paused almost a second, a very long period of contemplation for a Krall of his high status.

"Impossible!" he was emphatic. "There are tales of disgraced Krall that suffered a mind or brain defect that have gone to join the enemy, but over our long history it is but a few hands of them only, and always acting alone. This theory requires many such insane traitorous warriors acting together. The soft Krall are securely contained, and do not have the means or the physical capability to defeat us talon to talon. They are old warriors of the time of the Olt'kitapi. We passed them on the Great Path a thousand breeding cycles ago."

Kaldot was tentative. "Is the alternative that non Krall did this?"

The backlash he feared did not happen. Pendor considered this possibility for a moment, before making a conditional rejection.

"If it were not also impossible, I could consider that. That enemy would need to carry newly dead warriors, for activating the clanship and the weapons, as humans have sometimes done and replace them as the quantum locks detected death and refused them access. Where could they obtain so many dead for a long day of fighting? All but one Darpot corpse was counted."

He quickly decided on a course of action that moved the problem from his talons. He could not solve the mystery, but he could report this matter to a leader that was famed for his new thinking, and for adapting to this changing type of war.

Tor Gatrol Kanpardi, the overall commander of the war with humans would be informed of this strange event on the current invasion planet. Kanpardi was actively planning invasions of two other human worlds, as the next phase progressed to involve more clans and, pressure humans into more desperate resistance and effort.

****

Kanpardi was in a joint clan planning session on Telda Ka, when the urgent courier report from the Gatlek on Poldark arrived. He was relieved to have an excuse to leave the room full of bickering clan leaders. They were supposed to be preparing to open two new invasion fronts on human worlds, one a heavily populated and long settled colony, which had considerable industrial and technological capability on the planet. That world, the colony of Alders, would be the first real test of human ability to resist, when a world of very high value to them was threatened.

However, the council was not discussing what resources were needed to support three invasions, such as increased weapons production, expanding clanship building, or making more of any of the tools of war that were required. Instead, for three days they had argued over the fighting roll that should be granted to each of dozens of finger clans. The smaller clans were demanding greater access to serious fighting. They were client clans that major clans had spawned in the last three thousand years, to increase the number of sympathetic voices supporting the parent clan's interests in joint clan meetings.

Now came the time for the major clans to pay back those millennia of finger clan's support, with status earning combat opportunities in new invasions. The obligation was heavy on the tips of all their talons. It blunted their ability to strike at the real problem Kanpardi saw. Logistics and supply, versus which small clans would receive significant rolls in new invasions, was moot when the equipment to give to them was limited.

Once out of the council room, he spoke only with his trusted Graka clan mate, Telour. Kanpardi voiced his dissatisfaction with the lack of efficiency the joint clan council displayed.

"Clans that recently fought thousands of years of restricted interclan warfare, have been deluded into believing there is no limit to the materials of war, which they now waste so quickly. In clan wars, we did not tolerate pointless material destruction for pleasure, and preserved more weapons and ships for repair and reuse.

"The humans, as worthy enemies should, do not grant that tolerance, and we have pilots and warriors that recklessly risk ships that belong to all Krall, as if they have no responsibility to bring them back for reuse. Their own wasted low status lives are not worth the price we pay when they do not return with the tools of war."

Telour, slow to grasp just how annoyed his mentor was, commented, "The reckless dead do not earn status to reproduce, and their genes are removed from the Great Path. The new cycles of warriors are growing smarter, and learning to detect and avoid the devious ways that humans fight."

Displaying his irritation, Kanpardi snapped back. "Humans are changing how they fight faster than our warriors are adjusting. We will win because we have the ability to destroy all of their worlds. However, to increase the culling of good fighters from weak we need more fronts in the war. We lose war material at the rate it is made. It is not easy to expand a war this way. The clans that have control of production worlds think replacing losses is enough. The only production increase was of clanships and single ships, after the humans attacked Telda Ka twice.

"If they attacked what they call K1 again, even stronger than before, the losses would limit us to fighting on Poldark for years. We would have to waste the invasion possibilities of several human worlds, by total destruction, as another lesson to them. A large war on three worlds will divert their fighters and material to prevent such an adventure. We need to build for those other invasions."

To demonstrate his grasp of the politics to Kanpardi, Telour said, "The controlling great clans do not want to take K'Tal and warriors away from fighting, to open new worlds for production, or to increase it where we have trained slaves now. This thinking slows us on the Path."

Annoyed by his subordinate's effort to show he agreed with his leader, Kanpardi told him, "Cleaning my cloaca for me will not serve your status well, Telour."

Telour decided to ease away from the subject that had his leader agitated. "Then it is good I brought you a report from Poldark, to remove your thoughts from clan politics."

"Tell me."

The briefing of the information from Pendor was followed by information that Telour had thought was also interesting, and which he had gleaned from another unusual incident report, two or three hands of days earlier than when the one on Poldark started.

"My Tor, I was previously aware of a minor event here, at a Dorbo clan dome, of two lightly staffed clanships taken by force, and the watch standers and some of the occupants killed. On one ship, an octet had been engaged in physical training inside, and most of them were found dead. There were bodies and discarded body armor found charred on the ramps after the two stolen ships launched, but several bodies were missing, as if taken. This sounded similar to me of the story of the missing commander of the destroyed clanship on Poldark.

"Dorbo clan blamed their incident on some other clan, because of an unexpected landing of a clanship close to the two that were taken. They all departed together, so they believe it was a new finger clan that wanted additional clanships, but had no influence to have any assigned to them."

By Kanpardi's rapt attention, Telour was satisfied he had drawn the respectful interest of his superior with his additional research. Then he was asked, "Have you any explanation as to either of these two events, or a means to connect them as actually related?"

"My Tor, the sequence and timing of the two similar incidents permits the action on Poldark to have directly followed those on K1. I use the human name for Telda Ka for a simple reason. I suspect a human involvement in this. The only other alternative that could be shaped to fit the facts, which Gatlek Pendor completely rejects, is that a number of warriors have abandoned the Great Path and joined with humans against us. His rejection of that unsupportable theory is justified beyond any possible doubt, in my judgment."

Kanpardi looked at him with greater interest. "You would say this because in our long history there have been no organized traitors in our ranks?"

"Yes. There have been reported only a few hands of brain damaged warriors with mental aberrations, caused by some head injury, that have ever rejected our destiny to rule the galaxy."

"Can your rejection of traitors as a possibility explain the ability of these attackers to bypass quantum encrypted locks on our ships and weapons, if it was *not* done by one of us?"

Telour realized Kanpardi was testing him, and had formed an opinion of his own, even though he had only just now heard the details. That meant Kanpardi's own theory must be one that could be reached quickly, based only on the facts presented. He was leading Telour with the questions he asked.

"Humans may have learned how to bypass our locks, or have discovered that the key is in our tattoos. Since we must still be living for the tattoos to work, they might hold warriors captive to use them. That would be difficult, however, because they would need multiple live warriors, even though we can force our own death, and we are very difficult to capture and hold… No!"

He stopped himself short, as if for a moment of consideration. "The clanships that were taken have operated at normal acceleration levels a human cannot accept or survive. They would need to be as strong as we are, and we have never encountered humans like that in combat, where such capability would be more valuable to them than stealing three clanships they cannot use efficiently. Not even a powered suit can protect them from acceleration. It is either traitors of our own, or soft Krall."

Kanpardi didn't seem surprised at the soft Krall comment, an indication he had thought of that. He had an alternative answer to the subject of opening their quantum locks. "Humans probably have acquired Katushas from dead warriors or destroyed clanships, and may have learned how to apply a tattoo. This would provide them their own access to our equipment and weapons. However, as you have proved you understand, our ships perform at levels that we cannot use when we have human prisoners onboard. The inertial force would make them unconscious, as when they do the false death at night. Or it will kill them if we use high acceleration." He twitched his left shoulder, to indicate there was a question or problem he still saw.

"The soft Krall could fly our ships, and even if they are no physical match for warriors that have followed the Great Path for twenty-two thousand years, they are still stronger than humans. We still give them the tattoos so they can operate the higher Olt'kitapi designed ships for us, when we force them to do so. I question if the Tanga clan has perhaps grown lax, and let some of them escape their prison world?"

Telour, pleased the soft Krall idea had not been immediately dismissed said, "It would be very dangerous to their captive offspring and mates for soft Krall to come to Telda Ka or Poldark, where we have forces on alert for human attacks."

Kanpardi could be cautious for a Krall, a contrary trait in a Great Path warrior, but one that had actually helped elevate him to lead this current war. "No matter if it is dangerous for them to come here, there are at least three clanships no longer in our control that we must somehow explain.

"None of our clans on the Great Path would ever yield to a threat by any enemy, even if the threat was against a planet *covered* in warriors and nests of our own clan. We would *never* let a foe control us as we control the soft Krall." He extended his talons in response to a new thought.

"Some of the soft ones may finally have grown the bones in their backs to resist us. If some were free, could they be hunting for the ancient Olt'kitapi ships? They are never allowed to enter one of them unless they, and their offspring and mates, are in our total control. Otherwise, *we* would be the one's watching our clan worlds explode, as when the Olt'kitapi killed our first home."

Telour sensed the opportunity he had maneuvered to create was finally there, for him to earn higher status, by pretending to offer a personal sacrifice of his own time for his mentor. "My Tor. We have discussed unilaterally increasing clanship production at the world our Graka clan controls. However, we would gain no more than our normal share of clanships for our placement of additional K'Tals and warriors there, to push the slaves to work faster, to deliver more ships. We can recover that diversion of our warriors in status points many times over, if the new invasions can take place sooner, after you convince the joint clans that more material is required for new invasions."

Now for the proposal. "My Tor, send me as a representative of our clan leader. I should also go as a personal representative of you, as Tor Gatrol's second in command. The *first* level of authority, as clan representative, would permit me to order Graka clan sub leaders to increase clanship production." He let the reason for his proposal to represent the Tor Gatrol, a promotion to second in command, to hang in the air unexplained. He anticipated the question, which he'd made inevitable.

"How would you use the promotion you have just proposed for yourself?" Kanpardi liked the proposal's brashness, and suspected Telour's answer would match.

"My Tor, I could force Tanga clan to show me the precautions they have in place for containing the soft Krall, and account for them all. This would embarrass the sub leader they placed in charge, who was moved far from the war he wanted to be able to start."

Next came the most pleasurable part. "Parkoda, our mutual antagonist before we departed Koban, was sent there by Tanga clan for his political blunders and other mistakes, which gave our Graka clan the right to start the war with humans. You know he tried to provoke your resignation as Gatrol, in order for you to be allowed to answer dishonorable remarks made to you, if you challenged him to a death match."

Kanpardi initially sounded sour in his response. "You explained my grudge with Tanga clan, and with Parkoda, as if I had forgotten them within a single breeding cycle. I well remember his failed attempt to provoke me."

Then his tone became more enthusiastic. "I will forgive your unnecessary reminder because you have offered an excellent means to force a symbolical lick from him on my cloaca, in front of his warriors and K'Tal. Having a soft Krall watch him be humbled would not increase his pleasure either." Kanpardi appeared fixated on the topic of butt kissing today.

"Telour, you obviously knew in advance that the long travel to our clanship yards would pass conveniently near the planet where we keep the soft Krall. That was careful planning on your part, and provided me with an excellent inducement. You do show promise." It was high praise, from a hard to please Tor Gatrol.

Kanpardi wasn't finished. "I have another suggestion to humiliate Parkoda more, who will not dare to offer you a challenge after I give you the promotion you have cleverly extorted from me." He snorted in amusement.

"When you Jump from the soft Krall world, for our shipyards, I want you to insist that Parkoda go with you to inspect the living Olt'kitapi ships where they are hidden. They are not Tanga clan's responsibility to protect, but you have evidence for legitimate suspicion that soft Krall may have escaped. That is even less possible than saying humans somehow raided us and took our clanships, but use that excuse to your advantage. Naturally, a soft one would want to seek out those four old ships to try to force us to free his people.

"After seven thousand light-years, it is but a small side trip for verification of the security of the Olt'kitapi ships. Make Parkoda escort you inside all four ships, to prove they are all alive and still awake, and no soft Krall are hiding inside." They both snorted in amusement at Parkoda's upcoming humiliation.

Thus, a fateful confrontation was set in motion, although not the one Telour had carefully arranged.

Chapter 12: Haven

A month into the cultural contacts, and Wister had convinced more of the village to see and meet these strange people, some of whom spoke with their minds if you let them touch you. This was an amazing ability to them, and there were no stories from his people of other races with this ability. That was significant, because stories among the long-lived Prada went back many orbits of many planets around many stars.

He wondered if the Rulers should have left the humans alive. Did they know of this ability of the mind, of their great strength for their small size, and particularly their speed? Entire species, which were much less of a threat to the Rulers power, had been ruthlessly destroyed as quickly as possible. The most recent species they had killed, that Wister knew of, were the Malverans. Annihilated by a single clan in less than a hundred orbits.

His grandmother had seen some of these insect eating intelligent reptiles, which resembled half-sized cousins of the Rulers. The Malverans had lived in this part of the galaxy for thousands of years, and expanded very slowly. They had known of the planet the Rulers later described as Koban, the training world. They knew too of this safer world, which Wister had learned to like greatly. The Malverans used only warm, relatively dry worlds with lower gravity, and neither of the planets in this system was to their liking for colonization.

Despite long affiliation with the Rulers, he and the elders of other Prada villages did not understand the minds of their masters well. Their words of contempt for all other species was one thing, but their actions appeared to show a greater fear of weak, peaceful species (whom they defeated quickly).

They were most tolerant of those that fought them hardest and offered them the greatest risk (fighting those species could last a thousand years or more, when the Rulers could have been victorious much sooner). It was as if they enjoyed the *conflict* of becoming the elder dominate species of the galaxy. Why would such an elder rational species want constant war? The motives of this harsh senior race, apparently too complex for the Prada to grasp, had followed their Great Path over many millenniums.

All other species were destroyed or dominated by the Rulers eventually, as was their right as an elder species. They performed other acts incomprehensible to his people. The survival they granted to the Prada and the Torki were examples.

The Rulers, as ancient, as large and powerful a species as they were, could have built anything they needed on their own. Instead, they had granted the lowly Prada continued existence in exchange for their doing what they had always done, build and make things, and obey their elders.

The Torki often did not act as grateful to the Rulers as they should. Nevertheless, they built for them the delicate electronic and quantum mechanical parts of the machines that controlled the clanships and their weapons. Some parts they had created from their own science, others they copied or learned from the races the Rulers did not choose to save.

Wister saw no understandable pattern to Ruler behavior in this respect, but every Prada was grateful for their generosity in allowing them to share some of the many worlds the Rulers controlled.

The Raspani had somehow pleased the Rulers greatly, because they lived on all their worlds. They had hidden their great minds, and now existed only to feed the Rulers with their bodies. The Prada were granted this honored purpose on rare occasions, proof that they could please the masters this way at times. Hard work was all that was normally asked of them. An insolent Torki would be killed if it displeased a Ruler, as they deserved, but as an insult to them, the bodies were never eaten.

There was no way the Prada would understand that the lack of red meat was the only reason Torki were off the dinner table for the Krall, or that the pallid lean meat of a Prada was repulsive to their Rulers.

Unlike the Rulers who chose their planets more carefully, the humans apparently used almost any world, like an infestation, if their mind pictures of populations and type of worlds could be believed. Just as the Prada and Torki had survived on this gentle planet when left alone for a time, the humans had miraculously survived on terrible Koban, even when left without Ruler protection. They had managed to do on heavy savage Koban what the Rulers had not chosen to do, and the Prada and Torki could never do. They made it a safe home. They had brought two of Koban's smartest most deadly predators with them, as proof they had become partners. Thousands of Prada had died in their huge jaws, over the many orbits it took to build the domes on that deadly world.

Wister, because he had directed some of the construction on the two domes the Kobani now used, knew humans were recent arrivals to Koban, just as they claimed. They told the Prada that the Rulers had left this star system, intending to be gone for many orbits before they returned to live on Koban. (The humans insisted on disrespectfully calling the masters by their species name, the Krall). They urged the Prada to work with them to build cities on this world, without waiting for the Rulers to direct them in their wisdom.

There was no need to rush. The Rulers had disappeared from other worlds many times in the past, and returned to some of them eventually. They would surely come back for many of the loyal and faithful Prada they left behind. The Rulers had only been gone from this system for perhaps a full breeding cycle, certainly less than two complete egg-to-novice-to-warrior cycles.

Compared to the Prada's indefinite life span, this was a trivial interval. There was no reason to activate the underground production facilities now, which they maintained with their surplus population, awaiting the Ruler's return. It was two orbits early for him to replace his older sister in the vast factory complex, but he wanted her advice on what to do about these rash, pushy, and irreverent newcomers. His older sister, Nawella, would guide him as she had for over a thousand orbits on three planets.

The little "diplomat," as he thought of the Kobani named Maggi, had claimed the Rulers would be surprised to find this world full of people when they returned someday. She said it had room to hold Prada, Torki, and humans, all preparing for their return. Wister took the word "surprised" to mean the same as "pleased." He did wish to please the Rulers, without having to wait to do so.

The distinction when Maggi sometimes said human, other times Kobani, for her people, was confusing to him because the mental images and visual evidence suggested they were exactly the same species, but different somehow. Humans lived on many worlds, yet Kobani only lived on Koban. Since he could mind share only with those humans he knew were from Koban, a tiny minority population compared to the many billions on other worlds, it was easier to think of them all as simply humans.

They had a leader of the small human village living inside and around the clanship they used, and she named herself as Captain Marlyn Greeves. A triple name, as only a great Ruler might use. He understood that the first word was a rank position word that granted her authority over other humans, and her last name was something like a clan name. Like Dr. Maggi Fisher, she too preferred the middle name in conversation.

Marlyn often used Maggi as a mind-to-mind connection to communicate with him, providing more detail than the Ruler low speech could. She said the Kobani humans would find more Prada and Torki left behind on worlds the Rulers had left. They would bring them to this world, as a haven for them.

Just as the word for the deadly training world was "Koban" in the Ruler's low speech, the humans used that same word as the world's name. The word haven, meaning "a safe place" in the human language they called Standard, was being used as a name for this world.

Maggi told him, "Haven is where as many of the Ruler's servants as we can find and rescue will be taken to live."

The word "servants" was one that Maggi told him she had substituted for the actual descriptive word in her own language. She said the low speech Krall word for their role, under the rule of the masters, actually translated to another word in Standard, as slave, which implied ownership of the servants. A servant could choose not to serve anyone, but a slave could not refuse to serve a master.

Wister considered the distinction strange. He could not think of why he would choose not to serve the elder Rulers. Had any Prada sinfully chosen not to serve, the Rulers would quickly simplify their choice. A new living Prada would serve in that one's place.

However, knowing the Torki as he did, he thought it possible that some of them might choose not to serve. The word servant, versus slave, would do for a compromise description, he decided. The Ruler's rightfully owned the service of all races anyway.

The justification the Kobani put forward for the construction of cities on Haven, to house the new arrivals, was based on the Rulers having told the Prada they wanted to make Koban their new home world someday. If that were so, then many of the Rulers would return there to live. Where would that living take place?

Marlyn asked, "Where will the servants come from, to build new domes for them, install fusion plants, air handlers, assemble equipment, trucks, new clanships? Haven would be the natural place to find them," she said, and it sounded reasonable.

Wister was concerned that the Rulers did not want their servants living in larger gatherings than a village when they were away (he said the Rulers limited them to an octal 3400 residents each).

That accounted for the now confirmed 1,792 Prada in this village, and remote aerial surveillance of two other Prada villages indicated similar numbers there. Wister was waiting for the diplomat, Maggi, to arrive this morning to discuss the population limit he had told her about the day before, as she proposed larger cities.

He sat in the shade at the edge of the forest, idly rubbing Jelko's long ears, scratching his chest. The marsh dog resembled its namesake, with a panting pale white tongue lolling out of the side of its mouth.

Maggi said humans had latched onto several socializing pack animals on various worlds that filled the ecological niche that wolves or coyotes filled on Earth, humanity's home world. Most of those alien animals did not look anything like a dog, but if taken as pups they bonded with the human social creatures from outside their pack. The marsh pack animals had taken to the Prada very well, and humans seemed to like them as well.

The clanship, which the humans had strangely given the name Beagle, per their custom, was now parked on the half dirt-covered tarmac by the old dome, the construction of which Wister had overseen.

The Torki were another people that named inanimate objects. The stories his own people told of the Prada's former existence, *before* the Ruler's came, contained names for places and things. That naming tradition apparently stopped because the Rulers did not name things, and the Prada wanted to please and emulate the older species.

He saw the truck coming from the dome when it was several miles away on the mostly flat scrub brush and grassland. It was the same style as the hundreds of thousands of identical trucks he had seen previously, which the factories could produce any time the Rulers instructed Prada to make more. Jelko stirred, and growled. A bump, protruding over the back of the cab of the truck was the head of one of the two giant cats the Kobani had brought with them.

The rippers were well behaved, other than a predisposition to enjoy making anyone that wasn't a Kobani feel like they were potential prey. He calmed Jelko, with soft words and petting. The marsh dog had been near a ripper before this. The one named Maggi had brought a smaller female one with her for the second meeting, and for several others. It initially had stayed back by the shuttle they used to fly here, before moving the clanship closer. Maggi said the cats were "partners" with them, but that marsh dogs were Prada pets. He did not intend to call any of his pets closer today, while that *killer* "partner" was so near. He even warned his people to stay as high on the trees as possible at first. It was only after repeated safe visits and some mind picture exchanges that he relaxed his caution.

He learned on that second day that these intelligent predators were connected with how the Kobani had learned to speak with their minds. He knew obviously that it wasn't a taught ability. It had to be a genetic change, as his people once had done to themselves. They had never ever considered using genes from non-Prada, but it was possible in principle.

The few genetic changes he was aware of for his species, was that they had made themselves live indefinitely, providing them with even older leaders they could respect, follow and trust. There were some other trivial gene changes he thought, to make them resistant to infections for example, or cancers, but they had never achieved the near physical perfection of the Rulers.

Rulers did not live long lives. However, they did not desire an old age as warriors that could not fight as they did when young. Dying in battle was so likely, that longevity was a pointless trait for them to select via breeding anyway. Nevertheless, they had marvelous bodies that could suffer considerable damage, and could repair and regrow itself, and they employed redundant organs. They were impervious to many poisons and infections. This was achieved without use of any artificial changes to their genes. It was the result of their ancient heritage, and high reproductive rate, matched by the attrition of their own weakest.

That ancient bloodline for their species was the trait that made them so admirable to the Prada, who apparently did not think selective breeding, and culling undesirable genes through war, was merely a slower form of genetic manipulation and improvement. Exterminating other species was their prerogative, as the senior and wisest life form in the known galaxy. Newer species could not fully understand the long-range plans of the elder races.

The truck stopped a hundred feet from the tree line, and the small female Kobani human stepped down. She was alone today, except for the ripper of course. Not that she needed any protection from the Prada, and little even from the marsh dogs. Not with her surprising speed and strength.

When the cat jumped down from the back of the truck, its size was evidence that it was the male of the two rippers. The Kobani all called him Kobalt, and the creature actually considered the leader of the group of humans to be his mother's sister. His biological sister, Kit, thought of the leader as her real mother. Harming any of the two cat's extended family would have a *bad* outcome for the perpetrator. Their brief mind pictures made that amply evident, bringing an involuntary shiver to Wister.

Wister had actually seen the Rulers flee from these predators on Koban. They would bravely stand their ground to shoot the large blue humped animals with long nose horns, from which they loved to eat cuts of raw red meat, except when rippers were near. From the top of a partially completed dome, Wister had seen a pride of five rippers move to ambush three hunting Rulers as they focused on a herd of the large meat animals too intently. The wind was wrong, and they never smelled the doom closing from their rear and sides.

All three of the hunters were killed that day, with only a wound to one of the large male rippers. The fast agile beasts took them all down in a coordinated attack from three sides, avoiding most of the hasty brief gunfire with relative ease.

Afterwards, they all took turns standing over two of the badly injured yet still living Rulers, and lowered their heads to touch them. Next, they roared a challenge before killing the two survivors and carrying the mangled bodies away to eat.

His memory was jerked away from its dark musing by a voice. "It is a bright and good morning, Wister," Maggi called to him as she approached. She had one hand on the small ring of blue flesh around the ripper's neck.

Wister suspected that it was the equivalent of the mindreading hand touching for the Kobani, to sense and send mind pictures. The pride that killed the Rulers that day long ago must have sensed their pain and fear by touching them.

"It is a good day, so far." He was conditioning his reply on how the negotiation would go between them. He had a firm hand gripped in the neck fur of Jelko, who was trembling fearfully at the approach of the huge cat. The ripper outweighed the dog by probably a factor of seven or eight. Its long upper fangs were casually exposed in a manner that was deliberate, since at other times they were not easily seen.

In previous (very fearful) contact, Wister had clearly sensed that the predator used its mind reading ability to sense its prey's fear, and savored the terror and thoughts from its kills as they died.

Wister had been surprised and shocked when once Maggi touched both himself and Jelko's ear simultaneously, when neither of the cats was present. She fed him the mental pictures that Jelko had in his mind, of tearing out the throat of this creature that was touching its master and itself. He knew this creature had hurt and frightened its master and itself only days earlier. Jelko was looking passively at her this time, yet wanted to kill her in a vividly gruesome manner.

Maggi had told him in low speech, "Do not be concerned. All predators have violent thoughts like this. For anyone they do not like or trust, or they perceive to be prey, they think of attacking them. I am not bothered by his thoughts, because I also sense his emotions are fully in check, due to your comforting presence." She told him she had not sent Jelko images of her own thoughts, because it could frighten and confuse the animal, causing a violent reaction. It may not like her, she had said, but she liked him and his type.

Wister had discovered that day, that her liking Jelko, even if the dog did not like her, was a factor in her favor in his mind. He trusted the judgment of Prada that liked the marsh dogs, more than he did the Prada that did not like them. He was suspicious of their sincerity or motives if they could not empathize with the animals that worshiped them as their masters.

Maggi, who had picked that from his inexperienced unshielded mind, had toyed with pointing out the incongruity in his thinking. She wanted to ask him why he didn't expect empathy from the Rulers, in exchange for Prada devotion to them. She considered bringing one of the captives held on Koban, a typically and completely arrogant and unsympathetic Krall mind for him to sense.

She was tempted to try a mental relay between a Krall and a Prada. However, it would not be a Prada as important to them as Wister was. Not yet, without some predictability for the probable outcome. She certainly wasn't going to tell any of the

Prada right now that they had multiple Krall “Rulers” as prisoners.

She offered Wister a small clear container that held eight white grubs, dug fresh from the bark of “grub” trees, located on the other side of the old dome. Bradley had used his new ripper sense of smell to find the grubs. The trees near the village were foraged more frequently and had fewer and smaller grubs. The small offering was one she thought would please the Prada. The pre breakfast search had certainly *displeased* Bradley. She now owed him a chocolate cake when they returned home.

She provided an explanation. “The grub trees on the other side of the dome have not been checked, and have many of these in their bark. I thought you would like them.”

“I will enjoy them later, and share with some of our young ones.”

He accepted the gift with more grace than he had rejected previous technological gifts she had offered. Those appeared to offend him slightly, and he acted suspicious as to why she did that. It required explanation of human culture to ease the tension. He explained that they could easily employ electric lights if they needed them, and solar powered lights were not needed for them to see at night. The same for a gift of battery powered communications devices, and motorized trucks (presumably made by some long dead Prada on Koban). The Rulers preferred they live a simple village life here, so they did.

To Maggi, it was frustrating to offer to free someone that didn’t seem to want the freedom.

“Wister, have you considered how you will help the new Prada that will arrive here? More small villages are not an effective way to house many of them, and they do not know about this world, its foods, and its dangers.”

He delivered a shimmy of the shoulders, a Prada shrug. “The arriving Prada may have leaders older than I am, or older than my sister, Nawella, of our village. They would decide what we all do. There is room in the factories and in the living quarters for many more Prada. There is no need for that many maintenance workers, but there may be room, without violating the village size limit, or the number of villages on the surface.”

Maggi was brought up short by this remark. “What factories and living quarters?”

“The ones under our feet. Far below the forest and that old dome. Where my sister has been the elder leader of the maintenance workers and of the schools for the last three orbits.”

To her credit, her mouth only hung open for a second. “There are factories underground here?”

His pointed nose darted forward and back in a Prada nod. “Yes, of course. Under almost every large dome. The same as you have on Koban. Because you have not met Prada before, they must not have survived there. The factories will not be ready for production now.”

It was fortunate that the large bird population of Haven kept the insects under control. An open moist mouth, held that way for several seconds was a definite invitation. She closed her mouth before one of the flies buzzing near Jelko's head found a new home.

She felt a bit dim, repeating what he said, but couldn't stop herself. "There are factories under the largest domes on Koban?"

There were limits to even an elder Prada's patience with a member of a junior species. "It is surely how you made the things you brought with you, such as the truck you just drove. To make the parts to repair the domes and fences, to repair the walls. To make the weapons I see that most of you carry. I did not know of the factory to make clanships on Koban, but some of you must know. You have one.

"The Rulers would surely not leave those things with you if you would not follow the instructions to limit your village size and live a simple life, as we do."

She didn't think now was the time to tell him the "benevolent Rulers" had left all of the humans to die, so they never expected them to be around long enough to make good use of what they left behind. Now she knew where the excess Prada population went, to account for the children here in the village. She was partly right.

"When you have children, some adults must move below to the factories to keep the village population constant. Is there a limit placed on the factory population?"

"No, but with no production ordered by the Rulers, there is not a great work need below. Over time, we do have deaths up here, and some accidents happen down there. We accept maintenance workers back into the village to keep the population at the level instructed by the Rulers. When our workers below grow too few for adequate maintenance, we have as many replacement children as needed up here, and send adults below. When the children are old enough, they rotate below to learn how the factories work, about Prada history and knowledge, and an adult will come up here. There are often more than twice as many of us below as there are in the village."

"If you can have babies anytime in your life, and you live so long, why aren't the factories full of Prada? You only die by accidents or predators. Are there that many accidents and predator kills?"

"No. Except why would we have babies when we do not need more workers? After many orbits, we were close to the minimum workers for proper maintenance below, and so I permitted six babies to be born over the last two orbits. When they go below for training, I will allow more babies. This will continue enough orbits until we have twice as many workers below as we will have in the village."

This explained their apparent rigid population in the villages, because an excess or deficiency was corrected by population shifts to or from the factories. In addition, an apparently well-regulated birth rate supplied the buffer required. With twice as many below ground as above, there were roughly 5,375 Prada per village.

"What can the factories make?"

"Everything the Rulers need. Uniforms, some furniture, dome construction elements, construction equipment, fusion power modules, trucks, projectile, plasma, and laser hand weapons, swords and knives, computation devices, heavy body armor, plasma cannons, mini-tanks, laser defense systems, ground and air transports, orbital shuttles, freezers for food, radios…" Maggi placed a hand on his, to send a "stop" image. This sounded something like the orbital factories that humans used, but perhaps on a larger scale and more flexible, although apparently less well automated than we used. Human orbital factories did not require so many maintenance workers.

She explained why she had stopped him. "That seemed like it was going to be a long list. What is left for the Torki to make or build?"

"The Torki build the security and controllers for all of the complex equipment. Many weapon systems are quantum keyed, just as some doorways have keypads. Clanship systems and shuttles, and single ships use quantum encryption to activate. The Torki also modified the Malveran orbital defense platforms for the Rulers, and gave them remote piloted single ships with Jump Hole projectors in the nose. They know how to build the Hammer craft, the quantum interface controls and tachyon drives to operate them as Jump ships. Naturally they understand the quantum mechanical methods to make stable collapsed matter for their outer shells."

"Hammers?"

"Yes. The Torki can make hollow balls of matter that are very dense, using delicate control of strong gravity fields, to compress the material to form as a single crystal. Only the Torki know how to make openings in them as they take shape, using a Rolperry; that is a small quantum atomic dispersion tool the Raspani once knew how to make. Even the word for the tool came from the Raspani language. That was before they sacrificed their minds to feed the Rulers."

"You said that before, about the Raspani, that they had great minds. They have been food animals a long time. How do you know about their minds, and that they made this tool?"

"The Torki are smart," his head darted forward once. "Yet they say they do not know the science of that Rolperry tool. The basic quantum rules, which make the tools work. The Raspani hid their minds after the Rulers claimed their worlds, and that science was lost."

Maggi told him she had seen the Krall use a Raspani tool. "They held them in their hands to make small holes through any material. A human that came to Koban recently told us there were missile weapons that use those tools in their nose, to bore holes through ships. Is that the tool that you called a Rolperry? Who else makes those tools for the Krall?"

"There are no more of the tools. We Prada placed many of the last of them on missiles for the Rulers. When they are gone, there will be no more, unless the Torki learn how to do that."

"Have you seen the Katusha tools? The ones that are used to give the Rulers their tattoos. We think it works on a similar principle to the Raspani Rolperry tool. The Katusha gives the Krall the key, in their tattoo, to operate the machinery the Torki make for them. That tool was created by an ancient race called the Olt'kitapi. We have some of them, and I wear a tattoo that was originally placed on my chest by the Krall (she patted below her throat)." She opened the top button of her tunic to show the solid black oval.

"The Krall said the Raspani were helped by the Olt'kitapi. Did the Raspani learn their quantum level control of physics from the Olt'kitapi?"

The Prada wiggled uncomfortably, and his head made back and forth sideways motions several times. Maggi, as usual when they talked, was touching one of his hands. She sensed his mind was confused. She also concluded that his sideways head motion signified that mental state.

"Do you know the Krall say that they destroyed the Olt'kitapi?" she asked him.

A head dart, followed by a sideways movement came in succession. However, he did not speak and she received no mental images at all. His face was very still, not even the usual nose or whisker twitches. The little Prada had gradually learned how to hold back thoughts he did not want to share, and this appeared to be one of those times. He was apparently straining to keep his thoughts private.

Nevertheless, the combination signal of affirmation, followed by a probable sign of confusion was a clue. She had planned to bring the subject up later, but this seemed like a good opportunity now.

She prodded him gently. "The Prada respect the Krall as Rulers, because their species has been in space since ancient times, because they are older than your own race. You accept that these Rulers have the right to decide the fate of the Prada, the Torki, and the Raspani, by virtue of having existed longer, and being an older species. What of the Olt'kitapi?" A sideways head wobble was his only sign.

"The Krall told us, and I heard this myself, that the Olt'kitapi was older than the Krall. That this species wanted to help the Krall to change, but they thought they were making them weak. How do you *know* which are the older species? The Olt'kitapi also helped the Raspani become great, and that species learned a science that even you and the Torki do not fully understand."

The sense of confusion increased, as Wister's head moved side to side more sharply. He spoke, with no mental pictures to reinforce his words. "The Olt'kitapi species is gone, and are not able to speak. If they were older and had greater science, the Rulers could not have, would not have been able to defeat them. The Rulers defeated the Raspani, so they must have also been older than that species to overcome them. The Rulers say they are destined to rule the galaxy, and they have vanquished all they have met."

Maggi stared at him a moment. "There is an expression in my language. It says that after a war, the winner writes the history. That means that only the winner's version of the reasons for the war is heard later, and the other side of the story is lost.

"The Krall are undoubtedly, undeniably, mighty warriors. Yet one of our own young Kobani can fight any individual Krall warrior, unarmed, and probably defeat that warrior. Are we then right to claim that we Kobani are destined to rule the galaxy, if the Krall cannot defeat us? If we somehow defeat the Krall in war, and say we deserve to rule the galaxy, you Prada will know that is false. Obviously, you know that strength and victory does not make us deserve the right to rule older species. I say it does not grant us the right to rule any species, younger or older."

Speaking hesitantly, Wister strove to explain. “There are none to speak for the Olt’kitapi or the Raspani. There have been doubts spoken in the past, but it is wrong to disobey an elder you know is senior to yourself.” That appeared to be the crux of their subservience to the Krall. That and the fact that to oppose them would lead to extinction.

She questioned him. “If an elder species became the eldest by removing those that were older, more mature, do they deserve the respect of a younger species as being wiser, as deserving to rule them?”

“Diplomat Maggi, the Prada understand this principle, as even a very young species such as yours is able to perceive. Yet the truth that the Krall are older than us is supported by all evidence. We believe that makes them better suited to rule the galaxy than ourselves, or the now mindless Raspani. However, a practical matter remains if we rejected our long held beliefs. The Krall are, as you stated, ‘undoubtedly, undeniably, a mighty race’ which has defeated all others.”

Maggi was as surprised by his pragmatism as she was his first use of “Krall” to describe the Rulers. He was largely successful at blocking his thoughts, but his lack of experience at mind sharing, and innate honesty, made it difficult to hold back all that he felt.

She shifted away from this uncomfortable subject for him, to one she expected to be better received. “Wister, on Koban we have been protecting over three thousand Raspani, which were kept in a covered compound by the largest dome, located by the ocean. Do you know of that dome?”

“Yes. I directed the early construction of that dome, the only one by the sea. My sister was present when it was completed under her direction, and I had returned here to rest. She described the Raspani protective structure. That completely covered enclosure is the only such we know of that was ever built. Other worlds were not so dangerous that a tough transparent roof was required, as well as sides for a compound. The Raspani were left behind to die?” He sounded surprised.

“Just as we were left to die, when the Krall left in their eagerness to make war with our other worlds. Had we not discovered the Raspani, and helped with their health needs and food requirements, they would have died in a hand of orbits, I think. We have a school where we are trying to teach them how to help themselves. However, the high gravity on Koban shortens their lives. We wish to bring them to Haven to live. Do you think they can survive here in the open?”

“Wild marsh dogs and their cousins would hunt them, and the larger ones that we also fear. The ones you have called werewolves. The large black gundolor is another hunter that would kill some of them. I heard the young Kobani named Bradley call a gundolor that entered the forest two days ago a giant wolverine. The skathers, the long legless water predators, will also try to eat them when they come to drink at the rivers. The Raspani will be able to eat the vegetation here safely, because they did that before, when the Rulers lived here for more than ten hands of orbits. A strong high fence will protect them, to keep most predators away, as was done then.”

“Do you agree that your people think the Raspani are an elder race to the

Prada?"

"Yes, of course." The thoughts she detected from him suggested he suspected this was a leading question. He was right.

"If the Raspani retained their intelligence, would they wish to be protected from the predators?"

"You ask questions that have only one answer from me. If they retained their intelligence, they would protect themselves. Say what you really mean."

"Will the Prada build the fences, and help protect that elder species if we bring them here, and try to restore their intelligence?"

"You Kobani want to give up the responsibility for protecting them?"

He's becoming a perceptive little devil, she thought.

"We do not have the materials to make a fence large enough, and we believe the other people here should share the responsibility to help this unfortunate elder species."

"Diplomat Maggi, you have a way to identify what motivates those you negotiate with, and make them do what their beliefs require them to do, as you intended."

"If that means you will help, then I was a successful diplomat and negotiator."

"The people of this village will help. However, you told me that there were several thousand Raspani. That will require a great deal of open land for them to browse, and the other two Prada villages should accept part of the work and responsibility. I believe even the Torki would wish to contribute in some way, but not in the same manner as your people and mine do. They do not have open land suitable for Raspani, and building a fence is not the best skill they could offer."

"What skills can they offer?"

"You were trying to teach them, and wanted to awaken their minds. We were told by the Torki that the Raspani deliberately submerged their minds. If they know this much, they may know how that was done, and how to reverse the process. The Torki may be better teachers than your people."

"How will I make contact with your other two villages, and with the Torki? I don't want the next village elder to send his dogs after me. If I'm forced to kill them, I may have a problem becoming friends with them." She smiled, trying to keep her teeth less exposed. Flashing your teeth was a Prada gesture of anger, since they showed their sharp little teeth when mad. The blunt teeth of humans were less threatening, but it was the gesture that was significant, not the potential bite.

"If you will provide transportation in a shuttle, I will send representatives to the other two villages, to explain who you are, and what we must do for the Raspani. After the way is prepared, you or another of your people can meet with them. I will go with you to meet the Torki at the one place I know they used to live, on the western shore of this land. They will not be very far from there, even if they have moved in the orbits that have passed. They do not regulate their population as we do, and move to avoid late arriving young. The young that the sea creatures did not consume."

"They expand their population indefinitely?"

"No. They eat many of their young when they return home too early from the sea to molt on land. The adolescents return to the waters where the millions of eggs were released. If they are late to return to the birth beach, after many molts elsewhere, they appear too much like a mature Torki to eat. However, they will never develop the intelligent mind of an adult. Therefore they move their tunnels and caves to avoid that problem."

"Uh…, OK." There wasn't much to say to that.

****

When Maggi parked at the base of the Beagle, Marlyn was waiting to meet her, as Kobalt ran to her to deliver a wet raspy-tongued lick, and a brief frill. "I heard what was said. Were Wister's thoughts as sincere as he sounded? Will they help watch after the Raspani?"

"Yes. It is an obligation they will meet, partially as a form of retribution for past neglect of a species they have known was senior to theirs. I believe Wister was concealing thoughts he has privately held that the Krall have been 'less than moral' in dealings with older species."

"Gee. Do you think so?" Marlyn responded sarcastically.

"I don't know how the extreme youthfulness of humanity will play out with the Prada in general. They don't exactly have ancestor worship, since some of those 'ancestors' have avoided accidents and still live with them, like Wister and his older sister, Nawella. But they took the pragmatic view that it was necessary to accept the rule of the Krall because they couldn't stop them, and the Krall apparently *are* an older species."

"I don't know about you, but human history seems pretty long to me. I've read about the fossils that link us back a few million years."

"Fossil lineage isn't the measure used for a species maturity, at least not by the Prada, and it appears not by the Torki either, if Wister described their viewpoint accurately. The birth of a mature species seems to be when they achieve space flight, and start to leave their home system. I frankly don't think I was believed, when I said we launched our first humans into low orbits just barely six hundred years ago, yet we have settled on more than seven hundred planets, in a slightly flattened sphere within a nearly five hundred light-years radius of our birth world, and extensively explored another twenty beyond that."

"What's so odd about that? That is far less volume than the older species we've heard about has controlled. The Olt'kitapi supposedly had colonized ten times that much in radius, except along the Galactic north-south axis, because of the thinness of the disk. The Raspani held sway over a small volume of space for an advanced species, assuming the Krall translators were accurate on the Flight of Fancy recordings I have heard. They settled only a four hands of worlds, it sounded like. That's only sixteen worlds."

"Apparently it isn't the territory you *own* that measures your maturity, it's how long you have owned it, or have been colonizing other stars. The Raspani were originally pastoral in nature, not much different than they are forced to live now. They were thinkers and philosophers, and had no drive to expand or overpopulate. Until the Olt'kitapi helped them advance farther, they were only in two star systems. That expanded to about sixteen before the Krall came along. Even if they were slow to expand, they gained maturity 'credits,' which I suppose is a term we could use. I can't find out exactly how long the Raspani took to get that far, because the Prada themselves don't know. They suspect it was even longer than they took." Maggi raised her eyebrows, as if to say you won't believe this.

"How long was it for the Prada?"

"All they have remaining is anecdotal evidence, since they don't even know where their home world is any longer. Not since the Krall took them along for the conquering ride. They believe they had been in space perhaps seventy thousand 'orbits' of their forgotten home world. The length of time for that mythical orbit is no longer remembered. They suspect they lived in a close planet to a red dwarf star, because of their dim light adapted yellow eyes, and liking for the nighttime. A cooler star with a closer orbit could make for a much shorter year than we measure for Earth. Haven's gravity is a bit higher than their preference, so that fits with most habitable red dwarf rocky worlds being smaller. The Prada were once sociable with other races. Those races are gone now so they have no other reference."

"Still, seventy thousand orbits of any star is a long time. Even with a six-month orbit measured in human terms, they have to be very old. How large a volume had they colonized? There are more red dwarf stars with small worlds than there are larger Suns and Earth-like worlds."

"The Prada did not, and still do not, crave territory, or desire large populations, and defer to the senior members of their society. Their natural predilections play right into Krall hands. We know that the Krall have only been in space for perhaps twenty-five thousand years, and were probably still on their home world when the Olt'kitapi discovered them as barbarians. I have no doubt the race that turned these pricks loose on the galaxy were far older and 'wiser,' and yet were taken down."

"OK, how are the Torki for maturity, in Prada eyes?"

"Brilliant adolescents. If they are speaking without bias for these crabs, the Torki were star traveling for four thousand years when the Krall ran them over, six or seven thousand years ago, making them perhaps eleven thousand years old as space travelers. They chose mostly watery worlds with ample seashores. They traveled in giant ships, built to accommodate their larger bodies with simulated internal seaside environments. This means a lot of weight and fewer ships, and less flexibility for exploration. They apparently had a six hundred light-year sphere of colonization, with only twenty water worlds. The Prada consider them galactic whiz kids."

"What the hell do they think of us then?"

"You see the pattern, I think. We have done more, and considerably faster than these other species. Humans don't pass up very many worlds, and we are driven to explore and settle. At least until an aberration three hundred years ago, when we almost eradicated ourselves, we have always been highly combative.

"Wister doesn't seem able to accept our own history time line. It simply doesn't fit the Prada view that intelligent species develop very slowly and spread gradually, becoming gentler and wiser as they mature over a long period of gradual expansion."

"He thinks the Krall have become more *mature and gentle*?" Marlyn's voice held a sour note.

"In Prada eyes they 'must' be older because they have been able to rule all others, and their motives are apparently too 'advanced' for younger species to understand. It's rather as if their power makes them 'right' sort of thinking. They think only a senior race could accomplish what the Krall have done. It's an odd blind spot in their philosophy of following the oldest and wisest leaders, which I think they unconsciously accept for the Krall, because there is no other option anyway."

Marlyn expressed bewilderment. "Damn, I never anticipated a hard sell being needed to convince the slave races to get free of the Krall."

"I hope it won't be as difficult to gain cooperation from the Torki. Wister has agreed to help us look for their settlement tomorrow, if you can get away to fly the shuttle."

"Sure, I can leave Francis in charge here. I'll bring Bradley and Hakeem. Do you expect to make contact right away if we find them?"

"I'd like to, but I'll let Wister guide me in that respect, since he has met them before. Apparently, the Torki don't exactly have a leader as such, and rule themselves by consensus of the population. That's what I gathered from Wister's description. I don't know how they can reach any kind of an agreement quickly, unless their population is held down to the same level as the Prada are. We may have to wait awhile for their decisions if they are spread out."

****

Wister was curious about the human made shuttle. He had seen non-Krall craft previously, but had never been inside one. He immediately appreciated the passenger windows, because Krall shuttles didn't have them, and the warriors themselves apparently lacked curiosity in the view, unless they could kill something they saw.

Maggi sat with him as they circled over his home forest once, then flew west at a suborbital altitude to quickly reach the coastline, a distance of over two thousand miles. Shuttle fuel was no longer an issue, with production in full gear on Koban, so they boosted high and fast.

Wister directed them to a large bay where he said the Torki had previously lived. There were numerous openings in the sides of cliffs facing the bay, but no signs of habitation or large crab tracks. Based on current flow along the coast, Wister suggested they fly farther north, where late arriving younglings instinctively returning here would not have drifted. He pointed out crab tracks in the sand from about a hundred feet up, but said these were too small to be adult Torki.

Wister commented, “The Torkada here will be pre-adolescent younglings, with brains too enlarged to become intelligent adult Torki.” He didn’t explain how a brain “too large” could be a handicap to intelligence.

“The younglings at this stage of development are called Torkada. They look similar to the adults, yet are half their size. They never properly mature, and live shortened lives, subject to being eaten by anything that can catch and kill a crab that large. They are less intelligent that a marsh dog,” he told them.

Maggi asked him, “They don’t seem to be very nurturing to their young. Prada and humans take care of their young from birth, and start to teach them at an early age. The Torki act…, uncaring.” She almost said *like the Krall*, because they too didn’t care for their hatchlings, until after they survived on their own to age five or six-years-old, and were ready to begin novice training.

Wister explained what he had observed. “Their early forms are so different in shape that the adults readily eat them if encountered on the beach or in the sea. It isn’t as if they are *unaware* of what they are, but they also consume their own dead if the corpse is discovered fresh. They have a compulsion to not waste protein and sustenance in their makeup. However, they are rigid in the belief that to kill one of their own mature members for food is a crime, and they would starve before doing so. It is the similarity of the Torkada to the adult Torki, which places them off limits.

“They will allow them to exist, and die by natural predation, but they will not kill them themselves. Simply moving away is easier when too many of them have arrived. The Torkada are tolerated for a time living near the adults, but at some point, the adults move and leave the mindless ones behind to fend for themselves. The immature ones can even reproduce, but the offspring never develop into Torki, and they keep returning to the beach of their spawning.

“Even a couple of molts earlier, before the young take on the general body shape of adults, they are acceptable as food. It is apparently the *first* molt to their adult form, before the purple body and amber legs appear after the next two molts, that is the only time they are welcomed home from the years spent at sea, growing. Too early or too late, either is ultimately fatal.”

Bradley called out, just as they were rounding the point of the bay to fly north. “I see several of them, at the water’s edge. They look to be feeding on a carcass of a large fish or dolphin-like creature.”

Hakeem asked Wister for advice. “Is it OK to look at them up close, perhaps get a tissue sample? They would surely have the same DNA as the adults, and we wouldn’t risk offending the Torki by asking later.” The Prada had willingly offered blood samples, after the subject was raised delicately.

Once its purpose was explained, Wister went first, having no objection to their learning more about his people. He requested the same in return, saying they had labs in the underground facilities to analyze the biological samples. He told them that they had not done genetics for thousands of years, but the pure scientific knowledge was of interest to them.

Wister answered Hakeem, with a sideways head motion. “The adult Torki will probably not object to your sample request, and I think they will ask for you to trade samples, as we did. However, approaching the Torkada is risky, and you will have to be prepared to kill some of them if you try. They are aggressive and not very smart, and the claws, although much smaller than an adults, can easily sever an arm. Some of you are extremely fast and strong, and perhaps are not in danger, however I don’t think there is anything to gain from the risk. If there are Torkada roaming the new location where the Torki have moved, you will still need to be very careful to avoid them.”

Maggi looked eagerly at the three to four-foot wide crabs, larger than any she had ever seen on any world. The bodies were a beautiful purple, and the legs on the smaller ones were amber, and on the foot wider version were a pale orange. They waved their larger claw in the air at the shuttle, as it passed over, apparently not frightened by the noise or presence of a large unknown flying object that was a potential predator. Perhaps walking up to them wasn’t such a good idea.

Marlyn, as they flew up the coast was engaged in a radio conversation with an earpiece, interfaced with her transducer. They were far out of range of Kap’s transducer system, but not the Beagle’s radio.

“I just heard. On Koban, they found entrances to the old underground factory below Hub City. The place is a dark, wet, moldy and rusty wreck. It obviously has had no maintenance for a very long time. That close to the ocean, there may have been pumps at some point to help keep it dry. There is flooding in the lower levels. It seems like a complete loss for ever using it again.”

Wister, hearing the exchange asked what they were talking about from Koban, the one word in the conversation he was sure he understood. Maggi told him of the find in low Krall, with mental images.

His head darted forward, “That factory was built, but little used, even when new. I suggested to the Rulers that the dome was placed too close to the sea to stay dry. My sister was told to build the factory anyway. It required several orbits to make, and much work to keep it dry. We had many accidents with the workers.”

That sounded typical of the Krall, indifferent to an animal’s recommendation, and wasteful of their work, lives, and resources. He had a more optimistic view of at least one other factory complex.

“The smaller factory, under the dome that belonged to Maldo clan, which you say you call Prime City, should be dry and cleaner if the fusion powered air system still works. It was last used to make the walls and electric fences for all of the compounds of the Rulers on Koban, and it made more ground transports and shuttles to move that material to the other domes. It will need much maintenance, but probably could be returned to service if you know how.”

Maggi told Marlyn to have Prime City look for the entrance in the same place Hub City found their own covered over factory elevators and down ramps.

Perhaps a hundred miles north along the coast, an even larger and deeper inset bay, with high ridges on one side came into view. Wister suggested this looked to be an excellent location for the Torki to have moved.

As the shuttle passed over the two hundred-foot ridgeline, where the wide beach could be seen below its shelter, they were amazed and delighted to see thousands of Torki on the sand.

Maggi was the first to comment. “They were all facing and looking up at us as we came over the top of the ridge. They knew we were coming. Look at the size of them. They must be half the length of a truck. Seven or eight feet wide, and five feet across. They are waving the smaller of their claws at us. Wister, is that a threat gesture, like the Torkada made?”

“No. They used that gesture to greet the Rulers when they arrived in shuttles, and to greet Prada when we would arrive to work with them. However, I have never seen so many outside in the sun at one time. Usually most are inside the tunnels and workrooms underground, out of the sun. They like the cooler nights, as my people do, on this hotter planet.”

“Do they have the same population restriction from the Krall as the Prada have? There must be thousands of them on this beach. Look, on the other side of the bay, there are more over there. Not as many, but I think over a thousand.”

“The Torki have a population limit set by the Rulers, but it is difficult for them to regulate it as closely as we Prada do. They never know how many larvae will reach Torkedia stage and survive to return home. They have often violated the spirit of the Rulers orders when left alone for many orbits. This looks to be far above their population allowance.”

“You said something different than Torkada. Is Torkedia the acceptable returning size for their young? Because I can see many small pale versions of them on the beach here.”

“I see them as well,” Wister said. He had a disapproving tone to his words, which Maggi had learned to recognize.

“Where should we land?” Marlyn asked. The beach was evenly covered by them, the watching eyestalks pivoting to follow them as the shuttle passed over and hovered above the water’s edge.

“They are making an opening straight inland of our position,” Maggi observed. They were skittering away from a cleared section of beach (that word seemed to fit their fast sideways motion). She saw them gently lift some of the smaller translucent shelled youngsters and carry them with them.

Marlyn looked back at Wister. She turned the shuttle so he could see the clearing from the side windows. “Is that an invitation to land in the middle of them?” she asked in low Krall.

“It must be. I have never seen this many outside before, there was never a need for them to make room.”

“Is it safe for us to get out with you, or should we let you introduce us first?”

“The Torki are not shy, or normally aggressive, and I have never seen them act surprised. I see no reason for you not to step out with me. There is no doubt this is not a Krall craft, and they will be able to see Marlyn as the pilot. They have very good vision because their top eyes are large, and they can separate them or bring them together to focus near or far. They have other smaller eyes under the front of their shells as well."

Maggi noted that the little Prada had again used the name Krall, rather than Ruler, something he had done more frequently in the last several days.

Marlyn eased the shuttle inland, down the center of the open strip of beach, keeping high enough to minimize the sand being blown around. She then quickly throttled back and settled fast with as little sand blasting as she could manage, and quickly shut off the thrusters.

Maggi took her hand set radio from her waist belt, and activated its transducer interface, checking to be sure it could Link through the shuttle radio to Kap on the Beagle. This was being recorded, Tri-Vid and audio, and there were many interested eyes and ears at the other end.

"Everyone Link with me, so we all hear what is going on. Kap will be trying to translate if we hear a different language than low Krall. I'll be unarmed as before."

Looking over at her young bodyguard holding the 50-caliber rifle, she grinned. "Bradley, leave that cannon just inside the open hatch within reach. You have two pistols as does Marlyn and Hakeem. Thanks to Wister's information, we have no reason to expect a hostile reception." Wister's head darted forward to indicate agreement.

Marlyn, at the rear hatch, reached up and keyed it to open. As it rose, they heard the breeze, and the chittering of chitin as claws clicked, and shells rubbed or scraped. As the hatch revealed the humans fully, the sound increased, the small claw waving increased, and the nearest of the giant crabs lowered its front carapace almost to the sand, as if bowing.

"Wister, are we supposed to react some way to that display?" Maggi asked him in a low voice.

"I don't know." He answered, equally low. "I have never seen one of them do that. Even to the Rulers."

The same Torki directly to their front, about thirty feet away, answered, proving they had excellent hearing as well. In perfect base pitched low Krall, sounding as if it came from a Krall clan leader, the crab clearly said, "We do not greet the Krall this way, and they are not our Rulers, but our masters. They do not deserve welcome. These other world visitors are welcome. The Prada, Wister, is also accepted." The Torki raised its carapace to level.

Maggi made a deep bow, and the other people in the party quickly followed her lead. Wister shook his head sideways in uncertainty. As she raised her head she said, "I return your welcome. I was told that any Torki is able to speak for all of the Torki present. Will that one be you?"

"It will be me, for now. I have the voice for all of the adults present," it answered.

"My people are called humans, we speak as individuals, and I am the one chosen to speak first. My name is Maggi Fisher. Should I know your name to address you?"

"Lacking a shell or claws, I do not think you have the means to click-hiss our names in our language. However, my sound replicator can reproduce all of the frequencies of Krall speech, and those of yours that I have heard. A low Krall word you may use for my name is Coldar, because that means quantum key, which is something that I often build. I believe your use of low Krall speech indicates you can make that sound."

Now that the Torki had lifted its front, Maggi saw that there was a black, nearly flat oval object, about six inches across adhered to the underside of its front shell. The object seemed to be the source of the voice she heard. Many of the other Torki had an identical black object on their shells, but in slightly different locations. There appeared to be intricate mouthparts, with numerous small mandibles and pincher equipped limbs around it, which did not move in a fashion that seemed related to the sounds. She also saw four black dots near the mouth that could be the small fixed eyes, which Wister said they had on their underside. Coldar did call it his sound *replicator*.

"I can speak the name 'Coldar,' although we are interested in learning your language, even if unable to speak it ourselves. We too have sound replicators that can reproduce what we cannot speak."

"We have detected electromagnetic signals between each of you, and a distant communicator. Is that a leader or a recording device?"

"Coldar, our leader on this expedition to this world is with me, her name is Marlyn Greeves." Maggi indicated Marlyn, and then introduced each of the others with her.

"There are too many of us to introduce if we are to have a discussion today." Coldar suggested. "Is this a breach of your custom to not say a name for all that will participate?"

Maggi smiled, certain the gesture had no meaning to the Torki. "No, I only introduced my fellow visitors because we are few, and that could be done quickly. The sounds for their names are obviously in our own language, called Standard, and not the low Krall language. The words themselves do not have a meaning, such as a builder of anything."

"That is much as the Prada take names, so it is familiar to us. You use two names, is that like the Krall, when they earn more names or titles by what they accomplish?"

"No, our personal names are given to us by our parents, and some of us earn titles to go with our names, by what we learn or accomplish."

"I have had fertilized millions of eggs." Coldar responded. "Most adult male Torki have done so, and our females produce millions of eggs, which receive no names as new larvae, and we do not know which ones are our own children when they return. They find a name for themselves." It waved its smaller left claw (still almost three feet long) at several pale, almost translucent shelled smaller replicas of the adults, off to its left side.

Maggi noted the early tint of the adult coloration was present in them, but she could see organs faintly, through the soft looking shells. Each of them had a dark looking angular object near the place between their upper eyestalks. It seemed artificial.

She suddenly noticed that Coldar's eyestalks had dropped and one was looking directly at her, the other towards the Torkedia she happened to be observing.

Worried that she might have done something inappropriate by staring, she quickly looked back at Coldar.

Far from offended, he answered her unasked question. "You can see the Olt's, our mind enhancers in our returned Torkedia. They are able to learn from the adults now, and have all of our libraries for reference. They are able to listen to us today, but do not yet speak with language. This is our gift from the old ones, who first helped the Torki become aware."

Maggi looked at Wister and the others, before asking the question that came to mind. The Prada's head was doing its side-to-side motion, an indication it was confused or unsettled. Old ones could have meant older Torki, until he said they helped them become aware. Marlyn and Hakeem looked puzzled, but they too had caught the reference to awareness. Bradley just nodded.

"Who were the old ones that gave the Torki this gift?"

"The Olt'kitapi, before we were fully aware and intelligent, gave them to us. The old ones were gone before the gifts had done their work, to make us a united people. We make Olts for ourselves now, because they have the instructions in them to make more. It is how we join the minds of all Torki together, to know what all think. It is where our young have the knowledge of all that came before stored, for them to find and learn. One of the first tasks for an adult, after the color molt, is to start work on making a duplicate quantum storage device, a new Olt, using the one in our heads as a reference tool."

Wister was pulling his head back now, in a sharp negation signal. Coldar noted the gesture.

"The Prada do not accept that we knew the Olt'kitapi in the youth of our species. We were nearly mindless Torkada, on the beaches of our home world before they came. They slowly lifted us, to reach the promise they saw for our species. We usually eat our own dead, and that was how the Olt'kitapi discovered the way to pass knowledge from elders to our returning young Torkedia.

"The Olt, which we named after the species that gave it to us, is a partly organic quantum storage device. I have my Olt from my own return as a Torkedia, located where you see it in these young ones, acquired the traditional way, when an adult had died and I ate of the body. It migrated to where my optic nerves enter my brain. I have a second inactive Olt inside of me, which I made through years of effort, and it is now placed in the muscles along my back. A place where the hungry young Torkedia will find it in my body when I die, as well as the one in my brain. Inside my body, I have the seeds for two young adults to learn all of our knowledge. We can also make new Olts to feed to the returning young ones if no adult dies before they must make the color molt, into the first adult form."

Maggi looked at Wister. "You have heard their story before?"

"Yes, all of the Prada know this tale. It does not make them older than the Krall, even if they started their own path sooner. They did not become aware and finish as quickly as the Rulers."

Coldar used his two claws, spreading them wide as the pointed tips made a spiral twirling motion. It apparently signified overall agreement with Wister, when he offered his explanation.

"The process to become fully aware, and to learn what the Olt really was, and what it contained, required many generations of slowly increasing awareness and learning. Until some thousands of years later, one of us suddenly was able to access more of the knowledge that the Olt contained. Perhaps that forgotten one of our race had reached some level of intelligence, or some other mark the Olt'kitapi had set long ago, to allow him greater access.

"After that, every Torki that the first fully aware mind of our kind met also found new access to a hidden library of information in their Olt. From that time, we flowered into a real civilization, and every new adult Torki had this gift of knowledge when they ingested an Olt.

"We do not know how long after the Olt'kitapi gave us millions of the original Olts before this happened. We only know that our benefactors were gone, and we had a hint of who they were within our Olts. They did not ask for thanks or for anything at all from us. They helped the Raspani in a similar way, and were apparently trying to help the Krall when their peaceful and trusting nature became their downfall.

"The Prada are correct, the Krall were farther along their 'Great Path' than the Torki were on our march to civilization, when they destroyed our mutual benefactors.

"Had our home world, and its early colonies, not been so far from the space the Olt'kitapi had settled, we would not be alive now. Undeveloped, we would not have been of use to the Krall at the time they conquered the Olt'kitapi, and killed the other near-neighbor species.

"Like the Prada do now, we agreed to make things for them that they needed. We are guilty of staying alive by building weapons for them, to kill others, and then stealing what the dead races knew, and providing that knowledge which the Krall wanted to keep."

"Your Olt devices allow you to share thoughts?" Maggi wondered how much this resembled contact telepathy.

"It does not permit us to converse as you and I do right now, or to share ideas or thoughts. The combined signals of a population renders a sense in each of us of what the majority favors, even if we individually do not share that group feeling. Not all of us wanted to come out to greet you. Many fear you could be more dangerous than the Krall. Yet the group feeling brought all but the sick or injured out to wait for you."

Marlyn couldn't hold back. "You knew we were coming here? That's why you were all out on the beach? How did you know?"

Coldar aimed both eyestalks at Maggi. "Maggi Fisher, you said you are chosen as first to speak. Is it proper that I answer her question?"

"Yes, of course. I wish to know this as well."

"We monitored energy bursts for arriving space craft. We know well the range of energies of all of the craft the Krall use. Clanships, and the huge ships we Torki created for our travel in space, which the Krall now use to move both Torki and Prada from one world to another, are the most common. We detected new energies of a few arriving ships, starting twenty-six orbits ago, that were not normal Krall ships. Then after the last fleet of Krall clanships were seen arriving here twenty-two orbits ago, followed by a long silence, we knew they had left this star system."

Marlyn nodded, another meaningless gesture to a hard-bodied crab, and told him of the Krall pull out, and their new war on humanity's worlds.

"However, we also sensed radio, radar, and laser signals from the heavy world next out from the star, where the Krall previously chose most often to live. This was after we knew the Krall had left this system. Therefore, someone not Krall was alive there and curious. In the last year, there have been new clanship movements, but only the first one behaved like the Krall do. They are not curious. We sensed your movements around the planets here, movements centered at the neighbor world, where you said you now live. We listened to your radio signals, and heard an unknown language."

Marlyn explained the sequence of events. "We captured a clanship earlier this year, when it returned for a visit to this system that the Krall joint clan council had forbidden. We used that ship for some of us to leave this star system. We call the departure a Jump, and the gamma radiation when we return is called a White Out. The ship I used to come here, and I used to practice Jumps recently, is a different clanship than we first captured. The world next door we call Koban, and it is now our home. We have three clanships we took from the Krall."

Coldar waved the small left claw in a spiral gesture, apparently in agreement. "We can detect differences between the energy of individual clanships when they emerge into real space. We knew your recent return had different energy, and detected that you came here several times to look at this world. Your first return came with something you brought with you, but we could not decide what it was."

Marlyn explained the cargo pod they had towed within the event horizon for the Jump.

"That explains the difference we saw. We have monitored your radio transmissions, and knew your unknown language was of a new species, compared to the data we have in our Olts. The triangulated signals from another Torki lodge told us you were at a known Prada village. When you went to our old lodge location, and turned north, your signals told us you were looking for us. Most of us decided we wanted to meet the new species that moved next to us."

Maggi, always feisty, asked, "How do you like us so far?"

"You are not a friend of the Krall, a factor in your favor, and you have at least two of their clanships, and you say a third. They do not share, so you had to take them. More factors in your favor. You also have lived on a world the Krall failed to make into a world they could dominate. All of the Prada and Torki that once were taken there for Krall use, failed to survive the gravity and the deadly life there.

"You soft looking creatures have lived, and seemed to have thrived on the 'training world' you still call Koban. There is clearly more to you than eyestalks can see. You also move as if the gravity here, which is greater than the Prada, or we Torki prefer, is almost invisible to you. Koban's greater gravity could explain some of your ease here, but we think there is more to know of you, if you wish to tell us."

Wister finally had something to offer. "I want to watch them, collectively, when one of you tries what you call a Mind Tap on any of them. Their collective surprise may be enough to atone for their looking down on my people. They might learn the Krall are perhaps still the senior species, but not the strongest." His head darted forward several times, in apparent anticipation.

Coldar made no response, but even eyes on stalks could convey curiosity.

"Wister is speaking of abilities we have acquired, via genetic modifications, from some of the life forms on Koban. Many of us have their strength and speed of reactions. Others have also acquired increased sense of smell, night vision, and can hear the high speech of the Krall."

Bradley promptly spoke up. "I can hear the words you just spoke Coldar, and understand many, but I am not fluent in that language. I am the only one present here that has all of the genetic modifications just listed."

"Coldar, we have an ability that seems to be unique to any other world except Koban, taken from creatures we call rippers. They are predators on Koban that hunt in groups of four to ten, and live mostly on the open grasslands, killing animals that live in herds. We have become friends with them, and have two of them with us, but they did not come on our shuttle today, for fear they would frighten you."

"We know of these animals, but because we never lived close to where they hunt, we may never have seen them. What is unusual about them that you have borrowed or copied? What did the Prada mean when he said for one of you to Mind Tap one of us?"

"The group ability you Torki have by use of the Olt devices, sounded similar to some of the things rippers can do to share thoughts and mind pictures, but only when they are in physical contact. We humans discovered this ability, and inserted the genetics for this into ourselves. We can exchange emotions, mind pictures, even words, by making physical contact with other creatures. So far, it has worked on any animal or intelligent creature we have tested. We sense their thoughts, emotions, see the images in their minds, and we can share our own thoughts with them. It has even been done with the Krall."

That statement virtually froze Wister. The subject of mental contact with a Krall had not been broached with him because of the questions that could arise about still having some of their "Rulers" as prisoners.

"When did you do that?" he demanded.

"Wister, it was not on this world. We can talk of it later. I want to satisfy the curiosity of Coldar and the other Torki, and my own curiosity. I don't know how this will work with their species."

The Torki had a question. "How is it done? You said physical contact. We have hard shells that are very insulating. Will it work through that?"

"I don't know, but it may work to a limited extent. We normally use our hands," she waved them, "because there is a high concentration of nerve endings there for good contact. It works on most tissue that has a high density of nerve endings. I'd think for a first test, a more insulated place, such as your shell would be best. We touch hands with the Prada. I point out that if you have thoughts you do not want me to receive, it is possible to block sending them to me."

In the first sign of exasperation she had seen from the usually patient little Prada, he said, "Excellent. Warn the crab before you touch him. Let the poor Prada look like a crazy animal."

"Excuse him, Coldar; he has not gotten over the shock of our first confrontational meeting. He tried to attack me, as he believed a good subject of his Krall Rulers should do, and I had to get rough with him. I then read his mind without warning him first, as I have warned you I will do."

"I would think he would have sent some of their animals to go after you first. The Prada are not good fighters."

Without saying anything, Maggi simply looked at Wister. He had the good sense to remain quite.

The Torki held forth its smaller left claw, and advanced closer for her to touch. "There is some sense of feel in the larger two claws, but if that doesn't work, my smaller maxillipeds or mandibles are very sensitive, as are my eyestalks."

Maggi noticed that the Torki had three pairs of fine little claws close to its mouthparts, and there were the four button size black eyes, inset slightly in its carapace, directly over where its small manipulators would meet. The Prada had said the Torki were masters at working with small delicate circuitry.

She extended her hand, and touched the backside of the three-foot pincher claw, deliberately withholding any transmittable mental image, opening her mind to receive thoughts. There was a murmur of mental sound, sort of white noise, and a faint sense of curiosity.

"Coldar, I sense many distant voices, and curiosity, but it is not very strong. I'll try to send a mental image of some plants of the countryside around where I live, and which I have studied."

She pictured a sunny morning on Koban, after a night shower, and the water dripping from the tall teal grass, into blue, yellow, and red six-inch wide bell shaped flowers, holding an inch or so of water in the base of the flowers. Beautiful looking, but the sweet tasting liquid was laced with a toxin that numbed the nervous system of insects that drank from them. Otherwise, the superconducting nerves made the insects too fast for the carnivorous Grabber plant's flowers to curl in fast enough to catch them.

Then she visualized the Fly Spear plant. It had a sweet type of nectar also, but it wasn't toxic. If the wrong kind of fly came to drink, the spring loaded three-inch shaft of the stamen would dart down into the narrow neck of the plant, and stab the unfortunate insect, letting the impaled creature die over the next day or so, as enzymes in the "spear" helped break down the exoskeleton to release the nutrients inside. If it missed the target prey, the spring reset in about ten minutes to wait for the next opportunity. If the insect were the pollinator that had evolved with that plant, it would stroke the spear before entering the narrow neck to get the nectar, leaving a spore-like pollen equivalent on the stamen from its last flower, the chemical contact keeping the stamen locked in place. If the spear was launched anyway, the long legs of the slender bodied insect held it well to the side. It was seldom impaled.

The biologist in Maggi liked these plants, and they seemed like safe images to try to share, which would be different from anything the Torki had ever seen.

"I sense colored plants and insects, and a surprise, but it is not clear." Coldar told her.

"Do you wish to try a more nerve sensitive area?"

"Yes." It extended the left side's three foot-long grasper, leaving the two shorter pairs held close to its lower carapace.

Not particularly squeamish, Maggi nevertheless did not grasp the hard two-inch pincher claw, thinking that it might not have as much nerve sensitivity as the "arm" to which it was attached. This was a wise decision regarding her fingers. The larger claws were another matter entirely.

The Fly Spear was the last picture she had tried sending. That being the freshest image in her mind, she started with that one to send this time. She was blocking the previous "white noise" input from the Torki, trying to impress Coldar with a clear mental image this time.

She sent the image of the delicate looking orange flower with the long slender neck, its curved yellow stamen poised over the flared bell of the flower, and the sharp "spear" aimed down the tube. She visualized an insect forcing its way into the narrow flower tube to reach the enticing nectar. The lack of a chemical signal to hold the spear's "spring" locked released the stamen. Her eyes closed, to allow the sharpest possible image to fill her mind, the deadly stamen stabbed into the body of the insect.

All hell broke loose, as she was knocked violently and painfully aside. Her eyes being closed had prevented her from seeing the huge right claw swinging at her left side, and the smaller right claw opening to reach under the Torki's body, snapping open and closed. Had the large claw not knocked her down, the smaller one might well have decapitated her.

Not knowing what was happening, she kicked up at the flat surface of the heavy crab, wildly swinging its claws under its abdomen, opening and closing convulsively. Using her Kobani strengthened muscles in this low gravity, she easily flipped the six hundred pound crab into the air and onto its back.

She leaped to her feet, ignoring the bruising she felt, and turned to run to the shuttle. That was when she realized that all of the Torki were behaving like Coldar. Bradley leaped over a Torki that was spinning between her and the shuttle, as it kept reaching under its carapace with its claws, snatching at something. He landed by Maggi and bodily lifted her and leaped back over the spinning crab and landed by the shuttle's open hatch and shoved her inside. She instantly saw that Wister was cowering in a seat, looking terrified. Marlyn was limping up the aisle to the cockpit, and Hakeem was closing the hatch behind Bradley.

There were a number of hard thumps on the shuttle sides, but Maggi needed to stop Marlyn from starting the thrusters. She was afraid she was trying to get them away, and might harm the Torki in the process. She was the only one that knew what was wrong.

"Everyone, stop! Marlyn, don't activate the thrusters. This will end in a moment."

"The Torki went insane," Wister said. "Before I could move, I was grabbed and shoved into here by your young male. The others were pushed on top of me. I did nothing wrong."

Bradley explained. "Aunt Maggi, you and I are the only TGs here. I had to get the others inside as fast as possible before I could help you. I was a little rough."

"Bradley, you did right, and the fault, indirectly, is mine. I started that mad house out there. I hope none of them were hurt." She looked through the side windows and the leaping, spinning and claw snapping had ended, and the Torki were each inspecting one another, top and bottom sides.

Marlyn called back, "What are they looking for now on their bodies? They seem to have calmed down."

Maggi shook her head in dismay. "They are looking for a giant Fly Spear sticking through their bodies. Coldar thought he had been pierced, and therefore all of them did as well, because of the Olt link they share. They all must have been trying hard to sense what Coldar experienced."

Hakeem stared at her. "What the hell did you show him?"

"Flowers. In particular, the Fly Spear the second time."

"That fits in the palm of a hand." Bradley pointed out. "Why did they all go berserk over that?"

"We need to give them another moment. All of you hold my hand and I'll let you see what I showed, so you will understand."

Wister was reluctant, but had experienced enough mental images that he drew confidence in his ability to comprehend what he would see. She had placed it in context. The flower was small.

They all watched as the plump insect forced its way into the flower, and saw the image of the spear plunging at them as if they had the insect's viewpoint. Then it pierced the body as if they were off to the side to see. Only Wister jerked, because he was not familiar with the plants actions, but the forewarning was enough to ward off real fear.

He made the telling comment. "It looked very large in the mental image when the sharp object struck, but you showed the flower as smaller first."

"Yes, this time I did. For Coldar, I only used the mental image I had when we used a miniature camera, to watch this in a recording. It looked huge to him, and I closed my eyes to keep the image sharp and clear so he could see how effective this form of communication can be."

Marlyn understood. "They all thought they had been pierced. Wow. How do we fix this?"

Hakeem had an idea. "If they will ever talk with us again, I can put that recording on my tissue sample computer. Kap can send it to me if we need the proof. It must be in his library."

"Do that Hakeem. In the meantime, Brad, open the hatch again please." Maggi owed some apologies, and already felt the bruising she decided she deserved for the miscalculation.

Coldar was standing thirty feet away again, and this time he and all the other Torki had claw arms elevated, with the pinchers rotated down, tips on the ground. To Maggi it vaguely reminded her of the positions of linemen in the now defunct sport of twentieth century American football, ready to charge forward.

Wister was helpful without being asked. "That is a position of shame. Not of you, but of themselves. They know their reaction was wrong."

Maggi stepped out, and knowing she looked ridiculous, bent over and placed her fists on the ground in as close an approximation to the Torki posture as she could manage, and held that pose for ten seconds.

Standing up, she called out. "I am sorry. The fault is mine. You have never experienced a mind-to-mind image before."

Coldar, holding his distance, replied. "I failed to detect the proper scale of the event, to see that it was on a very small size, as when seen very close. I have harmed you. In my fear I made all of those connected through my Olt react the same way.

"This has *never* happened with the Olt in this way, to share our thoughts so clearly, what one of us is seeing so sharply. My emotions became those of all the others, not just the sense of all of our feelings on average. It connected us more strongly than we have ever experienced. When we checked our memories for what we each saw, we discovered a new section of the library within the Olts, which has opened to us for the first time. We will start to explore that information now. This opening of a new part of the library has happened in times past, when we reached a new threshold of development.

"When we were ready for fusion power, and created it ourselves, the Olts of those involved in the work revealed new information on how to use the new knowledge. It happened again when we first reached space, also when we discovered how to draw energy from the Universe where all matter moves faster than light.

"The Olt'kitapi, through the Olt, has continued to help us each time we were ready. This mind sharing today opened another part of the library. We owe you a great debt for this wonder, and I nearly killed you in my panic."

"Coldar, it was a clumsy accident on my part. Consider it a gift if it proves to be good for your people. You may not have reached a new stage in development on your own, so you may not be as ready as you believe for the new knowledge. We humans have also leaped ahead in development, and may not be ready for where this ability will lead us. However, we know the ability will help us oppose the Krall, and perhaps save our species."

"You may be able to do what you say against the Krall. For a small creature, you almost broke my shell when you threw me into the air and turned me on my back." There was a general scraping sound all around them that raised the hairs on the human's arms and necks.

Maggi winced. "Wister, what is that sound?"

"I have only heard it described, I never heard the sound myself. You have amused the Torki. I think I can wait a very long time to hear this unpleasant laughter again." From a Prada, with an indefinite life span, that was saying a lot.

****

A day later, the Torki were at ease with the Mind Tap images from Maggi, and their Olts had considerable information concerning how to use the devices for electronic mind sharing between the crabs. Tellingly, the Kobani learned that the range of the Olt device's communication between Torki was 121 feet. The same range as for the Olt'kitapi made Katusha and the Raspani made Rolperry tools, which was a sign that this was also some short-range quantum effect. Coldar told them that there had never been any electromagnetic signals detected from the Olts, and that they appeared to require no power source. The Torki on the other side of the bay, being out of Olt linkage range, had not experienced the panic of those clustered around the shuttle.

Maggi posed a question. "Coldar, why do you think the Olt'kitapi built those complex devices to migrate to your brains when consumed, and then provide a connection and a source of information between your people? It would have seemed less invasive to simply teach you themselves."

"Our species was not a true community when we were found by the Olt'kitapi. We lived in groupings, but had no society, no cooperation. We believe the devices were how they helped us slowly to become a people, to share group feelings. They did not fill our minds with knowledge we were not ready to use before we had discovered the science ourselves. Then the information to use the new technology safely was revealed to us. They did not have to be present for those thousands of years as we developed a civilization."

"That was quite an involved invention, for a newly discovered species."

"The Olt wasn't invented for us. The Olt'kitapi already had more advanced versions in their own bodies. There was another version for the Raspani, and one for the Krall."

"What?" Maggi was startled. "The Krall have something like that inside them? I've seen scans of their bodies, and I never saw the objects I can see inside the translucent shells of your Torkedia."

"The Krall you have met, the same ones the Prada call Rulers, do not have them. They were only given to some of the early Krall that were working to become more civilized. Those Krall that first went to the stars to live and work with the

Olt'kitapi. They are the ones that the Krall you have met now refer to as the 'Soft Krall.' We believe it was the offer to help them develop mentally, with the guidance of an Olt device custom designed for their race, which pushed the barbarian majority of the original Krall to stage the surprise rebellion."

"Where is the so-called Soft Krall now?"

"I assume the barbarian warrior Krall destroyed them, along with the Olt'kitapi. Both were gone from the stars thousands of years before the Krall found us. We have no direct memories of either of them."

"How do you know about this if it all happened before you encountered the Krall?"

"There are references to them in old Olt libraries. When we achieved Jump travel, as you call it, we found we could access limited information about alien races near us that we might meet. The only species in our internal library that we knew of and which still survived when the Krall enslaved us was the Prada and the Raspani."

"If the Raspani have an Olt-like device inside them, why did they lose their intelligence? You have retained your knowledge after the Krall defeated you."

"We Torki have examined Raspani remains after the Krall have slaughtered them for food, here and on other worlds. We found no signs of Olts in any of their bodies. Without resources, tools, and knowledge contained in an Olt, they cannot make new ones, as we make ours, so they may all have been lost long ago when the original owners were killed and eaten."

"Wister hoped you might be able to help the Raspani recover their intelligence. As I explained, we will bring some here to live a more comfortable life than on Koban. We all should try to help them recover their mental capacity if we can."

Coldar made a tossing move with his smaller left claw. The humans had learned this was a Torki shrug, indicating he didn't know the answer. "If they still had the implanted devices it might be possible to do so. I think the Krall killed or ate all of the Raspani with Olt implanted devices, and force bred them to keep the species alive. Without the Olts to preserve their knowledge, they would soon lose civilization under the Krall. We know the Prada believe the Raspani hid their minds, and if they were nearly as advanced as the Olt'kitapi was technologically, they possibly could have used their Olts to record their minds in one of the libraries. However, there have been no new Raspani Olts made for many thousands of years, and the minds would have been lost anyway."

Maggi nodded, in basic agreement. "Nevertheless, with human, Prada, and Torki assistance, they may have the capacity to recover some of what was taken from their minds. I thank you for your offer to help us. We will be bringing the first of them here within a week. Wister has returned to speak with his sister, to activate a part of one of the underground factories to make fencing material."

"Your mental images must have been very convincing." Coldar complemented. "We have never known the Prada to do anything that was outside of what their Krall Rulers ordered them to do. The accomplishments of your species, despite your youth, may have sparked the Prada into their first independent thoughts in ten thousand years. You have certainly sparked thoughts of hope in our own minds. With the freedom to ask for materials from the factories, we can make some interesting things for your people. The Krall have never made use of all that we learned from other species. Perhaps we can put that knowledge to good use on your behalf. We wish there were more of you. The Krall have many more warriors than your small population, and can hatch many more in a short while. Even feral Krall are dangerous if they choose to turn them loose on your worlds."

Marlyn, who had been simply listening to the discussion until now, butted in. "What are feral Krall?"

"Like those on our smallest continent on this planet, which you call Haven. That place will not be suitable for habitation unless they all eat each other."

With a sigh, Maggi asked. "You mean there are Krall on Haven? When were you going to reveal this to us?"

"There is no danger, so long as they can't get to any of the other continents. They are surrounded by an ocean they cannot cross, which is filled with creatures that will eat them if they try. Our Torkada, bred for living in the sea are eaten in their millions by ocean life before they return here, and if they land on that continent to escape the predators in the sea, the feral Krall will eat them. They will also eat any Torkedia that land to molt. Except to hunt, breed and lay eggs that is almost all the feral Krall are capable of doing. They have no language, learning, or tools. They fight each other, and eat the losers. They have animal cunning, but never develop high intelligence or technology."

"How did they get there? Why did the Krall leave them?"

"That place was a nursery continent for several finger clans, with natural geographical boundaries to keep the clan populations separate. The Krall do not nurture or raise their cubs until the survivors reach age five to eight orbits old. Those feral Krall were left there by their parent clans as not worth the salvage of their bloodlines. Had the adult Krall remained there, the feral Krall would have eventually been killed and eaten by the clever and cooperating pre-novice cubs they select for initial training."

"How dangerous are they?"

"They killed a small Torki colony there many orbits ago. We don't know if there was a Prada village, but it would be gone by now even if it went underground. There may still be large animals that survive there, and large predators. Eventually the feral Krall eat most animals but themselves, growing weak and starving as their own population is unable to feed the dwindling survivors. There are abandoned worlds where this has happened."

Maggi wasn't particularly surprised. "Humans can't survive without adults to raise and instruct children, but it appears the Krall have also bred to the level where they require adults to intervene to select those cubs that are able to accept training. If all adult Krall were eliminated, or lost all of their technology, the species would not be able to make wars on any but themselves. This is a strategy we have considered, but was not sure if it could work. We want to leave the Krall without the means to use Jump travel, or make war equipment."

"You will have to eliminate their forced labor, or they will make more weapons." Coldar didn't sound any different in tone, but there was an obvious inference herc. He surely wanted to know how the Kobani were planning to do this. Was killing the slave workers part of their plan?

"Coldar, did Captain Greeves, Marlyn who is here with me, explain what the name Haven means in our language? That is the name we will use for this world when we speak of it to others of our race."

"I only heard the sound of the word in your language. You did not use a low Krall word. Does it have a meaning in your language, or is it only a sound that represents this place?"

"It has a meaning. The equivalent meaning in low Krall is a refuge, or a place of safety. We want to bring as many of the forced labor survivors here to this planet as is possible. If the populations on production worlds are not much larger than they were here on Haven when we arrived, that may be possible. However, we don't have ships larger than clanships in our possession now, and we only have three of those. We considered trying to capture the larger Krall ships we have heard about for that purpose, or find some in Human Space we can buy. To buy them will take more time, and raise questions we don't want to answer in Human Space. However, we will try to find such transports somehow. We intend to save as many of your people as we can."

Coldar had a ready proposal. "I can tell you where to find such ships in orbit, empty and ready to use. They are stored where they are built, and returned there after use. On your navigation system, I can show you the planet where the largest Torki ships are built, and saved for use by any Krall clan. They are not a Krall design. They were designed by my ancestors to travel the stars in watery comfort. The ships are thirty times larger than a clanship, although they will not carry fully thirty times as much.

"They can hold twenty complete Prada villages, or four or five Torki colonies like this one, with sea water for us. The length of time for crowded occupation depends on what provisions can be stored. The number of Torki they carry also depends on how much seawater can be loaded. A short Jump needs less comfort and less water.

"The description of our ships in our language is a series of clicks and whistles, but means the journey our spawn starts when we release them in the sea. We now use the low Krall words for migrating animals as the purpose of these ships. We no longer gave individual names to them, because the Krall will use none. However, if you can use them, we would like to name those that bring any of our people here. I will give you a list of ship names, with the meanings before your people do this. It will have symbolic meanings to the Torki you rescue."

Maggi didn't grasp the usual self-centered Krall motivation here. "What do the Krall do with such large ships? Why do they use ships not designed for their own use, like the clanships were?"

"The migration ships still are built only because the Krall want to move us when they build a new base, or colonize a new world for a clan or a new finger clan.

They can carry the Torki or Prada workers, and the factory sections for them to assemble a starter facility. That small initial facility is used to build the remainder of a full-sized production complex, and that factory then can make other complete factories if those are required, or to make weapons and ships. It is faster and more efficient for them to move us.

"To rescue our workers, you will not need to take the old factories apart, or load starter factory sections. You can destroy what you leave behind. This way you would be able to carry more workers inside each ship. Some of the past production worlds we have lived on would need no more than five migration ships to move all of the workers, Prada and Torki combined."

Maggi gave Marlyn a skeptical look that was wasted in front of the oblivious Torki. "Tell me again how huge these ships are that only five will carry all of the workers from an entire factory world?"

Coldar understood her confusion. "Expect to need less than five for a single world. I used a number that I hope provides for less crowding and faster loading. To your populous race, I know it does not sound like many beings to fill an entire world, and it is not. That is because the Krall do not want or need worlds full of workers. When they choose a new world to colonize for a finger clan, they take only the workers needed. None of the worlds the Krall inhabit will have many workers, or many Krall warriors. They may have many pre novices, but those are culled greatly between breeding cycles.

"If the old world is to be abandoned by an entire clan, those workers left behind are eventually food for millions of hatchings of feral Krall left behind, who reproduce without limits or culling. The underground factories are destroyed before a clan departs, so we cannot use them to build effective protection or sufficient weapons."

The wonderful Krall, thought Maggi, always a loving and caring species for their subject races.

"Why didn't this happen on Koban, or here? They left us there to die."

The Torki considered this question for a moment. "It may be that abandoned eggs hatched, and the faster native life ate the weaker hatchlings before they reproduced. It also may be that because the clans intend to return to this system to make a home world of Koban, they left no large nests of unattended eggs to destroy the balance of life. Their feral young consume most life on abandoned worlds, which is why the clans do not return to them later.

"In the time since they left Koban, over twenty orbits, ten thousand or more feral Krall should have hatched from a typical large nest in twenty or thirty days. In three hands of orbits, they would mature enough that survivors would reproduce and increase numbers by ten or twenty times. In two more hands of orbits, they would multiply enough usually, to kill even the large animals on any continent, or killing their young would be enough. A starting nest of a hundred thousand eggs might cover any continent of your world by now. Perhaps that couldn't happen on Koban, where even most herbivores are stronger and faster than a Krall hatchling, or faster than a novice aged cub."

He waved a claw. “Even a few clutches of eggs from low status females can create a dangerous population after twenty orbits. These would be left at random, in forests or grasslands by females with too low a status to produce cubs worth training up to novice level. An unmanaged Krall reproductive cycle is shorter when the young are left untrained, without ruthless culling by adults. Twenty orbits is a more typical breeding cycle for producing warriors that earn higher status.”

Maggi shrugged. “Then we escaped the fate of other worlds they left behind. So we only need ten or fifteen of your giant ships?”

Coldar expanded on the number estimate. “The actual ships needed may be two tens more than that, depending on how many worlds you will raid at one time. I named numbers that are even multiples of ten in our method of counting. We use a base ten system, the Krall use base eight. What is your system for counting, a base four number system? You have four limbs, and we have ten, when you include our claw arms.”

Maggi explained humans also used a base ten counting system, because of the number of digits on our two soft “grasper claws,” and that we did not count based on our number of limbs.

Marlyn had a Spacer’s question. “Coldar, are these large ships controlled and flown the same way as the clanships? Can one of us that know how to operate a clanship fly them?”

“Once in space I think yes, because the Torki navigation and control systems were changed to be like those on a clanship so Krall pilots can operate them. However, these large ships must land on a planet to load and unload, and that is difficult for pilots that have not been trained to do this. If the ship is to carry Prada, it must set down on a hard surface, and that requires very fine control. To carry Torki, it can land in the sea much more safely, and our people would go to the ship where it floats, close to their lodge. It is then loaded with considerable sea water before it lifts, so no more than one or two lodges could be carried without crowding.”

“Do you have Torki here that know how to fly one of these ships, using both dry land and sea landing sites?”

“Using information on our Olt, in principle all adult Torki can learn to do so. Though some will do that better than others. Will you want some of us to travel with you? We are not good fighters or very fast, but we can lift heavy weights for loading, and operate the landing systems manually if computer control is not flexible enough for landing on the ground.”

Maggi shook her head, before remembering the alien wouldn’t know the human gesture yet. “I doubt we would want to risk taking you along to try to capture those ships. There are maneuvers our people can make in a clanship that will probably kill you or the Prada. I may not look very strong, but remember that I kicked you high in the air and onto your back.”

Coldar moved his large claw under his carapace to touch the tender place where her small powerful feet had nearly cracked his shell. “I have not forgotten.”

“What we *can* do,” she proposed, “is to have the Torki most qualified to be pilots of a migration ship mentally go through practice sessions, thinking of all the things they would do to operate the ships, while some of my people use a Mind Tap, and learn from them. Then we can teach that flying technique to our other people much faster.

"I promise you, Coldar, that we want you and the Prada free of the Krall, and not only because we want the Krall to lose the ability to make war. We need your help in making this world, and Koban safer places for you and for our people to live. If we gain new technology from helping you, our chance of stopping the Krall improves. This is a case of mutual benefit. We can help each other."

Coldar waved a claw. "If you look around, you will see that the few Torki that can best teach you to fly our ships are coming to join us. I called them using the new Olt capability. If you will permit, I will show you on your ship, the Beagle, where our former worlds are located in your navigation system. One of our old colony worlds makes all of the migration ships, and other places are worlds that make many of the clanships. The clanships can be made by the Prada at any factory complex, but for efficiency, the Krall build them on only two worlds.

"You should also go to the single world where the Hammer weapons are made and kept in orbits. Just one of these is able to destroy an entire planet, but it takes many orbits to form even one. The Botolians invented them as a smaller solid ball of dense crystal, which they launched at Krall clanship formations at high velocity with a magnetic accelerator. They often missed their targets because they could not be guided, but were almost indestructible.

"The Krall admired the powerful balls, and ordered the Torki scientists to learn how to make them as larger hollow balls that they could fly and steer. Using the Botolian made gravity projectors and their compression techniques, combined with the Raspani quantum disintegration tools to carve them without breaking their crystal structure, our technicians made them hollow with a hatch opening. When equipped with a tachyon powered drive system, a Krall pilot can Jump one of them to any world, and gradually build a velocity close to light speed if given enough time."

Maggi told him they knew of these weapons. "They used one of them against my own home world of Rhama, I was told. It killed nearly a third of the population, and ruined the biosphere. We don't want any of those balls used against us again. We have high velocity, diamond-tipped uranium projectiles to fire at them, to try to crack their surface."

Coldar spread his claw arms wide. "We had not thought of that method of destruction of the hammers. They shatter if they strike a massive enough object at high velocity. You found an alternative, a high velocity small mass with the hardest natural tip possible. We understand how a small crack will cause the shell to rupture violently. In making these balls, some lose stability and explode before completion when we try to carve the opening. You must need to shoot many projectiles to hit one of them when they move so fast."

She explained the theory of defense. "There are hundreds of railguns around our planets, ready to fire in the direction of any of these incoming hammers, which we call Eight Balls for a reason not worth explaining. The hope is that we can kill them far enough away to protect the planet, using many thousands of high-speed, diamond-tipped heavy metal slugs. I was told our military has not had a chance to test the railguns against the real hammers, only against similar sized drones flying under computer control."

Coldar raised and lowered his carapace on his left side, in a gesture Maggi didn't yet recognize as equivalent to a human headshake. "To truly protect your worlds, you must destroy all of the hammers that are stored in orbit around the former Botolian home world. Then remove or destroy the gravity projectors the Krall made us operate for them, the Botolian machines that were captured after the war. Next, you must rescue the Torki there who may know how to rebuild and use the projectors. Without the projectors to focus intense gravity for producing the collapsed matter, no more hammers can be made."

Then Coldar abruptly shifted to a very different subject. "Would your fighters like armor that is lighter, stronger, and more technologically advanced than any the Krall have?"

Maggi looked up into the black eyes on stalks above the purple carapace, looking unblinkingly back at her. "I think this is the start of a beautiful friendship, Coldar."

Chapter 13: Beware of Accidents

Crager dismissed his ninth interviewee, after confirming the man's activities after dark with other troopers, video surveillance around the barracks, and through observation by any of the permanent cadre while the out-of-camp excursion was known to be in progress.

"Breaker, get in here." He called out loudly over the speaker system to the men waiting in the outer part of the auditorium. He had used the AI to configure the large space into a large waiting room with no chairs, his interrogation room with a single desk and chair, an access screen to the base AI, and a neurological sensor chair for the subjects under suspicion.

There was a temporary holding room connected to the interrogation room, no other doors or windows, with bench seats along the walls. The only way in or out was through Crager's interrogation room, and wearing his Booster Suit he felt much more than adequate to personally control anyone that decided to try and leave without his approval.

There were three spec ops guards on the larger room's double exit doors. Only men Crager had personally eliminated as the potential fence climber were allowed to leave. So far, he had placed only one man in the second holding area, with active surveillance showing him in a corner window of his large screen. The man wasn't particularly suspicious; he simply had not been where anyone could verify his presence inside the camp.

As Breaker entered the room, Crager's link to the camp AI automatically provided basic data and history on the man. A glance at the screen on his desk showed him Jorl Breaker's training evaluations (all good), and the few personal details that had been collected on the man.

Seeing Jorl's face triggered a recollection of this group's first day. He was one of the few men that had not panicked or even showed a reaction when the realistic Krall hologram leaped at the people in the front row of the auditorium.

"Sit." He pointed to the sensor-equipped chair.

What followed were a series of questions of his activities after sunset today. The responses on the display were no more erratic than most of the other men he'd spoken with that night. All of them were slightly nervous in the presence of the Top sergeant, with no clue as to why they were here. Except at least one of them certainly had a clue. One of them had left the camp to meet someone.

"So you went for a run after dark, and you say you were in the shower when we called you outside to formation?"

"Yes, Sergeant."

"You had free time. Why were you running?"

"I have done this on other days. I had permission from Corporal Ranken." He had not answered the question asked. Yet both his statements were accurate, and displayed no strong left-right confliction between brain hemispheres, as it should if he'd been strongly deceptive. Crager, not thoroughly an expert with this equipment, was unaware that the mental diversion Breaker had just used hid a minor reaction to the real question.

The technology of monitoring neural networks had never produced an accurate lie detection system, but it had shown that the process of analyzing a question, and formulating a reply involved both brain hemispheres. If the reply was deceptive, the act of concealment revealed some mathematically modeled responses. That permitted some comparison of the thought activity of the rational and logical left side of the brain, to the activity of the emotional and creative right side, and displayed a pattern involved with possible conflict between a fully truthful answer, and a modified reply. It was still partly an art form for the interrogator and not a pure science.

Crager paused to check with Corporal Ranken that Breaker had asked permission to run. That was confirmed.

"Did you see anyone near the fence or outside of it when you made your laps?"

"Yes, Sergeant. I did."

That could be helpful. Crager looked at the screen. Normal comparison.

"What did you see?"

"The patrol truck passed twice, on my first and third laps. There were rabbits humping outside on the road."

"You did not see anyone else near the fence, or that climbed over?"

"No, Sergeant."

"Did you climb over?"

"No, Sergeant, I did not climb the fence." Of course he hadn't, he jumped over. Going and returning. However, his brain knew there was something he was slightly concealing.

The peaks of the curves differed slightly, but the computer showed the contours of the waves were similar, with the one for the right side hemisphere (emotional response) nearer to the screen's top, partly out of view. Crager touched the scale factor icon on the touch screen, and both of the wave contours shot off the top of the display as the AI yielded automatic control of the scale adjustment to the human. A moment later, Crager had the curves back where they belonged. He wasn't sure what he'd done wrong, but shifted his focus back to Breaker's supposed shower alibi.

"You have a towel around your neck now, and your head still looks damp. You were in the shower you said when Sergeant Norris called the formation, you dressed and dried on the run?"

"Yes, Sergeant."

Crager pulled the video recording of the door traffic of Breaker's barracks. He watched the man stroll into the barracks door, passing other men standing and talking at the same entrance. He recognized one of the other men was someone he had already cleared, using this same Tri-Vid camera data. He checked the time stamp, and saw this was several minutes after the mystery man was assumed to have returned to the camp, when the patrol was chasing the rabbit. The shower story might be accurate, but it didn't clear this man.

"Wait in the room behind me. And dry off." He had more men to check before focusing on those he couldn't clear immediately.

The next man's shrunken waveform on the monitor made Crager curse and adjust the screen scale factor again. However, he quickly eliminated nineteen more men from suspicion, using video, and cadre as witnesses.

The scale factor problem returned when he interrogated a young man named Yilini Jastrov. However, a break room Tri-Vid recording proved he was inside the camp.

The next man repeated the too small-scale factor, which Crager corrected manually again, with more cursing. That man and eventually two more men were also sent to the rear waiting area, because they had no verifiable alibi for their whereabouts.

Then the monitoring equipment repeated its same scale factor problem with a trainee candidate named Fred Saber. This time it impressed itself in Crager's mind more firmly, because Saber was cleared by exactly the same video as had cleared the Jastrov kid, the most recent anomaly on the brain wave monitor. They had been sitting at a table together in the center of the break room, in conspicuous view of both cameras there.

He let Saber leave, but was struck by the fact that he was searching for some sort of irregularity in the candidates, and three men had triggered a seeming hardware or software glitch in his equipment. He selected the camera in the holding room, and saw the five men there chatting, obviously discussing what was happening tonight. Well, not all were chatting. Breaker was pacing, but wasn't really part of the conversation. He seemed nervous.

Crager had the AI reverse the surveillance recording to when Breaker had joined the first man. They briefly spoke, each professing not to know why they were being questioned or held. Breaker started drying off with the towel he had to carry with him when he ran from the shower.

As he paced, he opened the top of his jumpsuit to rub the towel around the back of his head and neck. That was when Crager saw what he first thought could be a bruise on his upper chest. He thought that whoever climbed the razor wire fence in the dark, under Heavyside's gravity, might have been injured. He froze the image and had Karp, the base AI zoom in to see if it looked fresh, or if the skin had been torn.

The palm-sized, sharply defined black oval looked applied, not the result of an accident or a bruise. However, he wondered why the size and shape seemed somehow familiar to him. He thought a moment before he fed the image to his personal AI, and asked it to run a compare to similar shapes he perhaps had encountered in the past. It had to be something he'd previously seen.

His internal visual projection system played a series of images in his left eye. They were mostly random small blobs he'd seen, which the AI had found in recordings of past missions. Conducting a live mission was the only time he made such recordings.

"Wait. Go back several images." Something belatedly caught his attention.

When he found what he'd seen, it was on the fresh corpse of a Krall he and his team had ambushed and killed. The upper chest tattoo had a black oval rim, and inside it contained several dozen colored dots. The oval was perhaps one-third filled with color, as an experienced warrior usually had. However, it certainly wasn't black inside, not even any of the internal dots were black.

The part that caught Crager's attention was the location, size, and oval shape. Breaker appeared to have a blackened Krall rank tattoo at the base of his neck, of the exact same dimension. It was odd, but he'd seen tattoos previously that represented a Krall face, or of a Krall being killed, or already dead. Tattoo body art had mostly died out as a fad centuries ago, although some military members were bringing it back into style, because it could easily be removed now. This marking didn't look very decorative, and it wasn't placed where it could easily be seen, as most military related body art was.

Based on this eccentricity, and the odd brainwave height he shared with two other men, Crager had the camp AI run an analysis of all three men, to seek possible connections or similarities. There could be some sort of implants that altered their neural responses in the sensor chair. The platinum nerve overlays that graduate spec ops troops sported caused similar anomalies. This would make someone like that identifiable when in a neural sensor chair if you knew what to look for. However, he was also looking for anything common in their past behavior. He was actually surprised at what he learned. He'd assumed there would be no obvious links or connections if they had been inserted by some other secret government organization to spy on camp operations.

One of the other two men, Jastrov, was seen on video bearing a duplicate tattoo, when his jumpsuit fasteners had snagged and pulled open on the training course during a testing run. Matching unusual tattoos would eventually be noticed for the three, after the remaining candidates were reduced in number. They all shared communal showers.

He learned none of the three men had passed through the spec ops prescreening, done on the orbital transfer station. That wasn't mandatory, but very few volunteers that simply walked into the terminal at Port Andropov to join the other arrivals made it through the next week, the "weeding out" process in the camp on the other side of the port area. Karp told him that none of the three men matched any of the faces that boarded buses from the terminal to the camp gate, over the two-day period their group was assembled.

They were truly "walk-ons," of which *none* like that had ever been good enough to make it to SOB-1, as far as Crager knew, and certainly none had ever passed "Hell Week." This, and their joint youthfulness, made them obvious standouts if anyone went looking at them hard, as Crager was doing now. It seemed to be a clumsy infiltration method, counting on a lack investigation on the camp's part. Although, why not? It had almost worked, and there was a well-known lack of interest in a volunteer's prior background and criminal history by the black ops section. It wasn't as if the Krall could slip a warrior by them.

The three men's performance ratings were spectacularly average for a selection of already superb physical specimens, placing all three on the top center of the bell curve distribution for the entire group. Farther back on the curve and they would be subpar, and if placed a little ahead on the curve they would be clearly superior to many of the already above average people being tested.

There was a bell curve distribution for running, for speed, distance, and sprints. Curves for pushups, chin ups, sit-ups, long jumps, rope climbs, and more. The three always seemed to fall in the middle range after a day or so of repetition. All three were noted as "team building" participants because they encouraged the poorer performers to do better.

None of them was physically outstanding enough to draw notice, but stayed free of the risk of being cut. Except that on several occasions, when the next cut was going to eliminate less desirable candidates, located slightly on the low side of the publicly posted average center points of the curves, these three men had spike performances on the day it was needed, and they were safely retained.

Having helped design the elimination process, Crager was positive that anyone who's effort was only average at Camp Port Andropov, would fall well below the final cutoff point during "Hell Week." Yet all three remained almost exactly average even for that week. It meant at Andropov, they had only put out as much effort as necessary to get to SOB-1. Then only enough sweat to get through "Hell Week." The competitive nature of the type of men that made it this far was such that they nearly always wanted to excel in competition against their peers. These three men did not do that, yet each was able to step up their physical performance when called to do so. In hindsight, it was clear they had been holding back all the way through.

At this point, following his instincts, Crager was prepared to assume any one of those three had been the person that went off base and returned. However, two of them had rock solid video alibies, leaving Jorl Breaker at the focal point of his attention. The other two were clearly here to support him or act as alternates. The implication to Crager was that these men were ringers, slipped in here to spy on camp operations. Now they were detected before they had a chance to learn anything.

The only spy worthy activity Crager knew of was the beginnings of the genetic research still being organized. There must have been a leak. If that suspicion were confirmed, this situation had potentially become a real life or death issue for the planners. The risk was worth taking.

Because of the physical benefits the scientists insisted could be realized, if they repeated three hundred year old genetic experiments, this had strategic implications for the entire war effort.

Washing out the three men immediately would alert whoever had sent them that the targets of the witch-hunt knew they were under suspicion. The government couldn't have any evidence, or there would have been no need for this subterfuge. The "Hell Week" break this weekend must have been the first opportunity for any of the three to make a report or meet their handler. There wasn't a single incriminating thing the three men *could* have learned from the camp instructors. Only he and

Colonel Dearborn were in the loop out of the military staff, and they were generally not directly in contact with the trainees at this stage, and had never discussed their personal opinions with their underlings.

If these three had official high-level help, they might have technology to back them up as well. “Karp, check the typical transducer frequencies used in the camp over the last week. Look for use that can’t be traced to any of our permanent party.”

“Sir, there have been daily transmissions to and from various points in the camp that did not correlate with training instructors, headquarters or support staff, or our civilian personnel with such capability. The transmissions always occur within thirty minutes either side of noon, and they were often centered where candidates had gathered. Following privacy protocol, I do not have recordings of any messages that were not routed through my own communication system, and I would require Colonel Dearborn’s approval to reveal any contents of those I have recorded.”

“I don't think I’ll need our own messages, Karp. Over what power range were these unknown transmissions made? Limited to within the camp or to the outside?” The power invested would suggest the distance of the possible receiver.

“Sir, the incoming signals were always quite strong, the outgoing much weaker. The stronger transmitter was located at high altitude, or in low orbit. The weaker outbound signals had a range of no more than one hundred miles, or less, depending of course on the sensitivity of the...” Crager cut him off.

“OK. That means they didn’t need to leave camp to communicate. However, one of them met someone outside. They gave them something, or received something that wasn’t simply a message. Has the recon team arrived yet, Karp?”

“Yes Sir. They are outside the fence now, where the tracks were found.”

“Link me to whoever’s in charge.”

“That would be Sergeant Claude Williams, Sir. Just a moment.”

A moment later Crager heard, “Sergeant Williams. Can I help you?”

“Claude, this is Bill Crager. Have you and your men checked the footprints I asked you to examine, and looked at that presumed air boat landing site?”

“Hey, morning there, Top. Still dark out here, however we have indeed been looking. There are two particularly odd factors, which I assume is why you are so interested in this. Whoever went out, and came back didn’t actually climb on the fence. The ground impacts, at least the ones your patrol boys didn’t step on or drive over, show that whoever came over the fence must have had a Booster Suit.”

“What? How do you know that?” He did *not* expect that.

“Their kickoff point left deeper impressions both ways, because they did not climb the fence, they jumped over. Only a Booster Suited man could have done that, and even so, it’s pretty damned impressive to clear a twelve-foot fence with two feet of coiled wire on top, and to do it on Heavyside. The landing print depth back into the camp supports that notion, although the landing point on the jump out was walked on and driven over by your intrepid patrol boys, as I mentioned.”

“Crap. This is getting weird, Claude. You said there were two odd factors.”

“I did. Multiply the weird factor by three or four. The landing craft impressions in the little ravine, where the footprints led, left distinctive size and shaped indentations, and the length and apparent weight also match."

"Spit it out. Match what?"

"I say personally, my onboard AI says, and even Karp agrees, that the indentations match that of a Krall single ship."

Crager whistled as a comment for his surprise. "I think the weird factor has just cubed. The footprints. What do they tell you?"

"The print size is an average sized boot of standard trainee issue, not the custom spec ops foot gear anyone with a Booster Suit would normally own. Three-quarters of any of your volunteers could leave these size prints. I don't have an exact boot size yet. Average weight is suggested, but I'll be able to do better when we make casts, measure depth, and test soil compaction. They appear to have crouched on the ball of their right boot to step into the low hatch on that single ship. Either it was opened for them from the inside, or they could key it open on their own. I have never met anyone that could do it on their own unless they had a freshly dead Krall draped over their shoulder."

"I don't think we'll find a dead warrior nearby, and I have not heard any rumors that we cracked the Krall equipment codes, but our scientists have been at it for years. Someone must have been inside to open the hatch, and then departed stealthed when the patrol arrived."

"Right. My supposition as well. Once alerted by the vibrations on the road, the patrol spotted the faint IR footstep signatures leading to the gully. It appears our sneaky one caught a rabbit, barehanded apparently, and threw it over and well past the patrol, apparently to use the rabbit's noise and heat signature to distract them when he ran back to the fence. The strides on the dirt road, when he started to run for the return jump were very long, and also suggest a Booster Suit was helping."

"Thanks, Claude. Keep looking. I have someone that I suspect for this caper, but he doesn't have a Booster Suit on right now. I can't see how or even why the Krall would possibly be involved. This is not at all like them, so my guess is we have some operational single ships in human hands. It's still good and dark out there isn't it?" He had an idea.

"I need my implants to see, but the faint glow on the horizon and my implant clock shows we have sunrise in less than two hours."

"OK. I may head out in that direction shortly with my suspect. I'll contact you if I have more questions."

"Roger, Top. If we find anything really interesting, I'll Link to you."

When the Link closed, he gave the AI instructions. "Karp, monitor the unusual transducer frequency we talked about a few minutes ago, and block any outgoing signals on that frequency and notify me."

"Yes Sir."

It was unfortunate, but Breaker, on the surface a nice kid and outwardly a patriot, was going to have a fatal training accident before daybreak. Even if he somehow survived, this "accident" would permanently remove him from the training program. The other two men would have some sort of "slip and fall" in the next day or week. Fatal if the evidence supported a need for that result, as he presumed it would. After that, there would be some new prescreening put in place, based on what Crager could find out about these three young men. At a minimum, there would never be another "walk on" allowed.

Breaker appeared to have concealed a Booster Suit somewhere in the camp. How he got one of the tremendously expensive custom-made items was a question for later. If *he* had one hidden in the camp then the other two probably had them as well. The carbon fiber suits could be folded up into a relatively compact size. Something like a medium tote bag could hold one of them, and they weighed only about forty-five pounds for a man of Breaker's medium size. Crager's suit, on his large frame, was fifty-four pounds of very powerful synthetic surface muscle.

Winning the war was vastly more important than following paranoid laws passed two generations ago, when the human race was recovering from the brink of self-induced near extinction. Humanity was on a different brink today, more difficult for non-experts to sense because it approached so slowly. Their fear of the last racial disaster was preventing the implementation of our best possible defense in time for it to be useful. Crager was prepared to make his opponents suffer the ultimate sacrifice, on behalf of this must-win war. A sacrifice he was perfectly willing to make himself.

From the comments made by the six scientists on the spec ops program that were part of the budding genetic development project, even the best humanity had *ever* done genetically to enhance clones was not enough to turn the tide against the Krall. However, genetic enhancements, combined with a new generation of Booster Suits and other hoped for technology were necessary steps that had to be taken. Moving forward, a future next step could be figured out *after* this step was taken.

Crager gave the camp AI instructions to continuously monitor the location of Jastrov and Saber, and when possible, record anything they said or did. They would likely discover soon that their transducers no longer worked. He then stepped out of his interrogation cube and released the remaining men back to their barracks, telling them (for the sake of cover) that he would talk to them later.

He released the three door guards and used the auditorium's configuration menu to lower the walls and desk, and flow away the top of his temporary interrogation room, leaving only the four men locked in the remaining cube room.

Walking to the holding room, Crager used his retinal pattern and thumbprint to open the single door.

Standing at the door, he said, "Everyone but Breaker return to their barracks. I'll have more discussions with each of you in the morning. Candidate Breaker here has some extra punitive training to complete tonight. It seems he climbed the fence and left camp, and lied about it to me."

He looked directly at Breaker, and delivered his cover story. "I don't care if it was a girlfriend you met, or why you did it, but you were not authorized to leave my compound. I'll work your ass ragged for that infraction, and more so for lying to me."

The others started out, with a curious look at Breaker, and a nervous nod to

Crager, avoiding his glare.

Jorl didn't know how he had been found out, but he wasn't going to waste time denying it just to avoid some easy extra exercise. He spoke so the others would hear. "Top, you asked me if I had climbed the fence. I did not climb over it, so I technically did not lie to you about that. I wasn't asked if I had gone outside the camp, which I admit I did."

"Well, that's confirmation enough for me, Breaker. You knew what I wanted to know, and you hid it from me by dodging behind the words you carefully selected in your hair splitting replies."

"Yes, I also admit I did that."

Good. He knew the other men had heard him say that, making the discipline he mentioned justified. "The front door is open men, return to your barracks. Breaker and I will spend some fun time on the obstacle course through breakfast, since he has so much energy to spare." It sounded innocuous enough. He'd stage the accident to look like the tragic result of a candidate trying hard to appease his Top sergeant after violating a rule. Breaker didn't suspect that he had figured out what the snooping was really after.

"Breaker, let's jog over to the track, shall we?"

The two of them left the auditorium, and Crager immediately broke into a trot, and waved Jorl to move ahead of him. "Keep ahead of me as I pick up the pace." He told him gruffly.

Whoever Breaker really was, and wherever he'd been trained, he was able to use a Booster Suit, which demanded a high level of physical ability to master. As he watched him run now, he noted how smooth and lightly he seemed to cover the ground. He didn't even hear that slap of his feet that most runners made here on Heavyside.

Crager wasn't surprised. Breaker's fifteen-foot vertical leap over the fence, plus the horizontal distance covered proved he was even stronger than many of his spec ops instructors. That leap, on Heavyside, was one that Crager would be hard pressed to match due to his recent reduced level of physical activity. That was caused by the needs of the job of running this camp.

However, Breaker was entirely on his own now, and Crager had the only suit. He was going to push him hard at the start, to judge how fit he really was. He wasn't going to let him stay on the middle of that bell curve any longer.

He picked the pace up to a run, shoving Breaker's left shoulder to go faster. They were only a half mile from the track, so he repeatedly increased the pace, forcing Breaker to run all out, taking long strides that matched Crager's. By the time they reached the edge of the track around the obstacle course, they were nearly in a sprint.

Jorl had easily stayed just a step ahead of Crager, matching every increase he heard in the Top sergeant's feet striking the ground. This was faster than he'd had to run in training, but not his best speed by any means. It also didn't seem like Crager had fully peaked either, but they were at the track now. He started around the course clockwise, and suddenly Crager put on a showy burst and passed him, and turned in front and placed a hand on his chest to slow him, as he too slowed while trotting backwards.

He looked at the slightly shorter and smaller built young man. “You have speed, I’ll grant you that. Your nightly practice wasn’t entirely to cover your deception, I suspect, since you don’t seem winded.”

Jorl wasn’t breathing hard, although neither was Crager.

“You seem comfortable in this gravity, Breaker. I know you have been pacing yourself, to stay in the middle of the pack all the way to this point. Your lack of early effort and ability to pick up your performance when necessary was a giveaway when I started looking. Where are you from kid?”

“The requirements to volunteer for this opportunity did not require me to tell you that, First Sergeant. I still choose not to do so.”

“That was the offer.” He agreed with a nod. “However, have you spent time in a heavy gravity orbital station? I’m not asking where, I’m curious how you managed to grow acclimated before you arrived here.”

“Heavyside isn’t the only high gravity planet, Sergeant.”

“It’s the highest one we’ve ever settled,” he countered.

“This sparsely populated, half-empty world is not exactly settled, First Sergeant.”

“Shifting direction again, are we? You do that a lot. The heavier planets are not considered livable, and need environmental suits because there is too little oxygen generation on those even more barren planets. I doubt if you got that healthy tan you arrived here with from inside an environment suit.”

“You are correct. I got my tan the natural way, under a bright hot sun.” Jorl knew this cat and mouse byplay was leading to something more than exercise. He wasn’t being called “candidate” any more. He wondered if he was about to be cut from the program.

Crager shifted subjects this time, back to his stated purpose of exercise. “Why don’t we race to the top of Everest? On my mark.”

Everest was a one hundred twenty-foot high steel and wood framework, with four steeply sloping sides, and a twelve-foot square platform at the top. There were six-inch diameter rough wood poles lashed to a four-sided metal support frame, and squads were timed for which ones could get all eight members to the top in the shortest time. Jorl had heard the apparatus was named after some mountain on Earth, supposedly its highest peak. It was certainly the highest point on the physical training course, located at its center. The candidates had not been permitted to climb that for the first two days; to be certain they had adjusted to the gravity. The next highest obstacle on the main course was a seventy-five-foot latticed rope covered wall.

Jorl was suddenly suspicious. They had never done the highest climbing parts of the course without lights, in the dark as they were now, and never Everest even with floodlights, because shadows made good handholds harder to identify when you were in a rush to win the race. A fall from near the top in 1.41 g’s would be fatal to most people. Crager had night vision implants and he knew Jorl did not, making it safer for him.

However, was that really what Crager thought? Jorl's high-speed thoughts raced over what Crager had said and heard tonight. He had not asked what Jorl meant when he said he had not climbed the fence. Tunneling under or tearing through the fence had obviously not happened, so if it was not climbed, jumped over was the remaining logical conclusion. His identification as a Kobani wasn't possible by Crager, no one on Heavyside knew Koban existed, or of its new breed of soldiers. The Avenger came here directly from Poldark, so no word of what was happening there could have reached here.

Only spec ops troops in their Booster Suits had the potential strength to jump that fence. In a flash of insight, Jorl decided Crager suspected him of being trained like the spec ops troops were, and perhaps even had their nerve and eye implants. That would explain Crager's apparent assumption of Jorl's night vision and physical ability.

"Hold on, Top. You asked me where I'm from, but who do you think I really am? You know I must have jumped over the fence if I didn't climb over, and you just challenged me to a dangerous climb in the dark. I'm obviously not wearing a bulky Booster Suit like you have right now, but do you think I also have your IR eye implants?"

Facing towards him, the camp lights were reflected in Crager's eyes, giving him a sinister look. "Breaker, if that *is* your name, I don't know where you're from, or who sent you here. However, if you don't start climbing when I say *go*, I'll drag your helpless ass up there myself."

Jorl smiled in the darkness, aware that Crager could see his face in infrared. "My name really is Jorl Breaker, and I was sent down here to find a way to help you. Not help you personally, but your Special Operations Branch in general. Although I'm confident you are not about to believe me when I say that. Not yet anyway. I'll turn you into a believer."

He's certainly acting cool and confident right now, Crager thought. I wonder if that smug look will last all the way down, when I toss his ass off the top.

"Start moving, Breaker or I'll carry you, unconscious if necessary."

Jorl laughed. "You certainly couldn't force me to go, but out of simple curiosity, I plan to beat you to the top. I'd even give you a head start, but you would never trust me to follow after you."

"*Go!*" was Crager's only reply.

Jorl, turned towards the obstacle course in the center of the track, and in a smooth burst of his maximum speed, he left Crager briefly gape jawed, believing he was trying to escape. Crager reacted and started after him, his Booster Suit failing to close that widening initial gap and he fell farther behind.

Jorl reached the base of the tower, and in a graceful leap landed fully twenty feet up its side, and in a flurry of hands and feet, found the inch-wide gaps between the six-inch thick horizontal rough logs in the dark. He swarmed up as if on a shallow flight of steps, glancing back to see Crager just reaching the base when he was over half way to the top.

He made an easy one-handed flip up and over the top, to stand and look down at Crager, making his best speed trying to catch up. He saw the man glance up frequently, watching for some trick. It was too dark for Jorl to make out his features, but he assumed the man was pissed. When Crager was within ten feet, Jorl turned and walked to the center of the platform when he knew he was being watched. It permitted Crager to complete an unchallenged spring over the edge, landing in a crouched defensive posture.

His starlit expression up close was confirmed for Jorl. Definitely a pissed off look.

"You're fast you little shit, I'll grant you that. You must have on some sort of skin colored slim-line suit." Spec ops had never done a skin color match on the black carbon fiber Booster Suits. In combat, they always wore Chameleon Skin flexible armor, or more rarely, a hard suit that covered the Booster Suit as well as their uniform.

Crager assumed Breaker had a lighter version of a Booster Suit, which had been colored to blend with his skin. It would have to be a thin version, because the kid didn't display the thicker body build or the heavier looking muscles, which the standard suit gave a wearer. That implied to Crager that the display of speed was the primary advantage this lighter suit could provide. The standard suit had a thicker mix of overlaid fibers, some at various angles, to produce strength as well as speed. It could be configured to increase running speed at the expense of strength, and thus forming a slimmer looking body suit.

Crager studied the younger man's unconcerned expression. Up here, on a twelve-by- twelve platform a hundred twenty feet high, there was no room for Breaker to run, fast or not. He should have used that speed to try to get away. As analytical as Crager thought he was being, he'd forgotten the jump Breaker had made over the fence, which had been more than a result of mere speed.

"Top, the advantage I brought with me is under my skin. It isn't anything I can remove. I suspect you think you lured me here, to eliminate me as a threat of some kind to your organization, or to the plans for spec ops in the future. Actually, I've drawn *you* up here to prove to you that you have greatly underestimated what I represent. You will have no choice but to listen to and believe what I'm about to tell you. I am already what I believe you want spec ops troops to become."

"Lying spies? I think not. You can't call for help either. I have your transducer blocked, and those of your two friends."

"Ahh ha. You know I didn't come alone. Are Yil and Fred being confronted the same way right now?"

"I'll take care of them later, myself. I won't let you three, or who sent you get in the way of our trying to win this war."

"Top, we are part of a group that has the best chance to turn the war around, and we came back to Human Space to seek help from interested parties, and to offer them biotechnology they don't have. We had reason to believe there were interested parties on Heavyside. That's why we're here."

"I know why you're here, and you won't take anything you've learned with you."

Crager had been sizing Breaker up as they talked, considering the ramifications of his opponent wearing a limited Booster Suit. There was a trace of lighter sky to the east, so his own night vision advantage, if Breaker didn't have eye implants, would be gone soon. He didn't have time to draw out more information from him if the "accidental" neck-breaking fall was to happen unobserved. He lowered his hands and acted as if he were about to relax, but had not straightened from his partial crouch.

"So you came from outside Human Space…" he didn't complete the question because he launched himself at Breaker without warning. His intention was to use his strength to grapple with the younger man, and pin his arms and take him down as he wrapped his legs with his own powered lower limbs. He didn't want there to be any marks on the face or body from punches or kicks that would dispute his story of a neck-breaking fall from near the top of the platform. He would reach around Breaker's neck with one arm and cup his chin in a powerful grip. A hard quick jerk and his neck would snap. It would be almost painless.

He saw he had caught him completely by surprise, because he wasn't reacting to the form coming at him out of the darkness, only six feet away. He suddenly spread his arms to engage in a bear hug, prepared to accept a punch or kick to secure his victim, and pin his arms to his side. Once down, a leg scissors holding Breaker's legs from kicking would hold him briefly while he moved his right arm up and around the back of the neck to grab his chin. He'd be dead, an unfortunate training accident when found at the bottom of Everest.

It didn't go exactly as planned.

In motions so swift they left infrared streaks on his adapted IR night vision system, Breaker's left hand, backed by a rigid straight arm, simply appeared in front of Crager's face. The iron hard hand went over his mouth below his nose, thumb and forefingers on his cheekbones, snapping his head back. His momentum, driven by his exomuscle legs forced him upright, and he felt his reaching right hand grasped as if by a crushing metal gauntlet that yanked him violently around to his left, the stiff arm in his face acting as fulcrum for the pivot point.

Crager's right arm was yanked so violently that he continued to spin around as Breaker's right hand, having pulled back under his own left elbow, released the numbed hand it gripped. The spec ops sergeant was suddenly turned facing away from his opponent, and then his elbows were slammed down and pinned to his ribs by two hands that exerted and maintained a painful vice–like grip. He was lifted four or five inches off the platform, held by his elbows being pressed crushingly against his ribs.

Crager kicked backwards and tried to twist his torso to free his arms. His boot heels were just barely able to make grazing contact, without a solid blow possible. He snapped his head back to smash into his opponent's face, presuming he was close behind to hold him aloft so tightly. He encountered only air. Turning his head to the right, he could see Breaker's extended right arm held straight out, his right hand the only thing grasping Crager's right elbow. A quick left glance revealed the same. It was impossible! He couldn't lift him this way!

Breaker was supporting the much heavier man by two hands, both arms straight out from his leaned back stance, keeping Crager's feet inches above the platform. This was against Heavyside's gravity, and despite strenuous Booster Suit assisted kicking and shoulder hunching to make the task that much harder to hold him aloft that way.

"Top, it doesn't hurt much, but I'd like you to stop kicking your heels back at my knees and shins. If you don't quit I might just squeeze in and break some ribs to make you stop. I can probably hold you like this until the sun breaks the horizon in thirty-five minutes, making you look damn foolish to the rest of the camp, and ruining any chance we have at secrecy. I don't want to hurt you, and I definitely don't want to make you look ridiculous, which would be more damaging."

"I'll break every bone in your body, you sack of spy shit." Crager renewed his struggling, making Jorl suspect his promise of holding him suspended at arms-length for thirty-five minutes was a boast he might not be able to meet.

"Top, bare handed I doubt if you can break any of my carbon nano tube reinforced bones. I'm sure if I allowed it, you could bend some of my limbs and joints painfully. However, despite your expertise at hand-to-hand combat, and your Booster Suit and drugs, you can't beat an unarmed Krall warrior can you? Well, I *can* do that and I don't even have your level of training. With your training I could do it a lot easier."

"What the hell kind of advanced suit do you have?" He was wheezing from the increased pressure on his ribs, and his hands were feeling numb from the circulation cut off at his elbows. There had to be skin colored gloves to maintain that unbreakable steel grip.

"Top, you really don't listen to me or believe me when I speak the plain truth, do you? I *said* I don't have a suit, and what I do have is built into me. I was born with part of it, the rest was grown with genetic modifications later, and more will be added soon. My children, if I live to have any, will inherit every enhancement I have. Does that provide enough to make you quit fighting me? I'd rather not have to break anything to get you to stay still and listen."

"I know perfectly well you are saying what you think I want to hear. To get me to incriminate myself. There is no such capability to modify humans to do even what I can do as a Special Ops soldier, let alone what you are doing now. It's new technology. It's something my men need more than a damned snoop like you needs."

Jorl sighed, but latched onto his last words. "You want your men, and yourself I presume, to have the ability to meet a Krall on even terms, right?"

"You frigging well know that! It's what the spec ops program was designed to do."

"No, the program you have now is destined to *fail*, because you can't match Krall reaction speeds with any technology that depends on your own nerve speed as the trigger. Did you notice I stood still when you charged at me just now, until you were literally at arms-length? To me you moved in extreme slow motion the whole way. A Krall is at least five times faster than you are, but they also move slowly, at least to my perceptions."

"What are you," Crager snapped, "some left over Clone War monstrosity?"

Jorl paused, unprepared for that deliberate, if off the mark insult, coming from a person he had expected to be more receptive.

The extended moment of silence did what talking had not for Crager's thoughts. "What? Are you a clone? Someone learned how to make them again? We might win this war if we can make more of you."

Jorl shook his head. "I went from monstrosity to man-made savior in ten seconds flat. No wonder Captain Mirikami was so reluctant to come to Human Space to get help. You Normals flip flop too damned fast. If we can find a way to help you win the war, you'll turn on us when it's over. And no, I'm not a clone, I'm a one of a kind me."

"OK. I apologize for that stupid thoughtless remark. I give my word that I will not renew my attack on you without advanced warning. Please set me down. I want to talk."

Jorl set him on his feet and released him. As Crager started to turn around, shaking his arms to restore circulation, he reminded the man. "I didn't have any warning the first time you jumped me, so it doesn't matter to me if you announce it in advance. Same result, except I'll just break an arm or leg next time."

Crager nodded. "It matters to me. I just gave you my word."

"I'll accept your word. However, before I say any more, Top, I want to hear something from you. What are your hopes for improving humanity's chances in this war? What do you expect that people with my ability can bring to the table?"

Crager decided to stick his neck farther out. This mere boy had him beat anyway. "I believe we have to improve ourselves genetically. Spec ops requested research to be done in that area, and we were turned down strenuously. I can't see any sign of a suit on you. Is your speed and strength really built-in, and can be inherited?"

"Yes, although thus far the degree of inheritance has only been proven to extend to what I received from my parents, who received a handful of the clone mods of three hundred years ago as the starting point for my own ability, and the ability of many of my generation on our home world. Then we enhanced ourselves greatly from that point, with new modifications that have made us superior to the Krall. Everything we have done can be passed on to our descendants, and we are capable of intermarriage with other, standard humans, or Normals as we refer to you. I am, in effect, an example of a new race of our human species, just as your heritage, if I judge your features and skin color correctly, is a mix of Caucasoid and Negroid."

Crager shrugged. "I'm even more of a mix than that. However, most people today are. Where did you find bio-scientists that know how to do this?"

"Funny you should ask. I jumped the fence earlier tonight to get the data cube and some tissue samples to sneak into the possession of one of your scientists here. It explains much of what we have done and tells how we did it, and what's required. I doubt you have the technical knowledge to ask me the right questions, which is fine, because I don't know jack about genetics. I'm just a messenger, and a living example."

A chilling doubt crept into Crager's mind at the mention of Jorl's reason for leaving the camp. "Who met you out there? How did they get there?"

"It was a remote piloted Krall single ship. Controlled by our AI, launched from a captured clanship, which we renamed the Avenger. We stole the ship in a raid on K1. I told you we could beat the Krall in a fight, one-on-one. Our problem is that there are probably a hundred million warriors for each person like me. We need to sneak up on them, and not let them know who we are or where we are based, something spec ops knows how to do. We have some of our people receiving training right now, on Poldark. Do you know Colonel Trakenburg? He's in charge of a small training camp that resembles this one."

"Frank Trakenburg?"

"I don't know his first name. None of us on the Avenger met him since we never landed on Poldark. That was a different captured clanship, which landed there. He was less than cooperative at the start. About as friendly as you have been tonight, frankly."

"He's a very by-the-book stiff necked officer. I was one of his trainers years ago, before he rose in the ranks. You managed to win *him* over?"

"When we left orbit, he was still organizing the training for more of our people, with the cooperation of General Nabarone."

"You claim to have friends in high places. I'll have to confirm this, you understand."

"Fine. If you can get anyone to admit it to you. They are keeping this as secret there as you are your own plans here. The Hub government isn't going to accept what we have to offer. Not until the war is much closer to being lost. Poldark will go down within two years, and then one or two other worlds will be next in line. We can't wait too long to go after the Krall where they live, and strike where their war material is made."

"How can you know about any plans we had here?" Suspicion again.

He avoided a direct answer again, not willing to reveal Fred's Mind Tap ability. "Dr. Lisa Markel is one of your scientists. She wants to do the work on genetics. We were going to try to leave our data in her private quarters, anonymously. Now I can just pass it to you and let you do that for us. We'll be leaving Heavyside soon. The three of us were never planning to finish your training program here. It would take far too long at the slow pace you set. We can be ready for missions in a month or less, if we meet up with those of us that have finished training on Poldark."

"You boys might be good, but you don't know enough to take on actual missions."

"Top, I don't know enough right now, that's true. However, aside from an accelerated learning ability, we also have a learning transfer method that is genetically unique to us. We can learn every combat related thing you know in a month or less, *if* you decided to share it with us. We can't force you to do that, and would not if we could. Besides, we don't have time to do that now. However, I hope we can meet again in the future."

"Breaker, you keep telling me you have a reaction speed faster than a Krall. I felt your strength, and I saw you run and climb up here faster than I could do the same, but I didn't really see your reaction speed. Although I never saw your hand coming. You split the inside of my upper lip."

"Too bad. I think you were trying to split more than my lip. I guess you want a demonstration?"

"Nothing dramatic or painful, but yes."

Jorl grinned. "There's a game we play with kids below age sixteen. They don't receive the gene enhancement that provides the linkage to a high-speed nervous system when they're any younger than that. Here's how it goes. I'm going to reach up and touch a single finger to the tip of your nose, with either or both hands, starting with my hands hanging by my side. You will already have your hands up by your face, ready to smack my hands away before I can touch your nose. If you so much as touch my hand or fingers in the process, you win. Ready?"

Crager looked skeptical, but raised his hands in a defensive position near his face. He'd already activated his chemical boosters when he was climbing up the tower. He was as fast as his suit and embedded platinum nerve overlays could make him.

"Go." Crager told him

His fruitless swiping at the blurred hands completely missed their targets. Jorl had tapped the end of Crager's nose not once, but twice, using one hand at a time, both before he could block either one.

"Crap!"

"Yes, I believe I will," Jorl agreed. "It has been a long night and hours since I ate. We have a high metabolism, and I'm sure you noticed how warm I look in infrared. It's close to sunrise, and we should probably get down. I'll have to ask Yil or Fred in person where they stashed the data cube and tissue sample. You told me you have our transducer frequencies jammed. They picked up the data cube from my bunk after I jumped back over the fence and hit the showers."

It was a subtle difference, but Jorl had slipped into an attitude of dealing with Crager as an equal, not as his Top Sergeant and a superior he needed to please. He was ready to get back to the Avenger and go home.

"I'll meet you at my barracks, with Fred and Yil and the data cube. I'm sure you could have some men meet us with weapons, but not only would that turn ugly for them, but your secret plans to improve spec ops capability will die as well." With that, he stepped backwards off the edge of the platform, to skim down the steep rough sloped sides at a breakneck pace, his boot toes tapping rapidly and loudly on the logs to control and slightly slow his drop. Near where the base flared out slightly, he kicked off and performed a neat double back flip and a twist to land on his feet at a dead run. He had been waiting weeks to show off.

Crager briefly was tempted to drop down the same way, but then told himself that his arms still tingled too much from the cut off circulation, and chose to climb down normally. This conveniently ignored the fact that Jorl had not used his hands and arms for his descent.

Jorl burst into Fred's barracks, but he wasn't in his bunk. He woke several other men in his rush through the doors. Most of them had been kept up late last night and the rumor that Jorl was somehow the cause for the precious loss of sleep on the first free weekend didn't make him exactly popular. He headed for Yil's barracks, one building farther away.

Midway between buildings, he heard his name called. It was both of his friends.

In a low voice Fred asked, "Jorl, what did the First Sergeant do?"

"Yea," Yil prompted. "We heard he was mad enough to kill you."

"You joke, but I think you're closer to the truth than you know. I believe Top is part of a small local conspiracy to develop genetic modifications for spec ops, to fight the Krall more effectively. Does that story ring any bells?" He laughed.

"Damn. Really? We have the cube and tissue samples with us. If they searched all the barracks, we knew we couldn't let them find them. We were discussing going over the fence by the housing area, and breaking into Dr. Markel's unit. Did you just walk away from Crager? It sounded like you had been consigned to exercise purgatory and doing penance. Missing breakfast would be the worst part of that." Yil chuckled.

"Crager thought we were spies, sent to find out about their beginning plans for genetics research. He was prepared to make certain no one lived to tell the tale. He sent me up Everest in the dark, and tried to jump me. I assume he intended that I have a fatal accident in the dark. I stopped him."

Fred sounded horrified. "Jorl! You didn't kill him did you?"

"Ease down on the panic. No, he was climbing down Everest the last I saw him, on my way to find you two. I sorta filled him in on our mission, and he is supposed to meet me at my barracks building in a few minutes. Besides, *Mister Outraged*, after he tossed me off Everest, he had accident plans for you two as well, because he knows we're together. Hold out your hand Fred, I can pass this on faster than the time we've already wasted talking."

They touched hands, and Jorl briefed them in less than a minute on everything that had happened after he and Crager headed for the obstacle course.

"What if he does show up with a gun or other armed men?" Yil wasn't particularly trusting.

"If the three of us don't feel we can take them, we could let them hold us for a short time. However, Fred can confirm Crager's intentions with a question and a touch. I don't want to kill anyone that can be an ally, but if it's us or them, they lose."

Fred agreed. "Let's go to your barracks. It's getting light in the east anyway. We'll be able to see better shortly. I can't wait to get the next mods. Dark sucks."

Crager was just coming out of the door, alone, when they arrived. He spotted them quickly, in the shadows between buildings. He waved a hand, and came towards them.

"Gentle Men…" He started. "Sorry, I don't think of you as candidates now, and Breaker here told me you all would be leaving once you hand over the data you came to give us. I'm not comfortable with you calling me Bill, so Top will still do, and in case we are overheard. As it is, you three will be passed off as voluntary training withdrawals to the other candidates."

Jorl nodded. "That's fine with us, Top. Let me formally introduce my friends."

He gave Yil's full name, perfectly aware that Crager had all their slender data files at his disposal. He shook hands with Yil.

As Fred was introduced and while they shook hands, Jorl asked, "What will you do after we give you the data, Top?"

"I'd actually like you to give it directly to Dr. Markel, and I've asked her and Colonel Dearborn to meet us in the company HQ. I honestly don't believe they will want to believe me without meeting you. We'll have more privacy there, and it's a timely moment to have you sign the electronic withdrawal forms. After tonight's activities, it's a good pretext to have Breaker here leave, and claim you other two were of like minds. I'll stick to the story you went out to meet a girlfriend, and violated the rules."

"Good enough for us I think. Right, Fred?" Jorl and Yil both looked to their friend.

"Yes. That will be perfectly suitable, Top." Fred agreed, his nod assuring his two partners that the surreptitious Mind Tap verified all was fine. "We'll be happy to meet the other two people, and perhaps fill you in on some historical details of how our people were able to do what they have done. The name and location of our world will be kept secret. If the Krall knew where we came from, we couldn't defend the planet. Much of our background is on the data cube. The most crucial genetic advances were not achieved overnight we can assure you, but your program can benefit from our experiences, and you won't have to wait a generation to get results. Captain Renaldo of the Avenger may be available to talk to you if you wish."

Crager now assumed that Fred Saber was the one actually in charge, based on the two other young men apparently deferring to him. Jorl had actually been granted overall responsibility for the mission, partly for his age (nine months older than Fred and six months for Yil), and because of his mastery of athletic ability and fighting skills.

The matter of which of them was considered in charge wasn't actually a concern for any of the young Kobani in general. They all had been exposed to some military structure, but not indoctrinated by years of service. Because of the way they mentally shared information by Taps, any of them quickly had the same information that others knew, and could make informed decisions. Of course, Crager was unaware that Fred spoke up because he was providing confirmation of the sergeant's genuine intentions, via the Mind Tap he'd just used to sense the unguarded thoughts. Unethical, but then Crager had recently been prepared to kill all three of them, to protect his own secrets.

"Mr. Saber, I had not thought of that possibility. Let me remove the block on your transducers." He Linked to the camp AI and had the restriction removed.

"Dr. Markel was awakened, but not provided any details. She was getting dressed, and she'll be at the HQ building shortly. Colonel Dearborn was already up because of the fence incident, and should be there by now. If you'll follow me we can have breakfast sent over and some coffee made."

Jorl responded eagerly, on behalf of his stomach. "Breakfast sounds great, Top, but you don't need to make coffee for any of us. Our home world isn't in Human Space and none of our generation ever had coffee prior to this mission. Most of the older generation likes it, and are delighted to have a supply again. However, excuse me for expressing our generation's commonly held opinion. We think it tastes something like bitter brown piss."

****

Noreen was satisfied things had worked out better than expected, even though her plan had gone awry. "Colonel Dearborn, I have recently received word that we have had a lot of interesting things happening back in our home system, and we want to return there as soon as practical. I'd like to collect my three young men. Sending them to Andropov won't help. I can't just set our captured clanship down where everyone can see it and panic, and we don't want to land near your training camps. Can you drive them to a point midway to the spaceport, where I can set down stealthed to meet them?"

"Captain, I will send First Sergeant Crager with them to do that. However, I'm certain I'll receive some questions as to why my Top sergeant is turning bus driver for three withdrawn candidates. We may just hide them in the back of a staff car. Would you have time to let him walk through the ship for a short tour? Frankly, I'd like to go along, but I can't come up with a pretext that will explain both of our being gone. We'd each like to see inside an operational clanship."

"I can do that, Colonel. I'm confident one of our ships will return to give you another opportunity. It might be a fast tour, Sergeant, if we see any traffic coming our way. Even stealthed, we are not eyeball invisible, and there's a big burn spot when we leave."

"I understand. Thanks." Crager answered. "I'll be starting the drive in the next thirty minutes. Do you need one of your men to call you?"

"No need. Our sensors can see a military marked passenger vehicle parked next to the HQ building, if that's the one you plan to use. We'll see you drive off."

"Pretty good sensors you have there."

"Yes. The Krall have some nice technology. Your left front tire is low, and the car is dusty." She laughed.

Dr. Markel had to offer her thanks again. For the last hour, she had been skimming the data and reading the synopsis of what the data cube contained. "Captain Renaldo, this information cuts literally a decade of research from what we needed to learn, and takes us much farther than we would have managed on our own. Thank you. I hope we can contact you for more help as we go."

"We intend to stay in contact with you. It's dangerous to have all of our genetic resources for humanity on one planet, our own. Very shortly, the Krall are going to know that we are attacking their supply lines outside of Human Space, and we hope to move very fast.

"Our information is that they have grown so confident about their security over thousands of years of dominance, that their most critical manufacturing centers are concentrated on relatively few worlds. Major items like clanships, single ships, the Eight Balls, Dragons, the heavy battlefield armored transports, artillery defense systems, and the largest heavy ships they use to move their slaves and factories are made on only one or two worlds each.

"There are many worlds where they make trucks, personal armor, plasma rifles and cannons, and other small-scale war production items. They can even make those on Poldark, and do. However, moving warriors to fight takes clanships, and we can reduce those over time as they waste them.

"If we knock many of those production centers out quickly, we think they will start to feel the pinch on combat worlds like Poldark, and have to drain supplies from K1 and other worlds they control. They have a great deal of war material already at their disposal, but they use it up as if there was an endless supply. We want to cut that supply."

Dearborn had an obvious question, wondering if Noreen and her people had considered the answer. "If the Krall start to run low on materials to fight a slow protracted war on human worlds, what do you think they will do?"

"We don't think for a moment they will call a truce or pull back. If they reduce raids and invasions on new worlds, it will only be because they can't get to the point of attack, because they have a fewer number of clanships. We expect they will stop holding back in restricted wars like the one they are running on Poldark, and do what they have always had the means to do. Crush their opponents quickly, and move to another world and repeat.

"They surely must have other more potent world wrecking weapons you have not seen, equivalent to the power of the Eight Balls. Railguns may be able to stop those collapsed matter weapons, and we learned they don't have many of those because they are made very slowly, by a slave race on one single planet. We expect those and new weapons to come out of storage. We'll have to find and destroy each as they appear, or find some counter measure. We may lose planets, but that was going to happen to all of them anyway, if we let the Krall do what they want."

"OK. I wasn't sure if you understood that your raids, if successful, would not go without consequences for other human worlds. The Krall will try to exterminate every human settled world if they sense they are losing. A scorched Earth policy, in the most literal sense."

She answered back sharply. "What were you people hoping to do with a beefed-up spec ops program, Colonel? Obviously much the same as what we are going to try to do. Fighting the Krall face-to-face on planets with troops that are their match, or even superior to their warriors, isn't going to win for us in the long term. We take eighteen to twenty years to produce a child that becomes a soldier. Those egg-laying bastards can produce cannon fodder killers at a hundred times our reproductive rate. If we can take away their ability to travel and spread, isolate them on the planets where they are now, we have a chance." She sounded ready to argue more.

"Captain, I'm not disputing your opinion or understanding. What you said isn't significantly different from what I've heard come out of the Army and Navy think tanks. I simply wondered if you expected it to be as simple as knocking out the Krall factories. I see you *have* thought past that point. We need more miracles, and I see your people's existence as one of those. The ability to modify people genetically to become like you is another one.

"We have an enormous population of one trillion, and if even a fraction of one percent of our population opted to receive your genes, we could have billions capable of fighting the Krall. Somehow, we have to get our own side to move out of the way of our own survival."

"From the opposition I saw on our own world to what we were doing genetically, I fear billions on Rim Worlds and New Colonies will die before the massive Hub world populations feel frightened enough to accept us. However, we may not have to rely only on ourselves to fight this battle.

"In the last month we encountered two new alien species, Colonel, one is definitely an ally, and we believe the other may become one. They are two of the Krall slave races, and they know things we need to learn. We have made first contact with the Prada and the Torki, as they call themselves. They have sparse populations, and control no worlds, so we don't know where cooperation could lead. They might hold the keys to open doors to some of the miracles we still need."

Dr. Markel was amazed. "Two intelligent species? My God! Are there others?"

"There were." Noreen acknowledged sadly. "The Krall eliminated another thirteen star traveling species. A third slave species is a meat animal for the Krall. We are the seventeenth or eighteenth civilization unfortunate enough to meet them. This all has happened along a volume of perhaps six or seven thousand light-years length of a cylindrical section of the Orion spur and Sagittarius arm, spinward of where we are located. Our human explored region is relatively small. We assume there are many other intelligent peoples in the galaxy. With a race like the Krall around, I'm not surprised those nearby keep quiet."

Markel sounded eager to meet aliens. "Will you be bringing any of these races here to meet with the Planetary Union Government?"

"Most of my people are death penalty worthy genetic freaks to your government, as you will be if you use the data we gave you. I'm personally not going to introduce them to the aliens. Besides, we don't want the Hub government to know where our world is located, and the aliens might spill the beans. They don't have planetary governments of their own you understand. They have been slaves for thousands of years. Even if I trusted the PU to leave us alone, if the news leaked of where we are from, a fleet of clanships will soon appear on our doorstep. There are millions of stars and worlds out there, and we like our anonymity for now."

The three former candidates had been listening quietly after the introductions were made and the questions and answers had started. Now Jorl was impatient to start his journey back to Koban. He knew he'd be receiving the next round of mods, become a TG1 at least, and possibly a TG2 if all the mods were ready. Mind Tap the lessons learned on Poldark, and then prepare for the first real combat mission.

"Captain, I'll be happy to guide the First Sergeant around the ship, and I believe we are all ready to get started." That was a bit pushy, but he'd been pushed around a lot the last few weeks. He wanted to get home.

****

Standing at the bottom of the ramp, Crager was impressed with what he'd seen inside the Avenger on his thirty-minute whirlwind tour. He made sure to record it all for showing to Dearborn and the civilians, in the soon to solidify group of earnest conspirators, preparing the first steps in building their own genetic supermen. They had not been left with all of the Kobani gene secrets, but enough to prepare for future steps, when they were offered.

He'd been swarmed by other youngsters, amazingly strong and graceful in their movements, like the three he had driven back to the ship. It was hard to get in his own questions between their eager ones, until their truly gorgeous, raven haired Captain Renaldo ordered them to calm down, and let him ask his own questions.

Now he was waving at Jorl, Fred, and Yil, accepting the use of their first names now (he remained Top to them). All he could think of for the moment was how he could finagle a trip to go with them to raid a Krall planet when they sent the next ship back. They promised to deliver some equipment and supplies that their camp scientists didn't presently have. He was completely unaware of the fact that, even at his age, he could actually receive the gene mods these kids sported. Had he known of that possibility, it's likely the staff car might have been found abandoned a mile from the rough road, its driver off on an adventure.

He trotted away from the ship as its ramp retracted and its portal hatch slammed down in a flash. His pleasure at running in a Booster Suit was now forever spoiled, knowing how slow he appeared to be to those young men that had watched him turn away. He ached to have what they had.

Chapter 14: The Good Old Days

The Mark of Koban did a one day diversionary Jump to an intermediate uninhabited star system, to throw off any follower. Ethan was on the Bridge for the White Out, occupying one of the extra four acceleration couches they had permanently placed between the four couches in front of the actual control positions.

Using the Normal Space drive, they were still at a high rate of acceleration. Mirikami was allowing Jakob to build up a matching velocity that the Krall navigation system said would place them in a thousand mile orbit, moving along with Koban at their next White Out.

Ethan had been focused on intercepting any messages left in Tachyon Space by either of the other two ships. He appeared to be having trouble sorting something out, suggesting there *had* been a message. Carson was below, tasked with sending a message of their own at the time of transition between Normal Space and Tachyon Space.

"Uncle Tet. I picked up two message strings meant for us and for the other ships, but I haven't sorted them out completely. One was from the Beagle of course, the other from Avenger. I think part of the problem is that the Avenger's signal is a day or two fresher, and it was from Alyson, who really hoped to reach Carson. However, Carson was busy sending our message. We need to come up with a better system than blanket broadcasts for just anyone that's listening."

Mirikami, not having experienced the long-range mental communication process had to take Ethan's word for the problem. "Do we need to do another quick Jump in and out to catch the full message streams?"

"It won't work, Sir. When the messages are received, they are gone. The other ships were not waiting for us to respond live. We have to try to piece each data string together, and the other TG1's aboard will have gathered parts that I may have missed. We'll do a group ring Tap and share what we each sensed, then sort out who said what to us." However, he laughed at one thing of which he was certain.

"You won't believe this. Aunt Maggi has ripper frill ability! There is no possibility I could have mistaken her mental touch, and that is part of what distracted me."

"What?" Dillon displayed a flip-flop of emotions. "Aldry and Rafe actually figured out how to use the new nanites and med labs for that? That's wonderful. Damn! Maggi has the frill gene mod from the rippers." He promptly slipped back to a state of shock as the implication struck home.

"Oh no! She's able to Mind Tap now! Damn, that's going to be scary for me until I get the same mod. She'll know what I'm thinking. I don't block my thoughts very well yet."

"I think it's more than that, Uncle Dillon." Ethan was grinning. "I saw a mental image of her making a jump from some sort of high aerial rope bridge, which could only have been performed safely with the same muscle mods and coordination I have. She might have the full set of TG1 mods."

Thad had a hilarious thought. "You'd better get a stronger athletic cup than the plastic one you have now, or learn to hold your tongue. One wise crack from you and she might accidentally knock your balls up by your Adam's apple." Tiny Maggi often struck back after a smart aleck remark from Dillon, using a playful and very light low blow. It would be less light if it were a knuckle to his hard head.

Dillon was unusually tall and Maggi was unusually short. His crotch was a perfect and effective target area for her. He no longer behaved like one of society's male breeding studs, which the handsome science geek had previously imitated, before he met Noreen. However, Maggi had a long memory of his many randy years as a successful Ladies man. Most of his former dress suits had a palm-sized, floridly colored male passion patch on the "package," as advertising. Due to the war, the second-class citizen role for males had changed dramatically. Maggi's favorite bull's eye had not.

"You had best just hide when we land. You can't stop yourself from mouthing off to her," added Sarge, his grin matched by the others.

Mirikami, as was often the case, shifted the men's irreverent interplay back to practical matters. "Ethan, go down and ring-up with the other TG1's to compare messages. Then let us know the overall gist of the messages from each ship. We'll be Jumping in another couple of minutes. We have nearly five days to sort out what they each sent to us and to each other."

The desired Normal Space direction and velocity established, parallel to Koban's expected orbit at White Out, they winked out of Normal Space again, for five days this time.

Shortly after the group Ring Tap was completed, Ethan and Carson, as the two senior TG1's (plus being sons of four parents in leadership positions), reported excitedly to Mirikami. The captain then called a meeting, with selected participants coming to the conference room, and Jakob would broadcast to the remainder of the ship. Everyone would be interested in this.

All ten spec ops volunteers were invited to the conference room. They would be more stunned, and presumably pleased, at what they were about to learn than anyone aboard. The TGs would all discover how things at home were about to change in ways they never expected with their parents.

Mirikami started with the update from Heavyside. "Gentle Men, Ladies, we received updates from both of our other ships. The Avenger, at Heavyside, has confirmed what Colonel Trakenburg suspected and hoped was happening there. A cabal of people at the main camp, a number of scientists, base commander, and the top NCO were planning to venture into the realm of genetic engineering. They were essentially attempting to start a genetics program, much as we did twenty-two years ago on Koban, right under the noses of the Krall. On Heavyside, they need to fear the PU authorities. They still face imprisonment or death if caught." He paused to look at their ten new volunteers.

"Colonel, Captain, and you other eight men just heard me use the name of our home world, Koban. It's a Krall word that if they heard it used often enough might lead them to us. Be aware that the Krall associate it with a place they someday want to call their own home, and they don't want it contaminated by humans. I'll let some others fill you in on our history there. The ship you are in is actually named The Mark of Koban, and not simply the Mark.

"The ship was named for the tattoo marking I received from a Krall sub-leader, just before they departed Koban, expecting us all to die shortly after that. He thought that I was a *worthy enemy*, and hoped to find other humans to make their war worthwhile. My tattoo was made solid black at that time, as all of us now wear.

"For any of you to operate even simple doors on this ship, you need these tattoos as well. They actually contain some sort of quantum device or mechanism, which is a key to your using every piece of complex Krall equipment we've encountered thus far. Colonel Trakenburg and Captain Longstreet already have them. It doesn't have to be placed at the base of your throat, although mine was placed there by the enemy, where they wear their own markings.

"I *want* to display mine to the enemy someday, as we defeat them." He'd opened his tunic top to reveal the black oval. "You can place them on your butts if you wish. However, I wouldn't care to drop trousers and turn my back to show them." He got the chuckles he expected.

I doubt you will be the only spec ops forces to join us either. "Captain Renaldo sent us a message saying they had made contact with the people pushing for genetic enhancements at SOB-1 on Heavyside. She provided them with a data cube of our genetic upgrades, and some tissue samples to prove they work, and to help them get a head start on their own program. It will be conducted in secrecy from the PU government and out of the public eye, of course."

He addressed a puzzled look he saw on Trakenburg's face. "Captain Renaldo is Noreen Renaldo, Dillon Martin's wife, and Carson's mother. She kept her last name, per the usual social custom, and Dillon, breaking with that custom, kept his own last name when they married. Carson has the option I guess of using either last name, or both. It hasn't been an issue on Koban, but we are breaking with so many three hundred year old customs it's hard to keep track." He grinned.

"Anyway, the Avenger has departed Heavyside, and like ourselves, is on her way home. We should arrive within a day of each other, if not on the same day. Like I did, she chose a departure day at the start of a long range message window." He paused while there were some cheers from his crew, loudest from Dillon and Carson. Then he continued.

"The cooperation with another section of spec ops is gratifying to me, and eases one of my great worries for the future of our species. Not all of our genetic enhancement eggs are in just the Koban basket now. From Heavyside, humanity can take another independent step towards meeting the Krall head on, thus reducing the overall odds against success if Koban went down." He bore a serious expression.

"However, we mere handful from Koban will have the greatest burden for years, in facing the Krall threat."

Then in another turnaround, his face beamed with a broad smile. "That burden has just been eased a bit by the med labs and nanite technology we sent home with Captain Greeves." Now he looked at the eight new spec ops men, who didn't know who he meant.

"She's Thad Greeves wife, and she *really* broke with the fem tradition and took *his* last name. Ethan over there is their son. He doesn't care what you call him for a last name so long as it doesn't make him late for a meal."

The last was a reference to the large plate of breakfast food he'd brought with him to the conference room. The location for the TG1's Mind Tap Ring had been in the mess hall. Ethan's face turned red, which drew a laugh.

Mirikami was still primarily addressing the eight newest spec ops members of the group. They were volunteers, and taken aboard with little advanced information furnished. It was time to share more with them.

"Our TG1's have a limited form of a mind reading ability, which requires physical contact, strongest with hand-to-hand contact. I know that Colonel Trakenburg and Captain Longstreet briefed you men about that capability just after we lifted off, which means you have had less than two hours to think about this. There's actually a bit more to it than that, which even they didn't know about.

"That extra bit explains how we *know* what our two other ships have been doing, even though we are hundreds of light-years apart. A surprising long-range mental connection can exist as well, but *only* between two TG1's, under very limited conditions, and it is very brief."

He saw the flash of distrust return instantly to Trakenburg's eyes, and he continued quickly to allay that feeling. "We discovered, quite by accident on our journey to Human Space a couple of months ago, that TG1's can somehow link briefly with the minds of other TG1's that they know, for a moment as we enter or leave Tachyon Space. The messages seem to exist in that alternate universe for as long as five days. We set up a contact schedule, which was the message window that I mentioned for our day of departure. If messages are not received in that time span, they become garbled and lost. The exciting aspect is that separation distance in Normal Space does not appear to matter. Only that the target of the message, the other TG1 you intend to reach, is known to the sender's mind. Our TG1's were jointly *listening* and *sending* as we entered and exited Tachyon Space today.

"We frankly don't know how it works, but we assume that their minds have some sort of modulating effect on the lowest energy, nearly infinite velocity tachyons that harmlessly pour through us and the ship as we enter and exit the Jump Hole. Their thoughts seem to be impressed into that immense flow of a vast sea of low energy tachyons that we know is there.

Distance is of course irrelevant to an infinite velocity tachyon. If the mind patterns of the parties are familiar to each other, communication is possible. Data is also transmitted and received very fast, because the entry into a Jump Hole is quick, and so is a White Out.

"Believe it or not, that is how we obtained the information I'm briefing you on today. Stuck down in the gravity well on Poldark, we were out of that communications loop for two months. Happily, we have caught up on the news.

"Let me tell you the part of that communication that will ease your suspicions concerning this mind reading ability, and all of the other capabilities of the TGs and TG1's." He paused, employing his often-criticized *waiting for the other shoe to drop* method of ensuring total attention.

"Thanks to the nanites and new med labs we sent home to Koban, our genetic modifications, *all of them,* can now be given to *any* human who chooses to accept them. That means SGs can now catch up with our kids, and so can you men."

Longstreet spoke first, hardly able to hold back his enthusiasm. "You mean more than just the muscle mods from the clone genes I was expecting, but the superconductor nerve mods, carbon fiber muscles, and nano tube reinforced bones?"

On a rising tone of voice, he added, "Then, as a bonus gift, we get to read minds as well? Damn, do I at least get a *donut* while I have to *wait* for all this crap?" That cracked up the entire room.

Laughing along with them, Dillon added some more icing to the cake. "Joe, there are three gene mods that the TG1s with us don't even have yet. We learned that they *have* been applied at home to our people there, to SG's like us included. They not only worked but they were implemented in much less time than our previous mods. They have transitioned SGs into TG1's in a few weeks, and TG1's into what are being called TG2's in two weeks.

To do so many mods, starting from scratch with you men, we may need to do these in several stages, but we have now mastered all of the various processes." He listed the three new mods that had been waiting in the wings.

"There is a set of genes to furnish us with ultrasonic hearing, possibly not as keen as that of the Krall, but we at least won't need ears that pop out of our head to hear those frequencies.

"We will be able to smell the world almost the way the tiger-like rippers do, and we will have the night vision of those same predators. They partly use more of the ambient low light than we do, and their range reaches well into the infrared. It also includes the fringes of ultra violet frequencies.

"Understand this truth, my normal human friends. If you choose to become a Kobani, it means you will become one real dangerous badass in combat." He didn't think a sales pitch was needed, but there it was anyway.

"Excuse me, Dillon. I think we ten may have a problem." It was Trakenburg. Doubts and sour notes were often ready at hand for him. He felt relief that he and his men were being included, but the vision and nerve mods worried him. "We have eye implants for IR vision, and a retinal data display that is interfaced with our onboard AI. We have platinum alloy overlays for nerve system control of our Booster Suits. I think they might get in the way of some of your gene mods."

"You may have a valid point about the vision modification." Dillon nodded. "We'll have to study those before we mess with something you have that works. It does what we can't duplicate biologically, with your internal data projection system.

"However, I'm on the design team for the mods, and the parallel nervous system of organic superconductors won't care about those extra wires under your skin, any more than yours or our existing original nerves care. You automatically learn to use the faster responding superconductor set.

"Besides, I don't think you will need the wire overlays to control those Booster Suits once you can see how much more you can do without wearing the suits. The suits can't make you move as fast as the superconductor nerves and new muscles will, and I'll bet you'll find that even if the suits add extra strength, they will nevertheless slow your reaction speed down. We will have to see how that works out as we go. You may find ways to use both."

The colonel was satisfied. "Fair enough. I also want my men to know that their acceptance of any of these gene mods is entirely their own decision."

Mirikami stepped in again, to reassure them. "Please understand. We have thousands of people on Koban that have opted not to receive *any* of these mods. Others that wanted children only accepted the minimum number of clone mods that enabled that to happen in our gravity. We respected their wishes, and we will respect yours. They have paid personally for that choice by suffering under the gravity of Koban. Our 1.52 g's is seven percent higher than what you experienced for your Heavyside training. You may already have noticed that we have increased gravity internally to 1.25 Earth normal. By tonight, it will be at what we consider normal at home. We need to readapt from Poldark's low gravity.

"Incidentally, the talk about the gene mod improvements led me off track. Mentioning the people that refused our genetic mods helped me recall other news."

No dramatic pause this time. "There is a second habitable planet in the Koban system, which Captain Greeves started exploring when she returned, just before we started training with you men on Poldark. She named it Haven.

"It has gravity slightly less than Earth's. Its name is appropriate, because it is where we will send some of our people to live. Those without gene mods that want out of Koban's gravity well. It's where the three alien races that the Krall enslaved will live, if we are able to rescue any of them. The biggest news to report is that there were representatives of two alien species living there already, in small numbers."

Sarge, who had been quiet, spoke up immediately. "I'd love to meet an alien that isn't out to kill me. It could be an interesting conversation if someone can translate."

"Sarge, once you have the ripper frilling mods, you can sit down with them and ask your own questions, mind-to-mind. Maggi implies the Torki in particular are easy to work with, even if they are giant purple crabs with yellow legs."

Mirikami enjoyed the startled looks on the ten spec ops men, as they wondered what kind of bizarre new life they had agreed to accept. Their reaction to these aliens might be a chance to see how the rest of humanity would react, once there were aliens to meet that didn't want to kill you, or wouldn't try to eat your nasty flavored butt if they needed food, and then complain as they chewed.

"For my part," Mirikami continued, "Using our original genetic procedures, I was prepared to try the risky muscle and bone mods to increase my ability to handle the acceleration a Krall ship like this one can dish out. That was before we had the new nanites. Our previous roadblock to risk free full genetic upgrades has been removed. I can't speak for anyone else, but I damn well intend to be a TG2 when I take the Mark of Koban out after those Krall bastards."

"Can we newbies get all of the mods in time for that mission?" Longstreet asked. "I damn well want to go. I joined you for the opportunity to fight them on their turf, even though I expected to be a physical liability. I was going along as an advisor in exchange for what I could teach you. This is more than I expected, but exactly what I wanted."

His sentiments were echoed by Trakenburg and the other eight troopers. Not that Mirikami and his team were surprised by their attitude. The interview Mind Taps had revealed that all of these men sincerely wanted TG ability, but had come anyway despite thinking it could not be achieved, being limited to the less effective clone mods.

"I'll have some of our TG1's provide each one of you with one-on-one briefings of what the Mind Tap ability is like to use, and they will spend hours with you in the next five days passing along the history and specifics about Koban. I want you prepared to meet our rippers, how they look, think, and act. They are our most important partners on Koban, and if you hadn't figured it out yet, some of our most vital genetic enhancements were derived from them. Thanks to rippers, you will be faster, stronger and more deadly than you ever imagined. Oh…, and you'll be able to Mind Tap." Their eyes reflected their eagerness to get started.

"Another cooperative species, not as intelligent as the rippers but smarter than any animals you have encountered anywhere else, are the wolfbats, a large flying mammal and a predator. Their genetic contribution is providing us with the means to hear into the ultrasonic range. Our TG's carbon nano tube reinforced bones come courtesy of a dinosaur-like raptor, which can run at speeds and leap heights you wouldn't believe in that gravity.

"Carson and Ethan told me a short time ago that an unexpected offshoot of the wolfbat modification is still being investigated. It seems the hearing mod gradually changes how efficiently people organize and save information in an organic superconducting neural network. It appears to be a result of how efficiently the wolfbats store and retrieve mental pictures. It was evolved to process echolocation data, and to organize the massive amount of information they receive.

"We can't process echolocation sounds, which we can't make anyway, but the superior data organization realized in the much larger human brain leads to an improvement in our memory storage and learning, with faster recall."

Thad told them, "Not only will you love Koban's beauty, but being a full Kobani means you can go outside and enjoy its beauty with far less risk. Don't get me wrong, it's still a dangerous place even after you have these mods. Don't face off against a white raptor unarmed, or try to pet a rhinolo.

"However, it's probably no more dangerous for a TG on Koban than it was for the weak, naked apes we once were in the forests and on the plains of ancient Africa. After you've lived on Koban, I think you're going to find there aren't many dangerous species you can't get away from, or even beat one-on-one when you meet them. It will make being friendly and trusting safer."

Mirikami wrapped up the briefing. "We have some planning to do, Krall targets to consider, and we need to set a time table for conducting our first raid to hurt the enemy. I hope the aliens on Haven will be able to advise us on where we should go first. Let's split up into groups and get started."

****

Five days later, the Mark of Koban performed a White Out a thousand miles above the equator of its namesake. The blue seas a shimmering contrast with the lush teal foliage, the occasional red-browns of deserts and dunes, with the white capped gray mountains and volcanic ranges. The additional view screens they'd had installed around the ship furnished the entire complement with the images. It was Home for most, and a new home for ten.

"Sir, the Avenger and the Beagle are both in close polar orbits." Jakob informed Mirikami.

"Call them and Link them on viewer's number one for Beagle and number two for Avenger." He would use the ship's unique skin coating to have a joint meeting between all three ships, assuming Noreen and Marlyn were aboard. They might have taken a shuttle down.

Mirikami didn't see the Falcon, which Chief Haveram was bringing home with the last of the consumer goods and clothing they had bought for the fashion starved residents. Homespun clothing got old for many residents, who craved stylish, colorful, and durable attire. Hundreds of bolts of Smart Fabric, and a programmable Tailor Made brand machine had thousands of preloaded patterns of past and current fashions. Any would-be designers had the ability to innovate their own local styles.

Dillon, Thad, and both of their sons clustered near the screens as they lit up. Looking as if they were in an adjacent room, Marlyn and Noreen appeared smiling, looking at their husbands and oldest sons.

"Captains, hello" Mirikami began. "I didn't expect to see you both in orbit. I wasn't sure the Avenger would beat us here. Why the orbital gathering? I don't see the Falcon. Chief Haveram was bringing home a small freighter we bought at Poldark, with consumer goods aboard."

"Hi, Tet," Noreen responded. "The Avenger has been here almost four hours, and I radioed Marlyn, who Jumped back from Haven to join me. The Falcon beat us both home, Tet. That's a speedy boat, according to the chief. He had landed at Hub City even before I arrived. He'll head to Prime City after unloading the goods for those local textile merchants.

"Don't plan on landing immediately. Maggi left word with Jake to ask that we stay in orbit until all three ships could rendezvous. They knew our two ships were both due sometime today, via our Jump Tap messages, and Maggi has a celebration planned at Prime City."

Marlyn, her face beaming, sat on an acceleration couch on the Beagle. "Welcome Home, Gentle Men. Maggi thought it would be great if all three ships landed in formation in a triumphant joint return. The Beagle has been here, of course, but seeing the three ships land together will be an event for everyone. We have visitors from Hub City coming, or they may already be there. I understand you have ten new members for our community aboard. Maggi has a welcome all arranged for your guests, and for hers below."

Smiling back, he told them, "Ladies, I'll be delighted to have us all join the celebration. We haven't had much in the way of formal ceremonies here over the last twenty years, so things might be a bit screwed up, but let's go for it. When do we land, and how did Maggi plan to have us clustered?"

The details were simple and Marlyn outlined them briefly. "The Mark will land closer to the south entrance, between the dome and the Flight of Fancy. The Avenger and Beagle are to land with the Fancy at the center of our triangle points. Many of the family members of the returning TGs and TG1s are already waiting inside the Fancy. Other guests will come out of the dome when the dust and vapors blow away in the afternoon breeze."

It was the middle of autumn for Prime City, so the temperature on the tarmac would be cool and comfortable for those not genetically adapted for Koban's summer heat.

Mirikami repeated the conversation to the rest of the ship, and the TGs were thrilled to have a big welcome home. Other than high school graduation, they had never had a large gathering in their honor.

After that, he spent time talking with Marlyn about the aliens, what they were like, how they were reacting to us, and how they felt about the Krall. They were interrupted soon, when Jake advised that the tarmac area had been cleared for their arrival.

In a short amount of time, they were ready for landing. On cue, the AI's for the three ships started the thrust vectors to drop out of orbit, and form up for the landing.

As they dropped closer to the surface, the AIs reduced the main thrusters and shifted lift control over to the lateral maneuvering thrusters, located higher on the ship. The purpose of this less fuel-efficient method was to reduce the heat on the tarmac, where people would soon be walking. The Krall, with their tough feet and talons, always raced across blazing hot pavement at each landing, even when not on a raid. It took the finesse of the built-in automated landing systems of the clanships to accomplish this, rather than the usual Krall pilot's lack of concern for comfort, and a desire for speed. It was possible that none of the automated landing systems had ever been employed.

The three ships thundered down, surrounding the disabled Flight of Fancy. The instant their landing jacks touched, the thrusters all shut off simultaneously.

Mirikami and the Bridge group went down by elevator to the lowest deck, which was growing crowded as the TGs raced each other to stand on the deck or stairs at the bottom. They wore their normal range of personal clothing. They had been offered uniforms by General Nabarone, but it had been decided that the citizen soldiers of Koban would remain more citizen than they were soldier. Not even Captain Mirikami and the other three SGs normally wore a uniform. It wasn't as if the Krall drew a distinction between soldiers and civilians by uniform anyway.

With Trakenburg in charge of them, the ten spec ops men were certainly in their Booster Suits, wearing black dress uniforms, with black berets and boots. They looked sharp and sinister, and the color was in keeping with the carbon fiber body suits they wore underneath the uniforms. On Poldark, they had normally removed the body suits when off duty, except for straight-laced Trakenburg, who always seemed to wear his suit.

However, all ten had been wearing the Booster Suits for the five days in the ship's higher gravity, except when specifically exercising to tone muscles. Six months or more spent on Poldark had started to sap the muscles they had developed from their last refresher visit to Heavyside. A four-month rotation back there annually was needed to stay in combat shape. Soon it would be gene mods and Koban doing that for them.

It was prearranged that the Mark and the Avenger would disembark their people first, to allow families to meet with their sons and daughters, brothers and sisters. All uncomfortably remembered their six dead comrades, whose bodies had returned with the Beagle months ago. A ceremony was planned later for the returning TGs, to honor their fallen friends.

They waited for the signal that all was ready. On cue with Noreen, Mirikami had the AI open the portal facing the Fancy and extend the ramp. They were greeted by roaring cheers from the people that had gathered outside, pouring from the dome and out of the Flight of Fancy.

With over two hundred crew on the Mark, they quickly poured down the ramp to seek out their families. From the Avenger, those twenty-five also ran headlong to meet friends and family. Thad and Dillon went down more sedately with their sons, while Mirikami stayed with the ten spec ops troopers.

Sergeant Jenkins asked him, "Is this the usual greeting when you come home?"

Mirikami shook his head. "I can't say. It's the first time. It may be this way a time or two, but it probably won't last. It's the first any of these kids were ever off Koban. Some were never even away from home more than a few nights. We only have this Krall dome and another one for living space, each of which has greater capacity than our entire population.

"We're beginning to expand and explore, now that basic survival is no longer our main goal. We'll build human designed habitation soon, provided we can come up with materials the local animals can't destroy by bumping into it or trying to peel it open for what might be inside to eat." That comment drew some stares

Trakenburg offered a comment. "From what I can see, it seems very inviting. The air is fresh and fragrant the temperature is mild, a bit humid perhaps. However, I don't see anything but tarmac and the disabled ships you told us were here, and some blue-green grass past the pavement. Where are the animals I heard about?"

Mirikami pointed to the northeast. "See those groups of dots in the sky? Coming this way?"

"Sure. My eye implants show they are flapping like birds, but they must be larger based on their distance. What are they?"

"That is our air cover against scorpion skeeters. If you switch on your ultrasonic sound mikes, you can probably hear them. Those are squadrons of wolfbats. We have an agreement with them to furnish them meat in exchange for such protection, and to scout for us when we hunt or explore. They no longer consider us a prey animal and a food source."

"How big are they? They don't look like they'd be much of a threat."

"They range from the size of a midsized dog to a large one. However, their strength is greater than an average human, and they are a lot faster than you or I. If I tried to take a punch at one, or grab hold of a wing, I'd likely lose the hand or some fingers. An unarmed TG could take care of a squadron of five or six of them without a lot of trouble, if he or she was vigilant. You and your men, with just your suits and no guns? I don't think one of you alone would last a night against a squadron of five in the open. I sure wouldn't."

"Huh," was all Trakenburg uttered, obviously not convinced.

Just then there was a shot fired, which drew only brief attention from those outside. The spec ops troops appeared a bit itchy, ready to draw their side arms. Mirikami needed to convince them to keep their weapons holstered. "That was someone shooting down a skeeter with a buckshot load. You men have slugs. That is not what you want in this case. Even the buckshot would be dangerous if it hadn't been fired by that TG over there." He pointed to a young girl picking up the large dead insect she had killed.

"That has over a two-foot wing span!" Longstreet said. "That's a skeeter?"

"It's a *scorpion* skeeter." Mirikami amended. "There's a serious paralyzing sting in their tail. I guarantee that you will go down if stung. Three or four stings and you won't get back up, ever. They operate in small flocks of two to four bugs usually, so there are others still around that came with the dead bug. If you were paralyzed and alone, three or four will settle on you and drain you of blood in ten to fifteen minutes. We keep our eyes open and heads on a swivel on Koban. A Jazzer is the best weapon for them and crowd safe. However, I've seen more than one TG kill them with a well-thrown rock. We'll issue you some Jazzers later today. I have mine in my pocket."

One of the troopers called out. "Those closest five wolfbats are diving towards the crowd. They're making a hell of a racket ultrasonically." Corporal Dmitry Stepnov was clearly alarmed.

Mirikami looked where he was pointing. He saw that quite a number of people in the crowd were aware of them and looking up, but seemed unconcerned. Then the squadron leveled off three feet over their heads, and split up to dart around the sides of the ships, in chase of several skeeters that had been hovering for an opportunity to go after anyone not paying attention. That was not something anyone living on Koban for very long ever did when outside.

"I told you men, the wolfbats come when we have a ship land, or they see a lot of people outside, or if we whistle for them." He pulled out the stainless steel whistle he'd taken out of his duffel that morning and put in his pocket. It had not been useful on Poldark.

"They know we will offer them food for protecting us from the skeeters, or from a handful of other creatures that are brazen enough to come this close to us by the dome. Such as a pack of screamers that came after me, right on this same area of tarmac once. Those are two-and-a-half feet high miniature raptors, which operate in groups of six to a dozen. Noisy and superfast little monsters when they attack. They will eat your ass too." He grinned.

"Ok. I get the point of all your warnings," Longstreet said in a strained rush.

"Now please tell me that beast is a *tame* ripper running right at us!" He had placed a nervous hand on his pistol butt, and the other men did the same as they all started backing away from the edge of the ramp.

"Hands off your guns! That's Kobalt." His warning was more for their protection and the crowd's than for the big cat's safety. Their chance of hitting him was low, but there would be bystanders near him as he dodged. He slipped gracefully past them, coming at an easy lope, teal colored fur rippling over the powerful muscles underneath.

Mirikami stepped forward, hopeful the huge playful cat wasn't about to exuberantly bowl him over in his greeting, thus frightening the crap out of the ten men with guns, that were unsure if this was the least bit safe.

"Come on boy!" He said this as much to reassure the others, as to encourage Kobalt, who clearly wasn't going to be kept away from his Uncle Tet anyway.

The big beast bounded up the ramp in a single easy leap and reared his front paws enough to place them on Mirikami's shoulders, and planted a huge wet pink tongue on the man's cheek. He was perfectly aware that his uncle didn't like these wet "kisses," so he did it anytime he thought the absence had been long enough to pretend it was justified. Thankfully, Kobalt kept most of his eight hundred pound weight on his rear haunches. Even the weight of his massive forelegs and paws were as much as Mirikami could hold up as he was playfully mauled.

To those behind Mirikami, a small man anyway, he seemed engulfed by a giant blue-green tiger. The open mouth exposed the large fangs, and the long pink tongue around the side of his head made it seem the beast was in the process of chewing the hapless victim's head off.

Mirikami's squall of protest at the slobbery lick sounded awfully close to a cry for help to the watching men. Then the fanged monster suddenly dropped to the deck, rolled on its back, tongue still lolling out of the side of that fearsome mouth, and waited for the chest and belly rub it had learned to love back when it was a small cub, often delivered by this favorite uncle.

One hand rubbing at the chest and stomach, the other grasping the frill, Mirikami both scolded the cat's behavior with annoyed thought pictures, while rewarding it with the chest and belly rub it craved. It was a ludicrous combination of a giant fierce killer on its back, tongue hanging out, hind legs pawing the air as the belly rub tickled it into growling spasms of pleasure.

It ended too soon for Kobalt, but a frill thought from Mirikami promised more rubs later when they were in a less public place. Using his sleeve and shoulder, he dried his cheek, and a hand smoothed his short black hair back into place on the right, where it had been displaced by the lick.

Attempting to recover some of the dignity that Kobalt had just robbed him of in front of these fighting men, Mirikami took a deep breath and turned around to face them, bearing a thoroughly serious expression. It lasted all of two seconds as everyone burst into laughter. Theirs, mostly in relief they weren't facing a huge tiger's attack with pop guns and his, in embarrassment at this public display of affection. The latter was not something seen very often on reserved New Honshu, where Mirikami had been raised.

The laughter died down and Mirikami made an introduction to the ten wary spec ops men. "Men, I want you to meet Kobalt, the genetic origin of the most significant Koban derived modifications you and I will be receiving, and which the TG's and TG1's already have. He has a twin sister, Kit, whom I assume will be along shortly. The two of them were the first rippers we raised, as orphaned newborn cubs.

He glanced at Kobalt, and continued, "You should know that Kobalt and Kit understand perhaps eighty to eighty-five percent of the Standard spoken to them. It is the more abstract references they have trouble understanding. Such as, *this hot sun is burning my ass off.* They will look to see if that's true." That drew the laughs and chuckles expected.

"The limit to their vocabulary and understanding us better is largely because we humans did not have their genes for Mind Tap ability incorporated until a few months ago. That's when our ability to share thoughts and meanings with them accelerated, because our TG1's could explain meanings faster and better to them.

"Naturally, they don't have the means to voice our language, but they are very expressive in their own language." He looked at Kobalt, who sensed what was about to be asked. His large blue eyes twinkled.

"Roar for the nice men, Kobalt."

Kobalt raised his massive head, fangs exposed as his jaws gaped, and an ear splitting, deep base bone vibrating roar issued from deep in his chest, and it made even Mirikami step back and cover his ears. Everyone standing outside the ship was startled by the directed force of the reverberation, created in a metal-sided hold with only one portal open. They instinctively ducked down. It was instantly answered from half dozen places in the crowd, as Kit and some of her children, or offspring from other cats replied in kind. It quickly led to laughter among the people in the crowd, realizing it was a demonstration for the newcomers.

"Holy shit!" Longstreet shouted, half deafened by the effect in the enclosed space. "Warn us to cover our ears next time. I definitely don't want to hear that out in the wild."

Kobalt, pleased with the results, smoothly moved next to Longstreet, presenting his frill for touching. Mirikami explained what to do. "Joe, place a hand on that inch high fleshy ring around his neck. He wants to talk to you. We call that frilling, instead of a Mind Tap, but it's the same principle."

Longstreet tentatively touched the top of the ridge of teal flesh, and his eyes widened and he grinned as the thoughts poured from the cat. He visualized the cat's amusement at scaring the new arrivals. Then he was informed, partly with what seemed to be words spoken in Standard in Dillon's voice, which entered into his mind. He received images and emotions as well, explaining that rippers "tasted" the fears and emotions of others. The voice in his head seemed to be Dillon's, and it answered Longstreet's unasked thought question.

"I use my father's voice for thought words with people. He taught the world to me as a cub, and I wanted to sound as he does if I could speak. I was told by my mother and father, when I frilled them today, that I would meet a friend to my father where my uncle waited. I knew which man in black you were when my uncle touched my frill. I offer to hunt with you when you are ready. My father says you like to hunt."

Longstreet was surprised at the depth of this kind of communication. Every word he sensed came with images, and feelings, so it was difficult to separate actual individual words from the rapid stream. He sensed that sometimes it was his own mind forming words in Dillon's voice. They matched the images that came to him. It was astounding how complete the exchange seemed to him, coming from a nonhuman he had seen only as an animal minutes before. It was now hardly a surprise that the TG1's were able to share so much information so quickly between them.

Then the cat, lacking diplomacy and bluntly truthful, told him (in an apparent effort at encouragement), "You should not worry. You soon will learn how to think faster than a rhinolo when you have the frill changes. Rhinolo are stupid."

Joe had heard about hunting rhinolo from Dillon and Thad, and those beasts being brilliant and fast thinkers wasn't what he'd heard. He'd just been told the ripper found him to be slower witted than a stupid rhinolo.

He had the foresight to lift his hand from the frill before he formed his next thought. *They* told *me that a ripper couldn't lie very well. I wish this one had at least tried!*

Obviously, a predator that enjoyed its prey's dying thoughts of terror wasn't concerned about hurt feelings, or about conveying truthful perceptions that felt like insults to the recipient.

Mirikami invited the other nine men to "talk" with Kobalt, as he and Joe walked down the ramp into the milling people. Large outdoor assemblies were rare at Prime City. He estimated there must be at least five thousand people here. He suddenly remembered that he didn't have to guess, he could ask his old friend. Jake was always online. Jakob could answer as well, but he had spent many more years with the older model AI.

He spoke aloud. "Jake, how many people came out to meet us today. Please include Captain Joe Longstreet walking next to me in your reply."

"Yes Sir," answered the familiar bland voice from the Flight of Fancy's AI. There are four thousand eight hundred eighteen residents, plus the complements of the three ships present on the ramp area, with more people coming out, and others going inside. The number is constantly changing, Sir. I could…"

"That's fine, Jake." Mirikami cut off whatever he was about to say to expand his answer.

"Joe that was the AI that saved our butts on this planet, and provided a secret source of data and communications while the Krall were still here. The AI called Jakob, on my new ship, is far more powerful and sophisticated than Jake, but I could never part with this old friend."

Joe made an observation. "Dillon told me this old model AI software, and its obsolete computer host system was still more complex than anything the Krall appear to use. We must be well ahead of them in use of computers."

"True, but after learning what complexity a clanship is *really* capable of, now that I fly one, I believe it is the barbarian side of the Krall personality that leads to their disdain for anything that could think for them, or physically perform a task they can do for themselves. We hope to use that weakness to our advantage.

"The clanships were designed specifically for the Krall by a people called the Olt'kitapi, an advanced and benevolent race. They personally used a certain amount of computer and quantum technology within their own bodies. As a result, clanships have additional complex ways of interfacing with its operators. More than the purely manual direct method preferred by the Krall. I think the Krall were expected to evolve into a more sophisticated species over time, and their mentors gave them too much trust and leeway before they reached that point.

"Questioning the Krall translators before they left Koban, and recently asking the aliens Marlyn found on Haven, I think that a small portion of the Krall race had started to agree with the Olt'kitapi goals for them, and perhaps accepted some of the technological enhancements, either biological or electronic improvements or both, which were being offered by the Olt'kitapi. That action is what sparked the eventual revolt of the dominate warrior breed of Krall, determined to destroy their benefactors before the changes to their race became widespread."

Longstreet nodded. "Dillon also told me some of this. A more civilized Krall population might exist somewhere."

"We don't know if or where they live, but the aliens that Marlyn Greeves' expedition found on Haven may be able to tell us."

He concluded with a bit of sarcasm. "They might be worth finding, provided they don't share the genocidal aspirations of the murderous Krall we already know and love."

As they wove through the crowd, Mirikami was repeatedly greeted, and had to pause often to introduce Longstreet. Finally, he put people off, saying there would be a meet and greet later just so he could make faster headway to the Flight of Fancy. That was where the Inner Circle Members had decided to gather, in a meeting to share information with the city leaders of both domes.

Dillon and Noreen could be seen at the top of the ramp leading up to the Fancy's hold, talking to Rafe and Aldry. The taller Longstreet spotted Thad's head towering over most of the crowd, standing near the base of the ramp, surrounded by dozens of eager TGs that were probably wanting to know when they would get a chance to train and go on a mission.

Two rippers brushed by Longstreet from behind, giving him quite a start, and they pushed their neck frills against Mirikami's hands as they passed him, in an apparent casual greeting.

Mirikami glanced at Longstreet. “Those were Kit’s first two cubs saying hello. They seemed amused about something to do with their Aunt Maggi. Her image flashed at me, but was out of focus for some reason.”

“I heard Dillon say he was going to avoid someone named Maggi for a few days, until he started his next round of genetic mods. Who is she?”

“A small dynamo of a Lady, over a hundred and ten years old now, and a bio scientist. When she boarded my ship on Rhama years ago, she certainly could never have anticipated organizing a group of mismatched scientists and Spacers into a conspiracy to fight aliens. However, she is as much responsible for pulling our resources together as anyone. Before our trip, she’s the one that led the search for illegal copies of the old banned genetic research, from before the clone wars. Using that research on humans was never on her mind. The people she brought into the plan were only going to help make our food crops and livestock able to flourish on Rim Worlds and the New Colonies.

“She’s frail looking, and is actually starting to show her age after twenty-two years in Koban’s gravity. Don’t let that fool you however. She has a sharp mind and wit, and will shred most opponents in a debate.”

Mirikami thought about the two cat’s amusement just now. “The two rippers might think I don't know about her having some new gene mods. When I left Koban, we didn’t have the technology to apply ripper gene mods to anyone not *born* with the superconductor nerves. The nanites you spec ops types somehow magically *acquired* for us, and the med labs that General Nabarone sold us, obviously made that step possible for us SGs.

“Maggi received the same clone mods all of us SGs did years ago, as well as the redundant superconductor Koban nervous system. Many of us leaders, never planning to have children anyway, accepted the alien super conductor nerves first, as sort of test subjects.

“When Maggi left us a message in Tachyon Space, we knew she had received the gene mod from the rippers for frilling, which people have started calling Mind Tap. I suspect her big surprise is that she also has the muscle and bone mods to make her strong and fast. I’ll try to act amazed. She can be a real pain in the ass if you spoil her jokes. Literally a pain,” he chuckled, unaware that he was partly right, and more wrong than he suspected.

At the base of the ramp into the Fancy, he said his hello’s to Thad’s family, his other two teenagers, and allowed Thad to introduce Longstreet. As he hugged Marlyn, a twinkle in her eyes and a poorly suppressed smirk, revealed an undertone of amusement from her.

Of course, he thought. She’s been here with Maggi, and she knows what her surprise is today. I will certainly try to look amazed at her Tap ability, and at her new strength and speed. Forewarned is forearmed, he thought.

They went up the ramp and joined the others, and now that he was looking for it, he noted the occasional smirks on the faces of Aldry and Rafe. This was all a joke on him, Sarge, Dillon, and Thad. They would have to play their part.

"Where's Maggi," he asked innocently. "She didn't come over from the Beagle yet?"

"Oh, she wasn't on this trip to Haven. I was delivering the last members of the Raspani herd to their new home. The Prada and Torki are proud and excited to host them. They hope to help accelerate their return to full sentience. Maggi stayed here, finishing some preparations for our meeting today. I knew five days ago that you and Noreen had entered the Hole and were coming home. I've been making daily Jumps to Haven."

"Maggi is already in the large conference room," prompted Aldry. "She and Andy Johnson had Jake use some of that energy in Fancy's Trap fields to create a lower gravity field in there this week." Johnson was one of the Drive Rats for the Flight of Fancy, back when it was still space worthy. He acted as the ship's engineer when Chief Haveram was away.

The gravitational energy of a small star was held in the combined two-tachyon Trap fields of the ship, dating from the day the Flight of Fancy first entered the T-squared level of Tachyon Space, pulled into that Jump Hole by the Krall clanship that had captured them. That enormous level of tachyon energy had barely been reduced, even after all these years of providing power to all of Prime City. An adjustment to the curvature of a local internal gravity field in an area of the ship was not difficult, but it did eat more energy. In this case, the drain was trivial compared to how much they had stored. Mirikami's next question was clearly expected.

"Why?" His eyebrows rose.

Noreen, having arrived in orbit only a few hours earlier than he had, was nevertheless better informed. "It's a concession for our meeting today. We have multiple guests that have not lived under Koban's gravity."

Mirikami started to suspect a conspiracy here, to spring something on him, as he had done to them so many times in the past.

"The ten spec ops men that returned with me are not exactly guests," he corrected. "They are new residents and citizens that need to adapt. Besides, even though they were on low gravity Poldark, they have lived and trained on Heavyside, which I'm sure you know. They're wearing Booster Suits, and our gravity will hardly be a strain on them before we can give them the genetic upgrades."

Noreen grinned. "Oh, right. I wasn't even thinking of them. I'm sure they could manage fine. Are we all present?" She looked around. "No, I see the other troopers making their way through the crowd."

Sure enough, they were on their way, but encountering the welcoming greetings of the locals, and being introduced by many of the TG's they had helped train on Poldark. They were being greatly slowed in their progress. Mirikami stepped to the edge of the ramp and called out to the noisy, chatty crowd, but most failed to hear him.

"Jake, put me on external speakers please."

This time he was heard by all. "Ladies, Gentle Men, please allow our new arrivals to reach the Fancy, quickly please. We will have a social gathering in the Great Hall later, where you can meet them." The crowd opened space for the men and Trakenburg waved his thanks.

"Tet," said Noreen, an obvious co-conspirator on the joke being set up. "The rest of us will go up to deck 8 now. If you men will wait until you are all together, we expect you to join us in the large conference room shortly." With that, the others in the hold area left the five men waiting for the nine remaining spec ops men to arrive.

Thad watched the group walk into the ship's interior. "What have they got up their sleeves?" He noticed their demeanor as well.

"What visitors do we have that need the courtesy of lower gravity?" Dillon wondered.

Mirikami had sorted it out. "The Beagle has been back and forth to Haven all week, Marlyn said. Who did they find living there?"

"Hey," Sarge blurted. "We get to meet representatives of the Prada and Torki."

"That must be part of it," admitted Dillon. "However, it doesn't explain the funny vibes I got from Marlyn and Noreen, grinning like adolescents when I mentioned Maggi. She factors into this surprise some way, except we already figured out she has some or most of the Koban gene mods. I don't want her bench pressing my ass in front of everyone, or worse."

Mirikami laughed. "She might do that in private, but probably not in front of everyone. Surely not in front of aliens, who might not appreciate the childish level of humor you two engage in at times."

"Aliens?" Trakenburg had reached the top of the ramp with his other men.

Mirikami quickly brought them up to date on what he expected was about to occur in the meeting. Some of it would be humor directed at Mirikami and the other SGs, coming from a friend, Maggi Fisher, and the rest was probably an informal meeting with alien representatives, brought over from Haven.

Dillon offered the new men a caution. "I'm told the Torki look like larger-than-man-size purple crabs with large yellow claws and smaller mandibles for tool manipulation. They are supposed to be highly intelligent, and friendly towards us. The Prada are five-foot high furry bipeds, that I understand somewhat resemble an earth lemur. They too are intelligent, but still consider the Krall to be their legitimate lord and masters. They are standoffish, and have reservations as to whether they should cooperate with us."

Mirikami shrugged. "OK, I don't think we can get any more prepared for whatever surprises they have for us by standing here."

"How about asking Jake? He sees everything," Sarge suggested.

Mirikami brightened. "Good idea. That could be considered being a spoilsport, but what the hell. I'll give it a shot and we can all act as if we didn't know.

"Jake, reply on speaker, please."

"Yes Sir," came from an overhead grill.

"What surprises do the Ladies and Maggi have prepared for us in the conference room?"

"I'm not at liberty to tell you, Sir, without permission."

Mirikami almost sputtered. "What? I'm the captain of this ship. I'm authorized any level of access to your data." He had *never* expected this.

"Sir, you are now the captain of The Mark of Koban, a different ship. You may recall that this ship was decommissioned, and made a property of Prime City as the communal power plant."

"Of course I know. I did that myself, back when I was Commander of the dome and everything inside the compound. I certainly did not deny myself access to your data before or later. You have never refused my orders. Why now?" He felt as if a friend had turned on him, not an AI that obeyed impersonal rules.

"The Mayor of Prime City specifically instructed that I not provide the information you requested, for today only."

Mirikami fumed and turned red in the face. Trakenburg asked, "Who's the Mayor?"

Thad was laughing. "Maggi Fisher."

There was nothing left but to head to the central lift, and go discover what else the Ladies were holding back. Mirikami savagely mashed the summons button when he arrived. Once inside the lift, he pressed for deck 8 much harder than necessary. Dillon smiled, hoping that this meant that Maggi had another target for her humor today.

As Mirikami led the party to the set of double doors off the main corridor, they found them closed as they approached, manned by two of his former stewards, Nory Walters and Mel Rigson. They were in their old Interworld company livery tonight, their white vests looking bright and new, the black pants sharply creased. They nodded and pulled open the doors as he approached, saying nothing.

As he swung into the room, he saw there were only perhaps fifty guests present, of the two hundred people the largest room on the ship could hold. There were no living plastic chairs extruded from the floor today, but there were extruded tables holding snacks and drinks along the sidewalls.

Despite the forewarning, they each experienced a brief partial loss of equilibrium as the gravity field lessened when they crossed the threshold. It was as if the corridor behind them were trying to hold them back with its higher pull of gravity. This certainly supported the notion of guests that preferred a lower gravity.

They were greeted as they entered, and Marlyn and Noreen detached from the milling and clustered social groups and linked arms with their respective husbands. Aldry and Rafe were broadly introduced to all ten new comers, and Mirikami exchanged greetings with various city officials from both Prime City and Hub City that caught his eye. Nory Walters brought Tet his favorite drink, a glass of Death Lime juice with a bit more than a dash of rum. It seemed more like a purely social gathering than a diplomatic one.

Maggi was nowhere to be seen. However, a podium was in the back of the room, to one side of the seldom-used second set of double doors. Deanna Turner, Tet's friend and former combat team member, left a group of people and walked to the podium. She was the Deputy Mayor for Maggi, and often filled in for her at functions.

She tapped her finger on the gavel button to create a rapping sound for attention. A slender audio pickup extruded from the podium top towards her lips.

"Distinguished visitors, guests, new citizens," she nodded to the nervously clustered spec ops soldiers, uncomfortable in this civilian social setting, "and dear friends." She looked to Tet, and the Inner Circle's "movers and shakers" of Koban's past, present, and future.

"Today we are celebrating the return and reuniting of our intrepid heroes, who risked not only bearding the Krall lion in its den on K1, but also by entering Human Space. To contact and seek assistance from those that could easily have chosen to turn on them, as criminals guilty of Purge era crimes against humanity. They were successful in both undertakings, as our welcomed new citizens and wonderful new technology are proof that we can cooperate in our joint fight against the Krall." She beamed, and there was light applause.

"There have been strides made here at home, in a very short time using this new technology, the nanites and modern med labs. To more effectively and more widely employ the genetic enhancements that make our defeating the Krall possible. Not a guaranteed victory by any means, but now possible in principle."

More applause.

"Aldry and Rafe will speak with you individually about the marvelous steps recently taken in genetics. I'm certain you who have returned home today have heard rumors that the procedures used to create our TGs and TG1's, and now some TG2's, will function with more subjects than Koban-born children of Second Generation parents. Thanks to the war driven new nanites and med labs from Human Space, our gene mods also can be applied to their parents, who were not born with the organic superconducting nervous system. This means that any human, whether living on Koban or not, can be enhanced to become a member of the Kobani race of man."

That drew a loud round of applause, and Mirikami assumed that a triumphant and physically enhanced Maggi Fisher was about to come through the prominently exposed rear doors. Not yet, as it turned out.

Deanna addressed the ten newer men. "Your trip to K1 had the fallout of acquiring two more clanships to convert to our use. One of those, the Beagle, went exploring locally and found a second home for some of our own people and for the expected influx of Krall slaves, as we raid their production worlds. As you know, it was given the name Haven, and was found to already have a small population of left-behind races the Krall probably considered expendable, or replaceable."

Now Mirikami expected Maggi, and some aliens, to walk dramatically through those rear doors. Only partly right.

"Ladies, and Gentle Men, we have the privilege of presenting representatives of each race, the Prada and the Torki. We ask that you refrain from crowding them until they are more familiar with our customs, and we with theirs. Some of you here have met with them previously, or have seen them in Tri-Vid recordings. Our wanderers and new citizens have not. I present to you Ambassador Wister, of the

Prada on Haven, and Ambassador Coldar, of the Torki on Haven."

The rear doors opened slowly, and side-by-side stood the diminutive Wister, and Coldar. The eight-foot wide crab was standing offset to the side, to accommodate Wister's smaller frame in the doorway.

Wister's head darted forward once, as he walked into the room, seeing humans that he knew and had gradually learned to tell apart. As he cleared the doorway, Coldar sidled to the left and then was able to fit through the wide set of doors.

Trakenburg was intrigued by the aliens, but still had to whisper a nitpicking comment on the presentation to Mirikami. "This doesn't resemble any diplomatic function I ever attended, between the PU and colony worlds."

"Well, Frank, we aren't a colony world, and we don't have anyone still alive with us that was ever an actual diplomat. The same is true for these former Krall subjects, I presume. We can ad lib diplomacy as we go, just as we have done on the military side of things."

The last was a little dig at Trakenburg's gripe that the Kobani didn't choose to follow even a loose, let alone his preferred strict military rules of conduct. The closest they came to looking uniform was when they all wore their new Chameleon Skin flex armor.

This lack of military structure had its roots in the past of its two leaders with any military background at all. Tet had been in the PU Navy in his early Spacer career (not a satisfactory union), and Thad had been in a provincial militia on (the then Rim World) of Poldark, which had operated more like an adult Boy Scout troop with big guns. They had no desire to impose too rigid a structure on what was essentially an all-volunteer force of young and spirited, free-willed personalities, all with super human ability.

Mirikami still saw no sign of Maggi. He had grown fond of the sometimes irritating, older little woman. Over a private dinner tonight, he wanted to share with her the things he was planning, and to hear her tell of what she was learning from the aliens. The few months away from Koban had made him appreciate her counsel, advice, and company. They had been in near daily contact for over twenty years. He missed having someone he could confide in, on matters where he was uncertain.

He realized that Deanna was leading both aliens towards him, as the people in the center of the room gave the imposing looking Torki more room than they might have the smaller Prada. A four-foot long heavy right claw, and a smaller left one of three feet, tended to generate feelings of caution from soft bodied creatures.

Deanna made the personal introduction. "Ambassador Wister, Ambassador Coldar, this man is Captain Mirikami, our foremost citizen, who bears the greatest responsibility for our surviving our *interactions* with the Krall when they were here, and leading us as we sought to find ways to survive on Koban."

Wister responded first, in very well enunciated low Krall, if higher pitched than when spoken by a Krall. "Ambassador Fisher has spoken of you often, and provided me with mental images of you, and of things you have accomplished. I am honored to greet you." He bobbed his head vertically twice on his long neck, which

Mirikami took as equivalent to a human bow.

Replying in low Krall, he said, "I am pleased to meet you as well, Ambassador Wister. I look forward to our future discussions." He bowed deeply, certain he could not match the head bobbing motion on a shorter human neck. Besides, coming from him it might mean something completely inappropriate. He thought, *out of context, it might mean you look sexy for hairy squirrel.*

He suppressed a chuckle, not certain what provoked the random thought. Alien gestures would have to be studied, and human one's explained, before used or imitated. Simply looking into a Krall eyes could get you killed when we first met them.

Tet next was surprised to hear the Torki ambassador speak Standard, with no foreign inflection or accent at all. It was like hearing a high level AI speaking. "Captain Mirikami, your exploits and wisdom have been described to us by our mutual friend, Maggi. Her mind images are tinted with colors of fondness and admiration for you. I will be eager to mind share with you, after you achieve the genetic gift of what you call Mind Tap."

"Ambassador Coldar, I admire our friend Maggi greatly. I am eagerly looking forward to the next series of genetic enhancements, one of which will enable me to mind share, as you said." He repeated the bow, which Coldar emulated by lowering the front of his carapace, with a rustling and scraping sound as the hard surfaces rubbed together.

"I had not expected to hear you speaking Standard, Ambassador Coldar. That is quite impressive in such a short time after meeting us."

Coldar was humbly dismissive. "That was only a translation of low Krall into Standard, from a software program I downloaded from an artificial intelligence machine on your clanship named the Beagle. I speak to you using a sound replicator, because the Torki natural speech would be outside of your physical ability to replicate." The crab lifted its front to reveal a black six-inch oval device adhered to his shell.

"I also have an internal device of Olt'kitapi design, which has storage capacity for many things. One of those new things was a translation program from your intelligent computer, between low Krall and Standard. I already have a translator from Torki speech to low Krall and back. It seemed redundant for me to speak in the language imposed by my former masters. I was introduced as an ambassador in your language, although that is not a title among my species. I wish to be addressed in conversation as simply Coldar, a builder of quantum key devices."

"Coldar it is then. I prefer to be known to friends as Tet, which is a portion of my first name, and Mirikami is my more formal second name. Please call me Tet."

"The inference is that you wish to be a friend. I wish that as well. However, because the Prada do not know any language but low Krall, we should switch to that to be polite."

Mirikami nodded before he could catch himself. No telling what that could mean to an alien. He responded verbally in low Krall. "Coldar, I do ask that you call me Tet as a friend. Ambassador Wister, I have invited Coldar to be a friend, and I extend that invitation to you as well. Will you accept my offer of friendly informality?"

A forward head dart, and he said, "This is the arrangement I have with Maggi, and she addresses me as Wister. Tet, I believe we can act as friends as well. I have started to learn words of Standard, however, Coldar has said a smaller modified sound replicator disk can be made by his people, which will use the same program for translation that I believe he used with you now. My words in low Krall will be repeated in Standard to you, and I will hear low Krall from those that speak Standard."

"Excellent. We will have spoken words that we can share, and with my people, soon most of us will have the Mind Tap ability we gained from the rippers of Koban."

Wister shivered noticeably. "This is the first good thing anyone has ever received from those eaters of Prada and Rulers."

"Wister, at one time the wild rippers ate humans. Those that live near us no longer do that. We live with members of that species in our homes, and our children play together. We only use caution when we meet wild rippers, far from the domes where we now live. One day I think we will have a treaty with all ripper prides. You must also have had attacks from wolfbats when you built the domes here."

"Yes," his head darted forward, "but they were not as terrifying, because we could frighten them away with guns that the Rulers let us have."

"Humans have a truce with the wolfbats as well. They often work for us, in return for pay in food. We will make peace with any intelligent species when we can, and fight only when we cannot. We cannot make peace with the Krall, and so we must fight them. Not only for ourselves, but also for the Torki, the Raspani, and for the Prada."

"I have come to believe that your fight with the Rulers is what you must do. I even see that their claim to status as our Rulers is probably in question. That is only my own view, now that I have seen the mind pictures of what they do."

He explained how he had seen those images. "Maggi brought sixteen of your newest people, who arrived as Krall prisoners from the worlds where most humans live. I saw their memories of what the Krall have done to your worlds and your people. They did not know of my people until you brought them to visit Haven. They were frightened of us, and yet wanted to know about us, and to live on Haven because they cannot return home. They want to learn from us, as if we were the elder race. It was rewarding to feel that way, to have someone to teach. The other villagers are willing to help them make homes on Haven, if they do not live too close to us."

"Your world is mostly empty of villages and Torki lodges, Wister, so there is room right now for everyone. That will not last forever, as we bring more of your people and mine to live there. Can you learn to work with my people more closely?"

"When you say "you" I believe you mean the other Prada, and not only me. Yes?"

"I do."

It will be slower for some of my people, but with mind pictures to help, they can all learn to accept you as neighbors. I don't know how many can turn away from the Krall as our rightful Rulers, as the elder race in the galaxy. That is a difficult thing for us."

"Wister, you know more of the galaxy than do we humans, but even so the Krall, and the Olt'kitapi before them, occupied a very small part of the galaxy. There must be older races still to be found."

"If you find them, and we believe they are senior to us all, then we will reconsider. However, the practical problem remains that the Olt'kitapi were once senior, and now they are gone. Even the Raspani were senior to the Krall, but their minds have been lost. The Krall, in their drive to rule the galaxy will attack and defeat any race they find, even if my people accept another species as the rightful and wisest new Rulers. Your people's problem will not change, even if ours does. The Krall will win with or without the Prada"

"If the people of Koban, and any allies we can find, are able to protect other races from the Krall, then when you find an elder race you will be free to accept their rule. Will you build things we need, in exchange for payment?"

"For now, to help the Raspani, whom we know to be older than ourselves, we will build for them and for you, only if you protect them. That is a payment you can make to us."

"Good. We were doing that anyway, and your help is appreciated. Can we ask you to make major weapons and clanships for us?"

"No more powerful weapons than we feel are needed to protect the Raspani from Haven predators. That would be small arms, transport vehicles, and shuttle craft."

"Thank you for that. We need more but those things are helpful, and will ease the strain on our own supplies of similar items."

Coldar had been listening patiently, curious as to what the Prada would propose to do for the human leader. Now it was his turn to tell him what he had discussed with Maggi in the many days since they had first met. The Torki were not constrained by the notion the Krall deserved to rule anyone.

He began the presentation Maggi had discussed with him previously. "Our designers and engineers have reexamined older storage areas of our Olts, the quantum memory and data devices the Olt'kitapi gave us long ago, to help us become sentient. We saved scientific and technological information learned from species that the Krall defeated. Only those parts of their science that Krall clan leaders saw as useful were ordered into production.

"The Krall prefer weapons that permit individuals to attack alone, or even when part of a mass invasion assault, they normally want to fight and risk death based on a warrior's own capability. A warrior will often refuse cooperation with other individuals in a battle, or of offering support for warriors of other clans that are struggling with numerically superior forces. They are concerned mainly with their own status and breeding rights.

"Despite the stealth capability of clanships and single ships, most warriors would prefer to openly charge in and fight an enemy. Their stealth ability is actually an outgrowth of the overlaid skin material on their ships to absorb, deflect, or withstand various types of radiant energy in combat. When the outer skin is activated, the ships naturally become stealthy, but that is a side effect. It is not the Krall's desire to be sneaky because they are facing a superior foe. They will not accept that a superior foe is possible, and for many thousands of years that has proven true.

"Krall personal body armor uses visible *and* infrared background camouflage only because it is based on a design created by the Botolians, a former worthy enemy who preferred to fight at night. The Krall liked the armor because it made their interclan wars more interesting. They had selectively bred for infrared vision, and then found an enemy that could hide from them at night. They wanted to practice fighting an enemy they could not see in those frequencies in darkness.

"That armor could be more effective at other electromagnetic frequencies if they incorporated the stealth technology of the skins of the ships. It could be improved other ways. That quantum level of surface reflectivity control was created by the Olt'kitapi, and adapted and changed slightly by the Raspani. The Raspani version is what is used on single ships we build for the Krall and the original Olt'kitapi design skin is on the clanships. The skin on a clanship is tougher, and on the single ships, the skin has a wider range of radiation response and a faster reaction to multiple frequency energy weapons.

"There are built-in energy weapons available for body armor that the Krall have never requested, and which we did not volunteer to them as possible. Infrared beams, microwaves, multi-frequency lasers, and plasma pulse emitters."

Mirikami assumed Coldar was being more than merely informative, that he was approaching some sort of point in this discussion. "Are you saying it is possible to make body armor that is significantly better than what the Krall use now?"

This question had all of the men with Mirikami riveted to the conversation. The best hard suits were a better defense against projectiles and heavy plasma and lasers than the Chameleon Skins, but they were much more visible, particularly when moving, as when infiltrating behind enemy lines.

"Yes. I would not waste time explaining the possibility if we could not do this." It waved both large claws in a wide gesture.

"There are different energy weapons and communications capability for body armor, which the Krall have ignored because they did not need them. They decided to kill the Olt'kitapi because they were on the verge of making fighting too safe for the early Krall warriors to evolve on their ancient Great Path. They have moved far along that path now for many thousands of orbits. Yet, you humans have found a way to move ahead of them in a short time."

Mirikami looked directly into those jet black eyes on their slender stalks. "Humans will not take their path, because we intend only to stop the Krall from walking over the dead bodies of other species to achieve their selfish goals. I ask you and your people to create body armor like you described, so that we can test it against our common enemy."

"Your friend, Maggi, was convinced you would ask us to do that. She does understand you well, and I believe her explanation and description of this armor would have taken less time than mine did."

Mirikami looked around the room again. "I had expected Maggi to be here. She is the closest we have to a diplomat for this occasion, and she's good at logically laying out facts. She could easily have explained your proposal to me."

"She already is here." Coldar insisted. "It was her wish to demonstrate the new armor, for you and for the three other friends that she said will be fighting the Krall. She left the medical facility on this ship only after your ship landed a short time ago. After twelve of your number of days in the medical machine, she said she needed a short time to learn to use the armor we made for her."

Mirikami looked concerned. No one had told him she'd been sick or hurt. "Maggi was in the infirmary?" This was directed at Deanna, who had remained standing nearby. She reddened slightly, but smiled and said nothing.

Dillon noticed that both Noreen and Marlyn shared the same secretive smile as Deanna, with a gleam in their eyes that painful experience had taught him spoke of feminine mischief. "When is she going to show us this new armor? I'll bet she's late because she can't even stand up in the heavy damned thing." The wise crack was designed to cover his unease. An unease that was generally justified when Maggi was involved. He suddenly leaped two feet in the air and spun around, looking for whoever had just goosed him. Nobody there.

Then Dillon suddenly realized his crotch was getting uncomfortably warm, and he knew where the heat was localized. Standing in front of a roomful of gawking guests, dignitary's, and two aliens, he pulled a fastener loose on his Smart Suit's waistband, plunged his right hand down the front of his pants to the "formerly stylish" package bulge of that old suit's design, and with a hard tug yanked out a metallic athletic cup. The way he promptly dropped the thing, it either bit him, or was hot to the touch.

The sight and sound of the clinking cup bouncing on the deck drew laughter, but Thad had stepped away from Dillon and was looking around intently. Dillon hadn't jumped out of mere nervousness, although the height of his funny leap might have indicated some of that was present. However, the metal protector had not heated up all on its own.

Thad knew what he was looking for, and spotted it with difficulty. It was a barely detectable visual distortion between him and Dillon. He took two steps forward and appeared to wrap his arms around an empty place in air. Then the empty place in air suddenly broke his grip, lifted him and had him pin wheeling, about six feet above the deck. A handful of Ladies knew what was happening and were laughing hilariously. Of the men in the room, only Rafe laughed with them.

Thad squawked and yelled, "Put me down, damn it!"

A familiar voice, coming from a point just below him said. "You got it, soldier boy." He dropped to the floor, putting out his hands to catch himself, grateful now for the lower than normal gravity.

Sarge quit enjoying the other two men's distress, and spoke up before he became the next target. "Maggi, you got 'em both. You sure have the muscles to do it now." He nervously backed towards a side table's edge to keep her from getting behind him.

Longstreet leaned over to Mirikami. "That's one impressive suit. It works fast in real time, covering at least the visible light range and infrared. I can only detect a faint distortion from time to time. The heating of the metal cup must be some sort of radiant energy, because I saw the front of his pants start to glow in IR when Dillon turned around. I caught a faint shimmer in the air from him to where Thad made the mistake of trying to grab her."

Joe startled backwards when her voice, just two feet from him, asked, "Who's the good looking smart guy? And why's he hanging out with this bunch of puny male losers?"

Mirikami was grinning. He was relieved to know she was well enough to play jokes, and strong enough to rough house. Yet, twelve days was a long time to spend in a med lab for something minor.

She was getting along in years, and despite the fact that modern people stayed active until very late stages of their lives on Hub worlds, Koban had been harder on their bodies than would be the case on any other human world. He'd noted that Maggi had developed gray strands at the temples, and the outdoor, hot summer sun had added creases at the corners of her eyes in the last few years. She was a hundred and eleven he reminded himself. Hell, he was ninety-one himself. The same age Maggi had been when they were captured.

"Maggi, you've had your fun. Let's see this fabulous suit."

Suddenly, there was a brief shimmer in the center of the room, and a figure barely over five feet tall stood there, in a small smooth textured black and white suit, with an exotic rounded triangular face mask on a relatively small helmet. The helmet's front had strange multiple glowing blue lights, with something like earphones on the sides of the head.

Those six blue faceplate lights were centrally distributed around where her face would be, but none appeared to be placed exactly where you'd expect her eyes to be. Tet wondered how she could see the outside world.

The entire suit appeared snug and form fitting, even at what were joints on other suits. Here the elbows, wrists, hips, knees, and ankles looked like they flexed as if she were wearing a soft plastic layer only a couple of centimeters thick. The gloved fingers were far more flexible looking and slender than any hard suit gloves any of the men had ever seen.

The shoulders were less blocky than on most suits. However, there it did have small, articulated plates over the same flexible coverings of the other joints. It was an exceedingly compact set of armor, even when you allowed for the fact that it had been made to fit a small, slightly built woman.

The form turned and walked to the podium, passing through the people with a graceful motion that Mirikami recognized as typical of any of the TGs. She definitely had received that particular mod, so she had not needed a powered suit to lift Thad over her head.

With her back to the room, she reached for the helmet sides, which widened at the neck for her to slip over her head as she lifted. When she shook her head, medium length, disheveled blonde hair fell to cover the back of her neck.

For the entire time Mirikami had known the woman, she had sandy hair, always kept in a short, low maintenance style that required little effort. Dillon had known her for ten years before the fateful voyage to Newborn, and he'd never seen her with blonde hair, or grown that long.

"Who the hell are *you*?" he asked curiously, before she turned around. It appeared that the Ladies had pulled a switch on them, and he heard them snickering even as he asked the question.

Mirikami made the same assumption, and wondered why this seemed such a funny joke to them. It was mildly amusing, but not a laugh riot. Then she turned to answer Dillon.

Maggi's voice asked, "Who do you think, stud boy?" The question came from an attractive young woman's mouth, one wearing a touch of makeup and eye shadow that Maggi had never been seen to wear.

Dillon answered, "I don't know, that's why I asked, Tinker Bell." He glanced to his left to see that Tet was standing with the first slack-jawed expression he'd ever seen on the normally unflappable man. Mirikami recognized the voice, attitude, and resemblance.

"Tet, you look like you know who she is."

She answered for him. "Of course he does, you twit. I told him once that I had mentored a moron when I chose you. What a waste of my advancing years to train a scientist that can't see obvious evidence unless it hits him in his package." She started forward to demonstrate said action when Mirikami touched her arm and stopped her. He used his already open mouth to ask her a question.

"How the hell did you do this, Maggi? You look fabulous!"

"Why, thank you for noticing, dear." She said this with a bright cheery smile and a fake fluttering of her long eyelashes as, without looking at Dillon, she extended her left hand and casually flicked a center finger off the tip of her thumb, to feel it smack sharply on the previously announced target.

Dillon yelled and bent over as a laughing Noreen stepped close to tell him she still loved him, despite his inability to recognize his oldest friend.

Sarge and Thad started talking over one another. Sarge, the loudest, won.

"Holy crap, Maggi, you look decades younger."

Thad asked, "Are you a natural blonde?" Only to have his wife kick him lightly in his shin.

"What kind of question is that, you lunk head? Her hair got darker as she got older. It changed back. Mine used to be red before it lightened in the sun here. Shades change." She was strawberry blonde now.

"You didn't answer my question," Tet reminded Maggi. "This obviously isn't a face lift and makeover. Coldar said you have been in what must have been a med lab, based on his description. What happened?"

"The Prada happened." She answered, and then explained.

"We used a number of genes from Koban life, but we certainly aren't limited to that source. Wister is over a thousand of our years old, but this isn't a natural condition. They don't age after reaching maturity, and they reach that age in just under twenty orbits of this world. They still die from accidents, predator attacks, Krall wars, and diseases, but not from old age. Wister explained that due to his race's reverence for elders, that at some point in their distant past, they discovered how to modify their genes, adding some that they designed to prevent ageing, to produce the elder and wiser leaders they wanted to follow."

Dillon, coming closer to listen asked, "They solved the problem of preventing loss of telomere ends during cell division?"

"Not exactly," she said. She made an effort to explain to the others, "Telomere regions on our DNA deter the degradation of active genes near the ends of chromosomes, when cells repeatedly divide without creating a perfect DNA copy. As telomeres shorten, functional genes are lost over repeated cell divisions, so we start to lose genes we need to maintain our bodies, and we age in a variety of ways. About four hundred years ago, our own early geneticists found ways to slow the loss of telomeres, and thus delay the onset of age related gene damage. It keeps us younger longer, but eventually, after a hundred twenty or thirty years, the damage incurred by cell division progresses and accelerates to a point where the loss of genetic material is too fast, and we deteriorate rapidly in just a few years. What we colloquially refer to as RELP. Rapid End Life Process."

"What did the Prada do that's different?' Thad queried, certain he wasn't going to understand the answer.

"Their DNA was modified to create a permanent template of the original young telomere regions at conception, and stick it in the center of a section of evolutionarily unused, so-called-junk-DNA. These are areas found in most genomes, which at one time in the far distant history of life would have made proteins no longer used by the evolving organism. Proteins not needed in our case because we are not the primitive fish-coming-out-of-water creatures we once were.

"Much of the junk DNA doesn't do anything, it is excess evolutionary baggage. The Prada modifications make copies of their birth telomeres, and place the templates in this unused DNA. Then, in another active gene section, nearer the "safe" central regions of their DNA strands, they put an intelligently designed and functional gene complex that has the job of copying from that saved template, fixing any loss to the ends of the telomeres when there is cell division. That designed gene complex can copy the protected template from its own cell or from other cells, so there are zillions of copies of what the healthy end pieces of your original chromosomes should look like."

"Well, I was sure I wouldn't understand and I don't," said Thad. "That sounds like adding those Prada genes would end your aging by saving the telomeres you have now. Except that if you did that this month, you were already over a hundred and ten years old, with that many years of degradation. Isn't that how old you'd stay, using your old telomeres? You look a lot younger."

With her TG muscles, Maggi slapped Thad playfully and painfully on the shoulder. “People don’t smoke anymore or grow tobacco, but give that man a cigar.”

“What’s that mean?”

“Never mind, old reference. I only meant you asked the right question and deserved a reward. We now have nanites that we can program to scavenge for specific DNA segments. They were the answer for us old farts, and our age-damaged telomeres. I’ll let Rafe describe it, since he’s the brains that solved that problem.”

Rafe went to the podium and harrumphed twice to clear his throat, and then gave what he’d call a concise description. “None of us older people have completely original telomere copies, but the damage happens at different rates in various tissues, and there isn’t the same identical loss of telomere segments in each type of tissue. I sent programed nanites into Maggi’s body gathering telomere copies from multiple tissue types, and then used other nanites, and a standard gene-sequencing program, to assemble what her original undamaged telomeres most likely looked like when she reached maturity, at about age twenty-five. We used that process to create her personal template for use by the Prada repair genes. I made one for myself, and one for Aldry, and all three are different in each individual, unique for our bodies.”

Dillon’s face lit up in comprehension. “The Prada genes stop the aging process, but you used nanites to perform reconstructive DNA surgery on Maggi for the past week, restoring her telomeres and lost genes. The accumulated age damage.”

“Well…, twelve days, not seven.” Rafe corrected. “It could go a few days longer and lower her apparent chronological age by another five years, I believe. I think she may be at about where she was at age thirty. The transformation isn’t fully complete because not all of the cells were repaired, or damaged ones out of her tissues yet. The process can always be repeated, by the way if, there is age slippage.”

Sarge looked at the spec ops troops, grinning like a fool. “Ain’t cha glad you came now? We can make you young again.”

Sergeant Jenkins looked at him funny, and then chuckled. “You decrepit old geezer, I’m only twenty-five right now.”

There was a great deal of laughing and enthusiasm in the room, as people contemplated reversing their current ages. This was as momentous to many of them as the Koban genes had been. Mirikami saw that with Maggi’s appearance as a spur, even the recalcitrant Hub City clone gene recipients were now thinking of accepting a new gene mod, one originating in an alien species they had just met today.

Coldar, unaffected by the human’s enthusiasm, asked a pointed question. “Have you considered the implications for your species of indefinitely extending your lives this way, and of the reproductive issues and population pressures this will produce?”

Maggi had removed the remainder of the suit, which opened for removal much the way the helmet had. She was in a small jumpsuit that she had worn under the armor. It clearly revealed she had a fuller, if still slender figure. “Yes. Aldry, Rafe, and I have considered the possible long-term consequences for humanity, Coldar, yet we don't have an answer for your question.

"I was personally finished with reproduction, because I had delivered three children in my life, and desired no more. I recognize that I might change that position now. There are mothers in our society that produced five or six children, or even more, for the replacement of population after our brush with near extinction. Others did so for population expansion on our more sparsely inhabited colony worlds. We reproduce much more slowly than the Krall, but more of our children survive to adulthood, I think. At least they did before the Krall began killing so many."

Coldar added an observation. "Your species expansion into space was a very short time ago by the standards of every intelligent species we have encountered or learned about. In less than half the length of Wister's own life, you humans first left your home world. You then discovered and settled on over seven hundred planets.

"Consider that the Prada took nearly seventy thousand orbits to colonize a tenth of that in a volume of stars where light could travel for three-thousand orbits of this world, while crossing their space. They had a very slow moving expansion.

"My own species, even with help from the Olt'kitapi, traveled in the stars for eleven thousand years, and lived on many fewer worlds in a volume less than your mind pictures tell me your species control now.

"I do not know how long the Olt'kitapi was in space before the Prada. The Prada say they also do not know, but are certain they were exploring much earlier than they were. Yet the former settled worlds of the Olt'kitapi, taken by the Krall, were not as many as your people use now, even if their volume of explored stars is far greater. You humans live anywhere. Even the Krall avoid the most common type of habitable worlds, those with modest gravity less than Haven's, or that are too cold or too wet. Humans use those worlds.

"You are the most adaptable species I know of, and you occupy a range of worlds that other species would consider unsuitable. You use planets around a wider number of star types, with higher surface gravities, greater temperature ranges, and modify the existing life you find there, or modify your own plants and animals, to make them livable.

"I ask you this. If you survive the Krall war, how long before your species would become an eternal life plague, and swarm over all of the habitable worlds of the galaxy? Will you become more dangerous than the Krall? Are the Torki wise to help you defeat one evil, only to see it replaced by another potentially greater and swifter spreading threat?"

Mirikami gave the best answer he had. "Coldar, and you too Wister, I can't predict where my species will be in twenty or fifty thousand years, or if we will still exist. Whatever harm we may cause in our expansion to fill the many worlds we find acceptable, we will not wantonly destroy all those people we find ahead of us. We have hoped to meet other species. We met two initially antagonistic species on Koban, which thought of us as prey and tried to eat us. We made them friends and partners. We would make peace with the Krall if that were possible. We want to do that with the Torki and the Prada.

"I believe those of us living on Koban are representative of our entire species, because we came from many of our different worlds. Most of us are united in the belief that Haven, right next door to us, is where we want to place the survivors of the alien species the Krall have conquered. Some of our people want to live there, sharing that world with you. I believe that our unforced actions are a good example of our intentions, an answer to your speculations about what the pressure of our expansions in the far future will mean for the rest of the galaxy.

"Besides, if what we say isn't enough, and what we do isn't convincing for you, then we will continue what we are doing anyway. We do not *intend* harm, even if someday we do cause harm."

All Coldar said was, "You will have Torki help."

"That's all it took?" Mirikami asked, taken aback by the swift answer. "A speech by one human?"

"The example of your short speech is one no Krall alive could make. We Torki clearly understood that we could no more stop you than we were able to stop the Krall. We have helped the Krall because we had no choice if we were to survive. You give us the option, and ask for our help. Your species may prove to be an unintended plague on the galaxy, but certainly a more benevolent one than the Krall planed. We will take our chances and help you."

"Thank you. How about your people, Wister? Do you accept our word, and agree to work with us?"

His head moved side-to-side, in confusion or indecision. "I sense much of what Coldar says is a possibility to concern us, yet I do not believe you *intend* to do harm. However, our position was previously stated, and what help we can provide to you on Haven will still be given. I will urge other elders to do more to help you move our remote villages to Haven. The Rulers never told us other Prada villages were forbidden to live in this system, because before you came we did not have a way to do this unless they moved us."

"Fine, we can work with that degree of cooperation, Wister. Thank you."

Next, he rounded on his two ship captains with a stern look, and said, "Now I need to address this matter of insubordination, bordering on mutiny by my two highest ranking officers. You have concealed vital information from me." He glared at them.

"Like, when do I get *my* turn to become fast, gain super powers, able to leap over tall things?"

Maggi, butting in, said, "It's faster than a speeding bullet, able to leap a tall building in a single bound, and more powerful than a locomotive."

"Huh? What are you talking about?"

"God. You sound as historically ignorant as my moron protégé sometimes. You want to become Superman, and don't know who he is. I'll explain it to you over a home cooked dinner, at my place."

"I didn't know you could cook."

"The depth of your ignorance appalls me, Tetsuo." She shook her head, a grin indicating she had some sort of education in mind.

Chapter 15: Have Suits, Will Travel

Maggi was demonstrating new equipment for the four men, who were lying in adjacent med labs. Right now, she was showing how the helmets of their new body armor worked. The Torki had reopened their own smaller underground high tech production facilities, and had ordered fabricated materials per new specifications from the larger Prada factories, as parts of the new design armor. For illustration purposes, she held one of the new helmets the men would wear.

"The Torki are making the control modules, weapons, and power distribution systems for the new armor at a rate of ten suits a day from his home lodge. That will increase to a hundred per day he said, as more workers learn the new skills, and two other lodges join them in the work. The Prada are already at a hundred shells per day production for the basic suits and helmets.

Tossing the helmet lightly she observed, "The armor is thin and light weight, as also were the suits the Krall gave us for combat testing. Now, however, the articulation is natural feeling, as if it were a layer of flexible skin at the joints. It behaves much like Living Plastic, except it is flame and puncture resistant, air and watertight.

"This stuff has tremendous tensile strength, protecting your head, limbs, and torso, because few of the Krall pistol rounds we tested on bare shells would penetrate. The armor piercing rounds might get through. Plasma rifles will be less of a threat. It required two or three plasma bolts at the same point to burn through, and then finally it transferred the heat to the inside. The final outer stealth coating will reduce plasma and laser resistance even more. However, a fifty-caliber, armor-piercing round can still punch through, with much less penetrating power, but probably deadly. The real technology is in what the Torki added, and the quantum controlled layering of the suit skin surfaces. That provides stealth and energy weapon resistance, as I mentioned, but does more."

Tet, just recently awakened and still fuzzy headed, said. "Maggi, before Rafe put us under last month, you still had not explained how you could see out of your helmet. There are no eyeholes or a face plate on that one"

Mirikami, Dillon, Thad, and Sarge were undergoing TG2 conversion with Koban genes in the same room, simultaneously applied with the Prada age retention gene, and nanite age regression. It had been deemed more merciful to place the recipients into a state of induced coma for the month, while the most painful muscle growth and nerve attachments were forming. That period had now passed.

She gave her typical sounding reply. "Knuckle head! There are no peepholes or actual windows on the clanships, yet you get to see outside the Mark of Koban just fine don't you? The quantum level control of the surface material that coats the ships, and these suits, is what makes it possible for them to reflect, absorb, or pass and amplify selected electromagnetic radiation. The coating on the helmet fronts and on the inside is similar to the view screens on the Mark's Bridge. The zoom ability is amazing.

"For the helmet, there's a surface on the inside of the area in front of your face that presents the outside world. I don't know how they linked it to our unique superconductor nervous systems and ripper frill mods, but if you *think* at the suit, it will adjust the range of near and far vision in front of your helmet. You can select a portion of the incoming radiation from infrared to visible light, blending into ultraviolet, for presentation to our ripper level of vision. They initially tested it with Bradley's eyes, with his ultrasonic ears, then with all of his TG2 adaptations as signal sources for suit features.

"Inside the helmet, it's like looking out of a clear window with an automatic telescopic zoom, controlled by your thoughts. I can't even see these various energy weapon projectors mounted on the front of the helmet, although when I think of which one I wish to use, it displays one of five different shape recticles for each of the five energy beams. If you think of the plasma pulse weapon, which is the large center blue disk on the face," she pointed. "It places a round target symbol where you are looking, even if you are in zoom mode. It requires a specific thought sequence to fire a bolt, as a sort of safety. You teach it your own sequence for each weapon.

"For example, in my helmet I could think *plasma bolts, six, pulse fire!* Which, for me would trigger a sixty percent of maximum energy charged particle bolt, fired at the designated target. The amount of energy in the plasma can be adjusted by you through thought, just as it's manually done on a standard Krall plasma rifle. I arbitrarily chose ten equal divisions, with number one being the weakest nonfatal bolt for a human, up to a maximum strength armored Krall killer bolt of a ten for a head shot. You can custom set your own levels, dozens of intensities if you choose, and select repeated rapid fire. At least until the plasma chamber located near your butt empties and recharges.

"There are four directed energy weapons for electromagnetic radiation. Two are for red or green light lasers, chosen by which frequency seems to have the best effect on different armor or color of targets. To circumvent specific wavelength protections of various types of armor, you have a microwave beam, and an infrared beam. I used the infrared to heat Dillon's cup last month. I hit exactly what I'm looking at when the target designator is specifically over what part I want to hit. I only have to think of the coded firing sequence and strength of the beam I want.

"At present, we can't set a weapon to keep following the original target if we choose to look away at another potential target for a different weapon. When I mentioned that, Coldar says that is merely a coding change in the control module. I also told him about the PU Army having armor that can tell friends from enemy and permit the suits to fire or hold back when fighting in a congested area, with the enemy in among civilians. It can be done, he says. They simply never envisioned that situation. He said it was *wrong* to make war around innocent beings."

Sarge made a rather Krall sounding snort. "I guess he hasn't witnessed how the Krall normally conduct their organized slaughters."

Maggi went on. "Anyway, they will be reprogrammed to track and fire each selected weapon at the targets we choose, for the length of time we choose, or if set for free fire, to only target the Krall. Our limitation, of course, is the flow of energy that is available."

Thad made a critical comment. "The plasma pulse from that face gadget has no appreciable length. I don't see how it will have a tight enough beam focus for a long-range shot. We already know the Krall can see the warmth of the magnetic field as it forms, to focus a building plasma bolt. Won't they see where our heads are, just before we fire a short-range pulse they can duck?"

"Ethan and Carson passed that information along to Coldar, before they received their final TG2 enhancements. The suits will remain opaque to the outgoing plasma pulse until it is launched. They won't see it coming. There are also new add-on pre-flash suppressors for plasma cannons and pulse rifles. Small magnetic collars can conceal the heat escaping from the beam focusing fields, and you simply snap them around the muzzle ends. The Torki or Prada never knew about this advance warning feature because they can't see into infrared frequencies either."

Sarge's own professional critique provided him with other questions. "If the helmet plasma bolts have a short focal length, they will spread and have a shorter range. Won't we still need plasma rifles for long-range shots? Then, if we carry pulse rifles, as we have from the war's start, our armor's stealth is offset when the weapon and its heat profile give us away. To hide from a Dragon, for example, we sometimes had to disarm and drop our best weapon. I don't think the super stealth you showed us that first day will be as useful if we have to fight without our rifles."

Maggi looked exasperated. "God, you men are such a pain in the ass! We poor women could never think of all these tough warfare related questions, could we?"

"Don't be hard on yourself, Maggi. You haven't been in combat yet." Sarge foolishly thought this would mollify her.

Instead, she walked over to where the sample suit was hanging, next to a normal looking plasma rifle hanging on clothes hook by its strap. She lifted a thin elastic chord that extended from the rifle's quantum controlled trigger lock. She pulled it over to the suit's chest plate, and plugged it into a small slot there, twisted and locked it in place.

She slipped the too-large helmet on her head, sent the activating mental command, and the helmet, her head, the detached suit, and the hanging plasma rifle effectively vanished, except for the strap on the hook, holding the weapon.

"Is that sneaky enough for you moron level geniuses?" The acidic voice came from the headless petite woman. Then the helmet, suit, and rifle reappeared, as did Maggi's head when she lifted the helmet clear.

"The chord activates the same stealth coating on the weapon when the suit is in that mode. The rifle also provides targeting data to a different reticle on your visual display, so you can see what it is aimed at, and what pulse level you have dialed in for the shot. You can manually pull the trigger, or mentally command the shot."

"I stand corrected." Sarge offered. "You seem to have cleverly anticipated a battle field need rather effectively."

"You mean you lay corrected, you buffoon."

Then she offered an explanation that took away a bit of her seeming battlefield expertise. "It wasn't all my idea. The Krall have always had the automatic sighting capability between their armor and rifles. Evidently they distain its use, preferring the manual mode, which helps them select warriors that genetically survive better because *they* selected their own target, fired before the enemy could, and did it all manually. I suggested that a stealth coating be added to the rifle, and activated with the suit."

The buffoon comment canceled Sarge's previous offer of congratulations. With a grin he said, "I guess half an idea was better than none."

Before Maggi struck back, Thad said, "I don't see a power pack large enough for that skinny suit's plasma generator, let alone adding on the other four radiant energy weapons, which also need considerable power. How many shots do we have before we need to recharge or swap power packs on the suit?"

She shrugged. "Coldar says we don't need to recharge the suit, but we can't fire all weapons at maximum strength at the same time. The plasma pulse is the largest drain, and we can fire the directed energy beams at only partial power if we are firing plasma bolts at a rapid rate. All four of the other energy beam weapons will fire at their lower designed maximum power if you don't use plasma."

Thad looked bemused. "There has to be a replaceable power source if we don't recharge. That seems like a serious weakness. We'd have to tote a lot of whatever the power packs are, and that will spoil our stealth unless they are also coated."

Maggi shrugged again. "I don't know physics, but there are no power packs. Coldar says the suit uses small quantum controlled alternate universe energy taps, whatever the hell that means."

Mirikami asked, "Did he mention tachyons?"

"Oh no," she stated firmly. "He only spoke of an ocean of energetic particles that move faster than light, of which just a few can power the suits."

Mirikami looked at the other three men. "A sea of faster than light particles in an alternate universe sounds like a description of Tachyon Space. I think the crabs have a miniature Trap field built into the suits. They might be able to catch the most common low-level tachyons at a fast enough pace to supply suit power."

Sarge countered that suggestion, "I didn't think you could set up a Trap field deep in gravity wells. You told me you caught the massive energy of the tachyons that the Flight of Fancy still used for power when it was in space. If they were ever released, you said it could never capture any to replace them because it can't lift out of the gravity well to form a stable Trap."

"That's true. We can't *trap* any tachyons with the energy to form a stable event horizon down here. Otherwise, we'd repeat the early disaster on Earth's Moon, when they learned how, accidentally, to make a huge crater on its far side. That was when scientists tried to build a tachyon driven power generation station on the moon.

"In Jump Drive class I recall that any strength tachyon can randomly tunnel into a weak Trap field at any time, and tunnel right back out. The more tachyons there are, the higher the probability of one passing through. Low energy tachyons are the most common in Tachyon Space, like our microwave background photons. At velocities greater than light, in our Universe those particles represent high energy. However, in too strong of a gravity field we never found a way to trap and curve them to stay inside our fields so we could draw energy from the more powerful particles. It's possible the Torki learned how to extract low levels of energy for powering suits, via technology of some race that the Krall defeated. It isn't a new idea to us, actually."

"How's that?" Dillon questioned. "When did we encounter this before?"

"From two examples," Mirikami said. "We never learned how millennia old Katushas are powered, yet we know those are all at least twenty thousand year old quantum devices. The Krall killed their Olt'kitapi makers that long ago and there are no batteries or charging points on them. Then there is the Raspani quantum disintegration or drilling device that doesn't have an obvious power source either."

Dillon summed it up pragmatically. "Regardless of how the suit's power source works, it's a gift horse we don't want to look in the mouth. Accept it as it is."

Sarge looked at him strangely. "What the hell does that mean about horses? You sound like Maggi spouting one of her old lame brain sayings." He'd forgotten who was in the room.

"Any more smart assed comments out of you Garland Reynolds," Maggi said in a warning tone, using the first name Sarge disliked, "and you will learn a number of other old sayings, of which I'm sure you'd rather remain blissfully ignorant."

Chuckling, Sarge started, "Sticks and stones…," but Maggi suddenly stepped close and grasped his hand, interrupting *his* old expression.

"Sarge," her small figure leaning over him managed somehow to look menacing. "You are physically connected to that med lab right now, so I'd think you'd do well to recall that its original purpose was to heal *injuries,* not install gene changes. Let me be the first to help you with your new Mind Tap exercises." She displayed her most dangerous sweet smile as she squeezed his hand in a painfully powerful grip.

"Open your mind to the pictures I'll send you with this list of old expression, as you lay there immobilized, remembering that you are completely helpless: *An ounce of prevention is worth a pound of cure. Roll with the punches. The bigger they are the harder they fall. Don't play with fire and you won't be burned. The female of the species is more deadly than the male,* and *dynamite comes in small packages.* Do you sense a common thread in the mental pictures linking *those* old sayings, dear Garland?"

Sarge shivered briefly, his eyes widening as each illustrating mental image arrived with each old saying. "Why yes indeed I do," he announced, with a fresh sense of enlightenment. "Thank you greatly my Lady. The fountain of your wisdom has poured forth, and I have learned from you. I shall now lie here quietly and think on your words, and contemplate my own navel before it unscrews and my butt falls off."

She nodded, patting his hand, wearing the same sweet sinister smile. "A wise decision."

"You are becoming a smart man," Dillon agreed with a grin, speaking from hard-learned experience.

A youthful physiology had clearly not mellowed Maggi's feisty temperament, or altered her combative nature. Some outside observers would probably say her new ability to rip an arm off a gorilla *might* have emboldened her. Although, anyone that knew her would note she had never needed a physical advantage to win her previous battles.

Her tongue and wit were her primary weapons, with minor retaliatory physical acts as a *fun* means of interaction with her friends. The definition of a "minor" retaliation depended on whether you delivered or received said *fun* retaliation. Dillon had once received a nerve jangling, paralyzing Jazzer shot to his groin, after he pushed an embarrassing witticism too far with Maggi. The retaliation was quite funny to her and others. Not so much for him at the time.

Mirikami lay there quietly, offering no wisecracks of his own. Aside from wanting these upgrades to complete as quickly as possible for the upcoming combat missions, he had a new personal motivation to be tolerant of Maggi's jokes. He had been a bit sore with a pulled back muscle when he had climbed into the med lab last month. The dinner with Maggi had been more *educational* than anticipated.

This younger version of Maggi had recovered appetites *other* than food. The ninety- one-year-old Mirikami, with mere clone mods, couldn't easily keep up with the "dessert" an enthusiastic revitalized TG2 offered him, along with her home cooked dinner.

The two had shared affection for one another for years, and had conspired in private frequently, usually concerning matters regarding the future of the two domed cities of people they were determined to keep alive on Koban. However, their ages, responsibilities, and the tiring high gravity had conspired to keep their personal relations entirely platonic. Maggi was the first to experience this new lease on life that her Prada longevity and age regression mods had delivered, and she knew that Tet would receive them when he returned. She had placed other people's needs first for long enough.

She made her feelings known to Tet at dinner, offering him a marriage contract. He promptly accepted, it being only the second such contract he had entered into in his life, the first since leaving New Honshu as a young man. Thus, that agreement led to a late night celebration, which led to his pulled muscles and his subsequent insistence that he start with the new mods the *first thing* the next morning. At least as close to the "first thing" as Maggi would allow, and even then not until after a ten AM final breakfast "treat." He was definitely going to need his youth back.

Rafe stepped into the room to check on the progress of his "older" clients. "Gentle Men, how are you feeling now that you are awake? Any uncomfortable lumps I can add to your beds?" he asked jovially.

The med labs were designed to be as comfortable as they could be, and they shifted an unconscious body and moved pressure points to prevent bedsores.

However, after a month of lying there, the body's support points grew tender no matter how often they were changed.

"You can damn well move the huge lump that you put under my left hip." Thad griped.

"Well, good news friends. The month of immobilization, which I did for you four has proven more beneficial than I expected. Maggi, when she did the first Koban mods, was allowed to get up once a day for a real meal, and then returned to the med lab after an hour or two. She experienced some bouts of pain and discomfort when up and awake, and her movements seem to have retarded the work the nanites were doing when she got out, stretched and ate real food.

"You four have made faster progress, despite receiving more mods at once. I can let you step out after a few checks on your vital signs, provided you return to sleep here for eight hours per day for another week. The age reversal process needs more time to access every living cell, and to regrow youthful tissues. The Prada mod will hold you at whatever physical age you have when we stop your regression. Maggi took off another five years the first week you went into the tanks."

Sarge said, "Damn. Bring me a mirror. I want to see how young and good looking I am now."

Aldry had walked in while Rafe was talking. "Alas, Sarge, there are some miracles that even modern medicine and nanites can't perform. Unfortunately, you still look seventy- five."

"Hey! I was forty-nine when I entered your damned torture chamber."

"Oh, really? That is truly tragic. I must have inserted an IV needle backwards." That elicited general laughter and confirming, but false, observational comments of Aldry's assertion. Reynolds looked like a young recruit.

"Very funny. When do you and Rafe take your turns in these tubs? I want a chance to annoy *you*."

"We won't go in until we complete all of the upgrades on the TGs that are going on the first missions against the Krall. They don't need age regression, and they already have TG mods. We only need an hour to start them on the TG2 MEEN enhancements, which is what the TG1's are now calling them."

Before anyone could ask, she explained. "MEEN stands for Mind, Eyes, Ears, and Nose mods, from the Koban derived genes. They wait a couple of weeks for those to complete while they walk around. They won't receive the Prada age prevention mod until they reach twenty-five years of age."

"Well, I want to see how close to twenty-five I am now." Reynolds persisted.

Maggi sniped at him. "You definitely look more infantile, or perhaps that's only due to how you sound. Rafe just told you that you could get up in a few minutes. Be patient, or I'll shove you outside naked and let you sunburn. If you haven't noticed, the replaced, younger skin is pink, and your tans are gone."

Rafe had manually verified Dillon had proper vital signs, and was detaching some of the devices that had kept him fed, healthy, and his muscles toned while he slept. "The sunburn remark is valid, Gentle Men. After you wash away the dead cells, apply a cream I'll give you to induce rapid melanogenesis, to protect and darken your skin. It won't leave you as dark as your tan was before, but it will protect your skin from sunburn until natural exposure completes the job."

Rafe cleared each of the other three men to exit their med labs, handing each a tube of the melanin inducing cream. Mirikami lowered the side of his case to swing his legs out, wearing only a pair of white shorts. He looked at his legs, which were slightly darker than Dillon's pasty legs only because he was naturally darker by birth. Nevertheless, he looked more pallid than he had even as a Spacer, who spent little time under the suns along the routes he flew.

One pleasant surprise was seeing the flat stomach, and shorts that formerly stayed snugly in place about to slide off his hips. He might not have physically regressed all the way to his mid-twenties, but he was at the weight he held when he was in his late twenties.

He felt very light on his feet. "Why did you lower the gravity in here, Rafe?" They were on the Flight of Fancy, and he assumed the gravity was reduced in this expanded infirmary and rejuvenation ward for some medical reason.

"What do you mean?" Rafe looked puzzled. "We didn't adjust the gravity."

Maggi knew what he meant. "It's the new you, Tet. You didn't experience the carbon fiber muscle growth as it gradually infused your clone mod muscles. This is the first time you've felt the Koban carbon fibers at work. After you spend some time Mind Tapping with those of us that also have the ripper frilling genes, your thought processes will greatly speed up. For now, focus on your enhanced senses, such as hearing or sense of smell. They'll be working now, and you can sense things you never noticed before. You hear that high pitched thrum?"

"Yes. I assumed it was my tinnitus, which I sometimes experience due to an explosion and depressurization injury, which slightly damaged my inner ears in the Navy, many years ago."

"It's actually something causing a high frequency throb in the air handling system. I showed Chief Haveram the area where I thought it came from, since it's annoying as hell and in the ultrasonic range. He couldn't hear it, but he's in a med lab in the next room, and when he gets out, I'm going to push him to find the damn cause and make it stop. I can hardly sleep on the ship anymore because of that constant thrum. That is a gift of your new wolfbat hearing."

He raised his nose. "Another air processing issue is the smell. What *is* that?"

She laughed. "That's you, my dear man. It's also the three smelly brutes that emerged from cocoons when you did. The med labs remove your waste products, but you haven't bathed as the old skin was replaced. You wouldn't have noticed the sound or mild odor before you had a predator's senses. A group shower for all of you. NOW!"

As the four men meekly headed for the connecting shower room, Mirikami asked another question. "Rafe, Aldry, I have ripper vision enhancements, right? Why don't I see better now? It seems ordinary to me."

Aldry, still standing by the door, waved her hand over a wall sensor and the overhead light panels went out, leaving the only visible light source coming from the small readouts and telltale lights inside the four med labs. To Mirikami and the other three men, it grew dark for less than a second, when suddenly the room appeared bright again, with less intense colors, but everything and everyone easily visible. The ends of the med lab casings looked brighter now, a glowing shade of yellow versus the silver gray before the lights went off. He realized it must be from the warmth of their power supplies heating the outer shell.

When he looked back at Maggi and the others, he saw they also had faint yellow to red glows on their bodies, with shades of green to blue on their clothing and shoes. He knew they were in a darker area of the room, where his infrared senses must be picking them out. Above the med labs the internal small lights, as dim as they were, provided his light sensitive vision with enough photons to see clearly the fine-lined patterns in the cool ceiling panels.

The lights came back up, and his vision quickly returned to normal, without his being blinded by the returning glare. "The transition is faster than I'd expect," he noted.

Rafe answered the unasked question. "The superconducting links to your brain operate far faster than before, Tet. It's still possible to flash blind you for a moment, or to put you briefly into total darkness, but the TG2's we've tested say it lasts only a second at most."

Nodding, Mirikami was about to enter the shower room when Maggi, a mischievous look on her now youthful, pretty pixie face, *innocently* asked, "Want me to come in and scrub you down again, dear, just like before you went into that box?"

He glanced back quickly but didn't answer, and with a pained red-faced expression, turned and stepped through the doorway. Maggi naturally found a way to help her future contract husband get over his embarrassment. "Wow, we can see that blush all the way down to your butt, lover. Better put on a lot of that tanning cream."

****

The planning stage of Krall territory raids was finally underway. Between the Planetary Union scouting reports, and the information from the Torki and Prada, the three most critical weapon production worlds had been selected. However, those targets required separate preparatory raids, to enable the Kobani to conduct evacuations of the forced laborers from the manufacturing worlds. If they were left behind, the Krall would force them to rebuild the factories and resume production, or probably slaughter them if that wasn't possible, and start production elsewhere.

Coldar, standing on the Bridge of the Mark of Koban, which was now parked on Haven, described the first preliminary targets, two Torki shipyards, to Mirikami and his mission planners. The coastal shipyards were located on a former Torki colony world, left operational by the Krall after the conquest because their giant ships proved useful. "The only ships now built at Toborkiti colony are the largest ones of a very old design, which can be partly filled with sea water. They now are described only as migration ships."

He stated an often-repeated truism. "The Krall are very wasteful of ships, lives, and material. From previous reports that reached my lodge, back when dome construction both here and on Koban brought new workers from different Krall clan worlds, we learned that the migration ships were being replaced at a rate of two of them every five orbits of Toborkiti. The maximum rate of construction of one ship, per yard, requires nearly two orbits, so the Krall keep construction in progress at all times. Krall pilots recklessly fly them manually, rather than allow a Torki pilot do so with automation to assist. Therefore, rusting wrecks are to be seen on many worlds. Migration is a dangerous time for us.

"That type of ship design was used at the height of our own spacefaring era, thousands of years ago, and we have never improved the design because the Krall will not let us do so. They normally use them to move a lodge of my people, or several Prada villages, to a new world along with the technology we use, such as tools, instruments, and automated production facilities. If they do not need to fill the water tanks for moving a Torki lodge, they can carry several Prada villages, and one of their modular starter factories."

"Coldar, do those ships use the faster Krall Jump capability, using T-squared Tachyon Space?" Mirikami asked.

"No. We did not have that technology when we were conquered, and the Krall have permitted no basic modifications since. The Krall pilots and warriors that monitor and insist on flying them always complain of the lack of speed and efficiency. Clan leaders assign low status warriors to guard and fly migration ships. Their loss of time and of ours, or even of an entire ship because of a bad landing, is unimportant to the clans when they fight very long wars."

Mirikami looked worried. "Well, that low Jump speed creates a logistics problem for us when we raid production planets deeper into Krall controlled space. We can't safely use our clanships to tow even one ship that large and massive into the T-squared level, nor do we have enough ships anyway. We can't use our three modified ships to raid, or for pulling multiple migration ships for evacuation, or use them for resupply of those slow boats.

"We need to provide food, water, and sanitation for as many as twelve to fifteen migration ships if we conduct three raids at once. Those big ships will leave an easier to follow wake through Tachyon Space for the Krall, so they can't travel a direct route. They will have to take a longer more devious route to prevent them from being followed back here. That could take months, on overcrowded ships.

"I have plenty of volunteer Spacers that want to contribute to the war effort, and they can fly the migration ships back here, if we can provide them some resupply. Coldar, perhaps as a demonstration of your new freedom, some of your best qualified people would want the honor of landing them on Haven?"

Coldar bounced his body several times, in apparent excitement. "The capture of our ships from the Krall would make them human property, if we Torki understand your concept of victory and property ownership from warfare."

Mirikami shook his head, and then in case that wasn't understood, said "No. Those ships are the product of your people's labor. They are property that was taken from you, and you are our new allies. They will be yours when they arrive here."

The bouncing increased for a moment, and then halted. "We will have pilots practicing in a simulator we can build before you depart. This will represent an important event for us. We offer our thanks to you."

"Helping you is our pleasure, Coldar. How many reserve migration ships do you think are parked in orbit at Toborkiti? You previously told Maggi that perhaps five migration ships would be enough for evacuation at each planet where we will try to rescue Prada and Torki workers."

Coldar made a left claw twirl as he estimated. "There were previously twenty or twenty-five ships kept in storage orbits in reserve. The usual ship losses, caused mostly by bad, hard surface landings by careless low status Krall pilots, are most often replaced by new construction rather than refurbishing and using an older ship from the reserve. They keep the old ships in reserve except when a massive movement of Krall clans is planned, to move nearer a new war zone. I suspect that may have happened when the war with your species started, and our small neglected population here was not included. Most migration ships used in recent millennia, if intended only for a single planet's move of a clan are of newer construction. The older orbiting ships are saved, cold and powered down, for when a massive shift of many clan resources is required." He spoke of a recent use of multiple migration ships that he had heard described.

"Your human named Sarge told us of a world that the Krall captured for a base. If the Krall did as they have in other wars, probably eight or more migration ships would have been used to move warriors, workers, supplies, and factories of the major clans to that Krall base you call K1. Repeat trips would move lesser clans. When the invasions increase to more worlds, more clans will move closer to participate and they will capture other worlds for bases. They will need more migration ships to move the workers and factories.

"Unless human fighting ships attacked and destroyed the migration ships, they all will have been returned to Toborkiti for safekeeping. You will need a minimum of three rescue ships per raided planet, and four or five of them would reduce crowding, and increase speed of loading."

"Coldar, our information told us that the PU Navy never attacked the giant migration ships when they were at K1. The admirals held the belief that such huge ships would have powerful offences and defenses."

Waving a claw, Coldar discounted that fear. "They are slow and unarmed. The ships that would most recently have been used at K1 are going to be the easiest to awaken at Toborkiti, and will be the newest built. Those ships should be found in the highest orbits around Toborkiti, because the Krall follow old habits and traditions. The next newest ships will be in slightly lower orbits, where the previously used ships would be stored. The most ancient ships are parked in the lowest orbits, and after a thousand or more years will need many repairs before they can be used. Prada and Torki in suits would be sent to do that dangerous and difficult work."

"When these ships are shut down, how are they reactivated?"

"They use a different design fusion reactor from human and Krall ships. However, if you have the right mixture of heavy hydrogen for fuel, and a high current external power source, they are started in a similar way to Krall fusion reactors. To start the reactors, you fill their plasma chambers from a hydrogen fuel supply of double heavy hydrogen atoms, with a one percent trace of radioactive triple heavy hydrogen, and provide the starting current to build the magnetic confinement and compression fields. After that, fuel feed and ship systems operation is almost automatic if the computer controls are activated.

"All clanships have power terminals inside the lowest deck. Long power cables are kept on the migration ships, stored inside a large hatch close to the main reactor and fuel storage. Connect the power cable between the clanship and the main fusion reactor, and I will show you by your Mind Tap how to follow the startup sequence."

Mirikami touched a hand to a mandible Coldar offered. The information was transferred in seconds.

Mirikami saw one time constraint problem. "The ships can activate the Traps for tachyons soon after the main reactor starts. Heat and power to the rest of the ship can follow after a Jump energy tachyon is caught and a ship gets away. As you know, without reaching into the higher level of Tachyon Space, the time required to catch a random high-energy tachyon with energy for a minimal Jump of such a huge ship can average one or two hours of human time units. It sometimes will go faster, but not always. The fastest possible escape from Toborkiti is important if the Krall learn we are stealing the ships. I don't know if we can put crews on them quickly enough without their seeing. After they escape, we can fully supply the ships. I'm sorry, but we will probably be unable to rescue your people on the surface of the planet on this first mission. We can return for them later."

"That was explained to me by your sub leaders, Tet. Thad, Dillon and Sarge helped us understand how strategic planning decides the order of how the war is conducted. The greater good to my people will be to first save a large number of those on the clanship production worlds, delivering greatest damage to the Krall supply of war material."

"I'm glad that was explained. We are not abandoning your migration ship builders, but they will not be at great risk from the Krall. We are not going to leave any intact migration ships in orbit when we depart. Therefore, your workers will be needed alive, to make more of the giant ships, which is a slow process."

"My people understand that logic."

"I want to take as many of those migration ships as we can. There are many more flight-qualified officers than we need, eager for their chance to go along and bring them back. Particularly now that they have reached TG2 level. They are far less frightened of the Krall.

"Another aspect of the rescue mission is resupply of the migration ships for the long travel time from so deep into and out of Krall controlled space. If we capture unattended clanships from unsuspecting Krall domes first, we can use those to ferry supplies, and rendezvous with the big ships at intermediate star systems. The clanships can then return here faster, carrying some workers to ease the crowding. They would pick up more supplies on Haven or Koban and make repeat trips."

Coldar considered that proposal a moment. "You say you can't risk taking Prada or Torki on your three ships for the raids to destroy the shipyards and the hammers, because you had us remove the acceleration restrictors. In the event of space combat, if we were aboard we would not survive the stresses even if you remained within the Krall's own physical limits. However, I presume operations to capture empty clanships and migration ships will not require high velocity space combat. How will your people arrive to take possession of those ships?" He spread his claws wide.

Mirikami thought he saw where this was leading. "Our existing three ships will deliver the capture forces for taking the clanships, and the flight crews for those, and crews for the unguarded migration ships. Our fighting ships will provide firepower to protect them if needed, and a means of escape if required. However, these are covert operations that should attract as little attention as possible."

Coldar made the carapace bob that was intended to mimic a human head nod. "Could not representatives of Prada and Torki travel safely with you to Toborkiti, and transfer to the slow migration ships? We would already be present to explain to the workers you wish to rescue. After the fighting raids succeed, we can tell them who you are and where they will be taken. We will be living proof that you can be trusted. There will be trained Torki pilots on board for the more delicate hard surface landings."

Wister quickly agreed with that proposal, and offered another reason. "The Prada villages may refuse to go with you because the Rulers never told them of a new Krall home world, where they could someday serve them. Older and more senior Prada, such as my sister Nawella and I, might be able to convince them to board the ships if we tell them that the destination is to be the future Ruler home star system."

"Wister, you surely understand that we Kobani are dedicated to never allowing that to happen. Right?" Mirikami wasn't going to lie to manipulate potential allies into joining with him.

"I do understand. You also must understand that the Krall Rulers have actually said that Koban *will* be their future home. That will be the truth as stated by the Rulers. If you Kobani change that truth in the future, we Prada can deal with the new reality at that time." It was a technical loophole, but one the Prada and Mirikami could each accept.

Showing his agreement, Mirikami said, "We will need to coordinate the migration ship arrivals at the target worlds while the raids are still in progress and suppressing the local Krall defenders. You would have to start the Jumps before our attacks begin, since we can travel faster. Let me talk it over with my staff."

A quick consensus followed from Thad, Dillon, and Sarge, all in favor of that mission change, and thereby involving both species in directing part of their people's respective futures, and taking on some of the risk. Mirikami asked Sarge to handle the coordination between the Torki and Prada, and with the Spacers who

Mirikami would assign to the migration ship operation. Sarge and the aliens would have to work out the details of the secondary supply phase for the migration ships with the clanship crews.

The rest of the command staff now needed to focus on the actual raids. This was the most responsible job Sarge had accepted since his original rescue from the Krall. It seemed TG2 status had boosted his mental self-confidence as much as his body. His country boy slang talk was seldom heard now, unless it was at a poker table, trying to fool one of the spec ops boys into thinking he was some dunderheaded hick.

Mirikami, Dillon and Thad, left the Bridge and joined Marlyn and Noreen, who were with the spec ops group and the leaders of the young Kobani TG2 teams. They were already gathered in the conference room below the Bridge.

Mirikami explained the inclusion of Torki and Prada to them. "We have to capture additional clanships for resupply of the slow migration ships, and to get Torki and Prada representatives to the raid sites to obtain worker cooperation. The clanship theft will have to be done as quietly and sneakily as possible by stealing parked ships from tarmacs around Krall domes, using minimal noise and fighting, as we *tried* to do on K1. I don't think K1 will be as vulnerable a target as it was the first time, because the Krall don't take well to looking inept. They will surely be on guard there now. I think remote Krall worlds with low population finger clans could be prime candidates. Their ships sitting out on tarmacs might be completely unguarded.

"Wister gave me a list, by Mind Tap, of some Krall nest worlds for small clans that sounded like good candidates sixty years ago, the date of his last outside source of information. Even the Krall appear to change habits, homes, and social customs at a slower pace compared to us hyperactive and immature humans. Those small Krall colonies are probably still in the same places. Low population clan worlds should be the best bet for quick in and out operations." He turned to Trakenburg.

"Frank, I'd like you and Joe to plan and execute that particular operation, and I will deliver you there. You ten men have the most experience at stealth and bushwhacking. Please get back to me by tomorrow with a list of what resources in the way of additional TG2's and material you think you will need. Obviously, with Mind Tapping, the training of everyone involved will go extremely fast. Flight crews for each clanship prize have to be taken with us. At an absolute minimum, three more clanships are needed, but preferably many more if you can swing that. We need to provide full support for as many as three simultaneous rescue missions from the three Krall production worlds we will raid, and there could be up to fifteen migration ships involved."

Trakenburg was pleased to get a mission right out of the starting gate, which matched up with spec ops training. "This would need to happen first then, Tet, so the supply side can be ready for supporting the rescue operations that follow immediately after your raids. Those clanships will need to come here to get supplies."

"Yes. We don't want to initiate the three main attacks until we have the two pieces we need to provide for the rescues in place. However, to avoid spreading the word too soon to the Krall that humans are operating inside their territory, at widely separated planets, we can't let much time pass between the capture of clanships and migration ships, and the start of the main raids."

"Tet, you may have to start the raiders on their way before the other parts are in place."

"Probably, Frank. After I take you to get the clanships we need, one of the other ships will deliver the flight crews for the migration ship theft.

"The migration ships should be easier to take because they are in high parking orbits around a former Torki colony they called Toborkiti. There might be some investigation by clanships of the Tanga clan if we don't answer radio hails. Coldar says this old prestigious clan has had control of that world for many breeding cycles. However, the total Krall population on the planet was typically low, because it has low gravity, and is cooler and wetter than the Krall prefer. That's not surprising since it was a planet originally settled by the Torki.

"It's possible that the typical Krall's *mind your own business* attitude between clans will delay their curiosity, and put off investigation until the migration ships are ready to leave orbit. Coldar indicates that it might take less than half an hour to power up a migration ship, and I think it could require one to two hours to capture an energetic enough Jump tachyon for those big diameter ships to make a large enough Event Horizon to Jump. Since the Prada and Torki want to send representatives with the migration ships, they can handle bringing the craft fully on line, warming them up, and testing their systems. We'll place a human flight crew on board as well."

He didn't say it, but the human presence was for more than a backup flight crew. They could defend the ships from Krall boarders if that were needed, and any deviation from the intended use of the ships by an alien crew would be avoided. Trust them, but ensure compliance.

Longstreet had a question. "How will the two ship capture teams know when their separate operations have succeeded? Will you simply dart off to start your raids? Where will we meet each other?"

Mirikami grinned. "Ain't used that long range Mind Tap when entering and leaving a Jump Hole yet have you?"

Joe flushed. "Nope. I think we need to practice that locally before we do the real Jumps. We need to establish some sort of order to the windows for communication, and set up a way to subdivide the message workload to fewer individuals. When you Jumped back here from Poldark, you had a bit of a mishmash of messages from multiple people on more than one ship, targeted at too many different individuals. The information overlapped, and it required considerable sorting. We'll have more vital messages coming, and we don't want delays and confusion."

Thad pointed a gleeful finger. "I believe I just heard Joe, a former communications officer, describe how to set up better communications. Sounded *just* like a volunteer to me."

Longstreet laughed. "Damn! I thought I'd been in long enough not to do that anymore. Fine, I'll do the boring job and sort it out. I'll need at least three ships to Jump around the system to decide how many designated signal senders and receivers we'll need."

Dillon reminded him that the former smugglers ship and now a freighter, the Falcon, was also available for local Jumps. With out-of-practice flight crews, training on the Mark, Avenger, and Beagle, there would be opportunities in local Jumps to refine the message process in the next two weeks. Two weeks being the target date to initiate the first of their multiple offensive actions against the Krall.

"Now for the meat of the missions," Mirikami stated. "The three worlds we intend to hit the hardest will be to halt critical weapons production. We all agree that clanships are the Krall's primary tool for delivering warriors and single ships, defending their bases, hauling supplies, and engaging in space combat.

"There are two significant planets where the Torki and Prada know they were building and repairing clanships and single ships for at least the last several thousand years. Other factories on different worlds can switch to building them, but the needed supply of specific raw materials and metals requires those other worlds develop additional or new mining facilities, transportation for the raw materials, plus new plants for processing and smelting the ores. They would need to build more Torki operated high tech factories to manufacture the complex quantum control surface coatings for the ships, to keep them stealthy, as well as build the navigation and weapon control systems. The Torki that already know how to manufacture those and other key electronics will be gone from the old production worlds if our plans work.

"Migration ships to bring in worker replacements and factory modules from other Krall worlds will be in short supply, if not totally absent. We certainly will not leave any usable migration ships behind when we depart Toborkiti."

Carson, listening and learning had to ask a question. "Sir, won't the Krall make the Torki workers increase the rate of building migration ships? Shouldn't we destroy the ship yards and evacuate the workers there as well?"

"Reasonable question, but that's not worth the time and diversion of our limited resources to do that yet. Migration ships normally take over a year to construct, and are not immediately useful for conducting the war. What the Krall would need are workers moved to where they can quickly make more clanships and single ships. We won't leave the existing factories and facilities operational to do that where they currently build them, so putting new workers there isn't going to restart things quickly, even if they do have the mining and other infrastructure in place. They'd still have to bring in a modular starter factory, which also takes time to assemble and expand.

"I hope the Krall won't have many migration ships at their disposal to move workers to any planet for large scale ship building. Even when they do get workers to a designated new planet, they will be building infrastructure to prepare for building ships. In the time window we have for a surprise strike, halting clanship building and destroying Eight Balls takes away the greatest means the Krall have of directly applying offensive pressure on human worlds."

"What about the probably tens of thousands of clanships already built, Sir?"

Mirikami shrugged. "That's a problem Human Space has that we can't solve for them, and which only the Planetary Union can try to counter. They have to increase clanship attrition, while we try to prevent clanship production. General Nabarone, when we give him the word that we did what we planned, will start pushing for new ships for the Navy, to go after the roughly ten thousand clanships on K1 for example. I assure you, it's a position he will find most uncomfortable, because he's also made no friends with Lady Admirals."

They all smiled and chuckled at that accurate remark.

"However, his planetary defense forces have only been marginally successful at knocking down a handful of clanships per year at Poldark. The Navy needs to make a serious dent in their numbers while Krall pilots are still allowed to operate recklessly, as if there were plenty of material to replace losses. That attitude will not last long when the ship shortages are recognized by clan leaders."

He added, "The enemy can make Prada and Torki slaves build all the laser and plasma cannons, rockets, trucks, body armor and hand weapons they like. If they can't get them and the warriors that use them to new worlds to invade in massive numbers, the war will slow down. That could take years to accomplish, and we may lose more planets to invasions.

"If we are successful, and we find more people willing to accept our Koban gene mods, the ranks of the Kobani will swell, and we can expand our efforts to diminish the Krall's supply of war material."

Noreen, eager to discuss the role of the raiders said, "Tet, I'm ready for the nuts and bolts of how we will conduct the raids. Who goes where and does what?"

"OK. Here is the general outline. A raider will consist of each one of our three converted clanships, the Mark, Avenger, and Beagle, each packed with a thousand TG2s and their equipment, and four Dragons per ship. We have the ones we brought with us from Poldark and some that were assembled from what the Prada had stored as spare parts on Haven.

"I'll lead the raid to the shipyard on the planet I've labeled CS1, Noreen you have CS2, the other clanship site. Marlyn, you will have the Eight Ball production site.

"We will not do the Jumps to conduct the major raids before the extra clanships and migration ships are ours. However, after they are acquired, we three will Jump at staggered intervals to reach our target worlds nearly simultaneously, just before the migration ships can get there. The migration ships will proceed to the raid sites early, from where we steal them. They won't come here first. That would take too long, and the Krall might figure out we plan to steal some of their workers. I don't think they would guess where, but I don't want them to even suspect.

"The captured clanships are much faster, and they *could* make a round back trip here easily, if that particular operation moves as fast as I hope. I'll leave that decision to those flight officers."

He referred to a hologram chart of Krall territory, projected in the air of the slightly darkened room at the end of the long conference table. As Mirikami spoke, Jakob highlighted the described stars for visual reference from Koban, which was marked by an exaggerated size teal-colored light.

"Because the method we'll use to eliminate the shipyards on each of the two planets is similar, I'll describe what my own raiders will be doing, and you can extrapolate that to the other shipyard, Noreen."

"The Mark will go to CS1, designated as clanship production world number one. Not even the Prada or Torki know what the long dead species, called the Doloria, named their home world." A white light flickered at the proper location, deep in the Krall volume of space. Noreen, you will go to CS2, a former Raspani colony world, nearer to us than CS1."

A green light flickered for that star system, showing it was closer to Koban. "CS1 is roughly seven thousand light-years away on the far side of Krall territory. CS2 is three thousand light-years closer."

He gave them time to look at the relative locations, and then resumed his briefing. "CS1 was the main home nest for the Graka clan for five thousand years and had vast mineral resources for clanship and weapons production. The seat of the Graka clan moved about six thousand years ago to a cleaner world, inside former Raspani settled space. They did that to escape environmental pollution, and to move closer to some other war at that time. CS1 is a worn out manufacturing planet, raped of much of its natural resources, and its environment ruined. I'm told it is unpleasant to look at or to live there."

He dug into his newly organized mental notes for data on CS2. "The second shipyard is also on the coast of an ocean, on a warm and drier, almost one G gravity world that was the home of a race called the Piltcons, who never colonized another star system. The race's name and world is only recalled because they are described with snorting amusement in Krall clan histories." Humor made a rare and memorable appearance in that history of destruction, death and bragging.

"As K1 is a Krall base in Human Space, CS2 was also once a base for a long ago war with another nearby species, fought long after the Krall exterminated the hapless Piltcon people. Naturally, the Krall don't remember the planet's original name nor did they create one of their own. After the war of extinction of the next species, the Mordo clan claimed the right to maintain a clanship production facility on the former base. It had an agreeable warm dry climate, orbiting a slightly red star, plenty of untapped mineral resources, and the gravity was a bit higher than for an average habitable world. It has a rate of ship production and facility size similar to CS1, and its environment is now as bad as that of CS1.

"The following description of the CS1 facility is generic enough to CS2 that I'll leave the specific details and minor differences to Noreen and her staff to sort through." Mirikami saw Noreen, Dillon and Carson all nod. *The family that fights together stays together,* he thought dryly.

He continued. "Now that the biosphere has been polluted, the Krall don't maintain a large warrior presence on either CS1 or CS2, counting on their faithful

Prada slaves to toil on for them, and the Torki have no other option despite their lack of love for the Krall. Each shipyard typically would build, or repair, roughly a hundred clanships per year. That represented the normal Krall rate of waste, and a gradual population expansion. However, they could build at least twice that many clanships if the need arises. Humans have created a greater need. Because of losses in the war with us, they must be producing or repairing closer to a hundred and twenty clanships per year now, but well fewer than what they could build.

"The Navy briefed us that the Krall actually are still recovering from the thousands of clanship losses on K1, back when the PU Navy was willing to hit them there. They primarily moved reserves to replace losses. They apparently have increased production slightly, but not close to the maximum. After Rhama's near destruction, they believe they have taught us to follow the *proper* pace of exactly the type of war they want. We will disabuse them of that notion."

He looked around the room, picking out Thad and Ethan, who both would go with him to CS1. "Wister and his sister Nawella have never been to the remote CS1 shipyards, nor have any Prada they have ever met. However, it was told to them by Prada that migrated from near there, that Graka clan retains control, but never has more than ten thousand, in *octal* numbers, of warriors and pilots based there. That is four thousand ninety-six in decimal numbers. CS2, a Mordo clan world, maintains similar warrior and test pilot numbers. A thousand TG2's should be able to hold them at bay while we demolish the yards and parts factories.

"Clanship construction is spread out for miles along the coastal area, to provide multiple lodge locations for the Torki technicians by the sea. As you know, they move after several generations have returned to the original lodge from the sea.

"The Prada live underground in three large factories and many others in a single high domed aboveground facility, where the polluted air and water can be filtered and cleaned. They grow edible plants and trees for grub bark worms, and have taller trees for aerial housing support as they built on Haven. Each of the three factories branch off from beneath that Prada dome. This is true for CS2 as well. The Krall don't change things that work well for them, except for their own bodies, so that factory and dome arrangement should still be in place. We can push the Prada from the factories into the domes for evacuation to a migration ship, parked on the tarmac. The Torki will swim from their lodges to any nearby floating migration ship.

"The Krall inspect and test fly new clanships and single ships, and train novices from various clans that have completed combat training and have shown an aptitude to their parent clans as pilots. The Krall nearly all live in a single dome in an environmentally protected region, a two or three hour shuttle flight from the shipyards. The Krall train and test fly clanships and single ships at their own domes, and only go to the shipyards to take possession of completed craft after the Torki have installed the electronics and quantum controlled features.

"As soon as a clanship is ready for delivery, it is ferried to K1, or wherever a clan had been allocated a replacement ship. They don't store clanships in large numbers where they are built. That's unfortunate, because we could knock a bunch of them out sitting on tarmacs or in orbit. We will go out with a maximum load of anti-ship missiles, over a thousand twenty-four each. Most of those are reloads, so if we get into a shooting match, some TG2s will be very busy refilling the four stack missile feeders on the thirty-two launchers.

"The Krall also maintain a physical presence in the Prada domes at the shipyards, right at the top levels, reserved just for them, as they once did in Prime City back when it was called Koban Prime. They will be our first target, to kill or capture the Krall we find there, Mind Tap any that wear gray or blue uniforms for information, and to try to knock out any communications they have. The latter may be a waste of time if the warriors have their own com buttons. Those com sets have enough range to call for help from their home dome. We'll go in wearing our new armor in stealth mode, and presumably, they won't even know we are there until they hear the shooting. They will see us land a ship close to the Prada dome, but when the portals open, it won't look like anyone came out.

"While some of us rush to the top dome levels, dozens of demolition teams will go down to each underground factory to set explosives at key points. Coldar's engineers have built carry boxes with the same coating as our armor when activated. The real risk is setting the demolition boxes down and forgetting where they are before you switch off the invisibility.

"There is salvageable vital production equipment in the factories that cannot be easily replaced that we need to specifically blow up. The demo teams will also destroy the computers and databases that are used to direct the automated machining, fabricating, and assembly equipment.

"One particularly easy and destructive step is to open the underground factories to flooding by seawater. We will blow open the cooling water pipes and use the circulation pumps to draw in water. That will finish off the factories for good with saltwater corrosion. We found that in the abandoned and sea flooded factory under Hub City, and even in the freshwater intrusions below Prime City. The water caused considerable damage. Of course, on Koban they sat untouched for at least sixty years. However, on CS1 and CS2, we hope there won't be many workers left to recover anything, and pump them out. Possibly no migration ships will be found to bring more workers with new modular factories.

"Even when power fails to the cooling water pumps, Wister says the ruptured pipes will allow the ocean to continue to pour into the below sea level factories. This should completely flood all ten levels in a few days. That will ruin most of the machinery, instruments, and some tools. The factories are buried by designed, more protected from enemy missile and bombing attacks. However, the internal pumps to keep them dry will be destroyed by us. They can stand up to mild condensation with humidity control and Prada maintenance, but not flooding. Apparently none of their enemies were ever able to get inside to do what we plan to do."

He looked towards Marlyn, who had Maggi, Alyson and Jorl Breaker with her as staff. He'd been unable to keep Maggi out of the fray. It was tempting to tell her she was now too damned young to go. Due to her small size and pixie face, wreathed in the blond hair she had shortened again, she hardly looked older than the now twenty-year-old Alyson. He knew that if he even suggested she stay on Koban, even if he was motivated by concern for her safety, that he wouldn't be hurt physically (*probably, I think, I hope*), but his own twenty-five-year- old renewed urges would certainly take a serious hit tonight and for many nights to come. Therefore, she was going!

"Marlyn, your mission to the former Botolian home world, where the Eight Balls are made, involves fewer ships and people, and relatively few Torki to rescue. The Stodok clan, which controls that world and provides Eight Ball production, is one we have never encountered personally. It's an old small clan, and apparently in decline due to major losses from bitter interclan rivalries and subsequent status loss. This is their last remaining bastion, since they captured this planet from the Botolians."

A flash of blue light in the hologram map showed the planet's relative location from Koban.

"However, your success has a greater imperative and immediate need. Each of the Eight Balls you find and eliminate has the potential of wiping out the life on an entire planet if they Jump them to human worlds, and use Normal Space Drive to boost them to an appreciable fraction of the speed of light. The railguns we brought with us from Poldark, and the diamond tipped uranium slugs, can destroy the Balls with a single hit provided you accelerate the Beagle towards them at eight hundred miles per second before you fire. The railgun adds the rest of velocity required, since these Eight Balls will only be at a relatively slow orbital speed where they are parked. Coming at you at near light speed would make any collision with them destructive, but being able to hit one coming from a random direction is a matter of chance.

"Coldar examined the slugs, and using his Olt and knowledge of the crystal structure of the collapsed matter, did a calculation that factored in the mass of the projectiles and the shearing angle of a diamond's tetrahedral plane to determine the impact pressure if it occurred at the hardest part of the carbon crystal. It requires a dead-on hit by the diamond tip at over a thousand miles per second. The diamonds will always shatter on impact, but at a certain high momentum, the surface of the collapsed matter's crystal structure will also shift very minutely in a tiny region.

"Even a few neutrons slipping out of place in the quantum mechanical matrix are enough to radiate a spider web crack through the entire crystal at nearly the velocity of light. It will release the enormous pressure that pushed it together over years of repeated gravity compression cycles, all at once. You need to shoot accurately from a safe distance as you approach, and then Jump the hell away before the slugs hit, and the atomic debris rips off the ship's stealth and radiation protection skin. There will be penetrating neutron radiation if that happens, which would kill all of you within days or hours."

"Damn, Tet. Why don't you sugar coat it for us?" Maggi complained.

"I did. You need to blow the gravity projectors first, and evacuate as many Torki as possible from the orbital station to the Migration ship. The Krall will probably have one or more clanships coming after you before you can find and take out all of the Eight Balls. You will have to fight them off while you search, and you don't want Prada and Torki aboard to slow you down as you maneuver.

"Coldar can't say how many of the slow to create objects have been stockpiled in orbit, how many have been used, or have self-detonated over the roughly thousand-year half-life of one of the collapsed matter crystals. He said that in roughly eleven hundred orbits, half of the objects will have spontaneously exploded."

Marlyn nodded. "He told us that previously and also that the sensors on our ship can detect the mass concentration of the Eight Balls pretty easily. We should be able to find them in orbit quickly."

"Assuming they actually left them in orbit near the planet. Remember, they spontaneously explode sometimes, so they may be spread out in the system. When you eliminate the Krall garrison on the orbital platform that guards the gravity projectors, you can ask the Torki where the Balls are. They can probably tell you where they were moved after completion. Coldar says there is only one lodge on the planet below, as far as he knows. Perhaps there is also a Prada village and factory. Neither he nor Wister has that answer. The Krall also maintain a small dome there. If you can complete a rescue mission on the ground without an extended fight, fine. The Eight Ball destruction is your priority. No more of them can be made within the next twenty years or so anyway. Blow up the gravity projectors, even if you have to leave some Torki behind, and they will never make any again."

Marlyn told him, "I'm sure we can handle it, Tet. I don't want to leave any Torki or Prada at the mercy of the Krall if we destroy their ability to make one of their most powerful weapons."

"OK. It's your mission." He told her.

"After we have the migration ships in our control, and clanships for their resupply, they will divide into three groups. Ideally, into two main groups of four or five migration ships each for CS1 and CS2, with two or three clanships for resupply. The migration ships will promptly Jump to the three planets where we should be attacking when they arrive. When the fighting is under control, and the workers are free, our Torki and Prada representatives can land and talk to them.

"As I said, Marlyn, you'll have a smaller number of migration ships, possibly only one if we can't get enough. You will have a clanship for resupply. Two if possible. They will meet up with you near the moon of that former Botolian world."

"Yes Sir."

"OK. That wraps up the mission outline. You should break out into groups to plan your own mission details, and then we can have another group meeting in a few days to coordinate between us by Mind Tap. All of us will then know what everyone else will do. If there are questions or problems, come to me ASAP and we will find a solution. Let's get to work."

Chapter 16: Ship Shape

Mirikami was honoring a request for one of his captains. "Marlyn, since the orbital Eight Ball mission has no *planned* surface action to suppress Krall opposition, your team of TG2s can also take on the mission to deliver and protect the flight crews that will steal the migration ships from orbit. There is ample time to do that first, destroy the ships we can't use, and *perhaps* rescue some Torki and Prada to place on one of the stolen ships. That craft would need some supplies right away, which you can take with you.

"As we discussed, the capture of those ships has a high priority for performing the other rescues, even before you try to rescue any of the local Torki that built them. If you do attempt a local rescue there, you have to measure the risk carefully. You can't sustain damage to the Beagle that might prevent you from Jumping to the old Botolian home world, your primary raid site.

"To give the migration ships a head start, you'll have the earliest departure from Koban to capture them. Those big turtles of ships will be slow to reach the other raid sites. Particularly to CS1 which is deepest into Krall territory. You will be transporting the Prada and Torki representatives for the rescue missions, including Coldar and Wister. Don't let yourself be drawn into a clanship fight involving stressful maneuvers before they are off loaded to a migration ship. Dead allies are poor allies." He grinned.

Chuckling, Marlyn answered him. "I'll try to keep that in mind. My crew will be thrilled to have more to do. I almost called them 'the kids,' but half of them are adults that have finished upgrades just this month. The real kids that went to Poldark are Mind Tapping with them every day, teaching them what was learned from their spec ops instructors."

She actually laughed as she described the activities she was seeing on the Beagle now. "It is positively harrowing to move up or down the damn stairs, with all of the running, flipping, and pretend shooting going on. It's like those that have absorbed the experiences from Poldark by Tap, refuse to believe they have these new abilities until they test them out for themselves. I was scolding a reckless individual, whom I thought was one of the Hub City kids I didn't know very well, when it proved to be *old* Max Hallow, from Prime City. The age regression made him nearly unrecognizable until I heard his voice. He was about to sass me back before he realized I was his age regressed captain. We *all* look like kids again, and the older we were when we changed, the more childlike we seem to behave."

Mirikami joined her laughter. "I'm seeing the same reckless older generation activity on the Mark, although I have a higher percentage of the youngsters with me that went to Poldark. Noreen mentioned the same effect this morning, with a social twist that at first shocked me, for some puritanical based reason I suppose."

"Ahh," ahhed Marlyn, knowing of the event. "That must be the awkward liaison she stumbled onto, in what she expected to be an unoccupied anti-ship missile storage hold. She was verifying a missed inventory entry, and found Clarice Femfreid and Yilini Jastrov practicing missile firing and targeting, in the nude. A noisy bull's eye strike apparently."

After some heartfelt laughter and exchanging a few amusing remarks, he told Marlyn that Yil claimed they were going to sign-the-line for a short-term contract for one child.

Mirikami offered another observation and prediction. "Clarice's husband was killed in Krall combat testing before the Fancy even arrived here. She was a member of my one and only combat team, and we have stayed friends. I know she had a couple of parings with uncontracted male friends over the years, but nothing that was long term or reproductive related. Our future prospects were bleak most of that time, and she never expected to be young again. None of us did.

"She has at least fifty years of experience over Yil, but they nearly look the same age now. We are going to see more of this. It's no more surprising than the start of contract marriages of two generations ago, when males were in extremely short supply. Older women often contracted with mothers of teenage boys for reproductive rights, provided they were over sixteen and the woman could pay, and the mother received a seventy percent share of the hefty contract fee as dowry. We simply grew away from the necessity of wide age gap reproductive matches, once there were more males around."

Marlyn agreed. "It's odd how quickly we shift our societal rules and morals to match what we intend to do anyway, no matter what the rules were previously."

"Did you hear from Aldry, or perhaps Rafe, that we Kobani are already expecting our first eleven TTGs? Genuine and True Third Generation children. Three conceptions came while we all were in Human Space, three more happened quickly after you returned with good news on our progress, and the rest were not reported until after Noreen and I came back."

"Wow! I didn't hear about all of that, Tet. So many so quickly. Who are the expectant parents?"

"I have no idea. Aldry and Rafe refused to say before the parents elect to speak out. Even then, the fathers may choose to stay anonymous. The contract records are sealed from the public unless the signers agree to the release. According to Aldry, the mothers will start to show earlier than normal, because the fetus will grow faster in the supercharged metabolisms they have now.

"Aldry also says the first pregnancies appear completely normal, other than seeming to be 15 to 20 percent farther along than for unmodified humans. I'm sure you recall that you and Noreen delivered your three bundles of joy almost a month early each time, and you only had clone mods and high metabolism. These new moms also have superconducting nerves and muscles."

Marlyn had a practical concern. "If the mothers are any of our raiders, I wish I knew. I don't want them endangered, and I recall that a high metabolism in us SGs made for rapid onset morning sickness for many of us. I briefly hated Noreen because she never had that, and I did, twice out of my three children. The expectant moms won't be very effective, if they're puking in their helmets."

"According to Rafe, none of the mothers-to-be are on the teams we're taking with us, based on threat of medical disqualification if they tried to go. However, there might be some recent conceptions none of the medical staff is aware of, or even the future mother knows about yet. Hell, Clarice and Yil might just have started a little rocket man."

Marlyn displayed a brief pause with a puzzled expression, and then, "Oh! You mean because of where Noreen found them." She laughed at the pun. "If so, I hope a boy isn't named that."

"Anyway, back to the first part of your double mission. How soon will you be ready to Jump? We will time the other launches around the departure times of the migration ships when you tell us you have them. My arrival to CS1 should be the most delayed, because of travel time of the rescue ships. I expect Trakenburg's men to complete the clanship captures in a few days, and then I'll have to wait somewhere closer to CS1 for the expected arrival of the big ships.

"I may arrange to hold up some of the other rescue ships at unoccupied star systems, as I'm going to do, to keep our attacks as close to simultaneous as practical. We can't let slow and unarmed migration ships get to any of the targets first and give anything away."

Marlyn was curious. "Tet, why is the coordination of such widely spaced attacks so integral to your planning? If you hold off a week longer to attack, waiting for your rescue ships to cover the distance to CS1, and Noreen is ready at CS2, any Krall couriers with the news of her raid would not be able to warn CS1 in time. So what if we miss starting a raid by a few days or a week? They won't be ready for us."

Mirikami considered her question and comments. "We have only recently discovered instantaneous long range communication as we enter and exit Tachyon Space. As far as we know, the Krall don't have or even suspect this capability. However, in cautions passed to me by the Torki and Prada, they insist that we probably have not seen all of the Krall's captured weapons or technology. If it couldn't be copied or reproduced by their slave labor, then the Krall would hold onto whatever one of a kind weapon they had until it was needed.

"When I prompted Coldar for clues about possible technology or weapons that humans have not encountered, he spoke of an old event recorded on Torki Olts, of lodges in one star system where something important and secret was expected to arrive or to happen. Most of the Torki working there were placed on migration ships and relocated, as an *efficient* use of them as resources, or so they were told. The few workers that were left behind were never part of any later migrations, and no Prada village or Torki lodge has ever been sent back to that once well-populated Krall system. The secret, whatever it was, has been kept from their slaves.

"Krall surprises have a nasty habit of being dangerous." He listed some. "At K1, the PU Navy didn't know about Eight Balls, Worms, the old orbital defense platforms, or the traceable wave fronts created by massive ship movements in Tachyon Space. That ignorance cost the fleets and Rhama dearly.

He pulled at his lip in deep thought. "This first strike of ours is too important to have it go badly. We may never have another chance as good as this one to hurt the Krall as seriously, and to do it without any advance warning. It costs us nothing to coordinate it this way, and it *might* possibly cost us dearly if we don't. Why take any risk not required?"

Seldom had a tug of a lip led to so prescient a thought, and yet indirectly brought unexpected destruction to so many victims, simply by the application of caution that the thought suggested.

****

The Beagle had been gone three days, and was within three more days of reaching Toborkiti. It was time for the Mark of Koban to lift for the first and closest of three Krall planets, each lightly occupied by specific minor clans. The Maldo, Dolbrin, and Kordak were finger clans with only a handful of domes on the conquered worlds they were given to settle, and they had only a minor presence in the joint clan council. They were mostly relegated to conducting raids on human worlds. On rare occasion, they had participated in an offensive on Bollovstic or Poldark. They had few resources beyond small weapons, armor, and vehicle manufacturing, and the original gifts of a nucleus of clanships, provided by their parent clans. Those were considered the softest targets for theft.

Between successful raids and culling weaker warriors, their ships would be parked on tarmacs, as they trained the next generation of novices, genetically the best they had produced or procured recently. After the surviving breeders of multiple raids had mated and nested, and the natural savage culling of the resultant thousands of cub hatchings had reduced their numbers to the toughest, the six to eight-year-old young killers were forcibly placed in training.

The pre-novices that were temperamentally incapable of submitting to a superior opponent, the adult trainers that captured them, were admired for their spirit and killed, as lacking the ability to learn when to obey those with higher status. The remainder entered a form of basic training to become better killers and to learn how to earn their own status.

For any clan, this meant intensive one-on-one attention for the early novices, which received their first empty oval of a status tattoo. A high percentage of clan members in a smaller clan would largely be occupied with training, with few spare warriors to assign to guard clanships that couldn't be entered by other than a Krall anyway. With interclan warfare presently forbidden, there was no need to guard against theft by a rival clan.

Based on the last of a series of raids by any specific minor clan, the timing of their next nesting, hatching, and the start of several years of novice training could be forecast with reasonable accuracy. Data provided by Nabarone from reports about raids in Human Space was given to Jakob, the Mark's AI, allowing him to predict which of three minor clans should most likely be "hip deep" in training young semi-wild novices right now. The Prada and Torki had identified where those worlds were located for the finger clans Jakob identified. That data was gleaned from their last contact with the Krall overlords sixty years ago; they knew where each of the finger clans had last been based.

Mirikami could reach the first of those planets in three days, sparsely inhabited by the Maldo clan, located in a volume of space formerly settled by the extinct Malverans. If too few of their clanships were found there, or conditions were not right, the next target planet was another two-day Jump to hit the Dolbrin, and the third option was within another three- day Jump, if the most distant choice of Kordak clan were needed.

They were ready to launch. Mirikami addressed the entire ship. "People, unlike the Beagle's liftoff several days ago, we do not have any Prada or Torki on board, and everyone that is aboard is a TG2. Please get prone and strapped into your couch or pallets for this launch. It will be under the control of Jakob, and I have programmed in an acceleration performance that will certainly strain us, and is beyond the maximum limits the automatic Krall control settings would have permitted." He let that warning register.

"This isn't the first one of these I've done in the last two weeks of testing, but the watchers on the ground have not seen one yet, and few of you were on board. I hope they have their ears covered and eyes shaded, and that you all keep your underwear clean throughout this ride."

After a suitable warning to onlookers, who all had retreated inside the dome, Jakob did a brief count down, and initiated the launch.

The main thruster and the eight attitude thrusters all ignited at maximum power, and the brilliant exhaust blast was the practical equivalent of a directed explosive. The hot thruster forces ripped small chunks from the resilient tarmac surface, as the Mark seemed to leap into the sky on an intense column of blue-white plasma. They tore through the atmosphere in a roar that rapidly went hypersonic. The heated streak of their trail began to collapse back as they forced their way through the upper atmosphere, the thunderclap of a near vacuum column formed behind them slamming shut, adding to the sonic booms at the nose and tail. They were out of the atmosphere in under a minute, then when they were out of the gravity well, the secondary tachyon Trap snared the first energetic particle from T-squared space, and they had power for their Normal Space reactionless gravity drive.

That was when the hard acceleration was applied. The reaction thrusters had been at their design limits before, in atmosphere, but they were shut down now. The Mark leaped ahead at almost two hundred and eighty-five gravities externally and at nearly thirty uncompensated gravities internally. All of the TG2s were struggling to push blood to their brains with abdominal muscle contractions, as Jakob monitored the sensors of every crewmember for problems. There was a reduction of external acceleration to lower the internal, uncompensated acceleration to twenty-six g's, to ease the strain on a number of people on the verge of losing consciousness.

The high level of acceleration was sustained for a minute, and then reduced to only twelve g's internally for another minute. The relief felt at the big step down was instant. The purpose of the highest g forces was to give everyone the experience of how it might feel when or if they found themselves in combat with Krall crewed clanships. Krall ships couldn't match that same performance because of the designed acceleration restrictions the Olt'kitapi had built into the clanship controls. Those safety limiters had been removed from the human ships by the Torki. The limits now were what the humans inside could sustain after the inertial compensation had done its best, and was monitored by the AI.

That acceleration level was a significantly greater force than Krall warriors could endure and remain awake and functioning. If needed, Jakob could control and fight the ship with most or all of its crew and passengers blacked out.

Mirikami ordered the acceleration backed down as soon as they had matched the orbital velocity of the clan world they were intending to raid for supply clanships. The primary Trap field caught a far more energetic tachyon, and they formed an event horizon and rotated into a Jump Hole, reaching the second dimensional level of Tachyon Space.

"OK, Colonel," Mirikami spoke to Trakenburg, who occupied a spare couch on the Bridge. "We now have three days in the hole. I suggest your men Mind Tap and teach a few more of the flight crews what you'll be doing. They may have to get involved and help you out if things get hairy on that planet when we get there."

"Tet, if we go in sneaky, there shouldn't be trouble," he rebutted.

"Our White Out gamma rays can't be concealed, you obviously know that. We could exit behind a gas giant to hide our burst, but that clearly looks suspicious when we come out from behind. A lone clanship popping out in orbit shouldn't raise any alarm. We aren't stealthed from *their* sensors in any case, and I don't see a benefit from even activating that capability when they would detect that if we tried. When we land at a dome, they certainly will visually see us come down. We could make landfall at some distance from the target dome, but they might get curious as to why we landed in the boondocks."

Trakenburg's sneaky remark prompted a belated comment. "Frank, I thought you and Joe had decided to simply use the new suits invisibility mode to boldly walk across the tarmac to the parked ships, with the flight crews in their suits tagging along well behind to stay clear of any shooting."

Trakenburg nodded. "That *is* the primary mode of infiltration we considered. However, if we could get in quieter, without the Mark being seen or heard, it might mean we get out with *all* of the ships we need before they even know we are there. We spec ops types like it when we can get in and out that way."

"OK. We'll see what the layout is when we arrive, how many ships there are per dome. As I know you are aware, I have the two Krall design shuttles that can fly you in low and covertly from a remote landing site, if that seems best."

"I agree. We put more emphasis on the actual ship take over's than the insertion process this week. We're using two men to ascend per ship as your youngsters did on K1, and the three-person flight crew to act as door guards below. We have the kids Mind Tap experiences from K1 and on Poldark as guidelines, and because that sort of technique wasn't even possible for us before our gene upgrades, we'll largely follow their example until we find ways to improve. Two of my men have elected to retain use of the Booster Suits to evaluate how they perform in the field with TG2 abilities. Each man is paired with someone not wearing a Booster Suit."

Mirikami was curious. “My own armor fits rather snug. I didn’t know there was enough room inside for the added bulk of those other suits.”

Trakenburg waggled a hand with splayed fingers to indicate there were pros and cons. “We found that the armor has a limited adjustment capability. Apparently, in case the owner bulks up more or losses some weight. When we clamshell closed, the armor’s seams can extrude or retract at the edges, enough for a snug fit with the Booster Suit bulk if we wear them. I don’t think I’ll be wearing mine much anyway. Before, my Booster felt like a powerful second skin to me, but now it seems to slow me down. You give up some significant speed for a little more power.”

For two of the three days of transit, armored men and women were flipping up and down stairwells, practicing. Other than the slight sound of their passage and some degree of visual distortion to the naked eye, they were unseen, even to the ripper level of vision. That is unless the observer was wearing their own helmet, with its suit ID mode synchronized with those suits and activated. Mirikami ordered all suits aboard to be set up this way, in case anyone needed to find or help another otherwise invisible member of the crew.

On the third day, an hour before White Out, Mirikami ordered everyone into armor, even if not expected to participate in the ground action. Aside from making them available as a ready force if needed, the suits doubled as airtight protection if they took any penetrating hull hits if the operation went bad while in vacuum.

When the outside universe reappeared, they were roughly a thousand miles out from the largely tan world with mostly red and orange vegetation, already moving in the right direction to establish a nearly circular orbit. The clan world orbited a reddish-colored star, much closer in than was the case for brighter and hotter stars. The AI quickly located several Krall domes on this hemisphere, with three continents visible, one dome on each. It was obvious yet again that the Krall, even when it was a finger clan with a low planetary population, didn’t care for crowding and close proximity to neighbors.

Two of the domes were smaller than the typical size, indicating a small warrior population at those sites. There was a single clanship parked on each dome’s modest half-mile diameter tarmac, and one dome had two shuttles parked near the larger ship. The largest of the three domes was a bit smaller than the Prime City dome on Koban, but would have room for a population of twenty or thirty thousand Krall, except, there was only three clanships there, and a shuttle. That might suggest that there were less than three thousand Krall living there, or that they had departed for a raid or were at war on Poldark.

The Mark, receiving no challenge or calls, continued its orbit. In thirty minutes, a fourth dome, on what proved to be the largest continent came into view. It was a coastal location, and was the size of Hub City, the largest dome on Koban, and capable of housing twenty thousand Krall without any crowding. It also probably meant that there was a Torki lodge nearby, and a Prada village in the local forest and an underground manufacturing center below the dome.

The most interesting and exciting observation was the twenty-six clanships parked on the mile wide tarmac ring around the big dome. That was a bonanza of ships, if unwatched and unguarded. They made several orbits to observe for a time.

Finally, Mirikami decided he didn't want to make another orbit if he didn't need to do so. "Frank, you've seen the main assemblage of ships. The dozen we want are there, and we have crews to fly them. There hasn't been a launch or landing of a clanship on the entire planet since we entered orbit two hours ago. Jakob reports intensive training activity in camps on all four continents, located within a hundred miles of each of the four domes. It appears the Torki and Prada predictions of extensive novice training were accurate.

"The choice of where to get the ships is obvious, Frank. My question to you is do you want me to shuttle you and the flight crews over from a remote location, or land near the dome and you walk across the ramp?"

"My men and the forty-five crew members would require five or six round trips total, divided between your two shuttles. That would increase the chance of being noticed anyway with so much ground activity. The big novice training camp is only ten miles from the main dome, and they have octet level activity spread all around the area. The novices might not be suspicious, but their trainers could be. Even if armed with only pistols and plasma rifles, there has to be ten thousand trigger happy, young warrior hopefuls running around, with an equal number of trainers." The decision was obvious.

"Take us down to the dome. Right in the middle of the hornet's nest."

"I'll set down in the center of a cluster of clanships, and only open the portal on the side away from the dome, with the ramp left retracted. They probably won't question why no one got out if they don't see a door open. Your people will have to clear multiple ships with just your five two-man teams. I'm assuming you and Joe are on a team?"

"We'll be paired with one of the other men, not with each other, in case one of our two leadership teams went down. But yes, we get to work a ship or two ourselves. Ideally we won't fire a shot."

The Mark twisted to drop down from orbit, using power as a Krall commander might do, rather than follow a more energy efficient slow descent using atmospheric drag. The dome came into view on the screen as an icon, from around the curve of the planet. They soon flipped to a tail first approach and powered their way down in a typical waste of fuel most Krall pilots employed.

At this low level of acceleration, only four g's, Trakenburg unstrapped and went below, to join his men and the flight crews on the lowest deck. When he trotted down the last flight of stairs, Joe handed him a plasma rifle, which he attached to the power and targeting umbilical cord. On his command, everyone in the hold activated their armor's stealth mode, and all of the men going outside rippled into invisibility, including the ten rifles the spec ops carried.

Then Joe Longstreet's disembodied voice on speaker called out, "You six gawkers down here with us either need to climb up a level, or activate your stealth! Even if they can't see *us* when the portal opens, you'll stand out like sore thumbs. You can't plan to stay hidden behind one of the Dragons the whole time. Pass the word. So long as a portal is open, nobody moves down here unless stealthed."

Suddenly, the hold looked largely empty, except for some cases stacked to the sides and strapped down to deck anchor points, and the four equally secured one-man Dragons they brought for the raid on CS1. Joe's voice returned. "If we call for any of those cases to be carried out, don't forget to plug your umbilical into them before you move them, to make them invisible."

Mirikami's voice came to the entire ship's complement. "One mile up. I'm sending everyone a feed from the scene outside, channel two. I'll keep that channel visual active after landing, looking in the same direction of portal three, which is the one you will be opening for the exit. That one faces away from the dome."

There was a sound of the landing jacks absorbing the ship's weight as the thrusters were cut, and their weight cut to .85 g's in the lighter gravity.

Trakenburg stepped to portal three, and looked around the hold before pressing the codded keys. He saw the ghostly images of every suit of armor on his visor, with a designator that could provide specifics on each person if he thought about their icon. He pressed the four-digit combination, which they kept simple, but different from what the Krall typically used. The Torki had ensured that keypads on human ships wouldn't work for a Krall. Quantum encryption had favored them long enough.

The heavy door whisked up in its usual manner, revealing a pale pink sky with the red sun hidden around the curve of the hull. The nine clanships in view had a ruddy pallor from the reflected light, and all seemed closed and deserted. There were no Krall in sight, and less than a quarter of a mile away was pale orange-red grass at the edge of the tarmac, with red and orange leaves on clumps of shrubbery sprinkled around. Despite appearing to be the advent of sunset, here it was actually early morning, with the local sun still low on the horizon.

The ten spec ops jumped lightly the fifteen feet to the ground in pairs, each man pivoting to cover the side away from his partner. They left their plasma rifles hanging from the straps that supported them in front, and used their helmet target designators to look for threats and zoom in on anything of interest. The flight crews would stay in the hold until cleared to disembark.

Trakenburg quickly designated a team for the closest five ships that his range finder picked out. He and Sergeant Jenkins went to the left-most ship of the five, as the other pairs headed for their assigned targets.

Longstreet and his team partner, Private Blitman, went towards the far right designated clanship. As they cleared the bulk of the Mark and a landing jack, the dome could be seen a half mile away. The sun was just barely above its top, with the Mark almost within the dome's shadow. There were lights on for most levels of the dome, which were a lighter color than the ambient solar light. The Krall preferred a slight rose tint to their light, but this sun was apparently dimmer and a bit redder than that.

Resisting the temptation to crouch as he trotted, Longstreet reveled in the freedom this armor gave them to march right into the enemy's stronghold. He saw that his invisibility extended to not creating a shadow. The incoming light from one side was redirected or reproduced on the other side. He wasn't sure which term was right. Nevertheless, it resulted in no detectable shadows.

He glanced left to see that Blitman was crouching low, as he also maintained his head on a swivel, covering his side of the approach to the designated ship. He briefly considered using their secure tight-beam lasercom system to ask him why an *invisible* ghost would crouch low to make a smaller target.

Instead, he reached over to place fingertips on his shoulder and sent a mental Tap image of Blitman standing vertical and more comfortable, having a higher viewpoint, and a larger field of view when his head had a wider angle in which to turn.

He sensed the man's slight embarrassment in his return thought, as he assumed an upright posture. "Sir, it's hard to ignore the work habits that got my ass kicked when I forgot them in training."

His hand still on the shoulder, Longstreet thought back, "They still aren't bad work habits, but we need to be able to flex to use what our new capabilities give us. I personally feel as exposed as you did, but I believe I have a small but definite improvement in scanning the area with my head held higher, and no shoulder to block as much of my side peripheral vision."

"Yes Sir. I don't see anythin…" The thought cut off as Longstreet removed his hand, as a deliberate act, to see if it was noted. It was.

Without missing a beat, Blitman finished by lasercom, "Don't see anything moving but our people, and the orange grass waving in the breeze."

Also switching to lasercom with a thought to his suit, Longstreet said, "When we reach the ship, you jump up and open the portal, I'll be right behind to move through the door as it lifts. Don't overshoot and splat on the wall."

The latter comment was a flash of humor, because Blitman was wearing a Booster Suit under his armor. The running joke was that the users wouldn't judge their own strength properly, and over react.

Longstreet allowed Blitman to gain a step and a half on him by the time he leaped to the left side portal keypad. As preplanned, they had circled around the clanship to use a portal facing away from the dome. As light on his feet as a high leaping dancer, the private reached out to press the standard keys to open the portal even before his suit's toes touched the narrow rim at the base.

Longstreet, now also airborne, ducked slightly as he passed under the rising door panel, the timing seeming in slow motion to his senses now. His eyes adapted to the darker interior in less than a second as he stepped into the hold. His ripper vision, fed the full spectrum of light his new eyesight was capable of using. He saw the outlines of equipment in the dark hold of empty Krall armor hanging on supports around the central thruster shaft, and storage cases stacked against the walls. No movement was detected, and he and Blitman, both looking up now, split to reach the base of a set of stairs on each side of the portal.

They each promptly jumped to the next level, performing the flip and ceiling rebound, to land with hardly a sound on the soft flexible soles of the armor. They could clearly see each other, by the ghost image and designator on their visors, and the area had ambient light from the open stairwells. Some residual heat permeated the ship, but it was evenly distributed, showing no signs of warm spots from recent footsteps or any activity where life would have made one spot significantly warmer than any other spot. It was at thermal equilibrium, a strong indication the ship had not been occupied for days.

Longstreet made the hand gesture Blitman was expecting. Make a rapid ascent to the top, performing cursory checks as they passed through each deck on the way there. They found themselves standing on the empty command deck in under a minute. Longstreet sent the simple double click pulse signal on the frequency assigned to his first flight crew, waiting at the Mark of Koban. The double click in reply told him and Blitman they were on their way.

Longstreet activated a console and the external view screens to show them what resembled a glade of fat, red icons for clanships around them, and his visor saw the ghostly image of three forms rushing towards this ship. He saw two other crews on their way to two different ships. They were on schedule, and he and Blitman needed to get down quickly on the same assigned stairs, so they would not run into the three people rushing on their way up different stairs.

It was only as he was headed down that Longstreet questioned how he had seen the ghost images of the flight crews through the ship's screens, using his helmet visor. He understood how he might see them directly from his own helmet, with the ID feature activated. However, his view from the command deck was second hand, relayed through the ship's viewports. That suggested there was some information about the stealthed suits passed through those viewports that his helmet visor detected and displayed. The implication was that some sort of a signal was also picked up and repeated through the view screens. He'd have to make sure that information reached Mirikami and the others, and some of the Torki.

In thirty minutes, they had flight crews on the command decks, or quickly ascending there, on ten of the twelve clanships they had selected. These were the closest ones to the Mark. The last two spec ops teams were about to enter the final two clanships as their new flight crews were already running across the tarmac from the Mark, even before the ships were declared unoccupied. The empty status of the first ten seemed a forgone conclusion for all of them.

Trakenburg and Longstreet had saved those final two ships for their own teams, as their right to capture, and the other three pairs of spec ops men had returned to the Mark, to perform a secondary task that Mirikami had requested of them.

It was during the occupation of the last two ships that Mirikami suddenly broke radio silence and made a transmission, encrypted of course, but a flag to any Krall that intercepted it that someone was transmitting on their ramp, and didn't want to be understood. It also wasn't on a frequency that the Maldo clan generally used in raids.

"There are a large number of Krall coming in fast on foot from the woods, and some are now on the tarmac. They stayed concealed behind other ships from the Mark's line of sight as they approached. They obviously knew we were here from our landing, but probably didn't see anyone moving around and didn't react at first.

Not until they saw the portals open and close on their ships. We expected any attack to come from the dome, so they got close before Jakob spotted shadows moving under the bases of ships on the tarmac.

"Button up your ships, but remember, they can manually operate your portal keypads. One or two of each flight crew needs to guard the doors on the bottom deck until you can lift. I think most of you should be ready to go. Launch the instant you can. The Mark's doors have been recoded and are safe from entry, and we have the most defenders. I'll wait until all of you have launched."

Over the next minutes, Mirikami continued to urge every ship to launch as soon as possible. Eight of them responded within thirty or forty seconds, the exhaust blasts burning and vaporizing the warriors that had rushed towards their bases. Warriors actually made it inside four of the ships, two of which had previously closed their portals when the spec ops team had left. The lead warriors manually reopened a portal, and they and a few others jumped inside as quickly as they could get close enough. There was a belated response from the dome now, with trucks loaded with warriors streaming from the closest two entrances.

Two of the ships the crews had taken possession of had only the flight crews on them, and managed to get airborne with only a few warriors inside. Per the flight crews after they lifted, the airtight doors shut and kept the Krall below the critical deck levels, where the thruster engines were located, and far below the Jump Drives. They would be able to Jump to the nearby rendezvous system, only a half day away, where those Krall could be rooted out.

The final two ships were in more imminent danger. Longstreet's third ship take-over was farther from the dome, which after hearing Mirikami's warning, assumed that probably placed them closer to the Krall attacking on foot. He and Blitman were less than half way back down to the base, so he called up to the woman that was the leader of the flight crew, Tabora Saldivar. "Tabora, close the portal now and launch with us as soon as you can. We'll guard the lower decks."

There was a brief pause, "OK, Joe. I just activated a console and..., I found the portal controls. I closed it."

"Good, we'll try to keep them closed." However, even as he said this, he heard screams of rage from more than one indignant Krall somewhere below him, already inside.

Staying on that same frequency, he spoke to Blitman, knowing the flight crew would also hear. "Blit, I hear warriors already inside, and they can manually override the command deck to open the portals. We'll continue down. You take deck three, and I'll drop to deck two. Try to kill any that can get past me, and Tabor's two extra guys can take any out that slip past you."

He had only reached deck four when he caught motion at a stairwell a quarter of the way around that deck. He used one of the trigger thoughts he'd worked out for his suit. *Red, 10, shoot.*

A full-power, red laser lanced out and burned through the face of the Krall looking around as it ran up the other stairwell. He saw a blue flash from the far side, where Blit was descending, and knew he had fired a plasma pulse, from suit or rifle he couldn't tell.

Another head appeared over the deck at the same stairwell he'd just fired on, which was not a smart move for a Krall warrior to make. It also was left a smoking ruin as something about those warriors registered in his mind, and how easy the two kills were. Then he heard a high-pitched sound from directly below him, and he moved aside just as a pulse bolt came up and singed his suit. It had to have been a blind shot as he heard the rifle's power pack activate, but the choice of which stairwell to fire a bolt up would have been determined by the assumed origin of the two lasers shots he'd just made. He needed to move away from that stairwell for a moment.

He jumped to the side and removed the sling and umbilical from his plasma rifle. He activated the power pack as he set the now visible rifle down and stepped away. He heard the faint ultrasonic whine as it came online, using his wolfbat hearing. He also heard the Krall below order a warrior to look over the deck at another stairwell. Just as he anticipated, a head popped up at a different stairwell, but he didn't fire at that head. Instead, he thought *blue, 10, shoot,* as he put his target designator on the edge of the stairs next to him.

A warrior with a rifle surged into view, ready to kill whoever had shot at that other warrior. He aimed towards the rifle on the deck but had no target, at least that he could see. He died as his head ruptured from the excessive heat from a suit bolt that entered his left eye socket. Not waiting for the spatter to hit the walls, Longstreet dove to pick up the charged rifle and placed a shot through the head of the other warrior that had foolishly continued up that third stairwell. It shared the same characteristic of his first two kills.

"Blit, some of these warriors are grey head novices, with trainers wasting them to get a shot at us." The grey head reference was about how Krall started life with grey-colored skin, and turned a ruddy color as they matured.

"I just caught on to that difference, Cap'n. They sent two after me on different stairwells when a red head tried to pop me. He leaped up the stairs, and didn't shoot when he couldn't see me. Fatal mistake. I also popped the two rookies."

"I can't see *you* on this obstructed deck level, Blit, but I can cover five of the stairs. Can you cover all of yours?"

"Yes Sir. I also see five stairs, and if I move I can see six…, oops." There was an actinic blue flash and a Krall scream. "I wonder how many of 'em got inside, Sir? That's five for me."

"I got four. Blit, but by now they may have reopened another portal. Tabora, get us airborne."

"Ready, Joe, but two portals are open and won't close. The lower decks will lose air as we lift or fill with toxic fumes."

Longstreet recalled that the ships were designed with airtight doors that automatically closed on alternate decks at the stairwell deck openings.

"Launch now. We're in suits, they aren't, and we're still on deck four. We never reached the bottom. The airtight doors will lock them out."

"There are at least eight ships lifting now, all around us. We might collide."

She sounded frightened.

"Tabora, do your best. They're probably pouring warriors inside our lower deck right now. Go or we'll die here!"

He first felt the vibration then he heard the thunder of the thrusters through the open portals below.

Longstreet easily picked off two more grey-heads in midair, as they leaped up two stairwells simultaneously.

The acceleration wasn't as hard as he had expected, or had hoped it would be. Perhaps that was out of consideration or proximity of the other ships or because of the drag of portals that were apparently locked open.

Several plasma bolts were fired up stairwells before the inevitable happened. The automatic airtight doors activated in typical Krall fashion. No gradual closing here. They slammed shut in an instant, trapping the Krall below. Those on the lowest two decks would be exposed to near vacuum in thirty seconds at the present acceleration if the portals remained open. No air at all in forty-five seconds.

Let's see how good they are at holding their breath, Longstreet thought happily.

Any Krall left on the still pressurized decks three and four would have to be cleared the hard way, once the humans or the Krall figured out how the airtight doors were reopened. Since they still had pressure on both sides, there had to be a release. The other two members of the flight crew joined Longstreet and Blitman, to help them cover the hatches when they were finally opened. While not experienced with firefights, the Spacers had received Mind Taps of what to do, and they had the reaction speed required. It wasn't a clean operation, but they had gotten off planet with their prize.

****

Trakenburg and his teammate, Sergeant Jenkins, had just reached the command deck when Mirikami's warning came.

Jenkins, reacting instantly, used his radio to call to their flight crew, whom had been enroute from the Mark, and the portal below had been left open for them. Radio silence was pointless now. "Lieutenant Badar, you heard that. How close are you?"

"Too late I think. I see two Krall in the hold now and more are running towards it."

Trakenburg intervened. "Badar, the Mark is too far from us for you to return there, and this boat is your only way out of here. You three are TG2's, you're fast, invisible, and you are well armed. Jump in and kill the ones in the hold, and shut the door behind you. Trust your Mind Tap training sessions." He looked at Jenkins and shrugged, as if saying what else could he tell them?

Jenkins thought of something else. "I'm on my way down to help, you get your asses on this ship any damn way you can!" In a Krall-like move, the sergeant leaped over the rail by the stairwell and dropped to the deck fifteen feet below.

Trakenburg activated all four consoles, using what he'd learned in reciprocal Mind Taps done with various flight crews they had trained. "I'm working my way through the startup sequences for the launch. When you get up here, all you'll have to do is fly this bitch."

Jackie Bader was not an aggressive person, which explained why she had remained a lieutenant with her former cargo haling company for six years before her capture and stranding on Koban. However, she'd since had over twenty years of life on Koban under her belt now, and afraid of Krall or not, she hated them enough to have volunteered to help on this mission. She took command of her flight crew.

"Annie, Pieter, both of you think of how to fire the weapons you want to use. I'm choosing plasma because I want to blow their heads completely off. The Krall won't know where we are until we shoot, so move to the side as soon as you do, just like they taught us."

She turned away from the two ghostly figures on her visor, and started a dead run at the open portal a hundred feet ahead of her. In the low gravity, she was covering ground in long leaps at a respectable speed any sprinter would have envied. The other two in her crew scrambled to match her speed. Fear of being left behind here exceeded the fear they felt of the Krall ahead of them.

Bader, as she closed with the ship, no longer saw the two warriors that had already entered, but three more were coming towards her at a dead run. She finally noticed that they were moving slower than she was, not lifting as high from the ground with each step, and two of the three were armed only with long knives. The lead warrior had a plasma rifle, but it was slung across its back to permit more efficient running as it pumped its massive muscled arms, which were larger than her thighs.

She wasn't going to let it beat her to the ship, and she increased her speed as adrenaline pumped her ripper-derived muscles to new effort. Her improved vision and fast adrenaline driven super conductor thoughts saw the heavy breathing of the three Krall, and the strain on their muzzles and lips as they labored for air. They had been running all-out from the trees she saw far behind them, which was a considerable distance. They were tiring! It was uplifting to see that they had a level of weakness she could actually see.

It was as they drew within fifty feet of one another that her racing thoughts recalled the advice she had given her two friends. She thought of the weapon she wanted to use, and then how to make it fire. She locked her eyes on the fearsome gapping maw of the lead Krall, open to get more air, revealing its yellowed teeth and a purple tongue.

Plasma, 100, fire she thought, and was startled when a bolt of blue instantly shot from in front of her own face, and an expanding ring of fine red and gray particles appeared where her vision had been locked. The brute actually seemed to take another step as its momentum propelled it towards her on a leg that only *looked* as if it moved the corpse forward.

It fell forward in seeming slow motion, the arms making no move to catch the heavy torso from slamming onto the pavement, and finally sliding to a stop. The warrior to her left side, with a long machete-like blade raised, looked down at its dead trainer in what had to be the only look of surprise Bader had ever seen on any picture of a Krall. It was short lived, literally, when a red laser and a blue plasma bolt hit it simultaneously, originating from behind her.

The laser carved the shoulder off where the arm attached, that held the big blade. The surprised expression vanished with the same crimson particulate ring as Bader had just admired for her own target. She had continued to run for the ship, and because her attention was morbidly on the two dead Krall she and her companions had just produced, she almost forgot to jump up through the open and beckoning portal.

That wasn't all that she forgot. The third warrior, with a knife, leaped at the same opening. In their inexperience, her two companions had not split their firepower between the two remaining targets, and they had managed to double-kill just the one.

She slammed into the leaping lizard at full tilt, and her armor protected her from injury, but her mass, compared to that of the novice she hit, was roughly one-third. Bader was knocked sideways, and the Krall, unaware of what unseen thing it had struck, dropped its knife and grasped blindly at the hard feeling object, pulling it to the deck of the hold as it fell.

It rose to its feet quickly, holding onto what proved to be Bader's left arm, and she hung there suspended and terrified. She knew what had *her*, but *it* had no idea what it held. It reached for the unseen object with its other large hand; talons extended, and unknowingly appeared to be going for her face.

In a panic, Bader brought her right hand up swiftly to protect her face, and grabbed with desperate strength at a finger, which was small enough for her smaller-than-average woman's hand to wrap around the digit.

It was quite desperate strength. The bone of the finger first snapped, and then the pressure pinched the digit until it crushed. The Krall naturally screamed its pain and tried to pull its hand away. This had the effect of leaving the thick detached finger evidently floating in the air. The Krall dropped whatever it had hold of, and the finger fell to the deck as Bader let the gory thing drop.

This provided Bader with the first inkling of just how her strength compared to that of these extremely large, fearsome monsters, which had given her a lifetime of nightmares. She looked at the hand that had just ripped a finger off her nemesis. With growing confidence, she stepped towards the now unarmed creature. It heard the step, and backed away from…, what? Something it didn't know and couldn't see, but it feared.

She looked it in the eye, and knew that unarmed as it was, she could tear it apart with her hands if she chose. *Why waste the time?* Therefore, she thought, *plasma, 100, fire.*

As it fell backwards, its head missing, she had another justifying thought. *Why should I mess up my pretty armor with his gore?*

Her two companions had now joined her, and Annie tried pressing the keys to close the portal, only to discover that it wouldn't respond. Some alternate code had been used to force it to stay open until the proper counter code was entered.

They heard some firing above them, and in a moment Sergeant Jenkins dropped through a stairwell opening, prepared to fight off more Krall. He found his flight crew instead, and messy, dead Krall inside and out.

"Lieutenant Bader, please go help Colonel Trakenburg, before he tries to fly this thing himself. Your two buddies and I will keep the Krall out." Even as he said that, he used his plasma rifle to blast a warrior in mid-leap as it tried to enter on the fly.

Bader raced to a stairwell and started her rapid scramble upwards. "Colonel, I'm on my way."

The three people staying behind spread out and continued to knock Krall back out of the hold, or dropped them in their tracks as they entered.

There was another broadcast from Mirikami. "You need to get that damn thing airborne. I'm about to blow the support legs off six other clanships. I didn't see a need to carry all the boxed explosives away with us."

Jenkins knew now what the other six spec ops men had been doing while the last two ships were boarded. They had removed explosives from the cases on the Mark, planting remotely detonated packages on other clanships.

Bader's voice sounded on the radio. "Thrusters in fifteen seconds, people. You had better get a few decks higher with that portal locked open."

They scrambled to get to deck four above the second set of depressurization doors, and made it just as the thrusters fired. It felt good to be lifting, having accomplished everything they came here to do. The first eight "prizes" had cleared atmosphere and had Jumped, and three others would reach that point in less than a minute. There were two more ships to go, themselves, and then the Mark would follow.

Watching the last one of the newly captured ships rise, engine roaring, reaching two thousand feet, as if to thunderous applause for a successful mission, Mirikami ordered Jakob to launch the Mark, with instructions to trigger the six mines they left behind after they reached a thousand feet. He never quite forgave himself later, for not risking the blasts *before* they lifted. The six toppling clanships would not have been *that* close to the Mark, or have fallen over *too* fast.

****

Gotrak had heard a clanship land near the nesting dome, and assumed it was one of the clan's sub leaders returning from some political requirement. Perhaps, returning from the recent joint council meeting on Telda Ka. If so, it would most likely be Dorkda, sent there as the clan leader's representative. He had been gone since before the gathering of pre-novice cubs had started. Others were left to begin the arduous and impatient work of their training, over a year ago. Their clan leader could not leave their nest world at such a critical time, just to meet their status obligation to Dorbo clan, simply to vote as they instructed on clan council matters.

The debt to Dorbo clan could be fully paid in one more breeding cycle, when

Maldo, a finger clan that Dorbo had spawned a thousand years ago, gained enough status and proven warriors with battle tested skills, to demand the council grant them mature clan status.

After that, they would remain allied with Dorbo but more independent, and allowed to form finger clans of their own when they could afford the status points and furnish the material needs. One day they would vote to elevate Dorbo to Great Clan status, a success that would also indirectly benefit Maldo. However, without a status debt to pay to keep them poor, they could soon demand a greater participation in future invasions planned for human worlds.

In the meantime, they had to support their parent clan with their voice in council, and in private conversations outside the joint council. Dorkda had been sent in place of their clan leader to be that voice in the inefficient, self-serving pack, dominated by the existing Great Clans. It was apparently time to hear the results of the meetings, to know which clans had major parts in the new invasions. If Dorbo was one of those, it meant they had gained status, and in turn would offer more fighting to their finger clans.

If it were not Dorkda returning, then even a courier ship would bring more warriors to help in the task of training ignorant novices in the skills of combat. There needed to be much more culling to find the physically best performers out of the mass of angry, young meat they had to teach.

Despite Gotrak's complaints, he knew this was a better group of hatchlings than the previous two breeding cycles had produced. Greater status earned from successful raids had finally allowed them to purchase thousands of eggs from pairings of superior male and female warriors of other clans. They traded with clans with a surplus of high breeder status eggs, sold for status points.

There was no way for the temporarily isolated Maldo leadership, with all available warriors invested in intense novice training and culling, to have yet learned that on K1 (Telda Ka) that Dorkda had been captured on a raid to steal two clanships (actually he was presumed killed). Not even Dorbo clan, who had been humiliated to lose those two ships, knew that the ultimate shame was that it had been humans from the Mark of Koban performing the theft. Now this Dorbo finger clan was in line for even worse treatment from the same ship. Humiliation, like crap, did appear to obey the law of gravity, and roll downhill.

The hand of training octets that Gotrak directed was actually composed of nearly twice that number of Krall. There now was nearly one experienced warrior assigned to each inexperienced novice in a training octet. Later, as culling eliminated the poor candidates (the euphemism of "culling" standing in for the more accurate term "killing").

Last year, there had been three pre-novice candidates for each warrior to observe and instruct ("instruct" was frequently another euphemism for brutalize and punish). In absence of another clan's novices to fight with, the warriors forced their inexperienced novices to face low intensity beatings from them, teaching them via the "hard knocks" rule how to defend themselves, first from blows by feet, hands, elbows, knees, talons, and even the head.

Recently clubs, spears, rocks, then knives and short swords had been introduced. The discipline by now was such that challenge matches were permitted when two novices had a grudge. It was too soon to lose many promising novices in death matches, but death sometimes happened. At least the weaker candidates “accidentally” eliminated this way increased the rate of culling.

It would be months before the culling revealed the one-quarter of the original candidates who were ready to receive firearms training. Those that had physical skills and discipline to survive the temptation to kill so easily would live to enter tactical training and movements, and someday learn strategy.

However, right now they were mostly a rabble of thuggish club and spear users, with a few having proven capable and disciplined enough to be issued knives and short swords. There were always some that believed this ability to kill with sharp steel weapons gave them the ability to defy an instructor, or challenge them when they saw they had no firearms. They proved to be excellent examples, by their deaths at the hands of the instructor, or from his instructor clan mate if the first sneaky blow was one of decapitation.

Today, Gotrak had the four octets he was responsible for practicing infiltration through the woods, to find the camp of another hand of octets and attack them by surprise. Gotrak and the other instructors, on both sides, knew where everyone was, and simply acted as observers and advisors. They provided advice such as “don’t step on that dry stick and make a noise,” or “don’t let that branch swish back into your team mate’s face.” This phase of training went much faster, because by now their battlefield memory had developed, and the breeding and instincts of the nine or ten-year-old novices meant they remembered what actions had previously worked well. Some were innovating, and combining ideas that led to a better way of attack or defense in the training scenarios.

There were hints of the new tactics needed against humans. Cunning and trickery were no longer discouraged when seen, and more of the survivors of the human war had lived by exhibiting some of these traits. Their eggs, in future generations, would gradually become the model for smarter, better warriors.

It was at the edge of the woods that Gotrak was able to see the dome and tarmac, where most of the clans hard earned clanship resources were parked. His IR vision revealed which ship had just landed, by the hot ramp and thrusters, although his battlefield memory, if examined, would have helped him find the new ovoid in the plump forest of clanships.

Whoever had arrived, they had opened a portal, but not lowered the ramp. That suggested they had jumped down and were running to the dome. He looked under the maze of clanships without real curiosity, to see if he might see Dorkda running towards the dome, perhaps with news that would improve each of the instructor’s moods, if there were a promise of real warfare for them soon.

There was nothing moving on the tarmac. He looked away and checked with his octet leaders on progress towards the “enemy” camp, which because they had placed lookouts in the woods, knew about his approaching “raiders.” This could become an entertaining morning, even before the sun rose very high.

Looking back to the dome, he instantly noticed that four portals were now open on other clanships near the new arrival. Most of the parked ships had not been entered for almost a year, other than a cursory check of the command deck consoles and thruster engines for power left active or fuel leaks. Could this be a sign that a returning envoy was verifying the preparedness of some of their clanships for a raid? Gotrak would prefer to participate in activity such as that, instead of the tedious but required duty he now fulfilled.

As he watched, one of the four portals closed, but in seconds another ship's portal, on the opposite side of the new arrival ship, sprang open. There was no one in sight, no movement. These must have been operated remotely, from the dome or the new ship. He continued to monitor the activity in the woods, but checked the tarmac frequently. All of the original portals were now closed, but five other ships had one portal opened where he could see into the hold.

That very thought was interesting. He realized that looking through the one portal facing towards the woods he was able to see than none of the other portals was opened. The dome could not see this activity. That prodded him to remember why the ships were periodically checked. To ensure they were truly shut down, that no warrior that wanted to learn how to pilot had activated a console. No one could remotely open a portal if the consoles were inactive. However, he'd seen seven of them opened so far, and most were now reclosed. Only a warrior manually pressing the keypads could open the portals, but he had seen no activity or movement at any of the ships.

While he was watching, another portal facing him, on a different clanship sprang open. He didn't have a helmet or digital vision enhancers, but this was only two miles away. He could even see the outline of the keypads by the portals. There was no one there.

Gotrak called his fellow instructors and quickly told them what he'd seen. All of them had noticed the ship arrival of course, because it was uncommon during the seasons of novice training at a smaller clan like theirs. With their confirmation, he called the dome observers on duty at the top level, to ask if they knew who this arrival was.

They had not had contact with the arrival's crew, and had expected the pilot or commander eventually to enter the dome to report to the clan leader. Gotrak learned that Dorkda was actually not expected to return before the next winter.

When he mentioned the periodic portal openings and closings that he had seen on multiple clanships, the dome observers were surprised, because they said they had not seen any from their vantage point. There was a pause, and then a new voice.

"Gotrak, I sent no warriors to those clanships, this must be an interclan raid." It was clan leader Hashtok's voice. "These raids are forbidden by the council, but smaller new finger clans do not have clanships to go to the war on Poldark. They could try to take ours. Take a force and seek them out before they have a chance to lift. Move fast and stay hidden. They will be watching the dome if we move from here." Then he added, "For the Path and clan stop them."

This order demanded instant and maximum reaction, no questions. He stiffened, his left arm out with talons extended, and said, "I salute the Path and our clan." The only reply allowed.

His action and words galvanized the warriors that overheard him. They knew only one command justified that reply.

Gotrak repeated Hashtok's suspicion and his instructions. As the clan leaders designated voice for this action, the warriors near him each repeated the required reply.

"I salute our clan."

Gotrak addressed them all. "Send the most trusted novice runners to gather as many of the trainers as can be found and lead them here."

He had a simple basic plan, which he explained to several warriors. He singled one out now. "Fittdot, you will stay hidden inside the tree line to instruct how the movement to the tarmac will be done. One warrior will lead no more than three novices, who must stay directly in line behind the lead warrior until told to attack the enemy. A second warrior will be behind them to keep them in line. The lead warriors will use our parked ships as cover from the intruder clanship. You must cross the open terrain to the tarmac by running as fast as possible towards the enemy ship, with it always behind another ship. They must not see us coming from their view screens, or they could launch immediately with as many of our ships as they are able to steal. We must get inside our occupied ships and kill them all. I will lead the first line."

He pointed at an octet. "I want three novices to follow me, and another warrior behind them to keep them moving. They will not fully understand what we do or why, but the chance to kill a clan enemy will give them spirit."

He quickly shifted position in the trees until a parked ship blocked his view of the enemy clanship. He looked at the three novices, and the warrior behind them. "Follow me, as fast as you can run. We fight for great honor and our clan."

He turned and started across the expanse of pale orange grass at a ground-eating pace that seemed too fast for slightly bowed, muscular legs, which were a bit shorter than their arms. A second and third string of instructors and novices followed on that same path, and farther along the tree line, other strings started across, and using different parked ships to block a view of them.

It was a long distance in the open, but their opponents gave no sign they had been spotted. Even before he reached the cover of the clanship he was using for cover, Gotrak detected a flaw in his hasty strategy. His memory held the picture of which ships on the ramp he had seen with portals opened. Most had already shut those portals. He didn't know how their clan rivals had moved without being seen on the tarmac, but once inside closed ships that was irrelevant. He was the only one that could send warriors and novices to the correct ships, those he knew had been targeted.

Pausing behind a landing jack of the first ship they reached, he explained the problem to the trailing warrior. "That ship," he pointed, "is one of those they opened. Try to reach it by concealment and enter. I will direct the others to the targeted clanships. Go."

He repeated the directions for subsequent teams, but he had no silent way to inform the other approaches. Fortunately, there must have been warriors with them that had also seen some of the open portals, because they slipped around the landing jacks, going in the right directions. He cursed his rushed plan that had found a way to prevent him from making the first attack on their enemy.

Gotrak and every clan member on the ramp knew that the time for sneaking had passed when the first thrusters were activated. Some of these were ships he'd seen warriors and novices open a portal and enter, unopposed. At least two hands of warriors and novices died when the blast of thrusters of clanships ignited and burned them to cinders, which blew flaming over the tarmac. Some of their ships were being taken from them.

He started running towards where he'd been hearing sounds of shooting and screams of rage. He spotted a number of dead instructors and novices on the ground below a ship, with fighting continuing inside. He was on the verge of joining them when he heard the thrum of fuel pumps and knew the clanship was about to lift, and he could not get inside before that happened.

He stepped into the lee of a landing jack for protection and survived the heat of liftoff, singed and battered, as the ship rose with at least one portal locked open. He'd heard fighting inside, but unless they closed that portal, the fumes and then vacuum would cut the fight short. Another ship probably lost. He was enraged beyond measure.

There was still some shooting, but it was well across the tarmac from him, past the enemy clanship. If he ran over there, he would likely arrive too late again to help prevent another launch, and watch another lost Maldo asset roar into the red sky.

It came to him! There was another possibility. He might prevent the enemy clanship from escaping. It was surely too well defended for him to enter and try to overpower the crew. However, there was a more destructive and final alternative. It might permit them to find out who violated the interclan warfare ban, and give them a chance at revenge and compensation.

He leaped onto a portal rim on the cooler side of the clanship where he had taken refuge. The door rushed open and he raced and leaped up the darkened stairs closest to him. Half a life spent in clanships made even nearly total darkness no obstacle to a rapid ascent. There was a trace of warmth to furnish an outline of the stairwell.

Gotrak was confident that the last time this craft was used on a raid, it had returned with most of its defensive and offensive armament fully functional. After all, it was parked on *this* side of the ramp, instead of where the Prada and Torki performed most maintenance of damaged clanships.

Flying gracefully over the railing at the top, he rushed to the closest console on the command deck. It didn't matter which he chose. It came up nearly instantly after at least a year of inactivity. He gave no thanks to the Olt'kitapi designers, because a Krall thanked no one, for anything.

His former stint in pilot training returned dividends now as he quickly found the controls that had always interested him most, more so than flying. It was the lack of interest in flying that had ended his clanship pilot training. Instead, he became a weapons master, using the plasma cannons and heavy lasers on raids. One of his seldom-used tools of destruction was the racks of various type missiles. He had missed the fights with the human space ships when they twice attacked their base in Human Space, Telda Ka. Maldo clan was too low in status to have a dome there.

He would finally have a chance to use one of the missiles to knock the rival clan's ship out of the sky as they tried to depart. Its launch had to be imminent, and he didn't understand why they had not lifted the moment the counter attacks began.

A Krall could not grasp the concept of a leader staying behind to protect subordinates. Survive, or die was their typical attitude. All he had to do was be patient. No need to risk damage to other ships on the tarmac if he let it gain altitude.

Suddenly, he was presented with a golden double opportunity for destruction, as the last of the purloined ships started lifting with a tentative acceleration, and portals still open. The warriors he had sent had not been able to reach the command deck. This would be a mixed blessing, because he was about to destroy a ship that *felt* to him like it was still clan property, even if it was about to be taken.

He set targeting on it with two anti-ship missiles, which initially refused to lock on because of the close proximity. He would simply let it reach several miles and take it down with a double tail shot. That idea was promptly modified when he saw the flash and heard the rumble of another launch. It was his main target. He tried setting three missiles to track that hated target, but again the short range frustrated him. He'd have to wait. However, he'd make certain that commander would know what was coming.

The first ship would be high enough in seconds, and the other clan's mission commander would see it die, knowing his ship was next. He was poised over the firing command when suddenly he felt a violent jar, and heard a series of six external explosions. He instantly felt the deck vibrate and start a slight tilt. The noses of two other clanships in his view were also leaning.

In a fraction of a second, with a flash of understanding, Gotrak released all five missiles for launch, recognizing in a scream of rage that his enemy had managed to destroy this, and other ships on the tarmac with explosives.

Waiting for his own death to greet him, he watched as the first two missiles streaked out from side mounted ports. However, the other three missiles had interlocks that would delay their launch while waiting for greater range. He held onto the increasing slope of the console as he rapidly tapped the override to launch the last three missiles at point blank range. At least one of them should hit home.

He had the satisfaction of seeing both of his hypervelocity first missiles impact on the aft section of the higher ship. It blossomed at the rear, and started to fall off to the side. The direction of its drift suddenly became of critical interest to him. He realized with horror that it was descending close to the clan's main dome. Suddenly, the three other hypervelocity missiles blazed forth, as his ship's tilt reached twenty degrees.

They had such a short travel time, and the enemy ship was so low that it was under two seconds of travel time for them to reach their objective. Even without active guidance at this close range, Gotrak could see one exhaust trail was dead-on for a side impact, and the other two would miss by a small amount. With proximity fusing, they might still deliver significant damage. He could die knowing he took his killer with him.

The well-targeted missile hit the side of the rising clanship, and…, struck and crumpled against the hull without exploding. The other two passed it by, only to detonate when they had traveled far enough past it to exceed their minimal travel before the warheads armed. They were well beyond any threat to the intended target when they detonated.

Five seconds, to a creature bred to react in a hundredth of a second, is an eternity in which to experience despair and painful, wrenching, defeat. He had failed to do serious damage to the enemy ship, and it would escape. He saw on the now greatly tilted view screen that the ship he *had* managed to kill wasn't dying without a fight.

The main thruster and lower part of the ship was in shreds, pieces falling away, the main engine having automatically cut off. The pieces were *able* to fall away faster than the dying ship could have fallen, because the ship was using its undamaged upper attitude thrusters to delay its descent. On second consideration, he knew it wasn't a fight to delay the fall; it had repositioned itself for the inevitable crash.

He believed with certainty that it would no longer fall *close* to the dome containing his clan leader, the primary nest area, and the only below ground factory complex his clan possessed. Instead, it was maneuvering for a *dead center hit!*

The side thrusters gave their last flash of blue plasma support and winked off. He would not be alive to see it fall the nearly one mile distance, because he was within fifty feet of the sides of his ship rupturing on the tarmac, spilling the tens of thousands of pounds of thruster propellant and oxidizer, which would ignite on contact with one another. The other toppling ships near him would suffer similar fireball fates, because Krall efficiency maintained them all fully fueled for instant use.

He was privileged to watch these final events, which he had partly set in motion, and would result in the dissolution of the finger clan he had devoted his entire existence to expanding.

****

"Captain Mirikami, I have devoted all of my career and much of my life to destroying the Krall. This is a capstone to that career, helping to take a dome filled with them out with me. It was an honor and privilege, Sir."

For a man about to drop to his death, Colonel Trakenburg was remarkably calm, and sounded peaceful.

"Frank, I'm sorry. I should have blown those other ships sooner."

"And we might have lost you and the Mark in the process. War happens, Tet. Lieutenant Bader has made our end more than a fair trade, thanks to her skill." He let her have the last word.

"I lost my fear of the Krall, Captain. I tore a finger off a warrior with one hand, and then I blew off his head. He was actually afraid of me! My fear is gone. I know they can see us falling, and thousands more are afraid. You made it possible. Thank you, and goodbye."

"Goodbye, Jackie, Frank. If you can contact the others below, tell them how proud we are of all of you."

He knew from the severe damage to the lowest decks of the now freefalling ship that the other three had died instantly.

The final seconds were silent on radio, but the dwindling tarmac below the rising Mark blossomed in six huge, overlapping orange and black billows of flame, smoke, and spinning sections of clanships. That was followed by the devastating impact of the clanship on the dome, with a similar, single orange and black blossom of death.

There was no sense of satisfaction in Mirikami's heart or mind. Their losses, when weighed against the tremendous damage done to this Krall clan, might seem a fair trade to Frank and Jackie, and the other three. However, Mirikami measured them as friends, and by what else they might have accomplished in the future. This was only one minor clan.

He checked with Thad, who reported that the missile impact had penetrated the hull, partway into a compartment filled with missile reloads. Not that this would have made them any deader, if it had detonated those along with its own warhead. Automatic sealer had ended the atmosphere leak, and they could remove the shattered weapon and warhead at the rendezvous system.

"Thad, does the warhead seem stable? No risk to us if we jostle the thing?"

"Jakob told me that even though it didn't reach its maximum velocity, the camera and hull sensors show it crushed its warhead before the range failsafe was released. It's only the center of the missile, the guidance and propulsion systems, that its momentum managed to push through to inside. The explosive material is a type that can't blow up simply because you bang it around. It's smeared around on the hull, but safe. Why? What were you thinking of doing that will cause a jostle?" He had a suspicion.

"We've hurt Maldo bad. However, when they control the fires, they still have Jump ships that can get off-planet and describe what happened. I want to take another thirty minutes to make sure they *can't* do that any time soon."

"Let me know if you need any launchers reloaded, Tet." The grin showed that Thad heartily approved.

The Mark moved to a low orbit, just barely out of atmosphere so they would complete an orbit sooner, using thruster power to hold them low and fast. He quickly destroyed the clanships at the other three domes, and sent two missiles into each dome as well. Then in a pass back over the blazing main dome, he spent missiles on the remaining eight ships there.

Breaking orbit, Mirikami told Jakob to Jump them the half-day distance to the system where they would meet the other crews, kill any Krall that were inadvertently taken along, and clean up the messes.

“I also need to get this thorn out of my side,” he complained about the unexploded ordinance.

“Should I call someone from the infirmary, Sir?”

“Never mind, Jakob.” *Every* AI he’d met needed more work on their sense of humor. They simply didn’t have one.

Chapter 17: Migrating Headaches

The Beagle did a White Out at Toborkiti at a distance of nearly twenty thousand miles. This was the Torki estimate of the probable highest orbit of the most recently used migration ships. The passive scanners immediately began reporting the parked ship locations. All of the huge ovoid ships appeared to be in approximately circular equatorial orbits at different altitudes. However, they were naturally spread all around Toborkiti.

Those that were assigned long-range communications learned that the Mark had obtained eleven of the dozen clanships intended for resupply missions to the slow moving migration ships. However, they learned a ship had been lost to Krall missiles, with a loss of the flight crew and a spec ops team.

The Tachyon Space signalmen reported directly to Maggi, who was on the Bridge, and she passed the bad news to Marlyn and the other two watch standers. Alyson and Jorl were in couches on the Bridge, and like Maggi, they had Mind Tap training for backup piloting skills, but were primarily there for weapons control. Alyson had responsibility for the plasma cannons and Jorl controlled the heavy lasers.

They were told only that the loss of the ship to Krall action had cost the lives of five people that they knew. The message didn't say who had died, but the loss demonstrated to the crew of the Beagle how risky a mission like theirs could be, even if not directly involved with intensive ground fighting inside a dome or an underground factory.

The Beagle was immediately maneuvered close to the nearest high orbiting ship, and a swarm of crewmembers in their pressure tight armor went across on repair scooters of human design, trailing docking lines, and towing a container of a heavy hydrogen mixture to top-off or fill the fuel tanks of the ship's fusion generators. They attached the lines to maintain a fixed separation as the Beagle pulled away slightly, not budging the mass of the gigantic ship. The crew opened the hatches their Mind Taps with Torki told them were the correct ones to use. While some of the teams started refilling the main hydrogen tank, others uncoiled the power lines stowed inside a hatch close to the largest fusion generator. A scooter towed the connector end back to the open lower hold of the Beagle, and there it was plugged into a power jack on the converted clanship.

The migration ship's hydrogen tank proved to be partly filled, and when it was quickly topped off, the fuel scooter started back to the beagle with the container. Avoiding radio communication, a woman posted by the fusion bottle waved her arm to indicate the circuit was ready on her side. The man at the power distribution panel on the wall inside the Beagle's lower hold pushed the combination of buttons to send power to the now tethered migration ship. The magnetic field of the receiving fusion bottle quickly built up, as the superconducting magnets automatically focused, and passed a feed of heavy hydrogen ion plasma into the confinement chamber.

In less than five minutes, the heat and density of plasma reached the critical level and ignited the self-sustaining reaction when more energy was produced than the confinement field required. Several switches were thrown in well-practiced order, and although the control consoles and lights throughout the ship were inactive (an automatic protection feature at shutdown), the great ship only required their orderly activation. The Torki and Prada representatives and two Torki pilots were gently towed over by several scooters in a pressurized transfer module. It was equipped with a docking port for either a clanship, or migration ship, so the flight crew and alien liaison teams were already going aboard. They would handle the orderly warming and activation of the ship, and the startup of the other fusion generators. Five humans would remain aboard.

In barely eighteen minutes, the Beagle had recovered her boarding and startup crew, leaving those on the migration ship to retract the power cable and close the hatches. The Beagle moved to the second closest migration ship and repeated the process. This time the final detachment from the second ship, with TG2's gaining practice, and Mind Tapping one another concerning what worked best and fastest, powered up that ship in fifteen minutes.

They eventually reached a plateau of performance and speed, so that it required only about twelve minutes to activate another ship's bottle, and then move away before the ship was fully repowered, allowing the crew on board to finish more of the tasks.

It actually took more time to adjust orbits to reach the next ships than they had anticipated. After descending down to select several ships that were in quick and easy to reach orbits on the same side of the planet, they needed to step back higher to reach more of the newer construction ships in orbits ahead or behind them. They were averaging about thirty-four minutes to reach and leave ships. At that rate, they would require eight or nine hours to put crews on all fifteen they hoped to take.

Radio silence was maintained, and the lights in outer compartments with view ports were kept off on the still warming big ships. They were aware the Krall had sensors on the ground that would be able to see if the ships started to display internal lights through ports, or turned on navigation lights or activated electronics that sent any signals. The main control room or Bridge equivalent was internal, not at the nearly round bow, and used only electronic (and waterproof) view screens for information from the outside universe.

The air and surfaces inside the ships were so cold that the Torki and Prada wore what amounted to pressurized soft suits with oxygen refreshers as rebreathers. The Torki version was essentially similar to a large transparent bag that expanded very little in the ship's own air pressure, but required care on the crab's part, so as not to puncture the tough membrane. Not a serious concern with a surrounding atmosphere, even if it was icy cold. They kept their heavy claws tucked under the carapace out of the way, and wore padded foot covers on their relatively sharp feet. They walked with mincing small steps, but made a lot of them quickly. They moved faster than expected, when the humans first saw them don the gear.

There were small slender *arm-like* protrusions in front of their mouths and lower eyes for their manipulator limbs, to enable them to reach and operate equipment and controls. The main eyestalks were covered in a rigid tall bubble over the front of the carapace, so they could pivot them and look in any direction.

Unsurprisingly, the Prada soft suits were somewhat similar in shape to human suits, with a compartment along the back to coil their tails. Wister explained they hated the loss of tail use in the suits, but in a vacuum, a tail extension on a suit was too often pinched or cut, causing a leak.

Marlyn knew the Krall on the planet had to be aware of the Beagle's White Out, and presence in orbit. They no doubt assumed some clan was interested in the communal property in orbit. Why they went from ship to ship, without activating them and leaving orbit must be cause for questions among themselves. The visitors could perhaps be looking for one or two ships already configured specifically for Prada or for Torki use. So long as the migration ships stayed looking inactive, the number of them quietly preparing to leave would possibly not draw interest.

Maggi noticed how the process was taking longer than they had anticipated, because the ships were in wider orbits than expected. She called down to talk to the waiting transfer crews as the Beagle moved to intercept another ship. After consulting with them, and making some suggestions, they came up with a way to speed the process, freeing the Beagle from individually having to visit each migration ship.

There were two Krall designed shuttles aboard, which could hold three of the small scooters inside the passenger area, and cargo stowage for a hydrogen tank. They had brought spare scooters and tanks, so it was possible to increase their effort if the two shuttles made the visit to some of the big ships.

It would be crowded inside the shuttles, because there would be three Torki, a Prada, and five humans to stay on the migration ship, as well as a pilot to return the shuttle. The humans sat two people in the second seat in a cockpit able to hold two Krall, and let the three Torki stand on some of the armored people in the passenger area. The aliens were already in their soft suits, so the shuttle was slowly opened to space to let the atmosphere escape. This way, a human near the rear hatch could get out with a scooter, manually open a shuttle compartment hatch on a migration ship, and slide the Krall shuttle into a space meant for a far larger Torki space boat.

When that was done, the aliens climbed out and went to their designated stations through a manually cycled airlock. The humans pulled out the scooters, and hauled the hydrogen tank to the proper hatch. The shuttle pilot backed out and went to the hatch where the coiled power cable was located. Using the same type of Krall power connection plug as on the Beagle, the smaller fusion bottle of the shuttle had barely enough current to initiate the magnetic field of the larger generator. However, it all worked, marking another success of human ingenuity and improvisation.

The two shuttle pilots had to chase down the Beagle to repeat the process one more time, but overall, they shaved a bit more than two hours off the task if the Beagle had needed to visit those same four ships, one at a time.

It was finished none too soon. The last two ships were still warming their insides and bringing consoles to life when the Beagle detected a clanship launch. It came from the dome where they knew the resident Krall were based on this undesirable and isolated outpost of ship construction.

It had taken the Krall almost six hours to decide to check out the orbital activity of this unknown clan visitor. Had each of the ships visited shown early signs of power activation, Marlyn suspected there would have been a much earlier "inquiry" and more inquisitors. There were eight clanships parked outside that dome, and one each at the domes by the shipyards for the Krall overseers on duty there. The lack of a radio call to them seemed curious by human standards, but the less-than-emergency acceleration didn't indicate urgency on that ship's part.

A visitor making radio contact to those on the ground, from a clan that needed a migration ship, or even two of them, was not required or expected per information from the Torki. This was based on observing past practices of minimal Krall social contacts when different clans were involved. All clans knew which particular clan had responsibility for ship building here, and if you wanted to stay aloof and chose not to talk to them, you didn't have to do so.

The extended apparent ship selection could be the cause for interest now. What was wrong with the ships that they passed by so many? Switching on all fifteen Trap fields of the occupied ships could trigger hostile action, if the clanship pilot had bothered to set his sensors to detect those. If detected, that would surely provoke a strong challenge. Only a joint council decision could justify any clan or several clans appropriating so much of the race's communal property at one time.

Marlyn checked with Kap, the AI, to ask him when all fifteen migration ships were projected to be ready for compete systems activation, and tuning Trap fields for a minimal Jump. A roughly half light-year Jump was what the Torki claimed was the quickest tachyon energy that could be caught that would produce a large enough event horizon for the big ships, to do a rotation into a Jump Hole in safety. The probability for the time needed to snare a tachyon of that energy was an average of twenty minutes. It could be an hour and twenty minutes if you were unlucky. The fifteen ships were not going to be able to go all together. The Beagle could Jump in seconds if it was only going a half light-year, but she intended to be the last to leave, covering the back trail of the large ships.

Kap told her, "All of the migration ships should have powered up to the point where they can generate the required Trap fields. The previously designated time at which they all would do that is still two hours and twenty-two minutes in the future."

They had cut more than two hours off the time needed to occupy all of the ships and get them ready, but because of radio silence, no new Trap initiate time had been set. That was actually a good thing for the moment. The clanship coming up, if it was going to approach the Beagle, would not be suspicious and wouldn't become that way simply because time had ran out for waiting, and all the Trap fields turned active.

She made an internal ship's announcement. "All hands. A clanship has launched from the main Krall dome habitat, which was on the retreating limb of the planet from our orbital location. It isn't in any hurry, there is no targeting scanning of us, and it has not even started an arc towards us, assuming it's out here to ask what the hell we're doing.

"Per Krall standard behavior, they may be unwilling to give offense to a ship from a potential major clan that is looking over migration ships. Other than some heat that is starting to radiate from the cold hulls, I don't think they could know we put crews on the ships we visited. The high moisture content of the atmosphere down there will have absorbed most of the weak infrared radiation from up here. However, those heat signatures will be noticed soon. I want the Krall to get closer, and if I moved towards them, they might find that move to be on the aggressive side of the equation, and take a defensive posture. I want to keep them relaxed and comfortably on the toilet, their pants down by their ankles, if they wore pants that is.

"All launchers are loaded, and we have weapon consoles active, with tracking in passive mode, no scanning to alert them. If I suddenly need to move fast, I want you all secured. There are no aliens on board now, so I don't plan to be gentle. Suit up if you don't have your armor on yet. If I go to maximum acceleration without warning, you need to be well secured, so *stay* secured unless you check with the Bridge first. Captain out."

Maggi had noticed the clanship's track had adjusted course, but not towards the Beagle. "Hard to be certain without active tracking, Marlyn, but are they headed for that migration ship? It's one of ours, and in a middle orbit. Our crew has to be fully powered and ready to activate their Traps, because they've been on board for two hours. It looks like the Krall may want to know what was wrong with that ship that we looked at, and then evidently abandoned it to look at another ship. They'll see the heat increasing, and a sensor sweep will confirm the fusion bottle's magnetic field is active."

Marlyn shook her head. "I wanted them to march right over here to us and ask us what we were doing. If I try to intercept at that distance they'll know something's wrong when we charge over, and we can't get a missile there fast enough to surprise them. Plasma bolts and lasers are instant, but we can't hurt them seriously enough to disable them from several thousand miles away. We need to draw their attention away from the defenseless targets, and they'll remember exactly which ships we visited. If one powered itself on, they'll figure they all did. They don't even need to destroy them to make them useless for our immediate needs. A few laser hits on the Trap field emitters and they can't go anywhere, and they can always call for more clanships to launch."

Alyson offered a comment. "Sarge is down below, with the transfer crews. On the way here, he told us stories about the attacks on K1 by the PU Navy, and how the Krall broke into their defensive formation on the second raid. I think he said they micro Jumped in, from close range, instead of boring in from the outer edges of the globe of ships and bypassed their concentrated defensive fire."

"There are just the two of us up here," Jorl pointed out. "There's no defensive globe defending either side."

"I don't think that's her point," Maggi said. "Alyson, you mean us micro Jump over there, right? Good thinking."

"I've never tried one so short." Marlyn sounded doubtful. "In test Jumps for training at Koban we would go to Haven, or to the Ort cloud."

Maggi reminded her, "We did dozens without moving at all, to test long range Tapping for communications."

"Yes, but we applied no vector for those, or moved a significant distance in Normal Space. This is really a short hop. Even if I zoom in maximum on the console, there is a small uncertainty in destination coordinates. We might White Out as an intersect!"

Intersect was the term Spacers occasionally used to describe the extremely rare occurrence of a Jump terminating within a material object, fatally and explosively so.

Maggi, temperamentally disposed to make daring or aggressive moves, argued for the Jump. "The alternative is to let a single clanship destroy or disable our fifteen occupied ships before we can catch and stop them. We're faster in Normal Space drive than a clanship, but they can get off plenty of missiles and plasma bolts while we chase them. What if we fire multiple rockets as we come out, and let them self-seek?"

"Self-seek will go after any target. These are Krall missiles, not smart munitions."

"Kap can selectively disarm or self-destruct any missiles that chase after our own people. We have to do it before they close with the ship they're headed for. We can't wait if we're going to do this." Maggi knew, from past conversations with her younger friend, that it was to avoid making decisions like this that Marlyn had wanted to be an explorer. However, the luxury of safe choices was for other missions.

Marlyn stood up. "Kap, give me high magnification of that clanship on my front view screen, with a destination designator on the main screen when I tap the navigation display. I want see where we *should* make the exit. I'll try to get in his six o'clock position."

She obviously planned to use Krall manual piloting techniques.

"Mam, if you specify the distance behind the clanship you prefer as an intended White Out point, I will place a designator on your view screen, and move it as the target does." Kap just reminded her why they used AI's, rather than follow the reckless Krall examples.

"What is the recommended range for optimal target acquisition and tracking for a self-seek missile?" She was embarrassed, but adaptable.

"Recommended minimum distance is just over two miles from the target, which is a much greater distance than the half mile of uncertainty of such a short Jump. To ensure missile lock and arming after launch, that only requires a half mile of missile flight time."

"Kap, place the exit point one mile behind them, and show me on the screen." A red pip appeared behind the clanship, and the zoom backed out so they could see both.

"Kap, select four anti-ship missiles spaced evenly around the ship, and launch them all as we pop back into Normal Space."

"Ready, Mam."

"Alyson, Jorl, open all your gun ports, and fire any weapons that bear as we exit."

They leaned forward to tap at their own consoles, and kept their hands near for firing commands. Kap could do this as well, but they trusted their decisions better as to what part of the clanship to selectively strike first.

"Kap, Jump."

Even with their enhanced nervous system and eyes, they didn't see the galactic sky wink out and back, it happened so rapidly. The quadruple vibration of the four launches was felt, but that was a few hundredths of a second after they had happened. The orientation of the planet below had instantly shifted, and they found themselves one mile nearly directly behind the clanship.

Alyson immediately fired a finely aimed plasma cannon shot, which at near light velocity hit the cover port of the plasma cannon she could see on this side. Jorl, a thousandth of a second behind her fired two heavy laser pulses at as many enemy laser port covers. Their intent was to try to heat fuse them closed. The Krall would have sensor warnings of the four missile launches, as they each used active scans to find a target, but there would be no warning from the cannons or lasers before they hit.

The Krall reaction was still swift, because using a magnified view screen of the clanship, they saw one of the laser ports Jorl had hit manage to slide open. The other two ports remained closed, unable to fire on a missile that was inbound, coming from a position the one opened port could not fire at anyway.

The Krall pilot made a fine effort, as the attitude thrusters pivoted his ship hard, to allow open gun portal to bear on that missile, as well sight weapons on them. The hypervelocity missile was a small target, and it was unlikely to be hit by manual firing before its acceleration pushed it into their near side. Tracking showed a second missile had also selected the clanship, and was turning to intercept from farther away as it curved back.

Knowing what the Krall pilot was doing to gain a firing angle, Marlyn tapped for a short burst of Krall crippling thrust forward, and a hard sideways attitude thrust to bring their bow around to point at their enemy, creating a somewhat slimmer silhouette. The Krall laser gunner got off a beam just as Jorl put two of his beams on that now more visible gun port.

The Krall gunner had aimed where the Beagle was expected to be, but his target had shifted enough that when the speed of light beam was triggered by the warrior (a laser was something they could *not* dodge), it was aimed at a spot they had just vacated. He didn't get another shot with that weapon, because the portal opening suddenly glowed red and vapors and melted droplets sprayed into space. The beams themselves were invisible, but their effects were not.

Alyson was prepared to fire two plasma bolts at the already open cannon portal, rotating around on the clanship and coming into view, trying to come to bear on the Beagle. That was when the first missile spoiled the Krall's plan. The silent bright flash on the side of the nearly diamond-hard hull coating was evidence that a missile had stuck. If it worked as designed, the front part of the warhead, with its molten metal penetrator stream had opened a six-inch wide hole in the hull, and entering through that maelstrom of molten material was the bulk of the ultra-high explosive main charge.

A less bright explosion followed, because it happened inside, but the volume of debris and hull plating flying from the side of the clanship was impressive. The reaction of the ship to the explosive ejection of material halted its pivoting, or slowed it was more accurate, because the pilot had maintained the side thrust at the top, despite the major damage. This ship would never land on a planet, but it could still fight.

Alyson saw a blue bolt of ionized plasma from the cannon port she wanted to hit. However, the plasma wasn't directed at the Beagle since the weapon couldn't bear on them yet. She realized they must have detected the second missile arcing around as it sought its target. They missed hitting the fast agile missile, now up to a truly high velocity. On the zoomed in screen, Kap projected that it would impact near the bow, just below the command deck.

The angle for her to fire on that plasma port improved over the next second, as its plasma chamber would be recycling for a last effort to hit the now straight on missile. This was a better opportunity than they had on the first effort, to hit the missile as it was curving.

Alyson surely ruined the gunner's day when she blasted the plasma cannon opening with both of her bolts. Two seconds later, a second bright flash and then hull plates flew from the bulkhead of the deck immediately below the command level. That top deck did not have a decompression seal for the stairwells between those two decks. The pilot and gunners experienced the explosive overpressure, followed by rapid decompression. They were doomed if not in armor, which was unlikely for a flight up to orbit just to see what a fellow clanship was doing.

"Missile fired!" was Kap's warning, letting them know that the last act of the clanship was to try to avenge its own destruction. Unlike the Beagle, which had full stacks of missiles in all of its launchers on this raid, Krall ships normally didn't leave them loaded while sitting on the ground, as this ship had been, not expecting to find an enemy out here. They must have sent a warrior to load at least one rack, the closest launch bay being three decks below the command level, where it would be below the blast and decompression doors. A warrior there could have survived the hit that disabled or killed the crew above, and had launched a missile.

Marlyn realized if she applied emergency thrust, they would only close the distance, because their bow was aimed at the broken clanship. If the missile was on self-seek, they were the most probable nearby target.

On the captain's view screen, Kap displayed a computer track and prediction for the missile. It had been launched away from them, but like their second missile, it was curving around, obviously locked onto them.

Jorl recognized that manual firing in this case wasn't required for a human to select the best of several targets. There was only one. "Kap, take laser control and fire on the missile."

Instantly, the two invisible beams being fired were displayed on the view screen as representative of where they were focused. As soon as the intersecting lines met on the target icon, the missile activated its mirror finish, and twisted and turned to prevent any hot spot from burning through too quickly. The range was already so short that the seconds needed for laser penetration weren't available. The missile also happened to be inside the coverage area of the two plasma cannons that Alyson had just fired at the ship it came from. Her recycle time for those two cannons needed more seconds than they had. The enemy was either dead or dying. They would likely not see the results on the Beagle, but they had struck back effectively.

To TG2's, with superconducting thinking processes, the passage of two seconds before the impact was like watching a slow death coming. There was no way for thrusters or Normal Space drive to outrun a nearby hypervelocity missile as they overcame their massive inertia. Even dead or dying, the Krall could be dangerously fatal.

Maggi blinked and started slightly as the view screen picture suddenly changed, with no missile track shown. Had the missile exploded early, or the lasers gotten through? "Huh? What happened?"

"You didn't think I was just going to sit there and let them screw up my pretty ship did you? Close your mouth, and try to look smarter than that young face and blonde hair suggests."

"Marlyn! I mean, Captain, you Jumped!" Alyson shouted, almost in disbelief.

Giving her the *of course* look, Marlyn said, "I saw no reason to wait around, did you? I held onto the rest of that Jump tac energy because I was leery of getting so damn close to them to make our own shots count. That caution was right. Next time we go in, shoot at their asses, and we get out right away."

Jorl asked the obvious question that seemed to elude the other swift thinkers. "What's that missile going to do now? It'll seek a migration ship."

Marlyn agreed. "Right, let's Jump back and shoot it out of the sky."

They returned, with several hundred miles of buffer for time to take defensive action, discovering the missile had turned to seek a migration ship in a lower orbit. The new target wasn't one of theirs, and Marlyn decided to let it hit its new target. They didn't plan to leave it for Krall use anyway. She asked Kap about the other two missiles they had fired, and had left them in the AI's trusty digital and metaphorical hands. She had been so focused on self-preservation that those two had faded to unimportance.

"I placed their warheads on safe, Mam, and switched off their engines and seeker mode when both targeted migration ships. They have escape velocity from Toborkiti. Do you wish us to chase them for reuse? They are traveling in nearly opposite directions."

"Do they have fuel to reach some of the orbiting ships we don't have crews aboard?"

"Yes, if you do not delay very long to retarget them."

"Do that, Kap. However, choose ships that are as far from those we have in our control as possible, and in low orbits. They will be waiting for Jump tacs for some time, and I don't want them in the middle of a debris field."

Next, she told Maggi to broadcast to all the captured ships to prepare to Jump as soon as they were able, to the nearby rendezvous system. Then, to ensure they would get the time they needed, she had Kap take the Beagle to a lower orbit, and head for the main habitat dome for the Krall detachment based there.

The dome had been at the horizon when the first ship lifted, and the quick combat had taken place after the two ships would have been over their horizon. They probably didn't know that things had turned out poorly for their clan mates. She wanted to be the first to deliver the bad news, actually sent via more bad news in the way of "parting gifts," unknowingly repeating the same action that Mirikami had taken. She left no clanships untouched on the planet, and put several missiles into the habitat dome. The domes near the two shipyards received a single missile to the top center, presumably where the Krall monitors stayed. She didn't want to inflict damage too severe, if fires could spread to an underground factory filled with Prada workers.

In a communication Maggi made to Coldar and Wister on one of the migration ships, she apologized for the Beagle not attempting a rescue of their people on the ground there. There were two known Torki lodges, and the Prada must have at least one factory under either or both small domes at the costal shipyards.

She explained that the Beagle had risked being damaged or disabled in the fight, and the next mission was too vital to the human first-strike plans. If the mission to destroy Eight Balls, and the production facilities went well, one or two migration ships, with adequate space remaining, could return here to Toborkiti with one or two of their fighting ships for protection, and pick up the workers.

Coldar, when she told him how the older ships in orbit were to be destroyed, was confident that the workers below would be safe from Krall abuse, and they would be needed to increase production of replacement migration ships. There were two vessels already under assembly, visible in the huge support cradles in different stages of construction. Coldar said one ship looked to be within a half orbit of completion.

He told Maggi that the Olts belonging to the Torki in orbit, using the new capability discovered after they had experienced her Mind Tap, had a greater communication range and should be able to reach the Torki Olts on the surface, at least to send data. There was no reply yet from the more limited range of those groundside Olts, which apparently had not spontaneously opened the new library of data and ability as those on Haven had done. The data sent down explained the new Olt capability. If the data had actually been received, it was possible the Olts might soon undergo the change anyway. If not, a Mind Tap from one of the Kobani should unlock the new library of data for them, as it had on Haven.

Marlyn waited the almost two hours it required for the unluckiest of the fifteen migration ships to trap a tachyon of adequate energy, and Jump for the target system. The Beagle then put a missile in many of the higher orbit ships, which potentially could be revived with the least refurbishment. Plasma bolts and lasers targeted the hulls, propulsion systems, and Trap emitters of the oldest ships, thus destroying their maneuverability and making them useless in the short term while saving anti-ship missiles. Then she Jumped to join her prizes.

Her communications specialists sent the news into Tachyon Space that the migration ships were obtained, and that six would be dispatched towards CS1, six for CS2, and three for the Eight Ball production world. The captured clanships would return to Koban or Haven for supplies, and then Jump ahead to overtake the slow migration ships. They would meet them at the previously coordinated star systems, for initial supply transfers. There were enough migration ships to provide redundancy if there were technical problems with any of the older ones.

In return, they received word that the Avenger had passed through an intermediate star system the day before to leave the message, while enroute to the CS2 system. Noreen would wait at an uninhabited system short of her destination to wait for the migration ships.

There was no new message from Mirikami on the Mark, but he was in transit to his next waypoint. He would learn of the success of the migration ship capture when he made his next intermediate Jump. He too would wait at an empty star system closer to CS1, waiting for the migration ships to catch up.

The pieces were coming together for a coordinated set of attacks, and their loss of one of the supply clanships had been unexpected and tragic, but was included in the contingency planning, for taking more ships than required to provide redundancy. The additional migration ships were good news because it would speed the loading of refugees.

With only a thousand TG2s on each of the three raiding ships, there was no hope, or intent, to take possession of any part of the domes, factories, or orbital stations and hold them for very long. They were counting on Krall overconfidence by relying on a handful of warriors controlling their slave labor at the production sites, and most of those warriors staying in the small observer dome facilities near the shipyards.

The main Krall habitat domes were built well away from the polluted factory and mining areas. A heavy missile barrage on the way in to knock out any parked clanships and to make hits on the domes, to try to take out clan sub leaders, would disrupt and delay the Krall reply. They hoped.

The Mark of Koban and the Avenger would leave their raiders on the ground, and get airborne again to defend against any clanship that might have been missed, and to attack the slower shuttles the Krall would still have available.

The time of greatest risk to the rescue mission, would be the extended period of landing and loading the migration ships, and getting them back into space. The intent was to have them hold onto a tachyon in Trap field, with enough energy to execute a Jump as soon as the ship reached low orbit. The Torki, a safety conscious race, operated three independent Trap field systems on their ships versus the two that both humans and Krall used. They couldn't *Trap* a tachyon while in a gravity well, but like the Flight of Fancy had done for twenty- three years, they could hold onto any they caught out in space, before they landed on a planet. They then could form a stable event horizon shortly after reaching three hundred miles, and Jump to safety.

It was hoped the captured clanships would already be well enough armed that they could provide some orbital cover for the migration ships if needed. If not, there was a limited supply of anti-ship missiles on Haven, which the Prada were now making. Most had been loaded onto the three raiders. However, some of those newly produced missiles could be loaded when the supply ships picked up provisions on Haven. There would be little time for that if they were Jumping back to CS1, the most distant point in the raids.

Mirikami, anxious to reach his next planned White Out system, wanted to confirm the plan was working out for the rescue. If that part of the complex mission failed to come together, they were committed to complete the raids, even if the Krall exterminated the workers, which they couldn't move to another factory world and didn't need where they were.

He wasn't certain if their new alien friendships would remain intact if the collateral damage to their people was as horrendous as the Krall were certainly willing to apply. The balls were all in motion, now they had to keep juggling.

Chapter 18: Three Strikes and Out

A single clanship made an exit over Koban, broadcasting the recognition signal as it did so, and thirty minutes later another ten ships erupted into Normal Space, within two or three minutes of one another. Without the advance warning, some of the people below might have gone into a panic, learning so many clanships emerged together. Work crews quickly met them as they landed near the four entrances of the Prime City dome. There, some provisions for the human crews were taken on, and dozens more TG2s came on board to supplement the flight crews as supply loaders when they Jumped to Haven. They would remain aboard as added crew for the missions to support and defend the migration ships, which were still enroute to the systems where they would rendezvous with the three raiders.

The pause at Koban lasted only an hour, and all eleven ships launched in rapid succession for Haven, making the short Jump inward as soon as they cleared atmosphere. Having been forewarned by radio, the Kobani, Prada, and Torki waiting for them on Haven, had provisions ready for the refugee's needs, which were loaded as swiftly as possible. Some of the TG2's focused on loading pallets of anti-ship, and new heavy ground attack missiles aboard each ship, and using the internal hoists to place them in the appropriate launcher compartments. The designated TG2 gunners used a few minutes in Mind Taps with the Torki, learning how the new ground attack missiles worked, and their capability. The new larger rockets had just been produced on a recently opened production line.

The Prada seriously needed the refugees they expected to arrive soon, to increase their worker numbers. The factory was in short supply of the raw materials needed to make many of the weapons that were being requested. There were too few Prada to manufacture and to expand mining operations. They also needed workers to rebuild the old transport systems to bring the materials to the required locations. This entire process seemed much like the wartime migrations to new bases, which the younger Prada had heard about, in histories that described past Krall wars. They were eager to please, and knew what was required of them. However, those *being* pleased were not those that the average Prada thought they were serving.

For now, only a few of the elder Prada were aware that the production was not for use by the Rulers. There was no one openly lying to the work force about the purpose of this increased production. The deceit was one of omission. After thousands of years of working as loyal slaves on behalf of the Krall, direct explanations from the Rulers had never been offered previously, and that absence now wasn't questioned.

Mirikami, and the handful of Prada elders, accepted the guilty necessity of having the war material manufactured, which was needed for the rescue of Prada populations. Wister had cautioned Mirikami against trying to explain what was happening, when he had suggested that he wanted to be more forthright with the younger Prada.

Wister justified his actions this way, "Our people do not question guidance and advice from the elder Prada, accepting that we have the longer perspective and wisdom to make the right decisions for them. We elders are doing this for them now. It would be unwise to shake their confidence in a belief system that was bred into us before we met the Krall, and has been reinforced more strongly in us not to question the Rulers. Any Prada that questioned their right to rule us as an elder species has died. Such selective evolution applies to us as well as to the Krall. Now is not the time to try to modify those inbred instincts. Not when the first opportunity to do so in thousands of years is close to a reality, and is still fragile."

The workers probably thought the humans were taking the arms to the Rulers elsewhere. That presumption was accurate, if they were not to be as benignly delivered as they assumed.

The Torki had technical improvements to offer on some of the standard Krall weapons, and they too needed more workers and production facilities. Haven was swinging into a phase of growth that would create an inter species power base for the years to come. Unarmed Kobani supermen were far less effective than some armed with weapons only they could wield so fast and deadly, as no previous species in the galaxy had been able to do.

The Kobani spear point was being sharpened, even as their numbers (although still far too few) were increasing faster than anticipated. Humanity was in no way able to take the Krall on head-to-head. These first three strikes were only expected to wound, and with luck could prove crippling to Krall invasion plans for a year or two, giving humanity some breathing room, and time to prepare for greater strikes.

The eleven clanships were on the ground on Haven in as short a time as possible, and the first five ships were launched in a rush, going to join the six slow migration ships they knew were headed for distant CS1, and joining Captain Mirikami on the Mark. Within hours, the other clanships would be launched as well. Four of them would go in support of Captain Renaldo and the Avenger, for the CS2 raid. Two more went to the Botolian world where Captain Greeves and the Beagle would attack the Eight Ball orbital manufacturing station.

****

Marlyn's Beagle reached her rendezvous star system, six light-years from the old Botolian target world, twenty-two hours before the first migration ship did a White Out. The next two migration ship arrivals were staggered over a forty-five minute interval, matching the different tachyon capture times for their Jumps from Toborkiti.

Marlyn sent both shuttles to gather the three flight crews for a meeting on the Beagle, and to give them food supplies specific to both species, which she still had aboard from the journey transporting them all out from Haven.

This was only a contingency, in the event the two clanship loads of supplies from Haven failed to arrive before she had to depart. In order to coordinate her attack with those that the Mark and the Avenger would make, she had to Jump in two days.

Marlyn was still hosting the three Prada and three Torki representatives, furnishing them with a small buffet, when Kap told her the expected two clanships had all performed White Outs within minutes of each other. They were on the far side of the blue giant star, and had emerged transmitting their recognition signals. The wide separation distance was actually a security precaution to prevent an accidental emergence of all of the ships into any potential Krall ambush. That seemed incredibly unlikely, but it was another caution that Mirikami insisted on, and which cost nothing to implement.

Marlyn had been continuously broadcasting her own encrypted recognition signal, and the clanships had sent their own as they emerged. The intent was for them to allow enough time for her to have received their counter signals, and then they would Jump in-system to join the Beagle and the three migration ships. With Jump technology, the clanships arrived right on the heels of their own original gamma rays and recognition signals, popping out a few hundred miles away. Using Normal Space drives, they moved into a loose formation. They each had two shuttles, but rather than physically cross over to talk, they used their view screen systems for a conference meeting. Marlyn led her alien guests up to the Bridge to participate.

Marlyn took charge of her small task force. "Captains, I will Jump in a little more than fifty-two hours. I sent a message into Tachyon Space to both the Mark and Avenger, to let them know I was on schedule. I hope and expect to receive their messages, telling me the same thing, as I depart from here.

"The Beagle and our two shuttles will be here for two days to assist you in transferring supplies to the three migration ships." She paused a moment, looking at the Prada and Torki with her. "I don't know which ships are being used for which species to evacuate. Nor do I know the names you have chosen for them. I assume you have decided that already?"

Because the ships were to become Torki property, and each had a pilot, they had made the naming decisions on their own. In discussions with the Prada representatives, they had assigned which species would be boarded on each ship. Marlyn heard now what they had decided.

One Torki separated slightly from the other three. "I am Tathed, and have been selected to speak for us all. The ship names are in Torki, and are not pronounceable in your words. However, after we explained the meanings of our names to the humans with us, they suggested human terms that you can use to identify them. The Torki names are only symbolic, and logic does not care what you or the Prada use in your own words. Only that you know which ship is which."

Marlyn nodded, aware now that all Torki and Prada knew the gesture, from Mind Tap lessons of human speech and mannerisms. "I am pleased we will be able to return your ships to your control when we return to Haven." A subtle reminder that the three spacecraft had a human intended purpose for now, which probably matched what the Torki wanted as well. It didn't hurt to make certain there was no misunderstanding.

"What are the ship's names?"

Tathed told her his own ship's name, in Standard and in low Krall, meant Sea Wanderer. There was a grating clicking sound he made after that. Marlyn assumed that was the equivalent name in the Torki language. The other two Torki representatives bobbed their whole bodies in apparent excitement.

"The ship that Jatrup will pilot," he waved a claw, in a gesture to mimic a human's hand motion, and the indicated Torki did a semi bow by lowering her carapace, "is named Larval Drifter." A hardly poetic sounding name in Standard.

The third ship's name was announced for its pilot, Galrop, as Home Tide, which was a better sounding name to a human's way of thinking. Marlyn had already surmised, from overheard remarks from the human crews that flew the shuttles over and back, that they knew the names in advance, and had already "humanized" them. She didn't know the official names before now, but had already heard mention of the Wanderer, the Drifter, and the Tide.

"Those are fine names, and I am sure you will do them honor by your service to them. Have you decided which will be used for Prada evacuations if we are able to safely land on the planet?" With the bounty of three ships, they no longer needed to transport Torki and Prada together. The Torki would be drier than they wanted, and the Prada wetter if they had to share.

A small bow from Tathed, and he gestured to the Prada that had accompanied him from the Migration ship. The Prada spoke for the first time that Marlyn had heard. "I am Faltif Maltid, or just Faltif if you wish. Wister choses to use only one name, as do most of the Rulers, but I have taken my paternal name as second, as was our custom long ago." A Prada rebel, Marlyn noted with satisfaction.

"The Sea Wanderer will attempt to rescue the Prada that we believe are in a forest close to a small dome by the sea. Tathed will pilot the ship to land by that dome, and I will try to talk them into leaving the forest to join us. If there are workers in the factory under the dome, they may come as well. That is, if you do not need to destroy the dome first."

"Faltif, we can attack the dome without its complete destruction. We know where the underground entrances are, below the elevator shafts around the inner ring of the central great hall. We can fire missiles and plasma bolts to miss these areas. There will not be very many Krall inside the dome and most of them will be on the top floors. They always prefer the high ground."

She knew this from Mind Taps of their Krall prisoners on Koban, those that had not managed to will their own deaths yet. The higher the status, the higher the floor they were assigned for use. Blasting the tops of domes took out their highest status warriors and most experienced sub leaders. It was convenient that they always organized in that "top down" manner.

"There will be a delay before we can be assured you can safely land, Tathed. I can attack the dome and clanships we find there with a surprise volley of missiles they will not expect, from what they will believe is one of their ships. The underground factory is not vital so I don't need to destroy that, and I will be too busy to land troops there right away.

"My primary mission is to destroy the Eight Balls, and the orbital station that helps build them. There are Torki up there, which one of your ships will rescue when we take the station. There may be Prada up there as well. I don't know if the water in the station can be transferred to the migration ship quickly."

With a mental Olt signal from Tathed, Jatrup spoke now. "I will pilot the Larval Drifter to dock with the station when you say it is safe. Then when I have the workers, I can land at sea anywhere on the planet to load enough water for the Jump."

"It may not be made safe to dock there until I have destroyed all of the Eight Balls, and return." Marlyn told her. "I don't know where they might be located."

"The Torki inside will know. If you take the station, they can tell us where the hammers were placed."

"If there are hammers or Eight Balls, where I can see them, I will attack those first. Then I will take the station. Each of those weapons can kill a planet. However, we have two clanships, and one was not part of the planning. We hoped to have at least one, and we have two. I can place more TG2s on one of those for attacking the station, because I don't need them with me to shoot at Eight Balls."

This was an improvisation on her part, but the actual fighting at the station was all going to be done by the TG2s anyway. A missile or beam attack on that would open too many compartments to space, and kill most of those they were here to rescue.

One of the clanship pilots volunteered to deliver the large boarding party to the orbital station, leaving her free to track down Eight Balls. The Torki from the station could then tell them where more of the Balls were located, if spread around the system as she assumed.

The ground rescue might need all of their forces to take the dome and guard against a possible Krall counter attack while the Sea Wanderer loaded. The lodge evacuation on the other hand, would be easier. The Krall disliked water, and they were too dense to swim far or fast, and generally stayed away from cool, dank lodges.

The Home Tide was going to land in the ocean just off shore from the Torki lodge. It would take on water, and the lodge population could swim out underwater to get aboard. There were seldom Krall visiting a lodge, other than for picking up completed single ships, mini tanks, or testing other weapons that required electronics and quantum encrypted locks.

There would be a few dozen TG2s landing with Home Tide, to go ashore to provide protection.

Marlyn wrapped up the meeting, so the task of transferring supplies that the migration ships needed could start. She spent time with the three clanship pilots, whom she insisted on calling captains, despite their feelings they had not earned the position. All of them had the full complex of ripper genes, which meant they soon had the knowledge of how to fight their ships as well as fly them. If things went well, they would get to watch the Beagle do most of the shooting. Marlyn wasn't about to let on to them that she had gained no combat experience from her trip into Human Space, just more flight experience in a Krall clanship, which these former Spacers didn't have.

They were finished with the supply and crew transfers a half day before Marlyn needed to Jump. The newly christened Thunder, a name her new captain liked, would Jump with the Beagle. It would hold back while Marlyn made a pass at the unsuspecting planet, to take out the small number of clanships expected there, and hit the top floors of the dome where the lone Prada factory was located underneath. The Thunder would then follow the Beagle to the orbital station, and hard dock to let seven hundred TG2s knock on the doors, so to speak.

****

The Avenger came out at its waypoint system all alone. Noreen and her Bridge staff were informed by her signals section that there were two sets of messages for them. One, a day old message from the Beagle, which said all of its migration ships and clanships had joined her. Marlyn would be ready to Jump on schedule, as would be her rescue ships.

The second message was from Mirikami, sent two days ago, saying that the Mark of Koban was now waiting at its standoff point, but didn't expect his other ships to catch up to him before he had to Jump to CS1. He pointed out that he didn't need the rescue ships to meet with him before he started his raid, and he planned to leave a message for them to follow him as soon as they could. If supplies were not loaded by a day later, the transfer work could be completed *after* they left CS1. Saving the factory workers came first.

Noreen grinned over at Carson, monitoring a console on the Bridge. "Now if our own ships can get here before *we* have to leave. Our migration ships were the second set that Tet sent ahead, right after his group. I think they'll be here by tomorrow, and our supply clanships left Heaven early, and should arrive today.

"I'll ask your dad to organize our people below, to help prepare as many shuttle loads as we can before the big ships get here. Like Tet, I don't think we can get all the clanships unloaded into them before we have to Jump.

"I'd like to have one of the new clanships go with us, to add some firepower. Their message said they took on some of the new ground attack missiles, which we don't have. I wish we had known the Prada could turn those out so soon. Wister must have lit a fire under those bushy tails to get them so busy. I suspect Tet would have waited another day or two for those, if he knew they would be ready so soon. The Prada have not had tight deadlines from the Krall, who spent fifty years preparing to fight humans. They don't coordinate well with our impatient species, mostly because *we* are not the high and mighty *Rulers*."

Carson looked worried about her last remark. "Mom, if the Prada and Torki can gear up for faster production for us, can't they do it for the Krall if ordered? Are we really going to slow them down in attacks in Human Space that much? I know Uncle Tet is counting on our attacks to do that."

"Carson, your uncle Thad and General Nabarone understand this strategy better than I do, and they support it. Captain Mirikami has been so right so often on the big picture, that I don't doubt his overall plan. The Navy briefing they received on Poldark indicated the Krall were massing material on planets that were scouted out in their territory. It appeared they were almost in position to use the migration ships to transport a lot of war material forward to K1, or start more invasions.

"General Nabarone said the Army has tens of millions of soldiers in the training pipeline now, many of them from Hub worlds, and they can be placed wherever the Krall choose to go. The productivity of weapons and equipment is finally at a level to supply that many troops."

Carson saw where she was going. "After this week, the Krall can't deliver their new equipment to the front lines at the pace they need. They have already lost their migration ships, and the clanships they have now will have to last until replaced in a few years, from new facilities. If the Navy can take out more of their clanships it will force the Krall to slow down their advances, while humanity continues to build up forces."

Noreen was amused to watch her son pull at his lower lip, in an unconscious imitation of his uncle's thinking pose. His words also echoed the thoughts that could have come from Mirikami. "This is going to enrage the Krall clans. Berserker anger might be impossible to resist on Poldark, if they decided to punish humanity there."

Dillon, stepping out of a lift, heard his son. "Carson, it isn't as if they weren't winning the war the way it was going. Higher human casualties may result from our attacks in two days, but Krall recklessness and anger should also deplete their resources faster, buying time and saving lives in the long term.

"From the Prada and Torki we have learned they don't have the large slave population we expected. They only kept alive those workers they needed, to drag out wars for as long as they could for their selective breeding to succeed. High productivity has never been a requirement when they fought past wars. We are taking the workers that know how to build the most critical weapon elements with us. This will hurt them."

Carson asked the key question, which they all had been asking themselves. "What can they do to hurt us in return?"

The answer, when it came, would be worse than anyone had imagined.

****

Telour's visit to the soft Krall world was now paying the dividends he and Tor Gatrol Kanpardi had expected. Til Gatrol Telour, bearing his new title as Kanpardi's second in command, marched down from his clanship between two octets of his own honor guard. He had only permitted his title, and his inspection, to be announced in advance of his landing.

Telour relished the rare look of surprise on a Krall's rigid face, when Parkoda realized that the title of Til Gatrol had been awarded to his old Graca clan nemesis.

Parkoda, still a Tanga clan sub leader with one name, knew to expect a difficult time from any representative sent by Tor Gatrol Kanpardi, but he knew this inspection was going to be particularly brutal to his ego. There wasn't even the possibility that his clan would back him this time, in a death match challenge offered to anyone with such high status. On Koban, he now knew his clan leader had sacrificed him for a possible political advantage for the clan. A move that failed when Kanpardi had shrugged off Parkoda's insulting remarks, and had remained the Gatrol.

Protocol required Parkoda to walk up to a high status, triple-named warrior and salute, and ask how he could serve him. Determined to show no sign of his anger and resentment, he stood in front of Telour and raised his left arm; talons extended, and dropped the arm crisply.

He fervently wished he could have torn the flesh from Telour's muzzle, the stoic expression on his personal and clan enemy marred by a slight ripple of his flexible lips. The latter betrayed a sense of pleasure, as if Telour had just tasted some particularly flavorful Raspani meat.

Maintaining iron control over his own temper, Parkoda asked, "How may I serve you, Til Gatrol?" He omitted saying his base name of Telour, which conveyed no overt insult to the high status rank because the full title was spoken on his initial greeting. It was a trivial slight aimed at the holder of that rank, demonstrating that he wasn't currying the favor he knew wasn't going to be offered.

"Sub leader, you must personally show me how you verify every soft Krall prisoner's location, and demonstrate that they are all here." Telour knew well how it was done, but making Parkoda do it personally was part of showing to all that he was a low status flunky.

This demand surprised Parkoda. He anticipated criticism of how security was conducted, how guards were trained, and how many were assigned to monitor the compound where the soft ones lived. This demand was simple arithmetic, done mainly at the inconvenience of the soft ones, forcing them to pass in lines through a Katusha tattoo detector and having them counted. This was done periodically anyway.

"Yes, Til Gatrol." He turned to his own aide, to order the assembly siren to sound over the compound. He was interrupted.

"I said for you to *personally* show me all of the steps. If I was in error and you have been demoted in status again, and this warrior you turned to is now the sub leader in charge, I will order him to do as I said."

There, Telour thought in satisfaction. *One cloaca lick forced in public*. This was in front of Parkoda's next highest subordinate. The word would spread. The number two Krall always wanted his superior's status and job, if he could get it without exposing his own disloyalty or justify to the clan leaders that a death match challenge served their needs.

Parkoda's eyes narrowed and his deployed ultrasonic ears quivered to show his emotion, but all he said was, "Follow me."

Then he ran towards the armored blockhouse, placed outside the main entrance to the dome where the prisoners were housed. Because Krall generally ran from point A to point B if it was more than about fifty feet, it wasn't an insult to do this. However, doing so at top speed was pushing the envelope of proper respect.

For Parkoda's purposes, he wanted to dismiss the warriors inside to leave immediately. He would send them to help herd the soft one's towards the counting stations, before they could see what next humiliation Telour could think of to inflict.

When Telour stepped inside, the hand of warriors there were racing through the heavy airlock-like door, into the dome. Parkoda pressed the button to trigger the head count siren call the instant Telour entered, making certain he *saw* him performing the action. The wail of the alert through the open double doors diminished when the outer door closed.

That gave Telour his next opportunity to nitpick Parkoda's administration of the facility, but robbed him of his audience.

He noted critically, "Both doors were open simultaneously. A soft one waiting outside could have tried to enter the guard house."

Parkoda countered. "There were five of us in here, all armed, and we have twice their strength and speed. I assumed your time was too valuable to wait, so I opened both doors to send my warriors to gather the soft Krall faster. They will be tending their crops and Raspani herd." This was a Raspani dung pile of an excuse, but Telour couldn't call them back to witness another humiliation of their sub leader.

One of the two honor guard octets had followed Telour, at his signal, and the eight warriors were crowded at the outer entrance behind Telour. This gave Parkoda an opportunity to dig back at these Graka clan interlopers.

"I can call four of my warriors to staff this guard post so we can go inside, but if your octet can safely perform the duties of the hand I would call, you and I can enter the compound to observe the head count. Unless you require the protection of your honor guard from the soft ones once inside."

Bam! That was a double slight delivered in as polite a manner as possible for a Krall, which hit at both the octet, and Telour. The inference that an octet of elite Graka honor guards might not be the equal of a hand of ordinary Tanga guards provoked snarls from those behind Telour. The second slam was suggesting that Telour might need them to defend him against the non-aggressive soft Krall prisoners inside the compound.

This had not quite evened the scorecard, and Parkoda knew he would lose this game, but any victory for him loomed large today. He wished he'd delayed his guard's departure to witness his clever remarks. He lamented the fact that only Graka clan was witness to his cleverness, and the retaliation from Telour would only escalate now.

Telour left his guards at the blockhouse, awaiting replacements from Tanga clan, and accompanied Parkoda into the compound. As an experienced Krall warrior, with high status from combat, Telour wasn't personally concerned about any threat to himself. The same could actually be said of a novice with no kills. It was bred into Krall nature to relish combat, and to have no fear of the outcome.

Besides, Telour knew that if Parkoda failed to keep order in this compound, and a high status visitor were even attacked by a soft Krall, he would be fortunate if his clan leaders allowed him a berserker's death on some ice cold human world.

They moved quickly across a wide, grassy area, which lay between the structure that surrounded the ten-mile wide circle, and the inner dome. A hundred-foot high hollow ring, thirty feet in depth, had a mirrored surface inside the ring, where Krall monitors walked the four internal ring corridors, looking through the one way transparent armored walls at their prisoners. No Krall had ever heard of a frosted doughnut, which the compound somewhat resembled. The outer ring was the frosting for the unseen guards to patrol, watching their charges move about in the outside habitat where they produced their own food.

At the center was a sizable dome that housed over a hundred thousand of the "family units." That term stuck any Krall as bizarre, that these cousins to the present Krall species knew their offspring, and the mated pairs (usually) stayed together through multiple breeding cycles. The Olt'kitapi mental infection had taken these traitors away from the Krall's future on the Great Path.

These once typical "soft" Krall had allowed their minds to be modified by that damnable dead species, to make them behave similar to weaker species, to form alliances. Those were the mere animal species that all true Krall knew they were destined to dominate, or to destroy.

Whatever was done to them was permanent, and made a part of their genetics as a dominate feature. Cross breeding was possible with true warriors, in the early stages of Krall selective evolution, but the offspring of the mattings always retained the mental "defects." Namely, of the soft Krall's lack of aggression and loss of the intense desire to fight for domination. Of the most critical importance to the aggressive and warlike Krall, those long ago cubs of cross breeding, when they reached novice age, could be trained to fight but they still could not activate any of the ancient Olt'kitapi "living ships," even with a tattoo.

The inability of the modern and evolutionally improved Krall warrior to be able to operate one of those ships was the sole reason the older version of their species was permitted to exist. The ability to even cross breed was now lost, after twenty-three thousand years of genetic separation. However, only an unmodified soft Krall could arouse the last large ships the Olt'kitapi had ever designed.

Unless activated by a soft one, the ships seemed to slumber in a standby state for hundreds of years, occasionally activating on their own. They never tried to move from where they were stored, an act that would trigger their destruction. The great ships performed internal self-maintenance, rarely performed hull damage repair, and based on monitoring their activity they apparently did a massive data download, using their intricate sensors. Afterwards, they returned to the former standby state, apparently never requiring fuel replenishment. At least they had no fusion bottles the K'Tals could find.

The soft Krall could make the old ships respond to them, and to obey their commands. However, the soft ones claimed they didn't understand the technology of the ships. They professed not to know how they were able to get the ships to do what they did, or why the modern Krall, with the same tattoos as they had, were not able to do so. This denial was professed under conditions that even the warrior breed would consider extreme. The extended torture and dismemberment of the adults, and components of their "family units," would generate any concessions demanded but the one they wanted, which was, how to make the ships respond to the more dominate species. It was most frustrating, and required keeping the breeding line of the traitors alive, and healthy.

A viable-sized breeding pool for the soft Krall had to be maintained as well, something the selective breeding programs of individual warrior clans had proven was necessary. Unwanted, but useful, the early Krall genotype was maintained in captivity and guarded. Today, their numbers were being counted solely for the purpose of Telour to harass Parkoda. This was a way for Kanpardi and Telour, representing Graka clan, to rub Tanga clan and Parkoda's muzzles into the dirt.

It was a minor diversion from the more useful mission of increasing clanship production on Graca clan's former nest world. The roughly seven thousand light-year journey was already a long one, and the few light-years detour was well worth the time cost for the revenge.

Telour entertained himself most of the day, critical of any perceived infraction by Parkoda, or his clan's warriors. When he actually came face-to-face with one of the reviled soft ones, the pallid-grey hide appeared looser on her slightly smaller than normal frame. It made her resemble an underfed pre-novice. The red coloration all adult Krall sported now was a product of the gene selections that had led to the rapid stopping of loss of blood when cut or punctured. There had been greater sexual dimorphism between males and females in the early history of the race, and the soft ones retained that trait. The females were unusually small, and thus unfit for fighting. Not that the males were warriors either.

They looked like smaller pale Krall, but their talons were short and could not be retracted or extended, they could bleed to death if a limb were severed, they had but one heart and liver, and their lungs were smaller, reducing the barrel chests of the true warriors. If the lights went out, they had no night vision and little infrared capability. The ultrasonic ears did not retract for combat or when not in use, and did not have the more cup shape that permitted a more directional detection capability. Watching them move in the 1.3 g gravity of this planet, they obviously lacked the same muscle definition, speed, and strength of those that followed the Great Path.

Looking at the soft ones for the two hours it required for counting them all, Telour grew sick of seeing them. It was his fault for demanding the count, and then insisting he watch Parkoda as they passed by him individually. He relented on that decision, to complete the process within a full breeding cycle, or he died of boredom. It was another small victory for Parkoda when he permitted the line of soft Krall to pass by other Tanga clan warriors, each holding a Katusha mounted on a stand with computer attached. These did the actual counting, and the total from each station was linked and combined.

In the final tally, compared to the last census, taken monthly actually, there was a net decrease of two soft ones, despite the hatching of a cub that did not yet have a tattoo, and was manually tabulated.

Telour had never expected there to be any discrepancy in numbers, yet badgered Parkoda about how sloppy the process was if a new hatchling was only entered when physically seen. It implied some could remain hidden and outside their census. A ridiculous claim, but one it was impossible to prove could not happen.

That led to Telour's pretext to take Parkoda with him, to verify that none of those potentially "missing" and now grown cubs had not escaped from the planet, and were waiting to steal a great Olt'kitapi ship. The evidence to back that possibility were the clanships stolen from Telda Ka, and one possibly used on Poldark.

Not only did it allow additional time to humiliate Parkoda, thus relieving the boredom of long Jumps, his ambitious second in command would be in charge here while he was gone. If he left Parkoda on the Graka clan production world, forced to find his own way back to his assignment post, he may discover he had been replaced at even this backwater outpost.

They Jumped for the world where the powerful Olt'kitapi ships were hidden, with a clearly angry Parkoda in tow. It was a relatively short jump, because if these machines of ultimate destruction were ever needed, keeping them in proximity to the soft Krall was more efficient.

They were quickly challenged for identification on White Out, and a visual display of the mission commander and his command deck staff was required even before the boarders would dock with them. This was to preclude the presence of small gray-colored, soft Krall inside a clanship. At least none that had not been coordinated in advance to arrive as prisoners, in restraints. Five clanships met them, and four hands of warriors boarded and searched the ship, as the other ships stood by with missiles, lasers, and plasma cannons ready to fire. The borders efficiently and thoroughly swept every deck with Katushas, to verify that no soft Krall were in hiding.

Once cleared to move inward towards the star, they landed on a small airless moon and walked in vacuum suits to a shuttle made available for just Telour and Parkoda to go down to the planet. Visiting clanships, with their firepower and internal volume for carrying many warriors, were not allowed to land on the planet.

Calling the world a planet required a small play on words, because the habitable world was itself a large moon of a huge Jovian type gas giant, in a close orbit 1.5 Astronomical Units from its host star. A small moon orbiting a large moon, orbiting a giant gas ball five times the mass of Jupiter was an unlikely place to find a habitable world, with an eighteen percent oxygen atmosphere, and eighty percent nitrogen, with other traces.

Tidal stress and drag kept one face of the habitable moon pointed at the Jovian. Yet it received adequate light and heat from the star when exposed to its light, a star slightly larger and hotter than average. The planet-sized moon would sometimes fall in the shadow of the Jovian, reducing the stars heat and light for hours. However, the gas giant radiated more heat than it received, so temperature changes were not too extreme on the planet/moon.

The shuttle took them into the extinct caldera of a monstrous shield volcano. Parked along the inside rim of the crater, in shadow most of the time, were eleven ships, each five times the size of a clanship. They were smaller than the Torki migration ships, but could control immense power, and travel in a manner that no other ships in the experience of the Krall could match. Their shapes were oddly contoured, with all rounded edges, twice as long as they were wide or high, lying on their long side. They resembled a short plump sausage with a slightly bowed back that was lower in the center than at each end. There was no visible difference between either rounded ends of the ships, and in fact, either end was equally the bow or the stern. A trait it was said, that reflected its designer's flexible mental processes, the Olt'kitapi.

Of the eleven intelligent ships, only nine acted aware, or would respond and display signs of awareness. Five of those nine would no longer obey instructions from even the soft Krall. That was after those particular five ships had deduced that their power had been used for what proved to be acts of aggression or intimidation by the soft ones, against another species. This happened when the Krall had coerced their prisoners (using intimidation and threats to their families) into directing the ships to use their most destructive capability on uninhabited worlds as an object lesson. These were dead planets located in inhabited star systems, but some havoc spread to the inhabited worlds. The alien species that "earned" these demonstrations had used the type of weapons they were warned never to use against the Krall. Mass destruction weapons, usually nuclear, chemical, or biological, which precluded the clans from recovering viable breeders for the Path.

The two ships that, for thousands of years, had refused to respond at all had been directed to punish worlds that had proven to support intelligent life. Although they would power up when entered, these two were the first ships ever used by the Krall for such punitive purposes, and as typical for killers, they had pulled no punches. The ships each continued to function for a short time, only to return here. Their subsequent self-deactivation after landing convinced the Krall to restrict the use of the other ships as weapons. "Sparingly used" by Krall definition caused five more of the ships to become unresponsive to instructions, even if willing to wake up and interact when entered. Even though they had not directly targeted the subject worlds for the lessons to be taught, the impact on the inhabited worlds was noted by the ships used. The last four of the untraumatized ships were a precious and irreplaceable commodity, only to be used in extreme circumstances.

Required to disarm before they had departed the clanship on the small airless moon, Telour directed Parkoda to accompany him into each ship. As Til Gatrol, Telour was not required to explain his purpose here, and doing so would have given offense to the multiple clans that provided security for the great ships. There was no suspicion in Telour's mind that any soft Krall had escaped, let alone penetrated security and entered any of the ships. Only the four most tightly guarded operational ships would even have responded to one of them. The other five ships patiently explained, repeatedly, that they would not obey instructions or requests from a sentient species that attacked other nonaggressive sentient beings. Apparently, each ship had to experience this act itself, because five times in a row the now stubborn ships had Jumped where directed, performed the action a soft Krall directed it to do, and then soon refused any other commands and returned here.

The four ships that had never been used aggressively were now off limits to casual visitors, to preserve their use for future contingencies. Telour's title as Til Gatrol meant he was not a casual visitor like that, but Parkoda, with his low status was barred from visiting a functional ship. Even Telour was permitted to visit only one ship, and was accompanied by an octet of warriors.

As he approached the airlock, the ship sensed the group's approach, as would the other five ships, it dilated open as if it were a biological sphincter.

"Welcome," the ship greeted them, in perfect high Krall. The outer opening squeezed shut and the inner wall then dilated open to admit them. Telour wondered why the airlock was active while they were on a planet with a breathable atmosphere. Then, the purest fresh air of the most pleasant nature he had ever smelled, enveloped him. He drew in a deep breath of the refreshing combinations of gasses and scents. He was suddenly aware of the octet with him, watching his reaction.

He turned to the gray clad octet leader. "This is something you expected, and wished to observe my reaction. Is this some sort of drug I have experienced? The other ships did not smell this way."

"My Til, the other ships are said to have once smelled this way when we entered them, before they were used in a manner they found…, unpleasant." The octet leader had sought an uncommon word to describe the reaction of the other ships, those previously used for mass destruction. Telour had found the air in the other ships just like that of this world, despite the automatic activation of the airlocks when the group approached. Those ships no longer chose to please a Krall visitor.

Telour understood exactly what the unpleasantness referred to was, so he asked about the atmosphere he was now experiencing. "I have visited many worlds. None had as an agreeable scent as I detect here. What has been added?"

"My Til, study by many breeding cycles of K'Tals lead us to believe that this is the exact mixture of gases of our original home world. There are also added scents from growths and animals from there that we would experience if that world still existed."

Telour understood the human concept of irony at play here. An Olt'kitapi ship, of the same type that had wiped out the original Krall home world, had fabricated an internal atmosphere to match that of the lost world of the species the Olt'kitapi had tried to destroy in their last days. The same species that subsequently succeeded in killing off the Olt'kitapi that had built this and other identical ships.

If this were of a Krall design, assuming they had ever designed anything a fraction this complex, the atmosphere would be some choking poison for any visitors that had defeated them. It was another sign of the weakness of the Olt'kitapi, even when extended to their intelligent ships.

"Where is the command deck?" His question was directed to the octet leader, whom he had not deigned to ask for his name. His tattoo revealed he was Dorbo clan, and the octet was a mix of Graka, Maldo, Dolbrin, and even younger clans. A reflection of the mutual responsibility all clans had to preserve these ships.

The ship answered him instead. "Follow the gold strip on the floor, that path will guide you to my control center."

A gold colored, metallic looking two-foot wide strip appeared on the floor, passing through the inner airlock door and bent to follow a curving path along a tubular corridor.

A gold path, he thought. *I can't be the first Krall to see a comparison to the mythical depiction of the Great Path in our histories. How clever are the minds of these machines?*

It also had spoken of "my control center." It had a concept of "self," what it possessed, and who it was. He had heard that these artificial intelligences were literally aware, and that they were described as living ships that made their own decisions at times.

Human made AIs were shadows of what the Olt'kitapi had achieved. From a Krall perspective, man was foolishly following the same delusional path towards physical weakness. Trusting machines to help them make decisions or to think.

After all, it was because Olt'kitapi trusted machines to think for them that helped the ancient Krall to trick and defeat them. The ancient species had supplemented their minds with artificial devices in their bodies to help them think faster and remember more. They gave smaller, customized versions of this technology to the Torki and to the Raspani. Those species fell easily to the Krall as well.

It was an Olt'kitapi mind "gift," to a Krall clan seeking an advantage over the others, which had sparked the revolt and destruction of the givers. The devices began changing the way of thinking of warriors that accepted the implants. In a few generations they became the soft ones, able to operate sophisticated Olt'kitapi machines, and could directly use their minds to operate the clanships that all Krall were permitted to use. They began to avoid killing unless threatened.

Today the soft ones no longer had the electronic mind enhancement devices they once had. However, their minds remained different even when the tiny machines were removed from the base of their skulls. The last generation of ships the Olt'kitapi had produced was able to sense the differences between the soft Krall and the true Krall warriors.

The ships originally accepted instruction from the Olt'kitapi, of course, or the soft Krall. Even without the interface link between their brains and the ships, the soft Krall could still use verbal and manual commands to direct the ships. At least they could do that until the commands that were obeyed resulted in actions that the ships ultimately perceived to be a violation of their inbuilt moral restrictions.

It was incomprehensible to the Krall. How could a machine, however smart, be allowed to make a moral choice? To a true Krall, that was itself immoral. You pointed a gun, pulled the trigger, and it killed. It was not proper for it to decide if it should do that or not.

The degree of reaction of each ship varied, from total withdrawal from sentient thought, as had the two ships that had been directed to apply one of their "benign" designed functions on two populated worlds, many thousands of years ago. A deliberately misapplied function, which then led immediately to the deaths of large populations. A lesser reaction was displayed now, by five ships that had been used in a more indirect manner for destruction. A variation was tried each time to thwart their adverse reactions, a result of what they had been tricked into doing. For these ships, it was via a simple refusal to accept any further command inputs from a soft Krall. That seemed to be because the action taken *indirectly* caused harm to an intelligent species. There now were only four ships that were still willing to follow soft Krall instructions. They were a precious and dwindling resource for ultimate acts of war.

The Krall had never learned how any of the ships determined the deaths of the targeted populations, even if the mass murders were delayed for days after the triggering event, and the ships were safely parked here when it happened. The Krall were of course aware of the fatal weakness of the ship builders, a respect for intelligent life, which the Olt'kitapi somehow installed into the artificial minds of the ships. The ships refused to perform actions that would clearly harm planets that were obviously inhabited by a civilization. This was easily discerned from close-in observations.

The Krall exploited the same naive trust flaw that had made the Olt'kitapi vulnerable. They made the soft Krall order the ship to operate at a considerably "safe" distance from the targets, after previously having used the ship on a similar test target in a dead star system. The tests were performed under the pretext of obtaining a wealth of minerals to expand Krall civilization.

The fact that a Krall cared little for possessions that were not weapons, such as worlds to inhabit, cities to live in, property or mineral wealth to own, eluded the ships as it had their designers. A Krall valued status, earned by killing or dominating an opponent.

To fool the ships, they were directed to Jump into a test star system, perform the triggering event, and promptly Jump away. The action was then repeated in the target system, at a similar great distance (several billion miles), and then the Olt'kitapi ship was immediately Jumped away before the result was even visible, due to the speed of light limitation. The ships never communicated to the soft Krall what they learned later, or how they learned it, so it was a deduction on the Krall's part that the ships stopped cooperating because they somehow discovered how they had been misused.

The visit to the control center today was anticlimactic. There were roughly three feet in diameter, gray colored, circular places on the floor, where the gravitational restraint system would deploy for those in the control center, when the ship was in flight and involved in sharp maneuvering. Other similar restraint systems were located at multiple locations on the ship for other occupants.

For its large size, the ship didn't have the passenger capacity it would seem capable of holding. At five times the volume, it held only a fraction of the warriors that a clanship could carry. As evidence that they were not all expected to be of the same species, there were compartments that appeared to have wider gravity restraints that might accommodate a Torki, smaller ones that could better fit a Prada, and elongated ones that could have contained a Raspani. Those on the control deck suited the Krall, and presumably the Olt'kitapi.

The Olt'kitapi had not been interested in representations of themselves, so there were no statues or still pictures of them, and their digital records were indecipherable to the many K'Tal that had attempted to read them. One of the few clues to their shape was that they used the same size gravity restraint as fit a Krall. This left a great range of body shapes and heights. The soft Krall alive today had no anecdotal stories of the Olt'kitapi, and the Krall themselves had erased those stories, if ever they had them in their own histories.

The early histories of the warrior race, composed by the surviving Krall, invested no time discussing the appearance of the hated and physically weak enemy, but described how they had fallen to their fierce attackers by the millions, in only a few days. The hated enemy seldom was armed with anything that was intended to be a weapon, and only descriptions of their red blood, and brown, tasty flesh was considered worth mentioning. They were easily overcome if they permitted an aggressive Krall to approach them.

The Krall had established themselves as the fierce guardians of their benefactors. They protected them from every threat encountered, because not every species the Olt'kitapi met was welcoming. Some were mildly to strongly aggressive, and the Krall's natural tendencies were exploited to keep threats at bay. The Olt'kitapi didn't want fights, and preferred a withdrawal and separation to fighting, even if it were a simple rejection by another sentient species. They didn't impose their will on other intelligent races, and required an invitation to enter into trade and technology exchanges.

The sole known exception was the Torki, encountered when they were mindless sea creatures with a potential to learn to think. They helped them to become aware, even though they did not survive to see the results.

The clanships and weapons they built for the Krall were for performing their security duty. A task the Olt'kitapi recognized they needed performed, but one they were temperamentally unsuited to perform themselves. Recognizing that the unmodified Krall were too violent for the lesser need of protection from, versus annihilation of, other unfriendly species, they offered their new client race the advantages of advanced civilization, in exchange for diminishing their excessive aggression. A handful of the old breed of Krall accepted the offer.

A small gland in the Krall brain was the primary source of the addictive chemical that generated the drive they felt for constant combat. A new quantum mechanical based circuit, a small chip, provided some Krall access to parts of Olt'kitapi technology, and modified a set of genes that produced an adrenaline-like chemical. This was done with the permission of the recipients. It simultaneously made the aggression-inducing chemical non-addictive, and that eliminated the triggering of murderous impulses. That single biological trait had kept this species locked into violent internal clan struggles on their own world, and had prevented the development of an advanced society beyond that of barbarians.

The urge to reproduce, to make more warriors to join in fighting other clans had driven them to a callous disregard for their own young. There were so many of them that they needed to be culled to prevent starvation, saving only the best fighters. Those that produced the combat stimulating chemical were better fighters. The Krall were within a few hundred years of falling into total collapse, with the entire planet's ecosystem destroyed by self-consuming offspring. The Olt'kitapi's effort to save them, and open the Krall up to expansion to the stars and friendship, unleashed a scourge that otherwise would have killed itself off when it had nowhere to go.

Of course, none of this was in Telour's thoughts as he left the ship that refused to respond to him, other than to show him around. He couldn't activate any screens, or equipment. He knew that the bulk of the ship was given to massive generators of a type the K'Tals had been able to understand. They did something in Tachyon Space that required tremendous power to control, but in turn gave them greater ability to apply some of that power in Normal Space. The Olt'kitapi intended the power to be used to build a great civilization. The Krall saw a "better" use.

This ship could Jump from where it sat, in a gravity well, to any place it was directed to go. It reached distant destinations in hours, not in days. It would materialize without the revealing, and dangerous, burst of gamma rays to announce its presence.

It would do none of those things for Telour, or for any Krall. However, as every Krall had ever thought about when they were inside one of these ships, a true warrior would do anything required to a soft Krall, to force them to make the powerful ship do what the warrior wanted.

No wonder the joint clans kept the use of these ships under such tight control. Their use had to be conserved for the greatest need of the entire race, as they moved along the thousands of years of the Great Path still ahead. There would be many other enemies in the galaxy.

Telour collected Parkoda outside the ship, effused with the sense of power this craft placed in his mind. "Follow me. I will now go to complete my primary mission for the Tor Gatrol, so that he can increase the number of invasions we can support against human worlds. We can force the worthy enemy, which I have helped make of these animals, to speed our breeders along the Path. At least for those breeders that have earned the right to spread their seed, to make new warriors able to travel the Great Path faster." A fresh dig at Parkoda's sinking status felt good to him.

For the first time, Parkoda realized he wasn't being returned directly to his former posting. "Where are we going next?"

"To Graka clan's old base world, where we produce the most clanships of any clan. We need them built faster, to take the war to additional human worlds. The Prada and Torki have become complacent with the slow pace we allow them to work. They can do more, and my clan can earn status by making more ships available before the joint council even decides they are required. That is how a smart Krall warrior faces a worthy enemy."

That last boast to Parkoda would come back and kick him in the ass.

****

Mirikami looked stern and resolute, and then a slight smile touched his lips. "Gentle Men, we are ready to start kicking Krall ass, in a major fashion. In fact, I don't think the word *gentle* will ever apply to us males again, not as society has used it for the last three hundred years. The Ladies from Koban will also seem a lot less the genteel gender than women were once considered to be." That pulled a round of laughter from the mixed crowd of TG2s.

"I'm leaving a Tachyon Space message for the migration ships and clanships that I expect to arrive here shortly. I'll ask them to transfer what supplies they can by tomorrow evening, and then all of them will Jump to join us, with a White Out millions of miles from the planet. This keeps them out of danger, lets them see what is happening, and the supply transfer can continue as they drift inwards until we have made their landing sites safe."

From the stairwell, poised between decks 1 and 2, he looked over the assembly below him on the bottom deck, and over to those he could see on the second deck. They were already in armor, helmets under their arms. The four Dragons were opened for entry, and the explosives holding cases no longer secured to the deck for quick movement. All he had to do was get them on the ground and they would take the dome and factory. The Mark had a particularly short Jump from the binary brown dwarf star, which orbited the larger star of the nearby Krall system they had designated CS1. They would arrive in less than thirty minutes. The Avenger and Beagle should already be in transit, from their more distant holding positions.

"We Jump in five minutes. Good luck."

The three attacks on Krall war making capability were finally under way.

Chapter 19: Nothing's as Easy as it Looks

The Avenger emerged at two hundred fifty miles above CS2 on its night side, and Karl informed her, "Mam, as expected, the main Krall habitat dome is close to the approaching horizon."

They had ten of the new ground attack missiles loaded, transferred from one of the supply clanships. As soon as the number of clanships parked there could be ascertained and targeted, the attack would be initiated.

The second clanship, with another complement of missiles ready, did a White Out a hundred miles higher than the Avenger. It was the newly named Slasher, with Captain Anna Retief of the Old Colony of Suid-Afrika at the helm. Without the precision of an AI to help, Retief didn't try for as close a reentry as the Avenger. The Lady had been newly retired from a Rim world freight company when the mass ship capture by the Krall, done twenty-three years ago, had interrupted her flight home and left her on Koban. Definitely out of retirement now and rejuvinated, Captain Retief was ready to put as many Krall into early and permanent retirement as possible. She had been first and fastest to beg to make the Jump with the Avenger when Noreen made the offer, even though two other of the four clanship captains also wanted to join the attack Jump.

In an update, Karl said, "Fifteen clanships are on the tarmac of the main Krall dome, Mam. There is a hot spot on the ramp that indicates a recent launch, and contrails drifting away at high altitude confirms that a clanship recently departed."

Noreen immediately called Retief. "Anna, Karl says a clanship has launched and may be either nearby in space, in orbit, or enroute to the shipyards. Kindly power ahead in a low orbit to see if you can find and kill it, and any other targets we discussed. I'll hit the dome and the ships here."

A quick acknowledgement and the Slasher used its Normal Space drive to surge ahead.

Noreen gave her firing order to the AI. "Karl, launch all ten ground attack missiles at the dome, and then launch fifteen anti-ship missiles as the last of those leave the tubes."

The most likely source of communication would come from the dome, and taking the leadership Krall out first would reduce the chance of their warning the guards at the shipyards. The parked ships would probably be empty. Some were positioned relatively close together, and a single missile might destroy its primary target and damage others. However, clanships were tough and modular, and even serious damage could be repaired. The decision had been made to ensure complete destruction, so each would receive a missile.

As they rockets left the launchers, Dillon put the plot of missile streaks on the main view screen, ten in the front wave, fifteen trailing a short distance behind. Suddenly Karl made an unanticipated hurried report.

"Mam, a clanship has ignited thrusters and is about to lift."

There was little possibility that at a low velocity and altitude it could escape the hypervelocity missile that had it as a target. However, even as the warning was spoken, TG2 reaction time came into play.

Carson fired the only plasma cannon that could bear, directly at the bow of the rising clanship, and exactly in step, Yilini lanced two of the heavy lasers on the nose of the same target. At such a low angle to the target, the additional atmosphere the beams had to traverse would diffuse them slightly, but their purpose wasn't to try to down the clanship, a difficult task even at close range. The ship would probably try to use its instant-on lasers to target some of the incoming missiles. The two Kobani gunners intended to make that a problem for a Krall gunner, by putting a great deal of energy on the enemy gun ports, with the potential to damage them.

Only five more seconds were needed for the first volley to hit the dome, and one second after that the clanships would start to add their own flames to the fireworks display.

Either the Avenger's gunnery foiled the clanship's counter fire, or the pilot never managed to get the weapons on line in time. The clanship flared orange a half mile above the huge billows of debris rising from the dome, as ten strikes hit evenly around its top and sides. The rise of the dome fragments were quickly joined by the comparatively larger balls of orange of the fully fueled and undefended clanships, which surrounded the dome.

Then, Captain Retief, passing directly overhead the destruction on the dark planet below, offered a paraphrased fragment of poetic comment, as she witnessed the orange and black conflagration.

"Tyger! Tyger! Burning bright, in the forests of the night."

Carson's nearly eidetic new memory supplied a reference. "I doubt William Blake had this sight in mind, although in a sense, the stars threw down their spears."

The Avenger passed over her victim, the mushrooming cloud billowing with traces of orange flame still visible. Compared to the billion or more humans the Krall had already killed, this was but a beginning of the retribution they hoped would follow, in battles to come.

As Slasher was about to pass around the limb of the planet, Retief called out, "Tallyho, and missiles away. The missing clanship had just landed at the shipyard, its heat and descent contrail were visible. There is another one sitting on the tarmac. We sent two more bullets at the top floors of the dome. I'll finish a full orbit and look for other targets. Good hunting, Avenger."

Noreen increased speed to get the shipyards in direct view sooner. She was using a repeat image, relayed from a Slasher screen, but she wanted to be able to zoom and study the area directly.

The direct image on screen, when she powered around the curve of the planet, revealed two black mushrooms of smoke still rising above the shipyard dome in the early morning light, as they left the night terminator behind. The roof of the dome had collapsed in the center. If this had been a human facility, there would have been a chance they might find no watch standers on night duty away from a combat zone, or inattentive this early. Except Krall never slept and were always alert. Even if watch standers had been unable to escape the explosions on the top dome levels, there would still be an unknown number of Krall prepared to repel their assault.

From Torki and Prada estimates, it was predicted there would be roughly four thousand warriors on the ecologically ruined planet, but many should have been in the main dome and were now busy escaping the flames. They would have some shuttles available to them and the usual ground transports at their disposal, and all of them would certainly rush towards the fighting. Partly to defend the shipyards and factories that produced clanships and parts, but even more for clan honor. Mordo clan was a storied great clan, and they would likely fight with reckless abandon to defend their place in Krall histories.

Noreen swooped down into the atmosphere, rotated the ship tail first, and then let it fall at a rate that built a plasma envelope around the rear of the Avenger. Hot spots developed on the thick footpads of the four recessed landing jacks and the heat resistant main thruster port. The eight large attitude thrusters were folded into their nacelles for now, with only the eight small fixed thrusters keeping the ship in line with the desired trajectory. They were a falling, flaming, armored gray watermelon shape for the moment.

She was taking full advantage of the TG2's ability to accept higher stresses than the Krall. The friction of reentry was slowing them, but without a controlled burn, they would take out a part of the complex via the sizable crater they would make on impact. Except for the weather penetrating radar and sensors, the landing point was obscured by clouds. The atmosphere around the dome was full of smog particles, generated by the industry around the shipyards, and today was a rainy day.

At an altitude where any Krall observing would be forced to assume it was too late to save the ship, Karl sounded a loud warning horn once. Then he blasted the main thruster at maximum, pinning the humans to their acceleration couches, breathing with difficulty, and employed the Normal Space drive as well. This level of deceleration was calculated to put a Krall into unconscious. Because the enemy warriors didn't normally use acceleration couches, and held onto posts on command decks, or lay flat on the decks, some wouldn't have survived.

When velocity bled off enough, the movable eight main attitude thrusters rotated out of their protective slots slightly, and fired to rotate the ship into a vertical descent. They were still dropping fast, but under the control of the AI. On screen it was a frightful rate of last moment slowing, the column of blue thruster plasma blasting pieces of the tarmac away from directly below the ship as it grew close. The landing jacks extended later than the half mile height typical for a Krall pilot, when they were mere yards from the surface, and the ship settled deeply onto them, as all thrust shut off.

The bounce, as the jacks lifted the ship slightly, with less weight to support than the gravity field here required, made the upper decks sway with an alarming motion. However, it was exactly as they had practiced previously, all four lower portals slammed up into their recesses, and the ramps deployed automatically, all under Karl's control.

The TG2's were already in stealth mode in their armor, including the four inside the Dragons (in the event their tops got "popped," as Sarge described it). The mini tanks were not stealth capable, so the first four hundred Kobani poured out of the ship from each opening, and leaped past the ramps. The ramps were only for the Dragons, which would follow.

The only signs to Krall watchers that anyone or anything had made an exit from the ship would be the fast moving smoky, bipedal shaped holes in the steam and vapors lifting from the ramp.

The Avenger was mere yards from the closest garage entrance of the dome. Because of the two clanships still burning on the opposite side of the dome, they had relatively little debris to avoid as two hundred of the TG2's rushed the entrance in the first wave. Lying randomly around, there were dome struts, joints, and clear pieces of the shattered transparent window material, similar to human plazsteel, which had been blasted from the upper levels.

Two separate groups of seventy-five split away from the second two hundred in the assault force, and raced in opposite directions to the next two entrances, each located a quarter of the way around the sides of the dome. The final fifty Kobani troops jumped right up onto the sides of the dome, grasping struts, joints, and finger and toeholds on small ledges, to scale directly up the six hundred-foot sides of the gradually inward sloping structure.

The plan was to trap as many Krall inside the dome as possible, cutting off any easy exit point they could use to come out and attack the raiding forces. There was no consideration given to the possibility the enemy might look for an opening through which to retreat. Thesc were the Krall!

Fire and debris from the two destroyed clanships sealed one entrance, saving them the trouble of having to use a missile to close that one before they descended. Kobani were going to seal the other three entrances with troopers, and fifty more were going topside to pick off any warriors that attempted to get out via the upper levels, which were now open to the cloudy, gray sky and dirty rain.

The Dragons roared down the four ramps, and one each went to the entrances, to provide heavier plasma cannon support inside the dome, and eventually down in the factory levels. The large garage doors would easily pass them, as would the wide internal corridors.

The Dragon with the greatest distance to drive would cover the entrance near the still burning clanships, since they wouldn't burn forever. It had three stealthed TG2's riding on top, as mobile support elements.

The first four hundred in the assault force didn't carry plasma rifles, intending to rely more on agility and mobility, to execute lightning fast attacks with suit weapons, chosen over the slightly heavier firepower of the more cumbersome rifles. Four hundred of the Kobani behind them would carry rifles; a hundred of those would stay behind as a defense force for the ship, and establish a wide perimeter in a semicircle. They commandeered and drove a number of Krall trucks and tractors from inside the dome garages, to draw the attention of the attackers they expected from inside the dome. With their superior stealth capability, they would be waiting for the Krall some place they wouldn't expect them to be.

Three hundred troops with rifles, shoulder-fired single-shot tube rockets, and grenades, would provide cover and a way down into the factory levels for the one hundred two-person demolition teams. They were carrying stealthed-coated cases of explosives between them, to plant on equipment that might otherwise be salvaged later, even if exposed to salt water. Some of the explosives would be used to rupture the large coolant lines that ran from the nearby sea, and kept the temperatures in the factory and foundries comfortable.

****

The lone warrior on duty at the top of the dome, next to the main communications console and monitoring system, was less curious than was a typical warrior. He saw the double White Out signatures on a display, which were clearly labeled as two clanships. They were both on the night side of the planet, and apparently headed for the main habitat dome.

That was exactly where he wished he were now, so that he could participate in a mock combat session. The practice mission his leader of a hand of octets was going to conduct at first light at the main habitat dome. Daylight was just reaching this dome, at least if that smoggy, gray brightening through the heavy, gray clouds and rain was any evidence. He faced one more day of boring punitive duty after this one about to start, because the octet he commanded had failed to complete its mission successfully, in the previous exercise a hand of days ago.

Jagort and his entire octet were sharing the dull task of monitoring the activity around the dome and factories for this night. Seven other less than maximum efficient octets were patrolling the rest of the large dome, to watch for any Prada that tried to leave their shift of work in the factories below, before their rotation permitted.

There were more workers than productivity required right now, because a new transportation line from a more distant mountain range was not yet complete. Until the new ore supply could reach the foundry, parts production was less than that set by the joint council. The Prada would actually be happy when the work increased, but for now, they had less to do than normal, and wanted to return to their ridiculous family units early.

Jagort, in a command center near the shipyards, was in a mood to kill a few of the early returning Prada as an object lesson, and as a form of entertainment. However, production was supposed to increase soon, and Prada laziness would disappear. If the Prada were unable to make up for the sixty-four days of reduced production as quickly as expected, and it was because a bored octet leader had killed some critical workers, he would stay on punitive duty longer.

It wasn’t easy to elicit a cry of startled surprise from a Krall. Jagort managed a strangled sounding snarl of futile warning to the empty air, as he observed and heard a warning chime and flashing indicators of multiple missile launches from one of the clanships, directed at the main habitat dome. He immediately activated a radio channel to the main habitat, as required, even though the warning would be redundant.

The snarled reply was from a voice he knew well, Colwat, another octet leader, and he sounded exactly as Jagort would have spoken, if he had been on duty there.

"We see it stupid one! Gethok departed to deliver two test pilots to the shipyard a short time ago, and a second clanship operated by a novice pilot in training is lifting here now. I ordered her to intercept the ship that fired on us. Tell Gethok to turn back here to avenge us. We will not be able to stop so many missiles."

Colwat's insulting reply would have been grounds for a challenge match, except that both warriors were aware that only Jagort would be alive in a few more seconds. Twenty-five missiles, ten of them the larger more powerful ground target type would reach the main dome. As it happened, the pilot in training proved too inept to fire even a single weapon in defense of the dome, before her ship was blasted from the sky. The indication of laser and plasma fire on her craft still didn't excuse such an inefficient novice reaction.

Jagort was not simply standing around, using a talon to scratch the back portion of his lower torso. He had promptly tapped his shoulder com set to announce on a common frequency that the main dome was under massive attack, as were the clanships parked there. He lost his long-range feed on the incoming anti-ship missile tracks when the other dome and its sensors were destroyed, leaving a hole in his coverage.

He noted that the clanship piloted by Gethok, which Colwat had mentioned, had come into view over the horizon. It was flying low for the sub orbital trip, and his sensors could track it now. Gethok had significantly higher status than Jagort, or the now likely dead Colwat. He listened to the report from Jagort, of two unknown clanships that had just arrived, and of one's attack on the main dome.

When the out-of-favor octet leader, serving punitive duty, passed along Colwat's demand that Gethok immediately return to avenge the attack on the dome, he ignored him and told him what he would do instead.

"The ship that fired on the dome is far enough behind ne that I was below the edge of the planet. It cannot see me and I cannot see it either. It does not know I am here. I have two experienced pilots with me and there is another clanship parked next to your dome. The two clanships that you reported arriving together would have an advantage in our fight. I will hurry to land and transfer a pilot for that other clanship. Together we can defend the honor of Mordo clan."

On this small miscalculation was Gethok and the other clanship lost. Captain Retief's Slasher had surged ahead to seek him out, because he had overlooked the clues of his recent launch leaving a hot spot on a tarmac, and atmospheric contrails. He was caught committed to a breakneck landing of his own, as close to the second clanship as he could manage. The forces being exerted on Gethok and the two pilots with him, were too great for them to move to activate defensive weapons. One of the two hypervelocity missiles found him before he could complete his nearly amazing landing.

Jagort took small comfort in the demise of this particularly arrogant warrior, because he was delayed in delivering his own second warning to the warriors in his dome. He'd seen his own fate approaching in the form of two more of the larger ground attack missiles. Not that he simply waited for them to arrive. He scrambled out of the watchstanders compartment at the top of the dome, enroute to the nearest stairwell, prepared to hurl himself down, trusting that his body would heal if he survived. Hurled he was, but not down. The blast behind him helped move him along. He impacted one of the transparent armored windows, leaving a large red splat before the concussion blew the window and his remains out over the tarmac. At least his day was over, and he wasn't bored any longer.

****

Dillon expressed his first sense of relief. "We caught them flat footed. I've had this dreaded impression they were invulnerable."

"Why?" Noreen was puzzled. "You and Tet caught them by surprise on your first combat team. They had no idea how different things would be, and they sent in an octet from a finger clan that had never seen a human, and was known for their brashness and aggressiveness. It meshed with the booby traps and remotely activated weapons we had built and you left for them to trip over. Tet has surprised them again, by brashly attacking them where they couldn't conceive we had the ability to do so, in a place they were sure we didn't know existed. They had their pants down…, if Krall wore pants."

"I guess. Anyway, Carson has already started his teams down the stairs into the factory production complex under us. Yil is following a corridor towards the section where the stamp mills, foundries, and smelters are located, and Fred's teams are headed for the hull assembly site, and weapons mounting stations. The only Prada they've seen have run from their voices, back into the labyrinth of the factory levels. Calling to them in low Krall has no effect, not when it came from an invisible person. Yil said he had to make himself visible to get any response at all, which then was running away in fear."

Noreen had been following the progress of the fighting in the dome. "The teams inside have been killing Krall on sight. There appears to have been between fifty or sixty survivors that either were not on the top levels, or made it down ahead of the missiles. They encountered three that had donned their armor. It appears that we stay invisible to their visors, but we see them as ghost-like images, just like we see our own people with our helmets."

"How have the Prada in their housing areas been handling the fighting? Without a forest to live in, they don't have any trees to climb to get out of harm's way."

Noreen grimaced. "They don't dare come out of their compartments. The larger rooms were subdivided to hold multiple families. We have more living in the dome here than we expected. I hope that means there are fewer in the factories.

"The Krall, unable to see *our people*, killed a few of the Prada that dared expose themselves in hallways. I called for the migration ships to start down. The two coming to load the Torki will be out over the water, and won't have Krall to bother them. The Olts will let the Torki on the ships communicate with those in the lodges." She reminded him of that unnecessarily, because she felt nervous that the plan was on track.

"It's the Prada here that will be hard to convince to come out. They don't know who or what we are, they understandably fear us, and the damned Krall shoot them on sight when they move, since they can't see us. We need those elder Prada to talk to them."

"Hon, I was busy talking with the factory teams and didn't hear you make that call to the rescue ships. How many migration ships are landing total? Not all five of them, right?"

"No, only four. One is staying in high orbit as backup, and I called for two to land here by the dome, on opposite sides, to speed the loading of Prada. Their population will outnumber the Torki by a factor of four or five. Presumably, fifteen to twenty thousand if the number of workers per factory stayed at close to three or four thousand, and then we add in their normally small families. We'll have room to spare using two of those big ships, if we can just get them enough food. Two of the clanships Jumped to Haven as soon as I released them to go. We didn't have any more targets for them after they shot down six shuttles, and we'll need a lot more of those nasty looking grub worms." She shivered, much as a Prada did when a human bit into a rare piece of rhinolo steak.

He was down in the "catacombs," as Carson continued to think of the factory levels he was prowling, directly below the dome. He had seen and "greeted" three Krall. One managed to shoot him in the back, before he whipped around and put a plasma bolt through his screaming mouth. The Krall's plasma bolt had hit him in the center of his back, but at a glancing angle, which at first thought made Carson question the notoriously deadly aim of a warrior. It had deflected from his armor, and another TG2 confirmed there was nothing more than a faint scorch mark left behind.

"Yolanda, I was stealthed. Even if the bolt was to the center of my back and not my helmet, how did he even spot me?"

She looked back to where the dead Krall lay and noted steamy vapor jetting from an outlet valve of a press, which used heat and pressure to shape a hull or deck plate, and then used water to cool it down. "I think you walked through that stream of vapor. He saw the outline of your torso, and fired at the center of mass. If he'd used his head, and shot where yours is, we might not be having this conversation." The grin wasn't seen, but her tone certainly implied one was attached to her remark.

"Thanks." He offered her a high five. Her visor saw his ghostly move and she reciprocated.

"No problem. Alyson asked us to keep you from doing anything stupidly heroic today. Shot in the ass isn't heroic, so this doesn't count."

"It was in the back…, not my…" he trailed off, because she had turned and walked away. He wondered how Alyson was doing.

He selected a team channel and cautioned everyone to be alert for ways they could still be seen, such as the steam jet he'd passed through. Then he checked with the other team leaders, and passed that tidbit along. The catacomb thought he'd had earlier wasn't very accurate. It was actually well lit down here, with thirty-foot ceilings, except where a larger piece of machinery needed greater height. The entire place was set up for Prada to climb over the machinery, using ropes and aerial walkways, similar to how they did it in the forest villages. They were trying to keep working as the intermittent fighting went on around them, as faithful servants of the "Rulers."

However, the Prada couldn't help but observe the mysterious plasma bolts that suddenly flared into existence from a point in space whenever a Krall appeared nearby.

Sometimes, it was a red or green laser, which briefly flashed in the humid air. Those beams also originated from a point in space, and then came again from a new point located a short distance away. The sound of faint footsteps might be heard between the shots. It didn't require a leap of genius to know there were nearly invisible and aggressive intruders inside the factory. The intruders were behaving aggressively toward the Rulers only, and the Krall often fought clan-to-clan. The Krall that the workers *could* see, the particular clan of that "wiser" species they served, chose to kill some of the Prada today, for a reason their servants couldn't understand.

Carson's teams were placing their tamper proof explosives on the machinery Wister and other Prada on Haven had identified as critical for producing complex and vital clanship components. Such as thruster engines and fuel control modules, Jump Drive components, weapons consoles and weapons, and other parts that made a clanship more than an armored shell.

If the flooding with corrosive seawater proved successful, some of the planted explosives would be redundant. Other items, like giant presses, might be salvaged after the salt water was pumped out, so they were to be explosively converted to scrap.

Yilini and Fred were progressing even faster than Carson's teams, because there were a fewer number of things to destroy in a foundry and smelter, and the ship assembly work had apparently slowed recently, due to a shortage of large metal hull and deck sections, built as replaceable modules. Yil said that must have something to do with the low ore piles by the various crushers near the smelters. There was a shortage of raw material, which perhaps explained the lower activity in all three factories.

Yil was still explaining his theory of a temporary supply shortage, when Carson interrupted him. "Yil, I'm hearing one hell of a loud thundering sound, and the floor and walls are vibrating."

"I hear a roar too," he replied.

Fred had the answer they needed. "I'm outside, on a hull cradle in the assembly area in the shipyards. I can see two of those migration ships coming down near the dome. I can't believe fat tubs that huge can actually land on a planet. I see two more in the distance, coming down off shore. Those are the water landings for the Torki. Anyone hear from the teams sent out there?"

Two teams, in four ground transports, had raced out to see if there was a Krall presence around either lodge. Two of the fast moving Dragons had gone with them, since there had been less Krall resistance at the shipyards than expected. A convoy of over a hundred trucks and halftracks was on the way from the destroyed main dome, but they were at least two hours away. The roughly one thousand warriors crammed in and on them would have to be intercepted at some point, because the loading of the migration ships wouldn't be completed by then, even if the Prada all agreed to drop everything and come quickly.

Noreen had been speaking with Wister's older sibling, Nawella, before the descent. The fifteen-hundred-year-old Prada had experienced four previous moves by migration ships over the centuries, but was nervous. She knew of how some landings ended with a crash when the Krall pilot collapsed several landing struts coming down too hard, or off slightly from a near perfect vertical touchdown. On one of her landings, the pilot had allowed two of the ten landing jacks to come down off the edge of a tarmac into soft ground. The ship nearly toppled before the two jacks, at full extension, finally found solid enough support.

This time the landings were deftly handled, and delicately executed by Torki pilots. The first landings they had ever performed, but exactly as it had gone in the simulators they used for practice. The five large thrusters used ionized water as their reaction mass, once they cut out the Normal Space gravity drives at about one mile of altitude. Most of the remaining water in their tanks would be used for the departure, but that was far less than what they generally carried.

The departure weight of the ships by the domes would be far less, because they didn't need to retain a large and heavy volume of water for their Prada passengers to soak in, as did the Torki, to reduce acceleration stress. The Torki pilots assured Noreen that they would lift swiftly and lightly, much like a Haven insect that flew similar to a butterfly. How that description fit with a ship that more resembled a giant, silvered Earth pumpkin than a fragile winged fluttery insect, Noreen chose to ignore.

Nawella, true to her word, was among the first off the migration ship, accompanied by ten TG2s, in a Krall armored battlefield transport. The big trucks had ample room in the lower hold of the ships. It could be driven in and out using the wide sturdy ramp. In planning, they had allowed for possible sniper fire after the ships sat down.

The elder spokesperson, technically a "spokesprada," had to be protected if they hoped to convince the workers to come along quickly. Or even to come along at all. Once inside the factory, surrounded by TG2's, Nawella directed them to where she needed to be taken. There was an overseer room, which monitored all sections of a factory, and had a communications system. For the joint factory complex like this one, she could link all three public address systems together. The dome, as housing for the Prada, was included.

The problem Mirikami had seen was that they needed to disseminate the information widely, to every Prada, but after so many thousands of years, the Prada now spoke only low Krall. Any Krall in the dome or factory would hear and understand what was said.

The solution they wanted to try was to ask representatives of the various work sections to go to the "gathering" rooms, used during shift changes, to exchange information each day. Each division of workers had elder members that were tasked with learning what problems or issues had come up on the previous shift, and that was then passed along to the next shift of workers by the next shift's elder representatives. Wister and Nawella both believed that if the elder division members could be convinced to evacuate, the others would listen and follow them. The multiple gathering rooms, or conference rooms as the humans would call them, could be addressed privately, and via video link from the overseer room.

Nawella expertly activated the PA system for the entire complex. She'd done this many times as an elder Prada project manager. Her first announcement, audio only, was to request all elder division members, of every shift, to assemble in the gathering rooms.

They knew this would be a time of risk for the Prada that exposed themselves, and moved through the interconnected factories. The main avenues in the factories would have invisible TG2s guarding the way, watching for any Krall activity. Nawella identified herself and stated her age. She explained she was of Sither clan, a widely spread clan after thousands of years of migration moves. She knew not to reveal any detail that could identify her as currently residing in the Koban system. Her name and clan were matters of interest only to other Prada, and the Krall had never taken notice of them.

The Prada relied on honesty within their ranks, and accepted an elder's claim of age until proven wrong. If it was part of a deception, and revealed as such, that Prada was shunned and would die alone. Such a penalty was so severe to them that none could recall it being applied in over a thousand years.

There were several hundred Prada seen climbing down from the ceilings, or crawling out of hiding places. They were cautiously looking for any threat from their so-called Rulers, who displayed notoriously random violence at times. A Prada normally would obey any order from a Krall, but in the case of berserker rage, they felt justified to run and hide if no order was given specifically to them by name. It was convenient that few Krall knew any slave's name.

As they hurried along the corridors, some taking an "overland" route on machinery or elevated walkways, their long tails were constantly twitching at any sound. Three times the sound was from a sudden Krall attack scream, and a plasma bolt or laser cut it short. A few warriors were still prowling the factories, seeking a fast and potent hidden enemy that struck them down without warning or challenge. Three more completed their hunt with finality.

When the division leaders were in the gathering rooms, they were able to see the Prada female that had called them on screen. They were prepared to take her age on faith, and the social structure on this harsh world meant that every single one of them knew that her claimed age was centuries greater than the next oldest Prada among them. Dangerous work and poor living conditions had kept many elders from reaching truly advanced ages. They were prepared to listen.

After discussion with Wister, Nawella, and other elders, a strategy of avoiding the identity of the “alien” invaders was considered best. The location where they were “migrating” was to be another Krall world that was to be repopulated and factories rebuilt. Not mentioning the planet’s name was a no-brainer, and hardly suspicious. The Krall didn’t use them for places, merely a description of them, or the clan that controlled them. Those details weren’t provided.

Without stating this was interclan warfare, something many Prada had experienced in the past, or certainly knew about, Nawella reminded them that sometimes the Rulers made war on themselves for practice. She told them that production was now being ended on this old and worn out planet.

“Four great migration ships have landed,” she told them. “All Prada and all Torki workers will be efficiently moved. Today. Right now. Go tell your divisions, those on duty and those out of rotation in the dome, and their families, to take nothing with them and board the two migration ships you heard land above, and are parked on the tarmac. We will direct the flow to which ship has more room remaining. Food will be provided for you, and some is already present. Try to avoid the places of fighting. The Rulers do not need us to hinder their activity. The ships have been ordered to leave if fighting comes too close. Go now, as quickly as you can pass the word. Do not be left behind on an abandoned world.”

That reference, if any spur were needed, caused a near stampede to get the word out to board the ships. Every Prada knew that feral Krall hatchlings eventually consumed any world where they were not ruthlessly culled and then trained. The placing of explosives had been noted, even if those placing them had not been revealed. The factories were always destroyed on abandoned worlds.

Switching off the camera and audio pickup, Nawella turned to the TG2s with her. She couldn’t actually see them, but the strips of colored cloth tied to ankles and wrists let her see where they were. “They responded as I had hoped. I fear we may not be able to collect all of them in the time we have. The number of division elders was greater than I expected. This means there are more workers than we believed would be here. I need to meet the first arrivals to the ship I came on, and the Prada representatives at the other ship need to do the same, as we had planned.”

The eldest of the first arrivals would be sent back into the dome to direct the steady flow of Prada expected. Other elders would divide the loading equally between the two ships at the east and west dome entrances. That was why the huge ships had landed on opposite sides. An intact clanship could be seen at a third entrance, and the smoking ruins of two clanships blocked the fourth entrance on the north. The scene bore the hallmarks of clan warfare, as did a hurried migration of stolen property, the skilled slave labor to run new factories.

Dillon spotted the first of the refugees streaming across the tarmac to the ship to his right, on the east side. Then another cluster broke from the dome on the west side, and ran for the other ship. A plasma rifle bolt cut one of them down, fired from a point high on the dome.

"Damn it." He was about to seek a target for the smaller lasers on the Avenger, when at least twenty plasma pulses, and nearly that many red or green lasers turned the general area where the shot originated into slag. There was no repeat.

Instead, Dillon resumed sighting in two of the ships' heavy plasma cannons on the most likely entry point into the shipyards for the approaching convoy of Krall. The heavy lasers already had their target lanes designated, and would be under Karl's control when the AI was released to fire them. He had the normal AI restriction against risking human lives. However, there were no humans or Prada on those trucks.

The Torki had started leaving their lodges before the two teams sent to protect them even arrived. The only Krall that had been encountered were two hands of warriors, one hand per lodge, which had been on patrol in trucks. Both hands had already started back towards the dome when they saw it was being attacked. The Dragons took out their halftracks as they returned together, at a range of one mile. One warrior was still alive, and was easily disarmed by his unseen assailants. Then a removed gauntlet permitted a Mind Tap. The two patrols proved to be the only Krall presence there had been, near either lodge.

The warrior's eyes had widened when he saw a human hand appear in the air, and smack his own thick hand down painfully when he extended talons to rake it. The hand took a firm grip on a finger as its wrist was held in an iron grip by a second invisible hand. Questions came to it in low Krall, from a point in front of his face, in a tone of voice it recognized as also belonging to a human.

It had been years since he'd been part of the first invasion on Bollovstic, but he remembered the sound of weak human animals. However, his head, body, and limbs were being held as if by machines. He could snarl, but not shake free, try as he might. His missing lower left leg would not have prevented him from fighting, but he never saw his attacker and those that held him until the hand appeared.

"He has nothing else to share that we need," the voice said, in Standard this time, which the warrior understood slightly.

"Agar, do we take him back as a prisoner?"

"I saw his mental images of humans he's encountered before, as soon as he saw my hand and heard my voice."

"So?"

"So no, Jeni. The answer is, we won't." Then Agar Gupta put a more merciful laser beam through the warrior's right eye than the mercy his knives had granted his victims on Bollovstic.

An hour later, the two teams and the Dragons were back inside the shipyards, waiting patiently with hundreds of other TG2's. They were actually anticipating the arrival of the convoy of highly experienced warriors from the Mordo clan dome. Gupta had shown the others by Tap what the victory celebrations had been like for these clan members. It was a weeklong event, held using the helpless humans left trapped on Bollovstic when it fell. There were no Krall escaping from *this* convoy alive.

****

The Beagle was four hours ahead of the rescue ship flotilla, and accompanied by one of their two new clanships, the Thunder. They emerged close to the orbital station, and Marlyn was pleased to discover only two shuttles docked there, and no clanship. The shuttles were only lightly armed with medium powered lasers, and sometimes carried four anti-ship missiles in two external pods. These had no pods. Except for a possible ramming threat, they offered no significant defense for the station. She could ignore them for now, and would leave the gravity projectors tethered next to the station alone as well. The projectors and station couldn't get away.

Of greater interest was a partially completed Eight Ball, positioned next to a maneuverable work habitat, orbiting nearly ten miles from the main station. This separation was protection against a sudden spontaneous crystal matrix rupture, or a mistake by a Torki technician as the collapsed matter was sculpted with one of the Raspani atomic bond disrupter tools to make it hollow. She had been told by the Torki to expect to find one or two of the weapons under construction near the station, but far enough away that the main structure or the gravity projectors were not endangered.

She contacted the Thunder. "Captain Ralston, we can leave the station alone for now, those two shuttles have little offensive capability. I'll let you dock there with the assault force after we make certain there are no clanships that will come up here to interrupt you. Follow me down to the planet, and I'll target the dome next to the sea. If we spot clanships there, or at any other domes, we can split the targets. For now, provide me with cover in case any clanship is already aloft. I'll drop down to a hundred miles, just above the fringe of atmosphere. I want you at two hundred miles, and trailing a thousand miles behind me."

With Ralston's acknowledgement, Marlyn took the Beagle twenty-two thousand miles lower, leaving the station behind, in its geosynchronous orbit.

There was, as anticipated, no Krall challenge to the two arriving clanships. No matter which clan they represented, they *had* to be "friendly" because interclan fighting was now forbidden, with a worthy enemy to fight. This would probably be the last time the Krall displayed this level of laxity. After twenty-five thousand years of history, another species had come hunting *them*.

Once again, a dome was found with unattended parked clanships. Eleven this time. Tossing an opportunity to Captain Ralston, Marlyn told her, "You take all of the clanships, and launch five seconds after my salvo for the dome is away. I'll launch in thirty seconds when we are nearly overhead, to make the travel time short. I might catch more of them in the upper levels, thus fewer to fight later if we return to rescue workers."

The Beagle launched four of the ground attack missiles, and five seconds after that, eleven hypervelocity anti-ship missiles streaked from the Thunder. With the different missile travel velocities, the smaller and faster anti-ship missiles nearly caught up to the much larger rockets from Beagle. The bigger missiles were set for detonation twenty feet after initial penetration, which would be into the second level of the dome. They would destroy the top three or four levels of the dome, along with the clan leadership and most high status warriors.

The eleven clanships, almost simultaneously, went up in their orange and black fireballs, shattering the armored windows where they were parked close to the dome, on a smaller tarmac built for this undersized dome. Fuel cells spewed propellant and oxidizer alike into the gaping holes. The dome was going to receive more fire damage than Marlyn had expected.

The smaller landing area and fire might make evacuation from the factory below difficult for the Prada, at least when coming up through the dome. As she looked at the wreckage of broken clanships and dome debris still falling back to the ground, there didn't appear to be a safe place to set a migration ship down. They may have to land in the sea, close to the dome, and somehow get the Prada out to the ship. That would considerably slow the loading.

There was only one other clanship located on the planet by the AI, parked at a strip-mining pit where the red tint probably indicated iron ore was obtained for the factory. Marlyn destroyed that one herself. Thus far, this raid had been nearly flawless. They had control of the system, and now needed to destroy the Eight Balls, and rescue the workers in the orbital station first, and those down here if they could.

Marlyn led the Thunder back up to the orbital station, where the Krall there certainly knew they were coming now. As they drew within five miles, the shuttles launched, firing their lasers at the gun ports on the Beagle and Thunder, probably hoping to weld some of the ports shut from the heat.

Kap, Beagle's AI, immediately rolled the ship to distribute the heat over a larger area, and fired the heavy lasers, Marlyn having released control. The first shuttle struck started drifting in a sideways twist, as its attitude thrusters on one side were damaged. As its side was presented to the larger ship, Alyson fired double plasma bolts at the rear hatch, where the seam made the weakest point for the star-hot energy to force an entry. A jet of air proved the shuttle had been holed. The Krall pilot would have been in armor or a pressure suit anyway, so the loss of atmosphere wouldn't be fatal. The next shots from Alyson, at the exposed cockpit, as the craft continued to rotate, did prove fatal. The plasma bolts penetrated the forward view ports, and gutted the interior.

Captain Ralston, without an AI to shoot for her, knew her newly designated gunner was inexperienced and had not benefited from Mind Tap training yet. In a bit of overkill, she used another anti-ship missile for the second shuttle. It exploded in a smaller orange ball than from a clanship, and the flame faded swiftly in vacuum.

Marlyn sighed. Now there was a small debris field to navigate through, and it posed a slight risk to the TG2's as they boarded the station. No point in complaining now, it could wait for after action discussion.

"Alyson please put a half dozen bolts into the gravity projectors attached to the side of the station. If we take the Torki with us that know how to use them, or can build replacements, the Krall should be out of business to make more Eight Balls."

They had been told that the gravity projectors were of Botolian design, and one-of-a kind devices left from that species defeat. However, the Torki had resourceful engineers and scientists, and they might have figured out the alien design.

One minute later, Marlyn told Ralston she could close with the station to offload the seven hundred-fifty member assault team. They were presumably another example of overkill, but overwhelming force didn't seem like a bad idea. Sarge was in overall command of that force. A first for the reluctant leader.

Marlyn was now free to check on how many of the dense Eight Balls Kap had found with their gravity sensors, parked close to the planet and its moon. The partially complete object had four siblings detected so far. Two were in widely spaced ten and fifteen thousand mile orbits around the planet, and two were circling the moon, itself nearly three hundred thousand miles away.

Marlyn had the lower two decks manually sealed with the airtight doors at the four stairwells and the four elevator shafts at deck two. Thc pumps removed most of thc atmosphere, so the Kobani in armor could open a portal. A small amount of atmosphere was vented, but now the heavy rail gun could be rolled close to the opening, and locked securely into the clamps installed just for that purpose. The heavy slugs exerted a strong kick when the powerful current built the magnetic field, which pushed the ferrous jacketed, depleted uranium filled, diamond-tipped projectile along the thirty-foot acceleration track.

Despite the pleas of Jorl Breaker to let him fire the gun, all he would be allowed to do was place a "stick" of ten slugs in the autoloader, activate the telescopic camera, and switch on the Link to Kap. The AI also could position the ship, accelerate towards an Eight Ball, pivot and steady the ship as it moved sideways at almost a thousand miles per second, and fire a cluster of five precision shots at the target from over a thousand miles away. Then Kap would instantly apply acceleration at right angles to their motion to increase distance before the slugs could hit.

They started their first pass at a ball in the ten thousand mile orbit. The people in the hold were not even allowed to watch the weapon fire, in case a round fractured or a coil cracked. Fragments could penetrate the suits. Jorl had to settle for a suit visor image from behind the protection of the main thruster shaft through the hold. With Kap in control, it proved possible to track the slugs and zoom faster than he ever could have done manually. He had a good perspective down the length of the barrel as it fired.

If he had not been a TG2, he would have missed all but the result. As it was, the one point two seconds of flight time, and the intense light installed at the base of each slug let him see the projectiles close with the target in a beautifully straight line of white dots. The suits automatic dimming feature protected his vision, as the slugs all appeared to vanish in the same instant in an intense blue flash, which released a huge burst of gamma and x-rays.

The gun worked spectacularly well. After that one flash, the ball's material itself expanded in an invisible sleet of atomic particles, moving at a significant fraction of the speed of light. The hull of the ship was adequate defense against the particles, and in the second before the blast, Kap had rotated the ship to present its thicker base plate and blast shield towards the passing rain of mildly radioactive particles. The yield was a significant amount of energy, even if there were little matter around it for it to react against. For what was nearly equivalent to a small thermonuclear explosion, it was not terribly spectacular in the emptiness of space.

In analysis, Kap, who had faster and more precise visual processing than any organic being, even a TG2, announced that the first slug had done the deed. The other four backup rounds proved redundant. He didn't need to be that close for the next shots, or use so many.

The Eight Ball, in a fifteen thousand mile orbit was triggered by a single slug from two thousand miles away. The next one orbiting the moon proved the AI had limitations. The first shot struck a glancing blow from three thousand miles, and the Eight Ball failed to crack. The next shot at two thousand miles worked. The fourth one followed.

"It's like shooting fish in a barrel." Sarge transmitted from the Thunder, as it approached the orbital station. They had held off the assault until the nearby Eight Balls were vaporized, as a precaution against the sphere of penetrating particles and radiation from the explosions. Now they were about to knock on and open some doors.

They used a Krall strategy to cut their entrances. Attaching ten-foot diameter semispherical and pressurized domed devices at a half dozen places on the station's hull, they set remote actuators to activate thermite style, ring-shaped charges, which would burn through the bulkhead. It was a method of doing what the Krall did from single ships when they boarded human vessels or orbital stations.

The Torki had told them where there were internal compartments that would auto-seal with airtight doors if pressure were suddenly lost. However, the small domes they were using also sealed airtight to the hull plates, and they would not allow full depressurization in case the doors failed. They didn't want to kill the Torki inside the station by pressure loss. They merely wanted it to drop enough in the compartments to trigger the airtight doors to close.

Sarge had his entry teams positioned. He radioed on an encrypted channel. "I'll trigger the burns in, 3, 2, 1, now!" He thumbed the transmitter button.

****

Force Leader Therdak had his twelve hands of octets ready for them.

Whoever was trying to capture this large orbital station had already destroyed the habitat dome on the surface, and all of the clanships in the system. One of those had been scheduled to retrieve his warriors tomorrow. His force had participated in a week of training exercises up here, in preparation for a raid into human territory, to take control of an orbital weapons factory that had Jump capability.

The Stodok clan's plan was to Jump the entire weapons factory to K1 for study by their K'Tals, and to let the Torki study how humans produced so many weapons so quickly. This worthy enemy was clever, and there were things they made and did quickly that the Krall could order the Prada and Torki to learn to emulate, such as greater computer control of manufacturing.

The capture of one of those automated manufacturing stations would restore some of the honor that Stodok clan had lost in the last thousand years, before this new enemy was discovered. They were now a small clan that spent much time training on an orbital station, and therefore were well suited and experienced to conduct the raid they had planned.

This act would earn them respect and a larger role in the new war. Apparently, one of the vengeful clans they had previously fought had learned of this plan, and they were now in violation of the joint council's order to end interclan warfare. The intent was obviously to steal the hammers, the technology, and the workers. A pragmatic joint clan council might excuse them for this violation, if that clan had control of these powerful weapons, and could still produce them and make them available.

The shocker was what happened just before the assault force apparently landed (they had not seen them land, but the faint sounds on the hull proved they were outside). One of the attacking ships had destroyed four of the hammers, which had required multiple orbits each to produce, one at a time. It had also inexplicably destroyed the gravity projectors that made forming the hammers possible. The most valuable thing remaining for Stodok clan to protect was their Torki workers, who they believed had the knowledge to rebuild the projectors (even if that was denied), and resume production. There also were still four hands of completed hammers stored in orbits around the three outer gas giants, and their moons.

It was obvious that their enemy wanted the Torki alive, or else they could simply have fired missiles into the station. Now they were making the mistake of trying to take control of the facility, and they did not have a large enough force to do that. He had an octal *six hundred* warriors that had just spent a week practicing movements, and simulated combat up here. His warriors knew this station intimately. The normal complement of warriors posted here was two hands and rarely more than four hands, if there was an overlap for the day when duties were rotated. This miscalculation by the enemy would be the death of every warrior that burned their way into this station. They expected to meet only eight defenders, up to sixteen maximum. They were about to be hit by three hundred and eighty-four.

Two external cameras at the main docking station had observed two pressure domes being placed on the outer hull, part way around the curve of the station. The cameras did not reveal who was moving them, probably due to the curvature. They were of a type new to Therdak and his octet leaders, but their purpose was clear. Similar to when a single ship's pilot burned a hole in another ship's hull during a boarding operation, the opening was sealed to avoid air loss. These boarders were using a sort of rigid dome of a tent that could hold more than a single Krall. However, only a limited number of attackers would fit inside one of them. Probably, a crowded octet of warriors at most. One octet at each of the six points of entry, counted by the external sounds of attachment, suggested the boarders numbered about forty-eight warriors.

Therdak had already invoked the phrase "for Path and clan," to express that no quarter was to be given, and no yielding to a superior force was acceptable. It was this same phrase, used too often in past interclan conflicts, which had brought the clan to such a low state, and loss of status. However, this time there really was no alternative, and all of his warriors knew this.

When the boarders were killed, he intended to exit through the openings they had made, to swarm and capture the enemy ship, which was loosely tethered to the station with its portals still open. They had to prevent that clanship from pulling away and firing on the station, and it was their only way down to the planet anyway, unless they waited for shuttles to come up and ferry them an octet at a time.

His warriors were naturally all in armor, and some were waiting inside the six darkened compartments where the enemy had given away their intentions by the slight noises they made on the bulkheads. Clearly, they had not spent time practicing in the zero gravity outside, learning to move quietly. Burning through the hull would be the last successful thing they accomplished today. His massed warriors would kill them as they tried to enter, and then swarm out to take the ship, something they could never have anticipated.

The thermite, as it ignited, imprinted a glowing heat signature ring that Therdak and his warriors could see on the inside walls. He was standing just outside the largest compartment being breached. The enemy obviously knew where the larger compartments were located, and probably had intended to slip in multiple warriors before surging out into the corridors to attack what they believed would be few opponents. He wanted the surprise for the intruders to be complete. He offered a reminder that shouldn't be needed with these warriors.

"Make certain you have already activated your energy packs, the enemy will hear them when you charge the plasma chambers and be warned of the ambush." He snarled as he heard two packs whine as they came on. *Perhaps those two will die in the fighting*, he thought. *It would save me the trouble of killing them later.*

He had thirty-two warriors already inside this single storage compartment, and similar ambushes were set at the other five locations, prepared to fire from both sides into the openings, now being outlined in Infrared heat on the bulkhead. The burn-through seemed a bit slow, but perhaps it was their eagerness to do battle with a treacherous clan that made it seem slower. In any case, soon their charred corpses would be all that remained of the enemy.

There *was* a risk of depressurization, if his warriors punctured the air seal the enemy would be using outside, but his warriors were as protected as the enemy would be for vacuum combat. Even if pressure doors locked them inside the compartments by air loss, they would outnumber the enemy, blocking their advance. The cowardly crabs, which they needed alive, had been herded into central pressurized compartments, to preserve them for use after the fighting ended.

The sparks started to fly as various hot spots started to burn through. The spark color was different from the material used on single ship boarding operations, and the opening was forming far slower than good tactics called for. The defenders had ample time to gather their forces to repel these inefficient invaders. They would learn the fatal errors of poor planning.

****

Sarge, checking the timer displayed on his visor, readied his thumb again, and warned the boarding teams to be ready to go. “Three seconds, and the breeching charges go.”

Time up, and Sarge pressed the second contact on his remote, and six shaped explosive charges, placed on the center of each circle of hull section that should have nearly burned through by now, were triggered. The exploding breech charges flung the two-inch thick plates inward, against the internal atmospheric pressure. The vacuum of the rigid tent frames was instantly filled by a portion of the escaping air, and several vents in the tents permitted even some of that to escape. The venting would continue for a second or two before closing, to make certain the pressure loss inside caused the compartment doors to automatically seal.

Sarge pressed the third actuator, and said calmly on the general push frequency, “Let’s go people. We have Krall to kill.”

****

Therdak had positioned his warriors away from the expected inward blast of the hull sections, standing off to the sides. They were instructed to hold fire until the enemy started through the breeches. The instant drop in pressure was anticipated, as air rushed out to fill the containment domes the enemy was using. However, the domes apparently were not sealed properly, because the air pressure registered on his visor continued to drop rapidly. The automatic doors slammed shut, sealing his warriors inside with the outnumbered enemy, who would be pouring through the breech and into a hail of plasma bolts.

Through the thick door panel, Therdak heard the sizzle-crack of multiple plasma bolts being fired as his warriors sprang their ambush. The enemy must be coming through the opening, dying as they did so.

There was a puzzling momentary pause in firing, before a series of rapid, loud explosions caused the door panel in front of him to not only bulge outwards slightly, but it and the corridor wall panels rang with the sound of metallic hail. He noted that the heavy pressure door had small bumps randomly scattered around its surface, and the sounds of plasma rifles couldn't be heard.

An insightful octet leader, at the second door along the corridor, shouted out the answer. "Fragment explosion!"

"The enemy sacrificed themselves as well?" Therdak couldn't believe the invading warriors would die without trying to fight their way through. He promptly received a rush of reports from the sub leaders he'd sent to the other five compartments. They had heard the same self-destructive explosion by the invaders, and the now unresponsive warriors inside with them must be dead.

The enemy, outnumbered, had apparently blown themselves up with the ambushers, rather than die in honorable combat. Such cowardice and dishonor was inexplicable, more so than a clan attacking them when the council had forbidden such acts. The raid had a logical goal, even if the act were forbidden. The mass suicides, when honorable deaths were available, were foreign to a Krall's way of thinking. Why did they choose to die that way?

There was no time for indecision. The compartment door here was jammed shut, and it would require long minutes to open anyway with a vacuum on the other side. The same must be true at the other five sites. His six assault forces, poised in the outer corridors to join those in the compartments, couldn't swarm out through the breeches just opened, to overrun the clanship as he had planned.

He gave his orders to all six groups. "Move to the nearest cargo dock and go out that way, we have to reach the clanship before it pulls away." It wasn't much of a chance but it was the fastest option left to him. As it happened, it wasn't an option at all.

Therdak tapped his com set shoulder button, and called ahead to the hand of warriors he'd left watching each of the six locked and coded docking station doors. "Start the cycle to open the large airlocks. We need to get as many warriors as possible outside quickly, to capture the enemy clanship."

There was no acknowledgement. He suddenly questioned why the boarding points had all been located in equal distances between the six cargo docking stations. The plasma bolts he heard fired from around the wide curve of the circular corridor gave him the clue he'd been missing. The clumsily implemented burn-through points were a diversion, used to pull the most forces away from the normal entrances, which Krall boarding tactics always avoided anyway.

Somehow, they had entered and killed his door guards by surprise. The enemy still couldn't know how many were in the unexpectedly large force on this station, though he probably had lost close to a hundred ninety warriors inside those death trap compartments. He still had two hundred warriors to defend Stodok honor. They would wipe this foul clan from the station. In combat, the Krall were nearly always optimistic.

****

"How the hell many of them are up here?" Sarge wondered aloud, to himself since he had not *thought* to the suit to transmit to any of his squad leaders.

He had no way of knowing yet that they had killed far more warriors in each breeched compartment than they had expected to be posted on the entire orbital station. That serendipitous slaughter was courtesy of his Poldark experiences, of luring the enemy into poking their noses where they were sure they were safe. He'd packed ten modern "smart" grenades in each of six plastic buckets, one per breech point. These were some he'd had Tet obtain through General Nabarone. He'd had no idea what he might do with them, but having them was sure to spark his imagination. They had.

Each bucket of ten grenades was radio slaved to a "master" igniter grenade, and the bucket was attached by cable to a plate quick-glued to the bulkhead they were burning open. The breech charge blew in the circular section of hull, the bucket followed on the attached cable spilling the grenades. The master grenade in each bucket had a pin that was pulled as the bucket left the pressure tent. The nine other slave grenades were set for different but close intervals to detonate after the master grenade was activated. The compartments were suddenly filled with thousands of ricocheting depleted uranium pellets for several seconds. A simple and effective way to clear an area of enemy combatants, and no human had to be there.

Afterwards, when the assault teams discovered that all six large airlocks had four guards apiece, he realized that the number was already far more than the Torki had estimated would be here. He damn well wasn't going to trust their estimates any farther.

The airlock guards were more than mildly surprised when the coded locks failed to prevent the sudden opening of the smaller personnel entry doors, off to the side of the large cargo airlocks. The station was a refurbished holdover from the Botolians, which was where they made their own, much smaller, collapsed matter spheres, for firing from a linear magnetic accelerator at attacking Krall ships. No ordinary armor could stand up to the Balls, and if heavier armor did, the Ball fractured and exploded with the power of a tactical nuke.

The quantum-encrypted locks for the outer doors had been added by the Torki at Krall insistence. The Torki, from data contained in the Olts, explained how to *disconnect* the locks, which used unbreakable quantum codes on the Botolian doors. The dead race had not used complex locks on either their airlocks or external personnel doors for themselves, and they were simple mechanical releases, once the added-on complex Krall devices were physically disconnected. The Torki had done what they were ordered to do, place an encrypted mechanism on the mechanical latch system. For thousands of years the locks had served the Krall purpose, to lock out unauthorized and unimaginative Krall.

When the personnel door slid open, two of the warriors on this side of the cargo area saw and heard it instantly. Sarge was around to the side of the wall the door slid into, several other stealthed Kobani with him. They were pressed against the wall in case there were shots fired in reaction. There were not, so with trepidation, he mentally selected his weapons, and peeked around the edge. With another thought, he put a red laser through the eye of the closest warrior, and a green one through an eye of the other. It happened in barely five thousandths of a second. Once he told the suit to fire at the two eyeballs, target's which he'd locked into the new tracking system. It hardly seemed sporting.

Sportsmanship went out the window when plasma bolts started flying in his direction from the other two Krall. They had seen the now collapsing dead warriors suddenly pivot and point their weapons, but hold their fire when they saw no target. Suddenly, two lasers had lanced out from a spot just six feet above the deck, and killed them both. It didn't take a long analysis to deduce that the diverging red and green beams, seen faintly in the air, originated from the same spot.

The other two warriors started blasting at the place where Reynolds head was. Or rather where it would have been if the TG2 behind him hadn't been told to cover the other two warriors. Without an angle for a shot from inside the airlock door, Jason Sieko shouldered Reynolds out of his way to get his own shots off. The shove probably saved Sarge's life. The three bolts the Krall got off passed inches behind his helmet as he stumbled forward.

Sieko, a former steward from the Flight of Fancy, picked both warriors off deftly and said, "Sorry I spoiled your aim there, Sarge. No doubt you were going to shoot them just as soon as you finished introducing yourself." He could hear laughter over the frequency, so he knew the other squad members saw and heard what happened.

"Nah. I hate to be a hog and kill 'em all myself. I signaled those were yours, and I meant what I said. I was setting them up for you. However, thanks for shoving my dumb fat ass out of the way, Jason. I owe you" He owed him big time. Feeling invincible didn't mean you were.

"Sarge, nobody thinks your ass is fat." Jason was careful not to contradict the "dumb" part.

Maude Klinger had listened to the two of them talk long enough. "Hey boys, I may look younger now, but I'm still an impatient old fart. Is it safe to open the damned main airlock yet or not?" Another two hundred Kobani were waiting to get in, since the small personnel airlock would take too long to cycle them through.

"Cycle the lock, Maude." The large cargo airlock would have made more noise and taken too long. It would have alerted the Krall that someone was coming. The way they had diverted the Krall to the breech points allowed them to sneak squads in by the personnel locks, so they could clear the way to open the main doors. Now, a third of the force was waiting to enter. They had selected three of the six airlocks for bringing in their assault forces. Sarge's group was probably running late now, and the Krall would know they had been duped.

The larger volume airlock would be five minutes cycling, so Sarge divided the eight of them up to cover the three approaches to this airlock. Because the outer circular corridor is where the breeches were made, any Krall covering those points would be in that outer corridor, and would come running this way now. The radial corridor straight into the cargo area was probably less likely to be an avenue of attack. After all, how wide could the Krall spread their small force?

There were distressingly few places for concealment along the corridors. Invisibility was fine if you didn't shoot back and advertise where your head was located, as Sarge had just discovered. There was a corner at each branch to stand behind, but your back or side was exposed to any warriors coming from the other two directions.

The airlocks were the choke points, and just a handful of warriors could bottle them up here until the larger forces could get inside. If the airlocks were damaged and the inner doors jammed, they would have to be blasted open. The depressurization might kill any Torki not inside an airtight compartment. The squad only had to hold for about five minutes. That's an awful long time for even a few Krall to do damage.

What their external speakers were picking up, from both side corridors sounded like more than a *few* Krall. They had given up any semblance of a quiet approach and the padded feet of their armor was thudding heavily, and they were noisily scraping against the sidewalls in the packed advance wave that filled the halls from side-to-side.

Reynolds had four small grenades in stealthed compartments on his armor. He pulled two out and calling to Maude and Jason, each at another hall entrance, he tossed one to each of them. They deftly snatched them out of the air, such pitifully underwhelming help as they represented. They had left their pulse rifles with the main force, so they could crowd eight of them into the small airlock. All they had to help them now were suit weapons that negated their stealth capability when fired.

That gave Reynolds an idea. He activated the squad frequency. "I'm going up the hall to meet the ones running this way. They can't see me. I'll be in their midst before they know what hit them, and I can toss my grenades into the pack."

Before anyone could tell him what a stupid, suicidal notion that was, their visors showed his ghostly outline running up the corridor, leaving Kredman, his partner at the same corner holding the tenuous fort.

He pulled the two grenades out, and thumbed them for a two-second delay when released. He'd overlooked the fact that the devices themselves were not stealthed, and could be seen "floating" in air in his invisible hands. Before he moved so far around the curve of the ring corridor that Kredman couldn't see or cover him, he stopped, and placed both fists against the wall, side by side of a recessed light fixture.

"Hey Sarge, whata ya doing?"

"Kreddy, I'm making like a wall decoration. Get ready, they just came into sight."

Indeed, there was quite a mob rushing his way. Reynolds had no way to know this, but the surviving Krall forces had split again to cover all six large airlocks. There were thirty-two running right at him, not that he was counting.

He actually saw the eyes of multiple warriors glance right at him, as they automatically took in everything in the corridor. With relief, he knew his pose with the grenades had disguised them as part of the light fixture. In seconds, they closed to within twenty feet, and he lifted his thumbs, activating the timers.

With a flick of each wrist, the powerful little bombs flew well over the heads of the lead warriors who saw them coming. One rolled to the floor trying to bring her rifle up to bear, to try to shoot one of the unknown objects out of the air as it passed over her. While not Kobani fast, it was likely any Krall could have made that shot, had not the timers expired.

Reynolds, well past his former feeling of invulnerability, but still invisible, had dropped to the floor to reduce his exposure to the depleted uranium pellets about to fly.

The dual blasts rained perforating pellets through a dozen faceplates caught looking right at the two former wall decorations, which inexplicably had flown over their heads. The wounded or dying warriors in the forefront were falling, and several others had failed to clear the now dying warrior, face-up on the floor with two holes in her faceplate. The warrior, a pellet through an eye and into her brain, spasmodically pulled the trigger of her plasma rifle, the bolt tearing into the helmet chin of a warrior leaping over her.

Ten or twelve Krall fell either wounded or dead, and others, their headlong rush encountering fallen bodies were being tripped, and tried to leap over the tangle. The speed and momentum of the Krall caused bodies to slide into Reynolds. He used the confusion to pull a still living Krall over his own torso, and he looked up at four different helmets higher than he was, and commanded the suit to lock onto the quickly designated targets. He staggered the two lasers, and the microwave pulse to fire first, then the energy-hog plasma bolt. This distributed the energy released more evenly.

The two lasers penetrated the faceplates he'd designated and blinded or seriously wounded those two warriors, the heat of the microwave beam didn't kill its target, but the sudden red-hot heat of the helmet made it scream and tear it off and fling it away. The plasma bolt dropped the Krall standing next to him. In the distraction of three more warriors suddenly going down, and the strange action and scream of rage and pain of a fourth, had them looking about wildly for where the grenades and lasers came from.

Kredman, amazed at the havoc Reynolds had caused, took down four more Krall before they recognized the firing came from around the corner at the junction they had been trying to reach. They fired back at the edge of that corner to keep whoever was there from firing back again. Except, as his Mind Tap training had taught him, Kredman was already gone, moving towards the opposite corner, his motion invisible to the warriors.

Sarge, still under the weakening struggle of the wounded Krall that covered his body, positioned his own head under an armpit, and fired another microwave burst at another warrior. He realized that this intense microwave beam weapon, which he had distained previously, didn't leave a visible trail back to him. Another Krall ripped off a blistering hot helmet in a rage.

Over half of the former thundering horde was down, dead, or wounded, and their momentum dissipated. Kredman added one more dead to the mix, as he put a red laser beam through the toothy gap of the partly open mouth of the Krall that had just ripped off his helmet. Five plasma bolts promptly passed through the point midway across the open end of the corridor, where the beam had originated just a few feet above the floor.

Kredman had continued his crouching move to the other side, so his helmet was no longer at the apex of the concentrated return fire. Unfortunately, his left hip had not cleared that area. One bolt missed too high, two glanced upwards off the armor, and two hit and burned deep pits, which transmitted intense heat to the inside. Kredman fell to the deck, short of the cover he was seeking, and the burned spot on his armor lost its invisibility.

His scream of pain in his helmet was only heard by him, and he started crawling to reach the cover of the corner, only a couple of feet away.

Reynolds saw his icon flare yellow in his visor, indicating Kredman was wounded. He couldn't see him from where he was laying, but he could offer a distraction. He reached around the front of the weakening warrior he held over his torso, and grasped the plasma rifle hanging there on a sling. It was point blank range so he didn't need to aim. He pulled the trigger and shot one of the warriors in the side that had fired on Kreddy. Another trigger pull and he hit the knec joint of a second warrior.

Both turned towards the source of the attack, but saw only their clan mate, who didn't even have hold of his weapon. He appeared to be dead or dying. While looking directly at the downed warrior, a laser passed through the faceplate of one, and the other one's faceplate suddenly sagged with the heat it had absorbed.

Unfortunately, this didn't save Kredman. The other three warriors, not certain what they were seeing, put multiple bolts into the mysteriously moving spot that was a foot above the deck. He died in a blaze of agony as his suit was shredded at the hip. The suit's stealth capability failed, and the compact black and white armor suddenly shimmered into view. Their target was dead, but to be certain this unknown type of enemy was definitely dead, the three warriors engaged in overkill, and cut the suit in half with their fire.

Reynolds saw the icon turn red and fade, and he suddenly saw another one turn yellow. Jason was hit. He had been so busy here he had no idea what was happening in the other corridor. They had been fighting in quiet desperation within their suits. His attention was suddenly yanked away from the action elsewhere.

The Krall were less flexible in their thinking than were humans, and not quite as smart on average, but in combat they did pay attention. One of those warriors farther back in the corridor, having seen the body of some strange looking opponent suddenly appear out of thin air, looked for signs of other invisible enemies. A dead Krall hovering eighteen inches above the deck, which had somehow just shot two clan mates with his rifle, and then launched a laser beam from a type of weapon the Krall didn't carry, was a clue even the thickest headed lizard could absorb.

The armored body of the now dead Krall was suddenly snatched away, and the business end of plasma rifle was jammed down into the area where the corpse had been supported. The smart thing to do would have been to shoot first and probe later. Reynolds taught him that lesson swiftly. He snatched the rifle with one hand as his other grabbed and broke the armored arm that had extended the weapon. He tossed the weapon up and released it as he slammed down with both of his hands while he used his back to flip up from the deck, bringing him to his feet in one motion. He grabbed the rifle in midair, reversed it and put a bolt through the dumfounded warrior's faceplate.

He tossed the weapon up again as he dove away. The rifle became the focus for shots from the three warriors that had killed Kredman, and from two others farther back in the corridor. While they wasted multiple plasma bolts on a discarded rifle they had just seen kill one of them, Reynolds moved down the passageway, looking back.

Good shooting, he thought, all of them hit it.

He stepped behind the rearmost two warriors and fired the microwave weapon at one, and a plasma bolt into the rear of the helmet of the other. Neither was a kill shot, but were disabling. That moment was all that he needed.

He grabbed the rifle from the Krall that was more interested in removing the steaming helmet on its roasting head, and while standing behind him, he fired twice to kill two of the warriors looking back into the corridor. They were caught while looking at the thoroughly destroyed rifle they all had managed to kill.

The third warrior in the front shot the burned warrior he was standing behind in the head. This effectively took away Reynolds cover, and the warrior shooting towards him had dived to take cover behind corpses. He was blindly shooting over the top of one corpse accurately, using its battlefield memory of where his enemy had been.

Reynolds tossed the visible weapon in the air as he moved away, but it didn't draw fire this time. *Fooled them just once*, he thought.

He wisely didn't move towards the Krall he'd stunned with the helmet head shot either. It was down on its knees, trying to recover its senses, but the warrior up front had raised its head to get fresh information, and ignoring the falling rifle, fired into the empty space around the kneeling warrior. It had assumed the invisible enemy would go to cover behind the *next* closest Krall.

Suddenly, as he stepped over dead Krall bodies to get closer to the shooter, that worthy foe was shot in the back of its head. He first thought the main force had made it through, but no. It was Bill Coleman, the man paired with Jason Sieko.

With alarm, Reynolds realized that he had failed to note the missing icons. He and Bill were the only ones left from the squad. It had only been four minutes. The door wasn't ready to lift and the rest of the troops weren't inside yet.

"Bill, what's happening in the corridor on the other side?"

"They ran over us, Sarge." He sounded apologetic. "We needed more of those grenades. Maude followed your nutty example. God, she took down a dozen, but they are gathering in front of the airlock. They can't stop all of them, but they'll cut a bunch of our guys down. They know we have better stealth now, so they'll shoot as soon as the door starts to lift."

Mentally selecting the push for squad leaders for his group, he warned them. "The Krall had a shit pile more warriors here than we thought. At least a dozen are waiting for you when the airlock completes its cycle. If you have grenades, throw them under the door first."

"We don't have any. Seemed like a bad idea on a space station." That was Andrew Johnson's voice, and his ID appeared on the visor icon.

"Andy, I'll give you a diversion the moment the door starts to lift."

"OK. The pressure is almost equalized, we can start to open when you say go. We'll come out shooting."

"Good. Lock onto my visor image so you can see what I see. I'm headed for the entrance again."

He turned to Bill. "Cover my back. I'm going to get their attention."

"What can you do against so many?"

"Why play with dolls, of course." Staying close to the inside curve of the wall, he moved closer the corridor junction.

****

Therdak felt certain they were going to lose the station. The enemy was incredibly effective in battle, and had suit technology well beyond anything the Krall used. The stealth was nearly perfect. This new armor made the enemy essentially invisible at infrared as well as at visible light wavelengths. It was as if single ship stealth coatings had been applied to their suits, except the power needs for that material required a fusion bottle.

The only thing he was certain of was that this was not an assault by another clan. Not just because of the technology displayed. The one dead fighter's armor he could see was much smaller than a Krall's, and the stealthed armored corpses they could touch were the same size. The armor's integrity had failed when it was penetrated at close range, something that was harder to do than with Krall armor.

There had been a partial report from a leader of a hand of octets, voice cut off before it was finished, that an unseen enemy had poured out of an airlock on the opposite side of the station. His warriors were being killed quickly, from almost any point, even being shot from behind their formation in the firefight. The other sub leader at a different airlock had not answered him.

He was down to fifteen warriors at this particular airlock, only eleven were fully effective. None of the warriors that *should* have come from the opposite corridor had arrived.

There had been explosions heard, and multiple sounds of plasma bolts in that direction, but it was silent there now. He had one of his badly wounded warriors, without lower legs, working to remove the armor from one of the dead enemy. Unlike five of the six that had died, this one's stealth had fully failed when it was blasted into two pieces. He wanted to see the face of this new enemy before he died fighting them. He hated them even as he admired them.

He could see by the pressure indicator outside of the wide airlock door that it would open soon. He and his warriors, true to the "Path and clan" order he had issued, would take as many of the enemy as possible before they died.

"Force leader." It was the wounded warrior working on the dead enemy's corpse. "I have found the release for the helmet, it has partly opened and I can remove it now. You wanted to be first to see."

Therdak, knowing time was short, stepped close and bent to pull the strange looking object off. There had been no transparent faceplate at all. He didn't understand how it could see the outside world.

As he lifted the strange clamshell like helmet, he caught sight of the features, and drew in a sharp suck of air. A stab of fear, the first he'd ever recalled feeling, entered his mind. He was glad he still wore his helmet so his reaction wasn't seen.

His wounded warrior, however, had removed his damaged helmet to facilitate the task of visually seeing how to open the enemy armor. His shock was as great, and his blurted words were heard by all. "This is a human! We were boarded by humans."

Despite the circumstances, many of the warriors leaned over or stepped away from their place in the firing line to see. It was impossible that these weak animals had bested them in close combat.

Therdak had an answer to the strength they had demonstrated. The warrior on the floor, holding the dead human's torso could testify to that strength. His legs had been twisted and torn off at the knees in a hand-to-hand struggle, three against one human.

"Their armor must be powered. This gives them the strength that was not bred into them, as it is with us." He wasn't convinced that the slender armor had that ability, but what else could he say?

Just then, a hiss and clank told everyone, on both sides of the door, that the solid metal plate of the airlock door was about to lift.

Suddenly, a screeching banshee of a sound from the side corridor told them something insane was coming at them. Two Krall warriors, loosely holding their rifles came jiggling and wobbling towards them, looking oddly loose jointed. It drew the attention of every warrior. Four of them died, looking on in disbelief at the bizarre actions of their clan mates.

****

Reynolds used the rifle slings to lash them quickly to the hands of two dead Krall warriors. Then he grabbed them by the back rim of their helmet attachments and bodily lifted them. He sent a message to Johnson. "OK, raise the door when you see me reach the corridor junction on my visor. You had better shoot straight and often." He didn't wait for a reply.

Using a thought to activate his external speaker system, and setting it to high volume, he let out a screeching sound that echoed through the corridor. He ran around the inside curve towards the Krall, waggling the corpses like the dolls he'd mentioned to Coleman.

He instantly spotted one warrior standing over Kredman's body, holding his helmet. That one knew who they were for sure, and his first shot went through that one's faceplate. He didn't know he'd killed the Force leader, but with Krall, they weren't really disrupted much by that. It happened too often. He shot three more in quick succession.

Fortunately, for those in the airlock, the distraction worked. Ten troopers were lying prone, with plasma rifles ready and suit targeting set for auto fire on any target that didn't have a "friendly" icon.

Unfortunately, for Reynolds, the distraction worked. Half of the Krall opened fire on his "dolls," and his using them for protection only worked to a limited extent. That extent did not give his legs much protection. He was shot three times in his right leg. He went down in a tangle with his two "toys."

In seconds, the remaining Krall at this airlock were tangled bodies as well. Two of the ten Kobani in the prone firing line were killed by random shots to their helmets, one was wounded in the neck. All told, there were eleven Kobani killed at this forced entry point, seven seriously wounded, and five minor wounds. The Krall didn't miss often. Neither did the Kobani. The Krall losses were one hundred percent dead.

Three Torki were killed by decompression when in a panic, they forced open an adjacent compartment that had been breached. There was half a lodge present on the station, and even though they understood low Krall and hated the Krall, they didn't actively cooperate with the strange aliens until the migration ship arrived and docked. They received Olt communications, and shortly after the arrival of the Torki on the rescue ship, they all spontaneously underwent the experience of having the new internal library opened to them.

When it was explained that this library opening was a side effect of having communicated with the humans via their form of telepathy, the former slaves became most cooperative. As a token of their appreciation, they went along to direct their search for all of the Eight Balls they had been forced to build over the centuries. It was a pleasure for them to see things that had never been used for anything but war, destroyed.

With Krall resistance quickly eliminated on the planet and by the dome, the rest of the Torki lodge was taken aboard, and a second migration ship was landed to collect the one village of Prada. They were convinced by an elder to come along, just as the Prada at CS2 had been.

Marlyn came into the Beagle's infirmary to see the wounded, and lingered by one med lab in particular. "Sarge that was one nutty fine job you did on that station. You really managed to farkle up that bunch of Krall waiting at the door."

The nanites in his body had quickly eased his initial pain when he lost his leg at the knee, and now those of the med lab were starting the three-month task of regrowth. He was feeling no pain, and felt rather good about the mission. “Thanks. ‘Twern’t nuthin, Mam. And where’d you learn my home world cuss word, farkle?”

“From my Poldark husband, you twit. And, don’t say what you did was nothing!” she told him. “We’re going to have to create some sort of medal or an award, just for *your* actions today. Not to mention the heroics of so many others.”

“Crap. Marlyn, I don’t want a medal or award. It’ll just mean a promotion to some other position I don't really want. I’m happy as I am.”

Smiling, she answered, “You can’t mean that! Why there are people who would give an arm and a leg to be a decorated Kobani.” She started to turn away but stopped.

Looking back she added, “Oh, right... You already did that.” She laughed as she walked out.

Chapter 20: CS1

The Mark did its White Out at a thousand miles. It arrived alone, but left a Tachyon Space message for one of the four new clanships. The ship with the largest number of ground attack missiles aboard was instructed to follow him to CS1 as soon as possible. He had received the message about the larger missiles when he arrived at his waypoint. He wanted their firepower to help reduce the domes to rubble. The anti-ship missiles would do considerable damage, but they relied on high speed to hit and kill ships, and delivered less destruction to a dome.

While Thad watched the sensors for clanships off-planet, he talked. “Tet, do you really think our supply clanships will be that close behind us? The migration ships are probably another two days from the waypoint. Perhaps we should have waited for another clanship. Marlyn and Noreen will have had those available.”

“Thad, I don’t know that a day delay would matter, this far from the actual war. However, knowing a weapon I would have wanted is almost in my grasp makes me feel more cautious. I know I was prepared to go in exactly the way we’re armed now, but small things can make a difference that you didn’t foresee.” He looked over to Ethan.

“What do you see on the tarmac of the main habitat dome?” They had luckily emerged over the hemisphere where the main dome was located. It was in an oasis of green, compared to the considerable expanse of gray and brown wastelands of the metal rich planet.

The drab looking world had been strip mined for many thousands of years, making war materials. Smaller, more easily produced equipment was now made closer to where any war was conducted. However, the more complex and resource hungry ship production stayed put. The powerful two clans that retained the prestige of producing clanships, the backbone of their interstellar war machine, didn’t intend to lose status by giving up that control.

“Uncle Tet, there are seventeen clanships at that dome. One of them appears to be preparing to depart. It has a ramp down and its portal open. A row of warriors are lined up along each side of the ramp.”

Mirikami leaned forward in interest. “Put that image on screen. Your description sounds like an honor guard. That could be a high ranking visitor.”

A zoomed-in image flashed up on the view screen across the Bridge consoles from Mirikami. “I saw an honor guard like that on Koban, when Gatrol Kanpardi came to visit. I don't know if clan leaders get the same sort of honor, or if it’s even a common practice. I see blue, brown and gray uniforms coming out of the closest dome entrance, running to the waiting ship.” He chuckled.

“I once said I’d pay a week’s pay just to see a damned Krall simply walk some place.”

Jakob, placed on speaker for convenience, spoke up, when Mirikami would probably have preferred he talk to him through his transducer. “I believe you later told Maggi you would pay a hundred Hub credits to see them walk, right after Kanpardi and his guards left the Flight of Fancy.”

"Uhh…, thanks Jakob." They sounded different, but Mirikami knew that the newer AI on the Mark had a full set of Jake's memory bank data from the Fancy. He could have said that a hundred credits actually *was* a week's pay, but then he'd be promptly corrected with a quote of his considerably higher annual pay, divided into the monthly payments to his account, and then divided into weeks. *Pick your arguments carefully*, he thought, *and none at all with an AI. Or with Maggi,* he amended.

Thad had a suggestion. "Tet, do you think this is a chance to take out an important leader at the start of the fight?"

It was tempting, but Mirikami pulled at his lip, and after a moment said no. "The dome might be on higher alert to impress this visitor, and for all we know one or more of the other clanships could be staffed and ready to go with him. We might get into a shootout we don't want and may not win. Besides, if this leader safely Jumps out of the system, he'll report that all was well when he left. If we kill him, someone will come looking for a high status Krall much sooner. If we knockout all the clanships here in a surprise attack, the survivors might sit here for weeks or months before they get a visitor. Let's wait and watch. We need to complete this orbit anyway, to see what other targets we have."

Yet another logical-seeming decision that would have unimagined consequences.

****

Telour was satisfied with his inspection visit. The shipyards themselves were adequate to double production, the infrastructure to increase mining was already present, and an extensive transport system was already available, if they used refurbished older roadways and tracked lines. After all, this world had been under steady resource development and consumption for nearly eighteen thousand years. The Krall didn't build cities or need consumer goods (unless a mini tank was a work car, and a plasma rifle a credit card). The mineral wealth here was still sufficient for thousands of years of production.

The only bottleneck to quickly increasing production was the work force. The Torki and Prada bred at a slow pace, and required lengthy training to learn the complex tasks. The living conditions on the polluted world kept reproduction rates lower than on less ravaged planets.

The solution was trivial. Send one or two migration ships to worlds that had underused lodges and villages, and bring them here. If they died off too soon and were unable to breed quickly enough to repopulate, bring in more. It was just like mining any other resource.

The Graka clan already controlled multiple worlds with extra slaves that they could relocate within a month or two, using just one or two migration ships. No new factories needed to be built, so within a single orbit of this world, they could increase clanship production to double its current rate. All of the status points would belong to Graca when the joint council finally did the inevitable, and granted Kanpardi the material his additional invasion forces required.

Economics were *simple* when you sacrificed things that were unimportant, such as workers, ecosystems and material, and you gained something that did matter, status points for breeding more like yourself.

He left the dome knowing he had instilled energy in the sub leaders here, to prepare for the production increase in a few months, with a promise of a share of the status points that would result. These were largely low status warriors. Otherwise, they would not be stuck here, away from the war they craved to join. They would earn more status points soon, rank high enough to demand to go fight humans, then fail to be effective enough as warriors (as previously demonstrated). They would be sent to some *other* backwater production world to watch over slaves, still without enough status points to breed and continue their worthless bloodlines. The Great Path was served well in the long term.

As he ran towards the clanship, his honor guards lined up, he was accompanied by unfinished business, which he would presently conclude in a pleasant (for him) manner. Parkoda had been brought along for the sole purpose of allowing him to see what a successful high status Graka clan warrior Telour had become. He was still rising. He had already fostered thousands of (unknown) offspring, from mating's with high status females. A fact he had pointed out to Parkoda on occasion during the trip.

He pretended to thank Parkoda for the status points he had earned from the only raid he had shared with him, when Parkoda was the raid leader. This reminded his opponent of Telour's clever use of the humans on Koban, which Parkoda had captured, but which had given Telour and Graka clan ascendency over Tanga clan. He had out maneuvered Tanga clan, and arrogant Parkoda in particular, who then made the error of insulting Kanpardi.

Now, by offering to humiliate and punish Parkoda on behalf of Kanpardi, he had again created a status increase for himself at the expense of Parkoda. It was time for the final degrading step.

Telour pulled up at the base of the clanship ramp, standing between his two lines of honor guards, and turned to Parkoda. "I have found no indication that any of the soft ones have escaped your custody, despite the lax security I found at their compound. I now must return to report to Tor Gatrol Kanpardi. I must immediately tell him my mission to increase Graka clan's advance production of clanships for the new invasions will meet or exceed his expectations.

"Parkoda, you are free to return to the soft Krall compound. If no clanship of any clan arrives to take you there in the next quarter orbit, the migration ships arriving here soon will have ample room to carry you, and can perhaps take you in the direction of one of your clan worlds."

Telour had already left instructions with the Graka clan sub leader here that this Tanga clan worm had offended the Tor, and no Graka ships would be "able" to take him off planet. The slow migration ships would be his only alternative transport. When Parkoda eventually returned to his former posting, his second in command would surely have secured the sub leader post permanently. It was one more slap to the muzzle, and Kanpardi would enjoy a good snort at the retelling.

Parkoda, indignant, had expected to be dropped off on the return trip. It was only a slight detour, considering it would be a seven thousand light-year Jump. "Telour, you took me from my rightful duty station. You are obligated to allow me to return."

"I have said exactly that. Return as soon as you can."

"I can travel on this ship." It wasn't so much a demand as pointing out the obvious.

"No. Kanpardi was insistent that as soon as I knew the result of my primary mission, I should immediately return to advise him that his plans should proceed. As ordered, I will return directly to Telda Ka to inform him. That Jump would take you four thousand light-years beyond your destination. You require another ship."

Telour turned and ran up the ramp; his honor guard closing ranks behind him, cutting off any move by Parkoda try to follow, or to implore Telour to reconsider. However, Parkoda had accepted this new defeat. It had been obvious from the start he would lose a game so stacked against his winning. With his dignity in shreds, he turned and ran back towards the dome even as he heard the portal close and ramp retracted. He heard the fuel pumps activate. That meant they were launching immediately, and Telour probably hoped the thruster blast would "inadvertently" knock him from his feet and deliver painful burns.

The max performance departure was in keeping with the phony urgency Telour claimed for the return, but it didn't manage to knock Parkoda down. He ran at top speed to reach the dome entrance overhang, as the flakes of plasma torn tarmac bit into his skin. The trickles of blood halted almost immediately.

There was no indication yet that his bad day was only just beginning.

****

Thad leaned back again when the clanship Jumped. "Holy crap, Tet. They were in a hurry. I thought I was going to have to start a missile track the way they came off. I was afraid they were coming after us, as an unidentified arrival."

Mirikami had leaned forward too, in alarm when the clanship leaped off like that. "I was watching too, even though I was initially focused on the view on the tarmac after we had orbited past them. I think the lone, blue suit Krall that stayed behind received deliberate disrespect by that hurried launch. The ship buttoned up, and almost immediately did a maximum thrust liftoff. That blue suited VIP went up the ramp, followed by the honor guards, and didn't have time to reach even the third deck before the acceleration came. That should cause the loss of a pilot position, if not the pilot's life, if he did that without the VIP's approval.

"I believe it was done to insult the Krall left standing at the base of the ramp.

He ran out there as if he expected to get aboard, but then he was left behind. I don't know what he did, but he pissed off someone important, who could easily have said goodbye as they left the dome, and not out there on the ramp."

Ethan said, "Aunt Maggi claims she understands Krall politics better than human politics. The motives are simpler, and the actions and reactions more direct, she says."

"Nearly frying that one's ass on the Tarmac is certainly direct." His dad added.

Mirikami shook his head. "If he had stood there or just walked away slowly he'd be dead. However, running is how the Krall normally prefer to move. I think they wanted him to suffer the indignity of being blown over, or of having to hit top speed to avoid that. He did the latter. I stand by my guess that it was intended to be an insult, not to kill him."

"I wonder if there's something there that we can use to our advantage."

"Ethan," Mirikami smiled at the youngster. "If Maggi were going to engage in negotiations with them, she'd find a way to use it for sure. However, our only negotiating position here is going to be as simple and direct as the Krall prefer. Missiles down their throats."

As they were about to lose direct sight of the main dome and its oasis of greenery, Ethan saw something. "Captain, there are five Krall going out to another clanship."

"Thad, stay with passive tracking but keep ports for a couple of our missile launchers open. They may just be doing something the Krall leader that just departed told them to do."

That turned out probably to be the case, because the clanship stayed suborbital, and flew the several thousand miles to the shipyard dome, which had just appeared over the horizon for the Mark.

Mirikami decided it was time to move down closer. "OK, staying this high makes for a longer orbital period, and I don't see anything unusual happening. Jakob."

"Yes Sir."

"Take us down to two hundred miles, and do it before we pass the shipyards this first time around."

The ship rotated, and as thrusters fired, Mirikami gave the entire crew an update. "We don't see any unusual activity and we're dropping lower, as your monitors will show. A clanship just went to the dome at the shipyards, and…, I can see there was another one already parked there. We'll not take them out on this pass because I want to see the whole planet at least once. Missile loaders stand by your launchers for reloads. If everything looks good, on the next pass over the main habitat, things will be a bit more interesting."

Just as planned for CS2 and the Eight Ball raid, they would knock out all of the clanships on a single, fast, low orbit, and pound the main dome on the same pass. With the lighter warheads, more of the anti-ship missiles would be needed to cause heavy damage to a dome over four thousand feet across and six hundred feet high.

For the smaller dome at the shipyard, where the Prada occupied the lower levels, blasting the top Krall-used levels was all they intended to do anyway.

When they passed the shipyards, they saw five Krall, the same number they saw enter the ship that just landed, make the standard run into the dome.

Mirikami, dwelling on how open the Krall star systems were to infiltration by trusted spacecraft, thought this month might be the last time such clanships would be able to arrive unexpectedly over a Krall planet, and not be challenged or required to transmit some sort of coded reply to an electronic interrogation. The clanships were capable of this, as the Torki had shown them, but the Krall had rarely used the feature except in cases of authorized interclan warfare. The clanships humans captured would be set up to operate this way when arriving at the Koban system in the future.

Ethan, still conducting ground surveillance, said. "In the shipyards, there are a half dozen hulls that are half-built or greater, sitting in the cradles, and three more that appear almost ready to fly. I zoomed in on some of the Prada workers, and they are wearing filter masks. The brown-gray haze at low altitudes is thick around the shipyards and foundries. As I look towards the horizon in any direction, I see the haze is everywhere. There's no reason the mining and other industry couldn't have been done with scrubbers and filters to keep the air and water cleaner."

His father shrugged. "Planets have little value to Krall, you should know that. That's why they rape, use, and abandon them. Here they simply moved the clan to another cleaner world, and left an outpost to protect their interests and to keep the slaves working."

Mirikami was pulling at his lip. "There must be a swath of habitable but ruined worlds anywhere the Krall have been. Have you noticed how few domes, even old abandoned ones we have found on any of their worlds? We have only just started looking at worlds inside the space they control, but I'm seriously wondering how many of the Krall there are? The ones we Mind Tapped didn't know, since there's no census. They can breed like fleas, but they may be self-limiting in a sense, with their fixation on culling the weakest and breeding only the best."

"Tet, Coldar said according to Torki Olt records of races they have beaten, they have killed hundreds of billions, if not trillions. It seems logical to think they could only do that with a large population of their own."

"I thought so too, Thad, but look at what a few thousand of us are doing to them now, assuming that we *can* seriously slow their war with us. It could be that they too have only had a spear point of warriors all along, and didn't need much infrastructure or population to keep going. An army of ten billion super warriors is far more than the human race has, even with our trillion in population. The Hub's military forces are still below forty-five million, and about half of them are support personnel, not soldiers.

"If humanity can hold out and keep building forces and we win, we will have a great deal of habitable space to move into, even if we share some of it with the Torki, and Prada. Perhaps even share with the Raspani if we can put them back on the road to intelligence."

Thad sounded doubtful. "Places like this will need a lot of recuperation to be habitable again."

Mirikami nodded. "This world and CS2 may be worse case situations. The Prada and Torki say some worlds the Krall left with nests that ran amok, and hatchlings and feral adults ate every animal they could reach until they can only eat themselves. When the last of them die off, the plant life would support an introduction of new herbivores and grazers, and then the predators that eat them. Terraforming has been done many times." He paused, and put on a sly grin.

"But, let's not count our worlds before the hatchlings are dead, shall we?"

"Tet, you've been taking pun lessons from Dillon!" Thad accused.

"Can't help it. It rubs off on you."

As the ship moved around the planet, there were numerous strip mines sighted, partly automated, with transportation links that required minimal Prada direct supervision. However, it pointed out a tragic problem for the rescue. They could not take the time to try to rescue all of the Prada, spread so wide. As they again orbited towards the main habitat dome, Jakob suddenly made an announcement of some concern to them.

"Two clanships have performed a White Out together, at two thousand miles from the planetary surface, almost four thousand miles behind us."

Mirikami spoke quickly. "I think those must be ours. Our new captains won't know how to use the friend-from-foe interrogation and reply capability. Are they transmitting anything?"

"Yes, one ship is sending an encrypted message, saying they each have air to ground missiles, and request direction from you."

"Damn. There wasn't any other way for them to ask me? An encrypted message will be detected by the Krall. That might raise questions, particularly with three unknown and unexpected clanships arriving this close together. I should have waited for them and delivered instructions before the Jump."

Thad let him know that their firing run was already programed. "I have all of the parked clanships, and the dome targeted. If our people have enough of the larger missiles, they can take out the dome for us. We need to hit those parked ships quickly, in any case. That's where any return fire will originate."

"Ethan, tell them both to move in fast and unload on the dome from two hundred miles. We're well ahead of them. I'm going to make the Krall think the Mark is landing. That will make us seem less likely to be up to no good."

"Yes Sir."

"Jakob, make our flight path look more like a typical Krall pilot's landing. You have enough recordings of what they usually look like."

"I can try, Sir, but most Krall pilots like to come in vertically, fast, and apply hard thrust near the end. Should I go higher?"

"No, but boost speed, and then rotate and brake hard, as if we are landing. We will break off at twenty miles over the dome and climb out to orbit again."

"Yes Sir."

The thrust was immediate, and they leaped ahead.

"Thad, kill the dome launches by us of course. Fire on the tarmac ships when we reach twenty miles overhead and Jakob has rotated to return to orbit."

"Will do."

For the next minute, they accelerated at two hundred miles up, then the ship turned tail and applied hard thrust, wasting an excessive amount of fuel, exactly like Krall pilots did. They soon rotated to vertical, and started down at an altitude of fifty miles, nearly over the dome and tarmac.

"Captain," Ethan called to him. "About a dozen Krall came out as we approached, but when we rotated tail first for landing, they must have caught sight of our thruster glow, slowing hard. They stopped and looked, and are going back into the dome. I think you will get a harsh reprimand for flying worse than the average Krall, Sir."

Chuckling, despite feeling tense, he answered, "I hope the reprimand doesn't include my weapons officer missing any of his designated targets."

"We'll know in less than a minute, Captain." Thad answered. "My range finder says we are at twenty-five miles." For an optimum firing angle, Thad needed to wait for the AI to increase thrust and lay the ship into a roughly forty-five degree angle as it started to climb from a twenty mile altitude. The short range and missile velocity meant there would be little arcing needed to turn them towards the targets, and there would be mere seconds before impact.

The ship jolted as all fifteen missiles launched from the same five, lower side launchers, in three rapid firings, only one second apart from five launch tubes.

Unnecessarily, Thad said, "Missiles away."

In the next five seconds, the tarmac repeated the orange and black fiery spectacles that had blossomed on CS2 and the Eight Ball planet. The Mark of Koban was climbing and accelerating to enter a low and fast suborbital course to get to the shipyards as quickly as possible. There were two more clanships to reduce to scorched scrap metal as quickly as possible.

Ethan's startled exclamation gave them a frightful heart stopping moment. "Holy crap! Look at that plot!"

Mirikami, strapped into his couch couldn't see the console screen in front of Ethan very well. "Put it on a big screen." He pointed to one.

A glance and he agreed with Ethan. "Jakob, how the hell many are there?"

"How many what, Sir?"

"Missiles!"

"Counting those we fired and have detonated?" AI's could be so literal.

"No. The ones targeting the dome, damn it!"

"Oh. That would be eighty-eight, Sir. Forty-four from each of our fellow clanships."

"Yee gods," Thad muttered.

"Ethan, what did you tell those two captains?" Mirikami demanded.

Sheepishly, and more than a little defensive, he told him, "Exactly what you said to me, Sir." With his TG2 memory he was absolutely certainly he'd heard him right.

Mirikami, his own TG2 memory just as sharp, suddenly turned red in the face.

Thad played his own memory back of the half listened to words.

He exploded into laughter. “They fired every single one they had on board.”

Mirikami, recovering his composure grimaced. “It was a figure of speech. I didn’t literally mean for them *to unload on the dome*! Ten rockets would have been plenty.”

The subsequent explosions rumbled, one after another, for what seemed like a full sixty seconds, lasting for the extended time it had taken the ships to launch that many missiles. Finely divided fragments of the structure fell back, only to be ripped again by additional high-powered explosions. The granulated debris finally settled into a smoking, sunken looking pit at the center, with the upper dome struts having flown out over the tarmac and escaped being pulverized.

Thad, amused by the results shouted out in declarative sentences. “Sir! Shipyards in sight. Two clanships on the tarmac! How many missiles for each, Sir? We only have eighty- five left, Sir!”

Mirikami gave him a sour look, and held up two fingers. Too embarrassed and annoyed to speak.

Continuing in his loud military speak, Thad asked, “Two missiles apiece, Sir? Seems like overkill, Sir!” Thad was enjoying this rare slip by the famously near infallible captain.

In a false threat, Mirikami answered, “If you fire four missiles, I’ll send you into that damned dome alone and unarmed.”

“Yes Sir. One missile each.” He fired them. As they streaked towards their targets, he added. “One unarmed Kobani against all those Krall? Seems terribly unfair to me. The Krall might complain.” He and Ethan laughed, and finally Mirikami chuckled with them.

Before they passed over the second dome, with the fireballs still rising from the last two clanships on the planet, Thad put four anti-ship missiles into the upper levels. Their other two clanships passed above them as this was done, still in a two hundred mile high orbit, and requested instructions.

On the verge of forcing Thad to talk to them, Mirikami realized his two captains were former Drive Rats, and had not asked questions when the legendary Mirikami told them what to do. After all, they had Jumped into the teeth of things here with no knowledge of what they might face. They had volunteered to help steal the clanships, and then expected to fly only supply missions. Now they had a combat story to tell when they got back to Koban.

“Captains, I appreciate your help. I’d like to thank you by name if you would be so kind as to furnish them. Did the migration ships arrive before you Jumped here?”

“Sir, this is Francois Lebeau, and I have christened my ship the Pride of Gaul. The first migration ship did a White Out while we were enroute here. One of the other new ships did a short in-system Jump at the waypoint to send me a message in Tachyon Space. Carlos Fuentes, the captain of the Florence is a friend of mine and we were Drive Rats together. We learned we were able to make the mental connection when we do Jumps. He thinks the other four migration ships will be there soon."

"Thank you, Captain Lebeau. I take it you were from the Old Colony of Gaul before Koban?"

"Yes Sir."

"And who do I thank on the second ship?"

"Sir, it is Bob Danker. I've named my ship the Dagger. If I learn how to fight her, I'd like to join you on future missions."

"Captain Danker, I have no doubt we can find a use for your spirit, and with Mind Tap, you can gain the knowledge of how to fight with her. I thank you as well.

"With the arrival of at least one migration ship, and the security of this system in hand, I'd like you, Francois, to make the half day Jump back, and bring the other ships here as soon as possible. You can try to contact your friend when you Jump. Stop the transfer of supplies at the waypoint, and finish the job here. We want to get as many Prada and Torki off this world as we can."

"Sir, what about the Raspani, in the compound near the dome we destroyed?" It was Danker's voice.

Mirikami had never even *thought* about the Krall having them here as food. It was a moment of horror for his oversight. He couldn't leave them if he could somehow rescue them. "Bob, how many did you see and where were they? We were focused on the dome and ships."

"Sir, the fenced area was about five miles north of the dome, around a small lake and some buildings. Let me think a moment…"

Mirikami knew what he was doing. Sorting through his visual memory and counting or estimating how many he had seen.

"I would say over two thousand but less than twenty-five hundred. They were panicked by the explosions and running around. Sorry I don't have an exact count."

"Close enough, Bob. That many will fit on a migration ship, but we need to move them to where a migration ship can land on a hard surface. I'd like you to fly back there and see if there is enough clear space on the tarmac after all that destruction. Don't land, because we don't know if all the Krall were inside the dome."

"After that, Sir?" he obviously wanted some useful role.

"We need orbital cover, in case an enemy clanship arrives, or if you see any shuttle activity on the planet. If you do, don't shoot without talking to me."

After that, the Pride of Gaul Jumped, the Dagger orbited, and the Mark landed a thousand TG2s at the shipyards.

The Kobani spread out, as they had on CS2, some scaling the dome, others going through the four entrances. Teams went down into the first factory, and followed nearly the same tunnel layout to the other factories. Surprisingly, there were no Krall encountered in the factories below, and resistance was less in the dome than anticipated. It made Mirikami nervous. The Prada encountered obviously understood low Krall. Some of the TG2's had switched off stealth and had spoken to them. However, none would talk or answer questions put to them. We were clearly not "Rulers" so they would not cooperate.

Ethan was leading the assault to clear the dome, and Mirikami called him on his transducer. "Ethan, there are too few warriors being found, and I'm concerned they may have gathered someplace to make a counter attack. I'd like you to have your teams capture all of the warriors you can alive, for Mind Taps.

"Don't let anyone put themselves at risk, but with our superior numbers here and stealth, you should be able to wound some for capture. I know you have one of the needle guns, with the Death Lime thorn extract, but if they are all in armor, it won't help until you've already made the capture. Be careful."

"I will, Sir."

Thad was in charge of the demolition teams in the factory directly below the dome, and even though proceeding with caution, there had been absolutely no opposition. Mirikami finally decided on the intrusive step he had been so reluctant to employ on any of the Prada. He wanted them to trust humans after Wister arrived to try to talk them into cooperating. However, that would not happen for another day at best. He made another transducer call.

"Thad, if the Prada won't speak to us, we need to try to communicate with them before Wister gets here. If you can identify one of them acting like a leader, he will at least be an elder to those he's directing. Gently, and I do mean that, catch one of them, and with a bare hand do a Mind Tap. Ask questions in low Krall and let me know what you learn. I need to know were the Krall are that we expected to be in this dome. There were only a few dead ones in the upper levels, and only a few have been killed lower in the dome. Some of them finally figured out we can't easily be seen, and took shots when we made a noise. One clever devil set up water soaked walkways and shot his plasma rifle where he saw footprints appear. Our people saw his rifle's pre-flash and ducked to make him miss, so he never got another chance.

"The Prada might know what's been going on to pull the warriors away. That VIP visitor could be connected in some way. I'm happy we can bring down the rescue ships sooner, although I'd feel better knowing for sure we have no surprises."

The two teams sent out to visit the Torki lodges were at least able to talk to the giant crabs, and told them that others from their race would be here soon to explain what was happening. When a Kobani casually mentioned the new Olt library opening for others from their race, and how it came about, they were suddenly eager to try a Mind Tap.

Mirikami warned the teams about how intense the Mind Tap effect had been on the Torki on Haven. It was decided to allow a representative at each lodge to undergo the mental exchange, without the rest of the community trying to share the experience with their Olts.

This time, there was a definite consensus that only mild images, clearly nonviolent and properly scaled images would be transmitted.

It was while Mirikami was discussing performing Torki Mind Taps that Thad received a surprising transducer call from Ethan, who had been informed by

Jakob that the captain was too busy to talk.

"Dad, Uncle Tet is busy with something to do with the Torki, but I just captured a Krall, not wearing armor. I hit him with the needle gun, one tap in the neck, and now he's too numb to move. I think the captain will want to see this blue suit for himself, and do his own Mind Tap. This one knows who the VIP was, and personally has something to do with his mental images showing me another *type* of Krall."

"Are you able to send him out to the ship? We can't risk the captain going in there, away from the Mark."

"Sure, I can take him myself. How about your work below the dome? Are the cooling systems set to blow and flood the place? I mean if we can get the Prada to go to the surface of course, or up here into the dome."

"Son, I have people Mind Tapping several elder Prada leaders right now. Even if we don't convince them to trust us, we can surely get them to spread the word to evacuate the complex, so we can detonate the explosives, and flood the lower levels. There is a central office where they can make a public address announcement. Despite not being willing to go against the Krall, they appear to accept that they are a valuable asset for their Rulers, and they must preserve themselves for rebuilding. Whatever gets them to leave the factories is fine with me."

"OK, Dad. This Parkoda character is actually pissed off at the Krall big shot that just left. He wished we had blown up his clanship before it left. He's that Krall we saw running back to the dome as the VIP's ship lifted. He had just flown over here before we attacked in that second ship."

Thad, on hearing that name, responded quickly, "Meet me at the elevators in five minutes with your prisoner. I'm going with you to see the captain. The Krall probably reuse names often, since they normally give themselves only one. However, this name is one used by a Krall that all of us older generation have reason to remember. It can't be him, because this is a Graka clan world."

"He naturally can't speak right now, of course, but he doesn't like Graka clan at all. What was the clan for the other Parkoda? If I caught this one's thoughts correctly, he's from Tanga clan."

"Holy crap! Meet me at the elevators in two minutes, not five. I want to see and Tap this Krall myself. The Parkoda that captured the Flight of Fancy was from Tanga clan, and he was the one that blew open the outer gates at Koban Prime, which let in the animals and predators to kill people."

****

Once Telour had left him stranded here, Parkoda had no desire to wait for off-planet transport in the hostile atmosphere in the main Graka dome. He was still on the lowest level, near the exit, when he saw four Krall coming towards him. One of them was a brown suited K'Tal he recognized as being the pilot that had flown Telour's party around the planet and to the shipyards, for the inspection tour. Telour had ordered the ramping up of production even before the additional slaves arrived. This could be the task these warriors were assigned.

He hurried up to the K'Tal. "I request transport to the dome by the shipyards."

Thistok looked at him with distain. The instructions passed down to them from Til Gatrol Telour, was that this Tanga clan low-status worm could only leave the planet on one of the migration ships, which would be coming here.

However, a sub orbital flight to the other dome was not off-planet, and besides, the environment in and around the other dome was far less pleasant than here. Therefore, he consented, thus unintentionally saving the worm from imminent pulverizing death.

When the clanship landed, the other four Krall made certain Parkoda made his exit first. The K'Tal openly reset the code to enter the ship, and sent a warrior to the other nearby ship to do the same. Parkoda had not even considered the possibility of stealing a clanship, since that would definitely eliminate his chance of regaining his position as the commander of the soft Krall compound. The thought certainly was in his mind now.

He decided to look over the middle levels of the dome, when the four Krall went up to the top levels to discuss Telour's orders. There were Prada living here, which made the place stink. The last forest around here had died thousands of years ago so the central hall was filled with grub trees, artificial light for them, and an earthy smell.

The Prada paid proper respect to him, so it wasn't as bad here for him as it would be in the main dome surrounded by hostile warriors. He was looking for a suitable set of quarters, just below the top three levels reserved for Graka clan, where he could evict a Prada family unit and take their home. He would force them to clean it, and bring in anything he needed, such as a cooler for storing Raspani meat and jerky.

At least his rations would be no problem. There were even a few Raspani inside the dome, wandering among the grub trees, eating grass and ferns that the Prada prepared for them. These animals were brought over from the grounds around the main dome for convenience. The histories said this world was once home to the long gone Doloria, so it had never been a colony of the Raspani. However, he commented that the meat herd here produced the best tasting meat he'd had.

A Graka sub leader bragged that the herd here had been imported from the original Raspani home world. That was why they had a richer taste. Thousands of years of breeding them on other planets had caused some of the natural flavor to diminish, forcing the Krall to feed them the spicy plants that made them more appetizing.

Parkoda was walking through the third Prada household, trying to decide which to take, when he heard the explosions of the two clanships, followed almost immediately by explosions overhead. He was considering this particular compartment because of its proximity to a stairwell, so he was able to start down ahead of the collapsing levels above. The destruction didn't last, and there were no more explosions above. That meant only the high-level talks of the local Graka leaders were casualties, and were probably dead now.

That image was hardly unpleasant to him, but whatever clan was attacking here would not care that he was from Tanga clan, and would willingly help them in their destruction. He'd be killed as well. He never questioned that it was another clan doing this. This far from the joint council, enforcement of distant rules could sometimes breakdown.

He was armed of course. No Krall went unarmed. Parkoda had two standard pistols at his waist, and knives in his utility belt across his chest. These were of small use against a force of armored warriors, and this was not his clan's territory to defend. He decided to avoid the invaders, and wait to see if they would stay around or if this was a hit and run raid. He assumed the latter, because the attack could not be one that was sanctioned by the council of clans.

If they had a strong enough force and were thorough, they might kill all the Graka warriors before leaving. He might be able to force the Prada and Torki to finish one of the clanships in the cradles, which were waiting only for electronics and fuel for a test flight. He envisioned a Jump back to his duty post with an unassigned clanship to his credit. *That* would help his status in his own clan.

He took refuge in an empty Prada compartment, which had a corridor window. He didn't consider this to be hiding, merely avoiding having to fight and kill an enemy of his enemy. From a corner of his observation point on the third lowest level, he could see most of the central hall and its trees. A warrior in armor came into his view, crouching and working its way between trees. He saw it shot with a green laser through the faceplate, and fall forward. The color of the laser was unusual. The Krall, with a vision preference towards the red part of the spectrum, generally didn't use laser weapons in the green frequencies.

Parkoda was familiar with Graka clan weapons, and they preferred red as well. He assumed then, that the dead warrior was from Graka, and that a raider had shot him. Then something unusual caught his attention. Lower branches of the trees were pushed aside, as if someone were casually moving through the trees, not trying to be subtle. Three different such pathways were made through the trees this way, and they all converged on the corpse. The body was turned over, apparently to confirm that the warrior was dead. This would have been unexceptional, if whoever had converged along those three pathways had been visible.

Paying closer attention, Parkoda could see grass and leaves being pressed down, leaving a footstep impressed in the vegetation as the unseen attackers moved away. The size of the foot impressions were too small, and shaped wrong for a Krall's four splayed toes with talons. Krall armor replicated their talons on feet and hands, for a more natural feel when in a close up unarmed fight.

These unseen raiders did not seem to be Krall-sized. He let his mind briefly dwell on Telour's suggestion that some of the soft Krall had escaped. However, the soft ones were only slightly smaller than standard sized Krall females, and had the same shaped wide feet. Besides, he had proven that none was missing from his guardianship. This must represent some alien species, with a technological advance in armor. If he could kill one of these creatures, and return with their armor *and* a clanship, he'd certainly receive more than a little status increase. He didn't have armor himself, but being less encumbered, he could move quieter, and stay lower. Knowing what clues to look for would help him spot other aliens moving through the trees.

He crawled out of the compartment, staying as low and flat as his thick-muscled chest permitted. The railing wall wasn't solid, and had a one-inch gap every few feet, permitting him to see down into the grove of trees. He wanted to see one of them moving down there again, coming more or less towards him. He had selected a magazine from his belt with armor piercing rounds. He'd stitch shots up and down the upper half of whatever came his way. One of those rounds should find its way through the more fragile helmet faceplate, and he'd have his prey.

He saw his opportunity when a startled Raspani blundered through the trees, using its pudgy arms to part branches away from its face as it hurried pass. It could have bent its upper torso to almost horizontal and in-line with its squat gray body, thus passing its short-legged centaur-like body *under* the branches, making less noise and branch motion. It was too stupid to recognize that it made itself a subject of interest, and could draw fire.

An unseen follower was either herding the Raspani, or trying to catch sight of the frightened animal. It also pushed through the branches recklessly. Parkoda hadn't heard plasma bolt firing in the upper part of the dome for some time. Perhaps the raiders believed all resistance had been eliminated in the dome.

Parkoda made an estimate of the height of the creature, based on what was the highest level of branches that whipped back as it passed. He sighted ahead of its path, as it followed the Raspani's flight, and just as the branches started to move between the next two trees, he fired half of his clip through them in rapid succession, right where he expected the head and chest to be. The whoosh of the rounds leaving his weapon was followed by the sight and sound of them tearing through the leaves and branches along the way. He heard three solid sounding impacts. That was accompanied by a cessation of movement through the tree branches, and a thump as the body struck the soil. He had his kill!

He watched and waited, to see if there would be any activity to go check on the corpse, as they had checked the dead warrior, visible a hundred feet to the right through the trees. He noticed that his target remained frustratingly invisible under the trees where it fell. It wouldn't have been fully visible to him anyway, with the leaves obscuring his view.

He went to the nearest stairwell, as always, ignoring the elevators as a lazy transport. It would be much too noisy in this situation anyway. Parkoda kept his toe talons retracted and the tips up, to avoid any scraping. He went down the steps utterly silent, for a four hundred pound killer. His red pupils blazed in anticipation of recovering this alien and his armor. The Tanga clan's Torki slaves could reproduce nearly any technology they received.

The stairway's last flight exited into the large central hall, with a ten-foot wide strip of bare surface around the sides before the dirt pit started. The hall was almost fifteen hundred feet across, which was filled with the soil for the trees, grass and ferns to grow.

Using his battlefield memory, Parkoda sighted the tree with the bark pattern he'd seen from his hiding place on the third level. The dead alien was two leaps beyond that and one leap to the left, from his present position. He looked around the hall for movement, and saw a Raspani at the edge of the trees well to his right. It could be the same meat animal the alien had been following. Staying low, and waiting a moment for the Raspani to look away, to avoid causing it to run from his sight, Parkoda darted swiftly into the trees, staying well below the branches, and avoiding clumps of ferns that he would disturb in passing.

No way would Parkoda stupidly blunder through the low hanging branches, as the otherwise invisible alien had foolishly done. He crept in the direction he knew the body laid, taking a circumspect route to avoid fern clumps and fresh drops of leaves. The Prada kept the dead fallen branches and most leaves cleaned away, but had been distracted from that duty today. He was close enough now that he could see where the creature had fallen.

Looking carefully from a short distance away, he still did not see the armor, but he could see through to the rectangle of grass under it, pressed down where it lay. He started forward, but stopped to reconsider what he saw. A *rectangle* of grass?

The phifft sound of air just behind him coincided with a sharp prick of minor pain in the right side of his neck. He whirled, ignoring what had struck him, and pointed his gun, held in his left hand, under his right armpit to shoot exactly where he'd heard the sound originate. He squeezed his finger, to send armor piercing shells whooshing at whatever was so close behind him.

Except his finger closed on air, the weapon having been snatched from his hand as he went to aim it under his right arm. He saw the weapon suspended in air an instant before it was crushed, then the broken weapon flew through the branches. He'd instantly reached for his right side weapon, only to discover it was already out of its holster. He was rewarded with seeing it follow the first pistol, just as broken.

A voice in fluent low Krall sounded a few feet above and to his right. "Got you. Did you really think someone that could take on a Krall world would be so clumsy as to stumble through these trees?"

The instant the voice started speaking Parkoda had tried to pivot and lunge at where the sound originated. He found himself lifted by his throat and slammed backwards into a tree trunk. He hadn't really heard the last words, which was understandable. It is highly unlikely that any Krall warrior would have paid attention anyway.

He was reaching for his longest knife when his opponent suddenly flickered into sight. The black and white form fitting armor was topped with a roughly triangular shaped helmet with no transparent faceplate. Instead, it had a number of blue colored bulges or bumps that Parkoda couldn't decide whether they were for multiple eyes, or for sensors.

He got a quick answer to the unasked question when a red beam of a low energy laser lanced out of one of the blue bulges to strike his blade, turning it nearly molten hot. His fingers and hand blistered, he dropped the knife and extended talons to stab his left hand forward, as the right hand swung across to swipe at the blocking move he expected to be made.

What he got was a fast hard smack to the muzzle as two talons on the left hand snapped off on the hard armor. His enemy's hand and arm had darted past his swinging right arm in a move so fast that it registered even on his enhanced vision as a blur. He felt a tooth fragment fly back into his mouth, nicking his slender purple tongue.

He thought his enemy was adjusting his stealth capability, because the area away from the helmet was hazy. He glanced to where a holster with a gun would be, at the creature's waist, and realized the head and feet were all that were hazy. It was his vision that was being affected.

He pushed away from the tree at his back, only to discover his legs would not take the step forward his mind commanded. He couldn't even feel his legs or arms. The pinprick to his neck must have somehow severed a nerve. Only there were redundant nerve pathways that should have given him control. He was falling forward, and the creature stepped aside to let him fall face first into the dank grass.

"OK, guys, he's finally down. That dose will keep him still for at least an hour, unless you pull the dart out. Frank, collect that empty demolition box. We'll carry it back to the Mark for reuse."

Parkoda, barely able to move listened to these words in fluent Standard in disbelief. This was the human language, and their shape and size matched their body structure. He managed to roll his head to the side and found he was looking with tunnel vision directly at a large rectangular box when it flickered into view. It was where he had assumed the enemy he had shot had fallen. There were three deep dents in the case where his slugs had struck.

Frank, a finger in one of the inch deep slug gouges asked, "Ethan, how did you know the bullets wouldn't go all the way through the box?"

"It has the same hard stealth coating our suits have. I didn't think any of their rounds would make it through two layers of the stuff on the box and then penetrate my suit. I carried it right in front of me, but I was afraid he might shoot at my legs. I counted on his wanting a head shot."

"You want me to Tap him while you move on to do something else?"

"Nah. We have this dome under control. I don't have anything else to do unless the warriors we expected to be here show up suddenly. I'll do the Tap myself."

Parkoda saw some armored feet step into his vision, and then kneel down. He was rolled onto his back, based on the swirl of vision and the new perspective. He couldn't feel his body or limbs. His head was repositioned to look at the same helmet he'd seen before. The bare hand grasping his couldn't be felt, but the odd images that floated into his mind caused him to think of things he'd seen today and the last several days. The images were reinforced by questions in Standard, asking about how many of his clan was on the planet, how many here at the dome.

He instantly thought of his hatred for Telour and the Graka clan, and hoped the large gathering of warriors in the main dome had also been attacked. They had gone there at the order of Telour, probably to let him bask in the authority he now had. Not only in his own clan, as a representative of their clan leader, but over every Krall clan as Til Gatrol, second only in war to Tor Gatrol Kanpardi.

Ethan stood up. “There are probably no more Krall here. They all went to the main dome to meet with that high muckety-muck Krall leader. They were going to double production here.”

“What does mucky-muck mean?” Castro asked him.

“Muckety-muck. It’s something Maggi says sometimes about people that think they are more important than they are.”

“Let me call the captain and tell him what we have.”

After Jakob informed him Mirikami was in a high-level discussion about the Torki, he called his father.

He signed off, and told his team of four they were rushing this Krall back to the ship. “This one may be important to us. His name, Parkoda, and his clan match that of the Krall that captured the Flight of Fancy. We need to meet up with my dad over by the elevators. He’s coming up to join us.”

****

Still in armor from the neck down, Mirikami jumped down the last flight of stairs from the Bridge in the low gravity. He realized he had seldom used the lifts since he became a TG2. They were too slow, and he felt so energized.

“I’m off the Bridge, Thad. Why did I need to come down just to see this warrior myself? The migration ships have arrived, and will be setting down. I need to pick some people to go over in a clanship to round up those Raspani by the main dome and ferry them here to the extra migration ship.”

His helmet also off, and a lopsided grin on his face, Thad swung the chair around. Slumped in an upright acceleration couch was a blue suited Krall. “Recognize this one?”

Thad and the other Kobani present were rewarded with the rare jaw drop, and a shocked expression from the famously unshakeable Captain Mirikami.

Ethan said, “I’m so glad I asked Jakob to record this. Aunt Maggi will pay me anything I ask to get her hands on the playback.”

Still amazed enough to ignore Ethan, Mirikami asked, “How did Parkoda wind up *here*, on a *Graka* controlled world?”

“Funny you should ask.” Thad teased. “Another old acquaintance of ours forced him to come, just to humiliate him and leave him stranded here. Remember the charming fellow that gave you that final tattoo?”

"Telour? Was he that VIP I allowed to depart unmolested? Damn!"

"Parkoda wishes you'd killed him as well, although now that he's seen you, I suspect your death is also strongly on his mind."

"I saw him blink rapidly when I started talking. I look younger in the face, and I'm concealed inside this suit, but he reacted to my voice. Let me remove a gauntlet."

He grabbed a hand, and promptly pushed a conversation to the Krall of the last time the two of them spoke on Koban, just before and after he destroyed the compound gates, around what was then called Koban Prime. Thad had the other hand so he could "listen" in on the interrogation. Mirikami was making certain Parkoda knew exactly who held him captive now.

The return images from Parkoda, with low Krall words embedded said, "I should have destroyed you in your ship that day, and not permit Telour to leave you there. His weakness has cost all clans the ships being built here."

"We have destroyed not just the ships here, Parkoda, we have attacked the ships the Mordo clan produced, and the hammers the Torki make for the Stodok clan. We are not simply blowing up the ships and hammers; we will also destroy the factories. We captured or destroyed all of the migration ships. We are using them to carry away the Prada and Torki that know how to build your weapons. Thanks to you and Telour, your weakness has allowed humans to cripple all Krall war-making ability." He wanted to rub salt in the wound, despite how petty it made him sound and feel. It was the sort of taunt that a Krall would find most infuriatingly painful, coming from a prey animal.

The flash of hatred that returned was tinged with a sense of impending vengeance. It wasn't of personal retribution, although there was an impression that somehow, if not Parkoda directly, Tanga clan would have a roll in some important capacity. His thoughts were focused on racial revenge, and total human extermination. *It involved the soft Krall.*

Again, a reference to a variation of the Krall species. Simultaneously hated and needed by the clans. "What are the soft Krall?"

The visual images of them he and Thad saw looked much like novice Krall, until a modern Krall from Parkoda's memory was seen striking one of them. The "soft ones" were a bit smaller, and were uniformly gray, with no red tinged skin as they aged. They all went unclothed. The age difference was apparent because they were seen in family groupings, with small ones held, or seen standing within an obviously protective circle of adults.

"How will they help you attack humans, and why would they help you?"

The unexpected image of the plump, organic looking ships was something very different from anything ever associated with the Krall previously. The scale factor was impossible to judge at first, until in one image they realized Parkoda was standing on a rugged volcanic-looking landscape, looking up at one of them from nearby. It was shaped far different from a clanship or migration ship, and sized somewhere in between the two.

Parkoda, being directed to answer questions, and having received mental images from Mirikami, had an inkling of their mental ability. He was trying to hold information back, but not very successfully.

"Why will the other type of Krall help you? They appear to be captives and abused. Are they forced? Why do you need them anyway?"

The return thoughts came out confused and mixed.

Mirikami was asking too many questions at one time, he was too agitated, and this threat seemed too real. The Krall would brag and exaggerate, but they mostly did not lie to prey animals because there was no reason to fear them or to worry about what they knew.

For some reason those ships felt like some kind of weapon to Parkoda, but one that he did not understand, and could not use himself for some reason. The "weapon" apparently didn't *like* him, or perhaps it didn't like Krall in particular. How did a weapon have likes and dislikes?

"Where are those ships you saw?"

There was no thought leakage of that location at all, only the same scene of the ships. At first, Mirikami believed Parkoda had done what no other Krall had managed to do. Hide his thoughts. He asked in another way. If I take you to the navigation system of a clanship, can you find where the star system is located?"

An image of a control console appeared, but the galactic map he recalled did not suggest any star system.

Another approach was tried. "Where do the soft Krall live?" There was instantly a stellar system in his mind, and they knew that he could go *there* if he wished. He had feebly tried to hold that back.

"Tet, I don't think he *knows* where those ships are located. I saw at least a half dozen of them in one mental image, with an enormous gas giant planet in the background sky."

"I saw that, and the reflected light from what would normally be white or light gray cloud tops on a gas planet that size looked red. That world where they were parked, side-by- side, has to be a terrestrial-sized moon of a super Jupiter. The giant world is probably orbiting a red dwarf star, whose red light was being reflected."

Thad shook his head. "Hell, that doesn't narrow the search much. Red dwarfs are a dozen for a Hub credit. They're the most common mass star class in the galaxy. Probably half of them have a close-in Jovian planet."

"Not many of those systems would have a habitable terrestrial-sized moon that close. It would have to be tidally locked, one face always towards the Jovian, and there was a breathable atmosphere with decent pressure, and plant life."

"OK. It's so not like looking for a needle in a giant haystack, but a long search nevertheless, in a large volume of space that humans have never been inside before. Parkoda apparently wasn't high ranking enough to know where those ships are kept, which does suggest they are important. However, Parkoda knows that the soft Krall are needed, and they damn well don't trust them. I don't know what the connection would be."

They had not paid a great deal of attention to Parkoda. He was secured in an acceleration couch that a Kobani could not break away from if secured, and would stand up to acceleration that would render them unconscious. The Krall wasn't going anywhere, and he was no longer a physical match in strength or speed for any one of them, let alone the eight TG2s standing around outside the conference room.

However, he was a physical match for two prospective opponents that he knew he could control. He had gradually felt sensation return, from whatever agent they had used that nearly paralyzed him. They were pulling information from him that he had not spoken, but were discussing the answers to their questions they asked, as if he had told them. They put pictures and words into his mind. They must be doing the reverse, and obtaining information from him. He hated Telour, despised the Graka clan, but he *KNEW* his species was destined to finish walking the Great Path, and to rule the galaxy. He would not let this prey species slow the Krall's march. If they spoke true, and why lie to a warrior they certainly would kill once he was of no use, they had struck a blow against the war effort against them. The ultimate weapons would destroy them, but he was not going to let them find out any more from him.

He started his final battle, the enemy being his own body. He used his will to shut off blood flow to duplicate organs, such as his two liver-equivalents, a pair of adrenaline-like organs that provided the rage stimulus to fight on despite any physical damage, his blood cleaner kidney function was also a target, but was too slow to be effective quickly. Then he willed his two hearts to slow to a stop. He could shut down his brain, but once unconscious, his body would restore all functions automatically, and he'd recover. He maintained a steady pattern of breathing, and left his eyes fixed straight ahead. Soon he won this last battle against the prey, and his two hearts. He quietly expired.

Thad grasped Parkoda's hand, with the intent of asking how long his travel had been from the planet where the ships were visited, to reach CS2. That would provide a distance, if not a direction. The echoes of the final random thoughts of a dying brain was all he detected, and that was of gloating satisfaction.

Seeing Thad's surprised look, Mirikami touched the other hand, and detected even less of Parkoda's final thoughts. He shook his head. "We lost our fear of them and let him slip away from us. We know they have one more super weapon, more destructive than any they have used on our worlds. They require the soft Krall and those ships, in some capacity, to apply that weapon."

"We don't even know where to go, to strike at these ships." Thad said, worry showing on his face.

Mirikami was pulling at his lip. "No, but we may be able to find the soft Krall that somehow are part of using those weapons. They could be our next rescue mission."

"What do we do right now, Uncle Tet?"

"Ethan, we will finish our own mission, gather the Torki, the Prada, the Raspani, and get them away from the Krall, safe on Haven. I'm confident your mother finished her mission and Noreen her own. The Krall never even conceived that humans might have the ability to strike them this deep inside their space, and to do so this effectively. It may take some time for the impact to drive home the point we made today, that we can and will do more than simply defend our worlds.

"I anticipate there will be severe retaliation, using the same weapons they already have at their disposal. They have plenty of them. Some of their vital supply lines are cut, but what they already have available is deadly. If we can keep cutting the supply of clanships down, and spur the PU Navy to go after their existing ships in great enough numbers, we can start to turn the tide of battle."

"What do we do about their apparent super weapon on those ships?" Thad asked.

He pulled at his lip. "One step at a time. I don't think they will bring them out the first thing after they learn what we did. We attacked K1 twice before they took a hammer to Rhama. They can't walk the Great Path very fast if they destroy the finest worthy enemy they have ever faced too quickly. They need more attrition from the war they started for that purpose, and by their long-range standards, it is barely under way. We still have over seven hundred planets and a trillion people. I don't think they will feel rushed.

"There must be Prada or Torki that know something than can help us, and we can go after more Krall prisoners, now that we know what we want to learn. We can scour their histories, stored in the minds of every Krall. They blabber about any of it if given the chance. They might not know how the weapons work, as Parkoda didn't know. However, the Krall are braggarts. I mean, what could they have? Something to blow up an entire planet?"

Chapter 21: I Think, Therefore...

"My Tor, we should blow up one of their planets now!" Telour was livid with rage.

His brilliantly planned mission to increase clanship production was now worthless. He and Graka clan would earn no status increase, and both had suffered a loss of respect from some clans, as had the Mordo, and Stodok clans. Clanship production was essentially halted, the hammers were destroyed, and the ability to make more hammers was probably lost forever.

Kanpardi was adamant. "No! You would react by using up one of our most powerful weapons at the first real set back to the war. In the past, our greatest and irreplaceable weapons were wasted on weak opponents, before we understood how the Olt'kitapi ships would react. Unless the Torki learn to copy their capability, we only have one use of each of them. We may be able to destroy multiple worlds before the ship we use learns of the consequences, because the others did not quit talking to us right away, after a single use. But they do learn of the deaths somehow, of what we have made them do, and they will no longer respond."

He, like every Krall, was bemused by compassion for an enemy. He could not comprehend how the Olt'kitapi had managed to instill this alien concept in a machine.

"We have been at actual war for barely five orbits of this base world. The first fifteen orbits we spent in ever larger, more frequent raids, pushing our enemy to prepare to fight better. Now they have *done* so, and like a half-trained novice, you want their aggression to stop before we have advanced but a single step along the Great Path.

"The clans will now end their lazy ways. They agree, now that the means to expand our invasions to other worlds is diminished, that we always needed more material. A lesson that I too admit I have now learned from a worthy enemy, is that we needed far greater vigilance on our own worlds. We *let them* sweep in and attack our most vital resources, because no other enemy was ever able to do that."

He outlined his new strategy, until the damage to their clanship production was repaired.

"We will use what clanships we have built now, and recover what parts we can from the production sites. A major offensive on Poldark will push back the humans, permitting us suddenly to move half of that force, to invade another nearby Rim world.

"We will also consolidate other widespread forces on Telda Ka for a third invasion, of one of their heavily populated inner colony worlds. We must be seen as advancing the war if you and I are to survive this momentary reversal. I want the fault of this lack of preparation to be placed on the clans that opposed my decisions earlier. Your trip proves my decision to have Graka clan unilaterally increase clanship production was the right one. However, it was delayed by jealous and selfish clans, who could not see the need as I did. Graka will come through strong and shrug off this loss. Our status is less damaged because of the mission I sent you to perform, which no other clan considered necessary. The other great clans that were struck look weaker in comparison.

"Stodok clan is gone, of course. They have needed culling for many breeding cycles. They alone had the advantage of surprise forces on their orbital station, and were totally defeated."

The Stodok clan leaders would not suffer the humiliation they earned. Their past reckless mistakes had caught up with them and they had apparently all died in one last "for the Path and clan" resistance. An old clan, but no stronger than many finger clans, they had too few warriors on their single planet to resist the attackers, due to previous foolish interclan battles where they were over matched. This time, forbidden to withdraw or to submit, there were none left alive on their home world. Perhaps a handful that were on other worlds for clan business still survived. At least until they were all eventually killed, by demanding repetitive death match challenges, triggered by the derisive remarks from other warriors.

Tanga clan had fifteen migration ships taken, and the remainder of stored older ships was destroyed. They could still make the Torki construct more of the slow to build big ships, but it would take almost two orbits to complete even two, assuming the work could be accelerated to that level. There had never been a need for more of the new ships than to replace those that Krall pilots "wasted" periodically.

To increase the insult, the captured ships were used in the later raids, weeks later, to carry trained slaves away. That act was hampering restarting clanship production. The first Prada elders sent to do that were killed by angry Tanga leaders, when they told them the saltwater flooding had ruined the factories. Another group of Prada, sent by the Graka clan said the same thing about those factories. That group of elders was spared execution. They would assemble a new starter factory, being sent piecemeal, in smaller clanships.

The Maldo had lost what was probably of most immediate value to the raiders. Eleven clanships. A twelfth stolen clanship was shot down as it lifted off, but it managed to deliberately crash into the main dome, killing many of the high status clan leaders there. Twenty other Maldo clanships were destroyed, still sitting on tarmacs. That pattern of clanship destruction was repeated at every site the raiders struck. There had been no attacks on Krall planets, other than bases located inside enemy territory, for at least fifteen thousand years. It was daring, and unexpected.

It also had to have been humans doing this. Not a single intact body was recovered, because the raiders did a masterful job of finding and removing their dead and their armor. However, a few pieces of armor, sometimes with the accompanying human smelling and bad tasting meat inside, were found.

The armor surface had nearly the same hard quantum controlled coating as did single ships, which could partly account for the many reports that the raiders were invisible in the visible and infrared light spectrums. Single ships didn't quite have that detailed level of invisibility, and the power required for this feature demanded a fusion generator. The enemy certainly did not carry any of the bulky things with them on their suits.

A suit's leg, with limb inside, was recovered. However, it did not show signs of powered assist. The strength sometimes exhibited by the wearers implied there *was* such assistance. It was difficult to obtain good observational evidence, because the enemy couldn't easily be *observed.* Any warrior that got close enough to see a flaw in their stealth or engage the enemy directly, wasn't around now to describe the experience. It was hard to survive a well-armed enemy you could not see. Counter measures were being considered.

The suits were apparently a technological advance, yet one that was extremely limited in the scope if its use. This sort of human fighter had never been seen on the battlefield. It seemed their only effective use was in sneakiness and trickery, for which humans were noted.

In the last quarter orbit of K1 since the multiple raids, courier ships had been dispatched to every clan home world, and they then spread the alert to their forces on other worlds, and to their sponsored finger clans. No clanships were to be left unguarded. Even if only one or two were actively scanning and watching for intruders, no White Out would go unchallenged. The enemy had proven to be more worthy than any had in the past.

Telour wasn't giving up his desire for retribution so quickly. "My Tor, we can do the things you say. Yet, I believe humans need to see there is a price to pay, as when I hammered the world they named Rhama, where their fleet retreated after the second attack here."

Kanpardi shook his left shoulder in a sign of negation. "That was a different situation then. Construction and build-up on Telda Ka was not complete. We had not yet invaded the place they named Bollovstic. That first full-scale invasion was delayed full orbit because of their Navy. I forced the humans to leave this base alone, making that first invasion and the one on Poldark easier. We will now be able to invade two more worlds before this orbit ends on Telda Ka."

"My Tor, would the humans not fight more fiercely if we destroyed their home world? We did, when the Olt'kitapi destroyed our home with this same weapon."

Kanpardi looked at him sharply. The black orbs, with fire in the pupils, glared intently. "You grant this weak prey the belief that they could act with the same strength, ferocity, and honor that our race did?"

Telour's tongue was tied for the moment. He couldn't support the logical conclusion his half-thought-out statement implied. Kanpardi correctly deduced what Telour's actual motive was. It was simple, and came with harsh words.

"You want revenge because your personal plan for status gain was spoiled by them. Even if the revenge you want isn't in the interest of the Krall or our Great Path. I may have promoted you unwisely."

Telour knew in his two hearts that the first half of Kanpardi's words were true. He also knew that Kanpardi's time as Tor had just grown shorter. There now was a more aggressive Til Gatrol behind him, ready to replace the Tor's talons if anything happened to the war leader. Accidents happened to the smartest and best of warriors.

****

Mirikami had just Jumped in from a scouting mission into Krall territory. He called ahead to Haven, and was in conversation. “Maggi, I picked up a Tachyon Space message from Marlyn as I made my exit. Her raid to recover the Prada and Torki at the Toborkiti shipyards was a rough one. She needed all three of the other clanships I sent with her to keep the Krall on the ground away from the shipyards, and to hold off two clanships. If we didn’t have the acceleration limiters removed, we could have lost a ship. We are faster and more maneuverable, but the Krall have combat experience.”

She was apprehensive. “Did everyone make it back?”

He paused, letting her know there had been losses. “We lost Bill Murphy, Consuelo Dearborn, and Alfon Hanson. All of them were in a single defense pod mounted on the nose of a migration ship, The Blue Waters, operating lasers and missile trackers inside one of the six pods per ship. They were in the nose pod. Their hull pod was hit by an anti-ship missile.”

With the small population of Koban, any loss was of someone you knew at least by face. Alfon was a more painful personal loss for Mirikami. He had been a steward on the Flight of Fancy, and had served with the captain for over thirty years.

“Maggi, I’ll want to tell his contract wife myself. She’s expecting a daughter in four months; otherwise, she would have gone with him. Can you go with me to talk to her? I’ll see the families of the others with Marlyn, when she gets back tomorrow morning.”

“Sure, hon. I’ll take the Scorcher and Jump over to Koban when we get off the radio. I’m on the Bridge now. It’s parked next to the Raspani lands, where I’ve been working. I came up here as soon as your White Out was detected and announced by the AI. What happened to the Blue Waters?”

“Those huge slow ships are hard to defend. Had we not equipped them with point defense pods and missiles from General Nabarone, they might not have made it out. A Krall clanship Jumped in from the next rocky world out, so it wasn’t expected. Marlyn and two of our ships were covering the departure from below. The Krall had set up portable missile launchers and tried to hit the migration ships from below. Those tries were all picked off before doing damage.

“The Bad Girl was flying escort, eight hundred miles ahead of the migration ships as they tuned their Traps for a minimal Jump tachyon, headed away from Toborkiti. The new Krall clanship did a White Out right behind Bad Girl, who was out of position that far ahead.

“The Krall took advantage of the opening in the formation, fired a salvo of eight missiles total at all three ships, six were aimed at The Bad Girl to keep her busy or kill the main threat. The AI on Bad Girl automatically nailed all of those six. *One* of the two remaining anti-ship missiles, each targeted at a migration ship, was knocked out by a pod's point defense laser or a missile, or perhaps both. We don't know yet who got that one. It may very well have been killed by the same pod we lost. That last Krall missile altered course to target that pod. Those missiles are designed to seek active targets like that, if the pod had been the source of the counter fire.

"The clanship had obviously discounted any return fire from *unarmed* migration ships, and had already pivoted and turned its back on them, to go after The Bad Girl. We have the first confirmed clanship kill for a migration ship. It will require data from the AI on Bad Girl to determine which ship and pod the kill shot came from, but it flew right up the tail pipe. I hope it was launched from the pod we lost before it was hit."

"I hope so too, babe." She answered him, knowing the archaic endearment from the twentieth century was mildly confusing to her husband. Mirikami had grown up on the once Japanese colony of New Honshu, and ancient American film lore wasn't an interest of his.

"I hope you have some better news for me. I mean Marlyn rescued most of the workers on Toborkiti, but I would like some cheerful news as well."

"I do have some, but you didn't tell me how your scouting went."

"We certainly didn't find the star system where those ships Parkoda witnessed are stashed. The Torki say the shapes and size of the images we showed them match that of the final generation of starships the Olt'kitapi were said to be producing, when the Krall revolt came. Naturally, they never saw the ships since they were not yet fully sentient at that time, and information about the ships are not in the Olt libraries. The Prada have only anecdotal memory records, and those don't describe the ship's appearance, only their destructive power. That type of ship was used to destroy the Krall home world, which based on Krall histories, was virtually shattered."

"What sort of bomb can do that?"

"Some of the freed Torki, grateful to us after the new arrivals had the additional library in their Olts open up to them, made a concerted effort to gather bits and pieces of information picked up simply by being around bragging Krall for thousands of years of their slave history."

"And? Do I have to cajole it out of you?"

"Maybe. Depends of what the word means. It isn't Standard."

"I think it was originally French, but how I apply it depends on how nice you are to me when we meet. I want to go with you if you are going to stay gone a month at a time."

"Fine, kajule the hell out of me then."

With a sigh, "It's cajole. Tell me about the bomb."

"It doesn't sound like a bomb as such. Not like one that you would drop on a planet. The Olt'kitapi had mastered a branch of applied quantum physics, and we already know they had remarkable control of small-scale quantum features. When applied over a broad area, like ship hulls or our suits, it can control light reflection and propagation. The Torki know some of this, at least how to make and use it, if not how it's done.

"I know that, but.,." He cut her off.

"I'm not finished yet. The Torki believe they had technology that could adjust quantum states of matter at the level of fundamental particles, such as quarks or electrons. There isn't a tremendous physical difference between matter and antimatter, the opposite electrical charges for example for the same family of particles, and they speculate that the Olt'kitapi found a way to create antimatter in a short time."

"That sounds like you're saying it was an antimatter bomb that was dropped, which was speculated about when we first heard how the Krall's parent world exploded."

"I don't think so, Maggi. From the Krall histories, the planet seems to have ruptured from the inside. Aside from the problem of how the Olt'kitapi would contain or handle antimatter to make and deliver a bomb, if it struck the surface much of the initial explosive force would blow the antimatter back into space, reducing the effect and mostly destroying one hemisphere. Certainly catastrophic enough, but not matching the description. The entire planet fragmented and made the star system too filled with debris to enter. The antimatter would appear to have been delivered to the core."

"Well, it isn't like we can make one, or defend from one either. We have to stop them from using the weapon in the first place. What about the prison star system for the soft Krall? Any clues?"

"Not so far. It apparently isn't kept as secret as the location of the ships, because Parkoda was in charge there, as a low-level resentful prison warden. We don't have any idea what the connection is between the weapon and the original model Krall. Only that they are essential to its use. Parkoda found one final way to cheat us of using what he knew against his species, by killing himself. I was overconfident that he was personally no threat to Koban."

"If they were going to use the weapon, wouldn't they do like they did to Rhama, hit Human Space right after the fleet returned from K1 the second time?"

"I just don't know. The high and mighty Tor Gatrol Kanpardi is moving to do what I speculated would happen. They seem to be grouping for a big assault on Poldark. Henry is calling for more forces from the PU, and Navy help. I don't know how quickly they can get significant reinforcements there.

"Hey, you keep pulling doom and gloom out of me. What is your cheerful news?"

"The new Raspani refugees, particularly those Noreen was able to rescue from their former colony world at CS2, are significantly less interbred than those we found at Hub City, or that you rescued."

"That means what? They are smarter?"

"They are talking to the Torki."

"Really? What language?"

"Torki."

"How would the Raspani have learned that? The Torki were still not a spacefaring race when the Krall beat the Raspani. And it's impossible for us to speak it, how do they?"

"It's sort of a pidgin version of Torki, because they can't make some of the sounds."

"OK, that seems promising for them. What do they talk about, the flavor of grass, or where they are?"

"No. They want the Torki to build them an Olt."

"What? How do they know about those? Did the Torki show them or they heard them talk about them?"

"The Raspani say the Olt'kitapi made devices for the Torki, for the Raspani, and for the Krall. Coldar says that what they called the devices in Torki, in the broken speech sounds they make, is nothing like the word 'Olt,' which the Torki say to humans and Prada in Low Krall, or us in Standard. They use sounds that seem like they are trying to say *mind makers* in native Torki. Coldar confirmed that by repeating the phrase *mind maker* in clear Torki, the new Raspani all became excited. Interbred Raspani herds paid no attention to the phrase. The Krall truly appears to have bred intelligence out of those poor creatures."

"Wow. Does Coldar or any of his people know how to make the device they want?"

"No, but the Torki that Noreen rescued from the same planet say their Olts record that they encountered Raspani thousands of years ago when the Torki were first brought there by the Krall. This was before there was a single Raspani herd restricted to a small enclosure, when the planet was still healthy. The Krall used to go on hunts, with bare talons, to kill and eat the poor creatures."

"I thought you were going to cheer me up. Hell, that's almost as depressing as what I told you."

"How about the fact that the Raspani gave those Torki a gift back then, and asked that it be kept safe. The Torki were told it was the skull of a great Raspani leader, and he contained the seeds for many of their dead to return."

"Sounds a bit like the legend the Raspani on Koban sometimes described, of their people returning from the stars to save them. This lot has a variation of the same sad story."

"I agreed, initially, until one of the Torki, from CS2, produced a crystal case that holds a round skull of a Raspani. It's encased in this solid looking cube, and he brought it along with some of their more portable tools. He was sort of the supply master, or tool keeper. He inherited the task from a Torki before him, and one before, and so on. The case was traditionally passed along with the tools to whichever new Torki got the job."

"Sounds like the story had a touch of truth to the myth."

In a teasing voice, which the older unmodified Maggi had never been heard to use, said enticingly, "Don't 'cha wanna hear what I found?"

"You threatened me once to stop dropping one shoe at a time, because it drove people nuts. Tell me, you little minx!"

She tossed her blonde hair with a teasing look and flutter of eyelashes. "I did a scan, and discovered a device attached to the top inside of the skull. In microscopic detail, it appears something like the insides of a broken Olt that Coldar allowed me to scan. It may be the Raspani equivalent to the Olt. Coldar says if the circuitry isn't too different, he may be able to examine what it contains, and either try to make another one, or copy its data to the equivalent solid state matrix of an Olt. In short, we might be able to recover some of what the Raspani once knew. They also were able to use some of the quantum physics that the Olt'kitapi taught them. They made the disintegrator, or boring tool, for example."

"Does Coldar think one of those devices can be inserted in a Raspani skull, to restore their minds to full sentience?"

She shrugged. "He doesn't know. The Olt'kitapi designed the things specifically for each species, and the healed over slit in the old skull suggests where it was inserted. However, that isn't how the Torki obtain theirs. They eat them when adolescent, and the device migrates to where it belongs."

"The Torki were discovered by the Olt'kitapi well after the Raspani, so they may have improved their methods by then. If it really is a plug-in brain enhancer gadget, and the Torki can make them, we may seek a Raspani volunteer."

"I don't think that will be a problem. They are really pressing the Torki, and they haven't even seen this skull yet."

Mirikami pulled at his lip.

Maggi saw him. "Uh, Oh. What are you thinking, you clever devil?"

"Have the Prada heard the Raspani try to talk to the Torki?"

"No. Not all of the new comers are the least cordial to us Kobani. Even Wister and Nawella have had to curtail their interaction with us, to preserve their influence as elders. The workers know it was us that invisibly fought and killed Rulers. The elders are saying this is similar to interclan warfare, but that falls flat when we obviously are not Krall clan members. How does that bear on the thought you just had?"

"What species do the Prada know is older than the Torki, themselves, and the Krall?"

That made it obvious. "The Raspani are second in their eyes only to the Olt'kitapi as the elder species, but they are no longer intelligent. If the Raspani recover sentience, the Prada have a new elder race to admire and follow besides the Krall. That could cause other fresh problems, but those can't be as bad as the Prada wanting the Rulers to show up here to set things straight."

"My love, kindly delay your departure from Haven to consult with Coldar and his other engineers. As much as I want to be cajoled by you, we need to push this project along."

****

Coldar passed the black-colored, flat rectangle to Aldry with a small manipulator claw. "We have two other device designs, either of which may have a better neural interface to their brains. Only they are empty of data. I don't know if we could transfer the data if the original fails to connect to the brain automatically."

Aldry accepted the solid-state quantum storage device, disinfected it in a solution, and turned to the eager Raspani volunteer. At least it seemed eager, and he had entered the Mark of Koban willingly, riding the lift to the infirmary. It had followed several Torki that had been talking to it, and doing their best to understand what it was trying to tell them.

Mirikami found it odd that it understood low Krall, but made no effort to speak words that would surely be easier to enunciate than the grating shell scrapes and clicks of the Torki. It also spoke a version of Raspani that differed from that of the herd on Koban.

Jakob had a slim vocabulary of what those much-abused creatures could say, and had identified possible words that sounded as if they were natural for the lips, tongue, pallet, and nasal whistles and snorts of a Raspani. The creature, recently rescued from their old and former colony, did not appear to understand any of the supposed Raspani words Jakob spoke. Probably the long period of isolation and use of a polyglot mixture of words and interbreeding had mangled the Koban herd's small vocabulary too far from the original meanings.

It was also possible the Raspani still had multiple languages when they went to the stars. Humanity had been like that, until the Collapse after the Gene War made reconstruction easier with a common evolving language, which became known as Standard.

Aldry had relied on extensive years of research on the Raspani at Hub City, and the medical procedures performed that revealed what worked as painkillers and antiseptics for a physiology completely alien from human or Earth animals. DNA decoding helped a great deal to understand how their bodies worked, but some trial and error had been involved.

The incision and skull slot were made to match that on the skull the Torki had saved for so long. That location proved quite rational when it was noticed on brain scans of the newest Raspani arrivals that, at the top of their brains were a concentration of neuron-like structures, which were part of higher thought processes for them. That area had not been as active an area for the former Koban Raspani.

Much as the Olt did for the Torki, the Raspani device had biomechanical structures that were expected to infiltrate the neural connections, and establish their own contacts. The amount of data storage, from what Coldar explained, was staggering to the human technicians and scientists. The entire vast human library of an AI like Jakob's would fit in this device a million times over. Jakob's memory unit was ten times physically larger than these compact items.

Looking to see that Rafe had the skull imager active, and the brain scanner ready, she took a deep breath behind her face shield, and gently inserted the device, exactly as she'd practiced with a dummy sample, on a mockup of a Raspani head.

The imager showed the lower edge of the device was slightly above the surface of the brain, and the translucent sheath that surrounded the brain. Then she shoved the top end down slowly until it was below the top of the thickened skull by a quarter of an inch. Soon, that opening would have a sliver of bone placed over it, and the skin edges glued together.

First, however, they watched for the movement the Torki said should happen, as filaments extruded from the bottom edge of the device and sought the appropriate neural junctions in a Raspani brain. The Torki said it happened inside them, once the Olt migrated to the correct location, and in only a few seconds. The half-sentient young Torki recipient usually responded almost immediately, and had access to data that it didn't quite know how to process or understand. At least for a day or two.

There were two other empty devices with slightly modified biomechanical neural connections if this one didn't work that they could test and remove. On the expanded imager, hair-like fibers grew from the bottom edge, and reached the sac around the brain. They penetrated into the brain tissue, followed some chemical or neural cues and made links that the brain activity monitor showed was doing something. The high-level brain functions were climbing rapidly.

Even though the Raspani's head was clamped motionless, the creature jerked, and tried to move, the eyes looking around in panic, until it saw a Torki off to the side. It kept looking that way, and the crab moved to where it could see him fully. It visibly relaxed.

It spoke a string of lisping, whistling, lip smacking words of what was either fluent Raspani speech, or the drooling blabber of a mindless idiot. It was hard to say, since none there, or the AI listening, knew any version of Raspani that matched the sounds.

Coldar, off to the other side, asked Rafe in Standard if the brain activity seemed abnormal. The Raspani immediately turned its eyes in that direction and Coldar moved to the front of the creature to be seen easier. The Raspani then tried Torki speech, which was clearer than it had used previously, but fell short of fluency, since its soft mouthparts were never going to sound like a shell scrape.

The Torki used its voice synthesizer to speak in low Krall. "We do not understand the language you used at first, and my language is difficult for you to make the words. Do you understand this Krall language?"

There was a pause, then, "I do, but we have no wish to speak it if we can find another common language. Do you know any of the Olt'kitapi language? It may be stored in the mind enhancer they made for you."

The humans in the room, all of them standing behind and out of the sight of the Raspani now, were hugely excited, but Aldry had already warned them not to speak at first. The Raspani had prior knowledge of the Torki, and it was thought best to let them interact with them, provided the device actually worked.

Coldar and the other two Torki appeared to pause for a time, probably seeking inside the memory storage of their Olts for a language that could be Olt'kitapi, or even of Raspani origin.

The Torki had linked to the Olts of all other Torki on Haven, to ask them to conduct simultaneous searches. After a minute, Coldar resumed speaking in low Krall. "I regret that we have not yet located a reference to the old ones language, or of the one you first used. The Olt'kitapi had all been killed before our mind enhancers lifted us to intelligence. We call them an Olt in honor of the makers, and they elevated our minds so we achieved star travel. The Raspani had met the Krall well before that happened, and were defeated. How do you know of us, and of our own language?"

The connections were obviously improving as the device continued to consolidate itself in the Raspani's brain. It spoke more certainly, smoother. "As a client species that the Olt'kitapi helped long before you, we assisted them in distributing your first mind enhancers, the Olts as you call them now, and monitored you without interference as your species made its first advances. The Olts helped you to think, but the Olt'kitapi never controlled how or what you would think. That was also our choice when they helped us, as it was yours.

"Most of the Krall did not want this gift, or want it offered to the few Krall that saw its benefit. Even though it was helping those that had their version of an enhancer to think past the bounds of their race's evolutionary dead end. Within less than a thousand years, the old Krall would have destroyed themselves on their one planet, with unlimited breeding and constant wars. To allow time for them to learn to accept the mind enhancers, and decide for themselves the direction their race should take, the Olt'kitapi gave them ships to reach the stars and room to expand.

"That was a mistake of kindness, which they paid for, and other races pay still. We believe this, because you choose to speak low Krall, as if it were an obvious choice to use with us."

Coldar answered. "There are other races that have lost wars with the Krall and are now gone. My people have been forced into slavery for the Krall, as has those called the Prada."

The restrained Raspani tried to gesture, but could only twitch. "We know only a little of the Prada. They were a young star traveling species when we were conquered by the Krall. Previously, the Olt'kitapi saw no need to step in to help them develop, because they were advancing on their own. They preferred to leave a species alone if they could. Our own people were not on a path towards high technology or star travel. The Olt'kitapi saw our potential, and helped us become more than semi-intelligent grazing creatures."

"The Krall continue to make war. Another young star traveling race has been attacked by them. They are the species that rescued your people from the Krall. They call themselves humans. They could lose the war and be extinguished. Some of them are here with us, behind you, because they were uncertain how you would react to a species you did not know. We knew you remembered my people, because long ago one of you gave us a mind enhancer for safe keeping."

Another twitch. "We do not remember who brought us here, only that we awoke, secured in place. We first assumed it was to force feed our new body with spices to make us taste better to the Krall, before our slaughter."

That was a gruesome and reasonable thought none of them had considered.

"The presence of a Torki then led us to believe it was to install our enhancer recording into the brain of one of our people. I regret if we have taken the mind away from one of us, but it is a sacrifice of one for the greater good. May we meet the other species that has helped us?"

Mirikami had noted the recurrent use of "we" and "us" from the Raspani, and the regret that they had damaged the mind of one of them. It could be like the royal "we," of third person self-address. He walked around to the front to be seen, but didn't speak.

"You have less hair and no tail, but your body is shaped much like what we recall of the Prada."

"There is some small resemblance," he acknowledged, in low Krall. He realized that compared to a Torki or a Raspani that would seem true.

"We call ourselves human, and as the Torki named Coldar told you, we are at war with the Krall. We removed some of your people from captivity on Krall worlds. My name is Tetsuo Mirikami, or a short version of my name is simply Tet. That is what I prefer to be called by friends. I hope humans and Raspani will be friends. May I know your name?"

"I have no knowledge of the name of the individual who gave himself to us, to let us awaken. We have too many names to speak in half a lifetime here, but as the original speaker for us all, when we were transcribed, I am…." Then followed some slobbery sounding lip smacks and a short descending pitch nasal whistle.

"This is in the Raspani dialect I spoke when my mind was transcribed here, but I now know all of our many dialects. A meaning of my name that you will understand, in this hated low Krall language you must use, is Blue Flower Eater. As your culture apparently expects, I may be called the short version of that name, or simply Blue."

Mirikami executed a slight bow. "I am pleased to meet you, Blue. We have your body and head secured because the process of insertion of the mind enhancer you now contain appeared to be a fragile and risky procedure. When we cover the opening for protection and sanitation, we will remove the restraints to permit you to move freely."

"We would all like that. It felt like we were being held for force-feeding. To make us taste better for a Krall slaughter."

The repetition of that fear brought a fresh awareness that the newly awakened mind of this Raspani knew how its race had been used by the Krall. With good intentions, they had held it captive as if it was to be fed the pepper spice fern before being slaughtered for more flavorful meat.

Aldry quickly completed the head bandage, covering the incision, as Rafe, rushing and clumsy, removed the restraint clamps as quickly as he could. His face was deeply red at what this unfortunate creature had initially though must be its fate.

It stood, on somewhat shaky four legs, over the short padded bench that had supported its low but long torso. It backed away in an awkward straddling movement until its short legs were clear. It raised its arms, to touch the top of its head, feeling the bandage. It was impossible for Mirikami to avoid thinking of its body style as other than a small hippo-like centaur.

"Blue, we know the body you inhabit was fed and had consumed water before it volunteered for the installation of the device. However, do you wish any food or drink, or need anything at all?"

The Raspani seemed to consider for a moment, then said confusingly, "Not all of you at once, and we were just told our new body does not require food or water."

Mirikami pulled briefly at a lip, and asked, "Blue, am I right in assuming there are other personalities with you inside that mind enhancer?"

"Yes, there are very many, and your offer of food made many of us crave tastes we have not experienced since the Krall made us their preferred food. We only were fed what made us taste better to them."

Mirikami, his supposition confirmed asked, "How many of your minds are in there, and how did they become stored?"

"There are millions of us in this one quantum storage system, and there were once many of these systems to preserve the minds of many more of our people. I hope they are not lost. We altered the linkage we had between our many devices, so that some of unique designs we created could receive and store the contents of the minds of those that chose to be transcribed and sent into storage. Few were willing to face the experience of being killed for food. We hoped that we might each be restored to a living body if our race survived extinction."

"So now that you have a living body, it's better?" Aldry asked.

The reply convinced Mirikami that humans would understand and like the Raspani.

"It's a bit crowded, don't you think? We can't hear ourselves fart."

The digestive track of the herbivore Raspani was prone to produce methane in generous quantities. The remark made at least the humans laugh, but the Torki, left completely fartless by nature, didn't understand the joke.

"Blue, if the Torki make additional devices for you now, I assume you can transfer individual minds into them. However, if the transfer replaces the mind of the host body, how did you plan to do this? I can tell you we have recovered several thousand Raspani from Krall captivity. It's true that most of them do not display significant signs of intelligence, not after so many thousands of years of inbreeding. However there are not very many bodies for all of you."

Blue made an elbow squeeze to his sides that seemed like a shrug. "If we can determine that those you described as having lost the power of intelligent thought can host more of the mass storage devices like this one, we can reduce the congestion of our group thinking. I am an individual, but I require the cooperation of all the other minds to stay focused and silent, in order for me to speak with you.

"We have the instructions within each device to teach us how to make others. We will spend years recreating the levels of tools and technology we need, but we will one day make devices for a single mind at a time." He hesitated as a though came from within.

"One of us rudely asked me if the Torki make their own enhancers, or if they are limited to those that are inherited. If they make new ones, they may already have the tools and technology we need."

Coldar played speaker for the Torki once again. "We used our own tools to repair the damage age had done to your storage device. This knowledge is stored on our Olts for us to do this. Without our help it would not have linked to your brain otherwise."

"Age damage? I heard the Tet human say some of our race had no minds after thousands of years. What measure of time is a year for humans?"

Coldar had a simple solution. "Our Olts have a time keeping function, and so does the device where your minds are stored. Yours was inactive and shut down for a long period. If I grant you access to link to my Olt, you will be able to synchronize the time. The master time is set by our galaxy's rotation compared to the location of the central black hole of a galaxy two million light-years away."

There was a moment of quiet, and the hushed reply from Blue Flower Eater sounded sad. "We have lost over eighteen thousand years. Coldar has translated the human measure of your race's home planet orbit for us, Tet. It has been far longer than we thought."

Before the day was out, the other two empty storage devices the Torki had built were placed in the skulls of two Raspani from Koban that were determined to be effectively mindless and hardly aware. The task of transmitting a third of the minds stored in Blue's new body to each of the two empty receptacles would occupy weeks of time. Blue assured them that the Raspani had the knowledge of how to produce more of the mind enhancers, and do it faster than the Torki were able to do now. There were thousands of Raspani herd animal candidates for the devices, but there were several million hopefuls for a new body to host them.

The only long-term solution seemed to be to wait for the birth of a Raspani calf, and before it developed as another mindless replica of a Krall-bred meat animal, insert a device in the skull of the infant. An adult mind would have to endure the growth of its new body, but a singular life was worth the trouble.

The group minds in Blue's skull proved an interesting source of information about the early Krall. Mind Taps had been a dismal failure, with more than a stadium's volume of thoughts to try to sift through, even when they made a concerted effort to stay quiet.

The reverse process worked well, however. The Kobani mind pictures sent from a single individual was like a night at the movies, for minds locked too long together with little new external input.

Their initial fear of the rippers was finally overcome, at least as far as not running from them any longer. Something the Koban raised Raspani never were able to do, even after the rippers abstained from deliberately scaring them so they could frill them.

The newly aware versions were intensely curious about the ripper's natural mental ability and the Koban nervous systems in general. They had no collective records of any life with similar abilities or nervous systems. The cats refused to receive from them as a group, for the same reasons the TG2s did. The Raspani, as a former prey category, didn't care for most ripper "conversations."

Mirikami was probing for more about the soft Krall, and the minds that had anything to say knew only that they once had a "chip" at the base of their neck that linked to the nerves there. They had been Krall that the typical warrior, with fighting on their mind, would have challenged as weak. They had been removed from the crowded Krall home planet as hatchlings, and some, with early training, were smarter than the pure, warrior-bred Krall, and had less of the adrenaline in their systems to drive them towards violence.

They stayed isolated from the standard population, but their example and privileges of off planet travel convinced the clan leaders that there was some advantage to finding room to expand. There was less fighting when the same clan had ample room to take what they wanted on habitable worlds of their own. The reduced fighting convinced the Olt'kitapi they were slowly "taming" the entire race. The conflict was only being postponed.

It was the mind-altering effects of the "chips" that helped organize the soft Krall into a new small subset of Krall society. Their aggression was being curtailed, to make them suitable galactic neighbors. The access to knowledge and technology made the other Krall resentful. The advancing Krall were able to do things with the mechanical "gifts" of the Olt'kitapi that a warrior Krall could not do. Even to use what gifts, such as clanships and weapons they were permitted, a standard Krall had to change their normal tattoo of status for one the Olt'kitapi provided. With that, they could operate the ships they were given, and use the weapons made available. There were other hostile races in the galaxy, and the gentle Olt'kitapi wanted capable bodyguards. If they could make them smarter, and with less of a hair trigger, they could become ideal.

No one knew how long the joint clan council had existed, but it was the body that coordinated the cooperation of the major clans, and kept them in line as they insinuated themselves into Olt'kitapi trust at every level.

The event that the Raspani said initiated the revolt was the next generation of star ships the Olt'kitapi invented. It permitted the upload of an Olt'kitapi mind pattern into a quantum matrix that gave the ships a degree of self-awareness. It accessed a level of Tachyon Space that even the Raspani didn't know how to reach, and the ships could travel thousands of light-years in hours. What was wrong from the Krall's perspective was that the soft Krall would have access to these ships. The standard Krall were told that their minds required modification before they could instruct the intelligent ships on what to do. They needed to accept the same chip as the reviled soft Krall had inserted. This they knew would alter their fierce warrior spirit. They had bred for many generations to develop that spirit.

The first of these new style ships were designed to be used for immense mining projects, to build what Mirikami deduced was to be a series of something like a Dyson sphere, or a ring around an entire star. An immense amount of material was needed, and a rapid means of transporting it to the construction site was part of the design.

The start of the first mining project was witnessed by a number of clan leaders, as an inducement to join the soft Krall in asking their warriors to accept the chips so they too could reap the benefits of the coming great galactic civilization, that the soft Krall would help build. The long developing plot for revolt was coordinated to start everywhere on the same day, before the new ships made it impossible.

"What did the ships look like?" Mirikami asked.

Blue pointed at his rear half. "Shaped something like my lower body, but without legs and a tail."

"Let me show you something." He took Blue's hand. He flashed the visual he'd taken from Parkoda's thoughts, sharing it with the roughly one million minds still in Blue's storage device.

Blue said. "We thought they had been lost in the fighting or deliberately destroyed. However, it is good if you have found them first. We had assumed they were destroyed, as the Olt'kitapi had said they would be, when they were on the verge of annihilation. The great ones were reluctant to use these tools as weapons. However, we Raspani fled from Olt'kitapi settled space, and from the fury of the Krall's insane rage.

"Those of us here, who the Krall eventually trapped on our colony planet, never knew what happened to those ships. Obviously, one of those mining ships was used to eliminate the Krall birth world, and then that ship, possessing an Olt'kitapi mind pattern, would have gone insane, and of course so would have any Olt'kitapi crew aboard, who ordered it to perform that destruction. Neither the minds of those ships, nor their makers, are capable of enduring mass murder. It is why they lost the war, by initially refusing to destroy worlds where Krall lived."

Blue made a deep vertical skin wrinkle between his eyes that looked exactly like a severe human frown. Mirikami had recently learned this sort of facial expression was the Raspani version of a big smile.

"That thought pleases you?"

"No. That image you showed to us does, because we see you have found those surviving mining ships. They must be kept away from the Krall. We are extremely relieved."

Mirikami asked, "What if the Krall had those ships?"

"Why, then all of your worlds would die."

Blue looked at Mirikami. "We are happy to see such a big smile expressed on your face."

****

DRAMATIS PERSONAE

HUMANS

Crew from Flight of Fancy

Tetsuo Mirikami

Captain of Flight of Fancy. From Old Colony of New Honshu, in the Hub area. Became Commander of Prime City after Krall left Koban

Noreen Renaldo

First Officer of Flight of Fancy. From Old Colony of Ponce, in the Hub area. Married Dillon Martin. Mother of TGs Carson, Katelyn, and Cory.

Jake (AI)

Advanced JK series Artificial Intelligence (AI) computer, installed on Flight of Fancy. Able to operate many of the ship systems autonomously. Repository of vast human library of documents, books, films, Tri-Vid shows, etc. A common capability on long Jump passenger liners.

(Chief) Mike Haveram

Chief of the Drive Room on the Flight of Fancy. In charge of the "Drive Rats" and conventional thruster engines.

Macy Gundarfem

Motorfem. One of the "Drive Rats."

John Yin-Lee

Motorman. One of the "Drive Rats."

Andrew Johnson

Motorman. One of the "Drive Rats."

Nory Walters

Chief Steward, of the ten such staff on the Fancy.

Mel Rigson

Steward and primary Medical technician.

Cal Branson

Steward and Medical technician.

Javier Vazquez
Alfon Hanson
Jason Sieko
Stewards.

Bob Campbell
Machinist Mate.

Neri Bar
Machinist Mate.

Chack Nauguza
Cargo Specialist, handy man.

Ricco Balduchi
Cargo Specialist.

Passengers from the Fancy, various other ships, and early captives

On the Fancy

Dillon Martin
Professor of biological sciences, sent to Midwife to study developing primitive life. Hidden specialty is forbidden genetics research. From Rhama, a New Colony, close to the Hub worlds. Married Noreen Renaldo. Father of TGs Carson, Katelyn, and Cory.

Maggi Fisher
Professor of biological sciences, Chairfem of Board of Director's on Midwife project. From Rhama. Organizing unofficial teams to recover lost genetic knowledge. Later, first Mayor of Prime City.

Aldry Anderfem
Professor of biological sciences, granddaughter of Claronce Anderson, a former President of Alders world. Supports secret Genetics research. Administered first human Clone mods in three hundred years, to make Second Generation Kobani.

Vincent Naguma
Professor of microbiology, from Greater Angola, an African Colony World at the edge of the Hub, settled just before the collapse. Studied Raspani in Hub City enclosure.

Sarah Bradley
Biologist that specialized in simple viral and bacterial life forms from Newborn. Became interested in the study of Raspani at Hub City, after the old Krall compound was occupied.

Rafe Campbell

Studied human genetic mutations from cosmic rays on Brussels, a New Colony. Wife Isadora killed on ship by a Krall, "exercising." Dove into Koban genetic studies when given a chance to make humans physically superior to the Krall. Administered mods to teens born as SGs, which made them first Third Generation Kobani (TGs).

Ray McPherson

Husband of scientist. Member of the Fireball Brigade of flame throwers.

Jim (Jimbo) Skaleski

Hydroponics expert for the Midwife station. Fireball Brigade.

Early Captives (at Koban Prime, later renamed Prime City)

Mavray Doushan

Was Poldark's Deputy Ambassador to Bollovstic's Republican Independency. Both are Rim worlds.

Thaddeus Greeves

Former Colonel of a Diplomatic Security detail for Poldark Ambassador. Married Marlyn Rodriguez. Father of TGs Ethan, Bradley, and Danner.

Marlyn Rodriguez

First Officer of Rimmer's Dream, arrived in mass capture of human ships. Married Thad Greeves. Mother of TGs Ethan, Bradley, and Danner.

Deanna Turner

Organizer of the first Primes to volunteer to work with the Flight of Fancy personnel. On Mirikami's combat team.

Frank Constansi
Clarice Femfreid
Juan Wittgenstein

Early Prime volunteers to work with Mirikami. On Mirikami's combat team.

Third Generation Kobani

Carson Martin

Parents Noreen and Dillon, born an SG, received Koban gene mods to become Third Generation Kobani.

Ethan Greeves

Parents Marlyn and Thad, born an SG, received Koban gene mods to become

Third Generation Kobani.

Alyson Formby

Born in Hub City as an SG. At eighteen, left home to request Koban mods, against her parent's wishes. Became first TG from Hub City, then first to be a TG1 from there.

Jorl Breaker
Fred Saber
Yilini Jastrov
Richard Yang
Their parents were early Koban captives. At sixteen, they become TGs.

HUMAN SPACE

Garland (Sarge) Reynolds

Sergeant in the PU Army on Poldark. Captured by the Krall, and in a fluke of circumstance is taken to Koban, and is there rescued by the Kobani, twenty years into the war with the Krall.

Henry Nabarone

Major General of the Planetary Union Army, in charge of Poldark's defense. Formerly in a local militia unit, and second in command after Colonel Thaddeus Greeves of that same unit.

Frances (Frank) Trakenburg

Colonel in a Special Operations division, based on Poldark. Dedicated to improving the capability of his troopers, via any means possible. Somewhat of a stuffed shirt, suspicious and secretive. Not under the authority of General Nabarone.

Joseph Longstreet

Captain of a platoon of spec ops troops, expanded to absorb remnants of units suffering losses from missions behind Krall lines on Poldark.

Heavyside

A Rim world planet, not considered suitable for human colonization. Located on the anti-spinward side of human exploration, on the far side of Human Space from the Krall invasion. It has 1.41 times Earth's gravity. Originally, it was named Andropov's World, after Admiral Elaine Andropov, a long dead war hero from before the Collapse. The nickname for the planet eventually became the accepted name.

Discovered long before the beginning of the Krall war, it was never actively settled. The high gravity precludes successful childbirth on its surface. Native plants and animals offered little commercial exploitation. It was considered unsuitable for long-term colonization due to the high gravity, and terraforming was too expensive for no significant payback. It had a livable biosphere, and simple plants, lichens, and algae had produced an oxygen nitrogen atmosphere. Three hundred fifty years ago, the surface had been cheaply seeded with plant life that would boost the oxygen levels, so that it now was at twenty-two percent. Sea life had been introduced that had taken hold in the three-fifths water covered planet, but only a small amount of shrimp was actually harvested for the protein, because there was too few residents to consume the bounty.

Some people, thinking of a source of meat protein that might thrive on Heavyside, introduced the jackrabbit from Earth. Lemmings and voles also did well, but they competed for the same food, and rabbits were winning that battle. Learning nothing of the Australian example, the rabbits bred, thrived, and became a nuisance, consuming crops on the limited farmland. However, they did make a decent meal.

Heavyside is now home of the Special Operations training program.

KRALL

Parkoda

Titled Harzax Kopandi for Krall, or “Measures the Enemy” and a Translator. From Tanga Clan of planet Merkrall. Leader of the Newborn raid that captured the Flight of Fancy.

Telour

Originally a Krall translator, of Graka Clan. Second in command of Newborn Raid. Placed in charge of captives at Koban Prime. Eventually was second in command to Tor Gatrol Kanpardi, with the title/rank of Til Gatrol.

Dorkda

Krall translator, of small Maldo clan, a recent offshoot of Dorbo clan.

Gatrol Kanpardi

General/Admiral of Graka Clan, Gatrol was his early rank and title. Later, Tor Gatrol, as High General in command of the war with humans. Based on Telda Ka, or “Base 1,” the former human Rim colony of Greater West Africa, which humans now call K1. All eighteen million people were slaughtered on his order, just to have a “clean” base.

Gatlek Pendor

Mordo clan. He is the Invasion commander on Poldark, Gatlek is his rank, equivalent to the lowest rank of General for the Krall.

EXTERMINATED ALIEN RACES

Olt’kitapi

Highly advanced and ancient people, determined pacifists, who first discovered the Krall. Mentored the violent race, hoping to make them more peaceful, but were betrayed and destroyed by the Krall, about 22,000 years ago. Never physically described by the Krall. They taught the Krall how to use the more simple parts of their technology, and designed ships and equipment specifically for them, to suit their personality and level of intelligence.

They were the first conquest described by Krall: "Our old bodies, even so long ago, could easily defeat their smaller and softer bodies. They were fruit and plant eaters that believed their artificially enhanced brains made them more powerful than we were. When we rose up to attack everywhere at once, we lost our first home world to them, and many Krall died before our final victory. After that, we owned their many worlds. We ate them all like the cattle they were."

Botolians

Aggressive omnivores, evolved from social pack animals that resembled Earth Primates. Good fighters, but controlled a relatively small six hundred light year radius of settled space, bypassing colder and higher gravity planets. Slow breeders. Was first Worthy Enemy. Larger than humans, the size of lowland gorillas, and nearly as strong as a Krall. Smarter than Krall, but slower reflexes and predictable pack hunting tactics made them easier for the Krall to surround and attack. Not tricky or subtle, and preferred direct confrontation over ambushes, and were out matched in such fights. Always refused to surrender, and were all destroyed.

Piltcons

Wiped out by the Krall a mere thousand years after the enjoyable war with the Botolians. The young species had relatively low technology, inhabiting only two worlds in their home star system. They did not have Jump technology, and fought poorly. That was hardly surprising because they resembled a chubby but fast running long legged flightless bird with long feathery arms and three fingered hands. Their small heads did not house their sizable brains, which were located in the torso where the slender neck attached, placed one foot below the beaked mouth, large eyes, and hearing membranes. The Krall found it entertaining to decapitate the creatures and watch them run around blind and choking on their blood, until the lack of oxygen or loss of blood caused their brains to lapse into unconsciousness. They would "steer" the hapless animals by plucking feathers as they ran, causing them to turn away from the threat, which they felt but could not see or hear. Their lean dark meat was edible and tasty when raw, but the creatures were so fragile that clan leaders decided they were a poor choice as meat animals to be raised with the hazards found on various worlds. The truth of the matter was that warriors could not resist the fun of slashing off their heads for the entertainment value.

Malverans

Rise of the Kobani

A reptilian race the Krall met and exterminated several thousand years before encountering humans. They were an insect eating race that lived only on warm dry worlds, with 0.7 to .8 Earth g's. Their slow metabolism made them easy prey for the Krall. The volume they'd colonized was about four hundred light-years in radius, adjacent to an area humanity would have been exploring in less than fifty years.

Discovery of Koban

It was a world in Malveran space, which had been far too hostile for the slow reacting Malverans to settle. They had a few dozen colonies, and those fell quickly to attacks by a single clan, the Dorbo.

Eventually the Maldo, a small finger clan of Dorbo, were awarded a choice of former Malvern worlds to settle. They selected an unused heavy gravity world, later called the Testing Ground, or Koban. They built an open compound on Koban. Native life nearly killed off the Maldo clan. They learned they could survive there only by building walls and electric fences and carrying weapons. This situation drew the attention of all the major clans, who tried and failed to settle on Koban without walled compounds.

ENSLAVED AILEN RACES

Raspani

A spacefaring, once highly intelligent and peaceful race, with only about a dozen colonized worlds in a small empire. They were another client race of the Olt'kitapi, advancing under their guidance. After their defeat by the Krall they became semi-intelligent because the Krall bred and used them as meat animals. They were raised in herds on many of Krall worlds. The grey creatures, paler on the stomach than on the back, looked somewhat like a pigmy hippopotamus from Earth. They are nearly three feet high at mid back, and five feet long in the lower torso. The upper part of their torso is vaguely centaur-like, which when held upright places their heads five feet above ground.

They have a pudgy pair of human-like jointed arms and dexterous looking hands. When grazing, they pluck tender grass shoots and fern leaves with their hands. They also eat fruits and berries if they can find them. They have the masticating side teeth of most herbivores, but sport two residual tusks, jutting up from the lower front jaw. These protruded three or four inches above fleshy lips, and facial features arranged much like on a human. They have a central flat nose above their lips, with two large nostrils, and large, forward-facing brown eyes under light brown furred brows. The head was smooth, rounded, and hairless, but there was some sparse brown hair growing along their upper and lower backs.

Blue Flower Eater

A Raspani spokesperson's mind, encoded on a modified quantum storage device along with millions of other Raspani minds, who sought protection from

Krall atrocities on their species.

Prada

Bipedal, forest and jungle living, eats fruit, nuts, insects, and small game. The creatures are black or brown, with white markings. Resemble a lemur or monkey-like mammal, with a useful prehensile tail. About the size of an Earth Chimpanzee, they can use their five fingered hands (with longer middle finger for digging out grubs) and long toes almost equally well. They retain some arboreal ability. The Prada have large yellow eyes, and they were originally nocturnal animals. They are the Krall's main assemblers and builders.

Their society took roughly seventeen thousand Earth years to colonize a volume some three thousand light years in radius. They selected moderate gravity worlds of 0.7 to 0.8 g's, and preferred dimmer redder stars than Sol. They befriended other races, unless such contact was rejected. Engaged in cooperation and trade with Olt'kitapi.

They are a long-lived species who place their eldest members in charge. This deferment to the elders is why they originally cooperated with the Olt'kitapi, the oldest intelligent species they knew. After they were all killed, the next oldest species they knew were the Krall.

Now they are loyal and submissive to the Krall, and they have lost their original language, so speak only "low" Krall. They are the largest group of slaves and can build most things the Krall want for war, or have copied from other races.

Wister

A male Prada elder, roughly one thousand three hundred years old, found in a tree village on the planet next to Koban, left there by the Krall when they departed the system.

Nawella

A female Prada elder, and sister of Wister. She is a bit older than her brother is and he seeks her advice. Together they manage a small village of their people, who preserve an underground factory complex where anything required by the Krall can be built.

Torki

A highly intelligent eight foot wide by five foot long, and three foot high land crab race with one large defensive pincher and a smaller one for grasping, and a hard deep purple shell with eight amber colored legs. The two in front of their mouths are small and used as dexterous manipulators. Their eyes are on two-foot stalks, and they perform fine assembly of tools and electronics for the Krall, copying from plans taken from other defeated races.

They had been star traveling for eleven thousand years when the Krall over ran them. Preferred worlds with ample seashores, and bypassed most worlds inside their six hundred light year sphere. They built giant ships for their large bodies, and simulated seaside environments for their own comfort. Huge ships carried only a few hundred Torki, but when used by the Krall they had room for ten thousand warriors, or even more Prada. Several thousand Torki could fit, with great discomfort.

As adults these land crabs are terrestrial and are found as far as ten miles from the shoreline, returning to the sea only to soak or breed. They sleep at night in cool burrows several feet deep, or at least to a level that will allow water to seep in for moisture. They are primarily vegetarians, preferring tender leavcs, fruits, berries, flowers, seaweed, and some vegetables. Occasionally they will eat fish, beetles, or other large insects.

Like all crabs, they shed their shells as they grow. If they have lost legs or claws during their present growth cycle, a new one will be present after they molt. If the large claw is lost, males will develop one on the opposite side until their next molt. Newly molted crabs are very vulnerable because of their soft shells. They are reclusive and hide until the new shell hardens.

Coldar

An influential Torki in his lodge, left behind on the world next to Koban when the Krall departed. The crabs can communicate electronically by a quantum storage device they were given prior to becoming sentient, by the Olt'kitapi. As they advanced, the locked libraries in the storage devices open to help them access new knowledge and databases. They know of the ancient race, but they never met their benefactors. They build new storage devices as their population expands, and copy the data they have into them, not knowing what new information they may contain.

****

Attention reader: This concludes our regularly scheduled broadcast at this time. I hope you've enjoyed the story.

****

Excerpt from Book 4:

Shattered Worlds

Chapter 1: A Raid Less Easy

The two ships of operation Fast One winked into Normal Space in the outer reaches of the Krall occupied star system.

Noreen Renaldo, captain of the Avenger and in charge of the raid, tersely instructed the second ship to start their passive scans. "Slasher, focus on the southern hemisphere region of the planet and the area below the plane of the ecliptic. We'll cover the northern half, and above the ecliptic plane. I'll check out the moon myself."

"Roger," Was the only reply. They had discussed this previously.

Noreen had taken a page from the Krall's playbook. Stopping in the outer solar system for a look around before Jumping the final billions of miles to their next intermediate stop, a moon, on their way to the real target. The range out here was too great to wait the many hours for *active* scans to return information that would be out of date before the return signal arrived. The speed of light round trip would require just over two days, and radar and laser scans at this range would contain too little detail anyway. Besides, actively scanning and then waiting that long for the signal to return would alert the Krall that someone was conducting surveillance well before the raiders arrived at the planet.

Instead, Noreen wanted to conduct passive observation of the inner system as it appeared a day ago, using the superior Olt'kitapi view screens on the converted clanships. If their plans went as laid out, the raid should be over by the time their gamma rays from the dual White Outs reached the inner system. Their next Jump inward, faster than light, would pass up their gamma ray wave front "announcement."

The Avenger, and the Slasher under Captain Anna Retief, carried four hundred Kobani each, all of them with spec ops training. Indeed, some of them were actual spec ops troops from Human Space, who were now fully gene modified Kobani. With Mind Tap abilities, the level of training of everyone on the mission went beyond the specialties of spec ops troops, but the mission was one that was closer to that mode of operation. In theory, each one of them could pilot a shuttle, the new four-man ships, or even a clanship. They all had the knowledge of how, if not the actual experience of piloting each of those.

Their mission today was to try to slip in close to the Krall planet undetected, assault the intended dome, and the weapons factory under it, with relatively few raiders and then extract them as quickly as possible. There would be no attempt to rescue the Prada factory workers on this mission. They would do their best to spare them any harm, but it was impossible to sneak in and land a huge, slow migration ship for an evacuation.

Wister, one of the elder Prada on Haven, had said convincing these Prada to climb aboard quickly, before the enemy rallied to knock the nearly defenseless tubs out of the sky, was highly unlikely if not impossible.

Not to belittle the value of the lives of the Prada slaves here, it was nevertheless recognized that they didn't have special skills that wasn't available on dozens of other clan worlds. Evacuated or left behind (killing them was never considered), their absence or continued survival would not affect the Krall nearly as much as the loss of the underground factory. That facility would require a year or two to replace, and more time to bring it back up to its present productivity. The workers would be of even greater use to the Krall after the destruction of their workplace, to prepare for the new factory's arrival, so they were relatively safe.

It had been slow to sink in for Captain Mirikami and his other planners, just how important the theft of the migration ships had been, as well as the destruction of those much older migration ships stored in parking orbits.

To replace a factory, a modular starter factory would have to be produced by Prada, usually on some other world, for replacing any that the Kobani raiders destroyed. Because there were no giant ships to deliver the bulky things already partly assembled, at least twenty clanships would have to haul the components for delivery in one shipment, and then they required more ground assembly. A successful Operation Fast One would have a greater impact than simply halting the weapons now being produced by this particular factory.

Clanships, in shorter supply than before, had to be taken from the fighting fronts and used for internal supply runs. Logistics problems were not something the clan leaders had needed to think about in their past wars of conquest, of weaker, less aggressive species. When you found a worthy enemy, they presented you with new problems.

The Krall had had time to notify all of their major clan worlds, and most of the medium status clans, of the human raids that had knocked out four crucial manufacturing sites. Those were planets responsible for most of their strategic weapons manufacturing, and for the ships that delivered forces and supplies. They had needed those production sites in order to expand their war with humanity. They lost the two most significant shipyards for clanship, shuttle, and single ship production, and the only yard that built the Torki designed giant migration ships, which were used to move supplies, large warrior forces, and slaves. In the case of the Hammers, (humans called the partly collapsed matter weapons Eight Balls, because they were black spheres), the Krall lost a tremendously effective means to punish entire human worlds. Accelerated to a significant fraction of the velocity of light, an Eight Ball could slam into a world with an extinction level impact.

This was hardly the first time a foe had ignored restrictions or rules the Krall had imposed on them, of course. All of them did that at some point. However, it *was* the first time a foe had been so effective against them, and humans had forever destroyed their second most devastating weapon, the Hammers. They couldn't replace the Botolian designed gravity projectors (not available from a species they had made extinct), even if they found fresh Torki slaves that could relearn how to produce the Hammers using those projectors. The partly collapsed matter balls they had laboriously completed over centuries of labor had been placed in storage orbits for future need. The humans had somehow destroyed them in place, despite their being tough enough to batter their way through heavily armored human battleships, resisting lasers, plasma cannons, and missiles, virtually unscathed. The method of their destruction had yet to be determined by the Krall. That was because the high velocity, diamond tipped, depleted uranium railgun slugs were also destroyed on impact, or the near misses had left that stellar system at escape velocity.

The problem now was that the Krall didn't have a quick and convenient means (for them anyway) of rapidly punishing human worlds, to make them regret these acts. There certainly were plans to make human worlds suffer, but all of them required time and some level of unprecedented Krall sacrifice. Such as limiting the scope of new invasions, being less able to focus some special level of intense mass suffering on entire human worlds. Radiation would make those worlds worthless for war by their Great Path breeders, and would encourage use of nuclear weapons by humanity, which was also detrimental to the Great Path. Pity the plight of the poor genocidal warriors, with fewer opportunities to earn status point kills.

The most devastating reply possible to humanity presented the Krall leaders with a great level of difficulty, a material sacrifice of one of their most cherished super weapons. The highest leadership levels were in a dispute over what was the best course to follow. In the meantime, preventing additional human raids was imperative, and the more important clan worlds were on a high alert. Minor clans and new finger clans would eventually learn of the human raids, as successful warriors returned home from combat to breed the clan's next generations. However, those small clans could fend for themselves until word spread to them. After all, they only represented yet unproven bloodlines for the Great Path.

The most damaging three raids by humans had happened in a single, well-coordinated day a couple of months ago, when simultaneous attacks destroyed the irreplaceable Hammer making facility, and the two shipyards that produced or repaired the majority of their workhorse fleet of clanships. In the process of preparing for these raids, a matter of days earlier, the humans had captured or destroyed all of the huge migration ships used to move supplies, slaves, and factories to the war fronts. They also captured eleven more intact clanships to use in the larger raids. In the process, they destroyed hundreds of undefended parked clanships on dome tarmacs, and leveled many domes themselves. It was a humiliating experience for the clans that were attacked, and it represented a loss of status for each of them.

In a final insult, the humans used the stolen giant Torki ships to remove the most critical workers for building these complex pieces of war equipment, and destroyed the factories. At least clanship production could be slowly ramped back up within a few years. In the meantime, an unpopular requirement that the joint council of clan leaders and the Tor Gatrol war leader was promoting, was for clanship pilots to be more conservative in risk taking. They were asked to avoid excessive damage to their ships and to be more on the defense.

In order that the joint clan council could approve Tor Gatrol Kanpardi's plan to expand invasions to two new human worlds, the edicts went out that limited some of the more aggressive clan styles of attack, which placed clanships at greater risk. Kanpardi promised to rigorously pursue the fight on Poldark, to push the nearly thirty million men in the human army back on their heels, so that half of the four million Krall force could easily and suddenly withdraw, for starting a new invasion on another more vital and populous human world. This request produced a great deal of resentment among high status warriors and leaders, to be told to limit their aggression to protect mere *equipment,* and for a *withdrawal* on Poldark. No matter if it was to expand the war, the reduction in resources that made this necessary went against the instincts of these warriors.

Fortunately, there was ample production of less strategic but nevertheless, essential war material such as mini tanks (or Dragons as humans called them), anti-artillery laser batteries, counter battery rockets, plasma canons, and the heavy armored battlefield transport trucks.

The particular Krall world being scouted by the Kobani today had a large high capacity production facility of exactly those types of essential war materials. Noreen's concern was that the midsized Sudok clan, who controlled this world, might have placed clanships in orbit around its sizeable moon, located in a relatively close orbit to the habitable planet. It was expected that there would be clanships in orbit around the planet itself, but they hoped not around that moon. The clan could also have brought in orbital defense platforms, like those few that had survived the two PU Navy attacks around K1. It had been over a year since the passive Planetary Union navy scouting mission had observed this system, and that was before any Krall world had been placed on alert. The unstaffed, slow reacting orbital platforms were not as great a worry to Noreen as clanships stationed around that moon.

The moon was the intended "shield" for the Avenger and Slasher, to White Out behind its bulk to prevent the Krall from detecting their close-in arrival. Evidence of random Krall White Outs around the planet or moon would suggest they were doing micro Jumps to make undetected infiltration such as that harder to conduct.

The two human ship's sensors should be able to detect the presence of clanships in orbits around that moon, and certainly random White Outs. Noreen only intended to use an hour of observation before making her decision to Jump inward, or leave here if not. The two ships had quietly departed a previous target star system, located much closer to Human Space, because of a high level of watchfulness. This alternate target was deeper into Krall territory, and protected by a smaller clan with fewer resources.

Anna Retief was from the Old Colony of Suid-Afrika, and had fought her newly captured clanship once before, backing up the Avenger when the CS2 shipyards were attacked. Her aggressive nature and competence made her a natural to participate in this next raid. The Slasher, as she had christened her purloined ship, had been partly modified for greater human comfort (no slow sissy elevators needed for the fully gene modified TG2s), and she had an AI similar to the Avenger's, delivered from Human Space by the Falcon.

Chief Haveram had surprisingly kept his command of that former smuggler's ship, now turned into a Koban freighter. The former Flight of Fancy's Drive Room chief made regular Jumps to Human Space from Koban, carrying precious metals to convert to currency for purchasing things the Kobani needed, such as AI's for installation on the eleven captured clanships. The chief-turned-captain, surrendering to the physical temptation, was a TG2 now. The age regression he had undergone, curtsey of the Prada longevity genes, the new med labs and nanites, transformed him socially, and he had become something of a dashing figure around the rough Rim world black market ports he visited. He also had a reputation as someone you *did not double cross in a deal!* He was apparently much tougher and experienced than the very young man he appeared to be.

After almost an hour of watching the day old inner system activity, Noreen thought they had seen enough. "Anna, I'm not observing anything moving close to the moon, and Carson has so far spotted only a single clanship in a polar orbit around the planet." She was on view screen with Captain Retief.

"Noreen, I'm seeing what appears to be another clanship, also in a high and slow polar orbit, and offset a bit from the other craft's orbit. It's just coming into view below their south pole. It's a bit hard to make out yet, because I see it through so much of the atmosphere. However, if those are the only two watchdogs, and their orbits stay timed much the same, we can slip our shuttles and four-man ships into the atmosphere from behind that moon, between their orbit overlaps. That moon is surprisingly close in, but it works to our advantage. Must make for some huge high and low tides on the coastal areas. That must be why there are no Torki lodges here. Their quarters and labs would flood and dry out daily."

"You're probably right about that. We also see the second clanship now. My AI says there should be almost a thirty-minute window between their coverage of the upper northern latitudes, where our target dome sits. That assumes they are following that same pattern once we get closer. Our small ships should be able to penetrate and get into the mountain passes and approach the dome in its valley that way, all without the Krall seeing them coming."

It was good enough for Retief, who had been ready to charge in without so much as a first look. "When do we Jump?

"Alert your assault teams to get in their ships. We can Jump in ten minutes, on my mark, now!" The two AI's would assure the two ships made their Jumps simultaneously to the designated region, only three miles above the backside of that moon. Their dual gamma ray bursts on exit would go undetected on the planet, and by the two orbiting guard clanships.

Carson rose from his acceleration couch. "Mom, I'm joining dad in his shuttle, Alyson will stay here with you. Do you want me to send anyone else up here?"

"No. Alyson and I can handle navigation and weapons here if needed, and Karl can help with that as well. I have people for reloading our missile racks that I can call up here if we need help." Truth be told, the AI could do nearly any of the tasks required on the Bridge, except make life or death decisions on its own.

"Son, I know you will find this tiresome, but please be careful. Tell your dad that as well."

He flashed the same toothy grin he shared with his father, "You know me. Always careful."

Alyson shook her head. "I know you too, and that's why we both are telling you to be careful." She and Carson had moved into a semi-formal relationship, and had discussed a contract, "signing the line" in modern parlance, to make it official. They had decided after this raid to make the surprise announcement, which virtually no one that knew them would be surprised to hear. Carson's daredevil reputation was well earned, and even his reckless father was shocked at learning of some of the risks his son took.

"Right." He kissed Alyson on the lips in passing, and then bussed his mother's cheek on the way to the Bridge railing, which provided an open view to part of the deck below. One hand on the rail, he lightly vaulted to drop the eighteen feet to the deck below. The ship was only at one g, so it was hardly a knee bender when he touched down on the balls of his feet. They had lowered internal gravity to match that of the Krall planet they were about to raid.

He continued down the stairs for two more decks, to reach the new launch bay of the shuttle he would occupy with his pilot dad, Dillon Martin, his Uncle Thad, best friend Ethan, and eight other Kobani. The original two launch bays had been increased in number and size, from the two shuttle bays and thirty-two single ship launch tubes that the Krall used. Now there were four shuttle bays with craft that held a dozen people each, and sixty-four larger tubes for the new four person ships of similar design to the single ships, commonly called four-ships now. From a distance, the two new small ship classes were almost indistinguishable from the original Krall craft, having the same shapes and proportional dimensions. It was expected this would cause some underestimation of the number of forces they actually were transporting.

However, these were all better armed small ships than the standard Krall models because of Torki and Prada modifications, redesigned at human request. Now the shuttles carried four missiles rather than two, and had multi-spectrum lasers of higher power, capable of defeating the hull active reflectivity protection of Krall clanships and single ships. They also had plasma cannons stowed on the aft section bulkhead, which could be swung into place to fire from the left and right side hatches, when a hatch was slid open at *low* speeds. Any combination of the four missiles they carried could be the light hypervelocity anti-ship variety, the heavier ones for ground attack, or a new Electronic Counter Measure (ECM) missile (or pod as it was called).

The smaller four-ships had heavier multi-spectrum lasers as well, and two of the small anti-ship missiles. The smaller missiles were described that way because that matched their primary design function, to destroy other spacecraft. However, they could as easily hit stationary surface targets, if a larger warhead wasn't essential.

Today, the target was a Krall dome, presumably with alert observers on duty in the upper transparent level, and ready to warn the dome and entire planet of an attack. This shuttlecraft, and the seven others, would launch fourteen of the larger ground attack missiles at the dome, even before they had the dome in sight, but would fire those slightly *after* the launch of two ECM pods. Which meant the Krall observers would not have seen any of them coming yet either, from their concealment in the mountain passes.

The two ECM missiles they would fire would broadcast an advance signal, a transmission suppression code, specifically designed by the Torki to shut down the operation of the standard Olt'kitapi designed com sets and radio transmitters. Those were communications systems the Torki made for the Krall, and had stayed essentially unchanged for thousands of years. The Torki assured them the ECM gear would suppress any radio transmissions from the Krall in the dome, and even block the personal com sets they carried when on duty. This was different than jamming the frequencies with a powerful signal, preventing communications by overriding the enemy transmissions with noise. That itself would be detectable from a considerable distance, particularly by the orbiting clanships. They were taking advantage of vulnerabilities in the original transmitter/receiver designs, ordering the equipment to shut off via a short-range, low power signal. If the Krall turned the devices back on, the transmitters promptly shut off again if the ECM signal was still present.

The humans had a set of frequencies set aside for their own use, which were seldom used by the Krall, and their own equipment would not shutdown. These transmitters were nevertheless set for low power by their armored suits and ship AIs, to avoid bouncing strong signals off the ionosphere, something nearly every habitable planet had. After cutting their foe off from calling out for reinforcements, they didn't intend to make that call for them (indirectly), by filling the air with strong encrypted transmissions of mysterious origin.

As the time of the coordinated short Jump neared, Noreen made a broadcast to all personnel on both the Avenger and the Slasher.

"Attention. This is Captain Renaldo. After White Out above that moon, the two previously designated four-ships, one from Avenger, one from Slasher, will launch and fly to the east and west limbs of the moon to observe the planet from a hundred feet elevation. The two orbiting clanships were conducting active radar scans a day ago, and we need to confirm if that's still the case, and what their orbits are today. Use tight beam laser to communicate with your mother ships. We will use Normal Space drive to follow you, but we will stay behind the moon. You are our eyes. Report what your passive sensors see. We Jump in one minute. Renaldo out."

On the coordinated fraction of a second, the two AI's sent their respective ships into the Jump Hole and almost instantly, for that short a distance, two White Outs occurred three miles above the backside of the moon. The pair of four-ships promptly launched and headed around the curve of the moon to observe the planet and it's environ. The Avenger and Slasher drifted along in-trail, until the curve of the moon would prevent their tight beam laser com communication, and there they held station with their drives. Just able to see one another by line of sight, and their own four-ship, which represented their "eyes" on the planet.

They remained this way for over an hour, to collect current information on the orbiting clanships. There still were only two, apparently in the same orbits, scanning the volume of space away from the planet with radar. Their moving target detection sensors were probably on automatic, to report any tracks observed. The AI's confirmed that there would be a window of opportunity of about thirty minutes, when the planet would place them in shadow of the two clanships radars. That would happen the next time in twenty minutes, and repeat every one hundred eighteen minutes, unless either clanship altered course or speed.

Noreen decided it was a "go" on the first opportunity. Using the laser com system, she again broadcast to all personnel, by a tight beam to Slasher, which couldn't be intercepted. "The two ship AI's will coordinate when each set of raiders race out from behind the moon on each side, as the clanship about to go behind the planet's curve loses coverage of us. The other clanship will not be able to see this moon for nearly thirty more minutes. Closer down by the planet you will have a longer shadow time because of the planet's horizon. Get there fast, then use your drives to slow down to enter atmosphere without blazing a visible entry trail. Stay on the course and schedule that the AI's have fed your computers, and you will be in the mountains well before the next clan ship comes over your horizon. Its radar will be looking out away from the planet anyway, but to be safe I want all hundred and thirty-six ships down in the passes of the mountains, downrange of the dome at least two hundred miles from it before then. You will have a total of forty minutes to do that.

"Launch as soon as I sign off. That will allow you time to reach the edge of the moon, and then wait for the AI's signal to head inward at max acceleration. Back off when the computer tells you to, and slow down to make your entry. If the Krall on the surface go to an active scan on you before you reach atmosphere, come back here fast and we'll try some place else. Good luck and be safe. Renaldo out."

This was rehashing what had been discussed and practiced back in the Koban system. Not this exact scenario of course, since it couldn't be predicted. The type of atmospheric entry and subsequent low altitude infiltration to the target had been rehearsed multiple times. Each Krall planet would be different, but they had discovered that none of the Krall worlds was heavily populated, not even when compared to human Rim worlds and New Colonies.

This world probably held a population of perhaps three or four million warriors, in roughly a hundred or so domes, all belonging to a single medium sized clan, the Sudok, who completely controlled two entire planets, and had a presence on a few others, such as K1. This was their base world, where most of their population lived, trained, and bred, when not actually engaged in war. Even so, there were only a little over a hundred domes on the entire planet, and for a cooler planet like this one, they clustered closer to the warmer equatorial regions to house their nursery nests and hatchling regions. It wasn't difficult to find an atmospheric entry route in the northern regions that avoided habitat domes. The domes in cooler areas were mainly low population outposts where factories had been established, preferentially built close to the raw materials and resources needed, without consideration for what climate the Prada might prefer.

On their screens, Noreen and Alyson saw the swarm of craft from the Avenger racing silently away. There wasn't even a back reaction as there was when they launched missiles. The reactionless Normal Space drives were quiet and powerful, and left the Avenger without even a vibration. From the screens, they could see sixty-three of the four-ships and the four shuttles, all moving towards the lone four-ship already on watch at the limb of the moon. There were an equal number of assault ships leaving the Slasher. However, Noreen and Alyson didn't watch any of those ships launch. Their eyes were locked on one shuttle in particular, as a husband and son, and husband to be, eagerly raced toward danger.

The AIs on the two "mother ships" continued to monitor the passive data fed to them from the two observational four-ships. Allowing another minute to avoid any possible radar detection, when the clanship passed behind the curve of the northern pole of the planet, the two small armadas were released to accelerate towards the planet's northern hemisphere.

The Normal Space drive of both classes of craft could reach greater than two hundred forty g's real space acceleration. Internal compensation of the inertial forces left the occupants stressed, but nowhere close to the blackout level of a TG2. Most Krall warriors would have been unconscious at the internal stresses placed on these crews, and a few Krall might have died, because they distain the use of acceleration couches. The two flotillas flew nearly parallel courses, slowly converging on the atmospheric re-entry area over an uninhabited part of the continent where the dome of interest lay.

As they reached the midpoint of travel, the two groups growing closer, they simultaneous rotated each ship end-for-end, where the reason for approaching from opposite sides of that moon became clearer. They were not bunched so tight that a minor error in positioning while rotating would cause a collision. Technically, the Normal Space drives didn't care *which* way the craft were oriented in order to apply the powerful deceleration forces, required to avoid a fiery atmospheric entry. However, the occupants stretched out on their couches and fighting the stresses, only found it tolerable when the uncompensated force was pressed on them from their backsides.

There was never a doubt they could reach the atmosphere well ahead of the second clanship rounding the southern pole. However, if they left behind one hundred thirty six ion plasma trails, even against a daytime sky, someone on the ground would surely notice. The residual streaks in the atmosphere would also point the way to the general area of the attack.

It wasn't necessary to come to a halt, merely to get their velocity down to where their passage would not strip electrons from the molecules of the thin upper atmosphere. They were still traveling multiple times the speed of sound initially as they entered, but would drop below mach one high enough that the sound shockwave would dissipate in the thin upper air before reaching the ground. At some altitude, they assumed their passage would produce contrails if the moisture content of the atmosphere were right. To disguise the multiple contrails, the now slowed craft clustered in formation closely enough that when or if the vapor trails appeared, the separate trails would all quickly merge in the turbulence of passage. It was hoped that a wide elongated white streak, if noticed after the fact, would resemble a high, cirrus layer of cloud. Only its sudden formation would be curious, if noticed. The craft causing it would be invisible, of course, because optical stealth was active.

Dillon, piloting the lead shuttle of the group from Avenger, was in formation with the lead shuttle of the group from Slasher. There were ships spread to either side of them to widen the contrail front if those formed.

Using a command to his armor to open a laser com link to the ship on his right, Dillon said, “Hey Sarge! Looks like my flying lessons for you were worth the money. You haven’t bumped anyone even once.”

The salty answer was prompt. “Nah. Your lessons were worth exactly what I paid for them. Absolutely nothing. Thad provided for my flying expertise.”

“What? He’s a crappy pilot. He has two left wings, making him fly in circles.”

“I didn’t say he *taught* me. What a horrible, if not fatal result that could bring about. I said he *provided* for the lessons. Cost him a lot too.” Dillon could hear the man’s laughter.

“He actually paid for you? Who was it? I gave you *free* lessons, for cripes sake.”

“I already told ya what yours was worth. Anyway, there was no actual money exchanged, although I’m sure he paid in other ways. Marlyn taught me all she knew in compensation, just to hold it over Thad’s head.”

“Compensation?”

“Yep. Thad still can’t play cards worth a crap. Marlyn found out about a bad poker night of his, and paid me with flight lessons. Now *she* holds his IOU. Worth every cent to us both!”

“Ouch. I can’t believe you told on him.”

“I didn’t. Honor among men, ya understand. She found out in an evening of passion. You can’t block your thoughts *all* the time, you know.”

“Ahh. Been there myself. Leaked a thought when I felt guilty about something. Oh well.”

Knowing that Thad, sitting in the seat next to him had heard half of that exchange, Dillon looked over at him with an eyebrow raised.

“I don’t want to talk about it, so fly your damn ship!”

Grinning, Dillon switched to why he really had called the other group leader.

“I’ll fire the two ECM pods, just before we clear the passes. How about we cluster all of our landings around the north, east, and south side entrances of the dome, and leave that west one wide open for the Prada, to evacuate to that grove of tall trees on the northwest side. They’re bound to have a village over there, and they’ll be afraid of us, and our ships.”

“OK. I’ll pass the word to the Slasher crews. The Prada will have underground exits in the woods that also lead to the factory. I hope they don't have many workers living in the dome. Fourteen missiles will bring most of it down you know."

"I know. They'll be unavoidable collateral damage if they do house families there. Fortunately, this world's environment isn't as screwed up as the shipyard worlds were. They can live outside and above ground here, so most will be in the forest I hope."

"I hope so too. Let me pass the word before we reach those foothills and spread out, losing laser com connections. We only have about five more minutes before we split up."

The onboard AIs had the mapping of the foothills from their observations as guides, and the two groups would take multiple paths to reach the dome, staying below visual or radar scans (if any) as they made their way closer. At the lower speeds needed in the winding passes, they had about five additional minutes of flying at low altitudes. Dillon's shuttle was to hold the lead of either group, and was given one of the more direct routes. They needed to launch the ECM systems about thirty seconds before the other missiles. That second launch should be when the forefront of the leading assault ships was fifteen seconds from leaving the passes, and entering the wide valley where the dome was located. By that time the ECM equipment, broadcasting its signal ahead of them, should have shut down all radio communications at the dome. The exhaust trails of the inbound missiles might be seen in visible or in infrared light, but the observers wouldn't be able to tell anyone by radio.

The seconds ticked down. Dillon tapped the yoke button that launched the two ECM rockets, which promptly diverged as they climbed over the rim of the ridge of the pass that was concealing the shuttle. They diverged just in case some fast reacting and super observant Krall fired a laser and picked one of the low flying objects out of the sky. Either ECM pod was adequate for complete radio suppression. There was a spare third such device in a cargo hold.

Thirty seconds later, the eight shuttles combined to launch fourteen ground attack missiles at the dome, which was only fifteen seconds from direct view of the attacking force. Each missile, part of a smart network, was programed to spread out their impact points to destroy not only the upper four levels; the ones most often occupied by Krall when they were on duty at a factory dome, but missiles were also to strike major structural nodes on the perimeter of the dome, to bring more of it down.

The deliberate arrival timing worked extremely well. The advance craft were out of the passes with the dome in sight, just in time to see it explode like so many tinker toy parts, pin wheeling up and outward, then falling back. The parts of the dome not hit directly began to slump awkwardly, in fits and starts, as one collapsing section pulled another down. By the time the entire assault force was out of the passes, the six hundred foot high, half-mile wide dome looked more like a fifty foot high broken pile of sticks and shiny armored glass fragments, sparkling in the bright cheerful sunshine, which beamed its way through the pall of dust. Because there had been no clanships parked here (that was a surprise revealed by observations at the moon), there was no billowing orange and black column of fire and smoke from an exploded fuel tank.

Thad, checking the AI's communications report on one of the screens, verified there had been no outgoing Krall signals detected. The two ECM systems were both online, and their drogue chutes were still lowering them gently over the wreckage of the dome. Surprise was complete, and no warning had made it to the rest of this world. Yet.

Keying a push for the entire flotilla, using their reserved low power frequency band, Dillon told them, "Set down on all sides except the west, to allow Prada evacuations there. Let's see if the missiles left us any Krall to kill."

****

No warrior would ever admit to boredom, because that suggested they were less alert than maximum. The Krall had bred the need for sleep from their species thousands of generations ago, without regard to how a long day of wakefulness could be filled, if the enjoyment of continuous personal combat were not a constant mental stimulant. To fill the time on duty when on alert and nothing exciting was happening, most warriors relived past combat kills or actions from near perfect memories of battlefields. They repeatedly analyzed their own performance, and that of warriors that had been around them. Considering how they and their clan mates could have fought better, or more efficiently.

Because their minds were extremely active, they considered themselves to be at maximum alertness, ready to instantly detect and react to any threat. In effect, however, they were retroactively replacing the Krall brain's equivalent of REM sleep in humans, where the day's events were dreamed about and moved to long-term memory. The Krall's brain wasn't disabled from muscle control, as humans were when dreaming, however, the bout of "daydreaming" did not truly make them more aware of their real surroundings than normal. That was an artifact of the daydreaming thought process, where they were keenly aware of the past battles they were reformulating, to do it perfectly the *next* time.

As a result, the four warriors placed on duty at the top of the dome were technically wide-awake, each constantly scanning their quarter of the observational hemisphere with their eyes and heads moving, more or less on autopilot. They were unconsciously relying on visual movement detection to cue their real world attention. This was far better than human ability, but short of the Krall's expectation.

The two ECM missiles, when they appeared barely over the top of a ridge at five miles distance, were flying directly at the point of view of the Krall observing that quadrant. Their apparent motion was effectively zero across her field of view. She finally noticed their increase in size at about the halfway point.

Her proper first response was to alert the entire dome, relying on the other three warriors to overhear her report to the warriors stationed below. The second response was to try to survive the inbound attack so she could fight back.

Fashtok keyed her com button for wide broadcast, even as she leaped down the adjacent stairs, speaking loudly as she dropped. “Two missiles, inbound low from south.”

She couldn’t see her clan mates, but knew they had heard her and would have reacted as she had, and be on their way down after a quick confirmation glance where she indicated. That would put them a second or two behind her, so she assumed they might not survive the expected impending explosions. As she dropped rapidly below the third level, still going down at max break-neck speed, leaping landing to landing as the stairs turned, she heard the echoing voice of one of her clan mates, at least a level above her in the same stairwell, reporting multiple missiles inbound from three quadrants. Leaving seconds later, he had seen more. However, there was something wrong here!

She didn’t hear his report through her com set, but by the echoing sound of his high Krall speaking voice, reverberating down the stairwell. Her own first warning should have been heard by him and every Krall in or near the dome, and in the factory below by radio. She had not heard an answer from her sub leader to her first broadcast. Not only that, but her warning should have resulted in this stairwell now containing warriors evacuating levels she had just passed. Where were they?

She tried another message, as she passed the fifth level below the top. The echo of that transmission should have reached her ears from her trailing clan mate’s com set speaker, when it repeated what she transmitted. She didn’t hear that. That meant none of the broadcasts had been successful. As she passed the eighth level from the top, something else she didn’t hear yet struck her as peculiar. There had been no explosions from those two missiles she’d seen, which had had more than enough time to strike the dome by now.

Her confusion was short lived. Fourteen other high-powered rockets answered her expectations that her three late departing clan mates would not survive. Unfortunately, the onslaught of explosions reduced her survival chances to zero as well. As the wall of debris that would end her life raced in from the sides, she hoped the warriors massed below ground, defending the factory, would avenge the dome’s destruction.

****

The eight shuttles landed on the tarmac and eighty four of their ninety six troops charged out the two open side hatches, with a pilot and two side gunners staying behind on four of them. The stowed plasma cannons were swung into place and the four shuttles lifted again to provide coverage of the dome rubble and surroundings from the air.

The hundred twenty eight four-ships spread out on three sides, as previously directed, and their crews, five hundred twelve strong, scaled the mostly collapsed structure to seek the warriors normally occupying the upper levels.

All of the forces had stealth activated on their armor, making them ghostly hollows in the settling dust and swirling smoke, and pale shadows with an icon displayed on their helmet visors. The initial task of the crews of the four-ships was to clear the dome of any still living Krall. Despite the destruction, experience had proven that the resilient Krall could survive what seemed unsurvivable, and even with major injuries, could fight back with significant effect.

The missiles had spared the lowest eight levels of the thirty-two level structure, but the collapsing weight of the upper stories, and the penetrating effect of the spoke-like support struts allowed many to stab downward to reach ground level. In some cases, the struts poked slightly below the ground level floor, because underlying the dome was the upper level entrances of the subsurface factory.

As predicted, there was sporadic plasma fire in the crumpled mess of the dome in the pile of debris overlaying the heavily damaged, but largely intact, bottom levels. Previous attacks on other domes had revealed that any Prada housed in the domes over a factory occupied the lowest levels, often the ground floor. The shorter distance to their work areas made this practical, and in this case, the relatively clean environment would suggest many of the Prada families would live in the nearby forest. That was the hope, anyway. The reaction speed of the Kobani meant they could hold their fire for a moment, to better ascertain if a motion detected in the wreckage was a Krall or a Prada.

The sporadic sizzle-crack of plasma fire up high proved Krall were being found alive in the rubble, and some of the shooting, from the slightly different sound, was from plasma rifles, rather than Kobani helmet plasma bolts. Because only the Krall would have those rifles for this mission, that sound drew Kobani attention to surviving clusters of the enemy. Most would be killed, but any found that appeared to have higher status, based on their tattoos, would be captured alive if possible, for a Mind Tap.

The shuttle teams carried the cases of explosives to use in the factory, and had a number of the recovered Raspani boring tools, found on captured clanships or recovered from weapons belts of dead high status warriors. The tools were to be used to destroy fusion bottles, both at the base of the dome, and down inside the factory, after first shutting them off. If breached while in operation, the fusion generators became potent "bombs." The Raspani invented tools could bore holes up to a hundred twenty two feet deep in any substance thus far tested. There had been a bonanza of the tools recovered at an orbital station, where the Torki technicians had used them to delicately dissolve away some of the collapsed crystal material of the Eight Balls, to make them hollow, and provide an opening to install Jump drives, fusion bottles, and pilot controls.

The Raspani name in their language for the tools, was three sputtering lip smacks, a snort in the middle, and a deep grunt at the end. That native pronunciation lead Sarge to suggest the human description of them to be loosely translated as some form of the sound of a "wet fart." His own rendering was made by blowing with his tongue between moistened lips.

He pretended to be greatly offended when the consensus on all of the solicited names proposed for them was chosen to be Q-rupters, for quantum disrupters. He complained, "What a boring name for a spectacular piece of equipment that turns anything into a burst of gas."

Dillon was flying one of the shuttles with side gunners. They had found only one target worth their plasma guns attention thus far. An unattended Krall shuttle was parked nearly under the overhang of the east dome entrance. The two gunners each got a shot at the cockpit, cautioned to avoid the reaction mass fuel tank at the rear and its fusion generator. Once in space and out of the gravity well, shuttle Traps could snare tachyons to power the Normal Space reactionless gravitational drives.

The Kobani shuttles and four-ships had all retained tachyon power in their Traps, and could launch directly back to space without using reaction fuel. The cleaner and cooler trail made for a more difficult to follow IR or radar signature if an anti-ship missile were fired at them.

Thad was in charge of the factory destruction, and Ethan and Carson were leading two of the teams that would descend into the factory levels. They had entered via the east entrance, just before the Krall shuttle was made useless. Sarge, his own shuttle left empty and on "idle," as were all of the parked four-ships, led his demolition team in from the north side. Others teams entered at the south dome entrance. All of the factory entrances were at the base level of the dome, reached either via the swift elevators, or by stairs. The elevators made for potential traps, so they would take the stairs, located at the inner large ring of elevators and stairs, surrounding the central hall. Every dome so far found followed the same unimaginative design that the Krall appeared to find satisfyingly efficient, if boring to a human.

Today, the frequently encountered collapsed ceilings and penetrating dome support struts required some detours from the well know paths to the ring of stairwell openings. Although the teams were encumbered with the stealth-coated explosives cases, carried between pairs of armored and equally invisible troopers, they were hardly unprepared for a fight.

The front of their helmets contained all of the firepower it was decided they would require on this quick in-and-out raid. A thought to the suit could initiate two types of laser beams, a plasma bolt, or a microwave heat beam in an instant. They would hit what you looked at, and had indicated mentally was the target. The suit could lock on and continue to fire at a target, even if the wearer looked away to lock onto another target and fire. The only limitation was that firing all weapons at once reduced the energy available to produce the most powerful plasma bolts, at the maximum fire rate.

The look, shoot, and forget, target tracking mode meant that a single spec ops trooper could take on multiple opponents at once, and focus on a different task while the first designated targets were under continuous fire. They each also carried a waist load of eight grenades, concealed under a disposable belt of stealth-coated material. While attached, or in contact with the suit, they could select the mode of operation of any grenade number by thought (small digits 1 through 8 could appear on the bottom of their inner visor, and brighten when touched for removal).

The timing before detonation could be set verbally, manually, or by thought. They also could choose the proximity mode and set the range for a booby trap (nearby friendly suits would block triggering), and there was a ten step range of explosive power. The lowest three levels threw the depleted uranium pellets with less force, so that their own armor could resist penetration, but a nearby Krall (out of armor) would be perforated like Swiss cheese. At higher power levels, which could kill a Krall in armor, their own suits were equally at risk if they failed to take cover or were too close.

As a precaution, based on recent experience, additional armor thickness had been added in two areas to reduce the risk of nearby grenade use. The top of the helmet and over the shoulders was thickened, and on the feet, butt and crotch. If you threw the grenade yourself, you could point the top of your head and shoulders at the impending explosion (arms at the sides), in presumably a prone position. The alternative was to lay flat in the other direction, with your feet pointed at the detonation. So far, this strategy had only been used on empty suits in testing; with mixed results if the explosive power was set at the highest two power levels and went off too near. You literally risked your head or your ass if you tossed them too close.

Thad and Ethan, each carrying a case of explosives approached the inner hall, their visors showing them icons of teams arriving from other directions around the hall. They both had cut off icons reports from more than thirty feet overhead, because of the clutter of overlying icons of the swarm of troopers searching and clearing the upper levels. There had been perhaps a hundred twenty warriors up there, and nearly a quarter of them had survived the explosions and collapse. That was more than had been previously found on the other raids on factory related domes, so perhaps this clan had beefed up its complement of guardians. That should have been a clue.

The two of them paused as a voice in low Krall spoke from the other side of the debris cluttered large hall. That it was spoken in low Krall, and was being helpful, proved it wasn't from an actual Krall. At their thoughts, the visor showed them it was Sarge speaking.

"Leave here by the east exit and go to your village. Do not return and you will not be harmed."

There was some scuffling noise from the other side, and a chittering sound that particularly young Prada made when frightened. Reynolds and his team had apparently found some of the workers, and he was trying to direct them to safety. Thad, as a team leader, selected a view from Reynolds' visor, which appeared in a small, fully colored translucent square on the lower left side of his own visor. He could see through the image, but saw a group of four frightened Prada, one was probably a female, with a child clinging to her fur and clutched to her chest. They were scurrying around fallen ceiling sections and broken armored glass pieces, looking back over their narrow shoulders, not certain where the orders came from. However, they were following instructions, and moving quickly towards the dome exit they were told to use.

There had been multiple feeding stations for Prada, set up in the center of the hall, and that and debris prevented an easy passage through the middle. The four went around, and were approaching the south side, where Thad and his teams were about to enter the huge room. To avoid spooking them, he spoke on his group's channel.

"All teams hold back, and stay quiet. Let these Prada pass. They won't hear us if we don't step on anything crunchy." The workers couldn't hear him speak of course, unless he selected external speaker mode.

That kindness and consideration was negated, when a shoulder fired rocket blazed out of a stairwell opening. The same one Thad had been moving towards for their descent. It was a high velocity, armor penetrating rocket. The same type that had nearly killed Ethan, when he was driving a Dragon on Poldark.

It didn't explode when it passed through the body of the mother and child because they didn't represent a hard enough surface. It tore them apart, however, then exploded against the top of an elevator door on the far side of the hall, where the molten copper core of the warhead instantly burned its way through the metal plate of the lift door. It likely splattered the inside of the empty elevator carriage with red-hot droplets.

There was no doubt the rocket would have killed any of the armored raiders. The Krall that launched that missile either didn't see the target clearly, or assumed an invisible human in stealth armor was walking with the Prada near the head of the stairs.

The other two Prada froze in terror and horror at the falling and ruined corpses of the mother and child. There was no way to know the relationship of the other two Prada to the dead ones, but any speculation was short lived. Multiple plasma bolts from Krall rifles blasted the other two into charcoaled remnants of smoking and burning gray and brown bits of fur.

On a general push, Thad heard Sarge state the obvious to all teams. "Ambushes set at the stairwells. They're waiting for us. Use grenades."

Thad was in overall charge of the ground assault against the factory, but that was sound advice. He let go his side of the explosives case nearly simultaneously with Ethan. Before the case could hit the floor, he had selected a grenade for level 10, a two second delay, as he detached and flipped the fist-sized bomb into the stairwell, where the known ambushers were concealed. Ethan's grenade was simultaneously clattering with his on the stairs when the one two punch of the explosions shot more dust and smoke out of the stair well.

The answering scream of pain and rage was a welcome sound, but they could hear many angry voices, and plasma fire was coming up out of all of the stairwells now, in actinic fountains of blue white hell. Multiple other explosions erupted dust and pellets out of all of the stairwells, briefly slowing the rate of fire, which somehow managed to increase the level of screaming rage. The Krall seldom went quietly when they fell off the Great Path. The rate of fire increased again, so it appeared they were trying to clear the way to rush up to meet the enemy.

Suddenly, out of the stream of plasma bolts flew dozens of smoking canisters that arced out and hit the floors, spewing a light gray smoke that was thin enough to see through. Thad selected the general push this time, “Seal suits. They may be using poison gas. Troopers up top, get down to the central hall, the Krall are trying to break out of the factory level.”

As he said this, he flung two more grenades into two stairwells, one from each hand. The other troops were doing the same, so a continuous barrage of explosions were erupting from the stairs, even as the thin smoke spread through the large volume, added to by the explosives and dust they stirred.

Human and Krall suits both could double as space suits, so the use of a disabling or fatal gas didn’t seem an effective weapon to use here. It wasn’t thick enough to conceal the Krall, certainly not as effective for concealment as the trick Carson had used in the clanship cleanout on Poldark.

The similarity must have triggered a memory for Carson. He called on a private channel. “Uncle Thad, this thin smoke isn’t to hide them; it’s to make *us* visible. Some of them used steam and water puddles to spot us despite our stealth on CS2.”

A correct supposition or not, Thad realized that this would be the practical result when the Krall broke out of the stairwells. They would see the “holes” in the smoke, where their enemy hid.

Using the general push Thad warned the others. “The smoke will let them spot us. Don’t count on stealth.”

They couldn’t count on grenades to keep them down below long either, because the eighty-four troops here were running low on them. The Krall were somehow maintaining a high level of return plasma fire despite the initial success of the grenades. The enemy plasma bolts were largely ineffectual, because they weren’t hitting any of the Kobani. It simply kept them back from entering the hall. That might have been another clue the Krall had additional plans. Holding a defensive position was not their style.

Thad knew the bulk of the Kobani reinforcements could not arrive from on top of the dome before the Krall got some of their warriors out of the stairwells. Then grenades would risk friend and foe alike. That happened sooner than expected.

Suddenly, the Krall sprang the next part of the ambush, apparently only waiting for the smoke to spread adequately. Even the concept of an ambush proved that the Krall were learning tactics from humans. They had rarely planned such actions in the past, and this one was obviously well thought out, at least for them.

The elevator doors suddenly rose nearly simultaneously, probably on some prearranged cue, because the Krall didn’t have com set use. Of course, their visors could show them a time hack they could all use, and pass via word of mouth. The armored warriors that swarmed out had infiltrated up through holes cut in the elevator floors. The Krall in front were carrying something that explained their continued resistance in the stairwells, despite hundreds of grenades lobbed down the stairwells. The warriors in the front ranks held floor to head height metal shields. The depleted uranium pellets couldn’t penetrate those, even if some made it under the bottoms or through the gaps. They obviously had learned from reports of the previous raids, and expected the raiders to head for the factory entrances.

This battle was turning into a melee of close infighting, just the type the Krall liked. The Kobani were more than a match physically for any individual Krall, but this could devolve into a disorganized struggle, with no way of knowing how many of the enemy they faced. Thad had started with only six hundred and eight Kobani, because they had assumed this dome would be as relatively unguarded as the others had been on the previous raids. Big miscalculation.

With direct targets to fire at, the Kobani were taking out some of the Krall behind the shield wall as they strove to peek over the top, when they fired at wispy areas in the smoke, seeking the nearly invisible enemy. More canisters of the smoke generators flew over the shields towards where human laser or plasma bolts originated. Without being told, many of the Kobani switched to the microwave beams, which generated heat at their focal point, but did not leave as clear a trail through the air back to the origin. Following their training, they were constantly moving, firing and changing position. Because they were on three sides of the hall, they had shots at the backs of some of the warriors rushing out of the elevators when they pushed too far into the open.

Shooting a shield holder in the back of his helmet with his microwave heat beam, Ethan was gratified to see four other warriors drop their shields to rip at smoldering hot helmets, as other troopers worked to eliminate down that particular advantage. Thad, seeing that happen, made a broadcast.

"Target shield holders. Then toss grenades you have left through the gap."

The level of thunderous explosions suddenly increased for short time, and rattling pellets filled the air with ricochets off armor, walls and floors. This was of some risk to the spec ops, and several were wounded when pellets penetrated their suits before losing momentum, via rebounding from an intermediary surface. The majority of the grenades were dropped into clusters of warriors, piling them up in a matter of seconds, but that depleted the supply of them and the explosions diminished. That was the cue for the forces down the stairs to rally and charge up, without the concern of running over a just tossed grenade lying on the steps, and detonating behind the shield wall.

Thad could see that the number fifteen appeared by a red icon, indicating there had been that many serious injuries or deaths among his eighty-four sappers. Now the warriors that had been held below the first landing of the stairs by the grenades were leaping up them, jumping out of the openings, as they went high to seek their enemy in what had literally become the fog of war.

With the turbulence in the room so high, their carefully thought out detection method for their invisible prey was much more limited than if they had been lying in wait, with the gas already deployed, floating and still, evenly distributed across the room and into the corridors. Movements through that would have been far more noticeable. The Krall would make an adjustment for the next time they used this tactic, but Thad's concern was his force surviving this time.

There were already several hundred Krall in the large hall, the volume of rifle fire pushing the humans back towards the radial corridors that led away from the dome's center. If that happened, the troopers along the back of that press would not see as many targets to shoot at and kill. The human rate of fire into the swarm of Krall, who were perfectly willing to absorb injuries and losses, could wear down those at the front of the massed human troops. Thad could see friendly green icons moving closer from behind them, to bring up support from the rear. However, they couldn't fire on the Krall with their own people in the way if they were forced down the long hallways. That sort of numbers game of attrition suited the enemy, not what the raiders could accept.

Thad was on the verge of ordering a rapid pull back from the lower level of the dome when he was amazed by a sudden blossoming of green icons. They were in a ring around the central hall, on the level above them. He had set his visor to exclude friendly icons that were much above the ground floor location, to prevent his confusing them with his own smaller force. Now the troopers searching the upper structure had started dropping or climbing through the broken levels and had reached the three-story ring of balconies that circled the central halls on all Krall domes.

Much of the shooting from the Krall had grown more concentrated as the sapper force had retreated towards the only points of retreat and cover they had. Now it was suddenly directed elsewhere. Upwards.

The spec ops on the rings of balconies, particularly those on the top two levels (above Thad's arbitrary vertical cutoff of icon positions), were higher than the layer of smoke that revealed movement through its translucent wisps. They were having an old-fashioned turkey shoot at the heads of completely exposed Krall.

Thad wanted to visit Earth someday, to learn where that ancient term originated. What the hell was a turkey that it was so stupid as to be killed so easily? However, he was pleased with the results here, wherever the term originated.

With no possible cover from incredibly accurate and rapid firing from all sides and from above, they had to retreat from the withering fire. Initially, never having had to retreat from a human attack previously, those trying to fight their way up out of the stairwells or climb up through the floor openings inside the elevators, resisted being pushed back by the withdrawing warriors.

Thad, who had a good command of low Krall, and some measure of understanding of high Krall, wasn't aware of a word for "retreat" or "withdraw" in either language, any more than they had one for "friend."

In several more minutes, the enemy had been forced back into the stairwells, where the first landings turned a corner, and gave them cover. Per his suit AI, Thad saw that there were over five hundred dead or dying warriors in the hall and elevators. There were an unknown number down in the stairwells. Shooting and killing wounded Krall as they approached, Sarge, with Carson beside him, stayed clear of the stairwells. Obviously, he wanted to know how they would proceed next.

Troopers designated for administering first aid were moving to the red and yellow icons indicated on their visors, to asses which ones needed evacuation for treatment at med labs in four of the shuttles. The suit systems proved depressingly accurate for the red icons. All but one of the eighteen indicated now were already dead, and that lone surviving woman would never make it to a med lab.

As Sarge, his second in command of the factory assault group joined him, Thad Linked to Dillon, as their air cover and in charge of the dome assault, and included his eight sapper team leaders. Those eight included Ethan and Carson, although he was shocked to discover that Yilini Jastrov was dead, and that Jorl Breaker now led that team. Yil had just “signed the line” with the much older (and now young looking) Clarice Femfreid last month. They had signed for one contracted child, and because Clarice had not made this mission, it was quite possible she had not cleared medical due to conception. Damn!

Shaking the loss off, knowing Yil was a close friend of Ethan and Carson, he didn’t look at them as the visors automatically registered Jorl as the replacement team leader. “We can’t take the time or accept the casualties needed to fight our way down those stairs, not knowing how many warriors we might face. We clearly caught them by surprise when we arrived, but just as clearly they had a reception planned, based on our previous courses of action. They know we take out the dome observers, blast any ships on the tarmac, and enter the factory to blow up the equipment and flood the works.

“I don’t think we can afford the time to clear them out and fight our way down. I’m open to alternative ideas. Sarge, you first.”

“We know the Prada have work entrances at their villages, or close by. We might try descending there.”

“The Krall know those are there too, and we can’t spend time fighting our way between levels even if those entrances could get us in unopposed. This time we know there are Krall down there in force.” He turned his head to look as new explosions from grenades blew dust up the stairs, and there was almost continuous if ineffectual Krall shooting around the stairwell corners of the landings.

He had a question. “Dillon, were there many Prada coming out of the dome after the fighting started? Four that Sarge directed to leave were killed by the Krall right at the start of shooting.”

“I saw perhaps a hundred run across the half mile of open ground from the dome to reach the southern edge of the trees. I saw hundreds more of them in the woods, and their IR signatures vanished deeper into the trees. I also saw a continuous stream of them pass from the northeast edge of the woods towards the west. I’m guessing they were coming out of the factory. They would have heard the explosions, and their merciful Rulers never care if they are caught in the crossfire. I believe they may have evacuated on their own.”

“OK. I think we have to take the chance that they were perceptive enough to get away from the fighting when they heard it start; The Krall fought each other for thousands of years, so this can’t be an entirely new experience in their long history as their slave workers.

“Let me hear ideas of how to flood and blow up this factory complex if we can’t go down inside and do it personally and thoroughly.” There was only a brief moment of silence, when the expected two most adventuresome and daring individuals both spoke at once.

"OK. I can't listen to both of you at once, and to avoid favoritism, which will rear its head anyway, I'll let Carson go first, then Ethan."

With a thumb up to Ethan, Carson made his suggestion. One he'd been considering ever since the Krall proved today they were better prepared to defend their factory.

"We need to flood the factory to ruin much of the equipment, and delay their restarting and repairing it after we pull out. We might be able to do that without blowing up the cooling water pipes from inside the factory. They pull cold glacier water in from that large lake a mile to the east, and pump the warmer water out into the river on the southwest side. There have to be large intakes in the lake. We may be able to float explosives into them to go down into the factory to the pumps, and explode when well below ground level. Water will then pour in by gravity, as it did at other sites."

Thad nodded. "OK. But they must have grill covers over the intakes, and we know they use pumps to move the water in faster than gravity flows and then back out. The outgoing pumps might prevent full flooding if they stay operational."

Carson had a reply prepared. "We can remove any grills, either by burning them off where they attach, or with smaller explosives. Our suits are as good underwater as they are in space or a hazardous atmosphere. It's my idea, I'll go in the water." No surprise there.

Ethan, who had had a different idea, suddenly saw a way the two could work together. "His idea will work better if we also do what I was thinking. The factory doesn't have to be entered through any of the prepared openings that the Krall are defending. Much of this entire area is overlying the factory, and we have the typical factory layout on our visor maps for navigation. The mapping will still work topside. If we blast holes through the factory ceiling from up here, at places where there is a considerable drop below those points, we can toss in our explosives.

"Many of them were going to be set to explode when water depth and pressure was high enough for hydrostatic shock to do more damage anyway. I'd suggest we drop one package down along the outlet pipes where they rise, to fall near the pumps that push water back up to the river. Carson lets the water in, I stop it from being pumped out, and our other explosives go off when the water is deep enough."

Thad liked what he was hearing. "It's slower, but that might work. We don't have to wait for the Prada to get out, and any that are still down there can still climb faster than the water will rise. I don't think we can wait for the water to fill the whole cavity anyway, since that could take more tha a day. Carson, take your team with you in a shuttle, and two of the Q-rupters to cut open any grills so you don't have to blast. Ethan, the factory roof is no more than a hundred feet below ground in most places. We can use more of those drilling tools to help weaken the rock and soil overhead to blast through easier and quickly. Toss in the explosives before the Krall even arrive to see what we did. They'll think we're coming in through those holes. We can blow a few holes in other places, just to keep them guessing and moving in the wrong directions. Let's get started, while our boys are holding them in their holes here."

An hour later, with joint coordination, several breeches were simultaneously blown in the factory roof, just as Carson sent several remotely activated bombs and one final timed device for good measure, down with the strong pull of water into the inflow pipes. He was fortunate to have had cables tied around his waist and chest. The current would have sucked him in without three strong sets of Kobani muscles to pull him back against that flow.

Ethan dropped in two sizable explosive packets where the outflow pipes rose up inside the factory. He wasn't sure now if they would drop all of the way to where the pumps were actually located. There were structural supports possibly in the way of a complete drop to the bottom. However, either one of the packets would blast open the pair of three foot diameter lines so that water, if pumped up, would spill right back inside.

Blowing several more holes from the surface permitted dropping more explosives on the upper levels of the factory, where the maps indicated key automated machinery was located. These were set for remote detonation, or sooner if tampered with by anyone. They had brought more explosives than they had expected to need, in case a couple of shuttles were lost on the way down. Now, because they couldn't go down inside to use all they had brought with them, they either left them behind, carried their weight back to orbit…, or blew something else apart. The choice was obvious.

The charges were set for proximity detonation, and placed near the stair tops just out of view from below. They were daisy chained electronically, so that if one went they all did. No one intended to continue suppressive fire until the last moment and then run for a shuttle or four-ship. They had eight tripod mounted double-barreled heavy plasma rifles, brought with each shuttle in cargo, which could be set for motion detection triggering, or suppressive fire at a specified rate. Instead of letting them traverse, they were locked into one azimuth, the butt elevated from up on the lowest balcony level to aim down into a stairwell and set to start firing when the troopers raced to get outside to their craft. Dillon would activate the remote detonation of the ECM pods as they left atmosphere.

The set up was clever, and almost worked like a charm…, except unexpected company arrived.

Breaking radio silence, Noreen suddenly warned them by narrow beam laser com, "Fast One raiders. Don't reply and risk revealing your location. A suborbital clanship launched from a dome about fifteen hundred miles west of you. It's obviously headed your way.

"The ship isn't under maximum acceleration, so I don't believe it's been warned about the raid. However, your presence there or lifting off will be a dead giveaway when they see you. You have plenty of anti-ship missiles, but going to an active scan too early will warn them, and you have at least five minutes before the overhead orbiting clanship passes the pole and out of sight. Whatever happens, that guard ship will see a big explosion in atmosphere, or hear a radio call from the inbound craft. Let them come in and prepare to fire at least four missiles when they are so close they have too little time to use laser defense or make counter missile launches. I'm coming down to cover your retreat. I'm hoping without any White Out gamma rays that they'll be slow to sound an alarm when I'm seen. The Slasher is also standing by for cover fire."

The mass departure of all hundred and thirty-six small craft had been scheduled to happen during another one of the imminent radar coverage shadows, caused by the non-overlapping and repetitive orbits of the two guardian clanships. Even with the final explosions inside the dome ready to "celebrate" their lift off, they couldn't risk climbing out in the face of a clanship that could pick many of them off even before reaching space, let alone reach the moon.

Dillon, waiting to detonate the ECM pods on departure, had an idea. "Thad, we can try moving all of the ships to the east side of the dome, parked close to its sides among the debris. We may not be noticed there. If that clanship comes in from the west and lands, the ECM will suppress their communications before we launch the missiles."

"How far out does the suppression work?" They didn't have much time to plan.

"The pods silenced the dome from about five miles away. Should be the same for the clanship."

"Colonel Greeves? I may know something about the inbound ship." His visor told him that it was Fred Saber, a squad leader under Dillon, who had been part of the dome assault group.

"Speak. We don't have much time Fred." With a thought to the suit, Thad put him on the Link with everyone.

"Sir, I was Tapping a dying warrior when you called us down to help counter the ambush. She was expecting their sub leader to return this morning from a nearby dome. This should be him. I never got a chance to report becau..." Thad made his decision and cut him off.

On the low power general push, Thad gave instructions. "Everyone, stay low but lift to get as close to the east side of the dome to hide as well as possible, the eight shuttles need to get the closest because they will stick out more. Park at angles among or under debris to make a jumbled appearance. Move now!"

The ships, already prepared for liftoff, moved quickly. The fast reaction speed of the TG2 pilots was all that prevented the small ships from banging into one another.

Feeling like he'd sounded too abrupt with Sabre, who had furnished good information, he gave him a responsible task as reward. "Fred, I want you to choose another four-ship to help you, and one of you move into the debris field on the south side, one on the north, so you can both cover the approach from the west with your missiles. Be ready to fire if I give the word, or if the clanship opens fire or suddenly appears about to move away. Got it?"

"Yes Sir!"

Shifting to broader icon coverage with his helmet, and selecting ships rather than personnel, Thad watched on his visor window as Fred's craft, and one flown by

Richard Yang, a former classmate of Fred's, moved to take up the designated positions. The ship icon movements got a bit confusing as his team ran to join Dillon in his shuttle, as it parked next to the dome.

They had all had moved into their new locations and were motionless for perhaps thirty seconds, just as the approaching sub orbital clanship's bright deceleration burn became visible. That's when they all were startled by multiple simultaneous explosions, which shook the ground and blew more fragments flying up from the center of the collapsed dome. The dust was still rising as the center of the broken dome slumped into the huge hole blown into the roof of the underlying factory.

Obviously, at least one Krall pinned down in the stairwells had gotten curious about the strange regularity of the automatic plasma fire. Like the proverbial dead cat, his curiosity was now satisfied. He had triggered a proximity detector.

The question now was, would the fresh column of dust, and a lack of response from the dome cause the approaching clanship to pull away?

The apparent answer was no, when the clanship continued its approach. However, Dillon and Thad had sensors that detected an encrypted transmission from the clanship. From Thad's visor, when he expanded the image, or selected views from other helmets, it was obvious a number of the closely packed smallest ships were now buried under fresh debris. The larger shuttles, sitting closer to the vertical wall of the demolished dome had far less scraps of structure tossed onto them. However, Thad realized that many of the four-ships would need to be uncovered before they could lift.

Just then, the side walls of the dome on the east side, with no attachments to the center to hold them in place, and leaning outwards from the force of the last blast, slowly leaned out to drape over five of the eight shuttles. There was no way of telling if the shuttles would have the lifting power to get clear, or to do so without damage.

They had arrived with additional passenger capacity, in the event some of the ships suffered damage. However, not as much space as they would need if they had to abandon all the craft that seemed trapped. The "huddle close to the dome" idea seemed a hell of a lot less brilliant in Thad's hindsight.

As the clanship moved more directly overhead it appeared to hover a moment, and Thad was about to order Fred and Richard to fire their missiles, which could lock onto a visually sighted target and alter course to climb up and pursue. It was nearly six miles up, and only slowly descending, as if looking the damage over. There was another brief encrypted transmission, before the thrust backed off and the pilot appeared committed to landing.

****

Droktad was disinterested in the return flight itself. This was not a duty posting that he desired. After a year of fighting on Poldark as a rising status warrior, his first sub leader assignment of more than an octet of battle-tested warriors was of leading many untested warriors, who only monitored willing slaves. Slaves who were building weapons he wasn't going to get to use in battle.

This was an unpleasant task, even if a necessary one. Particularly after the humans had displayed completely unexpected capability and initiative in attacking war production facilities. The war leaders had not believed the humans knew of, let alone had the ability to strike those facilities. He wanted more than ever to be back at war. Sharing time in combat with other clan mates in rotation was tedious.

He had just visited his next level leader, to request permission to join one of the new invasions forces, to escape the lackluster slow status building position he now held. The cursed human attacks, he was told, made his responsibility to his clan and the Great Path even more vital now. To defend the production of their tools for making war. He selfishly asked if the greater importance of his role in defending this dome would earn him more status points, to enable him to buy his way into combat sooner. The answer was no, and he was returning to spend another orbit watching his warriors watch workers. His force sat and waited to defend against an impossible human attack.

His K'Tal pilot was only slowing slightly for a typically rapid descent, on a suborbital path that would bring them down over the dome soon. It was the pilot's comment that drew him away from cleaning his plasma rifle for the hand of hand of hand times. He would wear out the sturdy parts cleaning them well before he wore it out in combat.

"Droktad, something has just happened at the dome. Dust or smoke is rising. There was none seen when we rose over the horizon."

The sub leader rose and tapped his view screen controls, and selected a zoomed image of the approaching destination, presently below and behind them as their main thrusters added its plasma glow to the edge of the image. There was a column of gray and white smoke rising vertically over the site, and he suddenly realized that the structure was far too flat, and even as he watched, and increased magnification, the center of the building sank farther, leaving the sides standing higher than the center. The dome was collapsing into the factory levels below! There was no way he could tell that this was the *second* round of destruction. To his mind, it had happened as they approached.

He selected the ship's radio on his console, and called on the clan frequency set aside for this dome in an attempt to reach his second in command. "Bolgar, what is the status of the dome? Was there an explosion in the factory?"

There was no answer, and he immediately thought of the subject he'd just been advised was so vital to be prepared for. A human attack. He been required, with other sub leaders, to observe recordings and listen (again) to descriptions of tactics used against them by humans in recent raids, and how carefully maintained Krall ambush postures would block the effectiveness of those attacks, should they occur.

He had a clan-approved strategy already in place, and there was no sign of human clanships on the tarmac, or of humans or warriors swarming over the broken down structure. The static sounds of plasma rifle discharges would also be apparent if there were fighting, and he had just checked the sensor that could detect if these were happening in large numbers. There were always some static or electrical discharges, which could pass as single plasma bolts, but a battle would be full of discharges. At this moment, there seemed to be no more than would be expected if there were electrical shorts in the factory and dome, from the collapse.

They reached a point over the disaster, one he knew he would be blamed for even if he were not responsible. He had been away from his post when it had happened.

He gave Fangar an order. "Slow our descent. If there are explosions from munitions from the factory, I do not want to land on a place that will collapse beneath us. The factory roof has given away below the dome's center. I will try to contact those in the factory on the emergency radio frequency."

He was reluctant to use that widely monitored frequency, because it would be picked up by the orbiting guard ships, and probably several domes at their present altitude. Not that this catastrophe could be covered up or hidden in any way. He simply wanted to be first to learn what had happened, so he could portray himself in the best manner possible, perhaps shifting blame to an underling, or better yet, claim it was a Prada industrial mistake. Those were exceedingly rare, but had happened in the past. His thinking now followed his preconceived notion that a human raid here was unlikely, and his own precautions had made it impossible for one to be this thorough. Besides, his K'Tal had seen it happen and there was no telltale human presence visible.

He made his broadcast. "This is sub leader Droktad. I observed what appears to be an accidental explosion as we approached for landing. The dome is heavily damaged. Is there any octet leader or warrior that can say what has happened?"

There was no reply, and from the heavy damage, it was possible that confusion and noise was a factor. He motioned to the K'Tal. "Fangar, take us down. Do not land too close to the dome in case there are other explosions, or the roof of the factory settles from the weight above."

As they sank within range of the ECM pods, the loss of the com light on their communications control panels went unnoticed, what with their attention focused on the jumble of wreckage of the dome and parts lying on the surrounding tarmac. There was an unheard return call to them, from the orbiting clanship nearly over the northern pole, who had replied to the emergency frequency broadcast. Droktad had neglected to describe *which* dome had suffered damage, and had said it was an accident. This would be a simple matter to remedy, if he had heard and answered that next communication, or realized that he now could not use his radios. The orbiting clanship only knew the transmission came from the northern hemisphere of the planet. Instead of reversing course, it continued its request for more information, because the ship that made the call could be ahead or behind them. The name Droktad, as a sub leader could be tracked down of course, but there was no reason he would refuse to answer an inquiry about an accident he reported, was there?

It wasn't until the heavy landing jacks were deployed, at the normal altitude of just above a half mile that the mystery of the events below grew considerably clearer to both occupants of the clanship. That was when Thad ordered the two waiting four-ships to launch their anti-ship missiles.

Droktad had his eyes focused on the tableau below, where some oddly smooth shapes were mixed among ragged debris, and seemed clustered more on the opposite side of the tarmac from where they were intending to land. He had just realized that they looked like single ships in form, but he knew the only such small ships available to warriors at this site were presently in their internal launch tubes, on this very ship.

Two such smooth forms suddenly fired four missiles at them. Droktad was standing at his console already, and rapidly activated the target decoys that sometimes drew missiles away from their original target, provided the incoming seekers saw the strong signal from a decoy when it was still close to the original target, and just slightly diverging away, as was the case here. He also activated the instant-on automated laser defense system, another new tactic ordered for clanship pilots and mission commanders to use.

This defensive procedure was imposed after the human raids had cost them so many undefended ships to missiles, some of which might have been defeated by the automated systems, even if no Krall were aboard. Any true warrior preferred to control their weapons personally, and this seldom-used feature of the weapons suite, designed by the Olt'kitapi, was normally ignored. Those ancients had thought these types of computer systems would protect them from an enemy, but those aliens were all dead at the hands of the Krall, weren't they? That was taken as evidence that the warrior's way was best, despite the fact that manual control cost them more warriors, and worse, cost them more clanships.

Control of *one* of the high-powered laser cannons was retained by the ship's commander, who masterfully targeted one of the missiles and fired, in less than two seconds. The multiple decoys managed to pull two missiles aside, where they detonated harmlessly via their proximity fuses, as they passed close to the false targets.

The automated defense system used a heavy laser, the only one of those it controlled that could bear on a rapidly approaching rocket, to disable steering on that third missile. As it veered aside, it was cut in half by the rapidly computer tracked laser. The four missiles had not reached their maximum hypervelocity capability in that short a distance, so the automated system had no problem, with the target it was able to attack.

The incoming missile that Droktad fired on was grazed and slightly deflected, making it a pretty darn good shot for an organic fire control system in such a short reaction time. However, that wasn't quite good enough, as demonstrated when the warhead detonated against the left inside part of the bottom of the bell mouth of the thruster nozzle. An automatic engine cutoff prevented the now missing section of the thruster from tipping the clanship over onto its side, from what would have been a horizontal vector of escaping plasma that the attitude thrusters could never have countered. The grazing shot had deflected the missile's warhead to hit the toughest part of the clanship, the hardened ceramic material that could absorb the near star heat of the exhaust. It saved the lower part of the ship and hull, at the expense of loss of main thrust.

Ironically, the automated defense system would probably have claimed that missile as its victim as well, since the laser it was denied use of was the only one that could have done the job. Droktad's ego could not relinquish full weapons control to a computer, so the laser that *could* do the job wasn't tracking quite as precisely.

As a result, the K'Tal pilot now only had the attitude thrusters, near the upper part of the clanship to slow their descent. The earlier arbitrary decision to slow the approach briefly now meant their speed of fall was far less than would have been the case for a typical Krall pilot's max performance landing. They still hit hard, heavily damaging the landing jacks, and they didn't rise back on them as the springy actions normally did. The damaged thruster bell shattered as it sank low enough to strike the tarmac, with star hot black fragments spinning away. For a moment, tilted slightly, it appeared the ship might fall over, but it stayed upright, with a pronounced list.

The two Krall, knocked to the floor by the landing, could have benefited from the human style acceleration couches that they distained (again for ego reasons). They sprang to their feet, ready to defend their grounded ship and avenge the loss of the dome, and possibly the factory.

****

Sarge was impressed. "How the hell did that pilot pull that off? Or the ship commander. Whoever did the shooting, and deployed the decoys that fast."

Thad, annoyed he hadn't called for eight missiles, shook his head. "All of the heavy lasers ports were open simultaneously, but only two fired. I think they may have activated the automated defense system. That has been one of our edges, the use of computers versus their fast reactions. Even now that we personally are faster than they are, computers still act faster. They obviously have learned from their mistakes. I wish I had learned from our successes, and not stayed with the same basic attack plan. They laid a *trap* for us, expecting us to head down into the factory through the interior stairwells."

Dillon added his comment. "I don't think they were expecting the actual landing, or we wouldn't have made it to atmosphere before they would have been after us. The ECM was a new trick that gave us a slight edge, but they'll be ready to counter that with land lines soon."

"Yea, but that's for the next raid. Let's dig ourselves out and get away from this one first."

"Colonel?" it was Fred Saber.

"Yes son?"

"Do you want another four-ship to try to finish the job? Rich and I are out of missiles, but the clanship looks like it can still shoot back."

"What? Hell, my shuttle is covered and I can't see. It's still *standing*? I figured it crashed and fell over." He had not heard an explosion from the clanship's reaction fuel, but the tanks didn't always rupture.

"Yes Sir. The laser ports are still open, and from our external mikes we picked up the faint high pitch ultrasonic whine of the magnetic coils of the plasma cannons, as they came on-line. The ceramic barrels are heating because I can see a faint IR glow behind those ports, which are still closed." The TG2 senses were paying dividends. Now what to do?

"No. There's no point in firing them from where we are. Any of us are too close for a missile to arm and detonate if we fire. We need more distance."

Thad, using his command override, selected a higher power narrow focus radio, by deploying a dish on one of the shuttles not buried under the collapsed wall. "Noreen, you saw what happened." It wasn't a question. He knew she was watching as she came inbound from the moon. "Did the orbiting clanship turn back?"

"Not yet, but he did try to reply to that broadcast on an emergency frequency. I don't think it knew where that came from, and it has gone around the curvature of the planet. I'll be down there before the next guardian rounds the southern pole. I can't even see half of your ships under the crap lying over top of you."

"I'll send teams out to uncover what they can. However, we'll need you for transport of some of us, and then blow up the craft we leave behind. I need you to blow up that tough assed clanship on the tarmac for us. We have plenty of missiles, but they won't arm and explode at this close range. If I send out a few four-ships to get some distance, that clanship will nail them when they move."

"Right, when I hit atmosphere in five minutes I'll fire a salvo of five, with more to follow if he knocks those down. Keep your people on the far side of the dome. The explosions will make a big fireball of ragged parts."

"Will do." Switching to his low power transmitter, he said, "Fred, Richard, don't move your ships or the clanship will fire on you for certain. All eight of you climb out and run like hell for cover around the side of the dome. The Avenger will blast that clanship in five minutes, then fire and parts are going to fly. Your suits will hide you. Go!"

Both four-ship pilots had kept their three companions Linked into the conversation. Without a word, the person in back activated the rear hatch on each craft, and they worked their way out of the tight confines of the reclined seats and into the outside debris. Each nervously checking the large deadly clanship as they made their exit, located only a quarter of a mile away with a clear view of the craft.

****

Droktad now shared weapons control with Fangar. She would operate the Plasma cannons as soon as the plasma reservoirs finished heating. The ceramic barrels were already hot. Unaware of an incoming enemy clanship, they were not actively running a radar scan above them, and so did not have missiles ready. That was what the orbital guardians were expected to be doing. He had not asked himself how these small craft had managed to elude that same coverage.

At close range, with the known size of the jumbled support struts from the dome as comparison, the two small ships he could see near the north and south edges of the dome rubble pile were larger than a single ship, but they looked almost exactly like them. They were the source of the four missiles fired at them. A single ship didn't carry two missiles, and these apparently carried only two each, or else he wouldn't still be here, wondering who made them. Actually, the "who" wasn't a valid question, because there was only one enemy he could suspect. It was more one of "how" they had built a larger version of a Krall slave product. It wasn't double the volume of a single ship, most likely because a typical human was smaller than a warrior was. He guessed the ship would hold three to five humans, depending on internal equipment and weapons they brought.

He intended to destroy both of them soon, but wanted any crew still inside to think that perhaps the crew or equipment on the clanship was disabled. It certainly would be if this were a human ship and crew. He was learning, and intended to use patience to see what else these ships might do. If they showed the slightest sign of lifting, they would be smoking piles of metal. He had them both targeted for tracking, a talon tip ready to tap the firing command.

A slight movement of debris, several leaps from one of the small ships, instantly caught his red-pitted eyes. That wasn't the first time his attention had been so drawn, of course. Pieces of wreckage were still settling on the dome, and wind would move lightweight pieces of fragments. However, being close to an object of intense interest, he zoomed one screen on the area where he'd seen the shift. There was a repeat of the movement, as a section of strut rotated down for a moment, then lifted again. Just beyond that location, some dust spilled from a nearly flat section of a wide piece of armored glass, splintered from the windows of the dome. There was a scuffmark in a layer of dust on the clear surface. The dust had probably settled before his ship crashed, so it was scuffed after that, and he just saw dust fall.

He selected one of the lower power lasers, and while it was still off, aimed it towards the scuffmark. As he was watching, the scuff widened and it was paired with a new mark, which appeared a half step to the right. He instantly fired the beam and then, with a talon tip on the image, made the red beam wander back and forth above the scuffmarks. Imagine his surprised pleasure when scorch marks appeared in the air not only over the section of glass, but in another area almost a leap farther beyond. Two different targets had been revealed, and they started moving very rapidly, in different directions, but the scorched parts remained visible to him.

Droktad put more burn marks on the original target, playing the beam on it for longer. It suddenly seemed to twist and drop into the debris field of scrap metal and plastic, seen only as a few visible marks that were not moving. He played the beam more thoroughly, with pinpoint accuracy all around the whitish and some black sections, which were quickly defined as the form of a biped, of roughly human form and scale, wearing some sort of armor.

The animal had clearly been stealthed to the point of invisibility. Something Krall armor couldn't do, and in his prior experience on Poldark, and a hand of other raids, neither did human armor. He tapped the waiting command on the main console, and the two heavy lasers ravaged the two small ships. Even *they* were much more resistant to his beams, deflecting their effect far longer than a single ship would have survived. He now believed the reports of how effective the human raiders had become.

Now he pulled back his view screen from its tight zoom to look for more of these stealthed humans, and noted with satisfaction that Fangar had watched him, and was already searching.

"Until I damaged the coating on the armor I did not see them at all. Try different detection methods. I didn't see them in infrared until the suit surface was damaged and burning hot." Following his own advice, he studied the control range settings for the view screens, which he was aware of, but had never found cause to adjust beyond the visible light or infrared spectrums. He shifted towards ultra violet with no motion or human shapes observed. Fangar, to his annoyance, and then reluctant satisfaction, apparently found them!

"I have one." She blasted it, with her now barely online plasma cannon, operating at minimal energy for that ship-to-ship weapon. He saw where the bolt struck and splattered, at an empty (to him) point in space near the edge of the sagging dome wall to the north. The flying limbs and head from the destroyed suit torso became visible, as the power source for the stealth technology was destroyed.

He couldn't *wait* to get such a shot. "How did you see it?" he demanded to know.

"I moved my talon down to where I have looked at radiation from stars in the radio region. A signal frequency that is far below infrared. Closer to the waves we use for communications." She was a K'Tal, so that perhaps explained her knowledge of what most warriors considered useless information.

He noticed that as his talon tip reached the bottom of his current range scale of electromagnetic frequencies, that meaningless (to him) Krall script numbers appeared beside his tip. When he reached the bottom, below infrared, the scale suddenly changed, with a red dot and the same number where he had been touching, now shifted to the top so he could drag down more. For the first time he realized there were more frequencies that the screens could select than he'd ever needed. There were a huge number of frequencies, and the numbers changed as his talon returned to the top and started down again. He could seek for a long time.

"At what number did you find them visible?"

"They are seen in a range between…" and she provided two numbers, one a higher wavelength than the other.

Droktad knew what the numbers were, but they had never had any importance to him. He moved his talon tip down rapidly and saw the number he wanted to reach counting down on the screen as the lower frequencies were passed, and thus longer wavelengths were indicated. There was another legend at the top that said he was now in a specific radio frequency range. He didn't care anymore about that label than runny droppings from his cloaca. Except human body armor could be detected in that range.

When he looked at his screen now that it was in the right spectrum, he was dismayed to see it very dark, with some movements indicated. He couldn't see how he could direct his lasers accurately if he could not see the target's surroundings. He told the K'Tal so.

Fangar, in a slightly condescending tone that he wanted to make her regret later, told him how to select and lock-in the upper and lower radio range, then return to visual light frequencies to overlay that signal on the visual light on screen. He did that, just as she confirmed the method when she blasted another suit he saw faintly and only partially outlined on her own screen.

"That one was motionless and hiding behind a large strut." She added with supreme satisfaction.

It wasn't hard to accomplish, and he was quickly looking out at the area on this side of the wreckage in normal light on his screen, with presumably the radio wave data included. He didn't see anything moving at first. Then, at the south end of the piles of jumbled material, he caught a ghostly outline moving quickly towards the edge of the dome wall curve. A human was making a dash for safety, where it would pass out of his view around the curve.

Proving yet again that the speed of light couldn't be beaten in a foot race, Droktad claimed his own second victim, as he burned the suit in half at the waist, and it became fully visible in normal light as it fell. The superimposed radio images were mere ghostly outlines, which one had to look at carefully to see them against the richer, color-filled surroundings on his screen. He appreciated the detection that Fangar had made of the hiding human he'd just seen her kill. He would still give her some unpleasant duty for her disrespectful tone to her sub leader, a moment ago.

They had found and killed four humans, but more could have been held within those two destroyed ships, and now would be hiding on the cluttered tarmac. There were certainly more of them on the other side of the dome. They had helped destroy the dome he was charged with guarding. He'd seen the shape of more of their ships on the other side before his clanship was shot down. He desperately wanted to kill more of these cursed attackers before the guard clanships figured out what was happening, and finally arrived to finish the task. He knew he faced some unpleasant duty of his own when *his* sub leader confronted him. This might be his last opportunity to kill humans for a long time.

With a grunt of satisfaction, he detected the shape of a foot, and the top of another human's helmet, making a fast peek over a particularly massive support node with multiple broken struts protruding. There were *two* targets there. If he had control of the plasma cannons, he could take them out with a single shot, but he wasn't giving this shot to Fangar.

The heavy lasers would take longer to get through the node, but two of them could be brought to bear at the same time. He was joyfully (for a normally somber Krall disposition) sighting not only the heavy lasers on the node to flush them out, but setting up two smaller lasers to personally sever the lower legs when they started to run. He'd then kill them slowly, a talon length at a time, by burning off small segments as they squirmed. It had been a year since he'd had human prey to enjoy.

His snort of amusement drew Fangar's attention, and she knew he had found a choice target. Envy and sadism vied to keep her looking for her own targets, or to relish the slow death he assumed her leader's snort implied. He tapped the console to trigger the two heavy lasers, centered on the thick and massive support node. It would only require a short time to generate enough heat to force the two humans to run for other cover. He would be waiting.

As it happened, the wait became the remainder of his life! Five undetected anti-ship missiles ended his and Fangar's hunting pleasure, in an orange and black fireball. One missile happened to blast the command deck level off the top of the clanship, sending it cartwheeling vertically into the sky. This gave them a few seconds, on backup battery power to their screens, to watch as they flipped over, to drop back into the rising orange flames. It was a terrible thing to behold.

****

To Fred, and Jason, hiding with him behind the node, it was a beautiful thing to behold.

They knew they were doomed when the heavy lasers proved they had somehow been seen and targeted. There was no safe retreat from where they crouched. The node, initially the best heavy cover Fred could find when the shooting started picking their companions off, had turned suddenly into a death trap. Now it had become their safe haven again, as flames washed past them, along with flying pieces of clanship.

They looked up as the wind drifted the rising column of black smoke to the northwest, and they could see the Avenger settling tail first, towards the east side of the tarmac. She would be closer to most of the spec ops troops that now needed transportation.

Fred's visor had reported the grim details to him as two of his own team died and their icons went red. Then he heard from Colonel Greeves about icons that he didn't have displayed, from Richard Yang's team. Richard was a victim of the first plasma bolt fired, caught completely in the open, trusting to his stealth capability for protection. Another bolt had caught another member of Richard's team. The first troop killed, his own teammate Astrid Brandauer, seemed to have been an unlucky case of making her presence known by moving some debris or kicking up dust. At least according to Jason's account.

She was following Jason, and both were hit by what seemed to be a random low power laser hit, which damaged a portion of their suit's stealth coating. Jason, in the lead, managed to escape, but Astrid was singled out for an agonizing, scream filled burning death. She had called for help, but when the beam found her continuously, her radio was left transmitting. It was horrible to hear before she mercifully fell unconscious or, he hoped for her sake, she was dead. The damned Krall had continued to burn the surface of her suit, which retained power and stealth for the undamaged sections. That apparently exploratory burning to see what they had caught, prodded them into somehow finding a way to detect their suits. That was because, in the next three minutes their shooting became extremely precise, rather than a random detection of side effects such as debris movement.

He would pass this information on when they had their after action debriefing, assuming any of them lived to do that. They had to get off this dirt ball before the orbiting clanships caught them on the ground. Jason was limping, but the suit had countered the pain from the burn on his left calf. He helped him hurry around the dome to reach the others. Some of them needed digging out, and some ships would be left behind to self-detonate, he'd heard Colonel Greeves say.

"Hang on everyone," Dillon warned unnecessarily. He was trying to use a combination of reaction thrusters and Normal Space drive to lift the shuttle enough so that some handy broken struts could be placed under the portion of sidewall that had sagged over the top of five shuttles and a greater number of four-ships. The smaller ships were free of the wall, but in their hollow, they had nowhere to go to get out from under the obstacle. Dillon, in concert with the other five trapped shuttles, was hoping to lift the still continuously connected hundred feet of wall high enough, so that multiple teams of TG2s could brace it with pieces from the dome, and hold it up long enough for the trapped ships to fly out from under it. The troops on foot had to brave the turbulence of the reactions thrusters, as well as doge falling pieces of the structure.

Sarge, outside with those manhandling the longest pieces of scrap struts they could jointly lift, told the five pilots, "Try to hold there as long as you can. We are propping the top edge first, then sticking some in halfway, at the middle sections."

"Sticking them in halfway? I feel so violated." Dillon quipped in a falsetto voice. "That's what all you boys promise." It brought some humor to a tense moment.

For the most part, the tactic worked. One shuttle was still left trapped, along with three of the four-ships, but their crews could all get out safely. Now that they had seven shuttles free, and most of the four-ships recovered, their plight was clear. The Avenger could only carry four shuttles, and had internal launch tubes for only sixty-four of the four-ships. All of the extra crews would fit inside her, of course. However, half of their fleet of small craft would need to be left behind.

The window of opportunity for a liftoff in the radar coverage gap of the two orbiting guard ships was missed. Waiting for another gap was out of the question. They had been here too long already, and either of those orbiting clanships, or others, could be coming looking for them at any moment. There *had* been some sort of encrypted emergency frequency broadcast.

The Slasher was still at the moon, providing long-range surveillance, and added firepower if needed. However, she couldn't slip in undetected, as Avenger apparently had barely done, using up more luck than they deserved. It would be another hour before the orbital coverage gap would happen again, assuming the two clanships would stay on schedule, after the emergency frequency transmission. A micro Jump by Slasher would advertise their presence immediately.

Another factor was that there were surely Krall that had survived the big explosion and cave in, and they would be climbing out some place, unless they were trying to stem the flow of water coming inside the factory. More than likely, they would go to the forest village and order Prada down to do that work. If the explosives were not triggered by rising water first.

Noreen had the lower hold portals all open, and while the four-ships slipped into their docking bays, and four of the shuttles did the same, the pilots that had to leave their rides behind set them for remote self-destruct, and via Alyson on the Bridge, Linked them to the AI, Karl, for an assured destruction after they were safely aloft.

This process was still underway when Captain Retief broadcast down to them on the general push frequency. Before Noreen even heard her say more than her ship ID, she knew it was bad news.

"This is Slasher. The clanship passing over you has started a deceleration burn. It may have seen the smoke and the destruction there, or heard something from a broadcast sent just a moment ago from another dome. We'll have to fight our way out I think."

This warning didn't really speed boarding, because that was already proceeding as fast as TG2 coordination could make things happen. The shuttles and four-ships had smoothly and swiftly, slipped into the empty bays. Only the pilots that had set the destruct systems on the abandoned craft were running to leap twenty feet into the open portals. As the last one entered, the portals were slammed shut, and Noreen selected passive tracking for the weapons system, and tied four missile launchers with five missiles in each rack to Alyson's console.

Noreen was about to tell everyone to grab their socks and hold on, when Slasher broadcast again. "The second clanship, or a first cousin, is coming back over the curve of the northern hemisphere, and also clearly coming your way. Somebody else will surely be coming out to the moon to see who the hell is talking in a strange encryption mode. You start your lift and I'll be at the outer atmosphere before they know I'm coming. Retief out."

Noreen warned them. "Get down now. Max performance lift in one second."

She was generous and allowed one point five seconds, which is considerably longer feeling to a TG2, at ten times the reaction and thought processing speed of a normal human.

The main thruster and attitude thrusters contributed slightly, but Noreen had retained tachyons in Avengers Traps for the Normal Space drive, which did the real heavy lifting this time. They left a plasma trail in a literal blue streak as the ship rose at close to the TG2 tolerance for this level of g force, limited only by the atmospheric resistance the hull could accept. That was when all of the personnel were in acceleration couches. Almost half were not, and if they survived the next five minutes without destruction, some of them would fly home in a med lab. Otherwise, a med lab would be superfluous.

Unnoticed behind them, the ECM pods went off in minor explosions on top of the wrecked dome, and oddly, the parked fleet of small craft lifted off as well and moved away from the dome. Before they were five hundred feet in the air and a quarter mile away, the ships still trapped under the fallen wall exploded powerfully, as their fusion bottles suddenly ruptured. The already shattered dome hardly suffered any meaningful damage, but more of the ground managed to fall into the factory below.

At an altitude of just under ten miles, Alyson used her suit communications to send a launch command, via Karl, to initiate the high scan rate targeting radar, and to start firing anti-ship missiles as the atmosphere thinned enough they could safely clear the launch ports. At the hull searing passage through the now diminished atmosphere, it wasn't possible to fire them even a mile lower. The stealth capability of the burned and damaged skin of the leading edges of the hull was ruined, and would have to be replaced. Stealth wasn't needed now, because there wasn't a thing sneaky about this departure, and the Krall could see other stealthed clanships anyway.

The clanship that had been overhead and decelerating may have thought it was coming to the aid of the supposed accident at that dome, which had been mistakenly declared that by Droktad, and he was never able to correct that error. It wasn't using high rate target scanning at all, suggesting it had not been expecting to need to launch missiles as it flew a possible rescue mission, and it needed a few more seconds to get ready, which it didn't have.

However, its commander or pilot activated its instant-on automated defense system, and it spewed targeting decoys, and started firing lasers as Avenger's eight hypersonic missiles used the twenty miles to build velocity. Another four missiles were launched after a brief few second delay, when Alyson recalled how the previous clanship had nearly survived four short-range shots, with even less time to react.

Next, an event that sealed the descending clanship's fate occurred. A gamma ray burst flared above them, only a hundred ten miles above the planet and less than thirty miles above the clanship. Slasher came out swinging. She quickly launched a stream of ten missiles, five at the clanship below her, and five in the general direction of the much farther away second clanship. That particular distant opponent had seen Avenger's hostile actions, and had just fired a hand of missiles towards her, but at five hundred miles of separation, Avenger wasn't at great risk from them. She and Slasher would both be able to Jump before those threats drew near. It was that nearby clanship that Avenger had to get past.

The closer clanship, caught between Avenger and Slasher, couldn't defend effectively from heavy attacks from two directions, dividing its laser fire, and two of

Avengers missiles struck home. One aft, and one at midship, and it blossomed into an orange and black lumpy bubble of fire, nevertheless a thing of beauty to the human ships. Their extra missiles, of no danger to the two human ships designated as "friendlies," were redirected towards the second clanship, in the event they could cover that distance before being destroyed.

It was Avenger and Slasher against a single clanship, which was a bit too far away to be a threat. Even though there were launches seen from tarmacs at several domes, initiated after the fighting just witnessed had started, they would be too late to join this battle. Slasher was high enough to Jump again right now, and Avenger would join her in less than a minute.

That was when the Krall commander in the second clanship reacted as they sometimes did, for "Path and clan."

The Slasher was positioned just above the atmosphere, relatively motionless after her micro Jump from behind that moon, and the Avenger, within the upper reaches of atmosphere, was deviating around the spreading pieces of the exploded clanship she'd killed, and was presenting a screeching fast and accelerating target to the approaching distant clanship. One too difficult to predict manually.

The unexpected micro Jump, now termed an "intersect maneuver" by the PU navy, had no known defense. The Krall clanship winked out of this Universe, and before the light from that event could arrive (therefore, even computer reaction speeds did not matter), it reappeared within part of the volume of the Universe occupied by Slasher!

The resulting staggering blast was only survived by Avenger because there was no concussion in a vacuum to transmit the force of the relatively nearby nuclear force detonation. There were no damaging radiation effects to worry about, which the ship's hull might have protected the crew from in any case, at a distance of seven miles. However, the larger high velocity fragments could have penetrated and shredded Avenger's hull had it not deviated around the previously blown up clanship fragments. Noreen had naturally chosen the direction away from the second clanship's missiles, and coincidentally farther away from Slasher. As it was, the sleet of the fastest fine particles of both friend and foe peppered and pitted her upper hull, as she barely slipped past the more dangerous larger debris.

Operation Fast One had become a costly success, and not as fast or so slick as planned. The underwater explosions in the factory happened a few hours later, as flooding reached the detonation sensors. At least that all-important goal was achieved, as a return on the lives invested in its destruction.

In a sidelight, where Alyson would never have confirmation, she would be pleased at the results from her last moment instructions to Karl. When she was about to release the AI to destroy the small ships they were forced to abandon, she had a moment of inspiration. She remembered how the AI had remotely flown a single ship down to the surface of Heavyside when they were there. This time, the AI was also instructed to program each of the flight capable ships to fly somewhere, providing them with navigational coordinates of an alternate target dome on the northern hemisphere of the planet. This was where production of other war material was conducted. The small craft were all sent at ground hugging altitudes, like ancient cruise missiles, set to fly into the dome and detonate their fusion bottles. They might not totally knock out the underground factory, but it was a good use of the sacrificed small ships to slow production there.

Mission completed, the Avenger entered a Jump Hole a hundred fifty miles up, and she limped home by a devious route, to foil possible attempts to trace the direction of her travel. Today, the majority of the raiders went home, with some very painful exceptions. The equipment lost also hurt the Kobani efforts, particularly the Slasher. In sharp contrast to the Krall, material was far less important to them than their people were. Koban and Haven had a small production base, so replacing the material would take months, but valiant friends could never be replaced.

About the Author:

I was born in 1942, so I'm an autumn rather than a spring chicken. I live outside of Tampa, Florida with my fabulous wife Anita, and one remaining son at home, Montana. I have three older boys, Mark, Gary, and Anthony, all of whom have married and presented us with terrific grandchildren.

My early reading interests were arguably all sci-fi related, from Doctor Doolittle, Captain Marvel, to Superman. I then transitioned to "real" science fiction on black and white TV, such as Captain Video and Flash Gordon. I read hundreds of books by the science fiction greats growing up, and thousands of fair to not so greats in dual novel paperbacks and magazines.

My education gravitated to science, starting out as a physics major and my depression era folks told me I'd never make a living as a theoretical physicist (probably right, and Cosmology wasn't a career field then), so I moved to Electronics Engineering. I did most of that in the aerospace field for MacDonnell Douglas Corp, in St. Louis, Mo. I worked on the F4 Phantom project, and briefly on Manned Orbiting Laboratory (MOL), before the fickle fates of government finance forced contract cancelations. I devoted (read: I was drafted into) two years' service for the US Army from 1965 to 1967. A great two years, and the Army, caring not a whit for my electronics background, offered this draftee a job as an Air Traffic Controller. Cool!

After discharge I spent a short time back at MacDonnell Douglas before the contract reductions laid me off, and was hired by Emerson Electric (1968), working on the design of a neat heads-up fire control system for the Army's new Cheyenne Helicopter (to be a 270-knot hybrid fixed wing/rotor craft). Never heard of it? The fickle fates of Army finance is why this time, plus Lockheed didn't keep the airframe part from crashing and burning at a crucial point in development.

I taught Electronics for about eighteen months (near starvation wages after the high pay), and finally decided to try my hand at actually supporting my family again. I hired on with the Federal Aviation Administration as an Air Traffic Controller in 1970. Thanks Army! I spent exactly forty years in federal service, deciding in 1979 to use my technical background to work on writing features for the software of the FAA's Terminal Automation Systems (for 28 of those 40 years).

Retired, I now work as a consultant/contractor for the FAA, supporting a software system I helped create. In anticipation of more free time in the future, I finally decided to try my hand at writing what I love to read, Science Fiction.

Thanks for reading my books,
Steve Bennett

Published Books
Koban (August, 2012)
Koban: The Mark of Koban (February, 2013)
Koban: The Rise of the Kobani (September, 2013)
LOOK FOR:
Koban: Shattered Worlds
Book four in the Koban Series, expected in early half of 2014.

****

Made in the USA
Lexington, KY
30 January 2014